French Tales of
Vampires
(Vol. 1)

FROM THE SAME PUBLISHER

French Tales of Vampires (Vol. 1)

by
Cyprien Bérard, Paul Féval,
Louis-Sébastien Mercier, Marie Nizet,
Charles Nodier, Jean Ray
and J.-H. Rosny Aîné.

Translated by
Brian Stableford
Ruth Berman
Jean-Marc & Randy Lofficier

A Black Coat Press Book

ISBN 978-1-64932-312-5. First Printing. August 2024. Published by Black Coat Press, an imprint of Hollywood Comics.com, LLC, P.O. Box 17270, Encino, CA 91416.
 Printed in the United States of America.

TABLE OF CONTENTS

Introduction

The theme of the resurrection from the dead takes multiple aspects, but can be roughly grouped into three categories: ghosts, vampires and zombies, to use a terminology dear to the horror film fans.

A ghost is nothing more than a dead person who refuses to cross the threshold of death and persists in wanting to continue living, in a form that ranges from the ineffably ethereal to the grotesquely repulsive.

The ghosts in Oscar Wilde's *The Canterville Ghost* (1906), R. A, Dick's *The Ghost and Mrs. Muir* (1945), Alfred Adam's *Sylvie et le Fantôme* (1945) or Daniel Pennac's *Messieurs les Enfants* (1997) are *revenants*—the word defines the concept's underlying notion: sympathetic, funny and loving. In contrast, the specters from Shirley Jackson's *The Haunting of Hill House* (1959), Richard Matheson's *Hell House* (1971) or Peter Straub's *Ghost Story* (1979) are abominations whose evil existence is a threat to the physical, mental and spiritual survival of the protagonists.

From Casper, the friendly little ghostly child to the terrifying Spectre of DC Comics, from the love-struck revenants of Marcel Brion to those thirsting for revenge in the novels of Marc Agapit, the ghost is, to paraphrase Clausewitz, simply the continuation of life on another plane. The ghost only exists because it is attached to life and the living. If this connection is broken, the ghost no longer has any reason to exist and disappears into the afterlife, re-establishing the natural order of things. The ghost thus symbolizes a victory, alas all too ephemeral, over death.

The vampire, on the other hand, is an incarnated ghost, condemned to a parasitic existence—he sucks the blood of the living, or sometimes their "psychic energy", to feed him/herself and keep on living. This makes him not a revenant, like the ghost, but a superior form of life. The vampire is a dead person who refuses to be dead; he asserts that he is not dead, but "more-than-alive."

Like the ghost, the vampire is a myth with two faces: erotic and thanatological. The first category of vampires includes, to name but the most famous, John William Polidori's Byronesque Lord Ruthven (1819), arguably the first vampire in popular literature, Sheridan Le Fanu's Carmilla (1871), Pierre Kast's Vampires of the Alfama (1975), Anne Rice's Lestat (1976) and Jean Rollin's Two orphaned girls (1993). The second category includes the famous Dracula by Bram Stoker (1897), and his even more monstrous cinematic alter-ego, Count Orlock from the film *Nosferatu* (1930), Barlow by Stephen King (1975) and all the various vampires fought today by Buffy, the endearing heroine of the 1997 TV series.

The moral ambiguity present in the literary treatment of the vampire, contrasting seduction and horror, is indicative of how the theme of survival after death is perceived by the surrounding culture. Is it a desirable dream or, on the contrary, a loathsome abomination? And what price must be paid for this survival? For the vampire is both superhuman and subhuman: a sexual predator yet impotent, a passionate romantic yet soulless, depending on the version... So many contradictions are embodied in the vampire myth. The vampire is our mirror of the afterlife, the embodiment of our choices.

The zombie, on the other hand, doesn't get the same preferential treatment. If the vampire is an "more-than-alive" creature, we could say that the zombie is a "less-than-alive" one. With the zombie, all moral ambiguity disappears. Any resurrection is an unnatural act, a sacrilege. Mary Shelley's Frankenstein Monster (1818) is, of course, the prototype of the future zombie, especially in its film version: ponderous gait, hallucinated expression, raw savagery. It was cinema, more than literature, that gave the zombie its letters of nobility. From the classic film by Victor Halperin *White Zombie* (1932) to George Romero's *Night of the Living Dead* (1968), Lucio Fulci's *La Paura* (1980) and Sam Raimi's *The Evil Dead* (1982), and all their predecessors and successors, the zombie has become one of the pillars of horror cinema, successfully combining two taboos: that of death and that of cannibalism.

The simplicity of the zombie theme raises the question of the quasi-divine prohibition of resurrection. This notion is brilliantly evoked in W. W. Jacobs' short story *Monkey's Paw* (1902) in which a couple endowed with a magic talisman capable of granting three wishes prefer to send their resurrected son back to the grave from which he should never have emerged, rather than lay eyes on the abomination he has become.

The same theme can be found in Stephen King's *Pet Semetary* (1983) and Brigitte Aubert's *Ténèbres sur Jacksonville* (1994). The zombie is the final victory of death, presented as preferable to the horror of resurrection. The -only exception to this chorus of protests is Robert Silverberg's *Recalled to Life* (1958), in which the resurrection of the dead (limited to victims of recent accidents) is presented as an inevitable advance in medicine, without any other form of morality.

Jean-Marc & Randy Lofficier

Louis-Sébastien Mercier: *The Isle of Blood*

Louis-Sébastien Mercier (1740-1814) was best known in his own day as a dramatist. He was a prolific writer and a relentless propagandist for his own ideas, in various direct and indirect forms, including the idiosyncratic genre of visionary fantasy. He was not the only writer of his era to employ that genre, but he was the one who did so most prolifically, most inventively and—eventually— most successfully.

The great majority of the books that are nowadays thought to have made a major contribution to French thought prior to 1789 were initially published illicitly. It is, of course, difficult to be sure, in the virtual absence of records, but it does seem highly likely that of all the illicit books produced in Paris before 1789 (all of which had false title pages, usually claiming to have been published in Brussels, Amsterdam, Geneva or London), the one that was by far the most widely read at the time was Mercier's L'An deux mille quatre cent quarante, rêve s'il en fut jamais *[The Year 2440, a Dream if Ever There Was One] (tr. as* Memoirs of the Year Two Thousand Five Hundred*), first published anonymously in 1771 and subsequently revised and augmented several times. At the time, it was sensational, and it remains notorious today.*

The reason why L'An deux mille quatre cent quarante *became retrospectively famous in the 20th century is because it was identifiable by then as the first significant narrative set in the future, and thus the implicit ancestor of all futuristic fantasy, including the modern genre of "science fiction."*

Before 1789, of course, very few of the book's readers could have had any idea that it was, in fact, an element in a long series of visionary fantasies by the same author, and when the text became famous again as a forerunner of futuristic fantasy, very few of its readers could have known that, or would have cared if they had. Indeed, it was not until the twenty-first century, when copies of Mercier's earlier visionary fantasies became available in electronic form on the Bibliothèque Nationale's gallica website and the International Archive Digital Library at archive.org that it became practicable for anyone to place L'An deux mille quatre cent quarante *in its true context, within Mercier's pioneering development of philosophical visionary fantasy—a genre whose subsequent development has been stuttering, to say the least, inhibited by the commonplace notion that any story that ends "And then I woke up" should be awarded an automatic F in the qualifying examination for literary respectability.*

Perhaps ironically, it is partly for that reason that much of Mercier's visionary fantasy still seems fresh and original, its exploratory zest not having been weighed down by an enormous burden of subsequent sophistication. In Mercier's work we can see the full effect of the liberation that the device of dreaming gave to his literary imagination, how it enabled him casually to toss aside conventional notions of narrative structure and conventional notions of narrative propriety, in order to become a genuine precursor of surrealism and to develop a number of what were to become conventional tropes of supernatural fiction in original ways. For instance the triply layered dream-portmanteau in Songes d'un hermite *(tr. as "Dreams of a Hermit")[1] featuring* The Isle of Blood, *is a very early and, in retrospect, very interesting, contribution to the development of the literary vampire.*

B.S.

One of my old friends, having learned the location of my dwelling, had brought me some black puddings; I ate too many of them, and that was the only sin against temperance that I have committed in my retreat. I went to sleep with an indigestion, which occasioned me dreams analogous to the heavy nourishment that was inconveniencing me. I beg the physicians not to call that analogy into doubt.

I was transported, I have no idea how, to a frightful island called the Isle of Blood. No expression can render the horror that the land in question inspired in me. It was governed by a chief known as the Sansudourph, who was its absolute ruler; he had other chiefs under him, distributed between the villages and those chiefs, known as Sansuminadourphs, each had a great authority in his own canton. All those important persons nourished themselves on human blood, but only the Sansudourph had the right to drink it pure; the Sansuminadourphs mixed it with goats' blood.

All the inhabitants, men, women and children, were obliged at every full moon to draw from their veins the blood necessary to the nourishment of the chiefs of the nation; the tax was in proportion to age, and from the age of forty until death it diminished.

In addition to that tribute there was another. The Sansudourph and the other chiefs assembled their subjects to occupy them with various labors; they were animated with blows of an iron rod until they fell, bathed with sweat; that sweat belonged to the masters, who appointed officers to collected it with sponges, and those officers had the right to three quarters of it. The liquid was particularly for the usage of the women of the country; they distilled it and made use of it in the composition of a kind of lotion for reddening the elbow and the heel. They also made a beverage with it to animate the color of their flesh.

The wives of the foremost chief wore in their ears the hearts of two little children garnished with precious stones, and that was a third tribute that the inhabitants owed to their master after a certain number of moons.

---

[1] Included in the collection *The Iron Man & Other Visionary Fantasies*, translated by Brian Stableford, Black Coat Press, ISBN 978-1-61227-759-2.

Unfortunately for me, it was on the very day that the Sansudourph demanded the rent of hearts that my deranged imagination took me to that execrable island. I saw him emerge from his palace, licking his lips, dripping with blood, of which he had just drunk a large bowl. The officers were drunk on it.

He sat down and the child was immediately brought to him whose heart was to be given to him. It was a little girl, twelve years old. I had never seen anything so beautiful; her hair delighted me; the skin of her face resembled white satin painted pink; she smiled as she looked at her mother, who was holding her hand, and that smile caused me to shed a torrent of tears.

The Sansudourph was asked whether he wanted the tribute of blood at the same time as the tribute of the heart; he replied yes, but that, by an effect of his ordinary benevolence, he only wanted half the tax of blood. Then a vein was opened in the child's right arm, and the Sansudourph, throwing away the bowl in which he usually received the blood, took a kind of siphon, inserted it in the open vein and drank thus, in such a way that it was impossible to know exactly how much he had taken.

I had not ceased weeping, and yet I could not turn my eyes away from that spectacle. The child fainted; she was rubbed with her own blood in order to bring hr round, and her beautiful face became horrible, as if a rosebud had been dipped in bud. When she recovered consciousness and the apparatus had been placed over the wound, the executioner approached; that was the name given to the man who was responsible for extracting the heart. When I saw him taking out his implements I tore my hair; I would have liked to tear off his arms. Wretched black puddings, what a cruel night you made me pass.

The little girl was in the arms of her mother, who was washing her with her tears, and her father was holding her head. All of that was part of the obligation. The first blow that was struck caused her to utter one of those screams that have so much effect on mothers.

I had the good fortune at that moment to lose sight and hearing; that is why I do not know how the operation finished. I recovered my senses when it was over, and I saw the unfortunate tottering parents carrying away their daughter, doubtless dead, but who would live again, because the executioner, under penalty of losing his position, was obliged to restore life to the children who perished at his hands.

The black ideas to which the black pudding had given birth in my brain did not end with that spectacle. I went into a cabin inhabited by a numerous family. The nasty odor that it exhaled made me nauseous. I counted twenty individuals, men, women or children; they all resembled cadavers; they all tottered as they walked and had almost lost their voices.

An old man was lying on the ground, ready to render the last sigh. He was the father of the family. He saw around him his little children of the fourth generation; he wanted to embrace them before dying, but he did not have the strength; he begged his eldest son to lift his arms and put them around the necks of his children.

At the moment when he was holding two of them against his swollen breast, I saw three officers of a Sansuminadourph come in. They had bronzed faces, and grim and barbaric expressions. They told the unfortunate old man that they had come to collect the arrears that he owed their master. The sum was exorbitant, because the man had not paid anything for ten years, either for himself or his family, because of several maladies that had exhausted them all, and the Sansuminadourph had given him credit.

The dying woman was unable to reply. He made a sign to uncover his arms and show them to the officers. Then all the family members threw themselves at their feet; a younger daughter spoke, begging them to spare a life that could not last more than a few hours.

"The blood you take from my father," she said to them, "will not be worth the trouble of opening his veins; only a few drops will come out, and they will be tasteless. Leave us the consolation of seeing him expire without violence. If you kill him, several of us, already desiccated by sadness, will die of dolor, and those who survive us will be in no condition to give you anything for a long time."

The impatient officers imposed silence on her. "Give us your children," they said, "We'll begin with them. It's time that our master was paid, he's waited for you for too long."

Immediately, they opened the veins of the children and the mother, and left them motionless. They approached the old man, but he had rendered the last sigh when he had seen his family's blood flowing. They continued their execution on all the others, only leaving one young man, eighteen years old.

I remained alone with him; I did my best to console him, and I dared, in spite of is grief, to ask him for enlightenment regarding the credit or loan of blood, and he had the courage to satisfy me.

"Our Sansuminadourph," he said, "is a delicate man; he only wants good blood. When he finds a few families in his canton weakened by maladies or poverty, he waits a few years without demanding any tribute from them. But he has slaves that he maintains expressly, and from whom he takes the blood that the exhausted families can't pay. That's the blood that is called loaned blood. It's necessary to return it, when one is able to do so, and the tax is double for as many moons as have passed without payment. When the head of a family is on the point of dying without having settled the arrears, they run to him in order to take all the blood he might have, and that of his children; but they leave one person or two in each cabin to perpetuate the race and the rent of blood."

"What horror!" I cried. "What injustice!"

"No," he replied, "There's only injustice in a few cantons of the island, not in this one. Our priests have made laws in order that the interest on loaned blood should be legitimate; otherwise, the Sansuminadourph wouldn't accept it, because he's religious and has a delicate conscience. We're very fortunate that he left us for a few years without demanding anything. The measure of blood that we owe him at each full moon belongs to him; it's his property; when doesn't demand it, that blood circulates to our profit in our veins; so it's only just to return to him what he has lent us and the advantage we've obtained from it. The weaker one is, the more considerable that advantage is; because leaving a dying man the only drops of blood that are keeping him alive is leaving him his entire life; that's why he owes the Sansuminadourph his life and something more."

"And that," I said to him, "is also why you have just seen your entire family expire."

Charles Nodier: *Smarra, or The Demons of the Night*

Charles Nodier was born April 29, 1780, in Besançon. In 1824, he was appointed to the position of librarian of the Arsenal Library in Paris, a post that made his personal finances more secure, and made it possible for him to offer hospitality to younger writers, holding weekly salons for story-telling and artistic discussion. He held the post of librarian at the Arsenal until his death, January 27, 1844.

In 1832, Nodier published La Fée aux Miettes *[The Crumb Fairy].[2] In accord with his belief in lore and legendry as a source of story, he drew from several cultures in creating it. From France came the title character. The word "fairy" is itself French in origin. French fairies became especially prominent among story-tellers such as Mme. d'Aulnoy or Charles Perrault in the Parisian salons of the last decade of the 17th century. Their stories, written down, resulted in a new genre of fiction, the* conte de fees, *or fairytale.*

The fame of the competition in horror-writing that produced the vampire stories of John William Polidori and Mary Shelley's Frankenstein *led Nodier to co-author a dramatization of Polidori's* The Vampyre *(1819)[3] and to write a horror story,* Smarra, ou les Démons de la Nuit *[Smarra, or the Demons of the Night] (1821), set simultaneously in contemporary Illyria and in ancient Thessaly, the home of witches, in the folklore of ancient Greece. He drew also on Slovenian legends of vampires—although not as extensively as he liked to claim, calling the story in his 1821 preface a translation of a story by a Ragusan noble, whose pen-name was Count Maxime Odin. Actually, the writer who went in for using this pen-name was Nodier himself.*

French education in the 18th century had stressed the values of reason and good taste, allowing no extremes of emotion, and the models of ancient Greek and Latin classics. Nodier rebelled against these values, feeling that they left out too much that was important in human nature, emotions that were felt rather than reasoned. He looked to dreams and nightmares as revelations of the non-rational side. In Smarra, *he had two levels to the action of the story—Lorenzo in modern Europe has an uneasy night, full of nightmares; Lucius, in ancient Thessaly, is the protagonist of Lorenzo's nightmares. Scenes and people shift around Lucius, in the manner of dreams. Nodier must have taken a mischievous delight in using this classical setting for his characters' thoroughly passionate,*

---

[2] Included in the collection Trilby & The Crumb Fairy, translated by Ruth Berman, Black Coat Press, ISBN 978-1-61227-455-3,.

[3] Included in the collection *Lord Ruthven the Vampyre*, Black Coat Press, ISBN 978-1-932983-10-4.

non-rational story, reminding even the most anti-Romantic of his readers that the admired Greek and Latin exponents of good taste had their own stories of nightmarish horrors, often locating them in Thessaly.

Lucius, his head cut off by the executioner's sword, experiences the agony of death. Nodier, in Smarra, *aimed at reproducing the experience of actual nightmare. Nelson comments, "It is precisely the attempt to simulate a dream or, rather, a nightmare, with its inconsistencies and digressions, its incoherencies and absurdities that makes the tale so markedly different from the usual tales of vampirism and terror of the time. Indeed, Smarra is unique and considerably ahead of its time in its attempt to give the impression that it is a dream... It is because of this tale that Nodier can be considered an important initiator in attempting to record the impact of the dream on man's psyche and, above all, on the psyche of the writer.*

R.B.

Prologue

Somnia fallaci ludunt temeraria nocte,
Et pavides mentes falso timere jubent.[4]
Catullus

The isle is full of noises,
Sounds and sweet airs, that give delight and hurt not.
Sometimes a thousand twangling instruments
Will hum about mine ears, and sometimes voices
That, if I then had waked after long sleep,
Will make me sleep again: and then, in dreaming,
The clouds methought would open and show riches
Ready to drop upon me, that, when I waked,
I cried to dream again.
William Shakespeare - *The Tempest*

Ah! how sweet it is, Lisidis, when the last chime of the bell, dying over the towers of Arona, has just tolled midnight—how sweet it is to come to you to share the bed that's been so lonely for a long time, the bed where I've been dreaming of you for a year!

---

[4] Accidental dreams play in the deceitful night, / And bid shivering, deceived minds to be afraid.

You are mine, Lisidis, and the evil genies that separate your sweet slumber from Lorenzo's will no longer terrify me with their magics!

It would be right to say, you may be sure, that these nightly terrors which attacked me and rent my soul during the course of the hours intended for repose were only a natural result of my stubborn examination of the marvelous poetry of the ancients, and the impression that some of the fantastic fables of Apuleius left on me—for the first book of Apuleius seizes the imagination with a grip so keen and so painful that even if it cost me my own eyes, I wouldn't want it ever to fall open under yours.

Don't let anyone talk to me any more today about Apuleius and his visions. Don't let anyone talk to me anymore about Latins, or Greeks, or the dazzling whims of their geniuses! Aren't you yourself, Lisidis, a poetry more beautiful for me than poetry, richer in divine enchantments than all of nature together?

But you're asleep, my child, and you don't hear me anymore! You danced too late this evening at the ball at Belle Island!—You danced too much, especially when you didn't dance with me. And here you are, tired as a rose that swung in the breezes all the day and waits, half drooping on its stem, for the first sight of day, to rise up redder than before!

Well, then, sleep beside me, your face leaning on my shoulder, warming my heart with the scented warmth of your breath. Sleep is overtaking me, too, but this time it descends on my eyelids almost as graciously as one of your kisses. Sleep, Lisidis, sleep...

There was a moment when the spirit, suspended in the wave of its thoughts...

Peace!—night has completely fallen over the earth. You no longer hear the steps of townsfolk as they return home ringing on the echoing pavement, or the shoes on the mules' hooves as they return to their stable for the night. The noise of the wind crying and whistling between the gaping joints of the wood planks of the casement—that's all that's left to you of the ordinary impressions of your senses. And within a few seconds more, you imagine that this murmur itself comes from inside you. It becomes the voice of your soul, the echo of an idea, indefinable, yet distinct, blending itself with the first perceptions of sleep. You begin this nocturnal life which passes (what a wonder!) into worlds entirely new, among innumerable creatures whose forms were conceived by the great Spirit, but without bothering itself to bring them into existence. It was satisfied with scattering these flighty and mysterious phantoms through the unbounded universe of dreams. The sylphs, in the confusion of the night-sounds, descend around you, humming. They tap your heavy eyelids with the monotonous beating of their moth wings. You can see the transparent and multi-colored dust that rises from them floating for a long time in the profound darkness, like a little cloud shining in the middle of the dark sky. They press against one another, they embrace, they merge in one another, impatient to renew the magic conversation of the preceding nights, and to tell each other of unheard-of events. These wonders take shape in your mind as if they came from memory. Gradually their voice weakens, or, rather, it reaches you only through an unknown organ, transforming their stories into living scenes and making you an involuntary actor on the stage they have prepared. A sleeping man's imagination, in the power of his independent and solitary soul, shares to some extent in the perfection of the spirits' powers of vision. The soul keeps up with them, and, transported miraculously into the aerial dream-choir, it flies from surprise to surprise until the instant when the bird of morning's song warns its adventurous escort of the returning light. Frightened by the omen of its call, they gather together like a swarm of bees at the first growl of thunder, when large drops of rain bend down the tops of the flowers which the swallow would have caressed without touching. They fall, spring back, and mount up, crossing each other's paths like atoms attracted by opposing forces, until they disappear in chaos in a sunbeam.

The Story

> *O rebus meis*
> *Non infideles arbitrae,*
> *Nox, et Diana, quae silentium regis,*
> *Arcana cum fiunt sacra;*
> *Nunc, nunc adeste...*[5]
> Horace - *Epodes* V.

By whose order do these angry spirits come to fright me with their clamors and their goblin-shows? Who casts these lines of fire in front of me? Who makes me lose my way in the forest? Hideous apes whose teeth gnash and bite, or rather hedgehogs crossing the paths to be found beneath my feet and wound me with their prickles.

> *[...His spirits hear me*
> *And yet I needs must curse. But they'll nor pinch,*
> *Fright me with urchin-shows, pitch me in the mire,*
> *Nor lead me, like a firebrand, in the dark*
> *Out of my way, unless he bid 'em; but*
> *For every trifle are they set upon me;*
> *Sometimes like apes that mow and chatter at me*
> *And after bite me, then like hedgehogs which*
> *Lie tumbling in my barefoot way and mount*

---

[5] O witnesses, not unfaithful, to my affairs, Night and Diana, you who rule over silence, when they perform the sacred mysteries; now, now, be here.

17

I had just completed my studies at the Athenian school of philosophers, and, as I was curious about the beauties of Greece, I was visiting for the first time poetic Thessaly. My slaves were waiting for me at Larissa in a palace ready to receive me. I had wanted to travel alone, and in the imposing hours of the night, through that forest, famous for the spells of magicians, which extends its long curtain of green trees on the banks of the Peneus. The thick shadows gathered under the immense canopy of the woods hardly allowed the trembling ray of a pale star circled by mists to shine through some of the thinner branches into a clearing—opened, no doubt, by a woodcutter's axe. My heavy eyelids closed in spite of myself over my eyes, tired with looking for the white line of the path, now lost in the brush. I couldn't keep from falling asleep except by following with painful attention the noise of my horse's hoofs, sometimes making the sand crunch, and sometimes making the dry grass rustle under the regular beat of his tread. If the horse stopped at times, the silence wakened me, and I shouted at him, for I was tired and impatient, urging him to speed up his pace, if it had become too slow. Frightened by I don't know what unknown obstacle, he jumped and bounded, snorted fiery whinnies from his nostrils, reared up in terror, and drew back again, even more terrified by the showers of sparks that the bits of stones struck up beneath my feet.

"Phlegon! Phlegon!" I told him, when my over-tired head hit his neck, as he reared up in fright, "O my dear Phlegon! Isn't it time we got to Larissa? There are pleasures waiting for us there, and especially the sleep that is so sweet. A moment's courage more, and you will sleep on a litter of special flowers—for even the gilded bedding that people gather for the oxen of Ceres won't be too fresh for you!"

"You don't see, you don't see!" he said, shuddering. "The torches those women are shaking in front of us kill the heather and mix deadly vapors in the air I breathe.—How can you ask me to cross these magic circles, and their threatening dances?—they'd make anyone pull back, even the horses of the sun!"

And yet the rhythmic steps of my horse still went on ringing in my ears, and a deep sleep suspended my worries for the longest time! Only, every few moments it happened that a shining group of peculiar flames went by, laughing over my head—and a deformed spirit, in the shape of a beggar or a wounded man caught hold of my foot and let himself be dragged after me with horrible glee. Or, rather, a hideous old man, who added the shameful ugliness of crime to the ugliness of decay, would leap on to the croup behind me and bind me with his arms, as bony as a dead man's.

"Let's go, Phlegon!" I cried, "let's go, you most beautiful of the coursers fed on Mount Ida—come, brave the fearsome terrors strangling your courage!

These demons are nothing but vain appearances. My sword, whirled in a circle around my head, splits their lying forms, and they dissolve away like a cloud. When the morning hazes float below our mountain-tops, and the rising sun strikes the fogs, they're outlined by a half-transparent halo, and the summit, cut off from the base, seems to hang from an invisible hand in the skies. It's like that, Phlegon, when the witches of Thessaly split up under my swordstroke. Don't you hear the far-off cries of pleasure rising from the walls of Larissa?— Look, look, there are the proud towers of that Thessalian city, so loved for sensual delight. And that music flying in the air is the song of the maidens."

Who among you, you seductive dreams that lull the soul, drunk with the inexpressible memories of pleasure, will bring that sound back to me, who will bring back to me the song of the maidens of Thessaly and the voluptuous nights of Larissa? Among columns of half-transparent marble, under twelve bright domes, reflecting in gold and crystal the flames of a hundred thousand torches, maidens, wrapped in the colored clouds given off by all the perfumes, appear to the eye as just one blurred and charming form that looks as if it's ready to vanish away. The wonderful mist swirls around them or makes all the inconstant tricks of the light play over their enchanting groups, in the fresh colors of the rose, the changing hues of the dawn, the dazzling confusion of the capricious opal's rays. Sometimes there are showers of pearls rolling over their light tunics, sometimes plumes of fire springing from every knot in the bands of gold around their hair. Don't be afraid if you see that they're paler than other Greek girls. They hardly belong to the earth, and seem to have wakened up from a past life. They are sad, too, whether because they come from a world where they've left behind the love of a Spirit or a God, or because a woman falling in to love has in her heart an immense need for melancholy.

Listen, now. There are the songs of the maidens of Thessaly, the music rising up, rising into the air, and as it passes like a luminous cloud, touching the lonely windows of leaded glass in the ruins dear to poets. Listen! They hug their ivory lyres, questioning the sonorous strings which answer once, vibrate a moment, stop, and, motionless again, still prolong a kind of harmony, unending, that the soul hears through all its senses, a melody pure as the sweetest thought of a happy soul, or love's first kiss before love can even understand itself; or a mother's gaze caressing her baby's cradle when she had dreamed the child was dead, but now sees he is there asleep, beautiful and peaceful. That's how it is when the last sigh of the sistrum fades away, abandoned to the breezes, lost among the echoes, hanging in the middle of the silence of the lake, or dying with the waves at the foot of the insensate rocks, played by a young woman weeping for her lover, who has not come to her. The maidens look at one another, lean consolingly towards one another, fold their elegant arms, while floating locks are tangled together. They dance to make the nymphs jealous, as their steps stir the dust that springs up, flies away, turns white, dies, and falls again in silver ashes beneath their feet. And the harmony of their songs runs on forever like a river of honey, or a graceful stream, all the lovelier because it murmurs so sweetly of banks kissed by the sun and rich with hidden turnings, of cool and shady bays, of butterflies and flowers. They sing...

One all alone, perhaps... tall, motionless, upright, pensive... Gods! how solemn and troubled she looks behind her companions, and what does she want of me? Ah! don't haunt my thoughts, you faded apparition of my beloved who is no more! Don't disturb the sweet charm of my nightly vigils with the vision's terrifying reproach! Let me forget, for I've wept for you for seven years. Let me forget the tears still burning my cheeks by thinking of the innocent delights of the sylphides' dance and the fairies' music. You can see them coming, you can see their groups mingling, twining together in wreathes that keep changing and shifting, now clashing, now racing, drawing near, flying away, rising like a wave in its cycle and falling again like the wave, as it rolls across its fleeting billows all the colors of the rainbow that embraces sky and sea at the end of the storm, when just as it dies away at the last point of its immense round, it breaks against the ship's prow.

But what do the fortunes of the sea, or the voyager's curious anxieties matter to me? For after all, a divine favor has been given to me, perhaps a favor granted to humanity in a bygone age, freeing me whenever I want it—the delightful gift of slumber—from all the perils that threaten you! My eyes have scarcely closed, the melody that ravishes my soul has scarcely ended, when the creator of night's enchantments opens before me a deep chasm, an unknown abyss where all the shapes of earth, all its sounds and lights, die away. He throws a narrow, slippery bridge with no promise of reaching the other side out over a boiling torrent, greedy for death. He pitches me onto the end of a springy, shaking plank, high above cliffs that are terrifying even to look at... Calmly, I stamp on the obedient earth with a foot accustomed to command over it. It sinks, it rebounds, and, well pleased to leave humanity, I soar. I can see the blue rivers on the land-masses falling away beneath my easy flight, and the somber wastes of the sea, the many-colored treetops, dappled with the new green of the spring, or the purple and gold of autumn, or the dull bronze and drab violet of the leaves shriveled by winter. If some astonished bird flaps his laboring wings by my ear, I shoot up, I rise higher still, longing for new worlds. The river is nothing more than a thread hidden in a somber green, the mountains nothing more than a blurred point, the summit lost against the base, the Ocean only a dark blotch on some kind of shape, astray in the middle of the air, where it twirls faster than the six-sided knucklebone that little children in Athens spin on the point of its axis down the arcades paved with stones that surround the Ceramic quarter.

Haven't you ever seen along the walls of the Ceramic quarter, during the first days of the year, when they're struck by the rays of the sun that renews the world, a motionless train of haggard men, their cheeks hollowed by want, their eyes dull and stupid, some squatting like beasts, and others standing up, but leaning against the columns and bent double under the weight of their starved bodies? Have you seen them, their mouths half open to breathe in once more the first influences of the life-giving air, to gather with mournful consciousness the sweet impressions of the mild heat of the springtime? The same sight would have struck you at the walls of Larissa, for there is misfortune everywhere: but misfortune there bears the imprint of a special fatality which is more degrading than misery, sharper than hunger, heavier than despair. These unfortunates slowly advance in the line, one after the other, and mark each step with a long pause, like the fantastic figures a clever mechanic sets up in a circle to mark the divisions of time. Twelve hours run by while the silent procession goes around in its circle, even though its length is so short that a lover who counted the hours on the tips of his mistress's fingers, more or less spread out, could read the time left to him till the longed-for hour of the night for his rendezvous. These living ghosts have kept almost nothing of the human. Their skin is like white parchment stretched on their bones. The orbits of their eyes are not animated by a single spark from the soul. Their pale lips quiver with anxiety and terror, or, more hideous still, they curve in a disdainful, savage smile, like the last thought of a bold man condemned to die as he faces his punishment. Most are shaken by convulsions, weak, but continual, and they tremble like the iron stem of the jaw's-harp, that ringing instrument that children play by setting it between their teeth. The saddest of them all, struck down by the destiny that pursues them, are those condemned to frighten the passersby forever with the repulsive deformity of their knotted limbs and their rigid stance. Nevertheless, those recurring periods in their lives between one sleep and another are for them a time when they are free from woes that they find yet more fearful. Victims of the vengeance of the Thessalian witches, they fall prey to torments that no other tongue can express, as soon as the sun, fallen beneath the western horizon, has stopped protecting them from the fearsome queens of the shadows. That's why they observe its course, all too swift, with their eyes always watching how far it has gone, in the hope—always deceived—that it may forget its bed of azure for once, and rest suspended between the golden clouds of sunset. Night has hardly come to undeceive them, spreading out its wings of black crepe, leaving behind not even one of the divine gleams which died out all at once on the tops of the trees; the last reflection, sparkling yet on the polished metal on the ridge of a high building, has hardly finished disappearing, like a coal still burning in the blaze that's been put out, as it turns white, little by little, under the ashes, and soon becomes indistinguishable in the bottom of the abandoned hearth, when a fearsome murmur arises among them, their teeth chatter with despair and rage, they draw together and then apart in the fear of finding witches and phantoms everywhere. It's night!... and hell is going to open again!

There was one, among the rest, with all his joints creaking like worn-out springs, and his chest heaving with a sound harsher and heavier than a rusty screw as it turns with difficulty in its nut. But some shreds of rich embroidery still hanging from his cloak, a look full of sadness and grace that now and then gleamed through the listlessness of his own features, a sort of mixture of inconceivable degradation and pride—like the despair of a panther in agony caught and muzzled by the hunter—made me notice him in the crowd of his miserable companions. When he passed by some women, a sigh was all that could be heard. His yellow hair fell in neglected curls on his shoulders. They could be seen—white and pure as a fabric of lilies—over his purple tunic. Yet his neck bore the mark of bloodshed, a triangular scar from a spear-head, the mark of the wound that stole Polémon from me in the siege of Corinth, when my faithful friend flung himself over me in front of the frenzied rage of a soldier already victorious but still eager to give one more corpse to the battlefield. It was Polémon himself, whose loss I'd wept over so long, and who kept coming into my sleep to remind me with a cold kiss that we must meet again in the immortal life of death. It was Polémon, still alive, but preserved in an existence so horrible that the ghosts of criminals and the specters in hell consoled each other by describing his misery, for Polémon had fallen under the rule of the witches of Thessaly and the demons who follow them in their rites, the inexplicable rites of their nightly revels. He stopped short, studied me for a long time, looking astonished at seeing a face he could remember, and came towards me with a steady, yet troubled pace. He touched my hands with a hand that shook and trembled in grasping mine. Suddenly he threw his arms around me and gazed into my eyes, his veiled eyes shedding a pale ray of light into mine, like the last gleam of a torch going away from the dungeon door:

"Lucius! Lucius!" he cried then, with a fearful laugh.

"Polémon, dear Polémon, my friend and savior!"

"In another world," he said, lowering his voice. "I remember that—it was in another world, in a life that doesn't belong to sleep and its phantoms."

"Phantoms?—what are you saying!"

"Look!" he replied, stretching out a finger into the twilight, "there they are, they're coming."

"Oh, my young and unlucky friend—don't give way to the fears of the shadows! When the shades of the mountains fall and grow large, bringing together from all round the points and lines cast by their gigantic pyramids, and embracing each other at last in silence on the darkened earth; when the fantastic images of the clouds grow long, mingling and fleeing together under the shelter of the night, like lovers, secretly married; when the birds in the woods clamor at funerals, and the frogs at the edge of the swamps sing their monotonous songs in their croaking voices—don't abandon your tormented imagination to the illusions of the shadow and the solitude then, Polémon! Fly from the hidden paths where the ghosts meet to cast black spells against the sleep of men. Fly from the cemetery grounds where the mysterious council of the dead meets, all of them wrapped in their shrouds to appear before their Areopagus, holding court in their coffins. Fly from the open fields where the grass is trampled down in a blackened circle, sterile and withered, under the witches' dancing steps. Won't you believe me, Polémon?

"When the light grows pale and retreats, dazed by the approach of the evil spirits, come with me and revive its wonders in splendid feasts and wild orgies. Don't I always have enough gold for my wishes? The richest mines open the treasures of their hidden veins to me! Even the sand in the streams transforms itself under my hand into exquisite gems, fit for a king's crown. Won't you believe me, Polémon?

"It doesn't matter if the day dies, so long as the fire that it lit for us still sparkles in the lights at the feast—or in the more cautious gleams that adorn the sweet vigils of love. Demons, you know, fear the scent of burning wax or perfumed oil shining gently through alabaster or spilling rosy shadows over the double silks of our rich tapestries. They shudder at the sight of the polished marble lit by chandeliers with crystal pendants that shed long rays of diamond around them, like a waterfall struck by the last parting gaze of the setting sun. Never a gloomy lamia, never a fleshless mantis dares to show its hideous ugliness at Thessalian banquets. Even the moon, though they invoke her, frightens them when she shines among them with those fleeting rays that give whatever they touch the dull whiteness of tin. Then run away, then, faster than a grass-snake alerted by the noise of a grain of sand rolling under a traveler's foot. Don't worry, they can't catch you in the middle of the fires that sparkle in my palace and shine into all corners, reflected by my dazzling steel mirrors. Watch how fast they run away from us, Polémon, when we go for a walk, lit by my servants' torches, through galleries decorated with statues, inimitable master-pieces of Greek genius! None of these images could make a threatening move to reveal to you the presence of those fantastic spirits that sometimes make them come alive when the last gleam shines from the last lamp, rises up, and dies away in the air! The stillness of their forms, the purity of their features, and the never-changing calm of their stance should reassure fear itself.

"If some strange noise struck your ear, my heart's dear brother, it's only an attentive nymph, as she pours over your tired, heavy limbs, the treasures of her crystal urn, where she's mixed perfumes never before known in Larissa. They're mixed with an amber liquid that I gathered on the shore of the seas that wash the cradle of the sun; with the honey of a flower a thousand times sweeter than the rose, which grows only in the deep shade of brown Corcyra;[6] with teardrops from a bush sacred to Apollo and his son, which spreads over the rocks of Epidaurus its bouquets of purple clusters still trembling under the weight of the

---

[6] I believe that is not a question here of the ancient Corcyra, but of the island of *Curzola*, which the Greeks called *Corcyra the Brown* because of the appearance given to it from a distance by the vast forests that covered it. (*Note from the Author*)

dew. So how can the charms of these magicians trouble the purity of the waters that rock their silver waves about you?

"Myrthé—pretty Myrthé with the black hair, the youngest and dearest of my slaves—you've seen her bending down as you pass, for she loves all that I love—She has some enchantments known only to herself and a spirit that confides them to her in the mysteries of sleep. She's wandering like a shadow now around the bath-house, where the healing wave ripples the surface; she's running, singing the tunes that chase away the demons, and sometimes she touches the chords of a wandering harp, and the spirits give way to it obediently, even before her wishes have had time to make themselves known as they pass from her soul to the expression in her eyes. She's walking; she's running; the harp matches her pace and sings beneath her hand. Listen to the ringing sound of the harp, the voice of Myrthé's harp: it's a rich, full, solemn sound that makes ideas of earth be forgotten, prolonging and sustaining itself, occupying the soul like a serious thought; and then it flies, it flees, it dies away, it comes again; and the tunes of Myrthé's harp—a ravishing enchantment in the nights—the tunes of Myrthé's harp, flying, fleeing, dying away, and still coming again—while she sings, while her tunes fly, the tunes of Myrthé's harp, the tunes that chase away the demon!—Listen, Polémon, do you hear them?

"In truth, I've undergone all the illusions of dreams myself, and what would have become of me then without Myrthé's harp to rescue me, or without her voice, so quick to disturb the grievous and shuddering repose of my nights?... How many times in my sleep I've leaned over a clear, still pool, a pool only too faithful in mirroring my altered features—my hair bristling with fear, my eyes as fixed and gloomy as the eyes of a man in despair, not even weeping anymore!... How many times I've trembled to see the traces of the pale blood running through my pale lips; to feel my chattering teeth loose in their sockets, my nails coming loose at their roots, ready to shake and fall away! How many times, frightened at finding myself naked, shamefully naked, I've been given up to the laughter of the crowd, dressed in a tunic shorter, lighter, more transparent than the one that wraps a courtesan as she sits on the edge of the shameless bed of debauchery! Oh! how many times, in dreams still more hideous, dreams that even Polémon doesn't know anything about... And what would have become of me then, what would have become of me without Myrthé's harp to rescue me, and her voice, and the harmony she's taught her sisters, gathering obediently around her, to charm away the terrors of the woeful sleeper, to make songs brought from far away ring in his ears, like the breeze blowing between a couple of sails—songs that join together, blending into one another, dulling the heart's stormy dreams and enchanting them into silence with a long melody.

"And now, here are Myrthé's sisters, who've prepared the banquet. There's Thaïs, recognizable among all the girls of Thessaly, even though most of them may have black hair falling on shoulders whiter than alabaster—but there isn't another with hair curling in such supple, voluptuous waves as the black hair of

Thais. That's her, leaning over the fiery cup where the wine is turning white, boiling in a jar of rare clay, while she lets fall into it, drop by drop of topaz liquid, the most exquisite honey ever gathered from the young elms of Sicily. The bee, deprived of her treasure, flies restlessly among the flowers; she hangs on the solitary branches of the abandoned tree, asking the breezes for her honey. She drones her grief, because her little ones will no longer have this shelter in any of the thousand five-walled palaces she built for them out of light, transparent wax, and they won't get the honey she's gathered for them from the fragrant bushes of Mount Hybla. It's Thais who stirs in the boiling wine the honey stolen from the bees of Sicily. And as for Thais' other sisters, black-haired like her—for Myrthé is the only blonde—they hurry in, submissive, eager, and caressing, and smile obediently as they run to prepare the banquet. They mix pomegranate flowers or rose leaves in foamy milk; or instead they stoke the oven with amber and incense that burns under the fiery cup where the boiling wine is turning white, and the flames lean far in, all around the circular rim, they bow to it, bend to it, draw near to it, graze it, kiss it with lips of gold, and end by mingling themselves with the white- and blue-tongued flames that float above the wine. The flames rise, fall, and wander like that fantastic demon of the wilderness who likes to admire himself in the springs. Who can say how many times the cup has gone round the banquet-table, and how many times, empty, it's been filled brimful again with fresh nectar? Girls, don't hold back on the wine, or the hydromel, either. The sun never stops ripening more grapes, and shining his rays of immortal splendor on the sparkling clusters that hang in rich festoons on our vines, among the dark leaves on the round branches that run in garlands along the walls of Tempe. Another libation to chase away the demons of the night! As for me, I don't see anything here now but the joyous spirits of intoxication fizzing up from the trembling foam, chasing each other in the air like butterflies of fire, or dazzling my heated lids with their radiant wings—like those nimble insects decked by nature with innocent fires, the ones you can often see, in the cool silence of a brief summer's night, shooting up in swarms from the middle of a clump of greenery like a shower of sparks under the blacksmith's redoubled blows. They float, carried by a little breeze passing by, or called by some sweet scent they feed on in the heart of the roses. The luminous cloud goes on, or changes its mind and lulls itself, resting, or turns in a moment and falls, all of them together, on the top of a young pine, lighting it up like a pyramid used for public celebrations, or on the lower branch of a great oak, giving it the look of a chandelier ready for the forest's vigils. Look how they play around you, how they tremble like the flowers, how they shimmer in the firelight reflected from the polished vases: surely they aren't enemy demons. They dance, they rejoice, as abandoned and as riotous as the spirit of folly. If they take the trouble sometimes to trouble people's rest, they only do it like a thoughtless child to satisfy their pleasant whims. They roll themselves up mischievously in the linen wound in a clump around an old shepherdess' spindle, they make the straying threads cross and tangle, and multiply the contrary knots in spite of the efforts of her useless skill. When a traveler has lost his way and searches with an eager eye across the whole horizon in the darkness for some point of light promising him a refuge, they make him stray from path to path for hours, by the gleam of treacherous marsh fire and the sound of a lying voice, or like the far-off barking of a watchdog that prowls like a sentinel around a solitary farm. That's how they abuse the poor traveler's hopes until at last, touched with pity by his weariness, they bring him all of a sudden to an unexpected place to sleep, that no one had ever spotted before in that wasteland. Sometimes, even, he is astonished to find at his arrival a bright fireplace that's cheerful just to look at, with rare and delicate things to eat, brought by chance from a fisherman's cottage or a poacher's, and a girl, fair as the Graces, who serves him, afraid to raise her eyes: for it seems to her that this stranger is dangerous to look at. The next day, surprised that so short a rest should have given him back all his strength, he rises happily at the song of the lark as it greets a clear sky: he finds out that his lucky mistake has shortened his road by twenty stadia and a half, and his horse, whinnying impatiently, with clean nose, glossy hide, sleek and shining mane, strikes the ground before him with a triple signal to depart. The goblin jumps from the croup of the traveler's horse to the head, he runs his clever fingers through the spreading mane, rolling it and crimping it in elf-locks; he takes a look, applauds himself for what he's done, and he leaves, glad to go amuse himself with teasing a sleeping man burning with thirst who sees a refreshing drink that flees, shrinks, and dries up in front of his lips, just when he's ready to suck it; who judges the cup by sight in vain; who longs in vain for the absent liquor; then wakes, and finds the urn full of a Syracusan wine he's never tasted before, which the tricksy spirit had pressed from the choicest grapes, at the same time that he was amusing himself by disturbing the traveler's sleep. You can drink, talk, or sleep without terror here, for the merry spirits are our friends. Only satisfy the impatient curiosity of Thaïs and Myrthé first, and the yearning curiosity of Thelaïre, who can't stop looking at you, with her long bright eyelashes and her big black eyes that roll like lucky stars in a sky bathed in the tenderest azure. Tell us, Polémon, the wild griefs that you believe you experienced under the rule of the witches—for the torments with which they pursue our imagination are nothing but the vain illusion of a dream which vanishes at the first light of dawn. Thaïs, Thelaïre, and Myrthé are waiting... They're listening... Well, go ahead!... tell us your despairs, your fears, and the mad delusions of the night. Thaïs, pour us some wine. Thelaïre, smile during his story so that his soul may be comforted. And, Myrthé, if you see that he's overcome by the memory of being lost and about to give way to a new illusion, sing, and strike the chords of the magic harp—Call out comforting sounds from it, sounds that banish evil spirits... That's how we free the somber hours of night from the tyranny of dreams, and escape through one pleasure after another from the sinister enchantments that fill the earth during the absence of the sun."

Episode

Hanc ego de cœlo ducentem sidera vidi;
Fluminis hœc rapidi carmine vertit iter.
Hœc cantu finditque solum, manesque sepulchris
Elicit, et tepido devocat ossa rogo.
Quum libet, hœc tristi depellit nubila cœlo:
Quum libet, aestivo convocat orbe nives.[7]
Tibullus

Be sure tonight that thou shalt have tremblings and convulsions; the demons, during all that time of deep night when they are permitted to act shall exercise on thee their cruel malice. I shall send thee pinchings set as close as the cells of a beehive, and each of these shall be as burning as the sting of the bee that built it.

[*... be sure, tonight thou shalt have cramps,*
Side-stitches that shall pen thy breath up; urchins
Shall, for that vast of night that they may work,
All exercise on thee; thou shalt be punish'd
As thick as honeycomb, each pinch more stinging
Than bees that made 'em.]
William Shakespeare – *The Tempest*

"You girls, you all know the sweet caprices of women, surely!" said Polémon, rejoicing. "You've been in love, no doubt. So you know how the heart of a melancholy widow, who lets her lonely memories go astray on the shadowy banks of the Peneus, sometimes is taken by surprise by the bronzed skin of a soldier whose eyes sparkle with the fire of the war, and whose breast shines with the splendor of a brave scar. He walks, proud and tender, among the fair ladies, like a tame bear trying to forget his regret for the wilderness in the pleasures of a happy and easy captivity. That's how a soldier likes to occupy women's hearts, when he is no longer called by the bugle to the battles, and the risks of combat

---

[7] I have seen her draw stars out of the sky. She turns the course of the swift streams with her song. She cleaves the ground with her chant and draws the spirit from the tomb, and she summons the bones from the warm funeral pyre. At will, she chases the clouds from the gloomy heaven; at will she calls snow into the summer skies.

no longer attract his impatient ambition. He smiles as the girls look at him, and he seems to tell them: Love me!

"And, as Thessalians, you also know that no woman has ever equaled noble Meroé in beauty. When she became a widow, she wore a train of long white draperies embroidered with silver—Meroé, the fairest of the fair of Thessaly, as you know. She is as majestic as the goddesses, and yet in her eyes is a sort of mortal flame that heartens the claims of love.—Oh! how many times I've dived into the breeze of her passing, the dust flying up from under her feet, the happy shadow that follows her!—How many times I flung myself before her when she walked, to catch a glance from her eye, a breath from her mouth, an atom of the wind that swirls around her, stroking and caressing her every movement! How many times—Thelaïre, can you forgive me?—I waited to feel that burning delight when one of the folds of her dress brushed against my tunic, or watched for one of the sequins from her embroideries to fall on the paths through the gardens of Larissa, so I could pick it up and press it to my eager lips! When she went by, you understand, all the clouds blushed as at the approach of the storm, my ears rang, sight darkened in my dazzled eyes, and my heart was ready to stop under the weight of intolerable joy. There she was! I'd greet the shadows that had floated over her head—I'd long for the air she'd touched—I'd say to all the trees on the banks of the river: Have you seen Meroé? If she lay down on a bank of flowers, how jealously I gathered the flowers her body had bruised, the white petals steeped in the red that decks the bending brow of the anemone, the dazzling arrowheads that spring from the daisy's golden disc, the veil of pure gauze that folds around a young lily before it smiles at the sun. And if I dared to hug that bed of fresh greenery to me—a sacrilege!—it kindled a fire in me more subtle than the heat death puts in a feverish man's blankets. Meroé must have realized it. I was everywhere. One day, towards sundown, her glance fell on me: it was cordial—she had gone ahead of me—her step slowed. I was alone behind her, and I saw her turn around. The air was calm, it didn't ruffle her hair, but she raised her hand, and was pulling it back as if to smooth her disordered curls. I followed her, Lucius, to the palace, to the Princess of Thessaly's temple, and night fell on us, night full of joys and terror!—If only that could have been the last night of my life and the end!

"I don't know if you've ever supported the weight of your sleeping mistress's body—with a resignation mixed with impatience, and tenderness, too—when she fell asleep leaning on your outstretched arm without realizing what you were suffering; if you tried to fight against the shudder that gradually seized your blood, and the numbness that chained your passive muscles, and tried to defend yourself against being conquered by death pangs threatening to overwhelm even your soul! That, Lucius, was how painful it was when the cramp ran swiftly through my nerves and shook them with unexpected tremors, as the pointed hook of a plectrum makes all the chords of the lyre jangle together under the fingers of a clever musician. My flesh twisted like a piece of dry membrane near a fire. My chest was heaving fit to burst and split the bands of iron around it, when Meroé, sitting up all at once beside me, cast a deep look in my eyes, and put out her hand to my heart to be sure it had stopped beating. She left it there a long time, cold and heavy, and then fled far away from me with the speed of an arrow when the arbalest rope shoots it off with a shudder. She ran over the marble stones of the palace, singing the tunes of the old shepherdesses of Syracuse who enchant the moon in its clouds of pearl and silver. She sped into the depths of the immense hall, and cried out now and then, in bursts of horrible gaiety, to call some of her friends—I don't know who, for she hadn't told me their names.

"While I was watching her, terrified, I could see a crowd of innumerable vapors coming down the length of the walls, pressing under the porticos, and swaying underneath the vaulting, an innumerable crowd of vapors—each was marked off from the others, but without having any life, except in the appearance of the shapes, along with a voice as weak as the sound of the calmest pool during a silent night. A vague color tinged it, printed there by the pattern of the transparent figures floating in front of it.—Just then a blue and sparkling flame leaped up all at once from all the tripods, and Meroé flew from one to the other, murmuring some frightening, indistinct words:

"'Here, the blossoming vervain—there, three sprigs of sage gathered at midnight in the cemetery of those who died by the sword—here, the veil of the beloved, which her lover put on top to hide the pallor and ruin after he had cut her sleeping husband's throat in order to enjoy her love—here again, the tears of a tigress worn out by hunger and inconsolable at having devoured one of her little ones!'

"And her averted features expressed so much suffering and horror, that she almost made me feel pity. Distressed at seeing her spells interrupted by some unforeseen obstacle, she bounded up in a rage, drew back, and came forward armed with two long ivory wands, tied together at the ends by a braid of thirteen horsehairs plucked from the neck of a superb mare by the same thief that had killed her master. And on that flexible braid she'd hung an ebony *rhombus*[8] with empty, ringing spheres attached to it that made a howling noise in the air and came rolling around with a heavy grumbling, and rolled on, still grumbling, and then slowed down and fell. The flames in the tripods stood up straight, like snakes' tongues; and the shades were satisfied. 'Come, come,' cried Meroé, the night-demons must be appeased, and the dead must rejoice. Bring me blossoming vervain, sage gathered at midnight, and four-leafed clover; give the harvest of the sweet bouquets to the Seeress, and the night-demons.' Then she glanced with astonishment at the gold asp twined around her bare arm; at the precious bracelet, made by the cleverest artist in Thessaly—who had begrudged

---

[8] See the section on the *rhombus* at the end of the story.

nothing in the making, either in the choice of the metal or the perfection of the craftsmanship: the silver on it was encrusted with delicate scales, and each one of a whiteness heightened by the brilliance of a ruby, or by the transparency—so pleasant to the eye!—of a sapphire bluer than the sky. She took it off, she cursed it, she fell into a reverie, she called the snake, murmuring secret words; and the serpent came to life, unwinding itself, and fled with a hiss of joy like a freed slave. And the *rhombus* still swung round. It swung, always roaring, and rolled like the distant thunder moaning in the clouds blown by the wind and spreading out with a wail at the end of a storm. Meanwhile all the vaults opened, all parts of the sky were displayed, all the stars fell, all the clouds spread out evenly, bathing the threshold and the square in front in shadow. The moon, spotted with blood, looked like an iron shield where someone had just set the body of a young Spartan, his throat cut by the enemy. The moon rolled, and her pale disk weighed heavily on me, still obscured by the smoke from the extinguished tripods. Meroé kept on running, striking the innumerable columns of the palace with her hand. Long beams of light shot out at her touch, and each column that split under Meroé's hand revealed an immense colonnade peopled with phantoms, and each of the phantoms struck a column as she did, opening up new colonnades; and not a column but was a witness to the sacrifice of a new-born child snatched from its mother's caresses. 'Have pity! have pity' I cried, 'on the unlucky mother who fights against death for possession of her child!' But this stifled prayer only reached my lips with the strength of a dying man's whisper as he says: 'Farewell!' It expired in inarticulate noises on my stammering mouth. It died like the cry of a drowning man who tries in vain to confide his last despairing cry for help to the silent waters. The unfeeling water stifles his voice: it draws him down, cold and gloomy; it smothers his outcry; it will never carry him to the shore.

"While I fought against the terror that had overwhelmed me, and tried to drag from my heart some curse that would awaken the vengeance of the gods in heaven, Meroé cried: 'Miserable fool! you shall be punished forever for your insolent curiosity!—Ah! you dare to desecrate the spells of sleep—You speak, you cry out, and you see—Very well, you shall speak no more except to beg in vain for the unheeding pity of the absent, you shall see nothing but scenes of horror to freeze your soul—' And as she spoke these words, in a voice higher and more fearsome than a hyena with its throat cut but still defying the hunters, she took from her finger the gleaming turquoise ring. It sparkled with flames like the colors of the rainbow, or like a wave leaping on the incoming tide and reflecting, as it curls over on itself, the fires of the rising sun. She pressed a hidden spring with her finger, raising the marvelous stone on its invisible spring, and revealed a golden casket. It held a monster of some kind, shapeless and colorless, that bounded, leaped, flung itself forward, and fell crouched on the magic-maker's breast.—'Here you are, my dear Smarra,' she said, 'the dearly-beloved, the sole favorite of my amorous thoughts. The hatred of heaven chose you from all its treasures to be the despair of the children of men. Go, flattering spirit: deceive him or terrify him, but go torment the victim I've turned over to you. Punish him with pangs as varied as the horror of hell that bred you, and as cruel and implacable as my wrath. Go and glut yourself on the anguish of his trembling heart—count the convulsive beating of his pulse as it races and halts—observe his agony of grief, and suspend it only to start it again! Once the dreams start, my faithful slave of love, your reward will be to fall again on the fragrant pillow of your mistress—you'll embrace in your arms the queen of the night-terrors!' She spoke, and the monster sprang from her burning hand like the round quoit the Discobolus throws. It spun in the air as rapidly as fireworks shot off from boats, opened its bizarrely patterned wings, and swooped up and down, expanding and shrinking. The deformed dwarf's hands were armed with metal nails sharper than steel to sink into flesh without ripping it, ready to let it drink blood, sucking insidiously, like a leech. Joyfully, it fastened itself over my heart, spread itself out, lifted its enormous head, and laughed. My eye was fixed in terror. I tried in vain to see anything reassuring in the area my gaze covered: the thousand demons of the night escorting the demon from the turquoise—stunted women reeling drunkenly—red and violet snakes spitting fire from their mouths—lizards with human faces raising their heads over a lake of mud and blood—heads newly cut from trunks by a soldier's axe, but watching me with living eyes and skipping away on reptile-feet —

"Since that fatal night, o Lucius! I haven't had a peaceful night again. A girl's perfumed couch, full of voluptuous dreams—a traveler's shifting tent, opened every night under a different darkness—even the sanctuary of the temples is useless as an asylum against the demons of the night. Almost before I can close my eyes, gloomy and worn out with fighting against the sleep I dread so much, all the monsters are there, as at the moment when I saw them escape with Smarra from Meroé's magic ring. They run around me in a circle, dizzying me with their cries, terrifying me with their pleasures, and dirtying my trembling lips with their harpy-kisses. Meroé leads them and hovers above them, shaking her long curls. Streaks of pale blue light fall from her hair. Just yesterday—she was even taller than I'd seen her other times—it was the same shape and the same features, but I was horrified to see that under her seductive looks, the magic-maker's complexion was leaden, and her limbs the color of sulfur, as if seen through a light and subtle gauze. Her eyes were fixed and hollow, all bloodshot, tears of blood left furrows on her sunken cheeks, and her hand, spread wide, left printed on the very air the trace of bloody fingers.—'Come,' she told me, just grazing me with the wave of a finger—it would have made an end of me if it had touched me—'come visit the realm I will give to my husband, for I want you to know all the domains of terror and despair!' And with that, she flew in front of me, her feet hardly off the ground, drawing toward the earth and away again by turns, like a flame dancing above a torch ready to go out. Oh! how frightful that path seemed to all my senses, as we went tearing along! How impatient the magic-maker herself seemed to be to get to the end! Imagine the funeral-vault where they heap up the remains of all the innocent victims that they've sacrificed, and there's not a scrap, no matter how mutilated, that doesn't still have a voice, a shudder, and tears! Imagine the moving walls— moving and living—as they draw together from both sides in front of your steps and gradually close in, snaring all your limbs in an icy, narrow prison.—Heavy-hearted, your chest pounds, shuddering and gasping to breathe in the air of life through the dust of ruins, the smoke of torches, the dampness of the catacombs, the poisoned atmosphere of the dead—and all the demons of the night there, shouting, whistling, howling, and roaring in your stunned ears: 'You'll never breathe again!'

"And, while I was going forward, some kind of insect, a thousand times smaller than those that attack the delicate fabric of the rose-leaves with their little bites—a graceless mite that takes a thousand years to imprint one of its footsteps on the universal sphere of the heavens, though they're made of a stuff a thousand times harder than diamond—It was going forward—it was going forward there, too. And the stubborn trace of its lagging feet had divided the imperishable globe right down the middle.

"We ran so fast and so far that human languages have no comparison for it. But after we had run like that, I saw some flashes of clear white light shooting out of the mouth of a basement window, a neighbor seeming as distant as the furthest star. Full of hope, Meroé dashed forward. I followed her, drawn by an irresistible power. Besides, the road back, as lost as nothingness, and infinite as eternity, had suddenly closed off behind me, impenetrable to human courage and patience. Between Larissa and us already there loomed all the debris of the innumerable worlds that had preceded ours in the attempts at creation since the beginning of time. And most of them had surpassed ours in immensity as much as our world itself exceeds in its prodigious size a butterfly's nest. A door like a tomb had received us—or, rather, which had breathed us in as we left that gulf— and opened onto a field with no end in sight, where nothing had ever grown. You could hardly distinguish in a distant corner of the sky the vague outline of a dark, unmoving star, stiller than the air, darker than the shadows reigning in that abode of desolation. It was the corpse of the oldest of all suns, at rest at the shadowy base of the firmament, like a submerged boat in a lake swollen with the melting snows. The pale gleam that had just struck my eyes didn't come from there. You could have said that it had no origin and no color, except the color of the night, aside from the little that came from the conflagration of some world far away, still burning as a cinder. Then—would you believe it?—they all came, the witches of Thessaly, escorted by those earth-dwarves that toil in the mines, with faces like copper and hair as blue as silver in the furnace; and by long-armed salamanders of unknown colors, with their tails flat as sticks, running down, nimble and quick, in the middle of the flames, like black lizards crossing a fiery dust. They were followed by Aspioles, with bodies very frail and lean, topped by misshapen heads. But they looked cheerful, balancing themselves on the bones of their thin, empty legs, like straws blown by the wind. Then came the Achrones with no limbs, no voices, no faces, of no age, weeping as they bounced over the shuddering earth, like wine-skins puffed up with air. And then the Psylles, that suck a cruel poison and, in their eagerness for poisons, dance in a circle, whistling shrilly to wake up the serpents and stir them in their hidden lair, the serpents' twisty hole. There were even Morphoses there, the kind you used to love so much, as fair as Psyche, playful as the Graces, as full of song as the Muses, with a seductive look, more penetrating and more poisonous than a viper's fang ready to set your blood on fire and boil the marrow in your charred bones. You would have seen them walking around, wrapped in their purple shrouds, those women veiled in clouds brighter than the Orient, sweeter than Arabian incense, more harmonious than the first sigh of a virgin falling tenderly in love, in an intoxicating vapor that fascinates the soul in order to kill it. Sometimes their eyes rolled with a liquid flame that charms and devours—sometimes they nodded their heads with a grace that is theirs alone, begging for your trust and belief with a caressing smile, a smile which is a treacherous but life-like mask hiding their joy in crime and the ugliness of death. What can I tell you? Drawn by a whirlwind of spirits that drifted like the cloud—like the blood-red smoke that descends from a burning city—like the liquid lava that spreads and weaves back again, lacing fiery streams together over a field of ashes—I came to... I came to... . All the graves were open—all the dead had been dug up—all the ghouls,[9] pale, impatient, famished, were there. They were breaking up the planks of the coffin, tearing the sacred shroud, the last clothing of the dead. They shared out the frightful remains with an even more frightful glee. Their irresistible hands—for I was, alas! held captive, weak as a child in the crib—forced me to take part—o terror!—in their abominable feast!"

As he finished these words, Polémon raised himself on his bed. Trembling and overwhelmed, his hair standing on end, his eyes fixed and terrible, he called to us in a voice with nothing human in it.—But the airs of Myrthé's harp were already floating in the air; the demons were appeased; the silence was as calm as the thoughts of an innocent man dropping off to sleep on the night before he is to receive judgment. Polémon slept in peace to the sweet sounds of Myrthé's harp.

The Epode

Ergo exercentur pœnis, veterumque malorum

---

[9] In Slavonian, *ogoljen*, "stripped bare," either because they are naked, like specters, or in antiphrasis, because they strip the dead bare. I write "ghouls," because that word, established in the translations of the Arabian Tales, is not strange to us, and it is evidently formed from the same root.

Supplicia expedunt; aliæ pandantur inanes
Suspensæ ad ventos, aliis sub gurgite vasto
Infectum eluitur scelus, aut exuritur igni.[10]
Virgil

[... *'tis a custom with him,*
I' th' afternoon to sleep: there thou mayst brain him,
Having first seized his books, or with a log
Batter his skull, or paunch him with a stake,
Or cut his wezand with thy knife.]
William Shakespeare – *The Tempest*

The vapors of pleasure and wine had dizzied my wits, and I saw in spite of myself the phantoms of Polémon's imagination pursuing one another in the darkest corners of the banquet hall. Already he had fallen into a deep slumber on a bed strewn with flowers, beside an overturned cup. And my young slaves, surprised by a gentler exhaustion, had let their heavy heads fall against the harps they'd been holding. Myrthé's golden locks fell like a veil on her face between the golden strings which paled next to them. And the breath of her sweet sleep, stirring the harmonious chords, drew from it a voluptuous sound I can't describe, just dying away as it reached my ears. Yet the phantoms hadn't left— they were dancing in the shadows of the columns and the smoke of the torches. Impatient with this counterfeit of a spell, the product of intoxication, I heaped cool branches of ivy on my head to bring me back to myself, and I shut my eyes tight, tormented by the light's illusions. Then I heard a strange clamor. I could hear voices by turns grave and threatening, or insulting and ironic. One of them was repeating to me, in a fussy monotone, some verses from a scene of Aeschylus; another, the last lessons that my dying grandfather had taught me. From time to time, like a puff of wind whistling in the dead branches and withered leaves in the intervals of a storm, a face I could feel breathing on my cheek burst out laughing and drew away, still laughing. Bizarre and horrible illusions followed that one. I believed that I saw—through a haze of blood—all the things I'd closed my eyes against. They were floating in front of me and pursued me with horrible looks and accusing shudders. Polémon, still lying beside his empty cup, Myrthé, still leaning on her silent harp, cursed me furiously, demanding from me an account of some assassination or other. Just when I was getting up to answer them, and stretching one arm out on the couch, which was cool from plenty of libations of drinks and perfumes—something

---

[10] Therefore they are harassed by pains, and they are paid the punishments for old sins; some are hung and stretched out in the empty winds, some, infected with sin, are washed under the vast whirlpool or burnt with fire.

cold seized the joints of my trembling hands. It was an iron noose, and it fell at the same moment on my numb feet, and I found myself standing up between two rows of pale soldiers, close ranked, their spears tipped with dazzling iron, looking like a long progression of candelabras. Then I started to walk, looking up into the sky for the flight of a dove going somewhere, so that I could at least confide a secret to her to sigh over, before the horrible moment I was beginning to foresee. I could tell her the secret of a hidden love, and she could re-tell it someday, as she soared near the bay of Corcyrus, over a pretty white house. But the dove was weeping in her nest, because the goshawk had just robbed her of her dearest hatchlings, and I was going forward, with a painful, faltering step towards the goal of this tragic convoy. A murmur of frightful joy ran through the crowd, impatiently calling for my passing: the murmur of people with their mouths open wide, their looks haggard with grief, gripped by bloodthirsty curiosity ready even at the furthest edges of the crowd to suck up all the tears of the victim the executioner was going to throw to them. —

"There he is," they all shouted, "there he is!" —

"I've seen him on the battlefield," said an old soldier, "but then he wasn't as pale as a ghost, and he seemed brave during the war."

"How little he is, this Lucius people said was an Achilles or a Hercules!" answered a dwarf I hadn't noticed among them. "It's the terror, no doubt, which has sapped his strength and is making his knees give way."

"Are they really sure that so much ferocity could be found in a man's heart?" said an old man with white hair. His doubt chilled my heart. He looked like my father.

"Him!" replied the voice of a woman, whose face showed great gentleness. "Him!" she repeated, wrapping herself in her veil to escape the horror of my appearance, "the murderer of Polémon and the fair Myrthé!"

"I think the monster's looking at me!" said a woman in the crowd. "Shut your basilisk-eye, you viper-soul, heaven curse you!"

During this time, the towers, the streets, the whole city fled behind me like the port left behind by an adventurous ship going to try its destiny at sea. There remained only one square, newly built, vast, regular, superb, covered with majestic buildings, overwhelmed with a mob of citizens of all classes, who abandoned their duties to answer the call of this alluring amusement. The casements were bright with the avidly curious, and between them young folk could be seen jostling with their mothers or their mistresses for room in the narrow window-nooks. There were spectators climbing everywhere, on the obelisk that rose above the fountains, on the mason's scaffolding that shook beneath them, on the temporary stage of the strolling players. Men panting with impatience and excitement were hanging from the palace cornices. Hugging the ridges of the wall with their knees, they were repeating, with joy unbounded, "There he is!" A little girl with madness in her haggard eyes, wearing sequins spangled in her blonde hair, and a wrinkled blue tunic, was singing the story of my punishment. Her words told of my death and the confession of my heinous crimes, and her cruel ballad revealed to my astonished soul mysteries of crime impossible even for crime itself to conceive. The object of all this spectacle was myself, along with another man who accompanied me, and some planks put up on some stakes, on top of which the carpenter had fixed a rough seat and a block of wood badly squared off that stuck out an arm's length. I climbed fourteen steps. I sat down. I cast my eyes over the crowd. I wanted to see if I recognized any friendly faces, to find some gleams of hope or regret in the wary look of this shameful farewell. I saw nothing but Myrthé waking up against her harp and touching it with a laugh—nothing but Polémon setting his empty cup upright, and then, half dazed by the fumes of the drink, filling it again with a wavering hand. More calmly, I gave up my heart to the sharp, cold sword of the officer of death. Never has a deeper shudder run down a man's spine. It struck home like the last kiss fever imprints on a dying man's neck, sharp as refined steel, voracious as molten lead. I was only distracted from that anguish by a terrible commotion: my head had fallen—it rolled, bounced on the hideous square in front of the scaffolding, and, ready to drop all battered between the hands of the children, the pretty children of Larissa, who play with the heads of the dead, it had fixed itself on a projecting plank by biting it with teeth like iron in the fury that goes with the pangs of death. From there I turned my eyes toward the assembly. They drew back in silence, but with satisfaction. A man had just died before the people. They all slipped away, expressing a feeling of admiration for what had happened to me without fail and a feeling of horror against the assassin of Polémon and the fair Myrthé. —

"Myrthé! Myrthé!" I cried, howling, but without letting go of my supportive plank. —

"Lucius! Lucius!" she replied, half asleep, "well, you never go to sleep peacefully when you've had one cup too many! May the infernal gods pardon you, and don't disturb my rest anymore. I'd rather sleep to the noise of my father's hammer, in the workshop where he tormented copper, than among the night-terrors of your palace."

All the while she was speaking, I was stubbornly biting the wood, wet with my new-shed blood, and I was congratulating myself, because I could feel the somber wings of death expanding to spread slowly out over my mutilated neck. All the bats of twilight were skimming by me, caressing me as they said:—"Get some wings!"... And with an effort I began with shreds of something or other that barely held me up. But all at once I experienced a reassuring illusion. Ten times I struck the gloomy paneling with the movement of that almost lifeless membrane I was dragging after me, like the flexible feet of a reptile as it rolls in the sand beside the water. Ten times I bounced up again, testing myself little by little in the damp fog. How black and icy it was! How sad the wastelands in the shadows were! At last I rose up as high as the tallest buildings, and I soared in a circle round the solitary column—the column my dying mouth had just grazed—with a smile and a farewell kiss. All the spectators had disappeared, all the noise had stopped, all the lights had vanished. The air was still, the sky blue-green, as cold as a sheet of dull iron. There was nothing left of what I had seen there, or what I had imagined on the ground. And my soul, astonished to be alive, fled with horror from a vaster solitude, a deeper obscurity, than the solitude and obscurity of nothingness. But I didn't find the refuge I was looking for. I went up like a moth newly broken from its mysterious wrappings to display the useless wealth of its purple, blue, and gold ornaments. If it sees the casement of a sage far off, up late writing by the gleam of a cheap lamp, or the window of a young wife whose husband lost his way out hunting, it flies up, tries to settle in, trembles and beats against the glass, draws back, returns, circles, drones, and falls, leaving all the powder of its fragile wings on the transparent panes of mica. That was how I was beating the gloomy wings death had given me against the vaults of a sky of brass—which gave me no answer but a dull echo—and I glided down again, circling round the solitary column—the column my dying mouth had just grazed—with a smile and a farewell kiss. The column was no longer empty. Another man had set his head on it, his head turned upside-down, and the neck revealed to my eyes the sign of a wound, the triangular scar of the iron lance that had carried Polémon off at the siege of Corinth. His wavy hair fell in its gold curls around the bloody mass. But Polémon looked calm, with his eyes shut, as if fallen into a happy sleep. A kind of smile—not a terrified one—passed over his parted lips, and he was calling to Myrthé for more songs or to Thelaire for more caresses. In the light of the pale day that was starting to spread within the walls of my palace, I recognized in shapes still a little dim all the columns and all the entrances, where I had seen the funeral dances of the evil spirits taking shape during the night. I looked for Myrthé; but she had left her harp, and, motionless between Thelaire and Thaïs, she fixed a cruel and gloomy gaze on the sleeping warrior. All at once Meroé leaped up among them. The gold serpent she had taken from her arm was hissing as it glided under the arches. The loud *rhombus* was rolling and growling in the air. Smarra, summoned to the end of dreams in the morning, had just claimed the reward promised by the queen of the night-terrors, and was trembling beside her with hideous love, beating his wings till they hummed, so fast that they didn't dim the clearness of the air with even the faintest cloud.— Thaïs, and Thelaire, and Myrthé were dancing wildly, shouting for joy. Near me, some horrible children with white hair, wrinkled brows, and dull eyes, were amusing themselves by chaining me to my bed with the frailest webs of the spider that throws its treacherous thread across the angle of two adjoining walls to entrap a poor lost butterfly. Some of them were gathering those white silky threads that give off little flakes from the fairies' miraculous spindle, and they let them fall with all the weight of a lead chain on my pain-worn limbs.—"Get up," they were telling me, laughing insolently as they crushed my burdened chest with a straw, bent like a flail, which they had plucked from a gleaner's sheaf. But I kept trying to free myself from the light bonds which held down my hands, so fearsome to the enemy, and so heavy to the Thessalians who'd felt their weight often in the cruel sport of boxing with the cestus on—my fearsome hands, my hands trained to raise the death-dealing iron cestus, had softened on the unarmed breast of the fantastic dwarf, like a sponge battered by the storm to the foot of an old rock which the sea has been attacking since the beginning of the centuries without being able to shake it. And so this globe of a thousand colors, a fleeting and dazzling toy for children, vanishes without leaving a trace, even before it touches the obstacle a jealous sigh blew it against.

Blood was flowing from Polémon's scar, and Meroé, drunk with pleasures, held up over an avid group of her companions the heart torn out of a soldier whose breast she had just ripped open. She wouldn't give it up—she quarreled over the scraps with the Larissan girls, changed by blood. Smarra with his swift flight and his threatening hisses protected the frightful conquest of the queen of the night-terrors. With the end of his trunk, which unrolled like a spring out of its long spiral, he almost caressed Polémon's bleeding heart himself, to keep the impatience of his thirst under control for a moment; and Meroé, the fair Meroé, smiled at his vigilance, and his love.

The bonds that held me had finally given way. I slid until I stood upright, awake, at the foot of Polémon's bed, while all the demons fled far away from me, and all the witches, and all the illusions of the night. Even my palace, and the young slaves who adorned it, the fleeting good fortune of a dream, had given place to the tent of a wounded warrior under the walls of Corinth and a sad escort of the officers in charge of the dead. The torches of lamentation began to pale before the rays of the rising sun; the songs of lamentation began to echo under the subterranean vaults of the tomb. And Polémon—oh despair!—My trembling hand searched in vain for any feeble motion of his chest.—His heart was no longer beating.—His breast was empty.

Epilogue

> Hic umbrarum tenui stridor volantum
> Flebilis auditur questus, simulacra coloni
> Pallida, defunctasque vident migrare figuras.[11]
> Claudian

I never can add faith to these old fables, nor these fairy toys. Lovers, madmen, and poets have seething brains, an imagination that conceives

---

[11] Here is heard the doleful weeping of the spirits of the dead, flying with a faint sound of wings, and the inhabitants see the pale images and the forms of the dead pass by.]

nothing but phantoms, and their conceptions, rolling in a burning frenzy, all stray beyond the bounds of reason.

> [. . . *I never may believe*
> *These antique fables, nor these fairy toys.*
> *Lovers and madmen have such seething brains,*
> *Such shaping fantasies, that apprehends*
> *More than cool reason ever comprehends.*
> *The lunatic, the lover and the poet*
> *Are of imagination all compact:*
>
> . . .
>
> *The poet's eye in a fine frenzy rolling,*
> *Doth glance from heaven to earth, from earth to heaven.*]
> William Shakespeare – *A Midsummer Night's Dream*

Ah! who will come to break their daggers? who can stop my brother's bleeding and call him back to life! Oh! what did I come here and find? Eternal grief! Larissa, Thessaly, Tempe, the waves of the hateful Peneus! O Polémon, dear Polémon!...

"What are you talking about—in the name of our guardian angel, what's all that about daggers and blood? What's been making you blurt out these babbling words for so long? Why are you shivering with a muffled voice—like a traveler who's been murdered in his sleep, and is awakened by death?... Lorenzo, my dear Lorenzo!"

Lisidis, Lisidis, is that you talking to me? I honestly believed I recognized your voice, and I thought the shadows were going away. Why did you leave me while I was hearing Polémon's last sighs in my palace in Larissa, among the witches dancing for joy?—look how they dance for joy!...

"Alas! I don't know Polémon, or Larissa, or the terrifying joy of the witches of Thessaly. I only know Lorenzo. Just yesterday—can you have forgotten so soon?—the day that saw our marriage consecrated first came round again; yesterday we'd been married a week.... Look, look at the daylight! look at Arona, the lake and the sky of Lombardy."

The shadows go and come: they threaten me; they speak angrily, talking of Lisidis, a pretty little house by the water, and a dream I had on an earth far away... they're growing, they're threatening me, they're shouting...

"What new complaint are you going to torture me with, you ungrateful and jealous heart! Ah! I know very well that you're playing with my grief. You're just trying to find an excuse for infidelity, hoping to justify on some wild pretext a break-up you planned in advance... I won't talk to you anymore."

Where is Thais, where is Myrthé, where are the harps of Thessaly? Lisidis, Lisidis, if I wasn't deceiving myself when I heard your voice, your sweet voice, you must be there, near me... you alone can deliver me from the spells and the vengeance of Meroé... Deliver me from Thaïs, from Myrthé, from Thelaire herself...

"You're the one, you cruel man, who's bringing a vengeance from far away!—you want to punish me for dancing too long yesterday with someone besides you at the Belle Isle ball. But if he even dared to talk love to me, if he'd been talking love to me!

By Saint Charles of Arona, may God preserve her for that forever!... Is it really true, my Lisidis, that we came back from Belle Isle to the sweet sounds of your guitar, to our pretty house in Arona—or from Larissa, from Thessaly, to the sweet sound of your harp and the water of the Peneus?

"Stop saying Thessaly, Lorenzo, wake up... see the rays of the rising sun striking the colossal head of Saint Charles. Listen to the sound of the lake that comes to die on the shore at the foot of our pretty house in Arona. Breathe in the morning airs that bear on their cool wings all the perfumes from the gardens and the islands, all the murmurs of the newborn day. The Peneus flows far away from here."

You will never understand what I suffered that night on its banks. May that river be cursed by nature, and cursed be that fatal illness, too, that had my soul astray for hours longer than a lifetime among scenes of false delights and cruel terrors! it must have left the weight of ten years of old age on my head!

"No, I swear to you your hair isn't white... but another time I'll be more watchful, and I'll link one of my hands in yours—I'll slip the other among the curls of your hair—I'll breathe all night the breath from your lips, and I'll keep myself from sleeping too sound to be able to wake you up before any evil can torment you or reach your heart.... Are you sleeping?"

Note on the Rhombus

This word, very badly explained by lexicographers and commentators, has occasioned so much singular contempt, that I will be pardoned, perhaps, for sparing myself more of the same from translators to come. M. Noël himself, whose sound erudition is rarely at fault, saw it as only *a sort of wheel used in doing magic*; still, he was luckier in his encounter than his homonym, the author of the *History of Fishing*. Misled by the similarity of name based on a similarity of shape, he regarded the *rhombus* as a fish, and bestowed on the turbot the honor of the wonders of that instrument of Sicily and Thessaly. Lucian, however, who spoke of a bronze rhumbos, is a sufficient witness that it is a question of something other than a fish. Perrot d'Ablancourt translated it "bronze mirror," because there were in fact rhombus-shaped mirrors, and the shape sometimes stood for the thing in metaphorical language. Belin of Balu corrected this mistake only to fall into another. Theocritus made one of his shepherds say: "As the *rhombos* turns swiftly at the will of my desires, Venus, command that my lover may return to my door with the same speed." The Latin translator of the priceless edition of Libert comes nearest the truth:

> *Utque volvitur hic æneus orbis, ope Veneris*
>   *Sic ille volvatur ante nostras fores.*

But a bronze globe has nothing in common with a mirror. There is also a mention made of the *rhombus* in the second elegy of the second book of Propertius, and in the thirtieth epigram of Martial's ninth book, unless it's an error. It is almost described in the eighth elegy of the first book of the *Amores*, when Ovid passes in review the magician's secrets as she instructs her daughter in the accursed mysteries of her art. And I owe him the secret of a discovery, otherwise quite insignificant, to this recollection:

> *Scit bene—Saga—quid gramen, quid torto concita rhombo*
>   *Licia, quid valeat, etc.*[12]

Concita licia, torto rhombo, point clearly enough to a round instrument with straps to make it spin. And one cannot confuse it with the *Turbo* [13] of the children of Rome, for that was never made of brass, and it no more looks like a mirror than it does like a fish. Besides, the poets would not have looked for the unusual term of *rhombus* to designate it, since *turbo* figured quite honorably in poetic language. Virgil said: *Versare turbinem* [to turn a top], and Horace:

> *Citamque retro solve turbinem.* [14]

I am close to believing that, in that last example, when Horace speaks of witches' enchantments, he alludes to the *rhombos* of Thessaly and Sicily—its Latinized name [*rhombus*] was not used until after his time.

I will probably be asked what a *rhombus* is, if anyone takes the trouble to read this note, although it is not intended for ladies and has very little interest for people generally. Everything agrees in proving that the *rhombus* is nothing other than the child's toy, which really does have something frightening and magical in its projection and its sound, and which, by a singular analogy of impression, has been renewed in our days under the name of DEVIL.[15]

---

[12] She knows well—the Seeress—what an herb can do, or the threads set in motion by a whirling rhombus...

[13] *Turbo* signifies what we call a top, a cone with a stick through it that spins on its point. In Burgundy the *turbo* is still called a *trebi*.

[14] Let the turbo loose, let it loose spinning backwards.

[15] In English, a bullroarer.

Cyprien Bérard: *The Vampire Lord Ruthwen*

Lord Ruthwen, ou les Vampires *was published in Paris by Ladvocat in 1820. It was an obvious attempt to cash in on the widespread popularity of John William Polidori's novelette* The Vampyre, *first published anonymously in the April 1819 issue of* The New Monthly Magazine. *A rumor had quickly spread that* The Vampyre *was the work of Lord Byron, and Henry Colburn soon issued a pirated version of the booklet bearing Byron's by-line, which helped domestic sales considerably. A French translation by Henry Faber, credited to Byron, was issued before the year was out by Chaumerot jeune. That translation was reprinted in a set of Byron's* Oeuvres complètes *published by Ladvocat in 1820, given pride of place in volume one, alongside* The Corsair.

Byron hastened to deny that The Vampyre *was his work, and the true author of the story was rapidly revealed to be Byron's one-time friend Polidori, with whom he had fallen out. Whether Ladvocat knew that when he included the translation in his* Oeuvres complètes *is unclear, but he certainly knew it by the time the sequel he had commissioned was delivered, as the fact is acknowledged in the notes thereto.*

Given these tangled circumstances, it is not particularly surprising that Lord Ruthwen *was also deliberately misattributed by its publisher, credited to the great pioneer of French Romanticism, Charles Nodier—who, it eventually transpired, had only written the "preliminary observations", the actual text having been supplied by Cyprien Bérard.*

Little seems to be known about Cyprien Bérard, except that he was the director of the Théâtre Vaudeville and that he founded a royalist journal, La Foudre *[The Thunderbolt], in collaboration with the prolific playwright Marie-Emmanuel Théaulon de Lambert and Armand Dartois. The only other publication signed with Bérard's name is an 1825 pamphlet analyzing innovations in performance at his theater, but he had almost certainly done hackwork for Ladvocat, and had probably tried to persuade him to publish some of his poetry and short fiction. (If the implication of the notes in* Lord Ruthwen *can be trusted, Bérard had made a translation of* The Corsair, *which might have been the one used by Ladvocat in the* Oeuvres complètes.)

Nodier certainly worked for Ladvocat as a translator—he was acknowledged as the translator of Charles Maturin's Bertram *in 1821—and it would be perfectly in accordance with the practices described by Balzac, if he had also done unacknowledged hackwork of that sort for Ladvocat, including unauthorized translations of Byron. Nodier was also acquainted with Théaulon de Lambert who adapted his novella* Trilby, *first published by Lavocat in 1822, for the stage, and may well have contributed to* La Foudre. *At any rate, a conspiracy of sorts was formed, and the doubly-deceptive* Lord Ruthwen *was the result.*

The protagonist of the original novelette The Vampyre *is a naive "young gentleman" named Aubrey, an orphan who shares his vast inheritance with his sister. Recently arrived in London society, he encounters the charismatic Lord Ruthven (sic), who invites him to join him on a continental tour that he is about to make—apparently in order to flee his creditors. The two eventually separate in Rome, where Aubrey's growing suspicions regarding Ruthven's bad charac-ter are confirmed by letters from home. Before leaving Italy for Greece, Aubrey frustrates one of Ruthven's schemes, whose target is an intended bride.*

In Greece, Aubrey encounters a beautiful girl named Ianthe, who quickly falls victim to a "vampire," and he becomes ill himself thereafter. He is, howev-er, found and cared for by a seemingly-repentant Ruthven. Ruthven is then shot by bandits, and while he is apparently on his deathbed, he exacts a promise from Aubrey that the younger man will never say anything to compromise his reputa-tion. When he eventually returns home, haunted by apparitions of Ruthven, Au-brey falls seriously ill again. This time, he is cared for by his sister, until she be-comes engaged to be married. He is told that her fiancé is the Earl of Marsden, but finds out as the marriage is taking place that Marsden and Ruthven are one and the same. He finally breaks his oath, but he is too late—the last line of the story reveals that his sister has already "glutted the thirst of a VAMPYRE!"

The events of the story are usually read as a sly transfiguration of Poli-dori's own relationship with Byron, who took him to the continent when it was politic for him to leave England, ostensibly to serve as his private physician. The two quarreled continually, allegedly as a result of Polidori's bitter envy of his benefactor's wealth and talent; Polidori was dismissed in the summer of 1816, although Byron had to get him out of trouble in Milan thereafter, and apparently tried to fix up various appointments for him.

Polidori was undoubtedly familiar with the scurrilous Gothic roman à clef *by means of which the scorned and furious Lady Caroline Lamb had attempted to pay Byron back for rejecting her,* Glenarvon *(1816), and it is obviously no coincidence that the name of Polidori's villain echoes that of Lady Caroline Lamb's protagonist, Ruthven Glenarvon. Exactly how much malice there was in Polidori's transfiguration is, however, open to doubt, given that he really does seem to have been a remarkably naïve and unselfconscious young man. It is equally dubious, however, that he really was surprised as he claimed to be when* The Vampyre *was published—a circumstance for which he disclaimed all re-sponsibility.*

Poor Polidori, alas, never had the chance to appreciate what he had wrought; he was knocked down in a traffic accident and suffered brain damage, before dying on August 27, 1821, at the age of 25. He was survived by two sis-ters, one of whom muddied the waters further by carefully obliterating all the passages in his diary relating to Lord Byron, apparently for prudish reasons, thus preventing further research into his apparent grievances. He died presuming that he would never get credit for The Vampyre, having carelessly and unjustly lost that credit to his bête noire, but Byron was very enthusiastic to return it to him, and eventually succeeded in doing so, although the poet was unable to prevent its supplementation of his own image with an extra measure of the sinister.

Although his contribution to Lord Ruthwen was minimal, Charles Nodier did make some contribution, in collaboration with Achille de Jouffroy and the director of the Théâtre de la Porte Saint-Martin, Jean Toussaint Merle, to a dramatic transfiguration of Polidori's story. The end-result bore only a slight resemblance to the original, but helped nevertheless in its popularization. The villain's name was further transfigured in that version as Rutwen, presumably for much the same reasons that the Ladvocat version had altered it, establishing a distinction while preserving an obvious link.

The Porte Saint-Martin play, which premiered on June 13, 1820, was a sensational success, and prompted several exercises in imitation, including a similarly-titled melodrama by Pierre de la Fosse, an opera by Joseph Ramoux with music by Heinrich Marschner, and a whole series of parodies, the most notable of which was a "vaudeville" co-written by Eugène Scribe.[16] It helped to found a tradition of fantastic melodrama at the Porte-Saint-Martin, which proved so stubbornly enduring that when one of Merle's successors ran into trouble thirty years later, he commissioned Alexandre Dumas—who had been present at the first version's première and claimed in his autobiography to have seen Nodier being thrown out at the intermission for heckling—to write a new version of it. Dumas' Le Vampire [17]—which retains "Lord Ruthwen" but not much else from its predecessors—premièred in 1851, and helped to spark a further wave of interest in literary vampires in France.

Within this hectic context, the published version of Bérard's sequel seems a frail and muddled effort. Seen from a purely literary viewpoint, it undoubtedly deserves the oblivion into which it rapidly slipped. This is not surprising, as it must have been compiled in a tearing hurry; the bulk of the text consists of unrelated stories that Bérard must have composed previously, which were shoveled into the text to bulk it out, under the pretext of employing the "Galland method" of nesting stories within a frame, initially popularized by the French version of Les Mille et Une Nuits (1704-16) and much-imitated. The fact that two of the interpolated stories are unfinished—one of them falling well short of its foreshadowed denouement—presumably results from the fact that Bérard had previously abandoned them in that condition rather than from any innovative

---

[16] Included in *Lord Ruthven the Vampyre*, translated by Frank J. Morlock, Black Coat Press, ISBN 978-1-932983-10-4.
[17] Published as *The Return of Lord Ruthven*, translated by Frank J. Morlock, Black Coat Press, ISBN 978-1-932983-11-1.

literary daring. The introductory narrative and the sections that Bérard wrote to connect up his fragments into an apparent whole are merely a reprise of the fundamental narrative device of Polidori's story, whose further potential (which other subsequent writers proved to be abundant) went largely unexploited—especially in the extremely hurried conclusion, which is little more than a synopsis; it must surely have been composed in confrontation with an exceedingly tight deadline. It is not surprising that the optimistic promise of a sequel appended to the narrative went unfulfilled.

There is also no doubt, however, that one should not, and surely cannot now, look at Lord Ruthwen *purely from a literary viewpoint; it is more accurately and more interestingly seen as a minor, but crucial, element of a rapidly-grow edifice of revisionist mythology. Despite its literary faults—and, to some ex-tent, because of them—*Lord Ruthwen *is a fascinating text, and its publication in English fills an important gap in the history of vampire fiction, which has lately become interesting to a considerable number of readers and scholars. Its gaucherie provides remarkably clear evidence of the perceived difficulties facing writers of vampire fiction in the early 19th century, which are spelled out explicitly in Nodier's preliminary observations. Thanks to Polidori, Nodier and Bérard—and also, albeit indirectly, to Lord Byron—later writers had a pattern of established clichés to guide them in their efforts (or, of course, conscientiously to avoid) and to give them and their publishers confidence in the acceptability of such narratives. The underlying fascination of the notion was never in doubt, thanks to the abundant borrowing of materials from Dom Augustine Calmet's pioneering dissertation on the subject, published in 1746.*

Lord Ruthven/Ruthwen/Rutwen's most obvious illegitimate children include the penny-dreadful villain Varney the Vampyre *(1845-47), Marie Nizet's* Le Capitaine Vampire *(1879),[18] and, of course, Bram Stoker's* Dracula *(1897) as well as numerous lesser individuals. It was, however, Bérard's text, rather than Polidori's, that foreshadowed the other major thread of subsequent vampire fiction, featuring seductive female revenants, as popularized in Étienne Lamothe-Langon's* La Vampire, ou la Vierge de Hongrie *(1825),[19] Théophile Gautier's* "La Morte amoureuse" *(1836; tr. as "Clarimonde"), Victor-Alexis Ponson du Terrail's* La Baronne trépassée *(1852)[20] and Paul Féval's* La Vampire *(1856).[21]*

For all its faults, Lord Ruthwen *remains a significant stepping-stone in the evolution of the modern image of the vampire, and warrants translation and examination of that score.*

B.S.

---

[18] Included in this Volume.

[19] To be included in Volume 2.

[20] Published as *The Vampire and the Devil's Son*, translated by Brian Stableford, Black Coat Press, ISBN 978-1-932983-55-5.

[21] To be included in Volume 3.

It is perhaps essential, when one publishes a novel of this sort, to reply in advance to the inevitable objection of criticism by means of a frank confession. The story you are about to read belongs to the Romantic genre that is so obstinately, and perhaps justly, decried. The only justification that can be made in favor of the choice is that no novel was known to the ancients that could be considered as a classical model, and that Aristotle does not appear to have taken the trouble to trace the rules of this kind of composition.[22]

Even the name *novel*, suggestive of modern language, modern literature and a modern era of the imagination and sentiment, excludes the obligation of the servile imitation of antiquity that is the universal and absolute condition of beauty in all the arts.[23] We are, in fact, too far away from the naïve ideas of early eras to take pleasure in the pastoral amours of Longus's hero, as recounted in the delightful story of Daphnis and Chloe, who has lost his plausibility along with his models. Thanks to the improvement of our mores, the majority of ordinary readers of novels reject the cynical depictions of the most elegant imitators of Lucian or Petronius. If one of these genres has long ceased to be classical, because it has ceased to be true, and if the other has never been classical for honest

---

[22] Although more than one contemporary compiler of books of advice to writers has attempted to draw upon the structural analyses contained in Aristotle's *Poetics*, those analyses focus specifically on Greek drama. The only other narrative genre to which Aristotle paid any attention was epic poetry, which has no particular structure, being long on story and short on plot. As Nodier observes, there was no long prose fiction available to him, but it might be worth noting that there was a structurally-interesting genre of short fiction, comprising fables and apologues, which he ignored completely, perhaps because his great rival Plato, with whom Aristotle made it a point of principle to disagree, had made constructive use of apologues in *The Symposium* and *The Republic*—a stratagem that Aristotle was unwilling or unable to adopt.

[23] This statement reads more convincingly in English than French, because the English word "novel" really is suggestive of modernity, whereas the French *roman*—which can equally well be translated "romance"—is not. The term *roman* was, however, an adaptation of the term invented to describe Medieval romances, which were still see in early-19th century France as example of essentially "popular" fiction rather than "classical" literary models. Modern apologues, such as Voltaire's *contes philosophiques*, were also considered to be mimicking the popular form of the *conte* [folktale] rather than Platonic models, although attitudes might have been different had Aristotle included apologues in his analysis of literary practice.

folk because it has never been moral, it is necessary to seek another type for the modern novel in the present character of our civilization, and another source of aspiration in our most commonplace sentiments, our most pronounced passions and our most poetic superstitions.

Far be it from me to consider as a theme very favorable to the imagination and good taste those superstitions which, regretfully admitted by peoples, offer nothing to the intellect but scenes of terror. Such subjects doubtless ought only to be approached with timid sobriety. However, the frightful fable of vampirism could not avoid being consecrated in all the nations that are familiar with it in a few romantic tales. It is found in several episodes of the Arabian Nights. It has furnished lyrical elegies, the solemn horror of which is further augmented by the monotonous gravity of a bizarre rhythm, among the Slavs of the Adriatic islands. Finally, it has recently transfixed the attention of Europe in favor of a name that recommends all the writings to which it is attached: that of Lord Byron. Today, for the first time, it has furnished a developed composition to our literary medium.

That is perhaps enough, and the delicate circumspection that distinguishes the French mind necessarily advises our writers that they should be miserly with the future of this bold resource, useful at most in the arousal of a blasé sensitivity or to irritate a reluctant curiosity to sensation. I thought, nevertheless, when I was consulted on this subject that two motives, which excuse everything in France, will excuse the author's attempt. One is the merit of pertinence, the other that of a difficulty overcome. I have no doubt that the public will agree with me on another kind of merit this novel possesses, which is rarer and more estimable. I think I also recognize in it a great richness of imagination, a piquant variety of episodes, and a sustained elegance of style, and I regard my publisher's invitation to associate myself with its publication as a favor.

C.N.

Part One
The Story of Bettina and Léonti

I

Venice, the bold situation of which seems beyond human imagination, rises up as if by magic in the middle of the sea. Its celebrity dates from centuries already remote, and, redoubtable to all peoples, its far-traveling flag has long advertised to strange lands its respected naval power, the number of its seamen and the imposing memory of a glory that is no more.

Simultaneously menaced and protected by the waves of the Adriatic, which surrounds it on all sides, Venice presents to the astonished eye a frightful spectacle of severity. Not far from its lagoons, however, by virtue of a contrast that enchants the heart and the eye, hospitable woods embellish an ever-lovely nature linking the Lido to a few striking and delightfully cool areas of verdure.

It is on this fortunate isle that young Bettina lives. It is there, impatient with hope and love, that she awaits the lover for whose absence she has wept, and with whom she would like to be united forever.

It is midnight. The beautiful Italian sky, pure and starry, still brightens the environs of Venice. The moon outlines in the distance the majestic architecture of the Doge's palace, a precious monument of the Middle Ages, and its melancholy light strikes falls upon the gondoliers' huts. At the Lido, the dwelling of their chief is distinguished by its extent, and shines with a new gleam. Garlands of flowers suspended from the trees, set tables, elegantly-decorated boats moored on the shore, and various preparations all around, advertise an impending fête.

All is calm; everyone is asleep. Only a light wind troubles the silence of the nearby wood. The hour is conducive to sweet dreams and amorous mysteries.

A window opens. Bettina appears. Alone in the middle of the night, no fabric veils her charms. The linen that protects them without hiding them adds to her beauty. Her black hair, descending over her shoulders, augments the pallor of her face, giving all her features a more touching expression. Her abandoned bed calls to her in vain.

What grief has wrenched her from slumber? What sentiment is it that agitates her? Is it regret for a possession lost without hope of recovery, or the intoxication that precedes a long-desired happiness? A vague anxiety is painted in her eyes. Attentive, scarcely breathing, she gazes at the sea, which unfurls an unknown extent before her sight. Every slight sound fading away in the atmosphere—the toll of a solitary church-bell, the cry of a bird in the woods, the swell that rises and the wave that breaks—presents to her an image that charms her, a hope that excites her.

Suddenly, her bosom swells, her face colors and her voice resounds. With her eyes and gesture, she indicates a distant object that seems to be coming closer. She thinks she is seeing a floating boat. She thinks so, and already she is calling out to an adored lover. Vain illusion! It is an isolated rock, whose shadow, reproduced in the water, seems at first to be moving, but soon remains still.

Bettina recognizes her error, and her oppressed heart lets slip a sigh.

O surprise, though! A gentle harmony is heard. Who comes at this hour to repeat a song of love? Why hide? Is it a foreign lover? Is it Léonti? The wood hides him from Bettina's gaze. What a mystery! She listens. Alas, the voice is unfamiliar.

> Ah, what a pleasant delight,
> On a long voyage home one feels,
> As one's native shore shines bright;

The distant horizon reveals,
Parading before hopeful sight
The village church, whose bell peals.
For the impatient returnee
All is pleasure, all is glee.
Everything charms his avid soul
Every element enchants the whole
Every step sets his heart ablaze
And reminds him of youth's days:
Woodland flowers, the green field,
The tree, the hill, the sacred stone
Where his first homage was sealed
And his first farewell was a moan.
Bettina!

"O Heaven!" Bettina cries. "Léonti!"

Scarcely has this cry escaped her than everything—the song, the harmony—ceases; and like a dream, a vague sensory delirium whose transient illusion is destroyed by an awakening, everything has disappeared.

Bettina lends an ear again. Profound silence. Only an echo replies to her voice, and Léonti's name expires in the distance on the shore. It is not him, then. But who is this mysterious lover who has fled at the name of a preferred rival? Will he be generous enough not to make her repent of being imprudently betrayed by a single word, the indiscreet confession of a heart too full of the one it loves?

To deliver oneself to sentiments that it is necessary both to hide and feel; to develop a need for apprehension; to make a habit of constraint; to find an accustomed charm in painful dreams and a continual torment in one's most cherished affections; to be saddened by a gaze, made anxious by a smile; to betray oneself with a word, console oneself with a tear, and, on the point of obtaining a promised happiness, to experience every day, at every hour, at every moment, a thousand dreads troubling hope—such is the fate of women in a life that, agitated by long periods of grief and successes of short duration, passes rapidly, leaving no time for direction, and who, beginning with errors, escape ennui by means of memories, flee through the forgetfulness of others, and lose themselves in regret.

II

Bettina loved Léonti. Born on the same shore, they had spent their early years together. Their love was deceived by time and obstacles. A quarrel over unimportant interests, a rivalry of state, divided their families, once united by an amity that appeared to be proof against all the stormy events of life.

49

Soon, Léonti, refused by his beloved's father and deprived, while still young, of an adored mother, left the abode of his forefathers and sought a refuge from unhappiness in a military career. He hoped that glory might one day wipe away the tears of love, and that Torelli would accord to a defender of Venice that which an unjust hatred had made him refuse to a simple gondolier.

To vanquish that resistance, he also had powerful support from Bettina's mother. The good Verina cherished her daughter, and protected the two lovers, so it was to that tender mother that the young Venetian woman entrusted the care of her happiness—and her happiness was entirely dependent on becoming the wife of the man who, in opening her heart to love, had given birth to her first disquiet and decided the destiny of her life.

Léonti had already fought for the fatherland, and his regiment, having been recalled, had arrived a few days ago. He had announced his return to Venice and promised to appear at the gondoliers' fête. He knew that everything was prepared for the celebration, and that in the midst of various games, tumultuous scenes of gaiety and Venetian dances, he ought to be able to offer himself to his beloved's eyes and obtain a secret meeting with her.

That was the matter that absorbed all Bettina's thoughts.

Reason sleeps when love awakes. Torelli's daughter has told her secret to the infidel winds; she has confided her distress to the calm of the night; and her impatient vows have anticipated the dawn.

Finally, day breaks. The atmosphere is split by cries of joy. Its oar rapidly plied, a gondola prepared by skillful hands flies away from the shore. The repetitive barcarole mingles with the lively music of the guitar, whose docile strings leap beneath the hand that presses them, and the distant echo of the shore, like an imitative instrument, asserts yet again that the inspirational soil of Italy is the fatherland of melodious song.

Everywhere, the scene is animated. Everyone surrenders to joy. Bettina alone is pensive. Insensible to the homages that her elegant figure and adornment attract, to the cries of admiration that burst forth around her, she sees and hears nothing. She does not suspect that her distracted attitude embellishes her, that her melancholy distributes a new charm over her entire person; when she dances, her lightness and magical grace are applauded, but she does not notice. Meanwhile, her troubled eyes are moistened involuntarily; a tear falls, and betrays the secret of her sadness. One sole idea possesses her. The fête is wearing on, and Léonti has not arrived.

Suddenly, a stranger appears. His costume and aristocratic mannerisms reveal an elevated rank, but his distorted features and wild gaze give the lie to the tranquility that he is striving to manifest, and his furrowed brow gives evidence to all eyes that his life has been tormented by frightful chagrin. He is greeted with respectful urgency; he is asked what he wants.

He replies in these terms: "Fleeing the unwelcome tumult of cities, I have come to the shore where you dwell. I was wandering in your woods—a sweet shelter, a cool refuge—when joyful sounds suddenly struck my ears. Scenes of happiness exert an attraction upon me that I cannot resist. That is why I headed in this direction. Continue your games; I have no wish to disturb them."

Reassured by what he has said, the dancers begin again.

The stranger has noticed Bettina immediately. At the sight of her beauty, which has the freshness of a new flower, his face conserves its livid pallor but an interior fire had reddened his lips, and his smile is frightful. He approaches her, questions her interestedly, divines the cause of the anxiety of a heat unskillful in hiding its rapid impressions. He sympathizes with her, consoles her, offers her his help, and, effortlessly captures her confidence, which is too prompt to surrender to hasty concern and kind attention.

Heaven's most beautiful gift is innocence, but it is defenseless against the poisonous charm of seduction, and, like a flower of the fields beaten by the autumn wind, is permanently wilted in an instant.

Meanwhile, the feast continues. While the dancers are resting, a Tyrolean woman has come into their midst. She gives an account of her errant life, her success in foreign lands, and says that her magical art allows her to predict the future. Immediately, groups form around her.

People pretend to listen to these popular oracles indifferently, but such is the attraction of everything that is outside the common run and touches on the marvelous that, on the word of a vagabond fortune-teller, chatelaines and shepherdesses are equally afflicted by the chagrin with which an impure mouth threatens them, and rejoice in an uncertain happiness announced with confidence. In this way, credulity has often been seen to bring fear into a palace, and hope into a cottage.

The Tyrolean woman's pronouncements awaken amusement and interest, but no one dares to consult her at first. Her presence inspires a thousand secret projects in hopeless lovers and faithless spouses, and more than one young heart, fearful of losing that which it loves, would like to find in the confidence of a propitious fortune the imminent end of the anguish that torments it.

Skillful in reading the thoughts behind the gazes that strive to interrogate her, Elmoda is aware of the hope and read she inspires. She waves her mysterious wand in the air, composes her gestures, her expression and her voice, and launches into a prophetic improvisation:

"O you who surround me, listen to my songs.

"I speak to you of the prodigies of an art whose origin is lost in the traditions of ancient times. The stars consulted in the fields of Chaldea, the mysteries honored on the Egyptian shore and the famous oracles of Greece have revealed their redoubtable secrets to us.

"Messengers sent to this earth of exile, a supernatural power has appointed us the arbiters of human destiny.

"Peoples, address your prayers to us! Kings of the earth, bow down before our savant inspiration.

"Our predictions are infallible. They say to the prideful who triumph, hope for nothing more from fortune; to the weak, hope once more; to the virtuous, you shall remain pure and respected forever, if you remain forever neglected.

"We predict a glorious death to courage, inconstant slavery to beauty, abandonment to unhappiness, success to intrigue, disgrace to fidelity.

"All of you, who wish to know your fate, appear before me! My gaze will penetrate the utmost depths of your hearts."

Elmoda's song has ended. The gondolier remains motionless, the young lover has shivered, and the voice of roving oracles, which appeals for confidence in vain, has already spread fear around. But the attention of the Tyrolean sibyl has fixed itself upon the distinguished appearance of the stranger. She advances toward him.

"My lord," she says, "would you like to know your future? I will even tell you everything that has happened to you before today."

"No," the stranger replies, in a severe tone. Then, turning to Bettina, he adds: "Open that beautiful hand and hold it out, young woman. Why are you trembling?"

"You are greatly troubled, dear child. You're waiting for someone. It's a lover."

"A husband," said Torelli.

"What! Father..."

"He sang last night beneath your window. I heard him. He was born in the next village, but he spent his youth among us."

"What is his name?"

"Tomaso. I have promised him your hand, and I'm astonished that he has not come to the feast."

"He will come," the Tyrolean woman says to Bettina.

"Who?"

"The man you love."

Bettina replies with a sigh.

"Wait—your fate interests me. I want to penetrate the entire mystery."

Elmoda takes her magical pictures from her bosom then, on which various characters are traced; she shuffles them, consults them, demands complete silence, and continues her examination. Vivid emotion is painted in all her features. Her eyes have become wild, her hands tremble, her mouth quivers.

"Great God! I see..."

"What do you see?" several voices repeat.

"A misfortune; a frightful crime."

"Speak!"

"This young woman..."

"Bettina?"

"Yes—soon, Bettina is going to die!"

At these words, a cry emerges from the woods. A young soldier clears a path through the crowd, launches himself forward and addresses the Tyrolean woman: "Wretch! What do you dare to say…?"

It is Léonti.

An extreme pallor covers Bettina's face. Her strength abandons her.

"Yes," Elmoda continues, "her days are numbered. Her blood will be drained, drop by drop. Tremble for her, tremble, O you who surround me! Flee, all of you."

"Let us flee!"

"Know that a vampire…"

"O Heaven!" says Léonti. "A vampire! Is it possible? Speak, where is he, then?"

"He is on this shore, among you, in this very place and he is…"

"Stop, imprudent woman," says the stranger, fixing her with a terrible gaze. "Cease these impostures. It's money you want—here it is. Earn your living without predicting the death of others. Go away, or fear my wrath."

"O Bettina!" cries Léonti, beside himself, "my beloved Bettina, wake up. It's me—me, your lover—who is begging you, hugging you, covering you with tears. It's in vain that your life has been threatened. Who would dare, when I live to adore you and to defend you? Come, have no fear; believe in my love and my rage. Before anyone could reach you, my arm would be prompt to avenge you, and this sword, more rapid than an arrow that cleaves the air, would have plunged into the heart of the guilty party a thousand times."

Everyone has fled. Even the Tyrolean woman has run away. Torelli and Verina are chilled by fear. Bettina has recovered consciousness. Her astonishment is extreme. Her smile, on which unhappiness imprints a divine sweetness; her virginal brow, tinted by modesty; her embarrassment and the agitation it causes—everything within her testifies that she has no thought other than for the lover she adores, and the happiness of being close to him, in his arms. The rest seems to have been effaced from her memory. An alarmed mother is supporting her. Léonti reassures her, lavishing the most tender names upon her. Her hand trembles in his. Her father sees that, understands it, and his gaze has nothing severe in it.

"Come," says the stranger, then, "let's get away from this unwelcome crowd. Forget a vain terror. Are you unfamiliar with the audacity of these women, who, avid for a shameful wage, will stop at nothing to obtain it? Not daring to judge the present, which is easier to interrogate, they charge a future impenetrable to all eyes with the disorders of their delirious imagination. By that means they interest timid minds in their deceptive predictions. How credulous humans are! How passion leads them astray! What weakness there is in those creatures, so proud in prosperity and so abject, so pitiful, at the slightest dread of an anticipated reverse! Let us be careful of young Bettina's sensibility, however. Her heart is only too likely to receive sad impressions. Come, Torelli, let's go to your house. I know everything that interests you, and I want to offer you the advice of a friend."

And both of them, engaged in animated conversation, have soon traversed the distance that they have to travel.

At that moment, Léonti cannot help feeling a surge of jealousy and suspicion. The stranger worries him. Bettina hastens to dispel his suspicions. "He will be our protector," she says. "He promised me that. As you see, he's speaking to my father, whose agreement is today a happy anticipation—and if, by virtue of his concern, his pleas and the respect he inspires, he succeeds in uniting me with all that I love, I shall owe him more than life. O Léonti, dear object of all my desires! O Mother...!"

She can no longer speak. She is weeping. They are tears of sweet joy.

Poor Bettina! Her throbbing heart surrenders to the most delightful hope. Perhaps...

III

Bettina and Léonti arrive at Torelli's house. They take their places around a table set for the evening meal—and there, by means of his persuasive tongue, the stranger flatters the generosity of his host, encourages the two lovers, calms a mother's anxieties, and charms all his listeners.

But all Léonti's thoughts, to begin with, are devoted to the danger to be run by his dear Bettina, calmer now; he recalls the tumult that brought the feast to an end. Elmoda's last words are incessantly present in his mind, and a deadly presentiment pursues him, obsessing him in spite of himself. He tries to guess who the vampire that she wanted to identify might be.

The word vampire, in itself, causes a secret terror within him that he cannot get over. He is in doubt, unable to comprehend that men exist capable of all the horrors that are attributed to those monsters, invisible destroyers of a sex, the admirable ornament of life, whose weakness is already subjected to so many perils.

He questions the stranger, who smiles, and hastens to reply to him in a friendly manner.

"History," the stranger says, "in unfurling before our eyes the overthrow of empires and the revolutions of peoples, progresses through successive centuries surrounded by great truths and various fictions. The former are lessons that are forgotten, the latter fabulous depictions that delight, and are reproduced in different forms. There are errors dear to popular credulity, and which even contribute to the recreations of the elevated social classes. On harsh winter evenings, when snow falls in billows, rain in torrents, or storm-winds shake the forest trees, the weary woodcutter takes his rest by the unsteady light of a flickering fire; he scolds his young family, huddled around him by fear, and even he, listing avidly to a gripping tale, believes that he sees phantoms wandering in ruins, while merry lies alleviate the evening tedium of the château.

"For a long time it was believed that vampirism was a symbol of the perversity of men and the fatality associated with virtuous beings. All too often, the word offers images of ingratitude and corruption, overwhelming with their unexpected success the innocence that succumbs and the fidelity that moans in oblivion. It is said that men betrayed, unhappy in life, dying with vengeance in their hearts, return after their death to advertise their passage everywhere with bloody scenes. It is more consoling, however, to think that Heaven, limiting the number of these pitiless beings, has wanted to show them to the world in order to engrave more forcefully upon the hearts of other men a horror of crime and the sentiment of an eternal life, and, as divine bounty is reluctant to produce such monsters twice over, has permitted the same souls, recovering mortal coil, to reappear to desolate the earth.

"Strangers to remorse and pity, vampires choose for victims those creatures who are most charming in their delightful form, most interesting in their weakness, and most enchanting in their beauty. Like a woodland bird which, subjected to a spell that attracts it, and whose danger it cannot avoid, hops regretfully from branch to branch, unable to take flight as usual, advances involuntarily, halts, utters a dolorous cry, and finally falls in front of the reptile that swallows it, the woman soon falls prey to the vampire that follows her step by step."

"O Heaven!" said Léonti. "Can the Earth not be liberated from these monsters?"

"There are no certain signs by which they may be recognized, and, by virtue of a bizarrerie whose counterpart in not unexampled in society, they hide their perfidy beneath the most attractive exterior."

"So they do exist?"

"I am obliged to believe so," the stranger continued, "as you may judge by an event to which I was witness. I love traveling, and in order to vary my pleasures, I never return to countries that I have visited. Nothing gives greater extent to human conceptions than the renewed depiction of the character, mores and customs of peoples. Intellect grows by means of the comparison of so many various objects, and the fire of genius reignites to pain in broad stokes the romantic beauty spots of Provence, the cheerful landscapes of Italy, the arid soil of deserts and the icy climes of Moscow.

"I had been travelling in the vast empire of the Czars, and when, on my return, I passed through the ancient city of Koenigsberg, bathed by the green-tinted waters of the Spregel, the horizon revealed to my sight clouds that were confused with the immensity of the Baltic. That imposing sea, rival of the Adriatic, ever replete with sailors and bold navigators, opens its industrious ports to the riches of two worlds.

"After devoting a few days to examining all the precious produce acquired by the insatiable cupidity of humans, I continued on my way, and, skirting the shady banks of the Vistula, laid my observant eyes upon the fertile countryside of Poland. That beautiful province, so jealous of its liberty, is populated by involuntary agriculturalists who are born and die in servitude. Beside a hearth suspended on heaped stones, a crude edifice constructed by unskilled hands, the Pole, enveloped in a thick fur, seems more numbed by sloth than by the harsh cold of winter.

"Sparse châteaux, the only habitations open to hospitality, announce that opulence is the prerogative of powerful families, and oppression the law that an invincible necessity imposes on all the rest. In the season when frost covers the earth, a profound solitude reigns throughout the fields of Poland. Nature there seems to be a vast desert in which one only finds trees whitened by snow, a few vestiges of half-erased footprints, and he breath of the north wind, a mobile compass often replaced by a rising breeze. The traveler, wandering without a guide, interrogates these feeble indications of a road for whose races, lost beneath the ice, he searches in vain.

"It is then that the troublesome aspect of inhabited countries inspires the soul with fearful meditations. That bleakness extends all the way to the gates of Warsaw. There, everything changes: an immense city, floods of people spreading out in every direction, varied scenes and magnificent palaces astonish the gaze everywhere. Only the gaudy adornment of horses obedient to the reins that guide them advertises from afar the raid passage of sleighs disappearing over the snow that yields to their imperceptible effort, and the elegant Polish women, protected by a costume around which shines ermine whiter than the moving ground that they tread with their elegant feet, display their slender forms and charming faces to the enchanted eye...

"Forgive me if I paint with enthusiasm places in which my heart filled up with memories whose sweetness nothing can disturb, allowing me to forget the story that I was about to tell you.

"Obliged to leave Poland, I was already twenty miles from Warsaw; my carriage, having gone astray on the snow-covered roads, suddenly came to a halt. It was dark; the horses could go no further. The postillion pointed out a château and urged me to go seek shelter there. I decided to do so.

"A door stood ajar; I went in. No domestic servant appeared. I called out; there was no response. The château was inhabited, though; bright light illuminated an apartment perceptible in the distance through the trees in the grounds. I walked in that direction, not without some reluctance. The silence that surrounded me even inspired a little fear.

"Finally, I arrived, and found, next to an elegantly-laid table, a young woman of dazzling beauty, inanimate in an armchair. Head bowed, as if surprised by sleep, she had surrendered to an involuntary drowsiness. At first, everything confirmed that initial impression: four children were with her; one was covering her with caresses and weeping, two others were calling to her, and a girl scarcely out of childhood was trying to make them be quiet. She ran toward me as soon as she noticed me, and said to me with touching ingenuousness: 'Mama needs rest, Monsieur; she has wept so much today; don't wake her up—see, she's asleep.'

"Surprised by the scene before my eyes, I interrogated the girl. She replied: 'We were at supper; a friend of Mama's was with us. He spoke, Mama wept. He drew nearer to her—and, I don't know why, that nasty man frightened me! At last, he went away. Mama went pale, and wrote briefly on this piece of paper. Suddenly, she cried *Elisca!*—that's my name—and I ran to her knee. She looked at me, and her expression scared me—and then…that's when she went to sleep.'

"A sinister suspicion took hold of me then. I took the piece of paper from Elisca's hands. I read it. It contained a few lines traced with difficulty. I remember them. This is what they said: *The monster! I have given him hospitality. I am doomed. He has betrayed me. I loved him, and he has murdered me. I no longer have any but a vestige of life…my strength is exhausted. My blood has been drained. O my poor children! What will become of you? O Heaven, have pity! Elisca!*

"I examined the unfortunate mother. I tried to bring her round. Vain assistance! She was no longer alive. She had been the victim of a vampire."

"A vampire?" said Torelli.

"I saw him, in person."

"In person," added Léonti, quivering with anger.

"He came back, picked up the girl, who threw herself upon him to strike him with her feeble hands—and soon that pretty Elisca, the image of a nascent flower withered on its stem by a scorching wind, had ceased to live. I hastened to run away from that frightful spectacle."

"What!" cried Léonti. "You didn't bury a dagger in the villain's heart?"

"Impossible."

"It was at least necessary to hand him over to the law."

"I had a reason that I cannot tell you for treating him with less rigor," the stranger replied, smiling. "But it's getting late. Let's withdraw, young man. Goodnight, worthy Torelli. Until we meet again, charming Bettina."

IV

To what confused sentiments has all that he had seen and heard given birth in Léonti's soul! An involuntary sadness, the indication of an imminent unhappiness, throws him into a profound distress. He follows the stranger; he is close behind him—and the path they follow escapes his attention.

This time, as he draws away from Bettina, he experiences an inexplicable anxiety. His heart beats faster, especially at the moment when the gondola that is to take them to Venice quits the cherished shore of the Lido. An inexpressible anguish grips him.

The immense sea that offers itself to his sight in every direction; the calm of the night; perhaps even one of those fatal presentiments, the secret warnings of Heaven that import a sharp disturbance into the soul's depths, against which the human mind tries in vain to rebel—everything enhances and redoubles his misery. But then, by virtue of a contrast that is only too frequent in the foreground of life, a joyous prelude becomes audible beside him.

The boat is flying, scarcely skimming the water's surface, and the gondolier has already sung the chorus of a favorite barcarole of the young women of the Lido. Soon he sings.

"The standard of Venice calls you to distant shores. Depart, O gondolier! But forget not the fatherland where you were born for glory where you were loved for your good fortune. If fate betrays your courage, to console yourself, remember the beauty that mourns your absence; and, if you return victorious in battle, fear not to entrust your impatience to the fragile hull in which you must brave the waves of an angry sea. Hasten; you are awaited. A loving kiss will be your recompense. Then, O gondolier, lay your armor down on the shore, take up your guitar, and sing the song of happiness again."[24]

At these lines, which seem to describe perils and hopes that he has known himself, Léonti emerges from his profound reverie. He listens. The gondolier repeats his chorus, strikes the waves with his oar, and continues a song that Venetian suffrage has rendered popular.

"Young lover! Hymen has crowned your vows. The virginal face of your beloved is covered at the sight of you by the charm of a transient modesty. Hear its song of love. Elegant and pure, its voice mingles your name, which causes it to shiver, with the religious oath. The flowing wave is less gentle in its course, morning birdsong no more touching, and already it is done; Rosella is yours. Discreet in love, she loves you without saying so; fortunate spouse, she might yet love you more and tell you always. O gondolier, sing your happiness!"

That said, ceding of its own accord to repeated efforts, the gondola reaches the shore.

On setting foot on Venetian soil, Bettina's lover sighs, as his heart has not strength enough to throw off the vague sense of sadness by which he is overwhelmed. The stranger, who has not said a word since their departure from the Lido, and has shown himself equally insensible to Léonti's groans and the gondolier's songs, finally breaks his silence.

---

[24] It is not obvious why these lines are not rendered in rhyming verse like most of the other songs featured in the narrative. It may be that this is a literal translation of an actual Venetian ballad, or the lines might be a rough draft of a poem that Bérard had not yet formulated in rhyme.

"I am going to cause you distress," he said. "A friend sometimes has a painful duty to fulfill; you interest me, and I ought to tell you your fate."

"Speak," Léonti replied, swiftly. "I'm ready for anything."

The stranger went on: "Bettina's fainting fit, and the fear that a miserable adventuress was able to inspire in all minds, initially quieted the unjust resentment that Torelli bears against you, but he soon reverted to his original resolution. It was only by virtue of my advice and my strenuous insistence that he consented to protect his daughter's threatened health and receive you in is home. You have tasted a few moments of a happiness that only had the duration of a dream. Thus it is that, in the midst of the gnawing anxieties of a desperate situation, the slightest glimmer of a less frightful fate momentarily puts to sleep the pain that seems far away, but which will soon return, keener than before, never to leave us again. Such, at any rate, is the misfortune that threatens you. Abandon all hope. Torelli has asked me to tell you to respect the wishes of a father, and not to return again to the places where your mere presence is a source of anxiety."

"What?" said Léonti, sobbing. "Nothing can change his mind! Well, then I shall go away, Yes, I shall go away…but what am I saying? What will become of Bettina? I know her. She will die, and I shall be the cause." In a distraught tone, he cried: "No. no! I will not betray her. I will never abandon her!"

"Well," said the stranger, "in order not to be separated from her, you have only one means remaining."

"What is it? Hurry up and tell me.

"You will have to abduct her."

"Abduct her! Great God! But how, without help?"

"You shall have it."

"Without money?"

"Make use of mine."

"Overgenerous friend!"

"I offer you service in the army of Scotland. You shall leave with a letter to the general in command of it. He is a relative and friend of mine. He will see to your advancement."

"But what about my regiment—my colonel, who holds me in esteem and has taken me under his wing?"

"Your flight will be concealed."

"But my honor!"

"Honor! Frightful reverses have taught me to know men and judge events. One day, you will no longer be led astray by the errors of an ardent youth; then, you will learn, from the cruel experience that age will bring you, that honor, a vain word and a true phantom, is merely the illusion of a disguised pride. Think of your happiness, young man."

"If I can only dream of it by becoming culpable, I renounce it."

"So you're renouncing Bettina?"

"Renouncing Bettina? Impossible!"

"Sign this pledge, then."

"Give it to me; I'll surrender blindly to your advice."

"I'll take care of everything."

"You'll cover our flight?"

"A boat will be waiting for you on the shore."

"When?"

"Tomorrow, at daybreak."

"Agreed."

"Count on me."

"Goodbye!" said Léonti, in a stifled voice.

V

The hours of darkness pass by slowly, however. While Léonti is subject to the most intense agitation, Bettina, ignorant of the fate that awaited her on awakening, and worn out by the day's painful scenes, yields to the pressure of a deep sleep.

A pleasant dream stirs her senses delightfully and flatters her imagination, which offers her the seductive imminence of a future full of charm. Her happiness is assured. No more obstacles. Léonti is at her feet, intoxicated by love and joy. He calls her his dearly beloved, his adored wife. Her father leads her to the altar. The priest is about to marry them.

Suddenly, a violent tempest looms. The storm bursts, lightning flashes, thunder rumbles; the portico of the holy temple collapses; everything shatters into smithereens—and Bettina, knocked down, falls unconscious...

She awakes with a start. A stone has stuck her window. She gets up. A voice calls out to her: "I'm waiting for you in the wood."

She opens her heavy eyelids with difficulty, and looks out. There is no one to be seen.

Momentarily, she remains motionless with astonishment. "Is it real? Is it a dream prolonged by illusion? She collects herself. The noise that she heard was no chimera; she recognized Léonti's voice. The words *in the wood* are still echoing in her ears.

Her father is absent; the moment is propitious for going to the indicated spot. She hurriedly puts on her light clothes, but such is the force of the desire to please in women that, even in the midst of a thousand confused ideas, Léonti's young lover devotes some care to the elegant simplicity of her adornment. Her beautiful hair blows free in the morning breeze. A simple ribbon, a pledge of love, retains the charming curls at her neck, whiter than ermine.

She finally leaves, with a tremulous step, for the mysterious rendezvous.

She wandered for some time without finding Léonti. Finally, she perceived him in a sheltered spot close to the shore. He was pale and pensive, his stare, fixed upon the Adriatic, seemingly measuring its extent.

Bettina ran to him and said to him, as she drew near: "What's the matter, dear Léonti? How is it that on seeing me, your dispirited features are painted with anxiety?"

"Say impatience, O Bettina! Today, in a moment, I shall know whether you love me."

"Alas, how can you doubt it?" she replied, with the most passionate abandon and recklessness "Since my mouth has sworn an oath to belong to no one but Léonti, I have never had any other desire, hope or idol but him. In our absence, I have languished in regret, dried up in tears. The anger of a father, so many vows disdained, so many obstacles braved and chagrins suffered—nothing, dear Léonti, has been able, and nothing ever will be able, to stifle in my heart the love that dates back to the cradle of our life."

"Well, arm yourself with courage."

"The time of proofs is past. A kinder fate leaves us nothing to fear, and everything to hope for."

"Disillusion yourself."

"My father saw you here yesterday, without reluctance."

"He pretended to, at least."

"Perhaps he'll consent."

"According to his orders, I must never see you again."

"O Heaven! Who told you that?"

"The stranger."

"The stranger?"

"We must leave."

"Leave! You want to abandon me, Léonti?"

"You shall come with me."

"What are you daring to propose?"

"It's the only course that remains open to us."

"You love Bettina, and you want to dishonor her!"

"I want to save her."

"You claim to be saving me, and you give me the deadly advice to betray my family and my honor? Dear Léonti, I beg you to come back from your aberration. Think of the misfortune that would pursue us everywhere."

"I'm thinking only of Bettina. Everything is prepared for our flight."

"Our flight! No, no—don't expect that."

"Farewell, then."

"Léonti! Don't you recognize this voice any longer, which is so dear to you? You're going? You're running away? You're leaving me alone in this place?"

"You're weeping?"

"Ingrate, that I loved so much!"

"Oh, Bettina, don't try to turn me away from a necessary course. If I stayed, I would be an obstacle to your happiness."

"What are you daring to say?"

"I shall go. I shall flee to distant climes, and there, on the harsh summit of some distant rag, or beneath some uninhabited shelter, the sky alone will be witness to my unbearable dolor. Unfortunate in having loved you, and in admiring you still, more unfortunate in no longer being able to tell you so, devoid of fatherland and refuge, awaiting death without seeing around me a single friend on whose tears I can count, my cries will still seek you in the solitude of the desert; ever day my sighs will take flight toward you; my sad voice will name Bettina, and my tears…"

"Stop, Léonti…you're breaking my heart. My blood is already freezing in my veins. Take my hand…can you feel it? It's trembling…it's moist with cold sweat. Léonti! In the name of Heaven, have pity on me!"

"We must part."

"I shan't leave you."

"Come with me."

"I can't."

"Time is pressing; I'm going—goodbye."

"Oh, stay! Listen to a lover who adores you, who is begging you… Look at me, cruel man! I'm dying at your feet."

At that moment, the stranger arrives hurriedly, and informs the two lovers that he has just obtained a favorable promise from Torelli. He urges Léonti to take advantage of this fortunate change of mind.

"He's waiting for you," he adds. "Don't lose a second. We'll follow in your footsteps. Go on ahead—it's necessary. I'll bring your beloved Bettina along directly, to the arms of her father, who is already half-disposed to bend his will and yield to our combined entreaties."

Léonti does not give him time to finish. Animated by the sweetest hope, he leaves—flies—and has soon traversed the distance that separated him from the place where he expects to find the assurance of a happiness so long awaited.

VI

As Léonti comes to the threshold of Torelli's door he slows his pace. He listens. A troop of soldiers has assembled around he gondoliers. Torelli is questioning hem. They are asking for Léonti. He introduces himself.

"We've come to arrest you," he is told.

"Arrest me? Me?"

"You must come with us; those are our orders."

"But what have I done?" Léonti replies, rendered motionless by astonishment.

"You have betrayed Venice by deserting your flag to take service in the army of Scotland."

"What? How can this be? Who has told you that?" says Léonti, paralyzed.

This scene, which has already sown fear, is interrupted by a confused noise that suddenly erupts. A gondolier runs into their midst. Breathless, gripped by terror, he speaks disjointedly. All eyes are upon him.

"Friends," he says, "I've come to tell you...a frightful crime...my boat, launched from the shore...found an obstacle in its path... I looked—O shock! I saw...I'm still shivering in consequence...I saw...a corpse floating in the water...and I recognized the Tyrolean woman who declared at our fête that a vampire was among us!"

"God!" cried Léonti. "What suspicion! What a flash of enlightenment! The Tyrolean woman lifeless, my secret betrayed...yes, it's him! Torelli! Soldiers! Gondoliers! My friends! You shall know everything. Run that way. Search for Bettina and the guilty man. I tremble at the thought that there may no longer be time. Great God! What am I seeing?"

Whimpering, colorless, her hair in disarray, scarcely able to drag herself along, Bettina appears, like a spectre frightful to behold, making one final effort...

"Father! Léonti! Avenge me...the stranger...!"

She is unable to finish. The words expire on her lips. Her last sigh escapes her, and she falls at her mother's feet.

Despair and fury then take possession of every heart. A general cry rises up: "Where is the stranger?"

Léonti can no longer see or hear anything. He runs, ahead of everyone else. Like a furious lion impelled by a devouring hunger, he searches for his prey. Torelli and the gondoliers race after him. His agonized breast can only exhale cries of rage. His voice refuses the movements necessary to speech. He indicates by gestures which way they must go, which man that they must strike down.

They search everywhere. Vengeance inspires every face. A thousand arms are raised to punish the guilty. They hurry, they call out, they run to the shore, they arrive. Vain efforts! The stranger has disappeared.

Thus, happiness is neighbor to extreme misfortune. How often has seen the favorite of an opulent court, heaped with riches and honors, forget that the breath of adversity might cause the blade suspended above his head to fall? All-powerful in the palace of kings, he triumphs, and everyone flatters his vanity at first, everyone smiles at his ambitious vows; in the dizzying whirl of a favor that still seems to be rising and becoming more solid, he is able to dare everything—but at the very moment when he thinks himself secure from any downfall, disgrace arrives, shiny prestige dissipates like a thin vapor; friends, courtesans and protégés all flee with the master's favor; and then, from the steps of the throne, he is thrown into the last asylum of the guilty, astonished by his terrible fall; he is overwhelmed, devoid of hope and unable to understand how he has reached that ultimate degree of misfortune.

Such is Léonti's distress. He sheds no tears, the feeble relief of hearts brushed by a grief that will not last. Great pains are silent. When the entire body is gripped, all the senses suspended by a devouring evil, tears cannot find a way out; the eye is dry, the heart on fire, and a delirious fever absorbs the impulses of a sensibility that lacks the strength to burst forth.

Léonti was on the point of becoming the happiest of men, or at least he thought so, and death has snatched from his arms the woman he adored, the only creature attaching him to the earth. He feels that everything he loves has been betrayed, struck down, annihilated. It is all over for him.

It is ended; Bettina is no more. Her angelic head is resting on the bosom of a mother who wants to follow a beloved child to her last resting-place. To have all the pleasurable attractions, all the connecting virtues, to be beautiful, charming, in the flower of life...and to die! Vain regrets! A layer of sand will soon cover Léonti's young lover forever. She lived 15 spring times for innocence and love. A single instant sufficed to steal her away from this earth of exile. Thus shine and wither the flowers of the desert.

Léonti has no desire to survive his Bettina. His wild eyes are fixed upon her discolored corpse, which the expression of life and the animated charm of her beauty delighted for a brief interval. After the initial collapse into mute dolor, nature awakes again and his tears flow in abundance. He calls out to a lover who can no longer hear him, his strength exhausting itself in sobs; and, yielding to the violence of his despair, he falls unconscious while pronouncing Bettina's name.

He is carried into Torelli's house; the most generous care is lavished upon him. A few days pass; his condition deteriorates; a continual delirium pursues him. His youth, however, battles successfully against the fever that is consuming him. His weakness, and the derangement of his thoughts, gradually distancing themselves from a deadly memory, return him to a life that nearly escaped him. He is deaf to all consolation, though.

In vain, he is told about his colonel—who, told of his misfortune, has given him leave and freed him from his pledge to Scotland, which an unknown hand caused him to sign. Far from calming him, the generosity of the leader who had protected him reminds him of the stranger's treason. All his fury reviving, he shouts loudly for his weapons; he tries to get up, to fight a shadow that he thinks he can see in front of him.

A profound exhaustion immediately follows these impulses of a heart that no longer knows itself. Finally, time brings a calmness that becomes more favorable every day to the reason that is recovering its empire.

With health, Léonti finds a new energy. He wants to live in order to avenge his lover; the first desire he expresses is to see the wood, simultaneously so dear and so terrible, again. He drags himself to it, and everything there excites him, enchants him and drives him to despair.

It is there, at the foot of that solitary tree, that he received Bettina's first oaths; that her trembling hand squeezed his; that he swore in his turn to love no one but her; and that a kiss given by love and received by innocence, sealed the secret promise of their marriage—but alas, these trees, these shelters, discreet witnesses to the sweetest mysteries, have also played host to the efforts of crime. It is there too that Bettina, the victim of an abominable monster, perished in the flower of her youth!

What intoxicating memories, what frightful regrets, the same locations recall! Oh, how violently his heart beats! He comes and goes, stops, re-examines, strides forth—and, bewildered and beside himself, finally arrives at the extremity of the wood.

But then, what a spectacle strikes his eyes!

He sees a man sitting there, silhouetted against the places in front of him. This man, the clothes he wears, everything about him reminds him of the perfidious stranger, Bettina's murderer.

Léonti falls upon him with lightning rapidity, raising his arm to strike…

The stranger turns round. His face is unfamiliar; his eyes are moist with tears. Weeping, he looks at Léonti, whose wrath gives way to the compassion that grips him involuntarily.

"Young stranger," he says, in an emotional voice, "Forgive me. The state in which I see you dissipates an error to which your presence initially gave rise in my soul, tormented by a frightful dolor."

"Ah!" the stranger replies. "You're unhappy, as am I. Sit down beside me, and we shall both soften the bitterness of our regrets by telling one another our troubles."

Léonti feels the need to listen to a heart responsive to his own, and already, drawn together by an indefinable sympathy, they are yielding to the effusions of a consoling friendship.

When men born under the same skies, but adrift in foreign lands, who have never met before, encounter one another by chance so far from their paternal fields, a sudden emotion brings them together. The mannerisms, the clothing and the language of their fatherland makes them quiver, and each of them thinks that he has found a brother, a friend, a companion of his youth. In this way, a rapid interest unites two hearts crushed by misfortune.

Léonti, persuaded to speak first, relates the story of his love, so faithful and so unfortunate: his departure; his return to Venice; his dreads; his hopes; the stranger's perfidy; and Bettina's death.

At this final revelation of his story, his friend interrupts him with a cry that echoes in the distance.

"It's him!"

"What! You know him?"

"He's the author of all my misfortunes. Come, let's run after him. You know all of our enemy's crimes. Let's not risk losing precious time, and join forces to avenge ourselves."

"But, please explain!"

"Come on, I tell you, entrust yourself to a devoted friend. Let's go, without further delay."

This said, he forces Léonti to follow him.

A favorable wind pushes the boat that carries them, and soon, superb Venice, shrinking before their eyes, no longer presents itself as anything but a distant fugitive dot, which finally sinks into the water.

Part Two
The Pursuit of Lord Ruthwen

I

Lord Ruthwen, the mysterious man who hid his dreadful secret beneath the perfidious appearances of an amiability full of charm, had profited from an imperious opportunity to extract from the unfortunate Aubrey, his imprudent travelling companion, an oath to be silent for a year and a day regarding the crimes of which he had been the witness.

One recalls with terror that fatal oath, whose extraordinary empire enchained all of Aubrey's faculties, at the very moment when his sister, affianced to Lord Ruthwen in spite of him, became the victim of a silence that a supernatural power and the violence of his illness caused him to keep until the end.

Finally, destiny, which presides over everything and counts our moments, completed the union of all that the world offers of the most virtuous and most amiable with the sum of the most perverse and the most odious, and the day of the marriage, that primal day, so pure and sweet, the deceptive presage of a happiness that is believed to be eternal and which is of such short duration, that day full of life, was the unfortunate Georgina's tomb.

An extreme dolor had robbed Aubrey of the use of his senses for some time. The fear of those around him spread the news of his death everywhere, and yet, by an effort of nature, after a long lethargy, his pulse revived, his eyes opened, and the beating of his heart announced his return to life.

Vengeance was the first need that he experienced.

Scarcely back on his feet, he leaves London and launches himself on Lord Ruthwen's trail. He knows that the beautiful climate of Italy is the object of the desires and the goal of the travels of men to whom fortune permits these voluntary emigrations. A secret inspiration directs his search toward those smiling lands that he had already travelled in happier times.

He disembarks in Venice, and asks everywhere if anyone has seen him, if anyone knows Lord Ruthwen. Vain efforts! He can discover nothing. Then melancholy draws him to the shore of the Adriatic, and there, filled with a dolorous memory, inspired by the enchanting places that he admires, he inscribes on a piece of paper bathed with his tears the names of the places where he would like to be able to spend the rest of his life, with the beloved sister he will mourn forever.

It is in that situation that Léonti finds the inconsolable Aubrey. Their hearts understand one another at the first whimper of a dolor that has the same source. They leave, animated by the same sentiments, swearing never to part again.

Léonti's heart is too dolorously affected, however, and the loss he had just suffered is too recent to find relief in the distractions of the voyage. His sobs, his stifled sighs and his profound reveries all reveal the sickness tormenting him, and when his long-contained grief bursts forth with greater violence for the very effort he makes to hide it, Aubrey takes him in his arms, consoles him and weeps with him, and it is by sharing his troubles that he softens their bitterness.

When they left the Lido, the gondolier charged with carrying them to the next shore gazed at Léonti for a long time without daring to speak to him, but the grief of Bettina's lover made such a deep impression on him that, more than once, his hand released the oar, confiding the care of his vessel to the motionless sea. Finally, weary of maintaining silence, he said: "Léonti, all Venetians have mourned your misfortune. You deserve a better fate. Having served your fatherland, you ought to find recompense on our shores for the perils of war. Like you, I have served the standard of Venice, I have braved enemy fire, I have fought on the plain of Olmutz."[25]

"On the plain of Olmutz?" said Léonti.

"Yes," Nadoli continued, "and it was there, surrounded by enemies, that I was about to perish. Suddenly, a soldier arrived, saw my danger, and raced to my rescue."

"What are you saying? Speak—who was that soldier?"

"He wore the costume of our region, and when he appeared, he was alone."

"Alone?"

"By night."

"By night?"

"And, as quick as lightning, his first action was to stop the blade that was about to strike me and kill the enemy who was menacing me."

"What's that?"

---

[25] As the text will eventually specify, Olmutz (the German spelling of Olomouc) was the capital of Moravia, nowadays one of the Czech Republics. It is not obvious why Venetian troops would have been fighting there at the time when the story is set—which will also be specified eventually, although Bérard might not have had that date in mind at this stage of his story, given that it seems inconsistent with the temporal setting of the Polidori story to which this one is a sequel.

"Do you know that generous mortal? Is he dead, a victim of his own courage?"

"He lives—he is still breathing."

"Who is he?"

"It was me."

"O Heaven! What—that young soldier who, without knowing me, risked his life to save mine..."

"Was me."

"Who was immediately pursued, overwhelmed..."

"It was me!" Léonti repeated.

"Whom I attempted, unsuccessfully, to rescue..."

"It was me, I tell you!"

"And who, in his turn, struck by a mortal blow, fell dying at my feet?"

"It was me, in person."

"What about the wound he received?"

"Here it is!" said Léonti, explosively, uncovering his breast.

"Great God!" cried Nadoli, "It was you, Léonti?" And he fell at the feet of his rescuer.

Léonti lifted him up and hugged him in his arms. "Nadoli," he said, "since the death of Torelli's daughter, this is the first instant of consolation that I have found, perhaps the only one for which it was permissible for me to hope. Be happy in the places, ever loved and ever regretted, that I am leaving forever. I shall perish under a foreign sky. That is what destiny requires, which destroys the vain projects of human beings at its whim. Goodbye, then! Goodbye forever!"

At that moment, the vessel reached the shore. It was necessary to part.

Nadoli wanted to go with his savior. "Dispose of my life," he said, dissolving in tears. "Take it—it's yours."

Léonti did not have the strength to reply. He received the other's embraces, forbade him to follow him, and drew away—but in a voice interrupted by heart-rending sobs, in that tone which is so true and expressive that it produces a rapid and irresistible effect, with that cry from the heart whose vibration makes an immediate penetrating impact, resounds with so much force in the hearts of others, Nadoli still persisted.

"Friend! My benefactor! You to whom I owe my life, may Heaven preserve yours! Léonti! Farewell! Farewell!"

And the sea breeze continued to carry that farewell to Léonti, who was already far away.

II

Aubrey shakes his friend's hand sympathetically; the latter, able to understand that mute statement, replies with a tear. Nothing is purer, more consoling, than the memory of a generous action. For the benefactor, there is perhaps a reward greater than the benefit itself, which is the delightful emotion that it leaves behind.

They are soon far from the estates of Venice, however. Pursuing an enemy who always escapes them, they pass through many countries without pause.

In a happy situation, everything takes on a pleasing color for our observing eyes. We contemplate the inexhaustible beauties of nature ecstatically. A picturesque location, the slope of a hill, the summit of a mountain, the pure air one breathes there, an avalanche suspended over a precipice, an open space prolonged in a fleecy wood, a distant perspective fading away, the sun that, by virtue of a magical opposition, covers all the objects that interrupt its rays with a thousand shades of gold and azure, and darkens the shadows adjacent to its floods of light—all these scenes, which an immortal hand has placed in profusion in favorite climates, possess an admirable harmony that reanimates the delirium of poets, the inspiration of painters and the idle curiosity of travelers. But a man pursued by misfortune seems an exile on earth; the faculties of his imagination weaken. When his soul suffers, everything around him is sad. Respiring nothing but dolor, he obtains nothing from life save sensations whose diminished compass rends him insensible to everything that reproduces the distractions he rejects.

Such were the sentiments of Léonti and his friend. The marvels of nature had no attraction for them. If hazard led their path to a naïve scene of village love—a noisy troop of joyful harvesters, young men celebrating their return from labor and young women dancing in the green meadow to the music of guitars and amorous voices—far from pleasing Léonti, the variety of those happy groups, inspiring in their turn the gaiety that they inspired, further increased his sadness.

Aubrey, however, was impatient to go to Florence, where he was expected by a Neapolitan banker he had met during his earlier travels. Only a few leagues distant from that city, they were both hastening their pace in order to arrive there when a singular adventure forced them to stop at the first village through which they passed.

As they were approaching Roveredo their eyes were struck by bright light. The night was well advanced; the village, illuminated at all points by torches placed at close intervals, was dressed for a fête, and yet everything was dismal and silent; no singing could be heard.

That absence of melody, in a country where it seemed to be renewed at every step, was not a fortunate omen. Aubrey and Léonti went forward without daring to confide to one another the reason for their astonishment. As they entered the village, which seemed deserted at first, a cry of alarm emerged from a high window.

"There are two of them!" cried a voice—and these words, repeated, spread fear everywhere.

Long moans reply to them.

Aubrey stops, and tries to understand what might have caused the terror that their presence inspires. Léonti knocks at the door of a house that is more prominent than the rest. It does not open.

After further attempts to get in, he reverts to pleading. "We are two distraught travelers, whom misfortune has condemned to a voluntary exile. Grant us shelter for the night beneath your hospitable roof. Venice is my fatherland, and if storm winds cast your ship upon our shore, our urgent help would save you from the wreck. Why are you manifesting less generosity than us? Inhabitant of Roveredo, open your door to us."

After a long silence, someone appears at the window, and replies, in an uncertain voice: "Alas, take pity on us. One sole vampire suffices to put the whole village in turmoil, and there are two of you. Go away, or our wives and daughters will die of fright on seeing you."

"Vampires, us!" cries Aubrey, in astonishment. "You're mistaken. Far from resembling such monsters, we are in horror of them, as you are, and it's to liberate the earth from one of them that we have directed our path this way."

On this assurance, Rodogni hastens to come down and let them into his dwelling. In a vast, elegantly-decorated apartment, women gathered there tremble at the arrival of the two travelers, but soon, reassured by what the newcomers say, they recover from their fright, and Rodogni, yielding to Aubrey's entreaties, recounts the reason for their alarm.

"Two days ago," he says, "a vampire appeared in the village."

"Was he a foreigner?" asks Léonti.

"No," their host replies, "he was a native of this country. We knew him, and this is his story:

"Roberti, a poor farmer of the village, was the tenant of a domain that belonged to a rich Florentine. A poor harvest ruined him. He left for Florence and asked for help, which was refused. Forced to pay what he owed without delay, misery caused his health to deteriorate. When adversity weighs upon us, it seems that it overwhelms us with various disgraces at the same time, taking pleasure in draining the cup of bitterness to the dregs.

"In Roberti's absence, the modest field that his forefathers had worked was sold; his beloved wife died of grief, and a daughter, his sole consolation, was carried off by a foreign soldier. Driven to despair by so much misfortune, he came to request from his native soil a second helping of the wealth that was irredeemably lost, but found nothing but futile regrets. Fever took hold of him; his illness grew worse, and it did not take long to lead him to the grave.

"At this point, a prodigy commenced that still confounds me. Three days ago, Roberti was carried to the last resting-place of mortals, and the earth was already open to received him, when he leapt from his coffin, alive, and disappeared over our fields. At that unexpected apparition, the frightened priests covered their faces, the holy crucifix slipped from their hands, the religious torches went out, and the terrified women ran to spread the incredible news.

"That miraculous event gave rise to a thousand conjectures. Everyone knows that an incident much slighter than that one, unnoticed in a great city, rapidly acquires great importance in a village. In this remarkable circumstance, in my capacity as the local *podesta*,[26] I assembled the resident elite and, after having consulted the savants of all centuries and all places by way of my books, it was decided, with unanimous agreement, that Roberti, suddenly returned to life, was a vampire, whose return it was necessary to anticipate.

"The danger was imminent. He had been seen roaming around the neighborhood. I gave orders. The men were armed, the women ran to the church, where public prayers were said, but the precautions were in vain, alas. Yesterday, at ten o'clock in the evening, the vampire ran through the village. His passage has chilled everyone's courage, and at this moment, we're waiting tremulously for the fatal hour to chime."

Indeed, scarcely has Rodogni pronounced these words than a great tumult becomes audible outside, cries coming from all directions. Léonti and Aubrey, hidden on the threshold of the podesta's house, precipitate themselves after a phantom that flees before them. Then, however, the mysterious man stops, throwing off the black cloak that had covered him, and renders them motionless with surprise by responding to their threats with repeated bursts of immoderate laughter.

They hasten to take the pretended vampire to Rodogni's house, where, as soon as he comes in, everyone cries: "It's Antonio! That madman Antonio!"

From that moment on, fear gave way to the most lively gaiety.

The two travelers were unable to understand anything of what was happening around them. They demanded an explanation from Antonio himself, who promised to tell the story of his vampirism, and began thus:

"Everyone acquires in being born a character that ordinarily accords with his physiognomy. Mine is not sad, and I am even cheerful to the point of madness. It was assuredly to punish me that I was imprisoned in an accursed place where I only found people who became furious when I spoke and who wept when I laughed. They're insane, I know, and I pity them—but at the end of the day, their society was not to my taste.

"My prison displeased me to such an extent that, surprisingly enough, I began to become serious. I felt that if I became bored, I was doomed, and I looked out for a favorable opportunity to save myself. It presented itself. They had for-

---

[26] A *podesta* is a local official roughly equivalent to a French *maire*; like the latter term, its precise significance evolved along with changing patterns of administrative organization. There is no precise English equivalent, although the local squire would probably have held a vaguely similar position in the era in which the story appears to be set.

71

gotten to close a secret exit. I noticed it, and left—and here I am, free. But that wasn't the end of the matter. Once my escape was discovered, people would set out in my pursuit.

"What shall I do? I abandon myself to my star, which always guides me marvelously. I run toward this village. I encounter a chapel on my route. It is open. I go in. I was alone. I approach the altar, and in a coffin, which I am curious enough to open, I recognize...guess who? My friend Roberti. He was a good man, and I'm pleased to see him again—but while I'm looking at him, I hear noises at the chapel door, and make out torches. They're coming to fetch Roberti.

"My embarrassment is extreme. How can I get out without being seen? Fortunately, a mind like mine is fertile in expedients. An idea occurs to me, unique, singular and charming. I slide on top of the poor dead man and, thus hidden, allow myself to be carried away with him. You'll understand, however, that I have no desire to have myself buried alive.

"So, having arrived at the burial-ground, the funeral procession stops and deposits me on the ground; immediately, I say farewell to my friend, reach out my arms, take possession of his covering, stand up, and, as quick as lightning, escape through the crowd.

"Apparently, the people around me thought that the dead man had returned from the other world, for it was necessary to see them grow pale, turn their eyes away, utter screams and run away at top speed—truly, nothing could be funnier.

"The adventure was too amusing for me not to take pleasure in seeing it through to the end, and my plan was to come back every evening at the same time, to frighten the good souls of the village, who have courage, as you know, and have taken me for I don't know what. I was making my second nocturnal run when you stopped me. After that, let them say that I'm mad. You've heard me, and seen me—judge for yourselves."

Thus spoke Antonio. His return and his madness were soon known to all the inhabitants of Roveredo, and that ludicrous object of general terror then became an inexhaustible subject of merriment. He was taken back, by winding paths, to the accompaniment of musical instruments, to the place from which he had fled. Eulogies were delivered to the courage of the travelers who, more fatigued than satisfied by the adventure, got up at daybreak the following day and took the road to Florence again.

III

In the city, Aubrey found the Neapolitan banker to whom he had written, explaining the reason for his journey to Italy. The banker's name was Alberti. He made manifest to Aubrey the great pleasure that he obtained in seeing him again, and welcomed Léonti with the abandon, always so pleasurable, of an amity fortunate to be felt from the outset. He forced them to accept shelter in the house in which he was living, and there he said to Aubrey:

"I'm leaving for Naples tonight, on urgent business. The unfortunate Palmire, the daughter of Ganem Ali, a merchant from Bassora, who was entrusted to my care died yesterday in Florence. A few days ago, I still hoped to save her life, and even to make her happy. It was with that in mind that an English lord whom I met here, and whom I once saw with you, has gone to Naples to bring back the lover that she adored. Now that voyage is unnecessary, and I hope to arrive in time to prevent Lord Ruthwen from undertaking it."

At the name of Lord Ruthwen a sudden pallor covered Aubrey's face. Alberti perceived his agitation and asked him the reason for it. When learned of all the odious vampire's crimes, he urged the two friends to go with him of his own accord. Indeed, all three of them were animated by such a desire to lay their hands on the abominable Ruthwen that they traveled with extreme rapidity.

As soon as they arrived in Naples they carried out the most active search in all directions, but it was futile. No one had seen the man they described anywhere.

Alberti no longer had any doubt that Palmire had increased the number of the monster's victims, who brought despair and death everywhere he went, and always escaped human vengeance by flight. Aubrey and Léonti desiring to know what had befallen the young woman from Jerusalem, he promised to tell them the story in his summer residence, to which he invited them.

They had already passed through the city and reached the sea shore when an extraordinary scene attracted their attention. A young woman was being pursued by the people, and a boatman who had accompanied her was assuring everyone that she was a sorceress, of whom it was necessary to beware. He was complaining of not having received the price agreed between them for the journey.

Aubrey asked what he was owed and paid him. At the same time, confused cries announced that the pursuit was continuing. Léonti ran to protect the foreign woman; her clothing was reminiscent of the young women of Venice, and her pallor was extreme.

He launches himself forward, parts the crowd, and swears that he will defend her if there is any further insult to her misfortune. But what a surprise he has when, hearing a voice pronounce his name, he turns round and thinks he recognizes, in the young woman who is the object of the pursuit...

Great God! Bettina!

He calls to her, and runs after her—but the crowd has come between them, and she has disappeared.

Astonished by his confusion and distress, the people surround him, pressing upon him and interrogating him. Believing him to be in danger, Aubrey comes running, takes hold of him, and drags him away to a place where they can eventually converse in safety.

Léonti believes that he can still see the phantom that appeared to his eyes. "Yes, I saw her," he says. "It was really her!"

Aubrey, who is familiar with the causes of mental disorder, tries in vain to reassure him and attribute his fright to the delirium of a preoccupied imagination. Léonti persists in maintaining that he has seen Bettina. He wants to talk to the boatman.

"Where is he? Where does he come from? Has he come from Venice?"

To calm Léonti down, Aubrey sends people to search for the boatman, but he is not found; all that is learned is that the man, either by virtue of malice or superstition, had said that the young woman, having been dead for a brief interval, had returned to life and had set out in pursuit of her lover.

Aubrey smiles at the boatman's tale. He thinks he understands now why the people, whose credulity avidly adopts anything that is marvelous, had chased the young woman. He regrets not having seen her, in order to rescue her. "She's doubtless and unfortunate woman, prey to poverty," he adds, "or perhaps a victim of seduction and love."

Alberti confirms this opinion, with explanations that pique the curiosity of the two friends sharply.

"Almost all the inhabitants of our region," he says, "have a disorderly excitement in their ideas that makes them prefer the strongest emotion to the calm of rationality. Here, the head and the heart act with equal rapidity, and the sharper sentiments stifle belated reflection. The people are more turbulent and less civilized than anywhere else. They have all the faults that seem intrinsic to southern climes without possessing the qualities that temper their effervescence. They seek arousal, no matter by what means, and it's that need for continual agitation which inspires such a keen appetite for extraordinary events. I'm convinced that the entire scene about which we're talking has no other cause than a touching story that is well-known in Naples. It's the story of the white woman, which I shall tell you:

The Story of the White Woman

A Neapolitan lord, exiled from court by a sudden disgrace, had retired to a château some distance from the city. There, in isolation, forgetting vain worldly pleasures and the people who had done him an injustice, he brought up a son, the sole heir to his illustrious name and vast fortune.

To begin with, young Mancini divided his time between study and rural amusements, but soon, having reached an age at which the imagination becomes excited, the blood seethes, and the heart leaps and sinks in response to sensations for which it is avid, his ideas took a new direction. A vague desire for change led him to prefer hunting to other, less active, pleasures. He left the château every day at first light, fleeing an ennui that followed him everywhere, and was driven thus to the most distant fields.

It was during one of these excursions that he encountered a young woman of striking beauty. Maria had the simplicity and rural freshness that is the charming adornment of a shepherdess in the flower of youth. Her embarrassment, the uncertainty of her gait, the sound or her voice, and her anxiety on seeing Mancini, all gave her a grace more piquant than her beauty. Even her flaws made her more attractive. Such is nature; she is inimitable. The art that seeks to surprise her always goes over her head; ornamentation veils her secret, and one destroys her charm in seeking to embellish it.

The amorous Mancini was no longer alive, save when he was with Maria. He obtained her permission to see her, to talk to her and to listen to her every day, at agreed times. These times, always too long delayed, became Mancini's entire life. With what impatience the beating of his heart echoed the ticking of the clock that anticipated them!

Who has not known the violence of first love, and the intoxicating illusion of a happiness whose outcome, often distant and sometimes inaccessible, always seems so imminent? Alas, that happiness, whose disturbance is so sweet, is no longer recoverable in the storm of passions, the inconstancy that follows them and the frightful emptiness that they leave behind; like a distant impression that never leaves us, however, its sweet memory consoles our entire lives.

Mancini effortlessly seduced a simple heart open to love. Maria became a mother, and from then on, her lover was everything to her. She saw in him her first friend and last refuge. Poor Maria! She did not know that happiness flies far away from a woman who has given everything to love, at the very moment when it seems forever fixed beside her.

Mancini's father, however, anxious about his son's morning excursions and the change in his temperament, had him followed and his every step watched. He soon knew the secret of his love-affair with Maria. Alarmed by a liaison that was contrary to all his views, he hastened to remove his son from the dangerous solitude that had doomed him.

Taken to Naples, Mancini was initially watched so closely that he could not get away for a single day to see the victim of his seduction. Surrounded by distractions and fêtes, avid for pleasures that were new to him, he forgot Maria, and only a few months had gone by since his departure from the château when his marriage was arranged to the daughter of Duc Orlandi.

While the ingrate Mancini was entirely devoted to his new wife, what became of the unfortunate Maria? Astonished at no longer seeing him, she did not know how to explain his absence, but the heart is quick to forgive the object of its love; it exhausts all appearances and all flattering errors before believing it to be guilty.

Finally, a disquiet that grows by the hour illuminates and destroys ever-deceptive hope. No longer able to resist her pain, Maria goes in search of her lover. Her maternal tenderness awakens, already giving her the strength to withstand anything. She conceives the stratagem of introducing herself to the château without letting it be known what has brought her there.

She knocks. "Open up," she says. "Open up! I'm lost...unfortunate."

She hears nothing. Are the doors of the rich so difficult to open to the tears of the pleading poor?

She knocks again. The same silence. "What!" she continues, with a dolorous sigh. "Is there no one in the château who recognizes my voice and will respond? Open up! It's a little bread that I'm asking for—take pity on my poverty!"

Vain hope! Her touching plea dies away around her, and no one seems to have heard it.

In fact, the château was deserted. Maria did not know that.

She does not call out again. Mute now, her heart heavy with sighs, she goes away, weeping.

The next day, she returns, as night approaches. "This time," she says, "he will hear me; sleep has not yet rendered him insensible to my cries. Sleep! Can he sleep while I suffer, while I am close by, asking for him, calling to him in the name of the child of our love? No, he will hear me. May my song reach him with a reproach that I would be only too happy to forget in his arms. Let's try."

So saying, according to the habit of the region, she picks up the guitar suspended from her shoulder, and, tremulously, sings the melancholy refrain f a ballad that Mancini had taught her.

In the place where I lived in peace,
When the seducer set his stall,
I often, on my discreet fleece,
Repeated his flattering call.
He said: if a love that's entire
Gives rise to a thrill of delight,
A desire not matched by desire,
Is the source of a terrible blight.

At the sentiment newly laid bare,
My heart, swiftly eager to bloom,
Still young, was as yet unaware
That love might be coupled with gloom.
Alas, I found out on my own
That love does not always shine bright.
While my love persists, his has flown!
And the source of a terrible blight.

Already tremulous, cast out,
I must and dare not flee this place;

My sore heart is oppressed by doubt
And tears are flowing down my face.
He has abandoned me to pain!
Mortal, Mancini, is my plight,
To die without seeing my love again
Is the source of a terrible blight!

Her guitar ceased to vibrate. The profoundest silence reigned around her.

She listens again, and, her foot suspended, holds her breath. All is silent. No more hope. She falls, her guitar hits the ground, breaks, and echoes in the distance like a groan fading away in space.

Attracted by the noise, a stranger came running. He had come down from his carriage. It seemed that his assistance was futile. On arriving in Naples, he was told that Maria was dead.

That news spread rapidly through the city; it was the sole topic of conversation. Mancini unveiled its mystery. He ran in search of Maria, saw her lying at the foot of a tree, inundated her with his tears, and tried to recall her to life.

Belated promises! Superfluous efforts! His lover is lost to him.

In despair, by virtue of his culpable neglect and its cruel consequences, he did not hesitate to confide his keen anguish and remorse to a spouse worthy of him. Emilia consoled him, approved his decision to live in the château from which his father had removed him, to Maria's misfortune, and went with him, pronouncing these touching words:

"Weep for your lover, Mancini. Weep for her always. Your attachment, your belated but generous regret, moves me to greater affection. Love me as you love her. Have your child brought, and I shall teach him to cherish you. He is a stranger to our love, but I shall always have a smile for him."

Since then, they have lived at the château—and it is said that every year, on the same day, at the same hour, a white woman appears by night. When ten o'clock chimes, knocking is heard at the door. More than once, someone has tried to discover the secret of that mysterious apparition, but, by virtue of a bizarrerie that remains inexplicable, when all the people in the chateau, placed on different sides, watch out for the phantom's arrival, they hear knocking, but never see anyone—and the door quivers several times, without anyone being able to make out the cause.

A thousand rumors have run around concerning that extraordinary adventure. Some claim to have recognized Maria, others to have heard her asking for her child. Credulity, which feeds on chimeras, has rendered that version popular, and it is because of that memory that the young woman who appeared this morning in the public square caught the general attention.

Such is the story of the white woman.

The Pursuit of Lord Ruthwen
(continued)

IV

"The story of Maria, which links genuine misfortunes to scarcely-credible events," said Aubrey, "reminds me of another adventure that happened in Moravia. People worthy of trust have assured me that a young Moravian woman, betrayed by her lover, returned after her death to pursue him everywhere. If one can believe everything that is recounted, that would be the first example of a female vampire."

"Ah!" said Léonti, struck by what he had just heard. "If an incredible hazard has returned Bettina to life, it must be to reunite herself with me, to protect me and to put an end to my torments that she is following in my footsteps."

"I can see," his friend said to him, taking him in his arms, "that the scene we witnessed this morning is still tormenting your thoughts. That distressing image bore too close a relationship to your misfortunes. We must leave this place, which maintains painful memories. We'll leave for Rome tomorrow. There, masterpieces of art and an inspirational environment will astonish our imagination, and perhaps restore a necessary calm to our distress."

The following day they said farewell to Alberti, who made vain efforts to retain them.

During the journey, Léonti abandoned himself silently to his sad reveries. For a long time, Aubrey could not distract him therefrom. Finally, by the lure of a conversation that was both compassionate and witty, he brought to his friend's eyes a gleam of that hope which the unfortunate never lose, and succeeded in mingling a few gentle consolations with his sadness.

What power a true friend has over us, by virtue of his generous concern, his pleasant discourse, his honest emotion and the abandon which is its surest testimony! His persuasive eloquence penetrates to the depths of heart, doubles the joys that it experiences, ameliorates the pain that it shares, embellishing both—and that voice, always so dear, often lost to love, is never lost to friendship.

There was talk in Rome just then of a young Arab whom misfortunes unknown to everyone had exiled from his homeland. Nothing brings men together more than a conformity of character or situation. Aubrey and Léonti sought out Nadoor Ali. Chance brought them to share the same dwelling.

Accustomed to seeing one another, and wanting to be together, they formed a liaison that grew closer by the day, and soon, fleeing the unwelcome gaiety of all the travelers that curiosity of the study of the fine arts attract to the immortal city, they finally formed a permanent company.

Nadoor Ali was in the full bloom of youth; he had a noble bearing and a handsome face, and his stern expression, his tanned complexion and his sparkling eyes gave his entire physiognomy a remarkable character. His new friends did not take long to perceive that, like them, he was nursing the memory of a great misfortune.

Mutual confidences succeeded vague conversations of little interest. Once confidence was established, their tears flowed over the misfortunes of a love reduced to despair by the loss of an adored object, and soon a sigh, uttered by Léonti and repeated by Aubrey, interrogated the dolor of Nadoor Ali. He spoke about a young Greek woman, captive in Arabia, and promised to tell the story of her misfortunes.

A few days passed without the Arab seeming disposed to satisfy their curiosity, although his sadness had increased.

One day, while they were examining the masterpieces that were Michelangelo's legacy to the admiration of the centuries, they noticed a Roman woman in the crowd whose clothing advertised the opulence of an elevated status. The lady's eyes were fixed upon Nadoor Ali, and she never ceased looking at him. Aubrey noticed it, but what astonished him more was Nadoor Ali's indifference, his attention being entirely devoted to the admirable ornaments decorating a ceiling, all of which had been animated by the breath of genius.

The hour was late, though, and it was necessary to leave. The unknown woman, who was following them with her eyes, made a gesture, gave an order to a servant, and climbed up into a shiny litter. The procession drew away. The incident made Aubrey think that Nadoor Ali had some amorous intrigue in progress in Rome, but, not wanting to penetrate a secret that did not belong to him, he did not share his observations with anyone else.

Rome is full of superb monuments, but, surrounded only by a few historically celebrated mountains, its outskirts offer few shady places where the heat of the day may be avoided. In that hot climate, the moment when the cool of a fine evening begins is impatiently awaited. Immediately it declares itself, the countryside is covered with elegant costumes, and in the city, the artisan seated on the threshold of his dwelling, glad to escape his customary toil,[27] celebrates in melodious song the pure air that he breathes and the joy of living beneath the beautiful Italian sky.

O evening hour so dear to lovers, whose return has been hastened by desire, whose pleasures are sung by discreet voices!

After wandering on the Palatine Hill, the three friends direct their stroll toward the gilded waves of the Tiber. Halted on the illustrious banks by so many ancient memories, they contemplate the distant effects of the Sun, which, now only coloring the Earth feebly, still strikes the water with its dying fire, and seems to be disappearing regretfully as the shades of night approach.

---

[27] Bérard inserts a footnote here: *"Dolce far niente."* [Sweet idleness.]

Nadoor Ali is inspired by this imposing spectacle. "O Cymodora!" he cries. "I believe that I see you still amid the ruins of Athens, tuning your sonorous lyre to the roaring waves of the sea!"

This said, he stops, confused by having betrayed his secret in pronouncing the charming name of Cymodora.

Aubrey gazes at him compassionately, and with a touching plea invites him to pour out his desolate heart into the bosom of amity.

Nadoor Ali seems momentarily indecisive; then, sitting down between them, he wipes away a tear trickling down his cheek. He is about to speak, and Aubrey and Léonti are already lending him attentive ears, when they are interrupted by the rapid arrival of a charger, which sends a cloud of dust flying up before them.

A slave hands a letter to Nadoor Ali and, without saying a single word, spurs the flanks of his agile mount again—which, taking the road back to Rome, soon disappears from view.

Nadoor Ali is quick to consult his friends about the letter he has just received.

"It is necessary," he says, "that I tell you about my situation. It is embarrassing. Being more familiar with the customs of the country we are living in, perhaps you can give me some useful advice. I promise to follow it blindly; but before anything else, I owe you a few explanations regarding that which preceded today's event.

"I belong to one of the most celebrated families of the Orient. A terrible misfortune had exiled me from the shore of a homeland that I still regret. On my arrival in Rome, I was forced to yield to the insistences of the principal lords of the court of the Christian pontiff. I was present at fêtes from which might profound dolor ought to have banished me.

"At one of these numerous assemblies, surrounded by tumultuous pleasures, I became the object of universal curiosity, doubtless excited by my foreign appearance. A lady paid me flattering attentions. Hazard had placed me next to her. My sadness intrigued her. She interrogated me about my misfortunes. I seemed sensible to the testimony of her benevolence, but I avoided telling her secrets that I was obliged to keep. My reserve increased her desire to know me better. Before we parted, she pointed out her palace and exacted a promise from me that I would see her again.

"I was withdrawing from the noisy place where I had met her when a man came toward me and, in a fit of fury whose cause I found out too late, made it necessary for me to defend my life from his attack. I emerged victorious from the unfortunate duel. My attacker died in my arms, telling me that he was the lover of the Duchess d'A***.

"That adventure, whose consequences I deplored, fortified me even further in the decision I had made not to see the Roman woman again. The death of her lover made a great deal of noise at court. His family is powerful; it wanted to avenge him, but no one knew whose hand had struck him down, and the details that I had an interest in hiding. My safety was compromised. The slightest indiscretion would have doomed me. In order not to awaken my enemies' curiosity, I have lived since then in solitude, not confiding my grief and anxieties to anyone.

"I learned that the relatives of the nobleman who had succumbed to my blows were still making inquiries. Meanwhile, the Duchess—who had doubtless guessed the identity of the guilty party, far from naming me and delivering me to the pursuit of my enemies, has not ceased to give me proofs of a veritable interest. I do not know why, and can only think about everything that has happened to me. She was close to us yesterday, at the famous monument we visited, and this is what she has written to me..."

Nadoor Ali handed the letter to Aubrey then, who read it. It asked the young foreigner to go at a certain nocturnal hour to a certain place, from which a devoted messenger would take him to the palace, where he was expected.

The reading of this note gave rise to a lively debate between the three friends. Aubrey and Léonti asserted that the rendezvous, for which no reason was given, was a plot hatched by Nadoor Ali's enemies, and that, in a country where perfidy often sharpens the dagger of vengeance in the shadows, one would do better to consult prudence than a bravery surrounded by dangers devoid of honor.

"Oh well!" Nadoor Ali exclaimed, "If someone has designs on my life, I know how to defend myself against vile assassins."

"Friend," said Aubrey, "Yield to our wise advice, and leave to our experience the task of rendering the blows that are intended to strike you harmless. I shall go in your stead to tonight's rendezvous."

"No, said Léonti, "accustomed to the language of the country, I shall present myself on your behalf. I shall be able to thwart any criminal attempt."

"I cannot consent," The young Arab replied. "I cannot permit you to expose yourselves to dangers reserved for me."

The tone in which Nadoor Ali pronounces these words does not permit any further insistence on the generous offers that noble pride had made him refuse. Aubrey thus has recourse to trickery to protect him, in spite of himself, from the danger that threatened him. He obtains permission to accompany him.

An expressive glance makes Léonti understand that he is counting on him for the execution of a plan that they have to concoct without Nadoor Ali's knowledge.

V

Everything being thus arranged, they go to the determined spot that night. In accordance with a plan agreed with Aubrey, however, Léonti has preceded them. He arrives at the rendezvous first; alone, but armed, he has no fear, and, proud to be risking his life to save that of a friend, his courage is ready to brave the expected danger.

The hour chimes. A slave, enveloped in a large cloak, presents himself and whispers the name of Nadoor Ali. In response to that name, Léonti takes his hand and follows his guide, who opens a secret door, introduces him into a vast garden, and disappears.

Léonti advances through the somber clumps of trees. He listens; light footsteps seem to be coming from the side. He stops. A hand presses his; it is a woman's. Is this the presage of a mysterious joy? He reproaches himself then for having deprived his friend of a fortunate meeting in which his heart cannot take part. He allows himself to be led through thick foliage, discreetly confident of amorous pleasures that are about to be offered to him.

"O you," says a passionate voice, "whom my gaze has picked out, whom my heart has chosen, tell me whether yours is ready to share all that I have felt for you since he day I first saw you. Speak—say the word and I shall fly into your arms."

Léonti, forbidden this speech, does not know how to reply. Suddenly, a noise some distance away, like the rustle of a tunic, frightens he woman who has just spoke. She huddles against Léonti and, with a hand that she rapidly places over his mouth, bids him to be silent. She dare not even breathe...

A dry leaf on the ground has rustled again. There is no more doubt; someone is walking stealthily. The person comes nearer, and a voice is heard close at hand.

"Léonti," it says. "Léonti! You're forgetting Bettina."

"Great God!" Léonti cries, beside himself. "What have I heard? It's her! It's her voice! Where are you, then, Bettina?"

At these imprudent exclamations, a sudden agitation is manifest in the palace. Torches circulate on all sides. Léonti, left alone, does not know which way to go. He searches for the path by which he has come, and finds the initial exit— but, just as he is about to make his escape, he is reached by armed slaves who fall upon him.

He defends himself furiously; Aubrey and Nadoor Ali run to his aid. Blood runs. Two men from the palace fall, lifeless.

A dazzling light appears in the distance, already illuminating the battleground. The three friends flee, without separating, ever ready to repel a further attack, returning home at a precipitate pace.

They confide their situation to the proven loyalty of their host, who hastens to serve them. He tells them that the Duchess A*** is the niece of the most powerful and most vindictive cardinal in the court of Rome.[28] His haughty char-

---

[28] It is not impossible that "niece" is meant literally, but it is probably significant that the ostensibly-celibate cardinals of the Vatican conventionally introduced their mistresses and catamites as "nieces" and "nephews."

acter is well-known and feared. No one can hide for long from the pursuit of his authority. The slightest delay in fleeing will be fatal. He therefore urges them to leave, making the preparations himself, and darkness is still covering the Roman countryside with its somber veils when they take the road to the Duchy of Modena.

Their guide conducts them to the home of a friend of the generous Roman. They find a discreet hospitality there. In a house in the countryside, some distance from the city, an untroubled rest, embellished by the most assiduous care, soon dissipates their all-too-justified anxieties.

They did not realize at first, however, that Léonti had received a wound while defending himself. Nadoor Ali was the first to notice it. He offered Léonti the most affectionate reproaches, lavished the most urgent cares upon him, and made him promise not to go out until he was completely cured.

That adventure, in which they had run the same risks, made the bonds that already bound them together even tighter. Only Léonti seemed to conserve a memory that troubled his reason periodically.

Aubrey obtained a confession of these new anxieties. The apparition of Bettina in the palace garden pursued Léonti everywhere. He saw her by day, spoke to her by night. Nothing could dispel the idea that Bettina was alive, but the more he thought about it, the less he understood the impenetrable mystery. Finally, to clear up his doubts, he asked Aubrey to tell him the story of the young Moravian woman who had returned after her death to follow her lover everywhere.

"Calm down, dear Léonti," Aubrey replied, "I'll satisfy your curiosity. I still have the manuscript of the story you want to hear, and I'll read it to you:

The Story of the Young Moravian Woman

1

Moravia, which extends northwards as far as the fields of Bohemia and Silesia, is bordered on the southern side by the powerful Empire of which it is a tributary. Its fertile lands are irrigated by abundant waters whose springs escape the numerous mountains that traverse them, and which add their agrarian acreage to the rich agricultural terrains of the valleys—and the blue waves of the Morava flow through the superb Olmutz, the ancient capital of Moravia.

The celebrated family of Alberg, whose origins are lost in the night of time, shone with a merited brilliance in the first rank of the imperial nobility. The Albergs had been rendered famous by an uninterrupted sequence of outstanding services and glorious perils. Thus, proud of the rights acquired by the exploits that create heroes and the virtues that cause them to be cherished, they wished to transmit their long-historic name, pure and respected, through future ages. *Sacrifice life to honor* was their motto.

There remained of that illustrious house two brothers—who, being valiant in war, sustained the glory of their ancestors—and a young princess, a model of grace and beauty.

Elzine lived in the castle of her forefathers in Moravia. Some time before, her two brothers had come back to her, but, impatient to hear the call to battle, they longed for its imminent return. To forget the ennui of a time of rest they found difficult to tolerate, they hosted tournaments that brought together the elite of Moravian knighthood. Elzine did the honors of these festivals with that delightful generosity which, indulgent to all, welcoming to glowing happiness but more occupied with the suffering of the unfortunate, wins gratitude and does not allow complaint to make itself heard.

Already, though, Elzine is seeking solitude. Wearied by homages, alone with Athalise, her closest friend and the confidante of her most cherished secrets—the generous Athalise, whose devotion to her is absolute—Elzine releases the tears that must be hidden from the suspicious pride of her brothers.

Soon, war is declared. The order has arrived to leave without delay.

"Sister," says the younger Alberg, on departure, "Called, as we are, to sustain the honored name of our house, you must live in retreat during our absence. Do not permit any impure suspicion to arise as to the virtue of Elzine. Remember that, for a young beauty, honor is the flower of life. If Fate betrays the success of our arms, you will learn that our amity has foreseen everything and forgotten nothing. Farewell, Sister…"

"Farewell!" repeated one of Alberg's followers, a young cavalier, his voice low and his eyes moist with tears. "Farewell, Elzine! Think of our love and the unknown pledges, so dear, that I leave behind me."

They are already far away, and that discreet voice still echoes dolorously in Elzine's heart as she falls into the arms of her dear Athalise.

Taken to her apartment, Elzine wants to hide from all eyes. She forbids everyone to approach the isolated dwelling that she has chosen. There, her tears flow in abundance. She bathes her bed in them, and covers her friend's bosom with them. Athalise weeps with her, consoles her, and lavishes the most tender caresses upon her, but cannot restore calm to that tormented soul.

"Oh, Athalise, dear Athalise!" says Elzine, "I'm dying. You alone remain to me for support is the most cruel distress. What can I do? What will become of me? O Heaven, take pity on me!"

A fever breaks out. Her condition deteriorates. Midnight chimes. The part of the castle in which she resides is deserted. The darkness favors a bold plan.

Athalise leaves. Alone, without witnesses, she shivers in fear. Her foot trembles at the slightest rustle of the foliage that she brushes in the darkness, but perhaps, by means of her mysterious withdrawal, she might save her friend. A woman's heart, weak in its own suffering, is animated by a divine courage and a sublime devotion in the service of unhappy individuals whom she loves.

The day after that cruel night, Athalise does not appear at the castle at all. The anxious Elzine counts the hours and, the minutes. A thousand obstacles loom up in her sad thoughts. The happiness of her entire life, perhaps her life itself, depends on the dangerous secret of a step that everything obliges her to hide and that nothing must betray.

Finally, rapid familiar footfalls are heard. The door opens; it is Athalise. Her assured gaze and soft smile announce good news. She has succeeded.

Elzine hugs her affectionately for a long time, and her expressive silence speaks to her friend's heart.

A few months have gone by, however, and Elzine is lamenting having received no news of the army when a courier arrives at the castle in all haste and hands her a letter.

"Go back to Elzine's brothers," Athalise says to the messenger, "and tell them that their long silence and the dangers of war have alarmed her tenderness and brought her to the state in which you see her. Their prompt return would restore her health."

The messenger leaves. Elzine breaks the seal and reads, in a tremulous voice:

Dear Elzine,
Success has crowned our arms. We have lost warriors dear to our friendship, but a glorious peace is the prize of our exploits. We shall arrive at the castle tomorrow with the governor of Moravia, who wants to see you. Prepare to show him all the pleasure that the honor he accords to us causes us to experience.
Until tomorrow, Sister
Eric von Alberg

"Do you understand, Athalise? *We have lost warriors dear to our friendship*, my brother says. Here, read it—I'm trembling."

"Don't worry," says Athalise. "War harvest warriors, but Fate sometimes spares the life of the object of our dearest desires, and you should not yield to cruel alarms in advance."

"Oh," the princess replies, "How can I hide my distress from my brothers' eyes?"

"You must—be brave."

"And why is Prince Adalbert coming?"

"He wants to see you."

"To see me! What does he want? I don't know why, Athalise, but everything is frightening me and tormenting me."

The next day, the castle fills up with riders. A cavalry troop precedes the arrival of the governor. Elvine has mustered all her strength to hide her sadness and greet her brothers.

They arrive, and fly into Elzine's arms—but she searches for the eyes of a cavalier that she could not see. She dare not interrogate any of those around her.

"Brother," she finally says to Eric, "I've been in fear for your life. You've triumphed, and I thank Heaven for that, but if you're to be believed, your friendship has suffered costly losses."

"Yes, Sister," says Alberg, "victory often costs the victors more tears than the vanquished."

"What about Fernand, your companion in arms?"

"Alas!"

"He had saved your life in battle."

"He was my faithful friend; I regret his loss; I weep for him."

"He's dead!" says Elzine, leaning on Athalise for support.

"He died gloriously, with your name on his lips...he was so devoted to our family."

"Fernand is dead!" Elzine repeats, her voice faltering.

"Such is the destiny of arms," Alberg adds.

At that moment, the governor arrives.

"Sister," says Eric, "here is the prince." He addresses himself to the governor and adds: "Please excuse her—the dangers that we have run have drained her strength, and her affection for us renders her even dearer."

"And more beautiful," says Athalise, looking at Elzine.

Elzine retires to her apartments. Even her brothers, alarmed by her pallor, demand that she avoids the fatigues of a fête. The governor watches her withdraw, regretfully, and expresses the sentiment so tenderly that Elzine is troubled by it—but everyone is mistaken about the reason for her emotion.

2

Elzine's fears were all too well-founded. Her brothers had been dreaming for a long time of providing her with a husband worthy of her and their ambition. They had spoken about it to their friend the prince, and his visit to the castle had no other purpose.

Adalbert had often heard eulogies sung to Elzine. As soon as he saw her, he found her beauty above its renown, and that same day he declared his desire to marry her. The Albergs gave him their word, and immediately warned Elzine to prepare herself for a marriage that would fulfill all their desires.

What reply could she make to brothers driven solely by ambition? What resistance could she mount to desires that were unshared, but which no obstacle could block? What confession could she make?

Obedience was the only course remaining to Elzine; with a heart heavy with regret and eyes filled with tears, she pledged a heart lost to happiness at the altar.

Her extreme depression, on a day when everyone ought to smile at her vows, however, troubled Adalbert's love. Hastening to take her to his palace in Olmutz, he was prodigal with all the pleasures of his court in order to please Elzine—but nothing could distract her from her profound sadness.

The prince attributed this constant melancholy to the reserve of a young beauty brought up in solitude, and soon, happier with an adored wife, he obtained a son from her, who was named Oscar.

Athalise had gone with her friend, but the governor tried in vain to keep her at court. She always refused to leave a delightful house, not far from the city, in which she resided. It was in that charming retreat, embellished by Elzine's friendship, that Athalise lived happily, bringing up with extreme care a young girl named Thelemy, who always accompanied her on her visits to the palace.

Oscar and Thelemy were nearly the same age. They grew up and became handsome together. Oscar was lively and turbulent, but generous and quick to repair any harm that he did. Thelemy, always mild and affectionate, seemed resigned to suffering.

Thus innate character announces itself and develops within us.

In the midst of their games, vain pleasures of an age unknown to others and to itself, the young prince, born to command, already wanted to direct everything. At the slightest resistance he lost control and demolished the inconstant edifices that had cost their impatient hands so much effort, but an amiable sensitivity followed close on the heels of his anger. He would fly immediately into Thelemy's arms, embrace her, console her, and swear that he would be good henceforth, and obey her. Thelemy would weep and say, with a touching expression: "How unhappy I am!"

Alas, this childish cry, uttered in a grief as slight as the object that had produced it, would perhaps one day by the only one that her heart would be able to repeat.

Thus pass the early moments of life, scarcely felt, as quickly forgotten; thus fly those happy years when, so close to nascent passions and so far from the anticipation of their storms, one enjoys a tranquility that, soon lost, never returns, and which one always regrets.

Thelemy had reached the charming age at which everything seems beautiful to our eyes. Every spring caused more grace to blossom within her. The friendship, so naïve and so pure, that had bound her to Oscar thus far, was a sentiment that became more tender by the day, and the need to feel it had given rise to the desire to hide it.

For his part, Oscar, more timid in approaching Thelemy, could not account for the new anxiety that he was experiencing. Both of them were increasingly silent, and more reserved. Apart, they made a thousand plans with regard to everything to say to one another, but together, they dared not speak. Forced to see one another more rarely, they desired it more, and it was then that, escaping from the customary effusiveness of childhood, the delirious recklessness of the heart, they yielded innocently to all the charms of a danger still unknown but ready to explode.

A ball given at the court informed them that a tumultuous love had replaced their ingenuous confidence. Thelemy appeared there with all the attractions of youth, making no effort to please and pleasing everyone. She was the object of all desires, the subject of all flattering remarks. Beautiful without wanting to appear so, she danced as nimbly as a woodland shepherdess; her grace was delightful.

Oscar was moved and enchanted. At each cry of admiration she excited, he shivered visibly, and when Thelemy was praised, one might have thought that the praise was addressed to him, so much did it flatter his love. In the midst of the varied groups in which everyone delivered themselves to the pleasure of animated dancing, however, every time that a strange hand clasped the hand of his beloved, he went pale and red by turns—and if he tried to form some steps with her himself, the desire that he had to please her augmented his embarrassment.

Thus, perpetually agitated by the hoped of being loved by her, and even more by the dread of not being, the young and charming Oscar forgot all his advantages. He became the most timid of men, because he was the most amorous of them.

O trouble of the senses, delirium of the heart; vague desires, such sweet torments, the delights of first love—what pleasures are yours! It is then that life is no more than the most beautiful of dreams. Why can it not last forever?

Meanwhile, Athalise, whose health was deteriorating by the day, was too weak to come to the palace. Elzine often went to console and look after her.

The young prince is tormented by not seeing Thelemy. No longer able to resist his anxiety, he begs and pleads, and convinces his mother to send him to Athalise's house.

He soon traverses the distance separating him from his young friend. The first thing that he sees is Thelemy, occupied in embroidering a scarf. Nonplussed by his arrival, and unable to find words to express her surprise, she gets up anxiously—and that embarrassment, the indication of a love that is betraying itself, gives rise to suspicions in the jealous Oscar that he still dare not allow to burst forth. His gaze speaks for him, though.

After a momentary silence he says: "I can see that my presence is troubling you—I'm being indiscreet."

"Indiscreet!" says Thelemy. "You? Why?"

"That scarf…"

"What's the matter?"

"That charming scarf is for a cavalier?"

"Yes, Oscar, it's for a cavalier."

"He loves you?"

"I think so."

"And you love him?"

Thelemy remains silent, and sighs.

"Ah!" says Oscar, with a resentful gesture. "If only I'd known!"

"Stop, prince, and don't insult your friend. Wounding jealousy is a senti-ment unworthy of both of us."

"Forgive me, forgive me, Thelemy! I dread not being loved by you."

"Oh, my God, do you hear him? He says that I do not love him! Can one ever forget one's first friend?"

"Your first friend—yes, that I am; but is friendship, dear Thelemy, still sufficient to our desires? Oh, I feel…"

"Speak."

"I love you like a sister!"

"I cherish you like a brother!"

"I'd like to see you all the time, at every moment, everywhere."

"I'd like that too."

"When I see you…"

"When you appear…"

"At first, my heart stops."

"Mine stops at the very sight of you; and then…"

"And then…it beats forcefully!"

"Dear Oscar!"

"Thelemy!"

A soft silence succeeds this animated scene, but the most tender confession is close to betraying them.

"Thelemy," Oscar continues, "I'm going away."

"You're leaving?"

"Tonight, for the army. My father commands it."

"O Heaven! For the army! You're going to risk the life that is so dear to me!"

"In three days I'll be able to come back to you."

"You promise?"

"I swear it."

"Oh well! Wait…take this scarf. I made it for you. Let it be your adorn-ment. Look under this pleat—it's your name. Read it: *For Oscar*. That's the cavalier for whom it was destined."

"Ah!" says Oscar, enchanted. "Permit my joy…"

Thelemy escapes from his arms, crying: "Don't forget Thelemy."

"Me? Forget her? Never! Never!" the prince repeats to his beloved, who is already no longer able to hear him.

Proud to bear that cherished scarf, he thinks himself invincible. He runs precipitately, arrives at the palace, goes back and forth, returns a hundred times over to the places dear to his earliest memories. He roams the beloved woods of his childhood. He sees the ancient chapel in which his heart, virginal still, made the first oath of love; and the solitary spinney, the discreet shelter of a happiness without alarm; and the white rose, her favorite, the simple ornament of a bosom more charming than the flower that adorns it; and the hospitable tree whose inconstant bark changes, reproduces itself, changes again, and still conserves the imprint of his amorous carving. Everything softens his heart, everything charms him, everything speaks to his excited soul.

Clad in his armor and decked with his scarf, however, he has had his father's orders; he has to leave for the army. He leaves. Already, though, more impatient for love than glory, he is dreaming about the moment of his return.

3

Athalise does not get better. Thelemy answers an order from Elzine, who wants to speak to her. She goes into the vast gardens of the palace, and advances at a slow pace through the places that were once so animated, but seem deserted now. Oscar is no longer there. An involuntary charm draws her toward an orange tree, her favorite, for which her young hands cared. Surprise! A piece of paper is suspended from a branch. She runs forward nimbly, grabs hold of the mysterious note, opens it tremulously, and reads:

Love for her!
To see her, to love her, to be loved by her,
That is my desire.
I think of her always, and everywhere.
I love her so much! She is so beautiful
That I repeat, night and day:
Love for her!
Love!

Faithful friend,
I always knew that she was beautiful.
Jealous lover,
Soon I shall make sweeter vows.
Is friendship sufficient to her heart?
When one repeats, night and day:
Love for her!
Love!

Love for her!
Is a charming cry, worthy of her,
It comes from the heart.
Far from her enchanting gaze,
I wait, I seek, I call to her,
And I repeat, night and day:

90

Love for her! Love![29]

She re-reads that the tender confession, which Oscar has written down but did not dare to pronounce, a thousand times over. Radiant with joy, she appears before Elzine, who says to her: "You're bringing me good news."

"Alas, no," Thelemy replies, blushing. "Know the cause of the contentment that you were able to read immediately upon my face: every time I arrived in the palace, where I spent the happiest days of my life, I cannot resist an emotion to which everything gives rise. These places recall so many sweet memories! Everything here pleases me, I love everything here...even the air that one breathes here."

"Go on, Thelemy, seeing and hearing you, I experience a particular pleasure! But tell me...in the midst of all these objects that flatter your eyes here, awaking your memories and interesting your heart, do you not sense any desire that attracts you and leads you to me?"

"I'm Athalise's daughter."

"Athalise's daughter!" Elzine replies, sadly.

"You're my mother's friend. That title is very dear to me, it inspires respect for you, and keen gratitude..."

"And nothing more?"

"The rest is for my mother."

"For your mother, Thelemy! And for me?"

"I don't have...I can't have the same love for you."

"Stop, Thelemy—you're breaking my heart."

"Forgive me, Madame..."

"Dear child!" Elzine went on, in an emotional voice. "So you love Athalise very much?"

"Who would not love a mother? A mother gives us life, opens our infancy, protects our first steps, dries our first tears, glories in our happiness. Her love follows us everywhere. She never abandons us...what's the matter, Madame? I see that you're growing pale and weeping."

"Continue, Thelemy—speak, speak again, go on speaking. I cannot weary of the sight of you, your speech, your sentiments. I love you too...perhaps I love you much more than I can tell you. So, then, Athalise?"

"Her condition still alarms my affection."

"May Heaven spare us such a misfortune—but in the end, if you lost her..."

"Oh, don't give me that cruel dread."

---

[29] As with most of the other verses that the author improvises, this one has a rhyme-scheme, but I have not attempted to reproduce it, because it cannot be done without too much injury to the meaning of the words—which is, in this instance, of paramount importance.

"What if she went away?"

"Her! Go away from me! Impossible. She would not want to. I would follow her anywhere. A mother never leaves her child."

"Cruel Thelemy," said Elzine, dissolving in tears. "No, you don't know, perhaps you'll never know, the harm you're doing to my heart. Listen. Sometimes, a mother is forced to leave her child. A misfortune, a terrible misfortune, powerful reasons…what can I say? In life, there are terrible, inexplicable situations of which you know nothing, as yet. A mother seems to abandon the child of her love. She swallows her tears, hides her sighs, and often…the victim of a rigorous duty, there where her cherished daughter lives, in the same place…close to her, in her arms…although all her senses are stirred, her soul excited, her heart broken by grief suffered in silence…even then, she cannot show…no one must see in her smile anything but a feigned indifference, anything in her eyes but a hidden sadness, anything in her face but a cold insensibility. Dear Thelemy, mourn for a mother forced to leave her child; pity her, weep for her. She is surely guilty, but she is even more unhappy. She languishes, she suffers; her heart might betray her; she is dead to life. Oh, my daughter…"

"You're upset, Madame. I don't know why, but I can see by your tears that you have much to lament."

"Of yes, much to lament—but at present, your voice consoles me."

"It will always console you."

"Always!"

"At least, I hope so. If you wanted to, you could take my mother's place, and be my mother too."

"Oh! What do you mean? Speak!"

"I love Oscar."

"I know that. Friendship binds you together."

"Friendship! No, it's much more now. Like me, Oscar also loves me, and it's…"

"Go on."

"Love."

"Wretched girl!"

"Great God, Madame, your expression makes me tremble. Listen to me—I haven't done anything wrong. It's Oscar who wants it. I haven't seduced him—but, seduced like him, I love him! Oh, I love him as much as my heart can love. My desires are pure, and if I could be his friend, his lover, his wife…"

"You! Oscar's wife! Impossible!"

"Alas, I know that. Oscar is a powerful prince. His mother reigns in a palace; mine lives on her charity. Me, I'm nothing…very little…I'm Athalise's daughter."

"Go away, Thelemy. I need to be alone. Let this secret remain between us. Renounce your love. Don't love Oscar any longer. I forbid you to. Don't come to the palace again. One day, I'll tell you…you'll know everything. Don't distress yourself. Embrace your friend. Go on, leave—return to Athalise's house, I tell you...but no, I'll come to see you, to console you. Goodbye! Goodbye...!"

Poor mother! Her sobs cut short her speech. She hugs Thelemy, makes a gesture bidding her to leave, and hides her tear-flooded face in her hands, repeating in a heart-rending voice: "How unhappy I am! My God! My God, have pity on me...!"

Confused and nonplussed, Thelemy goes away, weeping.

Already, though, Oscar has returned. He arrives, animated by the sweetest hope, and the first object that is offered to his eyes in the garden through which he is moving rapidly is the desolate Thelemy.

"Stop," he says. "Why these tears? They increase at my approach. You're not answering me, Thelemy—hurry up and speak, speak...explain yourself. I demand it, I command it...I beg you..."

"Oscar, we cannot see one another again. This is the last time."

"What a thing to say!"

"You mother..."

"Well?"

"Has forbidden me to love you. Our union is impossible. There is too great a distance between us."

"Dispel your fears; trust yourself to my faith. I shall see, speak to and convince my mother. She will be unable to resist my stern insistence. She will hear the voice of a son she loves, the prayer of a lover who adores you. She will unite us, I dare to assure you. Look, can you see her through the window of her apartment? Tender mother! She's following us with her eyes. She's looking at us with love; she's weeping. She's recognized me; she's calling me. Can you hear? Come on, Thelemy, let's run to throw ourselves at her feet."

So saying, he dragged Thelemy away. She made vain efforts to oppose him, but he heard nothing more. He had but one desire, one hope, one idea.

He fell at Elzine's feet, and presented Thelemy to her. "Mother," he said, "here is the friend of my childhood, the companion of my life, the wife that my heart has chosen. Consent to our happiness."

"Oscar, my darling son! Give up this madness!"

"Allow us to marry."

"Marry—you! What are you asking? Never! Never!"

"Well then, dread my despair. One more refusal, and I shall expire before your eyes."

"Stop, Oscar, I implore you! I'm trembling. You're forcing my hand. Know, then what the invincible obstacle is that is opposed to your desire: Thelemy is your sister."

"I'm Oscar's sister"

"Who, me? Thelemy's brother!"

"Yes, I'm your mother—both of you. My children! I've said it! I had to, to prevent a frightful crime. The terrible secret is out. Guard it well. My life, my honor and yours, everything depends on your silence. Athalise, that generous friend who has taken care of Thelemy...but nearby.... A noise...O Heaven! It's my husband! All is lost."

"Guards!" the governor cries. "Get rid of this young woman. You, Harold, take my son to his apartment. I confide him to your zeal. You'll answer to me for him with your head."

"Guards!" Oscar says. "Don't touch her—or fear my wrath!"

Elzine is carried to her bed, dying.

Adalbert has gone. Informed of his son's arrival, he was coming to see him when, as he approached Elzine's apartment, the discussion he overheard stopped him in his tracks. Struck by surprise on hearing it, he redoubled is attention. It was thus that chance disclosed a secret that a necessary prudence had rendered impenetrable for so many years.

What will the governor do now? The pride of rank, his betrayed trust, the mystery so long protected—everything irritates his troubled mind, and stifles the generous instincts in his soul. He can do anything, but already his sole desire is to abuse his authority. Retiring to his study, he thinks of nothing but plans of vengeance. He gives the strictest orders and refuses to yield to the pleas of Elzine, who wants to see him, to speak to him before dying.

Oscar learns of his mother's danger; a faithful friend has given him the sad news. His father has ordered him to remain in his apartment in vain. He seizes the sword of the guard who tries to retain him and threatens to strike anyone imprudent enough to dare to oppose his passage. The young prince, animated by anger and filial love, is allowed free passage; no one stops him. He runs to Elzine's apartment and open the door.

What a scene! Women in tears, a dismal silence, and his mother dying!

Elzine offers him her hand and points heavenwards. "Dear Oscar," she says, in a faint voice, "We shall see one another again in another world. It's the end; I'm going to die. Your father didn't want to hear my justification with my last sigh. You shall plead my cause with him. Oh, my son, come here, I can feel you still squeezing my icy hand. Receive my last embrace. Watch over the fate of Athalise and Thelemy... Farewell, Oscar, my dear Oscar! Remember your mother..."

Her eyes close and her voice expires on her lips while pronouncing Thelemy's name.

Oscar's despair is impossible to describe. The loss of a mother is one of those misfortunes that, absorbing all the strength of grief, leaves nothing for its expression. Oscar sometimes busts into jerky sobs, and sometimes, motionless next to the inanimate Elzine, his fixed stare considers her with that frightful calm, that stupor, which is the sign of a profound depression.

Finally, his sensibility awakes; he is drawn away from the apparatus of death that surrounds him. Furiously, he cuts through the tumultuous waves of people assembled in front of the palace, and shouts loud demands for someone to save his benefactress. Elzine is dead to them, but she still lives on in the unhappiness that he has consoled.

Oscar arrives at Athalise's house; he finds no more than debris. Frightened by what he sees, he cannot believe his eyes. He asks questions. He learns that an order by the governor, published several days before, has caused the house to be demolished, that Athalise and Thelemy have been banished forever from Moravia, and that no one was able to help them without incurring the prince's ill-favor.

Crushed, deaf to all that he hears, he no longer knows what will become of him, which way to turn. He advances at hazard along any road that offers itself to him. He questions everyone he meets in his passage, and hastens to pursue his search in order to save his mother's friend and his beloved sister, if there is still time.

4

Meanwhile, having been thrown out of their home, Athalise and Thelemy are fleeing before the guards who are pursuing them. Wandering, abandoned by Heaven and human beings alike, without shelter, without friends, they drag themselves along the road of exile, whose extent makes their hearts quail in advance.

Athalise, barely recovered from a painful illness, feels her strength ebbing away with every passing moment. Her soul alone still sustains her, showing itself superior to adversity. She has doomed herself for her friend. That idea gives her the courage to bear her suffering. The misfortune that degrades and humiliates timid characters revives the energy of nobler souls.

Thelemy, however, in despair at the prospect of so much misery, follows her adoptive mother in a flood of tears. "O God," she said, "the whole world has abandoned us. Look, all eyes turn away from us! People avoid us. Oscar too. Does he not know that I'm suffering?"

"You must forget him," Athalise replies.

"Forget him! When love is devouring me!"

"He's your brother, Thelemy."

"He only became so in my eyes a few days ago, and he was my friend, my lover since I first drew breath. Can the heart forget such a long happiness for a single moment of ill luck?"

"You're raving, my child—don't aggravate the torments of our situation. It's frightful, as you can see."

"O Heaven! Have you given me birth only for misfortune?"

"Calm down, I implore you," said Athalise, compassionately.

"Oh, it's only for you that I'm weeping."

"Dear child!"

"You have done everything for Thelemy."

"Be quiet! Silence, Thelemy!"

"I owe you everything. I owe you more than life, and it's me—me!—who will be the death of you!"

"Shut up! You're hurting me."

"You've never abandoned me! You weren't my mother, though, and the woman who was…"

"What are you saying? What complaint dare you make? Dear child, pain is causing your heart to sin. Don't blame your mother. You have only your own misfortune; she has two of them. One alone—yours—is the most horrible of all for her. Your mother cannot resist that. I know her. Perhaps, even at this very moment, on the brink of losing her life, she is blessing the child that is condemning her."

Thelemy utters a dolorous cry. "Mother! Forgive me, Mother! Forgive your wretched child. Kneel down, Athalise—let's pray for her!"

If a pure soul, a fervent prayer and religious tears please the God by whose command everything lives and everything suffers, the pleas of Athalise and Thelemy will reach him.

Two days pass thus. Already need is making itself felt.

"Let's stop," says Athalise. "I can't go on any longer. I'm cold, I'm thirsty…a little water!" And, as she pronounces these swords of distress, she collapses at the foot of a tree.

Thelemy realizes her friend's danger. Her exhausted body is reanimated. Her only thought is the desire to save her. She runs, searching everywhere for urgent assistance…perhaps the last. She would give her life to find a limpid stream, a spring, her only hope, her only refuge.

She advances into the fields, through brambles and stony gravel. Her delicate feet are bruised, but she feels no pain.

She covers a great deal of ground like that, but all her efforts are in vain. Finally, at the corner of a wood, beneath a solitary rock, she believes that she hears the gentle murmur of a cascade springing forth. She flies in that direction.

Clear water is sprinkling the greenery. She fills her two hands with it, and, breathlessly, covered with cold sweat, she hurries back to Athalise…

Great God! She is lying on the ground. Her head is tilted in the direction in which she saw Thelemy depart. Her lips are parted and seem to be repeating a final farewell. Thelemy thinks that she is unconscious.

She calls out. No reply.

"Athalise!" she says. "Wake up, dear friend, it's Thelemy! She's bring you life. Athalise! Can you hear me?"

All is silent. Thelemy is gripped by fear; the water escapes her hands. She takes Athalise in her arms, hugs her to her distraught bosom, inundates her with tears, and repeats her name in the most dolorous tone imaginable.

Oh, how heart-rending is the voice of Thelemy then! But vain efforts, alas! No more hope! Athalise will never see her again. Her breast is cold; her heart no longer beats beneath the hand of her desolate daughter; her eyes have closed forever.

Thelemy no longer has the strength to resist this final misfortune. She runs wildly along the road. A carriage goes by. She throws herself in front of the horses. The carriage stops. A stranger gets out. Thelemy does not speak, but her hand points to the object of her cruel distress. She drags the stranger, who studies Athalise attentively. Thelemy's eyes are fixed on the gaze of the protector that Heaven has sent her.

It does not take him long to perceive that all medical aid is futile. He pronounces death. Suddenly, Thelemy's colorless lips display a frightful smile. Her head swims. She babbles word that are the frightful indication of the onset of madness.

At that moment, Oscar, who has been following Thelemy's trail for a long time, perceives her from afar. He races toward her, shouting: "Thelemy! Thelemy! I've finally found you... O Heaven! What a state you're in! It's me, look—do you recognize me?"

Thelemy looks at him but no longer recognizes him. Oscar takes her in his arms; she loses consciousness there. While the stranger carries Athalise's body, the despairing young prince supports Thelemy. They climb into the carriage, and it draws away.

5

The stranger was Odolzi, a famous physician who devoted his universally-admired talents to the sufferings of humankind. In a château set in the foothills of a mountain chain, shaded by trees—an enchanting location favorable to the secrets of his art—he gave to poor wretches, whom unexpected disasters, various misfortunes and lost reason had exiled from the world, the most expert care, the precious fruit of profound study. In that dwelling, embellished on all sides by cheerful nature, dwelt insane individuals who had once been happy and envied; objects of pity now, though still full of life, they did not know that they had lived for a society by which they had been permanently forgotten.

A dolorous depiction of human destiny!

Alas, more than one woman, victim of an excessively heightened sensitivity, unjustly betrayed, still demanded from the mute echo of solitude the lost love of a lover still adored.

There it was that Thelemy was taken.

Oscar was inconsolable. He no longer wanted to leave Thelemy. He looked after her, followed her everywhere. More than once he whispered the sweet names of brother and sister in her ear, but Thelemy was insensible to everything he said. Nothing could extract her from her silent distress.

Several days passed, and Oscar's despair testified that he had lost all hope. Odolzi tried to bring some relief to his pain. "Come, prince," he said to him one day, Come and witness an interesting scene, which might perhaps momentarily restore the reason of the friend for whom you weep. There are few souls sufficiently lost to nature to be insensible to the effects of harmonious music. Various successful trials have already made me proud of a discovery by means of which a few days of genius may obtain surprising results. The future will complete what I have begun.

"In the frightful abandonment by others and themselves that the unfortunates to which I devote my cares are often found, dementia does not absorb all the faculties. The intelligence is dead, the reason absent, the mind asleep, but the soul is awake. There is a heart that lights up again at the first spark of a new sensation. Sentiment has a memory that is not lost. Love is the romance of life, and neither feels nor reasons in the passions of woman.

"Music, especially, exerts its active influence on tender souls. Who among is, in advancing through life, has not come across a song heard in a time already distant from us, but which recalls affections dear to our memory? The harmonious sound of a harp, the brisk sound of a guitar, a ballad sung in happier times by a woman we have loved…all these sensations reproduce themselves with a charm that penetrates us, seduces us, moves us. That is why melancholy songs soothe pain. Their softness restores calm to a heart tormented by a well-being irredeemably lost. You shall judge for yourself."

Immediately, a signal having been given, a shepherd appears on top of the mountain. An invisible music becomes audible. It is so delightful, so plaintive, that Oscar is moved by it, in spite of his somber sadness. The valley from which these delightful chords are coming seems to him to be a magical place.

Soon, Thelemy arrives. She climbs up the rock and, having reached the summit, sits down. Her crooked elbow is set on the rock and her abandoned head inclines toward the supportive arm. The shepherd begins to sing.

> Let laughter fade!
> Fair Elmire bade,
> Her shepherd swain.
> You dare complain
> Whene'er I sigh,
> And bid me try
> Love none but thee.
> All around me
> Declares, betrayed:
> Let laughter fade!
>
> Within the vales
> The echo hails:
> Let laughter fade!

The wave so pure
Cannot endure.
All form decays.
Cold winter slays,
The green leaf browns,
The wind discrowns
The woodland flower.
You see its power
Declares, betrayed:
Let laughter fade!

Within the vales,
The echo hails:
Let laughter fade!

My love, delight,
Look on, shine bright,
All once was charm,
His smile was warm.
There is no truth,
In dreams of youth.
Farewell, I say,
My flight away'
Declares, betrayed:
Let laughter fade!

Within the vales
The echo hails:
Let laughter fade!

"See!" says Odolzi. "Thelemy is getting up, asking for a harp. Let's move closer—but don't show yourself yet, and above all, don't interrupt. Let her give in to all that the music has just caused her to experience. Soon, perhaps, she might recognize you."

Transported by this hope, Oscar is obedient to Odolzi's advice. He hides behind her. Oh, how Thelemy's divine figure is outlined at the top of the mountain! What grace her touching melancholy gives her, with the pallor of her face, and her hair floating in the magical hand that causes the strings of the harp to quiver as they resonates in the wind!

Oscar admires her; he thinks he is looking at a celestial being, an angel inspired by Heaven.

"My dear Thelemy," says the physician, "what sentiment are you experiencing at this moment?"

"An illness that pleases me. My heart is on fire...my ideas are confused; but once I was very...exceedingly close to him. He loved me then! Now...I'm very unhappy!"

"Thelemy!" Oscar exclaims.

"Silence!" Odolzi says to him.

"Oh my God!" Thelemy continues. "I thought I heard...but no. I was mistaken. No more happiness for me! So I want to die, but I can't!"

"Do you want to weep forever, then?"

"To weep forever," she says.

"Calm yourself. Everyone here loves you."

"No, he doesn't love me anymore. He mustn't love me anymore."

"Why do you fear that?"

"Why, he asks! It's obvious that he doesn't know everything. Well, I'll tell you. Listen:

I still live on! Just now I said:
Weep forever, and never die!
Heaven wants me to live instead,
Farewell to joy, fine days goodbye.
They are no more, my tears I shed
For Oscar, and our love run dry.
I live on! And just now I said:
I'll weep forever, and never die!

I loved him so, my love's not fled!
But he was set to let me lie.
The ingrate thinks that I'm misled,
But I know him—I want to die.
I weep while wishing I were dead
For Oscar and our love run dry.
I still live on! Just now I said:
I'll weep forever, and never die!

I long to see him, hear his tread
But he'll no longer heed my cry.
My name was once his wine and bread
But now he wants to let me lie.
I'll always weep, despite my dread
For Oscar and our love run dry.
I still live on! Just now I said:
I'll weep forever, and never die!

How he loved me! "Until I'm dead,"

He said to me, "I'll ne'er deny
I'll always love your pretty head."
But then it was I had to cry
I'm crying still, more tears I'll shed
For Oscar and our love run dry.
I still live on! Just now I said:
I'll weep forever, and never die!

I was lovely, and he well-bred,
Our friendship easy to espy;
By equal example we were led,
No one doubted the reason why.
But you can see the tears I shed
For Oscar and our love run dry.
I still live on! Just now I said:
I'll weep forever, and never die!

Suddenly, all the good times fled
My mother told the reason why
He and I could never be wed.
Alone beneath the hostile sky,
Forgive me for the tears I shed
For Oscar and our love run dry.
I still live on! Just now I said:
I'll weep forever, and never die!

Devoid of kin, of blood dry-bled,
No brother's voice to say: "Don't cry."
No heart to call my heart inbred.
Unhappiness causes smiles to fly.
Alas, I dread the tears I shed
For Oscar and our love run dry.
I still live on! Just now I said:
I'll weep forever, and never die!

All life on earth moves on ahead
Let unkind fate my birth belie
Orphan me in my mother's bed
And o'er her tomb force me to sigh;
I'll not forswear the tears I shed
For Oscar and our love run dry.
I still live on! Just now I said:
I'll weep forever, and never die!

And thus it is, my fortune read,
Devoid of any human tie.
The love he owed me all has sped,
Wretched am I, the end is nigh,
And that is why my tears I shed
For Oscar and our love run dry.
I still live on! Just now I said:
I'll weep forever, and never die!

Thelemy's song has come to an end. Oscar reveals himself to her sight. He covers her hand with kisses and tears. "Dear Thelemy," he cries, "will you never recognize your brother?"

"You, my brother? Oh, if it were only true. But what are you saying, wretch? A brother, me? I have none. I have never had one." Then, in a whisper, she added: "Silence! Guard that terrible secret well. If anyone heard us, all would be lost. For the sake of my mother's honor, no one must know that I'm her daughter. Do you know it yourself?

I'm the child of her loving lie.
I still live on! Just now I said:
I'll weep forever, and never die!"

"Dear friend! My sister! You whom I love, whom I shall love forever, you recognized the voice of Oscar, then."

"Oscar! You? Oscar! Yes, it's him!"

After that cry, which echoes distantly in the valley, Thelemy runs away in terror, and the edge of the wood soon hides her from every gaze.

"Don't follow her, prince," says Odolzi. "Avoid the danger of prolonged overexcitement. She's too weak to sustain so many sensations are the same time. I'll send someone to find her; they'll bring her back to the château. Trust in my zeal, and be reassured."

Darkness fell. An hour earlier, various messages from the court had arrived. Prince Adalbert had discovered his son's retreat, and Harold had orders to bring him back, with Odolzi. Everyone was prepared to obey the governor.

Meanwhile, the search for Thelemy is in vain. She has not been found. She has not returned to the château. A horn is blown on the mountain. That signal brings everyone together. The search is resumed in the valley, in the forest and everywhere else. Thelemy does not appear. She does not reply to the voices that call her. There is no indication of the refuge she has chosen.

The night is exceedingly dark. Torches are shining everywhere. Guided by their distant light, they finally arrive at the bank of a torrent, and the first light of day revealed a clue that chilled all their frightened hearts. A veil floating above the waters of the torrent is hanging from a wild willow tree. It is the veil that Thelemy was wearing. This news is hurriedly conveyed to the château.

Odolzi orders silence to be maintained regarding a suspicion that time alone can clarify, and, in accordance with his advice, they take advantage of a profound slumber into which the prince had been plunged, by the fatigue of all the torments he has suffered, to transport him while still asleep.

The signal for departure is given. As rapid as the wind, the governor's chargers follow the road to Olmutz.

The Pursuit of Lord Ruthwen
(continued)

VI

Aubrey stopped speaking. His two friends had shed tears frequently during the story of the young Moravian woman's misfortunes. Nadoor Ali loved Oscar's character, sentiments and conduct, but Léonti had only been struck by the fate of Thelemy. He was still lending an attentive ear and seemed to be awaiting the end of an interrupted story. Aubrey remained silent.

"My friend," Léonti said to him then, "why stop at the moment of your story that is the most interesting to me? Tell us what became of Thelemy. All her links of existence and affection were broken. She was only bound to the world by misfortune. Betrayed in her hopes and detesting life, she ought to have died. But if it is true that the torrent had put an end to her troubles, what resemblance can she bear to the cruel man we are pursuing? You promised that, and that's what I want to know.

"A female vampire lover! My mind rejects an impossible horror. My friend, a woman is an enchanting creature. Ornamented with all the graces and beautified by all the generous sentiments, she is nature's masterpiece. Seductive by virtue of her beauty, more sympathetic by virtue of her weakness, always a victim, she yields to oppression and never oppressed. Forgetting the happiness she gives, she remembers only that which she receives, and her heart, which is so tender, replete with potential for loving, suffering and forgiving, has no impulse at all toward hatred, even less toward vengeance."

Aubrey resumed his story:

The Story of the Young Moravian Woman
(continued)

6

On returning to his father's palace, Oscar went over the story of Thelemy's flight into the forest a thousand times: the cruel night that had hidden her from all the searches; and, finally, the veil found at daybreak, still damp with the waters of the torrent. He did not doubt that those pitiless waters had swallowed the person who was for him both the most adored lover and the most cherished sister.

All the brilliant fêtes of the court, the splendor of a superlative rank and the perils surrounding glory could not distract him from his regret.

Time bears away all transient pleasures, but a profound anguish lives in memory, and, even in fleeing, it leaves a painful impression in the depths of the soul that is never effaced.

Several years went by. Oscar was still insensible to the desires of a thousand beauties desperate to please him—but the ever-increasing ambitions of power and the pride of a famous name made the governor of Moravia determined to choose a wife for his son. It was necessary to obey.

Already, everything is in preparation for the celebration of a royal wedding. The nuptial headband adorns the forehead of Princess Amélie. She is about to plight her troth. The altar is dressed. The hymn commences. Oscar pronounces the hymeneal vows...

Suddenly, the church door pens. A harp resonates. A voice sings:

I still live on! Just now I said:
I'll weep forever, and never die!"

And they see...

The Pursuit of Lord Ruthwen
(continued)

VII

"O Heaven!" Léonti cries.
"What's the matter?"
"It's her!"
"Who?"
"Bettina!"
"Yes," says Bettina, "it's me. It was me that you saw in Naples and heard in Rome, who had reappeared to your sight to tell you that the perfidious stranger is here, all-powerful in the court of Modena."
"Our enemy is in Modena?" says Aubrey.
"He is the prime minister, and calls himself Lord Seymour."
"Lord Seymour? Is that really his name?"
"It's the vampire, I tell you—I recognized him."
"Let's hasten to take our revenge."

"Stop!" Bettina adds. "The enterprise is difficult, let's undertake it with prudence. The moment has not yet come to carry our vengeance to its climax. The governor of the palace is the faithful friend of the prince, the Duke of Modena. He hates the insolent minister who is betraying his master's confidence. He has been forewarned of the important secret that I have just revealed, and I'm awaiting his orders."

"Dear Bettina," says Léonti, moved to tears, "is it really you that I see again? If this is not a dream, if you have returned to me, don't seek to flee once again from an unhappy man who loves you—remain with your lover."

"A religious vow forbids me that until the day of the vampire's death."

"But for mercy's sake, take pity my plight—explain to us the inconceivable mystery of your return. Tell us how, in what place and by what supernatural power you came back to live?"

In response, Bettina smiles and promises to tell that incredible story. She invites Nadoor Ali and Aubrey to sit down beside her, looks at Léonti lovingly, and begins in these terms:

"When, in haste to follow perfidious advice, and filled with the desire to persuade my father, you left me with the stranger, both of us, alas, being young and innocent, we did not know that crime often borrows the language of virtue, and that treason hides beneath the mild exterior of friendship.

"That odious stranger was the vampire announced by the prophecies of Elmoda. Having become his victim, I fell down dying on the sandy shore; but the desire to see you once more before leaving you forever reanimated my failing strength, and I dragged myself as far as the place where I heard the sound of your beloved voice. I saw you, my dear lover, and, less unhappy, my extinguished gaze was able to bid you a final farewell.

"Do you still remember that dolorous farewell...?

"But what was I saying? Whether animated by the rapid breath of divine inspiration, or by the burning of a love stronger than life, my heart outlived its faculties. Then, O Léonti, as I expired before your eyes, I did not believe that I was dying forever, and it seemed to me that my soul, as it escaped me, gave me the soothing reassurance that I would see you again.

"The lily and the white rose do not flourish in funereal fields. Their culture, beloved of Heaven, is only pleased to embellish the happy refuge of hope—and yet, their verdant stems were already beginning to rise up over my tomb, covered with a mother's tears and a lover's kisses, when, by means of a prodigy superior to the human mind, everything seemed to stir around me.

"I felt a fire in my veins that devoured me. My eyes shone in the profound gloom, my burning lips quivered, the quaking earth opened up, and like terrifying claps of thunder, these terrible words resounded in mid-air: 'Vampire woman! Emerge from the tomb!'

"I appeared then to a new life. At first, darting distressed glances around me, I saw nothing but dark scenes. I was alone, separated from other living beings, whom my presence chilled with fear. The moon, friend of our climes, was in its decline, and lit with its uncertain clarity a distant horizon that fled from my sight. The imposing calm of the night added to my mental confusion.

"I did not know what to do. My disordered thoughts only allowed me to comprehend a vague desire for vengeance. But on whom could I slake the blind fury that was making my blood boil? Who was the guilty party that I ought to punish, the enemy that I had to strike down?

"Forgive me, Léonti! I don't know what cruel divinity had upset all my senses, but of all the objects that I had known in my first life, I only remembered you, and this heart that had loved you so much—can you believe it?—this heart formed the barbaric project of driving you to despair. Yes, it was you, it was you that I wanted to pursue, and that is why, a docile plaything of an imperious, inexplicable, horrible destiny, Bettina chose for a victim the lover that she still adored.

"That frightful idea tormented my soul, however, and as soon as I had expelled all bitterness therefrom, a softer emotion calmed my bewildered senses, my tears flowed, my cries resounded, and my errant footsteps steered at hazard. There was a gondola close to the shore. I fell into it and, floating in the open sea, I abandoned myself to the divine influence that was guiding my involuntary movements.

"Dawn was breaking, coloring the surrounding mountains with its first fires. Everything came to life in the lovely valleys and the green hills. The morning laborers confided their hopes to the fertile ground. A pure and melodious song rose into the sky. Young women grouped on a river-bank shaded by trees replied to hymns repeated on the opposite bank. That sweet harmony, which rendered the majestic spectacle of the waters even more delightful, brought a delicious calm into my soul.

"In that intoxicating ecstasy, the first need I experienced was to offer my prayers to the author of nature. I was penetrated by that pious duty when a wood came in sight. I guided my boat to the shore and raced in the direction of a chapel consecrated to seafarers. My knees bent on the steps of a revered altar of a God whom misfortune never implores in vain—but at the very moment when my prayers were rising up to Heaven, I felt my eyelids becoming heavy, and involuntarily, a sudden drowsiness overtook my senses. It was then that a soothing dream gave me a glimpse of a happier destiny.

"A celestial angel appeared to me. I saw him. He was suspended in midair, an azure cloud sustaining his deployed wings, and his dazzling aureole announced the messenger of a powerful God. 'Young woman of the Lido,' he said, 'prayer has moved the Eternal. By virtue of a favor that can only emanate from divine grandeur, your soul, pure in its early days, will conserve its bounty in the new life that will open up before you. You shall not be the terror of mortals, like those monsters, the detested scourge of haven and humankind.

"'Woman, often misunderstood, always oppressed on the Earth of vain errors, proud of fulfilling a mission worthy of her, should only return here to be the terror of the guilty and the safeguard of virtuous lives. That is the will of the God you adore. Bettina, you will be destined henceforth to protect the object of our chaste love. Awaken and go forth; direct your steps eastward. Heaven will guide you, but you shall not be reunited forever with the lover you shall find again until the vampire whose victim you were is rendered to the earth of tombs, which will soon close upon him for all eternity. Promise to obey the celestial will.'

"'I swear!' I cried…and with those words, I woke up. My opened eyes searched the sky in vain for the images that sleep had presented to me. Palpitating and inspired, I left for the sea-shore. A boatman came in response to my voice. I ordered him to take me away. I don't know whether what I had just seen had imprinted a divine expression on all my features, but the dweller of the sea-shore looked at me in astonishment, and his boat, docile to the oar, immediately, fled over the water.

"During that journey, of whose duration I was unconscious, the boatman accompanied me everywhere. He was my faithful guide in the cities through which I traveled, but when we arrived at the extremity of Italy, his zeal slackened. He interrogated me as to my further course. My mysterious replies gave birth to suspicions in his mind that rendered my situation more difficult with every passing moment. I did not know myself where I was going and I was relying on celestial inspiration to head me where my destiny intended. It was in the midst of such uncertainties that we reached the Neapolitan shore…"

At this point. Bettina's story is interrupted by a sound that makes her shiver. A messenger comes in and gives her an order from the court. Bettina reads it and says to the messenger: "I will come with you." Then, turning to Léonti, she says: "Until tomorrow; I'll expect you at the palace."

"At the palace?" says Aubrey.

"Yes," Bettina replies. "The Duc d'Albini, who is the governor, will furnish us with the means to confound our enemy."

"Stay here, Bettina!" says Léonti.

"I can't."

"Stop!"

"Farewell!"

And then, as light as a shadow, she flees from the three friends, astonished that they can no longer see her, and even more astonished to have seen her at all.

Bettina's arrival and discourse had produced such an impression on Nadoor Ali that, more than once, while she spoke, his extreme astonishment became manifest. As soon as she has gone, he says: "I can't understand the mysterious crimes of the enemy you're pursuing, and yet, they remind me of a perfidious friend that I am led to believe to be the author of my cruelest misfortunes."

"And to what nation did the author of your misfortunes belong?" Aubrey asks. "Was he from your homeland?"

"No, he was English."

"English? What was his name?"

"I don't know."

"Nor do I," Aubrey continues, "but a presentiment suggests to me that we have to avenge ourselves on a common enemy. Let us join forces to crush him. Tomorrow we shall go to the palace. While waiting for daylight, let's take advantage of the time remaining to us. Tell, us, my dear Nadoor Ali, the cause of the dark distress that is devouring you. I remember that in Rome, sitting on the sandy bank of the Tiber, on the brink of gathering in the outpourings of a heart, we were already listening to you—and your voice pronounced the name of Cymodora."

That name made Nadoor Ali shiver again. His face went pale, his eyes flashed and he manifested a sharp agitation in all his senses that he struggled in vain to control. He stood up and opened a window that overlooked the fields of Modena. Dusk was beginning to cover the green of the surrounding countryside with its veils, but the sky was starry. Everything was calm, except for a fresh breeze agitating the treetops, and, like a string breaking on an idle harp, the occasional harsh cry of a nocturnal bird.

Nadoor Ali stared at the landscape unfurled before him, and remained motionless in that state for some time. Finally, he emerged from his profound meditation, drew nearer to Aubrey and Léonti—who, observing his emotion, had not dared to distract him—and said to them: "Friends, as you wish it, I shall confide to you my most dangerous secrets."

Then he put his hand to his brow, reflected momentarily, and began to tell the story of his life:

The Story of Nadoor Ali and Cymodora

1

To obey and tremble is the destiny of the peoples of our climes. Made illustrious by military glory, does a warrior enjoy shining favor? The foremost slave of a proud court, a single instant suffices to annihilate his numerous services. His suspect faith becomes criminal. Torture is near to triumph. The same voice that raises up a favorite to the steps of the throne remorselessly orders the horrible fall of a minister who ceases to please; a prompt, inevitable, terrible death is the perennial law of a pitiless master, and the price of a rapid elevation to grandeur.

Such was my father's fate. He was too powerful; he seemed culpable. A cruel command raised the guards of his own palace against him. He was slain, and such is the brutalization of soldiers of despotism that his companions in arms, whom he had so often led to victory and upon whom he had heaped rewards, did not hesitate to plunge a dagger into the generous heart of the leader who had protected them for so long.

At the time of that bloody catastrophe, which deprived me of an adored father and my entire family, I was in the army. Already proud to be testing my young courage, I was fighting in the valley of Firan.[30] A devoted slave, escaping the carnage at the palace, ran to bring me the terrible news. Outraged by my father's disgrace, in the first surge of my despair I wanted to precipitate myself through the tide of warriors and at least perish at the hands of an enemy, but the faithful Azem, retrieving me from that impetuous ardor, guided my charger far from the places where my life was simultaneously threatened by the blades of battle and the will of the prince who had condemned lives consecrated to his defense.

Forced to abandon my homeland, I wandered for some time as a fugitive, devoured by my misery and detesting life—but, having been born of a father who lad left to future generations a name redoubtable in war, an insatiable lust for glory reanimated my depressed spirits. I directed my steps to the banks of the Ganges.

The Marathas[31] had invaded the territory of the Rajah of Benares. The greatest disorder reigned universally among a people more accustomed to the peace of seraglios than the fierce clash of arms. Boats were trembling under the burden of heaped-up riches, and the frightened Indians were fleeing in haste with a precious burden that called upon them a danger that they wanted to avoid.

I entered Benares in the midst of the tumult. Impatient to risk new perils, my blood was boiling in my veins and seemed about to cause my heart to burst. I advanced toward the palace; it as deserted and already pressed by the approach of the enemy. Surrounded by guards who threatened to become disobedient to his orders, the Rajah was considering flight himself. Then I appeared.

"Prince!" I cried. "In the midst of the misfortunes that surround you and your unworthy soldiers, trembling before your enemies, permit a stranger to offer the assistance of his virile courage. Flight is the shameful refuge of the weak. Guards! Will you suffer that I, raised far from these borders, and yet ready to fulfill a glorious duty that belongs to you, should fight alone for a master that you have sworn to defend? Let my voice arm you. The Marathas, frightened by a surprise attack, will flee before us, I dare to assure you. Victory will crown our intrepidity. All of you follow Nadoor Ali; he will march at your head. Let's go."

---

[30] Firan (Bérard uses the alternative spelling of Pharan) is in the southern Sinai desert; the valley contains an important oasis.

[31] The Marathas (*Marattes* in French) extended an empire by means of the gradual conquest of much of the Indian subcontinent between 1674 and 1818, when it was overthrown by the British. This reference is inconsistent with the date that subsequently sets the story in the early 1600s.

At these words, whether because my name succeeded in reanimating their confidence or because they were inspired by the warrior ardor that my face and words displayed with a sudden need to repel shame and prefer a glorious death, I saw them gather around me and swear to win a victory or to die. Immediately, I led them forth. We fell upon the enemy ranks. The most immediate success surpassed my hopes. The Marathas were dispersed, and I brought his guards back to the Rajah's feet, astonished to be returning as victors.

In the intoxication of unexpected good fortune, the prince did not know how to express his gratitude to me. I refused the riches that he offered me, but I accepted the command of his army, and from then on, attached to his court, I became his counselor and his friend.

A long peace soon returned to Benares the soft idleness that reigns in the palaces of Asia. Aloes perfumed the air. The bayaderes reappeared. Their voluptuous dances were combined with the harmony of concerts, and love of pleasure, resuming its empire, dispelled the very memory of the Marathas, a bellicose people tormented by the turbulent spirit of conquest.

It was during a brilliant fête that I saw the Rajah's daughter for the first time. Surrounded by a company of young slave-girls, who presented the attractions of all climes to the delighted eye, Azolida was more seductive still: lithe, charming and universally admired, one would have judged that her beauty would have called her to the highest rank of all if her birth had not distanced her therefrom. Never had the amorous harp quivered more charmingly than when her hand plucked its harmonious strings.

I had learned the arts of Europe, and sometimes, beside Azolida, my lyre gave voice to chords unknown to her. Then, after a gentle prelude, I would repeat this Arab song:

> Flower of the morning, I feel adoration for you
>> When I see you, love devours me
>> My heart and my senses reel,
>> And my eyes search for you again
>> Although I can no longer see you.
> Flower of the morning, I shall see you no more.

> Flower of the morning, sole charm of my life,
>> You will soon delight me,
>> Honor calls, I must obey,
>> And in the fields of Araby
>> Do battle, perhaps to die.
> Flower of the morning, farewell, I must go.

> Flower of the morning, know my aspiration,
>> In the battles to which I go,

If Heaven should spare my life
I have the hope on my return
In loving you to be lover forever.
Flower of the morning, I shall love you forever.
Forever![32]

Attentive and delighted, Azolida loved the expression of my voice, and she was still listening when the song had ended.

Meanwhile, renown brought us the admired name of a descendant of those cavalier kings who had once appeared not far from the deserts of Arabia. I wanted to see a people so famous for courage and elegant mores. I promised the Rajah to gather knowledge precious to our region regarding European arts of war and politics. He consented to the useful voyage, but stipulated that its duration should be limited, and when I left, Azolida's tears urged me to hasten my return.

2

I am reaching a period of my life when further misfortunes, perhaps more frightful than the first, inflicted a cruel wound on my heat that has never healed. I had been in the beautiful countries to which my admiration for warrior peoples had led me for some while when an order from the Rajah recalled me of the court of Benares. I obeyed, but, yielding to a desire I had to travel through places rendered forever famous by heroic exploits, I initially headed for Athens. There I interrogated the sparse ruins, the illustrious land trodden by the charges of Attica, sprinkled with the blood of heroes whose graves, covered with wild moss, have disappeared from the sad view of those who seek their traces.

One day, lost in a reverie on the shore of the Aegean Sea, I was admiring the islands with which it is dotted, sitting beneath a solitary palm tree, I heard the rustle of a tunic. Like a nimble gazelle detached from the sprightly herds that inhabit the shady banks of the Euphrates, a young beauty hurtle forth, passing swiftly in front of me, and the sight of her left me a surprise and delight of which my expressions can only give an imperfect idea. She was tall, with a lofty head and a proud stride, her hair floating free. A bow and arrows were suspended from her shoulder. Her hand held a lyre, and she thus combined the various attributes of the fabulous goddesses of the Greeks.

My charmed eyes followed the daughter of Athens from a distance. I approached hr without being perceived and, hidden nearby, I listened to the wild chords that her bold fingers played on the shore.

---

[32] As this supposed song is allegedly translated from the Arabic, its French rhymes are presumably a superfluous artifice, so I have made no attempt to reproduce them in this literal translation.

"Impetuous winds, blow in the plain, raise waves on the sea. Fearlessly, I appear in the midst of ruins. I love the noise of tempests. My lyre resonates in the quivering of storms. I flee the air sullied by the presence of men. I am free."

Thus sang Cymodora. Her pride, her energy and the harshness of a language that seems only to belong to the courageous Greeks, the honor of heroic centuries, made a profound impression on me. Curious to know the fate of that extraordinary woman, I stood up and introduced myself to her gaze.

As soon as she saw me she seized an arrow, and her taut bow directed it at me. I ducked my head and asked her to listen to me. My supplicant attitude astonished and disarmed her. I advanced toward her—but then, resuming her swift course, she ran through the ruins, climbed the hill and disappeared.

No, I shall never be able to describe the delightful disturbance that was left in my soul by the charms, the voice and the absence of Cymodora. For a long time, I stared in the direction in which she had fled. I wandered along the shore. I looked for the soft sand that had conserved her footprints. I thought I could still see her there, running; I recognized a few traces of her passage, and my enchanted heart asked Cymodora once again she had come from.

Tormented by the pleasure of having seen her, and he dread of never seeing her again, I started to draw away. I walked at hazard, and an involuntary alarm drew me toward the place where she had panicked on seeing me. I was looking down at the ground. I perceived writing on a piece of paper covered with a few strands of wild ivy. I lifted them up and parted them, and found lines gathered from the Greek muse who sang of love and her unhappiness, and was seen to perish on a rock, famed for her last farewell.

I could not understand how Cymodora, who was irritated by the mere appearance of a man, had been able to read the delirious expression of the most tender sentiment without emotion. But new characters were traced after the immortal verses of Sappho! I was impatient to know the thoughts of the daughter of Athens; they were to remain forever graven in my memory. I read.

Cymodora's Pensées

Unhappy Sappho! What use was your genius? Phaon was an ingrate.[33] *All men are.*

Women! Shun love if you fear abandonment and unhappiness. It brings in its train the dolor that withers beauty, and the absence that leads to oblivion.

---

[33] In Greek myth, Phaon was an ugly old boatman in Mytilene, on the island of Lesbos, who was given a rejuvenating ointment by Aphrodite after ferrying her across the sea. The amorous conquests he subsequently made were said by Ovid, Lucian and others to have included the poet Sappho, who allegedly killed herself when he moved on.

With what haste you flee to your doom, Palmyra![34] A charming virgin who blushes on being admired, you follow an adored lover. He promises you happiness. You believe in an illusion that dazzles you, and, delirious and confused, you fly into his arms. Where are you going, imprudent woman? The intoxication of love only lasts as long as a dream. Oh, how painful the awakening will be! Soon you will be the image of a colorless flower. Your eyes will lose their gleam, your lips their vermilion freshness and your soft gaze, worthy of inspiring the smile of the gods, will no longer obtain any but the success of despair: the pity of mortals. Cruelly, they will pass by without looking at you, and, while still young, you will learn that, for a discarded lover, life is nothing but a slow agony.

And you, daughter of the Orient! Bayaderes who shine on other shores; young odalisques, vain ornaments of Asian palaces, what is your fate? Slavery.

I, a daughter of the desert, hate men. I flee from them. I am free!

2 (cont'd)

What reflections did I not make then upon that liberty, the sentiment of which is born with life, which leads so many generous hearts astray, and which no mortal possesses?

"I am free," Cymodora said. She believed it; she did not know that, condemned to be subject to the yoke of a superior force, a woman cannot escape her destiny, and that everything around her, even temporary successes, was preparing the chains of slavery for her weakness. We wisps of straw, slaves of an invisible power, blindly obey the fatality that guides us. It was that fatality, the ruler of the world, which had placed Cymodora's secret in my hands—and I would see her again!

Filled with that hope, I returned to the place to which my heart summoned me. My expectation was not mistaken. I heard Cymodora coming. She was searching anxiously for the *pensées* abandoned to the breezes of the shore. I followed all her movements. In haste to give rise in her soul to a new emotion, I began to play a lyre strung in the Lydian fashion, and enjoyed her surprise.

Oh, how disconcerted she is by the unfamiliar sound of a voluptuous harmony! How charming it is to see her trembling with agitation, her ears attentive, her hands reaching out, scarcely breathing for fear of disturbing the sonorous air that carries my chords around her!

---

[34] Palmyra was a city in Syria, destroyed in 270 AD. Its destruction is the subject of a famous lyrical lament by Thomas Love Peacock, published in 1806, but Cymodora cannot possibly have been familiar with that work (although Bérard probably was) and must be quoting a much earlier source, seemingly out of context.

Her charming attitude reveals both the desire to listen to me and the dread of being seen. She tries briefly to resist the impression she is experiencing. Vain effort! Her disturbance carries her away. She cannot help being seduced. Her light footfalls skim the ground. She comes nearer, to listen at closer range. I hear her; I see her. Suddenly, the tune ceases, and I appear.

"Daughter of Greece," I say to her, "don't be afraid. I am not seeking to trouble your innocence, to ravish your liberty. No, I swear it, and you may believe in a stranger who admires you, a voice that begs you; I only want to enjoy the delight of hearing from your mouth the story of the misfortunes of your fatherland, and will withdraw thereafter if you tell me to do so. Born to command, I shall be your slave. Speak, and I will obey."

This manner of speech, new to her, dissipated her fear. She looked at me with astonishment. Her emotion was visible.

"Stranger," she said, "tell me by what enchantment you produce sounds so pure and so touching. Your art is dangerous. It is full of charm, but harmony ought to awaken courage and not enervate by means of the intoxicating softness of its chords. Don't you know that, in the great days of Athens, a Greek was pursued for having invented a seventh string for the lyre."

"Yes," I replied, "but when Timotheus was led to the public square in order to be subjected to his sentence, he perceived that the statue of Apollo was holding a lyre similar to his own in its hand. At this unexpected protection, he uttered a cry, showed the people the instrument that had served as a model, and prostrated himself—and his judges dared not condemn an invention consecrated by the attributes of a god."[35]

My reply surprised Cymodora. She blushed, remained silent for a moment, then said: "I must admit that the virile pride of your manner, the gentleness of your speech and everything about you inspires a confidence in me that I had thought impossible. But what is your intention? What hope bought you to this desolate shore? Have you come to contemplate our superb temples, admire the ancient monuments to the glory of the Greeks? You will see that they are no more.

"No vestige remains of those famous Areopagi, and that tribunal of harangues in which the thunderous eloquence of Demosthenes roared, and the elegant chariot of Alcibiades made the dust fly in the arena of the Olympic Games.

---

[35] Cymodora and Nadoor Ali appear to be misquoting this story. Timotheus of Miletus (446 BC-357 BC) was an innovative musician who added extra strings (probably four in number) to the *cithera* [lyre], which had previously had seven strings. It is said that when he visited Sparta, the outraged citizens seized his *cithera*, removed the extra strings and hung the mutilated instrument up in the public square to shame him, in spite of his protest that a statue of Apollo in the same square depicted the god's *cithera* with the same number of strings as his own.

Like the devastating fires that devour everything they find in their path, the barbarians have passed over the soil of Athens, and ancient Athens has disappeared. They have ravaged our fertile fields, shaken our porticoes, profaned the tombs of heroes, delivered the inspirations of genius to the flames and smashed the statues of our gods. Like the unworthy sailor gripped by fear at the approach of a tempest, degenerate Greece has fled before the impiety of those people who are enemies of gods and humans alike.

"Personally, to escape their fury, I hide my wandering life from their sacrileges. Raised in the ruins of a Christian church, founded long ago by a French prince, on the most obscure pint of one of our river-banks, adopted by the savant Alcidamas, a virtuous priest who educated my youth in the religious sentiments of our forefathers and the hatred of slavery, I lived with him, in the woods, far from mortals who are ever oppressive and mendacious. Alas, Alcidamas is dead. The gods have closed his eyelids, made heavy by age. My eyes watched him expire, bathed with tears. My hands hollowed out the ground that received him.

"As I speak to you about that generous friend, though, I don't know what fear takes hold of my senses. I imagine that I can still hear his dying voice. He is saying to me: *Cymodora, flee from men and you will be free.* I swore an oath to do so on his icy lips. O Father! I shall hold to that terrible oath. I shall be pure and free like you, and my soul, which disdains the weakness of slaves, and is aroused by the mere thought of a generous action, conserves the energy that you were able to inspire within it."

Thus spoke Cymodora, and her animated speech had a magic, a splendor and a majesty that tended toward divinity. I was in an ecstasy impossible to describe. I could not weary of seeing and hearing her.

Surprised by my long silence, she stared at me. What a gaze she had! It embraced my heart. My disturbance increased. I could not help myself; my knees bent; I fell at her feet. She blushed and, rising angrily to her feet, tried to leave.

"O Cymodora!" I said. "Forgive me—I could not resist the ascendancy that your beauty and the expression over your voice have over me. Can the abandonment in which you leave me inspire fear? It's you who have given rise to the intoxication that possesses me, it's for you alone that I have felt the love that you condemn and which might itself condemn you, when it is you that it inspires. If you forbid Nadoor Ali, an admirer of the heroes of your fatherland, who has known battle himself, to raise his voice toward you, at least accept the aid of his arm. War might desolate these climes again, brigands infest these shores. Fear them. In the name of Alcidamas, whose memory you have invoked, in the name of the very gods you serve, O Cymodora, permit me to protect you against the perils that surround you."

"Protect me!" she said. "Have I not my long-proven arrows? Woe to those who brave them!"

"Leave this place, where your liberty is under threat."

115

"I am free!" she cried, proudly."

I saw then that time alone could dispose her reason to understand the as-yet-unknown dangers.

"Well," I said to her, "dispel your fears. Yield to my plea; stay; tell me about the misfortunes of Alcidamas, and explain by what remarkable circumstance an elegant daughter of Athens has become a solitary virgin of the woods."

"Tomorrow," she said. "Dusk is approaching. The horizon is veiled, the night darkening. I have to go away. Farewell!"

With these words, she escaped. Less impatient in her accustomed course, however, she slowed her pace, turned her eyes toward me, resumed her progress, reached the top of the hill, stopped, looked at me again, and finally fled the place that she might soon never see again.

What diverse impressions are produced by the departure of a beloved woman! What memories her absence recalls simultaneously to our confused senses! At the moment when she leaves us, it seems that our soul follows her and leaves with her. The foliage that shaded her head, the place that she occupied, the flower that ornamented her hair, the pleats of her floating tunic, the stone that her hand has touched, the places where she has walked, even the air that she has breathed, everything is filled by her image, everything seems to repeat the farewell that she pronounced.

Tomorrow, Cymodora had said. She had said that! She hated and shunned men, but my presence had ceased to irritate her. I had spoken to her; she had listened; she had permitted me...what am I saying? She had *ordered* me to see her again.

Tomorrow!

I would see her, I would be close to her, I would enjoy her gaze, I would be intoxicated by her smile, and perhaps then, a thousand times repeated by the lover who adored her, a tender confession, a word, a single word long retained on her charming lips, might finally escape involuntarily....

3

The next day, the heat in Athens was scorching. I waited impatiently for the evening breeze to refresh the air, and ran to the place I thought I would reach before Cymodora. But how can I describe my despair when, having reached the shore, I saw a boat ploughing through the waters, and Cymodora, already captive, reach out to me with arms laden with odious chains, to appeal for futile aid?

I recognized the kidnappers. They were mercenary pirates who reap, over the immensity of the seas, the gold of Asian harems. I displayed to their eyes a sign revered in our climes: a dagger glittering with precious stones, an indication of my elevated rank, but my terrible voice carried the cries of my impotent rage to them in vain. Their vile souls, closed to all human sentiment, open to the sole avidity of riches. Those brigands, pitiless devastators of coasts, were insensible to the repeated outbursts of my distress as they fled, and soon I could no longer see either the boat or Cymodora.

There are cruel situations in life whose bitterness one cannot describe. A terrible dart that breaks the heart exhaust our combined forces in the experience, and leaves none for its expression. The fate of Cymodora absorbed my thoughts entirely.

"I shall never see her again!" I cried. "What has become of that superb daughter of Athens, so proud of her liberty? A slave beneath a foreign sky, she will no longer tread the protective soil of her homeland. She will die far from the tomb of her forefathers."

Cymodora had delighted me. I no longer had any hope of seeing her again. I conceived a horror of he places that she had fled forever, and searching everywhere for a vessel to take me away, I embarked at Corinth and set out for Benares.

I made the journey rapidly. The news of my return soon spread in Benares, and when I appeared, the atmosphere resounded with the pompous noise of instruments and the joyous cries of an immense crowd that covered the banks of the Ganges.

The Rajah came to meet me in person. Azolida accompanied him. Carried by slaves in a rich palanquin, she stopped on the bank, and when she lifted her veil, I was dazzled by her beauty and the emotion that animated her features. I knelt down; she reached out to me with a hand I felt trembling in mine, and forced me to sit beside her.

The homage rendered to me resembled the honors of a triumph. It was with that brilliant procession, preceded by bayaderes performing graceful dance-steps, surrounded by my guards and Indians who were calling me their liberator, that we arrived at the palace. There, everything was laid out for a fête. A sumptuous banquet was ready.

The Rajah invited me to sit next to Azolida, and said to me, in the presence of his entire court: "Nadoor Ali, learn the reason that caused me to hasten your return. Azolida was unable to bear your absence. Her grief awoke my compassion. She confessed her love for you. I owe you a recompense worthy of me and the services that you have rendered my people, who love you, and I have chosen you to be the support and heir to my throne. Tomorrow, you shall be married to my beloved daughter."

The running gazelle struck by the hunter's arrow, the warrior struck by a mortal blow, the errant voyager struck down on the desert sand by the inevitable blast of lightning, are not more shocked than I was by that unexpected news. Azolida fixed upon me eyes filled with the softest hope, and seemed to be waiting for my response.

I realized the necessity. I collected myself and, forcing myself to smile, I bowed my head before the Rajah as a testament of my gratitude—but my heart, occupied by a love foreign to that which was offered to me in flattering homage, shivered involuntarily at the unhappiness that I undoubtedly foresaw.

Soon, the signal for music was given. The Rajah, yielding to the keenest joy, said: "Friends! Sing the exploits of Nadoor Ali!"

Scarcely had my name been pronounced than a scream emerged from the midst of the harem slaves, who were still some distance away. It seemed to me to be a bad omen. I was nonplussed. Azolida blushed and went pale by turns, and her anxiety as extreme. But then all the pleasures of the Orient surrounded us, perfumes rose up, the songs began, and my disturbance escaped everyone's eyes in the tumult of varied dances and brilliant chords that filled the palace.

Eventually, the Rajah ordered everyone to be silent, and asked me to tell the story of my voyage. I obeyed. I gave rapid descriptions of the various countries that I had visited since my departure from Benares: the enchanting landscapes of Switzerland; the glory and talents honored in the fortunate fields of France; the fine arts admired in Italy and the ruins of superb Athens. With what charm I recalled the places, so dear, that I had recently quit.

Carried away by a sudden inspiration, my heart stirring and my features taking on a more animated expression, my voice became louder as I talked about the famous heroes of Greece, the monuments raised by genius on the soil of Attica and, finally, the harmony of the chords heard on the shore of the Aegean Sea.

The Rajah listened to me with flattering attention. He was moved, and when I had finished speaking, he shouted "Selim! Have the new captive brought forward."

In response to his order, a young slave came forward, took the lyre, and struck a chord.

Her veil fell.

Gods! It was Cymodora!

The Pursuit of Lord Ruthwen
(continued)

VIII

Nadoor Ali is interrupted. Someone is knocking forcefully on the door of the house in which the three friends have taken refuge. It is opened. An envoy from Duc Albini comes in mysteriously, introduces himself and explains the subject of his message thus:

"I have orders to take you to the palace via a secret door. the governor is waiting for you."

"What does he want?"

"I don't know."

"Where shall we see the minister?"

"At the fête that is being held this evening at court. You will be there. That's all that I can tell you. Let's make haste to leave."

At that moment, dawn is beginning to break.

Nadoor Ali, Aubrey and Léonti follow their guide, who recommends the most extreme prudence to them, and, by a roundabout route, they soon reach the Duke of Modena's palace.

Part Three
The Duke of Modena's Minister

I

Alfonso II, Duke of Ferrara, who died childless in 1597, declared Cesare d'Este to be his universal heir in his will. The new duke expected to be crowned by Pope Clement VIII, but the court of Rome, for the most frivolous of reasons, claimed that the Duchy of Ferrara devolved to the Holy See. Far from recognizing Cesare as the legitimate successor of Alfonso II, the pontiff published a decree by which he declared him incapable of succeeding to the Duchy of Ferrara, excommunicated the prince, along with anyone who helped him to maintain himself there, and submitted the city to a prohibition.[36]

Papal troops, numbering 25,000 men, approached the Ferrarans. Duke Cesare, unable to obtain the help of any other power, decided to solicit an ecclesiastical order, and asked for a truce.

A clever man was required to conduct that important negotiation. The Duke entrusted it to an English nobleman who had captured his entire confidence. A statesman and profound politician, adorned with a brilliant exterior and that suppleness of mind which determines success at court, Lord Seymour had

---

[36] Save for a couple of mistakes that probably originated as typos (which I have corrected), this basic account is accurate. Alfonso d'Este (1553-1597) became Alfonso II, Duke of Ferrara, in 1559, after which he became an important patron of the arts and sciences, playing host to Torquato Tasso, among many others. When he died childless, the Holy Roman Emperor, Rudolf II, recognized his illegitimate cousin Cesare d'Este as Duke, but lacked the will to provide material support when Clement VIII (born Ippolito Aldobrandini) decided to annex the city of Ferrara to the Papal States, with the result that the papal army met no opposition. Cesare d'Este then moved his court to Modena, where his early years were troubled by disputes between the Ferraran lords who accompanied him and their Modenese counterparts. The rest of the story is, however, entirely fictitious; Cesare had married Virginia de Medici in 1586, but none of the five daughters she bore him—in spite of recurrent fits of madness—was named Eleonora; the eldest was Giulia (born 1588). Although history is rich in Ducs d'Albini, none seems to have been attached to Cesare's court.

arrived in Ferrara a short time before, and had become the friend and confidant of the prince. He immediately accepted an embassy that opened a door to his ambition.

Cardinal Aldobrandini, the pope's nephew and legate to Bologna, was transported to Faenza, the place chosen for meetings. Thanks to his skill, the Duke's minister obtained a capitulation, specifying that Cesare would be absolved of all censures on renouncing the possession of the Duchy of Ferrara and its dependencies, and ceding to the Pope half the artillery and arms that were in the city.

The Duke left Ferrara and went to establish his court in Modena. He devoted his cares to the embellishment of his new capital, and made it much more brilliant than the city he had abandoned to the pretensions of the Roman court. In a short while, Ferrara was depopulated and deserted.

Lord Seymour was appointed as the Duke of Modena's prime minister. At first, that nascent court had all the hopes that a new government usually entertains, but the love of novelty, light as it is, cannot resist the friction of rival parties. Partisan spirit, blunted, denatured and lost under a strong government, reawakens, grows and extends under a weak prince. In politics, the worst of systems is not to have one. An uncertain progress, which lowers tomorrow those it raised up yesterday, has all the physiognomy of perfidy, and perfidy leads to disorder.

Such was soon the situation of the Duke of Modena's government. The Ferrarans, who had left their forefathers' fields, wanted account to be taken of their voluntary emigration, while the Modenese bitterly criticized the desire of foreigners who aspired to all favor.

The prince abandoned the reins of state to his prime minister, who was accused of an irresistible penchant for evil. More than once he was seen to protect vice at the expense of virtue, to stifle the voice of justice, the cry of pity and the voice of honor. From then on, a discontent that became more extensive every day, might have led to great public calamity, but in those happy times fidelity recoiled from the abyss of revolution.

Duc Albini, the former minister of the Duke of Ferrara, was the governor of the palace of Modena, and his son was in command of the guard. Numerous services and an utterly proven devotion had given the respectable old man the right to voice the truth, whose language is all too often misunderstood in the courts of princes. He had seen, painfully, a stranger take possession of an authority that should have been his. Accustomed to unveil the intrigues of cunning politics, he anticipated that the new favorite would have a stormy administration, and sometimes warned the Duke of misfortunes that he feared—but his courageous voice was unheeded.

In the palaces of kings, virtue often appears criminal, while the perfidious language of flattery corrupts everything around it, conspires, triumphs and narcotizes the prudence of the monarch with regard to the dangers that the present is preparing for the future.

Meanwhile, Lord Seymour, having reached the summit of honors and power, saw everyone bend to his law. The severity of his gaze and the deleterious modification of his features appeared to be the effect of his application to public affairs, but in the fêtes held in the palace he showed so much readiness in his intelligence and so much grace in his language that all the women of the court were desirous of his attentions.

The Duke had only one daughter, whom he cherished. In accordance with his orders, gatherings were held in the princess's apartments, where witty and varied conversations embellished the leisure of fine evenings. On such occasions, everyone would offer a true or imaginary account of some recent amorous adventure, or some ingenious tale whose moral was always applauded when it was amusing.

One evening, when there was talk of witchcraft and of a vampire that had caused the death of a young woman in Florence, Lord Seymour, pressed in his turn to pay his tribute to the assembly, yielded gracefully to the princess's desire. The courtiers gathered around him. Everyone was listening attentively.

He began:

"It is well-known that all peoples have their prejudices and their superstitions. Some are bizarre. Such is the superstition of the *evil eye*, of whose influence the Sicilians have a singular dread. The evil eye, it is said, acts suddenly; it causes a sudden malady; it fills the imagination with lugubrious visions; it removes the means of continuing projects begun. The same superstition exists in Scotland; it existed among the ancient Greeks and is conserved by their modern descendants. I read in a Greek book this strange passage:

"I do not call the evil eye a superstition, but a certain venomous faculty of reason. I have personally witnessed several effects of the evil eye, in particular, one day when I chanced to find myself with one of these fascinators, whose eyes afflicted several children and, that same evening, a vine. I asked him many questions, but all that he told me was that during the fascination he felt a certain acridity and warmth in his eyes, and a impulsive desire toward the object.

"I wanted to see an experiment, and I asked that some handsome and well-nourished animal should be brought to us. A young water-buffalo, well-fattened and quite beautiful, was indeed brought to us. As soon as the sorcerer had glimpsed it, he asked me whether I wanted him to strike it with his gaze. 'Yes,' I said, 'I would like that very much.' And, as he fixed his eyes on the buffalo, it immediately collapsed, as if dying, foaming at the mouth and grinding its teeth. He quickly ran forward and touched the poor beast three times with his right hand. It was not long delayed in getting up, and was returned to the herd.'

"The most bizarre thing about this anecdote is that it is recounted by one of the most learned men in Greece.

"In France where everything seems to be reproduced with the lightness and chivalric grace that has made the powerful nation in question the most amiable and most admired of peoples, pleasing fables and established prejudices are distinguished by a piquant mixture of seriousness and gaiety. Tales of witches and revenants are no exception.

"There are also various superstitions in Spain handed down through the centuries. Some reflect the character of that religious people, and others were imported by the Moors when, drawn far from their native lands by the spirit of conquest, they invaded the kingdom of Grenada.

"The Orientals, especially, mingle superstitions with all the activities of life. In addition to the admission of fatalism, they have created god and evil genies, vampirism is undoubtedly another dream of their imagination extrapolated to extraordinary conceptions.

"There has been much talk for some time of a vampire who travels through all countries, leaving victims in his wake everywhere. Ignorance has accredited this news, and all women tremble when they encounter a vagabond traveler whom fear has made into a redoubtable monster.

"I will certainly not deny the existence of vampires; I have even seen, in a few periods of my life, misfortunes that might have caused me to believe in them. I think, however, that the horrible crime that signals vampirism is more an allegory, the moral of which has several applications—for example, a conqueror who ravages peaceful countries, and whose insatiable ambition sheds the blood of peoples; an ingrate and prodigal son who reduces to poverty a virtuous father whose sixty years of labor had assured his fortune; a woman one loves and who, by virtue of her imprudence, continually sharpens the dagger of jealousy for us; a cruel king; a perfidious friend; a minister who betrays the confidence of his master and brings about a terrible revolution instead of the wellbeing that he could have produced. Do not all these individuals, the scourges of society, represent vampirism?

"Indeed, if one could always part the clouds with which the inexplicable cruelties of men that are called vampires are surrounded, one would often see that the fear they inspire is only produced by misfortunes beyond the scope of our intelligence, or by misapprehensions that, once clarified, make us blush at our credulity. That idea reminds me of an oriental story that fortifies my opinion.

Here it is:

1

Not far from Baghdad, the superb city built by the Caliph Abu Jafar Al-Mansur, which served from then on as the residence of the masters of the Orient, in a hut on the edge of a little wood, lived a poor fisherman named Gia Hassan. The tools of his trade and a few reed mats woven by his daughter Phaloa were all he possessed. The Tigris, whose waters flowed a short distance away, furnished them with sufficient for their nourishment and their needs.

Every day, after the morning's fishing, Phaloa went to the city to sell the fish caught in her father's nets and the baskets rounded by her pretty fingers. It did not take Phaloa long to place her provisions. She was so pretty that the merchants came running to crowd around her, and she soon came back, singing, to deposit the proceeds of the daily sale and the evening's work in Gia Hassan's hands—who gave her a paternal kiss. A simple and frugal meal, and the evening prayer, terminated these peaceful occupations. Thus it was that, poor but honest, unknown but tranquil, Gia Hassan and Phaloa passed days without remorse or regrets, which might have been envied by the Commander of the Faithful.

In that era, the great and redoubtable Haroun al Rashid reigned in the Orient, a Caliph powerful not only by virtue of the force of his arms, which he had caused to be respected beyond his realm, but also by a combination of the rarest and most fortunate qualities, which had earned him the love of his people. Full of grandeur and generosity, Haroun did not entrust the duty of rendering his people happy to his ministers alone. He listened personally to their slightest protests, judged their disputes by making the interested parties appear before him—and, more than once, when justice gave him a duty to pass sentence on an unfortunate, the latter would go away laden with the Caliph's consolations, bearing a double indemnity for the loss that he had just suffered.

Peace had recently terminated a war provoked by the ambition of one of the provincial governors submissive to the Caliph. Haroun had covered himself in glory, re-established order and punished the guilty parties. His return to Bagdad excited a universal joy. His subjects welcomed him not as a king but as a father. The Caliph, moved by their rapture, felt more than ever the happiness of being loved—the sole recompense and sole pleasure that sovereigns ought to be ambitious to attain.

Among the soldiers who formed the Caliph's guard there was one named Khaled. This young man, long employed in a corps retained in a distant location, was recalled when peace was declared. The honorable advancement he received proved that his good conduct had been appreciated, but as his tastes inclined him toward trade, in which estate his parents had brought him up, he waited for a favorable opportunity to indulge that penchant and obtain from his commanders the initial provision necessary to his plans—liberty.

While walking outside the palace one day, Khaled saw a young woman pass by whose grace, attractiveness and—most of all—air of modesty, struck him to the point of disturbance.

"O Divine Prophet," he cried, "If the houris that you promise to true believers have as much feminine charm as that young beauty, what felicities you have reserved for them!"

And Khaled, in saying these swords, followed the young woman, who, as fresh as a morning rose and as nimble as a Lebanese kid, was hastening to reach the bazaar, doubtless to dispose of the burden she was carrying in her arms.

As she neared the end of her journey, the young woman stumbled, and was about to fall—but Khaled, who was following close on her heels, was fortunate enough to catch her in his arms. Several baskets full of fish slipped from her hands. A merchant to whom she was accustomed to sell her wares recognized her immediately and ran to her, saying: "Beautiful Phaloa, how often have I pitied you for not having the help of a brother or a friend! May our Holy Prophet send you a model husband, in order to reward your virtues."

Frightened by the prospect of falling, Phaloa has not paid any attention at first to the stranger who helped her, but now she looks at him, and her face is overtaken by a vivid red blush. The stranger is beside her; it is he who protected her from danger, and yet he seems to be trembling more than her. He has heard the sound of Phaloa's touching voice, and all the sensations he experiences are combined into one desire: to love her and be united with her forever.

With her eyes lowered, the daughter of Gia Hassan addresses timid thanks to the unknown who is proclaiming his devotion and his delicacy, and does not want to suffer her to return home alone. He takes the merchant as a witness to his honest intentions, and adds: "I am Khaled, soldier of the Caliph. May God grant that I never sully with the slightest stain an irreproachable conduct esteemed by all my commanders. I shall escort this young woman, and return her safe and sound to her father's arms."

Phaloa has already received the price of her merchandise. Khaled, on whose arm she is leaning, blushingly, has already passed through the city gate. A few more minutes and they are on the plain, no longer able to hear anything but the distant muffled rumor of the noise of Bagdhad, the cadenced roar of the waves of the Tigris nearby on their right, and the harmonious songs of the birds of the evening all around them—a thousand various cries resounding in the air.

Oh, how their love was stimulated! How deeply the imposing spectacle of nature—a spectacle of love and pleasure in those fortunate climes—plunged their souls into a soft languor! There were not saying anything, and only looking at one another clandestinely, but it seemed to them that the magical scene had a language known to sensitive souls, which no two individuals could interpret in a different manner.

They were still absorbed in these pleasant thoughts when the sight of her father's hut struck Phaloa's gaze. She thought she was emerging from a dream. Entirely given to the new sensation that had overwhelmed her, she was not singing the customary song as she approached the refuge of happiness. The old man seemed troubled on seeing his daughter with a stranger. He was quickly reassured by Khaled, who provided the necessary clarifications, but could not help allowing the ardor that he felt and the hope he dared to entertain to show through his discourse.

2

Khaled was endowed with a pleasant physiognomy. His regular features expressed gentleness. He had lived in military camps, but his virtue, which was not alarmed by pleasure, had a horror of licentiousness. His heart was pure, and when he spoke, the accent of truth seemed to emerge from his lips. He soon gained the confidence of Gia Hassan and the affection of his daughter. He returned more than once to visit the fisherman, but Phaloa, who always felt renewed pleasure on seeing him, did not perceive that he had become necessary to her existence had her happiness.

One morning, Khaled came at the time for fishing. That was not his habit; a somber sadness transformed his facial features. His pallor and depression threatened bad news. Phaloa shivered without knowing why; her hear froze with fear. Gia Hassan ran back as quickly as he could in response to his daughter's voice, and Khaled, a little calmer but not reassured, spoke to them in these terms:

"Worthy Hassan and charming Phaloa, you know what the dream of my happiness is. You know how attached to you I am, and my love for Phaloa is no longer a mystery. What you do not know is that, having resolved to make her my wife and certain of his consent, I asked my commanders for the honorable discharge that my services merited, and permission to take my bride to the Mosque.

"Nadir, the officer of the Caliph, under whose orders I still am, had promised me that. The days passed, however, and my situation remained the same. A secret presentiment caused me to be very fearful of that slowness.

"O fatal difficulty, deadly thought! It has been realized only too soon. Yesterday, when I returned to barracks, distressing news was spreading. War has broken out again, with greater fury than before, and the Caliph, who has had ample time to rest and enjoy all the pleasures with his numerous mistresses, is making preparations to depart.

"O Phaloa! O Hassan! I have to go with him, to leave you…perhaps to perish far from here, far from you and the beauty that has become my happiness!"

As he finished speaking, his voice died on his lips and his head slumped forward on to his breast. He was unable to weep, but the precipitate movement of his sighs and the languor of his gaze testified to the dolorous disturbance by which he was tormented.

The old man and Phaloa made no reply. Hassan's daughter thought she was dreaming, but waking up seemed so difficult that she dared not move for fear of acquiring a frightful certainty.

Eventually, she emerges from her stupor. It's really him...it's Khaled...he's going away...

At this idea, her heart breaks, and her beautiful eyes moisten with tears.

"Daughter," says the fisherman, "don't abandon yourself to sighs. Perhaps everything is not as desperate as you believe. The Caliph is not insensitive. I intend to take you to him tomorrow. We shall embrace his knees, and ask him for brave Khaled's liberty—and if the sight of my white hair cannot persuade his clemency, your youth, beauty and tears will obtain the beneficence of his noble and generous heart."

Thus spoke Hassan. The souls of the two lovers, like a sea whose waves are agitated and broken against the rocks by a furious storm, seemed suddenly to calm down, as if by magic. Smile reappeared on their lips, and soon, along with the smiles, a soft radiance of hope colored their cheeks.

Animated by this sweet hope, Khaled set forth along the road to Baghdad, where his service was required. The two lovers swore once again a fidelity proof against anything.

The old fisherman, who had no need to seek information about Khaled to judge his good qualities, smiled at the sight of the young lovers' innocent intoxication. He blessed them privately. They would be the support and consolation of his old age. They were his entire future—and an old man's future is so brief! Gia Hassan made Khaled promise to come back and share their modest evening meal.

Phaloa did not go to the city that day. Her lover's absence caused her distress. What if the Caliph were inexorable? What if he disdained a poor fisherman's prayer? She was beginning to feel that, although love has its sweetness, it is mingled with exceedingly cruel pain.

While absorbed in these reflections, Hassan's daughter, without being aware of it, went toward her lover.

She was alone in the middle of the plain when a stranger enveloped in a large cloak approached and, with an expression that radiated generosity, said to her: "Young woman, you're weeping. Who, then, could sadden such beautiful eyes? In the name of Mohammed, may the traitor who has caused your tears to flow perish!"

"My lord," the timid Phaloa replied, "the Caliph is the sole cause of my grief."

"The Caliph!"

"In person."

"By what hazard?"

Then, ingenuously, Phaloa tells the stranger the story of her love, her hope, and the bad news that has just destroyed it. She talks about the poverty and virtue of her father, the bravery and services of Khaled, and, finally, the plan that they have made to go and throw themselves at the feet of the Commander of the Faithful the following day.

The unknown man, touched by her candor, admits the interest that she had inspired in him. He picks up a brick that happens to be lying on the ground, and draws a portrait on it.

"Take this drawing, beautiful Phaloa," he says, "and when you go to the palace, be sure to show it. I am an officer of the Caliph, and I will make every effort to persuade him to show favor to your desires."

After saying this, he follows the young woman to the fisherman's hut. Phaloa introduces the unknown man to her father as her liberator. The old man hastens to invite him to share a modest meal. The officer accepts, eats and drinks with a hearty appetite, and intones a few verses from the Qur'an. Soon afterwards he rises to his feet.

"I regret being obliged to leave you so soon," he says, "but the hour is nigh when service summons me to the presence of the prince. Farewell, my dear friends; farewell, charming Phaloa—don't forget what I told you. Remember, furthermore, the name of Nadir."

As he concludes this speech the stranger is on the threshold of the hut; he squeezes Phaloa's trembling hand, and disappears.

Scarcely has he gone when Khaled comes into the hut; he has met the stranger, who hid his face. Khaled loves Phaloa passionately, and is certain that he is beloved, but, being young, ardent and impetuous he cannot help feeling a twinge of jealousy. His anxiety and his precipitate questions give him away. He seems to be contemplating a plan that he wants to hide. When Phaloa tells him about the affectionate interest that the unknown man has manifested toward her—the portrait on the brick, the supper, the tender manner in which he squeezed her hand, it is all reported with the simplicity of innocence. Then the young man asks whether the sympathetic individual deigned to give his name.

"My son," says Gia Hassan, "his name is Nadir."

"Nadir?"

"Yes, Nadir—an officer in the Caliph's guard."

"He's an impostor, a knave, a traitor. Nadir is my commander, and I've just this moment left him. O charming Phaloa, I suspected as much; your charms have seduced this stranger, whose bearing is not unfamiliar to me. I even recall...yes, I'm certain now of having seen him several times roaming the streets of Baghdad at dusk, and on the banks of the Tigris. He's a dangerous individual, I no longer have any doubt about that. Dread his perfidious designs. Do you know what this infamous seducer is capable of doing? Do you know what dangers his ominous presence can cause? Know that he is a vampire."

"A vampire!" says Gia Hassan.

"A vampire!" the fearful Phaloa repeats, pressing herself against her father.

"Yes, a vampire. He's one of those monsters that have long been the terror of this region, and whose victims so many young lovers and unfortunate relatives have had to mourn. Alas, I only required this misfortune to reduce me to despair."

The worthy old man and his daughter tried to dispel the alarm that had arisen in Khaled's agitated heart, but the young man, as impatient as all lovers are, informed them of a new subject of distress. The Caliph could not be seen the following day. The privy council had to discuss important measures required by the war. It would not be possible for them to get into the palace until the day after, and a day's delay might bring significant events.

Phaloa dismissed all these obstacles and, by means of a reasoning that was frail, but which desire succeeded in making seem sufficient, succeeded in restoring hope to her lover's heart. It seemed to her, whether because a secret voice promised her that her charms would win the Caliph's consent, or because an optimistic presentiment told her that her lover's fears were exaggerated, that she was very close to the moment of happiness.

Women have a kind of prescience and rapidity of judgment that serves them admirably, and hazard often leads them to that which they desire or that which they have foreseen.

3

The following day, but earlier than on the previous day, the stranger returned to the hut. Phaloa, who as alone at the time, could not suppress a fearful movement.

"What's the matter, beautiful Phaloa? Who can be causing you such dread?"

"Oh, My Lord, if one can believe what is said, you're an exceedingly terrible man."

"Exceedingly terrible in what way?"

"A monster."

"A monster? Who could have given you such flattering information about me?"

"Khaled."

"Khaled?"

"Yes, My Lord; he says that you're a vampire."

"Me, a vampire! What does he mean, a vampire?" And the stranger suppressed a surge of anger that almost escaped him. "Can you believe, charming Phaloa, that I mean you any harm? My eyes don't say so, though."

"Men are very perfidious."

"Oh well—go see the Caliph; you'll soon know how far my perfidy extends. I'll have my revenge on Khaled...but... Farewell!" Having said that, he disappears, as on the previous day.

Phaloa begins to tremble; the unknown man had terrible eyes when he pronounced Khaled's name.

Gia Hassan returns. Phaloa makes him party to her fears—and this time, they are well-founded. Oh, how slowly the day seems to go by.

Finally, dusk arrives. Khaled presents himself at the door of the hut, but scarcely has he set foot within it when guards, who were hidden nearby, fall upon him, take him captive and disarm him. Frightened by their sudden appearance, Gia Hassan and Phaloa utter futile screams. They throw themselves at the soldiers' feet. They are told that it is on the Caliph's orders that Khaled has been arrested. The bewildered young man asks what his crime is, but no one can tell him anything, except that he is to be taken to the palace prison.

At these words, the unhappy Phaloa falls unconscious. The poor fisherman covers her with tears and kisses. The unfortunate Khaled, whom the soldiers lead away in spite his resistance, has lost all hope of happiness.

The next day there was a public audience at the palace. Caliph Haroun al Rashid, surrounded by his senior officers and seated on a throne whose splendor dazzles the sight, rendered justice in person and listened to the claims of his subjects.

Khaled in brought before him, free but disarmed. His distressed face testifies to his despair. He lowers his eyes, prostrates himself and waits in silence for someone to deign to interrogate him. A murmur of sympathy rises up around him, but he is deaf. He does not turn his head to look at the crowd, or the young beauty beside him covered by a veil sparkling with gems, who is looking at him tenderly. One sole thought preoccupies him, which is Phaloa's anxiety, and even the presence of the Caliph cannot distract him from it.

Immediately, a voice makes itself heard. "What harm has the Caliph done to you for you to have dared proffer insults against his sacred person? Answer, Khaled!"

"My service beside the Commander of the Faithful, and that blood I have shed in is cause, answer for my fidelity to his person. My tongue has never been able to belie my heart. I swear as much by Mohammed!"

"You boast of your services; for some time, however, you have solicited the favor of being set free."

"I adore the charming Phaloa, the daughter of Gia Hassan the fisherman. I can only live for her. I thought that my brave arm had paid its debt to my master, and that I might live or myself now."

"A short while ago, you brought a serious accusation against an unknown man."

"A stranger introduced himself to my beloved. I was suspicious of him, and suspect him of harboring evil intentions. I admit that I believed that he was a vampire, and said so."

"Raise your eyes, and behold that vampire."

Heaven! The Caliph! Amazing!

Khaled falls to his knees.

"Get up," says Haroun al Rashid. "Receive a thousand purses for your good conduct, be free, and marry Phaloa."

At these words, Khaled turns his head, and the young woman takes off her veil. O joy! It is Phaloa herself! She is accompanied by her father. She falls into her lover's arms. All three prostrate themselves, moved by gratitude to the Caliph, and the sympathetic people manifest in applause the pleasure they experience in seeing justice and love triumph.

The Duke of Modena's Minister
(continued)

II

When the minister had ceased speaking, everyone gave evidence of what a pleasure it had been to hear him—the Duke by means of a flattering word, the courtiers by means of praise, the ladies by means of soft gazes, and he princess by means of a smile.

Thus, Lord Seymour's credit increased further every day, and he already seemed to be at the pinnacle of his desire, when an unfortunate event—but a favorable one from his viewpoint—gave him even more entitlement to the complete confidence of the prince.

Princess Eleonora has hosted a concert in her apartments that the entire court has attended. It is late; the singing has ended, the harp is no longer resounding, people are leaving and already, all is calm.

Everyone is asleep, but thick smoke, gradually increasing, has disturbed the Duke's sleep. The air that he breathes brings a weight with it that oppresses his breast. He sits up, calls out, drags himself out of bed, staggers and falls into the arms of a devoted subject who races to snatch him from the jaws of death—just in time.

A terrible blaze is revealed; a hidden fire explodes violently; the flames increase, devouring everything they can reach. The alarm bell chills everyone with fear; the fear increases the tumult; the burning doors collapse noisily, and smoking debris soon marks the place where the superb palace stood.

The Duke wanted to know who his rescuer was. It was his minister, Lord Seymour himself. He did not know how to show his gratitude for a devotion that other people interpreted differently. He led him by the hand to his daughter, and said to her as he presented him to her: "This is the man who saved my life; it is for you to judge the reward he deserves, and to pay your father's debt."

Left alone with Lord Seymour, the princess, disconcerted by the price's final words, stammered a few thanks, and then added: "The memory of such a service will always be dear to me, but the expression of my gratitude ought to be sufficient for you. What reward could a minister at the height of his power desire?"

"There is one far above the honors of the court."

"What?"

"It depends on you."

"On me?"

"My assiduous attentions, my respect, my haste to please you, to talk to you, and my silence when I am near you, ought to have informed you what it is."

"My Lord!"

"Perhaps you forbid desires too unworthy of you. Forgive me—I saved your father's life, and to save yours, I ran..."

"What! It was you who snatched me from certain death in the midst of the chaos of frightful darkness?"

"What are you saying, Princess? Who snatched you from death, when, how and where? Go on."

"The fire had made rapid progress. Isine and Placida, my faithful companions, had run in search of help. Frightened by the danger that surrounded me I had almost lost the use of my senses, and believed myself lost forever to the affection of a father, when I felt myself being carried away by an officer, who withdrew rapidly after returning me to the arms of my friends."

"Who was this officer?"

"I don't know—the darkness did not permit me to recognize him."

"Can no clue allow you to identify him?"

"The plume from his helmet remained at my feet. It proves that he's an officer in the palace guard. That's all I know."

"Well, Madame, we must find out. Duc Albini's son commands the palace guard; he'll be summoned, and he'll help us in our search. The man who risked his life for you cannot be honored too highly. Let the most splendid favors be the price of a peril for which I would have given my life. The Venetians have declared war on us; the army is under my orders; let us give its command to a warrior who was able to deserve it by saving the life of the Princess of Modena. Here's the order; you shall convey it to Albini. Your rescuer must receive it in your name. If the power that I hold on your father's behalf has precious advantages, it is at this moment that I appreciate them most of all."

This gesture of generosity on the minister's part was inspired more by the desire to get rid of a dangerous rival that his amorous desire feared than by a sentiment of justice and benevolence. Eleonora was deceived by it, and her heart was softened by it.

It was then that young Albini appeared. A black armband veiled his armor, and all his features were impregnated by a faint melancholy.

"Princess," he said, "I've received an order to present myself before you. Deign to tell me what the object is of such a great favor."

"My Lord," said Eleonora, "Before anything else, permit me to ask you why your arms are covered by funereal attire."

"Madame," Albini replied, with embarrassment, "Don't seek to penetrate a mystery that I cannot reveal to you. The mourning that surrounds me is dear to me, and I've sworn to wear it until the day I recover my lost plume."

"Your lost plume. Wait—it can be replaced by another. I want you to take it from my hand."

"What! Madame…"

"Here it is."

"Heavens above!"

"Do you recognize it?"

"Madame," said Albini, embarrassed. "No…I can't…"

"No!" Eleonora repeated, with a sigh. "To whom does it belong, then?"

"Perhaps, one day, you shall know."

"Albini," said the minister, interrupting, "that officer is under your command; it is up to you to discover him. The army is waiting for him; let him show himself worthy of the honor that the princess has solicited for him."

"You see, Albini," Eleonora added. "This is his reward—that he leaves."

"If you order it, he will leave."

"I'll keep his plume; I want to give it back to him myself."

Such generous gestures are all the more dangerous for being filled with charm.

"I shall pray for the success of his arms and for him."

"And for him!" cried Albini, enraptured. "Farewell then, Madame, farewell! He will die for you, or he will return victorious."

Before the end of the day, the princess learned that Albini had departed for the army. Was it, therefore, him who had saved her life? But for what motive had he made a mystery of his devotion? His anxiety in speaking to Eleonora, and perhaps the dread of explaining himself in front of a dangerous witness, gave rise to the suspicion of his love for the princess—and his silence, which proved his delicacy, gave an even higher value to the sentiments that he had not dared to declare.

Eleonora, in the flower of youth, shone with the beauty that brings with it an irresistible seduction. Her slender, elegantly-proportioned figure outlined, as if by magic, forms that were the perfection of nature. Her features were dazzling in their expression and vivacity. Nothing was ever more expressive than her gaze, more delightful than her smile, daintier than her delicate feet. Art would have searched in vain for faults in the piquant mixture of so many various qualities; everything was graceful. The charmed eye saw nothing but her. In sum, her entire person was an enchantment, and if she was not beauty itself, it was because she was a hundred times more beautiful.

The princess was absorbed in reveries of which Albini was the object when the Duke presented himself in her apartments and expressed the desire to see that she shared the love of the minister whose wife she was to be. A father's will was a command to her; not knowing how to reply, she promised to obey. The minister, enchanted by her consent, gave the most lavish fêtes to please her; he was amiable, and he succeeded in interesting Eleonora. Their marriage was decided.

Meanwhile, Albini lost no time in demonstrating his courage. Every day the court learned of the success of the army under his orders. For political reasons that no one could understand, however, far from rewarding the service of its officers, the favors refused to them were lavished on sedition-mongers, and the minister gave his support to the prince's enemies. The palace governor, an old friend of the Duke, sought in vain to diminish his credit. The Duke only saw through the eyes of his favorite, to whom he had granted his daughter.

The marriage was to take place the following day. A brilliant fête was in preparation, a hunting meet was arranged, to begin the pleasures.

III

They set forth; a numerous cortege follows the princess. They separate in the nearby forest. The horses support the ardor of the hunters; the heat is excessive. The princess draws away from her followers and pauses in a shady spot. There, solitary and pensive, she yields to memories that she had tried in vain to forget. A secret anxiety is pursuing her. In a few hours she will plight her troth to Lord Seymour. She does not experience any repugnance with regard to forming that bond, and yet a more tender sentiment causes her to regret the generous Albini.

Her mind is drifting in this fashion when a stranger appears before her.

"Lovely princess," he says to her, "I have come here to save your life. Fear the knot that you are about to tie; the day of your marriage will be that of your death. The husband you have chosen is a monster, and your life will be lost in his first embraces. This language astonishes you; alas, it is all too true. You see in me one of his victims; time will inform you of others. Don't neglect my advice, and flee the misfortune that is about to overtake you."

Troubled by what she has just heard, Eleonora tries to call the stranger back, but she has scarcely recovered from the stupor that the mysterious messenger's speech has occasioned when the entire court arrives in her vicinity. They surround her. Lord Seymour presents her with her charger. The signal for departure is given, and they resume the road to the palace.

133

After a sumptuous banquet, the dancing begins. A thousand varied games embellish the fête. The princess, tormented by the fears that she cannot dispel, avoids the homage of the courtiers, and beneath a disguise that favors her desire to hide herself from all eyes, she searches everywhere for distractions that flee before her.

Suddenly, a masked individual stops her, and says to her: "Listen, O most adorable of women! It's in vain that an impenetrable veil hides you from every gaze. Mine has followed, divined and recognized you. By that noble bearing, the grace that animates all your movements, and that enchanting lightness of foot, who could mistake the beautiful Eleonora?

"Forgive a lover who adores you a confession that might cost him his life. In your presence, his heart have not dared to declare itself, but his voice will make itself heard. A pure love like that you inspire, delightful as it is, might have betrayed itself before you, but it has kept silent, and it requires all the mystery with which it envelops itself at this moment to abandon itself to the pleasure of speaking to you. O Eleonora…!"

At these swords, the irritated princess snatches away the unknown man's mask. A cry goes up within the assembly. It is Albini!

"Young man," says the Duke, with a severe expression, "Why have you left the army without my order?"

"My Lord," says Albini, "I have often risked my life in battle for you. My courage, attested by glorious exploits, gives me the right to my prince's confidence, and I have left my soldiers in order to render you a more important service. I know that someone has poisoned your mind against me. I know my enemy, but, less anxious to defend myself against his blows than to enlighten you as to the misfortunes that threaten your own person, I have come to accuse explicitly the minister who is betraying you."

"Who, then are you accusing?" says he prince.

"Lord Seymour," replies Albini. "Yes, it is the minister himself that I accuse here, and you shall shortly hear the witnesses of his crimes."

At the same instant, a curtain opens, which reveals the stage on which the musicians and singers are placed, and Aubrey, Léonti and Nadoor Ali appear, disguised as troubadours.

Aubrey

All smile in delight at the lute of the troubadour,
Tender ballads expressing tender amour,
The so-called sickness devoid of cure.
Beside the object that makes his heart adore.
Happy, he sings of pain that makes his heart soar
Unhappy, he sings all the more.

Léonti

But our weary voices can no longer resound,
For happiness; what song can be found,
When the heart by love's uncrowned.
When love has fled, upon the hallowed ground
On which on hear its last farewell unwound,
The final dream of life is drowned.

Nadoor Ali

Beloved palm-trees, my homeland's blue skies!
Burning sand whose storms sting my eyes,
Cymodora before me flies.
In the desert where she heard my cries,
She is no more, alas, all beauty dies
To avenge her, I will arise.

All Together

Prince! Subjects! All of you pay us heed.
Rich, honored, you are the victims of greed.
It seeks in vain its lust to feed.
The king of the weak hears the wretched plead.
The vengeful cry of mortal virtue freed
Demands that the guilty should bleed!

"Stop!" says Lord Seymour. "Insolent adventurers, introduced into the palace to import disturbance and slander!"

"I recognize him," says Aubrey, forcefully. "Lord Seymour is Lord Ruthwen; he's the one who killed my sister!"

"It's him!" says Léonti. "He's the one who stole my dear Bettina from me."

"Yes," adds Nadoor Ali, "he's the one who left Cymodora lifeless in the deserts of Arabia."[37]

"He is also the one," another voice continues, "who gave the secret order to set fire to the prince's palace in order to promote his ambition with a reputation for devotion without running any risk."

"Beware of the vampire!" they all cry, vehemently.

---

[37] This is inconsistent with what Nadoor Ali told Aubrey and Léonti before he began telling them the (conspicuously unfinished) tale of his relationship with Cymodora, when he said that she was a prisoner in Arabia—but it is, of course, necessary to the symmetry of the narrative that Ruthwen/Seymour should have killed her

Fear and astonishment are painted on every face; everyone awaits the outcome of such an extraordinary scene. The prince seems anxious and irresolute, and already it is evident that, giving little credence to what he has just heard, he wants to listen to his prime minister's justification. He orders that the fête should continue and that the gates of the palace should be locked, and then withdraws to his study. Lord Seymour follows him, and such is the force of the ascendancy he has obtained over the prince that a few moments suffice for him to lead him astray again and persuade him to do everything he wishes.

Soon, the news spreads that the governor of the palace has been exiled, Aubrey, Léonti and Nadoor Ali arrested.

From that moment on, Albini senses that he will be sacrificed to the minister's vengeance. Surprised to be still at liberty, he follows a crowd of courtiers gripped by fear, fleeing in all directions. He does not notice that someone close to him is moving at a precipitate pace. He has already reached the palace gates when, just as he is about to go through, guards that had long served under his command block his passage, surround him and press upon him.

"Our worthy leader," they say to him in a whisper, "our companion in arms, our benefactor, old warriors that love you offer you their lives. Our arms are ready."

"Against whom?"

"Against your enemies."

"My enemies are those of the prince whom we serve. It is in battle that warriors like you ought to show their courage."

"Your life is threatened. Our recognition desires to save you."

"My honor is opposed to it."

"We are supposed to capture you."

"Obey, then."

"The minister has ordered it."

"And I forbid it," says the princess, forcefully, removing her mask. "Palace guards! Recognize my voice."

"Madame, it's what you wanted. I have no complaint regarding my fate."

"Cruel! The step I'm taking at this moment tells you what a mistake I've made. Time is pressing, Albini. Flee! It's me who is imploring you."

"Guards! Do your duty."

"Our duty is to avenge you. Speak—who is the victim it's necessary to strike?"

"Me! I have given you an example of valor; I must give you one of fidelity. The order bears the prince's seal; obey, I tell you."

"We embrace your knees. At least yield to our prayers, our tears."

"Ah!" says Albini, moved. "Get up. I order you to, friends, I beg you to do so. The prince has spoken, here are my weapons. Let's go."

"So the voice of Eleonora has no effect on the heart of Albini!"

"Eleonora!" He pauses, looks at the princess, then says as he draws away: "Farewell, Madame; I feel that it is sweet to die by your hand."

"He loves me, he sees my pain and he blames me!" says the princess, sobbing. "Alas, irritated by a declaration that offended me, I thought to punish the audacity of a lover unworthy of me, and it's Albini that I've doomed—Albini, who is dear to me, to whom I owe my life. Well, it's now up to me to save him. Yes, I shall save it, even at the expense of my own."

So saying, she runs to lock herself in her apartments. A thousand plans whirl through her mind, conceived one moment and destroyed the next. Finally, she settles on the hope of changing her father's mind. The night has gone by and sleep has not closed her eyelids. Pale and distressed, her eyes still swollen with tears, she presents herself at the Duke's door and asks to see him in private.

Introduced into his presence, she says: "Father, the commander of your guard, the leader of your army, the warrior so faithful in the service of his prince, who vanquishes the enemies of his fatherland and whose glory has given splendor to yours, Albini, arrested at the gate of a palace he defended for so long, has been treated as a vile criminal. I have come to demand justice."

"Daughter, why do you take such a great interest in a guilty man."

"Guilty? He is not."

"He has left the army."

"In order to give you important information."

"He has slandered my minister."

"He has been deceived."

"He dares to love you; he told you so."

"That was when my hand tore away his mask."

"The motive that directed your action accuses you."

"It justifies me. If I had known that it was him, I would have respected his secret."

"It's true, then that you share his insane love, and that, dishonoring your father and yourself, you have received Albini by night in this palace? His plume was found in your apartments."

"O Heaven! What outrage is being done to me? And you can tolerate it?"

"Your enthusiasm to defend him is sufficient proof that he is guilty, and will pay with his head…"

"Stop, Father—know my innocence and Albini's generosity. He is the one who saved my life when fire broke out in the palace; in the disorder inseparable from the peril to which he exposed himself, he dropped his plume, which I kept in order that I would one day know my savior and lead him to your feet. My Lord, deign to have Albini brought before you; interrogate him yourself. You will know everything; you will render him justice. Oh, Father, be not deaf to your daughter's prayers and the voice of truth. I embrace your knees; you are softening, I can see…I hope. I will run to fetch the proof of Albini's devotion."

She leaves precipitately, arrives at her apartments, demands and searches for the desired plume—but in vain.

IV

At that moment, someone comes to inform the princess that a tribunal convened by the minister will pass judgment on her savior. Gripped by fear, she remembers her father's reproaches. The plume can no longer be found—how suspicious! Who, then, has dared to take possession of it? Only one man, a party to the secret, and impelled by jealousy, is capable of making it serve his vengeful plans. She is, however, resolved to try anything to confound that odious imposture.

Indignation gives her energy, and she is already making preparations to appear in person at the tribunal when the minister appears, and tells her that Albini has been condemned to death.

"That sentence is unjust," said Eleonora. "He will not be executed. I shall go, I shall speak, I shall defend him, and my father will hear me."

"Abandon that hope. Your father has approved Albini's condemnation."

"Cruel! It's you who have arranged everything. You have too much power in the court, but you'll answer to me for Albini's life. You must set aside this odious sentence."

"What you ask of me is beyond my power."

"Enable him to flee, then; sign the order to set him free this instant, or fear my despair."

"If I betray my duty in order in order to refuse you nothing, will you refrain from giving the man any hope that you love him?"

"What are you demanding of me?"

"That you yield to the desires of your father, who wants me to receive your hand at the altar this very day, without delay."

"Sign, then—I'll consent to anything."

"If that is your wish."

"Give it to me."

"Remember your promise. You'll be mine."

"I swear it."

"Well, Princess, you shall have to obey. Here's the order you desire. This evening, at midnight, in the palace chapel."

Thus, everything cedes to the politics of the cunning Ruthwen. He orders and directs the preparation for his wedding. The entire palace is at his sole disposal, and his master has only the shadow of supreme authority.

There is, however, a noticeable anxiety in the Duke's mind that bodes ill for his minister. He seems to be avoiding him, listening to him with embarrassment and following his advice mistrustfully. With a single word, he could break

138

the yoke whose danger he did not foresee—but he does not have the strength to pronounce that word.

Since the condemnation of Albini, he has locked himself in his study, invisible to everyone except Lord Ruthwen, whom he no longer loves, but still fears.

Such is the fate of a prince who abandons the reins of state to a favorite. He bemoans the misfortunes that offend his generosity, but which his weakness authorizes. Severe with his most faithful friends, he is indulgent to those who are betraying him.

While everything presages an imminent catastrophe in the palace, Albini, shackled in irons, awaits the fateful moment that will reveal his scaffold. He had appeared before his judges fearlessly. Proud of his innocence and the services he had rendered to the state, he was impatient to justify himself—but when, after being reproached for his desertion of the army, he was shown his plume as evidence of his criminal attempts on the Princess of Modena, surprised by the unexpected attack, he thought that Eleonora had taken sides against him. That idea made such a profound impression on his consciousness that he refused to defend himself.

Now condemned, and without hope, his prison resounds to a single groan.

"Is Eleonora my enemy, then?" he said. She too furnishes evidence to have me condemned! And great God, what evidence! That which recalls everything I have done for her.

"Ah, mortal thought! This is the reward for my devotion. The pain has broken my heart, and yet that heart loves her still, alas! It will only cease to beat for her when I cease to breathe.

"But while I mourn her, the ingrate is perhaps in the midst of pleasures...what sobbing can I hear? Who is coming towards me?

"Oh you, unknown creature, who alone has pity on my misfortune, what do you want of me? Why have you come to this frightful abode?

"You sigh, you press against me, you bathe me with your tears—speak; who are you?"

"Can't you recognize me?"

"Heavens! Eleonora!"

"I've come to break your shackles."

"You! Here! Now!"

"Oh, you don't know what your liberty has cost me."

"Explain yourself, celestial creature."

"I have made a terrible, horrible sacrifice for you, because I love you, because I adore you."

"What do you mean?"

"Know that, as the price of the order I've obtained to snatch you from the scaffold, I must marry..."

"Who?"

139

"Your enemy."

"Great God!"

"I've promised."

"No—that frightful marriage shall not take place. Think what will become of your life."

"I'm only thinking of saving yours. Follow me. I desire it; I command it; obey, or I shall die at your feet."

"Very well, yes, I'll go with you. A new hope is gleaming in my troubled mind. It inspires me; it inflames me. It's the one hope that remains to me. Yes, adored woman, angel of heaven, I shall save you once more, and I'm hastening to do so."

"What is your plan?"

"Go back to the palace. Tomorrow, at daybreak, we shall be avenged. Farewell!"

The Princess cannot hold him back; she fears that the fury that animates him might lead him to his doom. A terrible silence reigns around her.

As she ran to her lover's prison she had but one sentiment, one idea; she forgot all the dangers. Now that he is free, she is alone; through the shadows of the night she steers an uncertain course, passing through deserted areas.

She wanders through the darkness in this way for some time.

V

Finally, confused and trembling, Eleonora reaches the palace. They are waiting for her; the ceremony is already prepared. Her late appearance is criticized. Her friends dress her against her will. Soon, led to the redoubtable chapel, pallor on her brow and her heart broken, she puts on the nuptial headband, the fatal headband, symbol of imminent death.

The Duke observes her despondency, and is alarmed. The minister attributes it to a transient illness, impatient for the moment that will render him the happiest of men.

Eleonora yields to her father's order, and her mouth allows a consent to escape that, scarcely pronounced, becomes irrevocable. One instant more, and the beautiful Eleonora, Albini's generous friend, will see her life extinguished on the marital bed where happiness ought to await her.

The following day, however, the greatest disorder reigns in the palace. The Duke is told that his daughter is expiring; the tolling of the church bell brings the faithful hurrying from all parts.

Public prayers begin, but they are interrupted by a general murmur. A woman launches herself on to the steps of the altar.

It is Bettina.

"People," she says, "listen to me. Last night I presented myself at the palace to warn the unfortunate Eleonora about the fate that menaced her. My voice was lost in the air, and an unknown hand suddenly struck me with a poisoned dart. A vampire is my assassin, and that of the Princess of Modena. It is the minister of your prince; your prayers for his daughter are futile. Eleonora is dying. Avenge me; avenge her."

Having said that, she falls, rolls on the sacred floor, and dies in horrible convulsions. Then the church doors are flung open, and a company of armed men runs in.

Léonti flies toward Lord Ruthwen, plunges a blade into his breast, and immediately withdraws it, dripping blood, in order to strike himself with it.

The tumult is at its height. A cry of vengeance rises up on all side. Albini shows himself, harangues the people, lays his weapons down at the feet of the prince and sears to defend him. His warriors do likewise, and in accordance with his advice, they run to the palace to render life to the Princess.

There was no longer time.

With her last breath, Eleonora pronounced Albini's name.

The mourning of such a great loss was increased day by day by further anguish. The most beautiful ladies of the court were dying, without any detectable cause. Edolinda, the flower of Italia beauty, Countess Azelina, the lovely Zerbina and the tender Petrilia were perishing of an unknown sickness.

After a thousand vain conjectures, memories were consulted. Aubrey awoke just suspicions against his enemy.

The genius of evil never dies for its crimes, and such is the horrible privilege of a vampire—but how could those tenebrous mysteries be penetrated? How could they be resolved? What could be done?

Eventually, they run to the place where the infamous Ruthwen's corpse has been deposited. The earth is dug up, the grave opened.

O surprise! A hideous pallor covers the face of the odious cadaver, but by a miraculous contrast, it offers bloody vestiges of life.

Its sparkling eyes shine with a terrible expression, launching darts of fire, and its bloodied red lips are moving, writhing, seemingly still feasting on a frightful meal.

At the sight of this phenomenon, the witnesses recoil in horror; the envoys of the court, forced the recognize the truth of an event beyond all belief, write the irrevocable proof of it on a piece of paper that will conserve the story in the annals of Modena.

The prince is informed and immediately orders that, in order to prevent further calamities, red hot irons should burst the eyes and traverse the heart of the monster.

After this execution, death ceases its ravages. The Duke is inconsolable for the loss of his daughter and so many misfortunes.

Albini heaps benefits on Aubrey and Nadoor Ali and persuades them, without difficulty, to settle in Modena with him.

Appointed as prime minister, he deploys every effort of his genius and zeal to heal the state's wound, but such is the frightful abyss left behind by the rapid transit of an evil minister that a long period of care and sacrifice scarcely suffices to restore order and peace in the Duchy of Modena.

Finally, Eleonora's generous rescuer did the same for the state; by sage but energetic measures he stifled the spirit of revolt and civil discord that then infested Italy—and history, which stigmatizes perfidious custodians of power and advertises virtue and fidelity to future generations, has transmitted in permanence, to the gratitude of the people of Modena, the honored name of Albini.

The End of Lord Ruthwen
A Manuscript Discovered

Lord Ruthwen did not imagine that his end was so near when he went to the church with the Duke of Modena; he had not taken any precautions. After his death, his apartments were searched, and beneath a marble slab cleverly set against a wall and hidden in an obscure alcove, a little iron box was found, securely locked. It was necessary to break it to open it. This mysterious strong-box contained a manuscript, which bore the singular title: *The Story of My Early Life*

This manuscript was deposited, in that already distant era, in the ducal library, and stolen by a Venetian during the Italian wars. The same family conserved it for several generations in archives abandoned to time and dust, and it finally became the property of as French artist who, learning of the publication of *Lord Ruthwen*, has just offered us this text. This is how it fell into his hands.

In 1797, on a winter evening, having returned to his lodgings to work on the views of Venice that he had been sketching for several hours in a gondola placed in the midst of the lagoons, he asked for a fire. In order to light it a servant brought a heap of old papers, among which were the story of Lord Ruthwen's early life. That title piqued his curiosity. He hastened to start reading it, and the events recounted in the curious history interested him so keenly that he took care put the bizarre manuscript away in his portfolio. We might perhaps be able to publish it, if we are encouraged to do so by some success.

Notes on Vampires

The singularities of Lord Byron, in his private life, have contributed no less than the originality of his talent to make him famous in England. Overtaken while still young by a black melancholy, sharpened by domestic misfortunes and unjust slanders, he renounced his fatherland and, wandering from one country to another, might have been thought to have become a stranger to the human species.

Independent by virtue of his fortune as well as his genius, he only wrote by virtue of inspiration, and, untroubled by criticism and praise, disdained the rules of art and the conventions of society alike. By a bizarre preference, he chose for his heroes men who set themselves above all laws and sacrificed all the rights of humanity to their pride. It was a new road that he wanted to follow.

In his bold compositions he loved to paint in dark colors everything that struck his imagination, and the virile energy that characterized his Muse sometimes degenerated into harshness. Through the darkened scenes in which he seemed to delight, however, he drew from his Muse details full of grace and freshness, which proved his talent for descriptive poetry.

Among the number of his depictions remarkable in that fashion, we shall only cite a single passage from *The Corsair*. When Medora describes for Conrad the anxieties of his absence, the story of what she has experienced while separated from him has, in the original version, an inexpressible charm. We have tried to translate the passage as follows:[38]

Oh! Many a night on this lone couch reclin'd,
My dreaming fear with storms hath wing'd the
                                               [wind,
And deem'd the breath that faintly fann'd thy sail—
The murmuring prelude of the ruder gale....

Lord Byron's works remarkable in that, combining poetic merit with the interest of prose romance, they are based on extraordinary adventures that, having sharply piqued curiosity, leave the ultimate fates of their heroes uncertain. They thus create an exaggerated desire for a denouement, which, in seeking to divine it, the imagination augments at will. This method, which is not exempt from reproaches, is very piquant and perhaps best fulfils the aims that are bound to propose themselves to an author who does not disdain to combine the inspirations of a poet with the less elevated schemes of a novelist.

Whatever place Lord Byron ought to occupy in English literature, however, our intention is not to address that question but to expand further on the beauties and faults of his works.

---

[38] I have only quoted four lines from Byron's text (beginning with line 369) whereas Bérard's "attempted translation" has eighteen. There seems little point in quoting eighteen because Bérard's version bears very little resemblance to the original; although it seems evident enough which passage he means, his version does not even qualify as an accurate paraphrase. Having tried to retain the rhyme and approximate scansion of some of Bérard's poetry, I am well aware of the necessities of improvisation involved translating verse from one language to another, but it seems to me that he is being deliberately disingenuous in naming his poem as a translation rather than an independent piece inspired by Byron's. I cannot see any point, however, in my attempting a back-translation of his verse into English.

The Vampire is, without a doubt, the most extraordinary of all Lord Byron's compositions. It is well within the compass of his ideas, but his style is not recognizable therein. It is one of those mental aberrations that genius dares not admit. It is said that Lord Byron, pressed by his companions to tell a story in his turn, improvised the adventures of a vampire which have since been collected and delivered to print by his friend, the physician Polydory.[39] The work in question bears none of the imprint of Lord Byron's talent. The story is bizarre and frightening, and that is doubtless what has secured its success. It is the extraordinary vogue that the romance has inspired that gave birth to the project of supplementing it with the sequel that we are now publishing.

We shall not seek to explain here the folly of the superstition of vampirism. That incredible disorder of the imagination of ignorant peoples is probably merely the result of an as-yet-unknown malady. The authors of dictionaries define a vampire thus: "A man dead for several months or years who returns, becomes visible, walks, talks, and drinks the blood of the living."

Addenda to Part Two

The adventure of Antonio came from Saint-Remy, a pretty little town in Provence renowned for its Roman antiquities and a lunatic asylum. That madhouse is in a delightful valley in the foothills of the Alps. Gardens maintained with extreme care, abundant springs of an admirable purity, a keen and excellent atmosphere that renders the wind buffeting the rocks more salubrious and enchanting beauty spots embellished by the beautiful southern sky all combine to form a perfect setting for a place that serves as a refuge for unfortunates lost to society.

Monsieur Mercurin, the famous physician,[40] devotes his varied talents to the prosperity of that fine establishment, which is inhabited by the insane of many lands, and to which even this country has sometimes paid tribute.

Independently of the pharmaceutical aid lavished on these unfortunates deprived of reason, however, two powerful resources collaborate in the numerous successes that obtain the physician's well-deserved reputation: music and the

---

[39] Just as the actual title of the work Bérard is discussing is, of course, spelled with a *y* rather than an *i*, and its author's name with two *i*s rather than two *y*s. If this alteration is deliberate, its motive is presumably similar to the one that led to the substitution of Ruthven by Ruthwen, but the probability is that Bérard was dictating to an amanuensis unfamiliar with the name.

[40] This is presumably the physician Louis-Étienne Mercurin whose marriage was registered in Saint-Remy in 1788, but he was neither the first nor the last physician with that surname resident in the town. The Louis Mercurin who donated an organ to the local church in 1845 might have been the same person, but was more probably his son.

meeting of the two sexes, for two hours every day, under the surveillance of the servants attached to the house. It is impossible to describe the impatience of these unfortunates while they await the moment that will bring them together in the vast concert-hall. Several of them are musicians; they sing; the orchestra accompanies them, and they applaud he pleasure they experience themselves.

An even more curious spectacle, however, is to see them dancing after the concert. They choose their partners for the quadrille or the waltz. A perfect decency reigns in these meetings, at which, to the joyous sound of drums, all the pretty Provençal girls throw themselves collectively, who form quadrilles indiscriminately with the inmates of the house or the young swains that accompany them. A meek joy shines on every face and, amid that pleasant tumult, which presents the most bizarre contrasts, it is difficult to recognize the unfortunates who are mad in the midst of those who pass for sane.

The madman who, in order to escape from his retreat, employed the extravagant means that we related in the story of Antonio, is still alive. His name is Renaud. Except for his madness—and perhaps because of it—he is said to be the most amiable, the most cheerful and the wittiest of the creatures that one might find in such an abode, where the absence of reason more frequently offers travelers the distressing spectacle of human degradation. It is also Monsieur Mercurin's establishment that inspired a few scenes of the story of the young Moravian woman.

We should not conclude this note about Saint-Remy without pointing out an essential error into which several otherwise-praiseworthy writers fall. It is a league from that small town that the ancient court of love presided over by the Abbess de Sade and the beautiful Laure is located. In the woods of Romarin one can still see the ruins of the château where that amorous court held its sessions. We do not know why Madame de Genlis, in her new novel *Pétrarque et Laure*, and the estimable author of *La Gaule poétique*, have placed the court of love near Avignon.[41] That monument to chivalric times is curious enough in itself and in the memories it recalls for its true location to be fixed with exactitude.

---

[41] There are several peculiarities in this passage, not the least of which is the reference to the *"Abbesse de Sade"* [Abbess de Sade]. The background to the reference is that the uncle of the infamous Marquis Donatien de Sade, Jacques-François de Sade (who was an Abbé [a priest without a parish]), wrote a biography of the Italian poet Francesco Petrarch, who spent his early life in exile living in the Sade's native Provence. He subsequently recalled catching a glimpse of a girl named Laure leaving a convent near Avignon on April 6, 1327, which became a lifelong obsession and the inspiration of all his work. The Abbé de Sade argued (convincingly enough to have the allegation reproduced as fact in most subsequent reference books, even though Petrarch's claim might well be pure fiction, inspired by Dante's account of his fateful glimpse of Beatrice) that the girl in question must have been Laure de Noves, who subsequently married

The White Woman is a ghost story accredited in a few villages in Normandy. We heard the story of that apparition told at a pleasant gathering at the house of the Comtesse de B***. The remainder is invention, and we have transposed the setting to Naples.

In Rome, as in all the lands of the south, the heat is so intense during the day that dusk is awaited with impatience. Then, like errant shades in the Elysian Fields, men and women walk abroad, while other breathe in the coolness of the evening at the doors of their houses. Singing and the music of guitars are heard everywhere, and if one combines that magical scene with the varied effects of the moon, whose white light filters through the trees, one will have an idea of all the pleasure that such a spectacle inspires.

It is from the piquant work of an Arab poet that we have borrowed the idea of a young female vampire.

Addenda to Part Three

Political, literary and religious almanacs have furnished us with the historical narrative of the Duchy of Modena, and a scholarly article in the *Journal des Débats*, which appeared in 1812 the curious details of the superstition of the *evil eye*.

The manner of death that we have chosen for our vampire in the denouement is described in *Les Préjugés de tous les peuples*, a work by M. Salgues.[42]

---

his ancestor Hugues de Sade. Donatien de Sade recorded his own inspirational vision of Laure, experienced in a dream after reading his uncle's text while in prison. The book by the Comtesse de Genlis to which Bérard refers was published in 1819; it is not a novel, although it is not an orthodox work of literary criticism either. *La Gaule poétique* was an oft-reprinted showcase anthology by Louis-Antoine de Marchangy, first published in 1813. The literary fame of the ruined château to which Bérard refers was subsequently renewed by a poem by the Provençal poet Frédéric Mistral, "Romarin," which in turn inspired a notable short story by Jean Lorrain, "L'Âme des ruines" (tr. as "The Spirit of the Ruins").

[42] The actual title of this work by Jacques-Barthélemy Salgues is *Des Erreurs et des préjugés répandus dans les dix-huitième et dix-neuvième siècles* [Errors and Preconceived Ideas Widespread in the Eighteenth and Nineteenth Centuries] (1811).

Paul Féval: *Vampire City*

La Ville-Vampire *was first published in book form in 1875, although internal evidence suggests that it must have been written eight years earlier, probably for serialization in a French newspaper. It is the third novel Paul Féval had written which employs the notion of vampirism, and by far the most extravagant. Like its immediate predecessor* Le Chevalier Ténèbre *(1860),*[43] *it is an alloy of comedy and horror fiction, but whereas* Le Chevalier Ténèbre *was framed according to the "Galland formula" of tales nested within tales,* La Ville-Vampire *is a parody of the classic Gothic novel, which appropriates as its heroine the most successful of all the authors in that genre, Ann Radcliffe.*

The flood of imitations which Mrs. Radcliffe's novels had provoked at the beginning of the 19th century had already begun to die away when she died in 1823, but the genre was to enjoy two further leases on life in England. The first came courtesy of the "bluebooks" which packaged condensed versions of the most famous Gothic novels and crude imitations thereof in cheap formats, usually retailing at a shilling. (Bound books usually retailed at 10s 6d, and novels were conventionally issued in three volumes to suit the convenience of the circulating libraries.) The second came with a new wave of part-work publications and cheap periodicals launched in the 1840s, which extended the reading habit to the working classes and became known as "penny dreadfuls." These were supplemented in the 1850s by single-volume cardboard-covered "railway novels" which provided cheap distraction for the middle-class traveler. Again, the classics were reprinted for a new generation and again they spawned new and even cruder imitations. It was this third flood of Gothics old and new—and especially the final vulgarization of the form—that prompted Féval's parody.

At the time of its first publication, the hybrid horror/comedy genre to which La Ville-Vampire *belongs hardly existed, and Féval may be credited with its invention. It was not a great success in its own day, but now that comic books and movies have made horror/comedy a familiar genre it is difficult to write "traditional" horror stories—especially those with Gothic elements—without a gloss of satirical humor.*

The spread of gruesome horror motifs from 18-rated movies to the universally-accessible medium of television has resulted in the restoration of a certain calculated coyness to the presentation of Gothic imagery, which is routinely combined with a calculatedly light note of stylized irony. With the aid of hindsight, we can easily see in La Ville-Vampire *the ultimate literary ancestor of the popular television show* Buffy *the Vampire-Slayer. Although the fictitious*

[43] To be included in Volume 2.

"Anne Radcliffe" is not permitted by her gentlemanly author actually to slay any vampires with her own hand, she is nevertheless the prime mover of the expedition to the Vampire City of Selene; she watches with a distinctly proto-feminist fascination as the Irish hero carefully excises the heart from the breast of a comatose vampire.

By virtue of this happy coincidence, the baroque humor of La Ville-Vampire *is more likely to appeal to modern English and American readers than it could have done had a translation followed hot on the heels of its first appearance in France. Even the stream of sly insults leveled at the English can be easily laughed off by the contemporary English reader, because they clearly apply to the Victorians and not to us.*

Radcliffe was the most popular British author of the 1790s, not merely in Britain but throughout continental Europe, where she became the most widely-translated English author of that era. Her first two novels were both issued anonymously; the Scotland-set The Castles of Athlin *and* Dunbayne *(1789), was a slender and rather weak melodrama but* A Sicilian Romance *(1790), although it was not much longer, presented a far more striking story cast solidly in what would soon come to be recognized as the Gothic mold.*

Although Horace Walpole's The Castle of Otranto *(1764) is nowadays recognized as the original template from which the classic Gothics were stamped, it was not a particularly influential work in the 18th century, partly because it was so obviously a joke. Although some modern critics have tried to affiliate William Beckford's gaudy Oriental fantasy* Vathek *(1786)–which is even more sarcastic–to the Gothic tradition, the quarter-century following the publication of* The Castle of Otranto *actually produced only two significant novels which employed its formula more earnestly, both of them written by women. Both were careful to eliminate the supposedly-archaic supernatural elements of Walpole's plot, but they greatly exaggerated and extrapolated the sense of veiled threat to which their heroines were subjected. These two novels were Clara Reeve's* The Champion of Virtue *(1777; better known as* The Old English Baron) *and Sophia Lee's* The Recess *(1783-85).*

Radcliffe took from these examples the firm resolution that all apparently-supernatural events in her works must eventually be given a rational explanation–an aspect of her work which Féval casually disregards, except for a couple of sly asides–but she certainly did not underestimate the power of apparently supernatural events to reflect and symbolize the terror to which her heroines were reduced by the interest shown in them by urbane but malevolent older males. She became expert in the art of impregnating descriptions of architecture, landscape and polite behavior with oblique menace.

Having undertaken a trial run in A Sicilian Romance, *Radcliffe allowed her imagination full rein in* The Romance of the Forest *(1791), the first book to which she attached a signature and the first which employed a charismatically sinister villain, the Marquis de Montalt. The novel's popularity was such that she was offered 500 pounds–an unprecedented sum–for the right to publish* The Mysteries of Udolpho *(1794), which became a runaway bestseller and the inspiration for a flood of imitations. Its villain, Montoni, became the archetype of his species. So successful was the novel, in fact, that the publisher broke his own record by offering 800 pounds for* The Italian *(1797; sometimes reprinted under its original subtitle,* The Confessional of the Black Penitents*), in which the villain, Father Schedoni, shelters beneath the protective disguise of a man of the cloth all the viciousness and violence of the ancient Inquisition. All sophisticated readers agreed that he was a more impressive figure than the infinitely less subtle villain of Matthew Gregory Lewis's* The Monk *(1796), but unsophisticated ones were not so sure. Lewis borrowed extensively from contemporary German tales of terror–which were not in the least ashamed of graphic supernatural devices–so* The Monk *achieved the greater* succès de scandale *and became the more powerful influence on downmarket Gothics.*

In the same year as The Italian, *Radcliffe published a version of journals she had kept during her one and only expedition to continental Europe,* A Journey Made in the Summer of 1794 through Holland and the Western Frontier of Germany With a Return Down the Rhine, To Which are Added Observations of a Tour of the Lakes. *Presumably, she might have obtained 1,000 pounds for her next novel, but she did not; she published nothing more during her lifetime, although she did not die until 1823, when she was killed by one of the fits of asthma to which she had become increasingly subject. She must have known by then that she had conferred such awesome power on her villains as to inspire Lord Byron to employ them as role models, but we can only speculate as to what she would have made of that perverse appropriation.*

William Radcliffe's obituary of his wife gives absolutely no indication of how she came to write the kind of books she wrote, and none as to why she quit while she was so far ahead of her field. Given that he was presumably partly responsible for the dearth of surviving documents, his comments may seem to the modern reader to be calculated to maintain a veil of secrecy. It is in this historical context that the modern reader needs to set Féval's calculatedly frivolous speculations about the nature of Mrs. Radcliffe's inspiration and his vividly excessive caricature of the formula that she brought to its peculiar perfection.

B.S.

Prologue

There are many people in England, especially English women, who are appalled when they are told of the acts of blatant piracy to which French writers are subjected in England. Her Most Gracious Majesty Queen Victoria once signed a treaty with France with the laudable intention of putting an end to these oft-repeated thefts. The treaty is very well made, except that it contains one tiny clause that renders its terms illusory. Her Most Gracious Majesty, in effect, forbids her loyal subjects to appropriate our plays, books and so on, but she permits them to make that which she is pleased to call a "fair imitation."[44]

This is nice, but not honest. My dear and excellent friend Charles Dickens said to me one day, by way of apology: "I am not much better protected than you. When I go to London, if I happen to have an idea about my person, I lock my notecase, put it in my pocket and keep both hands upon it. It is stolen anyway."

The simple fact is that the "fair imitation" clause dangles temptation before subtle pickpockets.

Mr. Dickens' charming friend, Lady B*** of Shr*** House,[45] has repeatedly asked me the same question every time that I have had the pleasure of seeing her during the last twenty years: "Why don't you get your own back by stealing from the English?"

"It is certainly not that there is nothing in your books that would be worth stealing, Madame," I used to reply, "but I fear that our national character will not allow Frenchmen to indulge even in fair trickery."

That response caused Milady to burst out laughing. She even went so far as to recommend some suitable candidates to me... but hush! I have a tale to tell.

One morning late last year, Milady generously sprang a surprise on me.

"I am taking you away," she said. "I have arranged everything with your dear wife. We depart this evening."

"And we are going...?"

"To my place."

"In the Rue Castiglione?"

"No, to Shr*** House in Staffordshire."

"I don't know about that!"

The weather was atrocious. If snow was falling and the wind was howling even in Paris, how rough would the crossing from Calais to Dover be?

---

[44] Féval's French version is "blond imitation", deliberately using the wrong meaning of "fair." His subsequent remark that it would be contrary to the French national character to employ *"blond escamotage"*–which I have rendered as "fair trickery"–presumably accounts for the fact that his own imitation of English Gothic novels is distinctly dark as well as blithely unfair.

[45] This character is, of course, fictitious but there is a clue to her inspiration in Scott's *Memoir of Mrs Ann Radcliffe*, whose French translation Féval had obviously read. Scott quotes from Ann's 1797 travel book a passage describing Hardwick in Derbyshire, which had been built by Elizabeth, Countess of Shrewsbury. Although the passage does not remark that the lady in question was better known by the nickname "Bess of Hardwick," Féval presumably knew that–hence "Lady B***, du château de Shr***."

Milady, brought up on Byron, was a lover of storms. "Don't be put off," she said, "just because you're afraid of catching cold. I have figured out a way to return, at a single stroke, everything that England has stolen from you. It's a red-hot opportunity. Mr X*** and Miss Z*** are already on the track, and besides, at Miss 97's age one simply doesn't have the time to hang about."

Mr X*** and Miss Z*** are two of the most sensational English novelists, always on the lookout for a good idea for a story. I asked for further details, but Milady refused to explain, being content to employ her extraordinary God-given eloquence to excite my curiosity.

"Do you trust Walter Scott?" she asked. "He was a passionate admirer of *The Mysteries of Udolpho* and wrote a biography of Mrs. Anne Radcliffe. Think of it: Walter Scott! Dickens himself once went to see Miss 97–in those days she was called Miss 94, but she changes her name every year on Christmas Day. I'm well acquainted with her stories, but this one is so extraordinary..."

I gave in, of course. We set out immediately. The crossing was hideous; it will haunt my dreams forever. All the demons of the air and sea played with that ferry as if it were a rubber balloon. The next day, we took a train from London to the northwest and stayed the night in Stafford. The day after that, Milady's landau conveyed us over a snow-covered plain into the hills on the borders of Shropshire. That evening, we dined at Milady's house.

This was what I had found out during the journey:

We were in the native region of the Mr. and Mrs. Ward who were the parents of the woman who was to become famous as Anne Radcliffe.[46] Miss 97– who was only three years short of her hundredth birthday–was a second cousin of the Wards. She lived in a cottage in the hills, just over three miles from Milady's house. This cottage had long been the residence of her illustrious kinswoman.

I do not use the word illustrious lightly and I am prepared to defend it against any claim of exaggeration. The fame of Anne Radcliffe was worldwide at one time, and her dark tales obtained a height of fashionability that our most successful contemporaries have been unable to equal. It was said that she cast her spell on cottage and country house alike. The Mysteries of Udolpho went through two hundred editions in England. In France the book was translated several times over, and one of those versions was reprinted forty times in Paris. Nor was it a brief infatuation; by now the fever has calmed somewhat, but The Mysteries of Udolpho and The Confessional of the Black Penitents still terrify thousands of young imaginations everywhere.

Now, Miss 97 knew of a personal experience of Anne Radcliffe, which Anne Radcliffe herself had told to her some seventy years previously. It was widely rumored in the region that it was this episode that had turned the placid

---

[46] Actually, as Féval knew perfectly well–just as he knew how Mrs Radcliffe actually spelled her first name–the Ward family originated in Leicestershire.

and rather cheerful temperament of Anne Radcliffe into the terrible gloom that characterized her work.

Walter Scott had had a vague inkling of this story, as is evidenced by a letter which he wrote on May 3, 1821 to his editor Constable, which contains this passage:

"As regards the manuscript of the Life of Anne Radcliffe, I shall delay its delivery until after my next interview with Miss Jebb, from which I hope to extract some useful and very interesting items of information. This woman is, it is said, the custodian not merely of a secret but of a 'significant curiosity' which will inject considerable interest into our story..."

This Miss Jebb was none other than our own Miss 97, who had now added forty-five years to the date of Scott's letter.[47] Like all the English, she had a weakness for the nobility, and Milady had persuaded her to put off Miss Z*** and Mr X*** because they were writers of a "common" stripe.

After breakfast on the day after our arrival, which was cold and grey, Milady invited me to climb into a carriage. We traveled for half an hour, then pulled up at a green-painted wooden gate which served as the entrance to a little old house, whose appearance was thoroughly respectable. The hills loomed above it on three sides, but the open countryside to the south was pleasant.

We were admitted to a parlor whose size was appropriate to the smallness of the house. Several portraits hung on the walls, mounted in decoratively gilded wooden frames.

A tall and lean old woman was sitting in the corner beside the stove. She seemed to me to be formed like a certain kind of bird, to which I couldn't put a name although I was sure I had once seen a regal specimen in a taxidermist's shop. Her nose had a razor's sharpness and her round eyes seemed half-asleep.

"How are you getting on, my dear Jebb?" Milady asked, affectionately.

"Not badly–and your Ladyship?"

I looked around the room to see who had spoken. There were only the three of us. Miss 97 was a natural ventriloquist. Her voice had circled around us and was heard as if from behind. She must have lost her looks a long time before, but she had conserved her strength well enough.

When Milady had introduced me, we sat down. The voice of Miss 97, resounding as if from the other side of the parlor, addressed me benevolently.

---

[47] William Radcliffe's obituary, quoted verbatim by Scott, records that "[Ann's] maternal grandmother was Anne Oates, the sister of Dr. Samuel Jebb of Stratford, who was the father of Sir Richard." It is the statement that the fictitious Miss Jebb "had now added forty-five years to the [1821] date of Scott's [imaginary] letter" which suggests that Féval–who has already said that all this happened "late last year"–wrote La Ville-Vampire in 1867, but I have not been able to trace the serial version in order to confirm that date.

"The Frenchman, monsieur, is brave and clever, the Italian wily, the Spaniard cruel, the German dull, the Russian brutal, the Englishman happy and remarkable in his generosity. She liked Frenchmen."

Miss 97 lifted her eyes to the ceiling as she pronounced the word She—which, upon her lips and punctuated with pious regard, always referred to Anne Radcliffe. The quotation which preceded it, with which I was unfortunately unfamiliar, was from A Sicilian Romance, the second novel which She had written.

"What style!" exclaimed Milady. "And what profundity!"

"I am honored," Miss 97 replied, "to express my gratitude to Your Ladyship."

From her overcoat, which she had removed on entering the cottage, Milady took a parcel containing four duodecimo volumes. It was the French translation of Sir Walter Scott's Biographies of Famous Writers, published in Paris by Charles Gosselin in 1820.

"You see that She is loved in France," said Milady earnestly, as she opened the volume which contained the Life of Anne Radcliffe.

There was evidently a certain tension within that poor old head, which suddenly eased. Miss Jebb's teeth became visible, the set still complete although they were yellow and strangely elongated. At the same time, a loud dry laugh sounded out of nowhere, and the voice of Miss Jebb—which emerged, this time, from under the table—said: "Very well, very well! Since the gentleman has come a long way and is Your Ladyship's guest, he shouldn't go away with nothing to show for his journey. I still hope that you will able to call me Miss Hundred one day, but I have been suffering from autumnal headaches for the first time in my life, and I don't want to carry this incredible story to the grave."

No sooner had she said it than we were all ears. Miss Jebb set down her cup and seemed to gather herself together. During the silence which followed, she shuddered briefly on two or three occasions, producing a sound like hazelnuts rattling in a paper bag.

"There has never been another tale like it," she murmured, at last, clasping her hands about her knees to prevent them from shaking. "I grow cold when I think of it, in the very depths of my heart. I don't know whether I ought to break my silence, but what can it matter? I should like Her name to be on everyone's lips one last time—and they will certainly talk, for it is terrible... terrible!"

I

Miss Anna spent her early childhood in the house where her parents, Mr. and Mrs. Ward, conducted their business. They were not rich, but they had very good connections. When Mr. Ward sold his establishment, in 1776 or thereabouts, he brought his wife and daughter to live in the cottage in which we are now gathered.[48]

Anna's adolescence flowed peacefully and happily by in this retreat, where "the mediocrity of gold"–as the poet has it–reigned supreme, sustaining that modest ease which is called good fortune.

During holidays especially, the cottage came to life. Then we would entertain Cornelia de Witt[49] with her governess, Signora Letizia, and a blithe young man named Edward S. Barton, accompanied by his tutor Otto Goetzi.

Anna, Edward and Cornelia were bound together by a firm friendship. It was virtually taken for granted that Ned Barton would marry Anna when he came of age. I remember that Mrs. Ward had begun to embroider, ten years in advance, a superb pair of muslin curtains in which the monograms of Anna and Edward were interwoven–but man proposes and God disposes. It transpired that Ned Barton and our Anna loved one another only as brother and sister. I am sure that was true of Ned; perhaps there was a little something more in the dear heart of Anna, but William Radcliffe was nevertheless the happiest of husbands–Sir Walter Scott says so in his account of her life.[50]

---

[48] The Ward family actually left London in 1772 and moved to Bath, where Ann might well have encountered Sophia and Harriet Lee.

[49] William Radcliffe's obituary, quoted by Scott, says: "[Ann] was descended from a near relative of the De Witts of Holland. In some family papers which I have seen, it is stated that a De Witt, of the family of John and Cornelius, came to England... bringing with him a daughter, Amelia, then an infant." The Christian name Cornelia is presumably derived from Cornelius, although one of the characters in *A Sicilian Romance* is a nun named Cornelia.

[50] This careful insinuation that the Radcliffes' marriage was not a happy one is utterly gratuitous. Féval surely cannot have known William Radcliffe, although William was, like him, a man trained in law who gave up that vocation to follow another career (as editor of the *English Chronicle*). Perhaps Féval regretted that Scott's memoir remained stubbornly silent regarding the motives of her writing save for the obituary-derived claim that William had encouraged her to begin it when she became bored because his editorial duties so often kept him late at the office. Féval was, of course, far too much of a gentleman to speculate that William might have been so intensely jealous of his wife's literary success that she had to abandon her career to soothe his wounded vanity, and that her detailed pen-portraits of domineering male villains might have drawn inspiration from the well of personal feeling. Even modern critics who would like to establish Ann as a proto-feminist have balked at any such suggestion, although Robert Miles, in *Ann Radcliffe: The Great Enchantress* (1995) does call attention to the unusual fact that the first signature placed on *The Romance of the Forest* was plain "Ann Radcliffe", to which an indication of marital status was only added

The world being as it is, there can never have been such natural grace as Anna's. And what exuberance! Wherever she went, the room filled with smiles. Her only fault was an excessive timidity. Never judge authors by their works! It is not a hundred but a thousand times that I have been asked where she found the melancholy inspiration of her genius. You, at least, when you have heard me out, will never ask me that question again.

The month of September 1787 saw the last holiday shared by our three friends. William Radcliffe had already added a fourth to their number. He had asked for the hand of Miss Ward in July of that same year. Ned and Cornelia had been engaged during the previous winter; they were very much in love with one another and the life that was in prospect for them seemed to hold every promise of success.

On this occasion, Monsieur Goetzi did not accompany his maturing pupil, who was already sporting–honorably, of course–the uniform of the Royal Navy. For her part, Letizia had stayed in Holland, where she was serving as house-keeper to Count Tiberio, Cornelia's tutor. To illustrate how beautiful Cornelia was, one must have recourse to the eloquence of my poor Anna, who was later to immortalize the charms of her friend in *The Mysteries of Udolpho*–Cornelia was the original on whom the character of Emily is based.

Oh, the memories! I was still a child, but I remember our long walks in the hills. Mr. Radcliffe had hardly a trace of romanesque precision; he was proper, well-dressed and polite to the fairer sex. Every time Ned and Cornelia lost them-selves in the woods, William Radcliffe tried to strike up a conversation with Anna that was pleasant and tender, but she would immediately call out to me and turn the discussion towards literary topics. At her request, Mr. Radcliffe would recite passages from Greek and Latin poets. Although she could hardly understand their meaning, She was in love with their learned music–and some-times, while the graduate of Oxford was declaiming Homer or Virgil, the soft gaze of our Anna would lose itself in the distance, where Midshipman Ned and the pale Cornelia were wandering, as if in a dream...

She would sigh then, and request Mr. Radcliffe to translate the text, word by word–which he did with a good grace, always happy to oblige.[51]

The farewells were sad, that year. They all knew that they would not see one another again until both marriages had taken place: that of Mr. Radcliffe and Anna at this very place, and that of Ned and Cornelia in Rotterdam, where Count Tiberio made his home.

---

in later editions. Féval presumably did not know this, nor could he have known that asthma is a stress-related (and sometimes stress-induced) condition.

[51] This detail is also derived, via Scott, from William's obituary, although the insinuation that Ann's interest in William's translations was occasionally de-flected to more inherently-interesting subjects is entirely Féval's.

In response to a delicate and sentimental impulse, they had arranged that both marriages would take place on the same day, at the same hour: one in Holland; the other in England. By that means, in spite of the distance between them, a kind of communion would be established between the two happy events.

From the end of the vacation to the time of the double marriage, a very active correspondence was maintained. Cornelia's letters were filled with the purest joy. As for Ned, he was as amorous as a whole battalion of lovers. I did not see our Anna's replies, but she seemed to me to be a little sad.

At Christmas, the plans for the wedding were set in motion. Throughout the month of January 1787, there was no other matter of discussion but the trousseau. The great day had been fixed for the third of March.

In February, a letter arrived from Holland which threw the household into turmoil. The dowager Countess of Montefalcone, née de Witt, had died in Dalmatia. Cornelia, her sole heiress, suddenly found herself in possession of an enormous fortune.

The letter was from Ned, who seemed disturbed and rather saddened by this occurrence.

Although the missive was very short, it found space to record the singular fact that Count Tiberio, by virtue of the bountiful inheritance of the dowager of Montefalcone, now found himself the immediate heir of his own pupil.

After this letter, no further news was received from Holland until the end of February. There was nothing particularly surprising in that: bad weather held sway over the Channel and the wind, which blew incessantly from the west, made the crossing difficult. Today's steampackets make a mockery of the stiffest wind but in those days weeks could pass without any word arriving from the continent.

Every morning, as was his habit, the excellent Mr. Ward would look up at the weathervane atop the cottage and say: "As soon as that cock turns around, we'll get a whole ream of letters all at once!"

The first two days of March also passed without news. The wedding was to take place the following day; the house was full of activity and noise.

An hour after dinner, as evening approached, the wedding-gown was delivered–and almost at the same instant, the bell at the gate rang. The joyous voice of Mr. Ward was heard proclaiming from the staircase: "I said as much the day before yesterday: the cock has turned around! Here's the postman, bearing a whole armful of letters!"

Truth to tell, the arrival of the letters was rather inconvenient, given that the house was in such turmoil. The packet's contents were abundant and the dates of the postmarks very various. There was only time to open the most recent, in order to ascertain that our friends in Rotterdam were well, before everyone went back to work.

Under pressure of time, Anna was the prisoner of the couturiers who had brought her dress. I carried a batch of envelopes up to her myself, consisting of five letters–three from Cornelia and two from Ned Barton. At her request, I opened the one which seemed to be the latest, and went immediately to the foot of the fourth page.

"All is well," I said, after having scanned several lines.

"God be praised!" cried our Anna.

"Now, my angel," exclaimed the dressmaker, "little Jebb must show us a clean pair of heels–you're getting in our way, dear treasure."

She smiled at me to ameliorate the harshness of the instruction that chased me away. She was like a martyr assailed by four harpies with mouths full of pins, who were securing her within her shrine of white muslin. I put the packet of letters on the side-table and I left.

I should call your attention at this point to an important item: it is at this precise moment that I cease to speak as an actual eye-witness. From now on, it is to Anne Radcliffe herself that you are listening, for it was from her own lips that I had the rest of the story. I only saw her again after the events had taken place.

It was about seven o'clock in the evening when the dressmaker and her assistants left the house, carrying the wedding-gown away one last time in order to make the final alterations

When she was left alone, our Anna felt so utterly exhausted by the commotion of the day that she lacked the strength to come down to the parlor where her father, mother and fiancé were waiting. She offered herself the excuse that she had to give proper attention to the letters from Rotterdam, but sleep claimed her before she had reached the end of the first paragraph of a joyous letter bearing the signature Edward S. Barton.

Our Anna's sleep was feverish and filled with dreams. She saw a little church, framed in an unusual style, set in a pleasant countryside filled with trees and plants that did not grow in England. There were blankets of corn in the fields and the cattle had hides colored like turtle-doves. Beside the church was a cemetery whose tombs were all white. There were two among them that seemed to be identical, from each of which–a simple but touching motif one often encounters in English cemeteries–an arm extended, sculpted in a substance whiter than marble. The two arms stretched towards one another, so that their hands clasped.

She did not understand, in her dream, why the sight of those two sepulchers made her shiver and weep bitterly. She wanted to read the inscriptions engraved on the marble headstones, but it was impossible to do that. The letters became jumbled and fled before her gaze.

At ten o'clock, when the noise of the returning dressmakers woke her up, She was still in tears. She had slept for three hours but the weight of a terrible unhappiness lay upon her mind.

"I shall not ask why you have such red eyes, Miss Ward," the dressmaker said to her. "Young girls about to be married always weep, and I suppose they are entitled. Try the dress on."

The dress was tried on. It fitted well, and they left her alone again. She bathed her eyes. The couturier's words had brought back the impression of her dream. Her gaze happened to fall upon the letters from Rotterdam which she had almost forgotten, and a loud gasp escaped her bosom.

It was as if she could suddenly read the names inscribed on the marble of the two identical tombs: Cornelia! Edward!

She opened an envelope at random. Her over-anxious eyes saw nothing at first but black dots dancing on the white sheet. When she was finally able to read, she was quickly reassured. The letter had been written on the thirteenth of February by Cornelia, who was happily making plans for the next holiday. By that time, the will of the dowager countess would have been sorted out. Cornelia intended to come to the cottage, not to stay there as she normally did but to collect the whole family and convey them to Castle Montefalcone, in the Dinaric Alps beyond Ragusa.[52] She had a huge estate there, with marble and alabaster quarries. She was beside herself with joy. Ned had fallen in love with a poor girl, but now she was suddenly able to make him a rich landowner...

"What would I have given him?" our Anna thought, as she folded the letter. "It is better this way—and William is a worthy soul, after all."

Because she had already slept for three hours, she no longer felt tired. She settled down in a comfortable armchair and resolved to read the rest of her correspondence through to the end.

The happiness of her dear Cornelia delighted her, and you will understand that although a few sighs disturbed the muslin of her bodice, they were not provoked by envy. Anna envious—what blasphemy! No, but it is certainly true that Corny dwelt a little too much upon her new riches, her finery—and, above all, on the ardor of the attentions lavished upon her by the enraptured Ned. Entire pages sang like psalms, and vaulting over the psalms of Miss Corny came the dithyrambs of Edward Barton. Joy! Love! Love! Joy! It became monotonous. You have a nice saying in France: If you are rich enough, eat dinner twice! Perhaps our Anna thought: "They should be married twice, since they love one another so much."

She began to take a certain pride in comparing the moderation of her own proper affection with the delirium of Cornelia. Then, when she had become philosophical, thoroughly imbued with the kind of sagacity with which Chris-

---

[52] The name Ragusa was then attached by Western Europeans to the city which is now Dubrovnik in Croatia.

tians regard pagans, she began to tell herself that an excess of happiness could easily be transformed into its opposite. Such is human existence: action and reaction. Whosoever wins will lose–and beyond every horizon there are clouds on their way to screen the brightest sun.

As soon as this thought was formed in our Anna's head, it established itself with a remarkable authority. It struck a chord there. She began to dread, in advance, the miseries which could so easily succeed that deluge of felicities, in the near or distant future. Dear Ned! Poor Corny! Sorrow is so cruel when it follows joy! I believe that our Anna shed a few tears after having discovered the serpent lurking beneath the roses of the voluminous correspondence–because it was there, in the letters; oh yes, it was there!

I said there were five, and that was no lie, but they were separated within like those Chinese boxes that are nested one within another, to the continuing astonishment of little children. Cornelia's letters contained Ned Barton's interjections, while his permitted hers to spring forth within, and our Anna read on and on. She was on tenterhooks. It seemed to her that she might have been reading forever–and at the very moment when the philosophical idea came to her– the idea that well-educated people render as "The Tarpeian rock is very close to the Capitol"–a corresponding change overcame the letters.

A cloud, distant as yet, appeared in the blue sky. She saw it grow, advance, darken, concealing in its skirts... but we must not get ahead of ourselves. The thunderstorm will break soon enough.

I don't know if you are like me, but every time within this incomparable story that She employs that formula, whose inventor she was–we must not get ahead of ourselves–my flesh crept.

Little by little, the correspondence of the two lovers of Rotterdam changed its character.

As chance would have it, Anna had opened the oldest letters first. The cloud rose above the horizon when she opened the earlier of the last two envelopes.

It began as a letter from Ned; the song had descended into a lower key. So far, Count Tiberio, that paragon of tutors, had never been mentioned by Ned's pen without a gesture of indulgence, kindness or generosity. This time, the not-very-august name arrived bare of any adjective. Even more disturbing, Ned had not much to say about love.

Vaguely–very vaguely–he hinted that the inheritance of the dowager countess might possibly cause trouble. Count Tiberio's demeanor had changed. Monsieur Goetzi, who was passing through Rotterdam, had insinuated peculiar things...

There followed a letter from Corny, who was evidently suffering from "nerves." She called Letizia Pallanti "that person." Yesterday's angel, that "perfect creature" Letizia! Why? It was unexplained–but between the irritated lines of the missive, our Anna's perspicacity divined one utterly shocking thing: Letizia, neglectful not merely of universal morality but even of the most common decency, had entered into a relationship with Count Tiberio which it would be superfluous to describe.

As for Monsieur Goetzi–this was a more recent letter–what part was he playing? He spoke very ill of Count Tiberio, saying that his scandalous conduct had thrown his affairs into chaos, and he passed entire mornings and afternoons locked in Count Tiberio's office! He was present at all the orgies (the very word written in the letter) and when "that creature" Letizia emerged sporting diamonds, Monsieur Goetzi would play up to her like a cavalier!

Think of the lateness of the hour! It was already long past the time when She had heard the chimes of midnight but she felt not the slightest need of sleep. Our Anna was consumed by a fervent desire to know what it was that had taken root in her good heart. She read on and on. A strange wedding-eve!

As the reading proceeded, the vague menace became distinct. Happiness and security induced boredom, but as the cloud gathered on the distant horizon, her interest reawakened.

As the first thunderclap sounded, She leapt suddenly from her armchair. A note of Ned's spoke of "delay"–and it was the marriage that was delayed!

The explanation was given by the statement that the inheritance was a splendid thing, but a little complicated, and that it was necessary to go to the place...

Why did the two not get married beforehand?

That was exactly the question that poor Ned posed.

She unfolded page after page, finding medium-sized leaves within the larger ones and smaller ones within the medium-sized. She read on and on. The most recent envelope had already been opened, when Mr. Ward had extracted from it the reassuring letter that had occasioned his cries of joy.

But do you know what that brave man had read? And I too, in my turn–for I had been similarly deceived.

We had read, here and there, two or three fragments of paragraphs in which the word "happiness" had been repeated one more time–but, alas, it was to express the regret of happiness lost!

"At the moment when all was smiles," poor Ned wrote, indeed, "when the future presented itself to us in the brightest colors: happiness, wealth, love..."

Mr. Ward had not inquired any further, and nor had I. But the sentence went on:

"...the storm burst. Yes, at that very moment; we were struck by lightning and cast down; we are lost!"

Lost! Imagine our Anna's state of mind.

Unhappily, there was no exaggeration in that fateful word! A note added by the unfortunate Cornelia read: "Torn from my bed in the middle of the night. Monsieur Goetzi seizes my hand at the foot of the stair and says: 'Courage! You have a friend!' Should I believe him? I am dragged away... The night is horrible and the tempest drowns my pleas to be sensible..."

She let go of the paper and fell to her knees.

"Oh Lord of All," she cried, between sobs, "why do you permit such heinous crimes? Where are you now, Cornelia? Where are you, my dearest friend?"

Other women usually faint in similar situations, but She was superior to the rest of her sex. Without abandoning her prayerful posture, she seized the letters again and continued to read through her tears. Ned seemed to respond to the last question which had sprung to our Anna's mind.

"Monsieur Goetzi had warned me," he wrote, in a few scarcely-legible lines, "but I did not want to believe him. What part is that man playing? This morning, I found Count Tiberio's house deserted. In the street the neighbors had gathered, crying: 'They have taken flight like thieves! The bankruptcy will be enormous!' 'You're wide of the mark,' replied Monsieur Goetzi, who had sprung forth as if from the ground. 'There will be no bankruptcy, and Count Tiberio will pay everyone, for he will marry the heir to the immense Montefalcone fortune!' "

One letter remained; a scrap of paper on which Ned had painfully scribbled: "Last evening, Monsieur Goetzi came to my house. He seemed to sympathize with my distress. He has told me that my beloved Cornelia, abducted by her infamous tutor, is on her way to Castle Montefalcone in Dalmatia. He advised me to hasten in pursuit. A saddled horse was ready and waiting outside my door. I set forth, although my strength was near-exhausted. No sooner was I out of town than I was surrounded and attacked by four men with their faces obscured by masks. Nevertheless, by the light of the moon and through the holes in one of the masks, I believe I recognized that green light which shines in the eyes of Monsieur Goetzi. Is it possible? A man who has been my teacher! They left me for dead on the highway. I lay there until morning, losing blood from twenty wounds. At daybreak, villagers who were carrying their produce to market took me up and carried me to a nearby inn, which bears the sign Ale and Amity. May God reward them! Not that I value my life, but Cornelia has no one but me to defend her. My bed is good. My room is large. It is decorated with prints displaying the battles of Admiral Ruyter. The curtains have floral designs. The innkeeper seems harmless, but he resembles Monsieur Goetzi from behind. He has no face, which produces a peculiar effect. He is accompanied everywhere by an enormous dog which has, by contrast, a human figure. In the wall directly in front of my bed, eight feet above the ground or thereabouts, is a round-shaped opening like those which give access to stove-pipes. In the darkness above the hole I can distinguish something green: eyes which watch me incessantly... I am, God be praised, quite composed. A doctor has been summoned from Rotterdam to look after me. He and his pipe must outweigh three Englishmen. There is a hint of green in his eyes. Do you happen to know whether Monsieur Goetzi ever had a brother...?

"A little boy five or six years old came into my room rolling a hoop. He demanded of me in an impertinent manner: 'Are you the dead man?'–and he threw a folded paper on to my coverlet. It was a letter from Cornelia... I scarcely had time to hide the paper. A bald woman came in, followed by the dog which now seems to look at me with the eyes of Monsieur Goetzi. It never barks. The innkeeper has a parrot that he carries everywhere on his shoulder and which says incessantly: 'Have you dined, Ducat?' The green eyes transfix me from the depths of the black hole. The child laughs heartily in the courtyard, crying: 'I have seen the dead man!' Around me, everything is green. Anna, my dear Anna, help...!"

II

She got up right away, for she had not merely read the final word but understood it.

Within and without her mind, a double voice that sounded like the reunited voices of Cornelia de Witt and Edward Barton distinctly pronounced the words: "Help us! Help us!"

She strode back and forth across the room, in the grip of feverish distress. Then her thoughts turned again to God. She felt calmer.

Having been called, what could she do but go? She must go to their aid. How? She had no idea. The consciousness of her weakness was crushing, but there was something in her that was great and indomitable: her will.

She would save Edward and Cornelia.

A powerful effort calmed her fever. She was able to collect her thoughts. Who could she ask for help? Mr. Ward was old and his prudence was notorious. William Radcliffe, her intended husband, was certainly young enough, but he was a lawyer. Doubtless there are lawyers who are as brave as lions, but it is not their calling. In the end, our Anna concluded that she should not approach Mr. Radcliffe.

It was the same with the other friends gathered in the house: peaceful folk best suited to backgammon and card-games. She was kind enough to think of me for a moment, but I was definitely too small–and yet, it was necessary to get moving.

The first light of dawn was illuminating the curtained window. She pulled a little case into the middle of the room and threw the necessary items into it haphazardly. I do not think that she had made an actual decision to set off secretly on a long journey on the very morning of her wedding–no, she had a proper respect for convention–but there are certain things that we do without thinking, and this was one of them.

It was about four-thirty or five in the morning. Everyone in the cottage was asleep as she slipped through the corridors, carrying her case.

Grey Jack, the handyman, slept in a room on the ground floor, next door to the pantry. She knocked gently on his door and said to him: "Wake up, Jack, my friend; I have to speak to you about something important."

The good servant immediately leapt from his bed, rubbing his eyes. "What is it, Miss?" he asked. "Today, we must all begin calling you Madam! What a day! What the devil are you doing up at this hour?"

She replied: "Get dressed quickly, Jack my good friend. You are needed."

Hearing those words frightened him. When the lamp had been lit, he could see her, and was terrified. She was paler than a corpse. "Has something bad happened in the house?" he stammered.

"Yes," she replied, "something very bad has happened, but not in the house. Get dressed, Jack, for God's sake!"

The old man was all a-tremble, but he put on his clothes with all due haste. When he was dressed, she continued: "Grey Jack, do you remember your friend Ned Barton, whom you dandled on your knees, and Corny, the little girl from Holland?"

"Of course I remember Mr. Edward and Miss Cornelia!" the old man exclaimed. "Aren't they getting married this morning, on the other side of the sea?"

"You liked them both very much, didn't you, Jack?"

"Very much indeed–and I still do."

"Good! Jack, Johnny must be harnessed to the cart and driven across country to town."

"Who by? Me?" cried the stupefied fellow. "I must leave the house on your wedding day! You'll get married without me!"

"I won't get married without you, Jack, because I'm going with you." He would certainly have protested, but she added: "It's a matter of life and death!"

Grey Jack, totally bewildered, ran to the stable without asking for any further explanation. Reluctantly, he did as he was told. From time to time, he looked back at the windows to see if anyone else had got up–but everyone was still in bed. The whole world was asleep.

She took her place in the cart.

Grey Jack climbed up on to the driver's seat. Johnny broke into a trot.

No one in the house awoke. She felt a constriction in her heart. Although she had not yet composed any of her admirable works, she already possessed the brilliant and noble style which Sir Walter Scott was to praise to the skies in his biography. Indeed, she could not help exclaiming: "Goodbye, dear refuge. Happy shelter of my adolescence, adieu! Verdant countryside, proud hills, woodlands full of trees and mystery, shall I ever see you again?"

Grey Jack, who was not in a good mood, turned to her and said: "Instead of talking to yourself, Miss, you would do better to tell me why we are going to Stafford so early."

"Grey Jack," she said, solemnly, "we are not bound for Stafford."

Grey Jack turned to her, open-mouthed. "Miss," he said, while his huge eyebrows drew together, "for twenty-three years you have been whiter than a lamb, but if you are using me to run away from your father and mother's house, I'll be damned..."

She cut him off with a gesture, and said: "Don't jump to any conclusions, Jack. Just go—to Lichfield!"[53]

Even the most beautiful girl in the world could only give what she had. I am recounting the tale to you as she told it to me. She did not bother to fill in certain details. For instance, no exact account of the cycle of day and night figured in her narrative. She passed over such mere trifles, carried onwards by memories that soared like the winged horse Pegasus, symbol of the imagination of poets.

You are entitled to suppose that She ate meals, for her stomach was of the same superior quality as the rest of her being. She slept too, equally well, but these diverse functions and all those which debase our nature we shall pass over in silence.

Another matter on which subject our Anna always disdained to furnish me with any details was the question of money. In that respect, Milady and Monsieur, you may formulate your own hypotheses with all the ingenuity of which you are capable. The journey was long and confounded by the most extraordinary obstacles. She was continually required to open her purse. Whence did she draw those expenses? I don't know, and wash my hands of the matter. The fact is that she paid her way and returned to the fold without having left a single outstanding debt.

Between Stafford and Lichfield, Grey Jack, who had had a good meal, became more inquisitive.

"I suppose, Miss, that Miss Corny and that strapping lad Ned are waiting for you down there with a third gallant? Am I right? William Radcliffe doesn't know about this, does he? It doesn't matter—here in England there's no shortage of vicars to marry two young people at the drop of a hat. But who would have thought it of you, Miss Anna? Not me."

Instead of replying, She asked: "What do you think of Otto Goetzi, Jack?"

The old man nearly fell off his seat with astonishment. "What! Miss! Is it for that scruffy devil that you have scorned such a gentleman? Master William is certainly a queer bird, but..."

"I beg you to speak more respectfully of my husband, Jack!"

"Your husband! Now I don't understand anything at all!"

---

[53] Féval says "Lightfield"; this and other slightly-fudged references to English geography might be intended to satirize the typical geographical infelicities of the English Gothic novel, but there seems little point in duplicating them in an English version of the novel.

"I asked you what you thought of Monsieur Goetzi."

"I think that I would like to be in Lichfield in order to get to the bottom of this," replied the old man, in a bad humor. "As for Mr. Goetzi, he's not the first scoundrel I've seen well-supported and well-nourished by good families while pretending to teach young children."

The horse shied. Grey Jack crossed himself. "See what happens when his name is spoken aloud," he muttered. "No one knows anything about the man, except that he is a vampire."

"I don't believe in vampires, my friend," said our Anna, disdainfully. She was above belief in the superstitions that flourished in the hills between the counties of Staffordshire and Shropshire.[54]

"Is that so?" replied the old man. "One has to believe in vampires. They come from the Turkish lands, a long way off, beyond the city of Belgrade. Only, I don't know exactly what they are. There's nothing you don't know–would you like to explain it to me, Miss?"

Like all educated people, She loved to instruct others. "Vampires," she said, "supposing that they exist, are monsters in human form, who originate from southern Hungary, between the Danube and the Sava. Their nourishment is the blood of young women..."

"That's right, Miss," cried Grey Jack, impetuously. "I have seen him with my own eyes!"

"Monsieur Goetzi–drinking the blood of a young woman?" said Anna, horrified.

"For want of a better word. It was Jewel, Miss Corny's little spaniel. What a darling! Do you remember? He stalked and drank the blood of the little creature, like the disgusting weasel he is. And he stole raw cutlets from the kitchen! And he got up at night to talk to spiders! And everyone knows that was how Polly Bird of the High Farm died–found asleep by the side of the stream and never woke up. And whenever he goes into a room all the lamps glow green. Can you deny or disprove it? And what of the tomcats which leap upon his back because he stinks worse than a she-cat in heat? And you ought to understand what the washerwoman says about him: all his shirts have a faded bloodstain in the place next to his heart!"

"My friend," she said to him, "those are the sort of rumors which circulate among common folk. I need something more definite. Don't you know why Monsieur Goetzi was dismissed from the house of Squire Barton?"

"Of course! Any child would be able to tell you that. It was because of Miss Corny. Squire Barton valued Mr. Goetzi highly as a man of learning, and he was like you–he didn't believe in vampires. It was because Miss Cornelia

---

[54] Féval's rendering might be more literally translated as "the shires of Stafford and Shrop"–another mild joke.

contracted a chest complaint and began to see green, and... that's odd, Miss Anna—look at the moon!"

The near-full moon had risen behind a screen of leafless poplars. Our Anna had the courage of a hero, but she could not help shuddering when she saw that the moon was green.

"Go on, I beg you," she murmured.

"That's what happens," Grey Jack murmured, "when one talks about him. One morning Miss Cornelia was found unconscious in her bed. Upon her left breast there was a little black puncture-wound, and Fancy, your chambermaid, saw a green spider of unusual size disappearing under the door. She followed it. The spider ran so swiftly along the corridor that Fancy couldn't catch up, but she perceived that it went into Mr. Goetzi's room. She found Ned Barton, the dear boy—who did not much like his tutor, it's true. Ned went into Mr. Goetzi's room and beat him so vigorously..."

"The wretch!" Anna put in, bringing her hands together. "Is this true? Did Ned really thrash that pernicious and vindictive creature?"

"With his fists, yes Miss, and kicked him too, and hit him with a cane and a chair. And Mr. Goetzi went to complain to the squire, who gave him a sum of money..."

They arrived in London that evening. She went, with Grey Jack, to see the Olympic Circus in Southwark. She was in no mood for frivolity, but there was no boat due to leave before the following morning and the idea of going to the circus was suggested to her by a peculiar coincidence.

One particular word leapt out at her from the extraordinary profusion of posters advertising the event: the word VAMPIRE.

Between the bills which advertised the clever horse that could walk on its hind legs, and the ones promoting the clown Bod-Big, who could swallow a mole and regurgitate it alive, there was inscribed in green letters:

MAIN ATTRACTION!!!
THE DEVOURING OF A YOUNG VIRGIN
BY THE AUTHENTIC VAMPIRE OF PETERWARDEIN
WHO WILL DRINK SEVERAL PINTS OF BLOOD
AS IS HIS HABIT
WITH THE MUSIC OF THE HORSEGUARDS
WONDERFUL ATTRACTION INDEED!!!

When She and Jack went in together, the immense circus-tent was full of spectators. They were watching an old woman painted with gilt, standing upright on a galloping horse. She leapt through paper circles, to the immense delight of the huge crowd. It was the famous Lily Cow.

166

Afterwards, the candles were extinguished–the age of gaslight had not yet arrived–and darkness fell, to be succeeded by a phosphorescent glow which reflected lividly from the faces of the spectators all around the amphitheater. Lightning flashed in the distance, and a pervasive moaning wind was heard. The music became grating.

An enormous spider, which had the body of a man and the wings of a vulture, was lowered down on a thread which hung down from above, stretched by its weight.

At the same time, a young Czech girl, hardly more than a child, dressed in white and mounted on a black horse, entered the ring. Balanced on her head was a garland of roses. She was sweet and beautiful, that young girl. She bore a slight resemblance to Cornelia de Witt, and–strangely enough–the resemblance grew the more clearly she was seen.

The spider curled itself up at the bottom of its thread; it no longer moved, but lay in wait. While it was thus immobilized, a distinct aura of green radiance could be seen surrounding it, most intensely at the center, weakening towards the periphery.

The young Czech played with her flowers and danced.

All of a sudden, the spider let itself fall from its thread. Its long and hideous legs flowed over the sand that carpeted the ring. The young girl saw it and made her fear manifest by means of diverse mimetic poses, which won her abundant applause.

The spider pursued the young girl, who fled as fast as she could to her black steed. The monster went after her, with uncertain strides. Unable to gain sufficient purchase on the surface, it adopted an expedient typical of its kind. I do not know exactly how to describe the manner in which it took her, but it carried filaments hither and yon, which appeared to emerge from its mouth. Within the blink of an eye, it had spun a web: a spiderweb!

The young girl was on her knees on the back of her horse. She threw away her garland, threw away her veils; clad only in flesh-colored tights she made a touching sight. Suddenly, the spider trapped her in its web. It was horrible. The horse, still free, darted right and left.

There was a sound of grinding bones.

It was not a spider, but actually a man who was seen to drink deep draughts of red blood through a blaze of green light.

The circus-tent shook with the volume of the applause, but Anna fell into a faint, crying: "Monsieur Goetzi! It is Monsieur Goetzi! I recognized him!"

There is no country in the world where the principle of liberty is so splendidly applied as in England. Nevertheless, I do not think that our laws permit the exhibition on the public stage of an authentic vampire crunching the bones and drinking the blood of a real girl. That would be too much.

I believe therefore that you can take it for granted that the administrators of the Southwark Circus produced the illusion by the means that they were accustomed to employ. The proof of this is that the young horsewoman, devoured by the vampire, was pulverized and drained in like manner every night for several weeks, and was none the worse for it.

As regards the question of knowing whether the monster was really Monsieur Goetzi, I do not believe it, although we are assured that these exceptional creatures called vampires or accursed wanderers have the gift of ubiquity—or at least of alibi-ty, if I may be permitted to invent the word.

Our Anna's error can be explained by virtue of one of those resemblances which are so common in nature. The majority of authors agree that all vampires exhibit a family resemblance, as if they were the sons or nephews of the same stallion sire.

It would be very foolish to suppose, no matter what was described just now, that Monsieur Goetzi could have taken the trouble to abandon the important matters which required his attention in Holland in order to perform as an acrobat.

III

The crossing was uneventful. Grey Jack ate and slept. She, on the other hand, propped herself up against the bulwark in one of those correct and noble poses which she naturally assumed, watching the frothy wake churned up by the vessel's passage. Her eyes were trying to penetrate the immense profundity of the sea. The waves were suggestive of infinity.

Once they had passed out of the Thames estuary Grey Jack woke up, saw the land on the horizon, and asked for a drink. She made him sit down beside her and recounted with marvelous exactitude the incoherent ravings that she had read on the eve of her wedding.

"Such is the sum," she reported, "of that unhappy correspondence. It turns out that Count Tiberio, the tutor of my cousin Cornelia, is a débauché, and also that his business is in a perilous state. As for Letizia Pallanti—a well-born person does not deign to mention creatures of that sort. The two of them have seized Cornelia and have taken her to the mountains of ancient Illyria. Do you think that such force could have any honorable intention? The infamous Tiberio is my cousin's heir. O Heaven! I dare not think of what might happen to my dear Cornelia in the wilderness of Dalmatia, which civilization has been so slow to penetrate."

"The fact is," said Grey Jack, "that the more one thinks about it, the more content one is to be in England. But who will sow the spring seeds if you take me off chasing all the devils in Hell? Will you have the goodness to tell me that?"

"While you are asking me frivolous questions, Edward Barton, stabbed by four hired bandits, has been delivered into the care of mercenaries. His last letter did not even mention Merry Bones..."

"That Irish rogue!" Grey Jack exclaimed, with sudden violence.

"The Irish are Christians, like us, my friend," Anna pointed out, gently. Try telling that to a man who is English to the core! Jack's fists had clenched at the mere mention of Merry Bones, who was Edward Barton's valet.

This Merry Bones, Old Jack's enemy, bore some resemblance to a bundle of firewood. His figure was defined by very big bones, which had hardly any flesh upon them, and when he laughed, his mouth split his face from ear to ear. A merry companion indeed! His right eye was huge and his left so tiny that it seemed to be the child of the other. His hair was so coarse that it was impossible for him to wear a hat; he plaited it like the tail of an American horse. He had once been a mariner, but he had spent the greater part of his career as a "nail-head" in a public house in Whitefriars.

A "nailhead" is the name given to those Irishmen who hire out their skulls for sixpence to test the fists and canes of gentlemen. They charge a whole shilling for a cudgel. If asked, Merry Bones would go as far as to take a saber-thrust for half a crown.

The boat put in at Ostend and then set out again for Rotterdam. Moving along the coast of that unique and celebrated territory, Anna could not help but think of the great historic events which bound England's past to Holland's; but as the vessel progressed northwards by degrees, passing the mouths of the channels one by one, the importance of the matter in hand reasserted itself.

Night was falling when the boat entered the estuary of the Meuse; by the time they reached the port of Rotterdam the darkness was complete. Innkeepers were eager to attract their custom, but they were not so tired as they had been the day before; in reply to the various solicitations, Anna said: "I don't want to stay at any inn in town, but can anyone tell me the location of a country hostelry known by the name of Ale and Amity?"

The men gathered by the quayside suddenly fell silent. Then one voice said: "Young lady, this is not a good time to go to a place like that!" And as if all their tongues had been loosened at the same time, a great murmur began in which only the following words could be distinguished: "Why choose the very inn where the Englishman has been stabbed?"

Although the talk was of murdered men, the Flemish tableau was not at all unpleasant. There were a dozen honest faces there, lighted as if in a Rembrandt painting by the lanterns of the hotel touts. She came down into the middle of the crowd, draped in her cloak and supported by the arms of Grey Jack. A few yards away flowed the Meuse, where galiots swayed heavily on the waves.

She repeated, coldly: "Does anyone know the way to this sinister place called Ale and Amity?"

The silence which followed these firm words was disturbed by the noise of dry derisive laughter.

"What's that?" our Anna demanded, losing none of her intrepid serenity.

Before replying, they crossed themselves.

"The wind laughs like that, ever since the Englishman was stabbed..."

"In God's name, young stranger, don't go out on the Gueldre causeway to-night, or you'll be sorry."

"Yesterday's high tide has broken the dikes."

"The road has crumbled away in more than ten places."

"It's impassable to carriages and horses alike."

"Do you hear, Miss?" Jack exclaimed. "Neither carriages nor horses! See!"

"I will go by water," said our Anna.

"The high tide has flooded the canal. No boats can enter it."

"Then I'll go on foot," she said. "There is no obstacle large enough to keep me from the road I want to take. If one among you will consent to guide me to the inn of Ale and Amity, I will pay the asking price–whatever it might be."

The crowd remained silent, and a distant echo could be heard of that laughter which had previously pierced the night.

At the same time, a peasant dressed in trews and a doublet of white linen suddenly appeared in the lighted area, pushing through the crowd. He was wearing a big Flemish hat, which was tilted over his eyes. The light of the lanterns tried to slide under the capacious rim, but nothing could be seen of his features: nothing at all. And–how can I put this?–that nothing induced a shiver.

"Who is that?" asked a chorus of low voices.

No one replied.

The peasant passed through the crowd and came to take the suitcase from Grey Jack's hands. The servant's teeth were chattering.

"The matter is settled," the newcomer said, with a voice that our Anna herself was never able to describe. "I will take you where you want to go. Follow me." And he set forth, as stiff as a man of stone but making swift headway.

She followed him, in spite of Grey Jack's supplications.

The shore was enveloped by the darkness of night, but in the distance a pale radiance could be seen, within which the group composed of the peasant, our Anna and old Jack moved with great rapidity.

It seemed that the radiance came from the peasant: it was green. The representatives of the various inns felt their flesh creep as they dispersed like a flock of ducks.

The travelers maintained a straight course, clearing the canals and fences whether or not there were bridges. It all seemed perfectly straightforward to our Anna, who went where her guide went–and Grey Jack followed in his turn. The town was behind them in the blink of an eye.

They left the town on the east side. Crossing a terrain where land and water alternated and mingled in extraordinary confusion, the journey proceeded with

170

scarcely any difficulty. There was certainly no shortage of obstacles: the ever-present canals, rivers and marine inlets were like tangled hair, but there was an excellent system of bridges which allowed them to keep their feet dry.

After some minutes, the scene changed. I beg you to do your utmost to imagine three individuals enshrouded in near-blackness, making their way by the muted light of the stars. A dense mist was gathering, hiding both the earth and the sky.

Within this mist the peasant shone faintly as if his body had been rubbed with phosphorus. He had not said a word since they had set out, but he went on and on. His Flemish hat was no longer on his head. The wind stirred and twisted his hair, drawing sparks therefrom.

Then, all of a sudden, the night became clear. The entire panoply of the stars was suspended in the sky. The road ran straight and level as far as the eye could see between two meadowlands flecked with puddles like polished mirrors.

How was it that the sound of a bell could extend into that place where there was neither bell-tower nor parish church? The twelve strokes of midnight could be distinctly heard. At the twelfth, the illumination of the peasant's hair was extinguished, and the air was filled with derisive laughter.

"Help!" lamented Grey Jack.

The earth suddenly opened up to engulf them, thus confirming the presentments of our Anna.

If you balk at believing in the instantaneous formation of a deep pit, I will freely confess that the personal opinion of our Anna was that a cave-in had already taken place, caused by the high tides of the new moon. The principal charm of a narrative like ours is its realism. And besides, in making further progress we shall encounter more than enough hyperphysical incidents.

She was fond of that word–which could, I suppose, be rendered "supernatural".[55]

The pit was as black as the ink at the bottom of a well, and lined with suffocating and acridly odorous marine mud. A dark silhouette was outlined above them, gesturing in cruel triumph, and the suitcase was dropped into the abyss, displacing torrents of mud as it fell.

Grey Jack–who was, after all, only a man of common extraction–seized the opportunity to address bitter reproaches to his young mistress. "See what a pretty pickle we're in now, Miss! You should have followed the good advice I gave you. I was certain that this rascally peasant was none other than Mr. Goetzi himself, or at least one of his kin. Now, we'll perish in this cesspit!"

---

[55] This is Féval's principal concession to the fact that Ann Radcliffe always provided rational explanations for the supernatural events in her stories, although the much later reference to the Countess Elvina's old Aeolian harps is a more accurate reflection of the author's strategy.

In the deep silence of the night, the cackle of demoniacal laughter was heard yet again, but so distantly that it was scarcely distinguishable.

Fortunately, at almost the same instant, sounds of a very different kind made themselves heard. Soft musical notes of a rustic quality became audible, mingled with bursts of cheerful laughter. At first, our Anna could not believe her ears, and Grey Jack thought that he was in the grip of the hallucinations which precede death.

Soon enough, though, it was impossible to doubt it. The sound of horses' hooves and cartwheels was approaching rapidly. The darkness, meanwhile, was relieved by brightening lights.

Eventually, at the edge of the pit opposite to that which had given way under the feet of our Anna and old Jack, a very agreeable sight presented itself. Firstly, there were young Dutch girls crowned with flowers and dressed for a holiday, whose smiling beauty was lit by the glare of many torches; a near-equal quantity of young boys followed in their train. Then came a respectable man in clerical costume–not the robes of a Catholic priest, but the dignified and austere habit of an Anglican priest. Then, last of all, came a young nobleman, a member of the finest aristocracy in all the world, no less: the English nobility.

This unknown person, fair of hair and pale of skin, with rosy-cheeks and sky-blue eyes, was positively comparable to a god.

She did not know the honorable Arthur *** from Adam, or Eve. She was certain, all the same, that she immediately recognized in him, firstly an Englishman, because the English "leap to the eyes" wherever one has the good fortune to run across them, just as Venus reveals her divine nature in every step she takes; secondly, one of the gentle folk, because every species of flower has its distinctive perfume; and finally, the son of a titled family, because none but the blind is denied the pleasure of classifying a star by its rays.

He was traveling incognito, perfecting his military education with a study of the historic battlefields of Germany and the Low Countries.

The young village girls crowned with flowers and clad in their Sunday best were contemplating the precipice in a somewhat crestfallen manner, saying to one another: "Look at that! We'll be late for the wedding!"

The clergyman, calm and serene, took up a position behind his pupil. "All well and good," he said, peering down into the pit. "Everything in life must be turned to profit. Tomorrow morning, I shall set you the problem of designing a bridge that would allow an army to cross this lagoon: thirteen thousand foot-soldiers, eight thousand horses and seventy-two artillery pieces of various caliber, with supply-trucks, ambulances and so on."

Immediately, the young unknown comparable to a god leaned over the pit, and lowered a torch so that he might see into it.

Our Anna could have contemplated that arresting spectacle for a lifetime, but Grey Jack–who was made of coarser stuff–had been knee-deep in mud for far too long.

"Oi!" he cried. "Are you going to leave us here, in the devil's name?"

There was sudden consternation among the villagers. The clergyman and our Anna, seized by the same thought, spoke in unison: "There's no need to such language!" Then the clergyman added: "Very well, My Lord, consider this question very carefully: given the situation that an unknown number of persons find themselves in trouble down below—by virtue of an accident, I suppose—what mechanical means would you employ to hoist them up to firm ground, if you had a rope but lacked a pulley?"

"I would take my purse," said the adolescent, matching speech with gesture, "and I would say to these brave people here: I will give ten French silver pistoles if you can bring that old man and that young woman here to me, safe and sound."

I do not know whether that response would be marked correct in the military examination at Eton, but the male wedding guests needed no further encouragement. In the blink of an eye, they leapt down from the lip of the landslide, and the two friends were carried up to the roadway.

She was then able to see the magnificently-equipped coach which had accommodated the young nobleman and his estimable instructor thus far along the road, having come from Nijmegen bound for Rotterdam.

The wedding-guests, interrupted as she had been by the landslide, undertook to find another way across—but because it was necessary to retrace their route, the young unknown comparable to a god gallantly bade our Anna to climb up into the carriage, and delivered her to the very door of the inn that was known by the singular name of Ale and Amity.

IV

The inn was a huge building framed by pilings, situated at the intersection of four roads. It was entirely black in color. There was no hedge around it, nor any trees nearby; it gave the impression of being lost in the middle of a desert. Above the door, the guttering light of a signal-lantern flickered in the night wind.

She felt her heart constrict as she lifted the door-knocker, thinking: "Between these walls, far from his homeland, my childhood friend Edward Barton has breathed his last!"

I have nothing to report of Grey Jack, whose mudstains extended as far as his armpits, but that he shook with fear and was in an exceedingly bad mood.

Although there seemed to be no light within the inn, the door opened at the first knock. Our Anna and Grey Jack found themselves in a low-ceilinged room which reeked of pipe-smoke.

There was a long table, furnished with benches. Empty pitchers stood upon it, their bases set in pools of spilled ale. There was a three-foot high counter de-

173

fended like a fortress, on which stood a clock in a fawn-colored cabinet encrusted with gilt, surmounted by the figure of a scrawny bird.

The hands of the clock stood at one hour, less two minutes, after midnight.

All this was apparent, even though no light burned in any of the candle-brackets and it was impossible to imagine that any ray of moonlight could have crept through the closed doors and windows. It seemed at the time that the objects emitted a dull and limpid light of their own, softened with a hint of green.

Unmoving beneath the clock, a group of people was gathered around a big man who seemed to possess only the outlines of a face: a frame of hair and beard. He had a long-tailed parrot perched on his shoulder. To his right there was a small boy of mischievous appearance, propped up on a hoop; to his left a monstrous flesh-colored dog whose form seemed nearly human, rigidly set on its four widespread paws.

Behind the counter, a bald and extremely fat woman was asleep, snoring loudly. Apart from the ticking of the clock—which was peculiarly profound—this was the only sound that could be heard within the inn.

She experienced an indefinable sensation, which was not quite fear. She had the strangest feeling, in consequence of this ominous emotion, that the people before her were mere accessories of the pendulum: parts of a mechanical system, like the figures mounted on the Strasbourg Clock.

"If you please," Grey Jack piped up, "we would like a fire by which to dry ourselves, bread, meat and ale!"

She bade him be silent with an abrupt gesture, although his requests were perfectly reasonable, and said in her turn: "We demand to be taken immediately to Edward S. Barton, esquire—an English subject, who is or was lodged in this public house—if he is still alive. If, unhappily, he is deceased, whether by natural causes or violence—which the forces of justice will ascertain—we shall claim his corpse so that we can ensure that it receives a Christian burial."

The inhabitants of the inn made no more response to these words than they had to Grey Jack's request. All remained silent—but the silence and stillness were soon split by a voice which sounded from every part of the inn, near and distant, high and low, and which cried out in a combative Irish accent: "I'll rip out your heart and eat your soul, begorrah! Vile spider! Do you think that the blood of a son of Connaught can be pumped like an Englishman's? See here!"

"It's Ned's valet, Merry Bones!" She murmured, hope mingling with astonishment. "He must have come to his aid."

Grey Jack shrugged his shoulders and muttered: "Or the devil brought the dirty rat!"

The cries of the Irish voice continued to echo, now from the attic, now from the cellar. Our Anna—who was valor itself—was just about to run out of the ground floor room when the inner workings of the clock emitted a rumbling sound, followed by loud chiming.

It struck thirteen times.

174

As soon as it began to sound, the comatose inhabitants of the inn finally began to move. The bald woman at the counter opened her eyes; the innkeeper shifted his weight from one foot to the other; the parrot combed his master's moustache with its beak, saying "Have you dined, Ducat?" The little boy spun his hoop, crying out "I've seen the dead man", and the scrawny bird on top of the clock-case spread its enormous wings and called cuckoo thirteen times.

In the meantime, a door opened between the counter and the clock. A tall bony body was framed in the opening, topped by a shaggy mass of hair, like an inverted brush of the "Turk's-head" variety. Behind Merry Bones–for it was he– came a second edition, complete and exact, of the various individuals who were in the ground floor room, to wit: the innkeeper without a face, the parrot, the dog with human features, the little boy with the hoop and the fat bald woman.

The only differences were that those from without were a little paler than those within, and innkeeper number two had an enormous bludgeon in his hand.

The latter's gaze–for the place where one should have been able to see his eyes was host to a gaze–was noticeably green; and when our Anna turned her own gaze towards innkeeper number one, she saw that a bludgeon had now appeared in his hand, and that his gaze also glowed green.

A terrible battle ensued.

Merry Bones, poor devil, was caught in a crossfire. The company that was already present and the company that had just arrived flung themselves upon him all at once, with angry ferocity. The two dogs and the two children seized him by the legs, the two parrots pecked at his eyes and the two old shrews grabbed him by the neck, while the two innkeepers, alternately raising and beating down with their clubs, hammered away at his head like blacksmiths at the forge.

Paralyzed by boundless horror, She bore witness to that hideous assault. As for the old reprobate Jack, rendered stupid by nationalistic spite, he merely folded his arms and muttered: "It's the Irishman's problem–he can look after himself."

As it happened, the Irishman did contrive to look after himself. He was unarmed, but his head was worth as much as a cannon. Each bludgeon-blow rebounded as if from an anvil, unable even to flatten the bristly mop of his hair. I don't know how he defended his legs, his throat and his eyes, but during the entire minute that the prodigious battle lasted, our Anna did not see him receive a single wound. To the contrary, the two parrots were fluttering their wings, the two fat women were sticking out their tongues, the two little rascals were kicking their feet like overturned crabs, and the two watchdogs were held at bay, growling threateningly. As for the two innkeepers, Merry Bones butted them in the stomach one by one, and sent them sprawling against the walls in opposite directions.

It was splendid to see, even though the worthy servant had not a drop of noble blood and had first seen light of day in a despicable country.

Then he leapt over the table with a mighty bound, zoomed across the room like an arrow and disappeared through the outside door. As he went, he found the time to blow a kiss to our Anna and made a sign of a different kind to Grey Jack, whose cheeks were swollen, as if he had had three teeth extracted.

As he disappeared into the night, Merry Bones addressed himself to our Anna, saying: "See you soon! I'm off to find the iron coffin!"

If She had ever devoted one of her masterpieces to the subject which presently concerns us, you would find therein explanatory chapters placed at the end of the text, which would provide detailed information about the notorious but little known social class of vampires. With that possibility in mind she had made copious notes; Monsieur Goetzi–who, apart from being a member of that species, was also a man of great erudition–had furnished some useful insights.

These notes cast some light on the inhabitants of the Ale and Amity, human and bestial alike–for the beasts here manifest were persons as well as the people.

I shall soon have to tell you some very remarkable things about the nature of these creatures which retain certain human characteristics although they are not human. For the moment, however, I shall restrict myself to pointing out, in passing, one of the most peculiar anomalies of the vampire race: the divisibility–or, if you prefer, the dividuality–of such creatures. She employed the more scientific term.

Each vampire is a collective, represented by one principal form, but possessing other accessory forms of indeterminate number. The famous vampire of Gran, which terrorized both banks of the Danube around the town of Ofen in the 14th century, was man, woman, child, crow, horse and pike. The history of Hungary attests that Madame Brady, the vampiress of Szeged, who passed also for an *oupire*,[56] was cockerel, soldier, lawyer and serpent.

In addition to this peculiarity, which already poses a considerable puzzle to contemporary science, it appears that each subsidiary form, like the dominant form, also has the ability to duplicate itself.

Thus, you have been able to observe that the innkeeper's family was both inside and outside the ground floor room at the same time–which made Merry Bones' situation very perilous indeed.

I shall explain one more thing, which was perhaps the strangest of all: the family of the faceless innkeeper, which you might consider, up to a point, to be a collective living being, could also be considered as nothing more than a mechanical system entirely composed of accessory figures, motivated as if by clockwork. The dominant form was not included among them.

---

[56] The text has *eupire*, but this is probably a misprint; Féval subsequently uses the more familiar *oupire*, which he had also used in *La Vampire*.

You will understand everything when I add that the chief of the clan, the very soul of the group, was...yes, you have guessed! The innkeeper, his wife, his dog, his parrot, his little boy, and perhaps even the cuckoo on the clock were all Monsieur Goetzi! I shall provide you with convincing proof soon enough.

It is necessary that you understand that this bundle of beings, singular and plural at the same time–which seems to be the most blatant realization of the most incomprehensible mysteries of our Christian era–was not created all of a piece. It was aggregated and rounded out by conquest, like the winnings in a game of cards, or a rolling snowball. The infamous Monsieur Goetzi, having drunk the blood of all the inhabitants of the Ale and Amity, had incorporated them all into himself. You will readily appreciate that this facility was extremely convenient.

V

I beg your permission, in continuing the story, to go back in time a little, in order to tell you what had already befallen those persons who are, in fact, the principal characters of this story: Edward S. Barton, Cornelia, Count Tiberio and Letizia Pallanti.

On the far side of the Rhine, to the east of the town of Utrecht and some distance from the low-lying countries which owe their existence to man's victory over the sea, the Château de Witt rose above a pleasant landscape of wooded hills. There dwelt Tiberio Palma d'Istria of the Montefalcones, who had entered into the illustrious house of de Witt by his marriage to Countess Greete, a second cousin once removed of our dear Cornelia.

Countess Greete was beautiful, well educated in letters and sciences, and as virtuous as the heavenly saints are said to be. Unfortunately, however, her education had not been extended very far in regard to the music, dance and language of Italy, which were then the height of fashion.

It was for that reason, when Cornelia's parents had died and the tutelage of the beloved infant had fallen to Count Tiberio, that she was obliged to consider appointing a governess.

Italy was then as well supplied with them as England is today. I do not know what references decided the issue in favor of Signora Pallanti, but it is certain that one could not have found another young person so accomplished had one searched the whole world. She knew almost as much as the Countess about Greek and Roman literature and had a thorough understanding of algebra and trigonometry; she could recite French tragedies, including Voltaire's, with surprising charm; she danced like Terpsichore and played the guitar, the harp, the lyre and the harpsichord; she could recite the entirety of *Jerusalem Delivered*[57]

---

[57] *Jerusalem Delivered–Gerusalemme Liberata* in the original–is an epic poem about the First Crusade by the Spanish writer Tasso (1544-95), first published in

starting at the last verse and proceeding backwards to the first. (It is said that for connoisseurs, the sound of that divine poem in reverse is a delight without compare.)

Signora Letizia Pallanti might have been twenty-five years old or thereabouts. The information she gave out regarding her past was rather vague, but she was her own recommendation and her arrival at the Château de Witt was an occasion for celebration. The good Countess Greete embraced her a hundred times over.

Only Count Tiberio welcomed her, in spite of her remarkable beauty, with a cold expression. He said that he did not like women whose busts were overly endowed–Letizia was, in fact, well-equipped to give nourishment–and that prodigies intimidated him. Besides, in his opinion, the beautiful stranger did not have enough hair.

Letizia was a brunette. Her dark tresses were a trifle thin, and Count Tiberio was spoiled in that respect by the luxuriant blonde tresses of his wife, which could have been woven into a cloak had they been shorn.

Letizia, seemingly at least, was not at all put out by the attitude of Count Tiberio. She devoted herself wholeheartedly to her duties as a governess, finding abundant opportunity to return the generosity of Countess Greete, on whom she lavished every care. Cornelia, in her hands, made marvelous progress. Every evening, the whole family would come together. Greete and Letizia would sometimes enter into learned discussions of Greek or Roman poetry.

In brief, the Château de Witt presented the very image of happiness.

Cornelia adored her beautiful instructress. She brought her along on one of the journeys which she made every year to England for the holidays, and the Ward family also fell in love with the charming young woman.

I was only a child at the time, but it seems that I can see her still. Never in my entire life have I encountered a woman more seductive than Letizia.

Our Anna was equally enthusiastic–but after the events of which I speak, she told me more than once that there was an element of vague and mysterious terror mingled in the feelings she entertained towards the lovely Italian.

One thing to which I can testify myself is that Monsieur Goetzi, who was then Edward Barton's tutor, consistently manifested an extreme antipathy towards her. For her part, Letizia averted her eyes every time Monsieur Goetzi came into the room.

Even so, I caught sight of them one evening in the old chestnut-grove. Like all children, I was curious. I crept up on them. When I arrived at the place where I thought I had seen them from some way off, there was no one there. I was frightened...

1581. Although the author repudiated that edition, and rewrote the poem under a different title, most critics prefer the earlier version cited here.

Letizia departed with her pupil at the end of autumn. She had been hurriedly recalled to the Château de Witt.

Countess Greete had been counting the days until her return. Even Tiberio looked more kindly upon her, and one evening when she had been singing, the Count said: "In truth, Countess, that young person would be a marvel, were it not for her hair."

Such things are said. There is nothing unusual in it. But for some reason, Countess Greete became very pale.

It was around this time that Count Tiberio ceased to hold forth on the subject of women whose figures were a little too opulent–and while caressing the Countess Greete's hair one day, he said to her in the manner of a pleasantry: "In truth, you could share these riches with Signora Pallanti."

I am quite sure that the good Countess would not have liked anything better–but what Letizia wanted was not a part-share.

One morning, our old acquaintance Goetzi arrived at the Château de Witt, carefully keeping to himself the information that he had been dismissed from the position of tutor to Ned Barton. On the contrary, he pretended that he had come out of his way to bring Cornelia news of her kinsfolk in Staffordshire. He was politely received and he accepted the hospitality he was offered, speaking at the time of the Wards and Barton as if he still enjoyed their amity and esteem.

This was, of course, an educated man, likeable and worldly wise. In addition, he played a good game of whist, chess and backgammon. His company could have brought a new gaiety to the life of the chateau–but as things turned out, it did not. Apparently without any particular cause, Count Tiberio became thoughtful. One could not say that he drew away from his wife, but their relationship became cooler.

Countess Greete, for her part, lost a little of her equilibrium. She was uneasy; she had dizzy spells. Day by day, somehow, she was seen to grow paler, thinner–and older.

This was, I admit, by no means unusual in someone of her age, for she was no longer in her twenties. Ordinarily, though, when a beautiful woman loses her hair, it is caught by her comb and her chambermaids commiserate with her every morning regarding the ruination of her locks. In this case, there was nothing of that kind. Not a single hair remained lodged between the tortoiseshell teeth after grooming, and yet they were removed. Oh yes, they were removed!

And behold! Letizia's hair chose exactly that moment to replenish itself. One might have thought that Count Tiberio's playful wish had come true and that the beautiful Countess was sharing with Signora Pallanti.

It was not possible, of course, given that one was blonde and the other brunette; but eventually, in quantity, at least, that which Greete lost, Letizia gained.

I should point out at this point that since the arrival of Monsieur Goetzi, Letizia had been using a hair lotion recommended by the learned man–but the poor Countess tried to use it too, and found it useless. Despite the excellent restorative result obtained by the governess, Countess Greete watched despairingly as her skull shed its covering. I hesitate to write the word, but in the end it must be said: she was bald!

And she began to entertain the horrible suspicion that la Pallanti had somehow stolen her hair!

How could she explain it? Countess Greete did not even try. She knew only too well that the moment she broached the subject, everyone would think her mad, such was the absurdity of the idea that would be set before them. In any case, in whom could she confide? Cornelia was infatuated with her governess, and poor Greete could already hear the bursts of childlike laughter that such an extravagant claim would call forth.

Then again, how could she formulate her complaint? What proof could she offer?

There was the good Count Tiberio. of course. She could tell her beloved everything–there are no secrets between lovers–but did Tiberio still love her? Tiberio was still young and handsome; she had aged ten years in as many months. Tiberio no longer looked at her with anything but pity. He avoided her. While her lovely hair had gone to furnish the temples of Letizia, little by little, Tiberio had forgotten the way to her bedroom.

Suspicion worked its way into the Countess' head like the point of a dagger. I don't know exactly how the idea became established within her wounded spirit, but she saw Letizia as a rival to be fought and destroyed, using some part of herself as a weapon. It was, after all, her magnificent hair that Tiberio loved, even though he loved it on someone else's forehead.

The Countess was alone in her room one evening, listening to the distant sound of the harp that was being played in the drawing-room, when she was seized by an irresistible force. For the first time in many days, she went down the staircase and came to the doorway of the room where the concert was taking place. What stories the paneled walls enclosing her favorite space could have told of her former happiness!

She did not go in. Cornelia was at the harpsichord. Behind her, Tiberio and Letizia were seated on the sofa, chatting. Tiberio's fingers were bathing in the curly mass whose waves now fell upon the shore of la Pallanti's shoulders.

Countess Greete clasped both hands to the breast which housed her breaking heart. Without saying a word, she made haste to return to her room–which she was only able to attain with the aid of her old nurse Loos, whom she encountered in the corridor.

When she felt her heart beating more soundly, she said: "Listen, Loos; when I was a little girl, I told you all my troubles; today, I am so very miserable that I shall die of it."

She spoke for a long time in a weak voice, weeping all the while. Loos listened with her hands pressed together. What shocked the nurse was not the intrigue recently entered into by Count Tiberio and Letizia–the whole chateau knew about that, except for Cornelia, who was as innocent as an angel–but another circumstance reported by the unhappy Countess.

Every night, at about midnight, the Countess' insomnia was relieved for a few minutes. She fell abruptly into a heavy slumber, which was pure torture; a dream would begin–the same dream every night–in which she sensed that a man came into her room and quietly approached her bed, and began to pluck hairs from her head with steel pincers, tearing them out one by one. She did not know who this man was, because she was never able to open her eyes in his presence. Once he had departed, her head was gripped by a burning sensation, and the nightlight beside her bed was reflected in green from every object in the room.

That was not all. Some minutes afterwards, distant cries would break the silence: a woman's cries, which seemed to come from the wing of the house where Signora Letizia slept.

After having told this bizarre story, Countess Greete fell asleep in the arms of the old nurse, exhausted and grief-stricken.

Instead of retiring, as was her habit, the nurse slid into the space between the bed and the wall and crouched down, well hidden behind the pleats of the curtain.

Towards eleven o'clock, the harmonious sounds of the drawing-room were silenced. Some time afterwards, the Countess' breathing became louder, like that of someone who slept profoundly.

At that moment, the bedroom door opened noiselessly, and Monsieur Goetzi appeared at the threshold. Loos could see him perfectly as he crossed the room and cautiously approached the bed. Monsieur Goetzi, believing himself unobserved, allowed himself to relax entirely into his vampire self. He shone brightly green, and his lower lip burned as red as a hot iron. His hair stood on end, flowing and trembling like a flaming punch-bowl. He was a fine example of his species.

He immediately leaned over the bed. Using a long gold pin which he held between his index finger and his thumb, he pricked Countess Greete behind the left ear and promptly applied his lips to the wound. He suckled for ten minutes, measured out by the clock. It was because of this treatment that the Countess had grown pale and aged. Her health had been cruelly affected by it–as can readily be understood, given that it was repeated every night.

Monsieur Goetzi drank, moreover, merely for nourishment, without any pleasure at all. His taste was such that none but the blood of young women could intoxicate him. When he had taken his daily allowance, he put away the gold pin and took out a little set of pincers, by means of which he plucked hairs one by one from the Countess' head. As he took them, he arranged them in a bouquet, as if he were a gleaner arranging a sheaf of corn.

The Countess moaned feebly in her sleep. Old Loos, petrified by horror, could not believe her eyes.

As soon as Monsieur Goetzi had finished his task, he cheerfully took himself away. He was humming a song in the Serbian language, which vampires generally use between themselves.

The nurse's first impulse was to awaken the Countess, Tiberio and everybody else, and make them throw Monsieur Goetzi into a white-hot furnace. Persons of little education suppose that one can get rid of a vampire by burning him, but this is an error. However, while the old woman was stretching herself, because terror had made her limbs go numb, she heard the distant female cries of which the Countess had spoken.

She was seized by curiosity—and what difference could a few more minutes make? She emerged from her hiding-place, left the room, and moved quietly along the corridors, guided in her course by the cries.

She soon arrived at Signora Letizia's apartment, whose voice she now recognized well enough. La Pallanti wept and wailed as if she were being flayed alive. Old Loos hastily put her eye to the keyhole to see what was going on.

Through the hole, she perceived that Letizia lay upon her bed, writhing in agony. Monsieur Goetzi was standing over her with the long gold pin in his hand. You must have guessed what he was doing—and you are absolutely right. Monsieur Goetzi was making little holes with his gold pin, and he was planting the Countess' hairs in Signora Pallanti's scalp, one by one.

By now, the wrath of old Loos knew no bounds.

"Ah!" said she. "A pair of demons to be brought to account! The furnace will burn hot!"

Her anger had made her speak incautiously. Monsieur Goetzi heard her, and stopped work. That did not frighten the old woman, who set out to implement the plan that she had already worked out—but no sooner had she got up to run than she found herself face to face with Monsieur Goetzi, who barred her way. She recoiled, stupefied, saying: "How did the monster get behind me?"

Monsieur Goetzi laughed and reached out for her as she set her back against Letizia's door. The door opened behind her and the noise made her turn around again.

It was Monsieur Goetzi who came out, laughing and reaching out for her.

There were two of them! She collapsed, overwhelmed by an excess of astonishment.

VI

There were indeed two of them. That will not surprise you unduly, of course, since you are already familiar with some of the mysteries of vampiric life, but you can imagine the stupefaction of old Loos.

The Monsieur Goetzi who emerged from the room and the Monsieur Goetzi who had arrived in the corridor were so exactly alike that one would have said, seeing them come towards one another, that one man was reaching out to his image, reflected in a mirror. The gold pin was also duplicated. Each of them clutched it in his hand.

Alas, Countess Greete's unfortunate nurse had no time to marvel at the prodigy. The two gold pins touched her temples at the same time, one to the right and one to the left, and she expired without a sound.

The two monsters did not care to taste her blood; she was too old.

"My dear doctor," said one to the other, "tell me, I beg you, what we should do with the body."

"Whatever you please, my dear doctor," replied the other.

They reached out their hands, and the corpse lifted itself up on eight paws. It was a duplicate dog–two dogs, if you wish, which had the same nearly-human form. Each of them went to set itself meekly beside one of the two Doctors Goetzi, who said in unison: "He is called Fuchs. Let's get back to work." Then they embraced and blended into one, while the two dogs entered into one another.

Thus came into being the strange creature that we encountered in the inn of Ale and Amity.

Monsieur Goetzi returned to Letizia's bed and completed the hair-transplant.

It was during the holiday season that Countess Greete died, abandoned in a deserted house. Cornelia was here, staying with Mr. and Mrs. Ward and making the final arrangements for her marriage to Edward S. Barton. On this occasion, Cornelia was unaccompanied by her governess, Letizia having excused herself on the pretext of having family affairs to attend to in Italy.

Only much later did it become known that she had immediately followed Count Tiberio to Paris, where they proceeded to go mad, eating, drinking and gambling to extravagant excess. A belated taste for debauchery had suddenly come upon the Count, and he threw a huge party on the evening of the day when Monsieur Goetzi notified him of the death of his unhappy wife. She had died devoid of hope, with not a single thread of her magnificent hair left on her head.

The following day, Monsieur Goetzi rented a small house in the port of Utrecht, in which he installed the bald woman we subsequently discovered at the counter of the Ale and Amity. This woman, who obeyed him like a slave, was the remains of the Countess Greete; in Holland, where she took care of Fuchs, the dog with the human face, she was called Madame Fiole.

When the Count returned to the chateau, there was a conference between Letizia, Monsieur Goetzi and Tiberio. They discussed the recent death of the Count of Montefalcone, the richest man in the country of Istria and Dalmatia, which faces the republic of Venice on the far side of the Adriatic.

Montefalcone had left a widow and a single child. In the event of the son's death, Cornelia de Witt would become the sole heir of the dowager countess—and if Cornelia were also to die, the entire Montefalcone inheritance would revert to Count Tiberio himself.

Count Tiberio was not the kind of person one would have described as a natural rogue, but he was now under the dominion of la Pallanti, and she was under the dominion of Monsieur Goetzi.

The conference lasted all night. It was decided there and then that Monsieur Goetzi would travel to Vienna on the business of the house—not commercial business, but bad business. It concerned the young Montefalcone, the son of the late count and the dowager countess, who was a captain in the Austrian army, attached to the Liechtenstein regiment at the court of Emperor Joseph II. He was a bad lot.

Monsieur Goetzi set out with Fiole, the bald woman, and the dog Fuchs. Our Anna did not give me details of their journey. I only know that on their arrival in Vienna they lodged at the house of a money-lender named Moses who had advanced funds to Mario Montefalcone. He held credit-notes bearing the young count's signature for more than a million florins.

He lived on the third floor of a big house in Graben with his grand-daughter Deborah, who let down a silken ladder from the balcony of her room every night for the convenience of Captain Mario.

Old Moses had a leather pocket in his overcoat, in which he always carried the notes of credit which were the cream of his fortune. He slept in his overcoat. The balcony to which the beautiful and sinful Deborah tied her silken ladder was made of iron.

One day, when there was a military parade between the hedges of the imperial castle of Schönbrunn—which were the tallest in the universe—Deborah pestered her grandfather so long and hard that he agreed to take her to see the parade. She put on her most beautiful attire and all the jewels that the captain had given her. She looked superb. Her pearls and rubies were worth exactly as much as the credit notes signed by Montefalcone, less Moses' commission. Montefalcone, for his part, had a brand new and exceedingly shiny uniform. They found one another so pleasing when the column passed by that the looks they exchanged secured the promise of a rendezvous that very night. Moses had his hand upon his leather pocket, pressing it against his heart. The whole world was happy.

But Monsieur Goetzi, Fiole and Fuchs had stayed behind to look after the house in Graben. They spent the entire time of the parade in the bedroom of the beautiful Deborah, whose blinds they had lowered. Monsieur Goetzi and Fiole worked in shifts on the balcony, with a whetstone, while Fuchs stood guard on the stair.

When Monsieur Goetzi and Diole finished work, the two upper edges of the bar that served as the balcony rail were as sharp as knives.

That night, at an hour when the square was deserted, young Count Montefalcone arrived, all wrapped up in his night-cloak and as happy as a lark. As soon as he appeared, the silken ladder fell from Deborah's balcony and the young count began to climb.

The ladder was very good, for the iron rail of the balcony, changed into a razor, took time to cut through it. It did not break until the moment when the captain had reached the second story.

There were two screams, one a woman's and one a captain's. Then the silence of the night reigned once more, like a river closing over a drowned man fallen from the parapet of a bridge.

At that very instant, Monsieur Goetzi woke old Moses to tell him that an evildoer was scaling the balconies of his house. The innocent went out, carrying a blunderbuss in one hand and pressing the other to his leather pocket.

Fuchs, the dog with the human form, strangled him on his own doorstep.

Monsieur Goetzi had nothing more to do in Vienna. Having emptied the leather pocket, he took to the road again, singing popular songs by moonlight with a light heart.

His escort was now further augmented. As well as the dog Fuchs and Fiole, the bald woman, he had a parrot and a little boy who played with a hoop as they went along the road. The parrot with the powerful beak and hooked talons was Moses; the urchin was the captain. This was all that had been found within the brilliant uniform.

Instead of taking the road to the Low Countries once again Monsieur Goetzi turned southwest, across the Archduchy of Austria, Carinthia and Carniola.[58]

She never specified whether he traveled on foot or by carriage, but here is a rather curious detail regarding the fashion in which vampires and their accessories adopt in order to cross running water. The entire family presses against the master vampire and enter into him. When the process is complete, the master lies down on the water and sails across feet-forward like a plank. No current, however strong it might be, can grip him. Whenever you discover a person crossing a river in this feet-forward fashion, take every possible precaution, because he is most certainly a vampire.

Monsieur Goetzi veered slightly eastwards when he reached Trieste, cutting through Istria, crossing Croatia and entering Dalmatia, committing himself to the Dinaric Alps until he reached the frontier of Albania, where the Castle of Montefalcone was situated. It was one of the most imposing in the world, and had served as a stage for some of the most dramatic episodes in history.

Everything hereabouts was unruly, tumultuous and sinister, from the grass on the ground to the clouds in the sky. The mountain peaks loomed in the back-

---

[58] Carniola is the western province of Slovenia.

ground with savage fervor; before them was a hurly-burly of towers, battlements and belfries, from which vast tresses of ivy fell into hundreds of ravines. Pine-trees could be seen growing in the walls, which seemed to spring up like bottomless precipices.

The overriding impression they gave was of the absolute impossibility of entering into them against the will of their master. Behind the long and narrow windows one sensed watchmen lying in ambush, deadly weapons at the ready. All the drawbridges were equipped with portcullises, hanging in the void like so many gigantic traps.

No sentinels stood upon the ramparts, but in the corner of a courtyard, lit by the horns of a moon half-immersed in a cloud as scaly and flat as a crocodile's back, there was the square frame of a gibbet, one of whose arms still bore a skeleton. Crows swirled around the other.

Monsieur Goetzi arrived some little time before sunset, pausing upon the summit of one of the highest peaks, whose face dominated the entire landscape. From there, he could see not only the castle but many towns and villages, uncultivated gorges and fertile fields, and islands in the sea. He looked long upon all these beautiful things–principally upon the domain of Montefalcone, which would indeed have suited a prince.

An indefinable smile played upon his lips, which glowed like the embers of a fire.

Suddenly he said, "Go forth!"–and his entourage of spectral slaves immediately set forth. The parrot took flight, the dog bounded down the mountain slope, followed by the bald woman and the child rolling his hoop.

VII

When his accessories had departed, Monsieur Goetzi duplicated himself so that he would have someone to talk to. He lit a fire, and anyone who lifted his eyes that evening from the valley floor to the summit of that inaccessible peak, untrodden by any human foot, would have seen two grey shapes squatting in the snow, warmed by a livid brazier.

Night had fallen when the emissaries returned. The Castle of Montefalcone had become nothing but an undefined mass lurking amid the mountains. Here and there, behind its girdling battlements, candlelight flickered.

Although Monsieur Goetzi had said nothing to his slaves at the time of their departure, each one of them had carried out his instructions. They all returned–but at the same time, they all stayed down below, at the different posts to which they had been assigned. The faculty of duplication allowed them to render him invaluable service.

All the half-demons sat down around the fire–except for the parrot, which perched on Fiole's shoulder–and Monsieur Goetzi listened to their reports.

Fiole spoke first. "Sovereign master, I have entered the guard-house at the main gate with a barrel of kirschwasser. It seems that I have not suffered too much deterioration, because all the soldiers are trying to embrace me and call me my dear. This is what I have found out: the castle is on a war footing because of a band of brigands which infests the mountains. The garrison is strong enough to defend the town. They have one significant artillery-piece. Woe betide anyone who tries to get in that way!"

"Where is your barrel?" asked Monsieur Goetzi.

"Sovereign master," Fiole replied, "it is in the guard-room, where I am still pouring out drinks for the soldiers who call me my dear."

The dog Fuchs burst out laughing and the parrot pecked the bare head of the horrid old crone.

"Good," said Monsieur Goetzi. "Your turn, poodle."

"Sovereign lord," replied Fuchs, "I have made a tour of the fortifications. There is only one weak spot, and it will need to be further undermined if we are to go in that way. It is a gateway where there is no sentry posted, but there is a dog as big as a bull. It's lucky that we are not the same sex..."

"You've played a serenade beneath his window?" Monsieur Goetzi put in, good-humoredly.

"Yes, sovereign lord. He became fiery with passion and I have strangled him—and it is I who presently stand guard in the courtyard."

"Good," said Monsieur Goetzi, again, stroking his servant tenderly. "Your turn, captain."

The urchin wiped his mouth, which was stained with jam.

"Colonel," he said, making a military salute, "my hoop and I have been admitted to the skirts of three beautiful girls who are the old Countess' chambermaids. They have stuffed me with sweets and are telling me that they will require mourning-dress, like widows' weeds, because news has arrived from Vienna that the son of the house—the only son, if you please—has broken his neck like a drunkard while scaling the balcony of a young woman..."

(If I have forgotten to mention it, you will understand now that these wretches retained only the vaguest memories of their former state.)

"Is that all?" asked Monsieur Goetzi.

"No, Colonel. The three maids have given me maraschino to drink. It seems to me that I know them; but the devil take me if I can remember where I have seen them before. Here is the garrison gossip: the old woman loved her innocent of a son very much; she does not want to stay in the castle, which is full of unhappy memories. Tomorrow, she departs for Holland to find the young girl who is now her sole heir, whom she wishes to have with her. The maids have also offered me *rosolio* ."[59]

"And have you left your double with them?"

"Yes, he's a little drunk. They have put him in a corner with a bottle of anisette."

"Good," said Monsieur Goetzi, for the third time. "Your turn, Harpagon."[60]

He was talking to the parrot, who was fluffing up his plumage to make himself seem larger.

"As for me, sovereign lord," old Moses replied, "my double is at this very moment with the dowager countess, who is in love with me. When she saw me fly through the open window just now, she ceased to cry and weep. She is almost consoled. I would have been able to tell you more stylishly all that the others have told you, but since that is ancient history now I will make you a more tangible gift. Take these!"

So saying, the parrot took from beneath his wing a bunch of ornately worked and gilded keys, which he respectfully placed in Monsieur Goetzi's hands, adding: "It's the old lady's key-ring. With these you can easily gain entry to her bedroom."

Monsieur Goetzi favored Jacquot[61] with a friendly pat and got to his feet, saying: "So far, so good. To work!" And he descended the sheer slope of the mountain, followed by his household.

The night was already well advanced when they arrived at the foot of the wall. In order to cross the broad moats, which were deep and filled with water, Monsieur Goetzi availed himself of the method described in the previous chapter. No sentinel raised the alarm. In the courtyard, the double of the dog Fuchs refrained from barking. All the closed doors opened to the Countess' own keys, and when they reached the antechamber where the three maids were, the maids were so absorbed in making the double of the little boy drink curaçao that they heard not a sound.

The poor dowager herself heard nothing, deafened as she was by the babble of Jacquot's double.

She was strangled by the hands of Fiole, the bald woman. Who would ever have thought that the virtuous Countess Greete could have conducted herself

---

[59] All the various substances which the mischievous maids give to the little boy are hard liquor. The cherry liqueur maraschino is reportedly at its finest in Dalmatia; rosolio is a sweet cordial made from brandy, sugar and raisins.

[60] Harpagon is a miserly character of Molière's whose name is used in France as we might use Shylock's, as a synonym for "skinflint."

[61] The French call all parrots "Jacquot" much as we call them "Polly"–the presence in the story of a Polly Bird makes it inconvenient to substitute the more familiar word here.

thus? The dog Fuchs–formerly the gentle Loos–was ordered to eat the face of the dowager, and Monsieur Goetzi sowed a beard around it.

It is rather extraordinary, but a fact, that the child was afflicted by a slight ill-feeling while he watched this ignominious treatment being meted out by his companions to one who had been his mother.

Monsieur Goetzi withdrew then, after having set fire to the bed-curtains in order to provide an explanation for the disappearance of the corpse–for I hardly need to explain that he took the unhappy Lady Montefalcone with him, and that she became the faceless innkeeper.

At the moment when Monsieur Goetzi left the castle, Fiole and her barrel disappeared from the guardroom. For their part, the three maids searched in vain for the child with the hoop, who had vanished into thin air.

The whole dismal troop, augmented by Master Haas–that was the innkeeper's name–was now traveling towards the sea. Once having reached the plain, Monsieur Goetzi turned round and was able to enjoy an imposing spectacle. The curtains had set the dowager's bed on fire, and the fire had consumed the room whose resident corpse had been taken away. It was splendid. The gorges, bizarrely illuminated, displayed the enigma of their mysterious profundity, the snowy peaks were ablaze with purple glints, and at center-stage the flames danced as wildly as a colossal torch. Our friend often told me that nothing is as beautiful as a fire in the mountains, but I cannot speak from experience.

Despite his habitual indifference to the wonders of nature, Monsieur Goetzi paused for a little while, but he soon resumed his course, crossing the Adriatic in an elegant tartan.[62] He did not stay long in Venice, so I shall not describe its carnival; She has devoted many pages to its astonishing magnificence. I shall only mention that Monsieur Goetzi, for his replenishment, set an infamous trap for the daughter of a Lido gondolier, and slaked his thirst with her young blood. She was completely drained.

It was during the time that Monsieur Goetzi undertook his voyage to Dalmatia that Ned Barton came to Holland to make preparations for his marriage. Count Tiberio was now living in the nice little house that he had bought in Rotterdam after the death of his wife. At the time when Ned disembarked, he still did not know of the death of his cousin, the young Count Montefalcone.

I shall not surprise you overmuch by telling you that neither Cornelia, who was fully occupied with her own affairs, nor Edward Barton had yet become aware of the relationship which existed between Tiberio and Letizia Pallanti.

It would probably be fair to say, though, that Cornelia was the only person in the whole of Rotterdam who was ignorant of the conduct of her tutor. Letizia, since her trip to Paris, had blatantly attached herself to him and her proud proclamation that "I am at home in the home of my former master" had been heard far and wide.

---

[62] A tartan is a single-masted Mediterranean coaster.

Things changed somewhat with the arrival of Ned Barton. You must remember that he was an Englishman–very young, to be sure, but age is immaterial. The English have a natural supremacy. His presence commanded respect and imposed a certain propriety.

Believe it or not, Tiberio was ashamed in his presence and Letizia was afraid. Their conduct reverted to its former pattern because of him, and a truce was declared in the scandal.

Ned was, however, accompanied by his domestic servant, a scatterbrained Irishman: a lazy unkempt braggart, improper from head to toe, who had not sixpennyworth of anything in his cramped brain but common sense.

Excessively curious, utterly indiscreet and having not the slightest sense of dignity, Merry Bones immersed himself so thoroughly in the gossip of the public house and the gutter that after a few days he knew the whole story better than those who had witnessed its unfolding.

Merry Bones could not abide Letizia Pallanti. This is invariably the way of things between valets and governesses. He had already tried more than once to spill the beans while he was shaving his young master, although Ned had not wanted to hear it, when one morning in January–having soaped Ned's jowls–he held his razor in suspense and said: "Your honor, Holland is not a bad place, although the beer is too flat, but the Meuse will wash up more than one dead dog before March–and take my word for it, sir, your marriage is not yet made."

He whipped the razor across the hollow of his hand, suggestively.

"Be quick," Ned ordered him. "I'm in a hurry."

"The hussy's in a hurry too," the Irishman replied. "A hurry to make mischief and to do you a bad turn, or may God condemn me to eternal fire! Have you seen how she looks at you, your lordship?"

"Be quick!" Ned repeated.

"She has already devoured I don't-know-how-many thousands of that imbecile's ducats–I mean Count Tiberio–and it's no longer Miss Cornelia who has the first place at the table."

"That's true!" Edward admitted.

"Nor the best room, any longer. Holland is a pretty funny country, where schoolmistresses wear clusters of diamonds! I'll bet two sixpences–and that's a whole shilling–that I can tell you something you don't know–because, praise God, your honor never knows anything. There's a vast inheritance come down to Miss Corny, the dear angel. Her cousin Montefalcone–I'm pretty sure that's the name–who was a captain, has already gone to his death, I don't know where–and it's the governess who received the first notification of it!"

Edward at last consented to listen. "Are you sure of that, lad?"

"The telegram was from that scoundrel Goetzi."

"You've seen it, then?"

"One looks things over, don't one? It's the way to find things out."

190

"In any case," Ned said, "it's the dowager countess who will inherit from her son the captain."

Merry Bones plied his razor and removed a swathe of hair. "No doubt, no doubt, your honor," he replied, "but do you want to know what I think? The dowager countess won't make old bones. And when the dowager countess is gone, it'll be look out Miss Corny, you mark my words! Count Tiberio's business is three quarters devoured, and the governess is still hungry. Now do you understand?"

It was in this period that the letters which Ned and Corny addressed to our Anna began to lose their joyous innocence.

It was not until the end of February that the death of the grand dowager of Montefalcone—which made Cornelia a rich heiress—was confirmed. Monsieur Goetzi had returned, but he did not show himself. He had a plan, which involved provoking Edward Barton to some act of violence which would provide a pretext for calling off the marriage, but Ned did not fall into the trap which had been laid for him.

Ned had held back from confronting Signora Pallanti with the contempt that she had inspired in him, and was careful to maintain her illusions as to his true sentiments no matter how unhappy this made him.

As for Count Tiberio, Ned continued to go to his house—the only place he could meet Cornelia. Every day, Tiberio treated him more haughtily—one might almost say scornfully.

The engagement of marriage had been so public that it could hardly be broken, but it became obvious that delays were being manufactured that would be equivalent to a rupture. Thus, the matter was raised, without discussion, of a journey to Castle Montefalcone—a journey from which Edward Barton was to be excluded. And Edward Barton made no protest.

This was, at least, the impression which emerged from the letters which were read all together by our Anna, on the eve of her own wedding.

I will tell you right away that these letters were not completely sincere. They held back from revealing the whole truth—a typically English scruple. In England, we have a particular horror of the scandal called "elopement." The more freedom we give to young women within the family, the more it is incumbent upon them that they do not break their promises. Decency is an essentially English virtue. I do not believe that our Anna included a single elopement in her novels—I mean, of course, an elopement to which the young woman consented; abduction by force is a less shocking matter.

Alas, the enormity of their dread was so powerful a motive that Edward Barton and Cornelia de Witt, having searched in vain for a preferable expedient, became determined to commit themselves to that reprehensible and dangerous course of which the gentry cannot approve no matter what the excuse (although

191

it is common enough in the lower classes). Knowing themselves to be guilty of impropriety, Ned and Corny kept their intention hidden from their friends.

Please do not think me capable of excusing in any degree something which is not done, but I feel bound to point out that they had to contend with an unscrupulous fraudulent bankrupt, a female living in sin and a vampire. It has to be admitted that their situation was difficult.

The Irishman Merry Bones played a considerable part in drawing them towards that evil path, but they were not in the end able to follow it, because frightful catastrophes had hastened upon them.

If they had only listened to the servant–who had, after all, a good deal of common sense–they would not have waited until the last minute; and once in London, under the protection of English law, they would have made fools of the vile bandits who simultaneously threatened their happiness, their fortune and their lives. When they finally made the decision, it was too late.

On the eve of the appointed day, the departing Letizia Pallanti treated Mademoiselle de Witt with such contempt that the poor noblewoman, bereft of prudence and patience, put her firmly in her place. On the same day–the second of February–Count Tiberio contrived at last to pick a quarrel with Edward Barton. The contract had been signed that evening. Nothing had been explicitly broken off, but when Ned presented himself at the house that evening, he was refused entry–and when Cornelia wanted to go out the following morning, she was kept prisoner.

Meanwhile, Monsieur Goetzi reappeared, playing an apparently helpful role–but you already know full well that he was not to be trusted. He gave Ned vague warning of a danger that he did not specify; he advised Corny to have courage–but he also attempted, treacherously, to drown Merry Bones in the Meuse while that good servant was guarding the boat until the hour appointed for the flight of Edward Barton and Cornelia.

You already know how the episode of the broken marriage and the interrupted flight ended. In the middle of the night, Cornelia was thrown into a carriage and taken away, not by Ned but by that infamous pair Tiberio and Letizia Pallanti, who took the overland route to the domain of Montefalcone.

VIII

At the very moment when Merry Bones had disappeared–in a fashion that will be revealed to you in the proper time and place–Ned, thanks to the perfidy of Monsieur Goetzi, took to the road in order to chase after his beloved and was stabbed beside the old road to Gueldre. He was then carried by villagers, dying, to the inn of Ale and Amity.

We can return now to that dangerous tavern where we left our Anna after the truly fantastic battle between poor Merry Bones and the double pack of sub-vampires who formed the household of Monsieur Goetzi, during which the clock had struck thirteen times.

After Merry Bones had left the ground-floor room, pronouncing the enigmatic words "I'm off to look for the iron coffin" everything was immediately put back in order. The various members of the Goetzi family re-entered into one another like folding chairs.

According to the laws of probability, I ought to be able to tell you that our Anna saw these impossible things with utter stupefaction, and that the mysterious phrase let fly by Merry Bones put her imagination to the torture. Well, not at all. Perhaps her spirit, by means of some exceptional facility, had already adapted itself to this kind of prodigy. Henceforth, it would require something more to astound her.

In any case, She became very calm.

Grey Jack was spewing forth maledictions while pressing both hands to cheeks inflamed by the slaps administered by Merry Bones, but She silenced him with a gesture. She recalled that Merry Bones was, after all, an Irishman, and wondered whether he might have been entirely in the wrong in the scuffle which she had just witnessed.

To tell the truth, now that things had settled down, the innkeeper and his family presented a rather peaceful appearance; one could easily assume that the bald woman, especially, was a good person. The boy brought a cup of beer to old Jack, who wet his cheeks with it and drank the remainder with pleasure.

Our Anna thought that this was a convenient opportunity to repeat the declaration that she had previously made a few minutes before the thirteenth hour.

"I demand," She said, in a distinct and firm voice, "to see Edward S. Barton esquire, who resides–or has resided–in this public house, if he still lives. In the unhappy event that he is deceased, whether by natural causes or in consequence of violence, I wish to be taken immediately to his resting-place, so that I can ensure that he receives the last rites, according to the provisions of the established church."

Hearing this, old Jack became tearful, while the innkeeper and his wife cried: "Ah! The dear young gentleman that God has blessed!"

For his part, the little boy said, "I've seen the dead man," and the dog howled softly, in the manner of a sick woman, while watching Anna languidly. The parrot, incessantly combing the beard of his master, repeated: "Have you dined, Ducat?"

Our Anna never could give me a full explanation of the motifs contained in these oft-repeated responses, which remain quite mysterious. Sir Walter Scott accused her of habitually leaving such explanatory gaps in her work.

The innkeeper offered her a nice room and to warm the bed therein. She accepted, not having slept contentedly since her departure from the cottage.

She was conducted to her apartment by the innkeeper, who brought a tea-tray, and the bald woman, who carried the candlesticks. The little fellow followed with the warming-pan and the dog brought up the rear. Grey Jack was not with them. At the time, She did not think to ask why she had been separated from her loyal but admittedly unintelligent servant.

I feel a little hesitant in relating this part of the story, in which our Anna's actions proved to be rather irresponsible. Should She really have so easily put her trust in people whom She had seen duplicate themselves, then sheathe themselves in the same skin, having not yet received any information about Ned? I can only point out that her greatest work, The Mysteries of Udolpho, is by no means lacking in similar episodes of thoughtlessness. She did not have a good memory, and the charming Emilia, her heroine, although endowed with extraordinary sagacity, is subject to singular fits of distraction. She was, moreover, overwhelmed by fatigue–and you can well imagine how terribly a young woman of good and tranquil family might be upset by adventures such as these.

The fact is that She got into the well-warmed bed. The bald woman carefully tucked her in; the innkeeper placed the tray containing everything necessary to make tea on the bedside table, and the little fellow set up two candles. Afterwards, they all wished her a good night and retired.

She was alone. Outside, a key grated twice as it made a double turn in the lock. The footsteps of the retreating company faded away as they passed along the corridor. The silence would have been total had it not been for the melancholy voice of the wind plaintively shaking the window-frames.

It was the first time since her departure from her father's house that our Anna had found herself in a comfortable situation, conducive to reverie. Her thoughts immediately turned to the pleasant countryside of Staffordshire. Oh how beautiful England, the gentle Queen of the World, seems when glimpsed through the tears of exile!

While She was dreaming in this fashion, half-asleep and in the grip of all manner of vague emotions, a dull noise came from downstairs: the harsh settlement of the clock's inner workings, which preceded the chiming of the hour. As soon as the chimes began to sound, a concert of wild cries and imprecations began again on the floor below, accompanied by the tumultuous echoes of a battle. The chimes sounded fourteen times, and fourteen times the scrawny bird sang cuckoo! After that, silence fell, except for the shrill voice of the little boy with the hoop, saying "I've seen the dead man!" for the final time.

That woke our Anna up with a tremendous start. The dead man was Ned! How had she contrived to forget that cruel sorrow, even for a moment? Ned, the laughing child who had shared his early years with her and loved her as much as he was able, like a brother: Ned, the dead man!

Anna suddenly recognized the room she was in. How could She have failed to recognize it before? It was the room of which Ned had spoken in his letter: the one from which he had cried: "Help! Help!"

By the light of the two candles, whose long wicks emitted more smoke than flame, She saw the floral curtains and the set of prints depicting the exploits of Admiral Ruyter, and the round hole opposite the bed, eight feet from the floor, which had once held a stovepipe...

It was here, on this bed, that Ned had yielded up his last breath.

The candle-wicks were further elongated, crowned with black mushrooms. Their smoke filled the atmosphere with a thick and sinister fog. What was hidden within it I cannot say, but the silence was disturbed by muttering and groaning.

All the while, the obscurity became worse, for the candles became thinner and thinner and the mushrooms of their wicks grew in monstrous fashion. The half-obscured prints seemed more like distant windows, lit from without by livid fires.

Having become no more and no less than a poor superstitious child, vanquished by the terrors of midnight, She hid her head beneath her bedcovers.

Scarcely had She taken that position when she heard a noise that seemed entirely natural. It resembled the footsteps of a man wearing shoes that were too large for him. As soon as our Anna heard it, She regained control of herself. She carefully removed the bedcovers and pricked up her ears.

She had not been deceived. A heavy heel ground metallically on stonework, mere feet away from her. Our Anna's dread immediately changed its nature, although it became more than mortal. One can brave death; even the idea of dishonor, horrible as it is, is conceivable; but hobnailed boots within the bedroom of a well-brought-up young woman... The first thought that occurred to our Anna was to run to one of the windows, open it—if she were granted time to do so—and to throw herself head first into eternity.

"Begorrah!" said a voice. "They've put her in his honor's chamber! Are you asleep, Miss?"

Was it a dream? She thought she had recognized the voice of Merry Bones, but no matter how hard She looked nothing could be seen within the room.

"Is that really you, Merry?" she asked.

"Yes indeed," replied the good servant. "It's me, my pearl. Give those two candles a little blow—a Christian likes to see clearly."

You will appreciate that poor Merry was not much concerned with modesty. Our Anna blew on her candles and soon worked out why she had not been able to see the brave Irishman until now, although her eyes had searched the lighted chamber in vain. He was lodged behind the stovepipe gap as if on a balcony; he had passed two long and stick-like arms through it, and was waving them as much as he could. His strange face, straightened by masses of hair but seemingly full of good humor, was split by a smile broader than a saber-cut.

"Where have you sprung from, Merry my boy?" our Anna asked, entirely reassured.

"Well," replied Merry Bones, "didn't I tell you, miss, that I was going to look for the iron coffin?"

"What is this iron coffin?" Anna murmured.

The Irishman had disappeared from the hole now, and could be heard moving something on the other side of the wall. Immediately afterwards, the hole was plugged again. but not by the woolly head of Merry Bones. The object made a metallic sound as it scraped the inner surfaces of the hole; it only just contrived to pass through.

In the end, one last push got the object clear, and it fell noisily to the floor. The widely-grinning face of Merry Bones immediately reappeared in the bull's-eye, framed by its shock of hair.

Our Anna tried in vain to see what sort of thing it was that had made such a noise while falling. When Merry Bones was comfortably reinstalled in the gap, his two arms extended therefrom like cardboard devils from a snuffbox, he noticed her anxiety in that respect.

"I suppose you can judge how heavy it is, my flower?" he said. "That's because it's made of iron..."

"It's the coffin then!"

"...and also because it's full."

"What's inside it, for God's sake?"

"That which one usually puts in a coffin, Miss."

"A body?"

"Exactly, Miss Anna."

"Whose body?"

"My master's body, of course."

"Edward Barton's body!"

"Precisely!"

She gave a heart-rending cry.

"What? Has the devil got you?" asked Merry Bones.

Our Anna, deafened by her own sobbing, could no longer hear him. Merry Bones had to shout at the top of his voice: "I'll get it open tonight, God strike me dead if I don't. You'd do better to listen, my pearl. If there's a body in that coffin–and there is, or I'll be kippered like a herring and chewed by the black teeth of all the benighted Hollanders–there's a soul too, and a good soul, for all that it's an Englishman's..."

She had heard him only vaguely until then, but the last words reclaimed her attention immediately.

"What do you mean, Merry Bones?" she demanded, urgently. "Are you trying to tell me that Mr. Barton is still alive?"

"Yes, Miss–that's exactly what I mean."

"Then why isn't he moving in there?"

"He's asleep."

"Asleep!" cried our Anna, her voice rising again. "Do you think he could sleep through the coffin falling to the floor?"

"Oh, I think so, Miss–in fact, I'm certain of it."

"Do you mean that he's been narcotized?"

Merry shrugged his shoulders carelessly and said: "I don't know about narcotized, but I know that His Honor's lettuce soup was dosed with poppy heads."

I don't know if you'll approve of our Anna, but She told Merry Bones to stand back from the bull's-eye and, throwing her cloak about her shoulders, She hurried to the iron coffin, which had a lock and key just like a trunk. She turned the key in the lock and lifted the lid.

On seeing her cousin the midshipman lying smiling within, as fresh as Jesus in the manger, our Anna immediately became happy again. While She contemplated him fondly, Merry Bones reappeared at the stovepipe-hole.

"He's very pretty and very slender, isn't he, Miss?" he said. "While you're amusing yourself looking at him, you can hear me well enough, I suppose, because we haven't much time and it's necessary that you should know how all this came about.

"On the day when Miss Cornelia should have been brought away and taken to your family in England, Monsieur Goetzi–spider that he is–had already spun his web. I was caught in it and could do nothing, and what could they have done, poor little lambs, once they no longer had my help? Miss Corny was sent to the devil like a pretty little parcel, and His Honor received half a dozen knife-wounds in his side. To cut a long story short, I was a prisoner but I jumped the man set to watch me and I escaped. I arrived here, at the inn of Ale and Amity, yesterday evening, dying of hunger, numb with cold and in a sorry state all round. It was before your arrival, but night was falling. I was about to enter the downstairs room, without suspecting anything, when I thought it advisable to put my eye to the keyhole first. I saw the bald woman throwing poppy-heads into a pan while the innkeeper ground lettuce-hearts in a mortar. And they were both lashing out at the brat, who was asking, 'Why do you want to put the dead man to sleep?'

"As you can well imagine, I immediately got the measure of this lot, and I had no desire to walk into the middle of a wasps' nest. I went around the house looking for a back door, and when I couldn't find one I clambered up the ivy to the roof and came down the chimney-flue like a sweep. Luckily, it got me into the room where I am now. It was empty and dark, but I heard talking in the next room, which is where you are. I saw the hole where light came through and I stuffed my head into it. I saw three men–or rather, one gentleman and two halves of a rogue. It's more than likely that His Honor had already been made to drink the poppy-drugged lettuce soup, because he was asleep. He didn't seem too bad for someone who had four or five stab-wounds. Two Monsieur Goetzis were with him: the real one and his double. The real Monsieur Goetzi was laying out material inside the iron coffin, while the double was using an auger to make little holes in the side-walls.

" 'A strange occupation for a doctor of the university of Tubingen!' the double said.

197

" 'It's not a despicable trade,' replied the real one. 'Anyway, if I can be an upholsterer, you can be a locksmith.'

" 'And what's the point of it all, boss?'

" 'I want to get out, my son. It's my intention to retire, to live out my years in Castle Montefalcone, whose proprietors we shall become.'

"'Good idea!' said the double, rubbing his hands together. 'But how shall we become the proprietors of the lovely Castle Montefalcone?'

" 'Keep pricking–I'll explain it to you. You understand well enough that the marketplace is run by greed. On the one hand, Monsieur le Comte Tiberio Palma D'Istria has bought the young Englishman from me, dead, and I need to bring him in his coffin. Do you understand?'

" 'Perfectly.'

" 'On the other hand, Signora Pallanti has bought the same Englishman from me, but alive.'

" 'What price is Count Tiberio offering?' asked Goetzi number two.

" 'He will give me the blood of la Pallanti,' replied Goetzi number one.

" 'Oh! And la Pallanti?'

" 'She will give me the blood of the lovely Cornelia.'

"The eyes of both halves of the vampire sparkled as the name of the lovely Cornelia was pronounced, and their lips lit up like hot coals.

" 'All of which says nothing,' Monsieur Goetzi's double said, meanwhile, 'about our becoming proprietors of Castle Montefalcone.'

"The real Monsieur Goetzi smiled. 'When we have drunk the blood of the lovely Cornelia,' he replied, 'how can I be prevented from incorporating her? And is there any law to prevent her from keeping her true form? She will be at one and the same time Cornelia de Witt and Monsieur Goetzi. Thus, Monsieur Goetzi will be the legitimate inheritor of Montefalcone. Can you see any difficulty?'

"The other Monsieur Goetzi could find none. It was as clear as crystal. By this time, their task was complete. The iron coffin was very comfortably lined and the last auger-hole had been pierced. The two Messieurs Goetzi took hold of poor sleeping Ned, one by the head and the other by the feet, and they laid him to rest within his bier, which was then closed and the key turned thrice..."

Merry Bones then continued to recount how he had seen all this through the stovepipe hole. His ears had been flayed by the friction, but it's said that such a process is good for generating ideas and Merry Bones searched every nook and cranny of his brains for one. How could he retrieve his master from the hands of these scoundrels? While he put his brain to the torture, the true Monsieur Goetzi passed a cord around the coffin and ordered his double to open a window. A branch of the Meuse flowed beneath the window, and there was a barge waiting there, manned by two sailors.

"Ho there!" shouted Goetzi.

"Ho yourself!" came the reply from below.

"Are you ready to receive the merchandise?"

"All ready."

"Good."

The two Messieurs Goetzi lifted the coffin and hoisted it on to the windowsill. I should tell you that Merry Bones had been forced to stand on a log of firewood to raise his head to the level of the hole in the wall–the room in which he was located served as a woodstore. His agitation caused him to make a false movement, which displaced the log. The resultant noise betrayed his presence.

The two Messieurs Goetzi immediately turned their heads and recognized him. They hissed like a pair of serpents. The inhabitants of the inn made for the room simultaneously, from every direction, and a terrible battle ensued, during which Monsieur Goetzi–the principal–continued to lower the iron coffin into the barge.

Merry Bones, being one against nine, did not have an easy time of it. Fortunately, there was a knock at the outside door of the inn. It was our Anna, with Grey Jack. The family of Monsieur Goetzi was obliged to split up, and Merry Bones was able to save himself, at the moment when the clock in the ground floor room sounded the thirteenth hour.

Once outside, he went around the building and ran after the barge which was moving down the branch of the Meuse, carrying the iron coffin. We may suppose that the two boatmen were drunk, as is usually the case, and that circumstance must have made the task of Merry Bones much easier. After several attempts, he contrived to take hold of the iron coffin and carry it back on his shoulders.

IX

During the entire time that the Irishman was telling his story, She was lost in contemplation of her childhood friend.

Merry Bones shook his huge shock of hair discontentedly. "Do me the favor of closing the coffin now," he said. "You'll have fewer distractions then, and we can finish what we have to do. I have a plan–but to carry it through I need to know whether you have a cool head."

She smiled with calm pride, and lowered the lid of the coffin.

"That's good," said Merry Bones. "Now listen carefully. When I came back, I couldn't climb up to the roof, because my load was too heavy. I came in by the kitchen and I heard that pack of villains plotting in the downstairs room. This is what I gathered: at the fifteenth hour–which will soon sound, I think– Monsieur Goetzi has invited them to a little family feast. They are quite content; they believe that the coffin is heading down to Rotterdam with His Honor inside, and after the little feast of which I speak, they plan to meet up with it so that they can all leave together and deliver the merchandise to Castle Montefalcone."

"What is this little family feast?" our Anna asked.

"The drinking of your blood," replied Merry Bones.

She did not fall into a faint. "The drinking of my blood," She repeated, tonelessly.

"Exactly," Merry Bones replied, adding, "it's true that they prefer young women less than twenty years old; but this was how Monsieur Goetzi put it: Miss Anna Ward, if needs must, will still be potable."

"Potable!" exclaimed our unhappy friend, wringing her hands. "Potable. In God's name—potable!" I think, My Lady—and you, Sir—that you can readily imagine the various sensations which disturbed her. There are very few situations as horrible as this in the annals of modern literature. Potable!

Our Anna's first impulse was to cry: "Let's get out of here, for Heaven's sake!"

"What?" said Merry Bones. "That would be silly. It's too good an opportunity. I've found a hatchet here in the woodpile, my pearl—a hatchet for chopping wood. I've a scheme that will make us laugh. Open the coffin, take His Honor out and put him in the cupboard beside the chimney-breast...

"Hurry up! It seems to me that I hear the groaning of that evil clock, and I still need to wake that innocent Grey Jack—we have need of him."

Anna got to work briskly and courageously. She was strong in spite of her small stature. She took Edward S. Barton esquire from the coffin. lifting him in her arms. Having opened the cupboard, She carried him into it.

Merry Bones applauded enthusiastically. "Close it!" he said. "You have a stout heart, true enough. Now, push the coffin far enough underneath the bed to hide it completely."

She did as she was bid.

"Now," said Merry Bones, "hurry back between the sheets and pretend that you are sleeping like a pretty little angel... Begorrah! There's the mechanism grinding down below, ready to strike... when they come, don't move and don't open your eyes... bye for now!"

The movement of the clock could be heard from the floor below. The head of Merry Bones disappeared precipitously from the hole, and the first stroke of the fifteenth hour sounded, sending sonorous vibrations through the shadows of the night.

As soon as the clock's hammer rose and fell for the first time, a muffled confusion of noises emanated from the ground floor of the inn. There was the sound of footsteps on the staircase. At the second stroke, the tread of the footsteps sounded in the corridor. At the third, the door rotated slowly on its hinges, and the room was invaded by a green glow. Like the odor of felines, the glow of vampires increases at critical moments.

Monsieur Goetzi entered, alone. He had the semblance of a human shape carved out of bottle-glass. The dim candlelight streaming past him cast his shadow on the door he closed behind him. The fourth stroke rang out.

Monsieur Goetzi came directly to the bed, and our Anna's heart stopped beating. Monsieur Goetzi leaned over the bedhead. Within his body, a tumultuous voice spoke, saying: "We are thirsty! Let the feast begin!"

The clock sounded the fifth stroke.

Monsieur Goetzi pulled back the coverlet a little, his scarlet lips becoming rounded, like those of a gourmet about to taste a vintage wine, and he said with sinister gaiety: "Patience, children! I think I have the right to the first glassful."

"Then hurry, master, hurry!"

It appears that vampires have sharply-pointed tongues, with which they can make the punctures necessary for the satisfaction of their hideous appetite. Once that lancet has penetrated, they drink after the fashion of leeches.

As the sixth stroke resonated, the door opened again and Merry Bones came in, hiding his right arm behind him. The crestfallen Grey Jack followed him, as meekly as a beaten dog. An Englishman always bruises easily, and the two slaps Grey Jack had received at the thirteenth hour had, it seemed, been of the finest quality.

As soon as Merry Bones appeared, Monsieur Goetzi whistled, and his entire family emerged from his flesh at one and the same time. At a second whistle-blast, they all split into two, including Monsieur Goetzi himself–and the seventh stroke sounded.

Monsieur Goetzi immediately placed himself behind his eleven emanations, and they all threw themselves upon the Irishman. Anna, who had kept her eyes shut until then in response to Merry Bones' instruction, opened them upon the most extraordinary melee that had been seen since the world's beginning.

Two dogs, two parrots, two bald women, two little boys, two innkeepers and one Monsieur Goetzi were positively devouring the unhappy Irishman, who was only using his left hand to defend himself, and was concentrating its use on defending his eyes from the attacking parrots. He grabbed those cruel creatures by the head and twisted their necks, but that did no good at all–and while he was thus engaged, the dog and the boy sank their teeth into his legs. The innkeeper and the bald woman, aided by Monsieur Goetzi's double, tucked into his sides, his flanks, his belly and his breast.

Although he was an Englishman, Grey Jack waited on the threshold. Don't blame him for that–such were his orders. He was the reserve force, and you will understand soon enough how extremely important his role was.

The eighth, ninth and tenth chimes sounded while Merry Bones marched towards the bed, advancing inch by inch despite the relentlessness of the male and female harpies. They tore at him like a pack of hounds which have brought down their quarry; I tell you in all honesty, no part of that poor creature was spared–and he was little more than skin and bone to start with. The whole vampire troop couldn't have found more than a mouthful of meat to chew on his entire body. Skin and bones, that was what he was made of—and it's worth repeating that their stoutness provides further proof the incontestable superiority of the English.

The Irishman bled from every vein in his sorry body, and the jaws of all those jackals were reddened; but little by little he advanced nevertheless, and when the eleventh stroke sounded, there was none but one of the bald women between himself and the true Monsieur Goetzi.

Merry Bones suddenly shook his shaggy main, let loose a resounding Begorrah! and lifted the horrible old crone from her feet with a kick which I do not hesitate to call heroic, for the shrew became firmly lodged in the stovepipe hole. His right hand, which had not yet been shown, was abruptly brought into view. The large blade of the hatchet sparkled, and—at the very instant when the twelfth chime resonated—the head of the Goetzi-in-chief fell, severed by a single trenchant blow.

Straight away, all the other heads of an inferior order were rolling on the floor as if the same edge had separated them from their trunks.

An indescribable but mute confusion ensued. Every one ran after his or her head. In the midst of that tumultuous silence, the commanding voice of Merry Bones erupted like a thunderclap: "Your turn, Jack, you old imbecile!"

And Grey Jack proceeded to march forward in good order, without haste or idleness—as our admirable soldiers always do. His mission had already been mapped out. He drew out the iron coffin from beneath the bed and opened it, and at the very instant when the double of Monsieur Goetzi recaptured his head, Grey Jack stuffed him into the coffin and closed it, turning the key upon him.

The others were unable to perceive this, because they were fully occupied in gathering up their skulls. The thirteenth stroke sounded and the fourteenth too, while they jostled one another like vile maggots in the summer mire of a sewer. Merry Bones watched them, laughing with all his heart—which prevented him from simultaneously keeping track of the efforts of Grey Jack and Monsieur Goetzi senior.

The two of them had achieved their goals at the same time—which is to say that Grey Jack sat down on the reclosed coffin at the very moment when Monsieur Goetzi recovered his head and replaced it between his shoulders.

Monsieur Goetzi whistled. The population of vampiricules, obedient to his order, reassembled their pairs as one. At the second whistle-blast, his family performed a second maneuver, promptly re-entering into his own body—but the execution of this maneuver did not have the desired effect.

"Is anyone missing?" Monsieur Goetzi asked—but without waiting for a reply, as the clock sent forth the fifteenth stroke, he contrived to throw himself through the closed window, and disappeared into the night beyond.

A piteous voice emerged meanwhile from the iron coffin, replying: "Monsieur Goetzi! Monsieur Goetzi! It's your double that you lack!"

It was too late. The clock had finished chiming and the cuckoo sang fifteen times in its turn, while the only thing of which our poor Anna was certain was that she was still alive.

After the cuckoo's final call, Merry Bones begged for silence in order that he might explain the rest of his plan of campaign—for you will understand well enough that the war had only just begun.

"Now, Miss," he said, "it's high time that we set ourselves on the road to Castle Montefalcone, but as His Honor is fast asleep..."

"Open the cupboard door," our Anna put in, but he ignored her.

"It will be a pleasure-trip, and I don't doubt that I'll recover while we're on the road. Grey Jack will carry the coffin..."

"May the devil take you if...!" that worthy began—but Merry Bones cut the speech short, saying: "The coffin is essential to us for more than one reason; firstly to keep the bird in the cage..."

"You're mistaken, good Irishman," Monsieur Goetzi saw fit to observe, in a soft voice, from within his bier. "I'll give you my word of honor that I won't try to escape, if you let me out."

"...Secondly," Merry Bones went on, without taking the trouble to reply to this suggestion, "to introduce His Honor into Castle Montefalcone when the time comes. It seems that the walls are as high as the dome of St. Paul's, but I have my plan."

"Ah, good Irishman," said the soft voice of the coffin, "you have plenty of spirit! You are wrong to refuse my offer. I am deeply devoted to you, and I could render you excellent service."

You will doubtless suppose that this was a trap. Well, not at all! The serious authors who write thick books on vampires are in accord on this point of doctrine: a captive vampire belongs as completely to his conqueror as the same conqueror would belong to the vampire if the outcome of their contest had favored the latter.

The only differences are that ordinary men very rarely make themselves masters of vampires, the general rule of human life being that Good is always much less powerful than Evil, and the fact that having accomplished the capture of a vampire, the moral and physical inclinations of the man will prohibit his drinking the blood of the vampire.

The absence of the latter detail prevents the perfect assimilation of the vanquished vampire to his human conqueror—but the vampire prisoner is no less the slave of his new master.

While Monsieur Goetzi's double was protesting his devotion through the holes in the coffin, there was the sound of wings outside, and the window-frame was shaken from without as if a big bird or a colossal moth was bumping into the panes.

"What's that?" asked our Anna.

The prisoner immediately replied: "Don't be fooled by that for an instant. It's Monsieur Goetzi, who has come back to find me because he cannot do without me."

"I'd like to send him on his way with a bullet in the head!" cried Grey Jack. He took the stance of a man holding a rifle, firing towards the window.

"Wait, old man," said the captive. "The monster who has launched innumerable evil endeavors against your young mistress and her friends is powerless from now on. I am missing from him. It would take too long to explain the matter in precise scientific terms, but a comparison will enlighten you sufficiently. I am myself, it is true, no more than the twelfth part of Monsieur Goetzi, but I have been detached from all the rest and my absence puts them in the situation of a necklace which has lost its thread. You see his difficulty."

This had a considerable impact on the audience–but our Anna, more thoughtful than is usual in one of her tender years, asked: "Prisoner, why do you betray your patron?"

"My dear child," replied the voice of the coffin, "and don't be surprised to hear me calling you that, for I have the right; I have many reasons for acting as I do. I will tell you two of them. The first is the universal law of conquest: the subjugated remains the enemy of his vanquisher. The second, in order to be fully understood, requires me to tell you a story. In the period when Doctor Otto Goetzi came to the county of Stafford to be the tutor of Edward S. Barton, he was still only an apprentice vampire. He had neither a double nor any accessories at all. Do you remember poor Polly Bird, the daughter of the High Farm, whose premature death set the whole parish mourning three years ago? Well, my friends, it is the unfortunate Polly Bird herself who is speaking to you. Monsieur Goetzi, when he received from Peterwardein the diploma of a master vampire, immediately chose me to be his double and the foundation of his interior mechanism."

"When I think," our Anna exclaimed, "that we have sat one beside the other in church, with the seven Bobington girls!"

Merry Bones had understood that Grey Jack would not easily submit to carrying the coffin. "All things considered," he said, "Polly Bird was a pretty good girl then, and the mistress has no chambermaid. If Polly will promise us to be good, and to carry the coffin, I don't see why we shouldn't amuse ourselves by putting up with her until we get to Castle Montefalcone."

Polly Bird prevailed. Merry Bones inserted the key into the iron coffin's lock and opened it. Monsieur Goetzi–for it was still Monsieur Goetzi–could now be seen, looking at the company in a sweet and modest fashion. On careful consideration, however, Anna and the others were able to perceive, behind the features of the despicable doctor, something of the physiognomy of Polly Bird.

The unfortunate thanked them profusely, curtsying as soon as she had been set on her feet. We shall employ the feminine gender in speaking of her henceforth, in order to avoid confusion with the real Monsieur Goetzi. You should not forget, however, that this was a man– and in consequence of that fact, the plan to confer upon her the position of chambermaid to our Anna had to be abandoned.

What is more, as a security measure, the coffin was attached to her neck by a strong chain. In the first place, Grey Jack and Merry Bones ensured by this means that she would carry it; in the second place, it seemed reasonable to suppose that the restriction of her movements imposed by such a cumbersome burden would make any attempt to escape very difficult.

X

Dawn was breaking when She dismissed her companions so that she could attend to her toilette. In the meantime, the former Polly set about waking Ned Barton, by means which I cannot explain. When our Anna rejoined her companions–having offered up a brief prayer, or at least made the appropriate gestures, in order to request divine protection from further perils–Ned had just opened his eyes and was looking around in a stupefied manner.

"Where am I?" he asked, at once.

She wanted to give him a full explanation, but Merry Bones insisted that they get underway immediately. "I have had a chat with our companion Polly," he said. "She has given me some good advice. We have a rather delicate task to complete before we head for Castle Montefalcone. While the real Monsieur Goetzi remains alive, nothing else matters."

They went downstairs. They saw that the clock in the ground floor room had stopped at exactly fifteen o'clock. The cuckoo had vanished.

As soon as they had crossed the threshold, their eyes were caught by a large placard suspended beneath the lantern. The sign read: INN TO LET.

Without pausing to contemplate this curious but unimportant detail, the little caravan took to the road. The former Polly was in the front rank, closely guarded to the right and the left by Grey Jack and Merry Bones. As agreed, Polly carried the iron coffin. Anna and Ned Barton–who was still a little weak and needed the support of his companion's arm–brought up the rear. The Dutch, being a ponderous race, watched indifferently as they passed by.

Their journey to the banks of the Rhine would have been incident-free were it not for some vague whistling sounds heard above the sound of the wind, and some confused movements in the bushes. Having been warned by the ex-Polly, who was anxious to display her perfect loyalty, Merry Bones explained to our Anna that Monsieur Goetzi was dispersed in the air and in the water behind the foliage, lying in wait for a suitable moment to recapture the double who was indispensable to his freedom of movement.

Once, our Anna felt something like a child's hoop brush her legs, and a shrill voice emanating from who knows where said: "There's the dead man!"

Having reached the Rhine, they hired a boat to take them upriver as far as Cologne. Towards evening, when the shadows of twilight descended upon the Rhine and its banks, a pale green glow appeared some two hundred yards in front of the boat. It followed the watercourse upriver, moving at exactly the same speed as the boat.

As the darkness deepened, the glow became brighter. It gradually became concentrated; having formerly been widespread, it eventually appeared no larger than a man's body. Now, Monsieur Goetzi could be distinctly seen, sailing feet first, shrouded by his vivid aureole.

While each of them silently considered this strange spectacle, the former Polly broke down in tears. When she was asked why she was so sad, she replied: "Do you think that I can look upon the monster who stole my honor and my happiness without being overcome by rage? Mark this: he will not give you an inch of leeway while you lack the means of destroying him utterly. I tell you this partly for the sake of my vengeance, but above all else for your safety. Every hour of the day and night, whether he be apparent or hidden, you may be certain that Monsieur Goetzi is always prowling around you. Consequently, I now intend to explain in every detail the plan which I have already suggested briefly to Merry Bones–which, if it is executed courageously, will permanently annihilate our common enemy. The moment is favorable, for while we can see him down there, we can be certain that he is not here, listening. While he does not have me, he is obliged to keep all his other parts within him, and you will understand how angry that makes him."

That response having silenced all objections, they gathered closely around the former Polly, each one paying close attention–except perhaps Edward S. Barton esquire. It pains me to say it, but the young midshipman was not yet fully recovered. He was still dazed and confused, in need of time and tender care.

The unfortunate who had been Monsieur Goetzi's first victim unburdened herself in this manner: "There is a little-known place which is undoubtedly the strangest in the world. The people who inhabit the barbarous lands around Belgrade sometimes call it Selene, sometimes Vampire City, but the vampires refer to it among themselves by the names of the Sepulchre and the College. It is normally invisible to mortal eyes–and to the eyes of each of those who contrive to catch a glimpse of it, it presents a different image. For this reason, reports of its nature are various and contradictory.

"Some tell of a great city of black jasper which has streets and buildings like any other city but is eternally in mourning, enveloped by perpetual gloom. Others have caught sight of immense amphitheaters capped with domes like mosques, and minarets reaching for the sky more numerous than the pines in the forest of Dinawar. Yet others have found a single circus of colossal proportions, surrounded by a triple rank of white marble cloisters lit by a lunar twilight that never gives way to day or night.

"Arranged there, in mysterious order, are the sepulchral dwellings of that prodigious people which the wrath of God has placed in the margins of our world. The sons of that people, half demon and half phantom, are living and dead at the same time, incapable of reproducing themselves but also deprived of the blessing of death. Their womenfolk are ghouls, also known as oupires. Some, it is said, have sat on thrones and terrified history. Following the example of those men of iron who were oppressors of the country in the Middle Ages— and who, when beaten back, retreated to their impregnable fortresses—they maintain this sinister and splendid shelter: a citadel and place of refuge, as inviolable as the tomb.

"Every time a vampire is severely injured, in a manner that we would deem mortal were we speaking of an ordinary human being, he makes for the Sepulchre. Their existence can undergo crises which are not actually death, but which resemble it. They have been found, in various parts of the world, reduced to the state of a cadaver, although the flesh remains uncorrupted and a mechanism set within the heart continues to secrete a warm ruby-red liquor. In this state, a vampire is at the mercy of his discoverer. He can be chained and walled up. He can make no move to defend himself until chance brings his plight to the attention of an evil priest who holds a key—a key which is the only means by which the workings of their apparent life can possibly be restored. To achieve this, the priest introduces the key into the hole which every vampire has in the left side of his breast, and he turns...

"Monsieur Goetzi is in exactly this situation; he is in pressing need of re-winding. As time continues to run out, he will be subject to a gradual but increasingly rapid enfeeblement, until he can obtain the requisite number of turns of the key. He is already on his way to the Sepulcher; only the passionate desire to recover me—his missing link, his synovia,[63] if I may be permitted to use the scientific term which he applies to me himself—forces him to remain close to us. While he still feels that his health is not too poor, he will make no move, waiting for a favorable moment to whisk me away by force or stealth...

"Come closer, I beg you, for a fog is beginning to form, and Monsieur Goetzi's glow can hardly be seen any longer. Be sure that as soon as he can approach us without being seen, he will slip into the body of one of our oarsmen...

"We are also headed for the Sepulcher. Don't worry that it will take us out of our way; it only requires a slight detour. I know the byways of that funeral hospital by heart. We will go in as far as Monsieur Goetzi's hidey-hole, and then...but the green glow is no longer perceptible. Look out!"

---

[63] Synovia—*synovie* in French—is the lubricating fluid secreted by the body to facilitate the smooth working of its joints. It seems likely, however, that the ever-innovative Féval, heedless of its pre-existent meaning, synthesized the word from syn—familiar in French, as in English, in such words as synonym and synapse—and vie, intending to imply something like "joined life."

"What?" said our voyagers, all at the same time. "What shall we do then?"

"Shh!" said the former Polly, putting a finger to her lips. "Listen!"

A suspicious splashing agitated the water around the boat, whose wash was brightened by a pale light.

"Tell us in a whisper," begged our Anna.

The former Polly agreed. She was a truly good girl, although that appearance was hidden by the features of Monsieur Goetzi. One by one, they lent her their ears and received her murmurous confidence.

"Excellent!" they cried, one and all. "That idea is worth its weight in gold."

Do you remember the burst of laughter which our Anna heard while disembarking, on the night of her arrival at Rotterdam? Something similar grated in the air, and at the same time, one of the oarsmen gave a sudden start.

"Look out!" commanded the ex-Polly. "The enemy is here! You have only one means of keeping me safe, and the fact that I tell you what it is will give you the measure of my good faith. Put me back in the iron coffin, and sit on top of it!"

They had no sooner moved to act on this suggestion than the possessed oarsman made another convulsive movement, releasing a huge sigh. At the same time, a sound like that of a body falling into the water was heard. Monsieur Goetzi, realizing that his strategy had scant chance of success, had gone back whence he had come.

The rest of the night passed peacefully.

The new day dawned while they were passing through Dusseldorf. Our Anna asked Merry Bones to find a shop selling musical instruments and buy a lute—which served, in spite of the circumstances, to relieve the monotony of their journey.

Monsieur Goetzi seemed to have disappeared; they were able to reopen the coffin to let a little air in to the unfortunate Polly.

At Cologne they abandoned the Rhine for the overland route, hiring a coach for that purpose. They crossed Westphalia, Hesse, part of Bavaria and took to the water again at Ratisbonne, this time on the Danube.

Nothing noteworthy occurred between Ratisbonne and Linz, between Linz and Vienna, between Vienna and the ancient Magyar city of Ofen—which is nowadays called Buda—or between Buda and the plains of southern Hungary.

It was one morning thereafter that our Anna and her companions saw the thick-waisted towers of Peterwardein set before the magical skyline of Belgrade, bathing in the glorious scintillation of the first light of the Oriental sun. Open countryside extended to the horizon on either side, perfumed by corn and flowers, through which the broad Danube flowed like a sea.

Since Vienna, there had been no sign to indicate the presence of Monsieur Goetzi, but the former Polly had never ceased to say: "He is there." And, indeed, in the last hours of their voyage, he became perceptible again, still floating feet-forwards, enveloped by a small cloud of pale fog–but he was considerably smaller, and so very thin! The livid haze which surrounded him flickered as if it were on the point of vanishing.

At some distance from Belgrade, he steered for the shore and made landfall in the reeds, seeming to be little more than a thin puff of smoke.

"The abominable villain is powerless now," said the former Polly, placing her hands on her good heart.

It was on the Christian bank of the Danube that Monsieur Goetzi had taken to the land, not far from Semlin in the banate of Timisoara. He could still be seen beyond the reeds for a moment, but then was lost in the tall verdure of a cornfield.

"We must land!" said Polly, who was now the leader of the expedition.

The boat immediately moved to the bank. They climbed ashore. Polly, taking her place at the head of the column, immediately headed for the little town of Semlin, the nearest to the Turkish border.

"Now that my infamous seducer is reduced to the last extremity," she said, marching rapidly, "he will undoubtedly be couched within his marble trough, for the Sepulcher is closer to us than you imagine. Now that we have no further need to beware of his espionage, I can fill in the last details of my plan. We have arrived at the terminus of our journey. When the hour is propitious, we shall be able to see the unique atmosphere which surrounds and veils Selene, the dead city. At present, the morning is too bright–and I am glad of it, because we must have time to make our preparations.

"You know that vampires divide the day into twenty-four equal parts, and that their clock-faces consequently show twenty-four hours. At the twenty-third hour–which is to say, at eleven o'clock in the morning–the mercy of God has allowed that their power is in abeyance for sixty minutes, as shown by the hands of the clock. This is their great secret, and by revealing it I expose myself to the risk of the most abominable tortures–but I'm prepared to do it, in order to achieve my vengeance. It's now about eight o'clock; we shall have three hours in Semlin, during which we must buy charcoal, a portable stove, bottles of Epsom salts and a box of candles. Don't ask me why–you shall see the utility of these various objects for yourselves. We also need a skillful surgeon, and I know just the one: Magnus Szegeli, the most learned practitioner for miles around. He will want nothing more than to follow us, for he has a score to settle with the vampires. Unhappily, I cannot take care of that matter myself."

"Why not?" asked our Anna.

"Because, Miss, Monsieur Goetzi has drained two charming young ladies whom he adored, and who comprised his entire family. Given that I am manifest in the form of Monsieur Goetzi, Doctor Szegeli could scarcely fail to recognize me, and you will understand that I would hardly inspire confidence in him."

She turned away, unable to conceal her repugnance, and murmured: "Unhappy creature! Have you tasted the blood of those poor girls?"

"In our condition, Miss," replied Polly, lowering her eyes, "one cannot do other than one must."

"And did you find it good?" asked Edward Barton, as curious as any seaman.

Perhaps for the first time, She thought of her fiancé with pride. William Radcliffe would never have asked such an unwarranted question.

Semlin, which is the ancient domain of Malavilla—a prize frequently taken and retaken by the infidels in the Middle Ages—still harbors the remains of the fortress built by John Hunyadi.[64] There our companions bought the various objects which would be indispensable to them, and our Anna had the idea of furnishing herself with a sketch-artist. She thought of everything. It is unfortunate that photography had not yet been invented.

The Slavonian surgeon Magnus Szegeli lived next to the Israelite school. Our Anna went into the house alone, while Ned Barton, Jack, Merry Bones and the unhappy Polly devoted themselves to the vulgar necessity of taking their morning meal.

Doctor Szegeli was still a young man, although his hair was entirely white. His figure, ravaged by pain, displayed the legacy of the deplorable history of his two daughters. Almost as soon as She began speaking—at the first word which informed him that he was required to fight vampires—he snatched up his case and brandished it with all the eagerness that the hope of vengeance inspires. Following Polly's advice, She also persuaded him to bring one of those large iron ladles used in poor houses to serve soup, having first sharpened its edges. The purpose of this instrument will be revealed to you in due course.

It is as well to put on record that the number of young women devoured by vampires in the immediate environs of their convent was much less considerable that one might have imagined. In order not to rouse the entire country to revolt, the vampires had agreed between them that they would not inflict any damage within a perimeter of fifteen leagues. Monsieur Goetzi had, therefore, broken this pact in slaking his thirst to the detriment of an inhabitant of Semlin—a prohibited town, like Peterwardein and Belgrade. In consequence, for fear of being reprimanded by his own kind, he had not dared enroll the two Szegeli girls in his company of slaves and had made mere art-objects out of their carefully-prepared cadavers.

When our Anna rejoined her companions, she found that Polly was once again enclosed in the iron coffin—a doubly useful precaution, firstly because the

---

[64] John Hunyadi (1407-1456)—Jean Hunyade in Féval's version—was the scion of a noble Hungarian family who became voivode of Transylvania and Captain of Belgrade, in which capacity he waged war against the Turks. He won a famous victory over Mezid Bey in the last year of his life—the year in which Vlad the Impaler first became ruler of Walachia.

Slavonian surgeon would be unable to recognize Monsieur Goetzi in her, and secondly to spare the unfortunate girl any temptation to flight or treason. Her repentance seemed sincere, it is true–but she had, after all, acquired some exceedingly nasty habits whilst in the company of her ancient master.

They departed on the stroke of ten o'clock–the twenty-second hour, according to the clocks of the Sepulcher. The weather was bright. Semlin, which is on the line of latitude which passes between Venice and Florence, has the same gentle climate as Italy. Our voyagers went gravely and silently across fields of millet and corn, whose hedges were made of oleander. She marched ahead, followed by Grey Jack and Merry Bones, who carried the coffin. Edward S. Barton esquire came next, carrying the charcoal, the stove and the box of candles. Doctor Szegeli brought up the rear, his paces moderated by grief. Don't think that I've forgotten the painter; he wandered away to the left and the right, as is an artist's prerogative.

Ordinarily, supernatural phenomena manifest themselves around midnight, under cover of complete darkness. If you will permit me to make the observation, Milady–and you, Sir–the episode I am describing, with due historical rigor, presents a remarkable character of originality. It was the middle of the day and the sun-bathed the natural world with its bluest radiance. No delusion was possible.

At three-quarters of a league from Semlin, in the direction of Peterwardein, the terrain underwent an abrupt change of appearance. No more oleanders could be seen, nor laburnums, nor lilacs. The rich verdure of green corn disappeared. The soil, so rich a moment ago, became dull, as if recently showered by ash. At the same time, the blue of the sky was veiled with grey, and something for which there was no word–a melancholy screen–was drawn across the face of the sun.

These symptoms became exaggerated with surprising rapidity. After five minutes, it seemed to our voyagers that they were separated by an enormous distance from the objects which had formerly surrounded them. They closed ranks instinctively, forming into pairs and searching the sky for the sun which had been hidden behind the falseness of that night.

"Go on," said Polly, within the coffin.

And they went, although their limbs were weakening, their heads unquiet and their bosoms oppressed by an uncanny weight. They staggered and bumped into one another. You would have thought that they had become heavily inebriated–or, rather, that they had suddenly been struck blind; for what surrounded them now was utter, impenetrable darkness.

"Go on!" said the voice of the coffin.

They went. Is there some darkness even deeper than the blackest night? That something fell upon them, as cold as a pall. All external sound had died away. Nature was no longer breathing.

In the midst of the nameless silence, the voice of the coffin spoke:

"Stop!"

They obeyed.

Suddenly, beside them—among them, I should rather say, so tightly did the sound enwrap them—a bell that sounded loudly, but as clearly as the note of a harmonica, slowly tolled the twenty-third hour.

At the twenty-third stroke, the shadows were rent apart and the Sepulcher appeared.

The company was in the very center of the Vampire City.

XI

The desolate city which surrounded our friends was entirely devoid of life, color and movement. Their spirits were overwhelmed by the silence and the spectral splendor of its marvelous scenery, whose melancholy richness was unparalleled and indescribable. Magnificent beneath the malediction of God, the city had been named Selene after the Greek goddess of the moon; most experts agree that the moon may be assigned to the vampire race as a fatherland.

Let's begin with the central edifice, situated in the middle of a vast circular plaza. Imagine an immense rotunda where the styles of antique architecture are aggregated one above the other in the service of a barbaric but learned fantasy, audaciously marrying the strangest archaisms of Assyria with dreamlike Chinoiserie and Hindu caprice. This was a temple, a tower, a gargantuan Babel constructed in pale porphyry, delicately tinted with a hesitant and dilute shade of green. Huge blocks of this stone, lusterless and yet as translucent as amber, were bound together by narrow seams of black marble.

The first section of the peristyle set around a circular flight of thirteen steps was composed of Doric columns, as thick as those of the temple at Paestum, but so large in proportion that they produced an impression of cyclopean solidity. Between the columns appeared Moresque windows with wildly excessive arches. The second series was Ionic, to the extent that the designations reserved by historians of art to characterize the exaggerated formulas of barbarism can be applied to it. It was equipped with trefoil windows. The third was corrugated by Corinthian columns and retreating walls, pierced by flattened Gothic arches. The fourth was Composite, but floridly displayed thousands of strangely regular ornamentations, shielding windows in the form of stars. The fifth and last was an efflorescence of veined colonnettes, a fountain of pearl-encrusted lianas, which supported a vaulted roof, partly leveled-off and crowned by another, smaller cupola from which a fountain of flames shot forth. It played with all the styles, denying all precepts and defiantly displaying the impossibilities of Faerie.

But what defined the character of the whole of that colossal chapel—at once grandiose and frivolous, magnificent but woebegone—was the inordinate protrusion of its capitals and their entablatures. The friezes and cornices of the Doric flared out; the volutes of the Ionic were swollen and extended; the acanthus leaves of the Corinthian and the Composite erupted in cascades; and the hectic vegetation of the final nameless order formed a huge and deep sheltering ladder, disposed in parasols which gave the ensemble a pagoda-like profile.

Under the peristyle, between each pair of columns, there was a crouching porphyry tiger, its claws tearing open the heart of a supine young woman.

Twenty-four pedestals were ranged atop the circular flight of steps, also mounted with statues of young women–all of them very beautiful, but every one assaulted, subdued and violated by an invisible enemy.

These statues bordered a large circular arena which filled in the heart of the rose beyond whose openings the six main squares of the Vampire City, with their subsidiary streets, were set. Each of these districts seemed enormous, packed to the limit of vision with innumerable buildings whose perspectives were lost in an opal haze. They were all different, but their design exploited clever analogies which persuaded the eye that they were in perfect harmony.

All this livid magnificence was redolent with death; it was soundless, motionless and breathless. Even the air seemed eternally asleep, undisturbed by the slightest whisper of wind. The grandeur of the necropolis was overpowering; words could not express its terrible solitude.

Although the gigantic assemblies of architectural marvels testified to the might of the hand of man, there was no one here. There was not even a shadow to be seen in the white expanses which stretched into the distance in every direction, nor beneath the colonnades which curved around them. The pallid blooms of all these flower-beds slept on their stems, unswayed by any breeze. The enchantment which had suspended their animation had power enough to freeze the water-jets of fountains in mid-air. You know how monotony enlarges everything by discouraging thought, even immensity itself; twilight as cold and clear as the face of the moon struck that symmetrical crowd of monuments–all built of the same stone, colorless and semi-transparent–from every side at once, casting not a single shadow.

Within the majesty of silence and death, there was a fugitive impression of wakefulness. In the debauchery of styles and the wild promiscuity of decorations, there was an orgiastic savor. The orgy was temporarily suspended–but who would want to be in that sepulchral Babylon at the hour when it was resumed?

The chimes of the crystal bell reverberated for a long time in the mute atmosphere.

The newcomers stood still, lost in astonishment. While our Anna tried in vain to measure these frightful marvels, Merry Bones muttered Celtic imprecations and Grey Jack peered into the distance in the vague hope that he might be able to discover the sign of a tavern somewhere in the depths of the panorama. The artist had taken up his crayons. Doctor Szegeli, the distraught father, studied the statues of young women with a moist eye.

213

"Let's go! Let's go!" said Polly Bird within the coffin. "There isn't time to waste in trifling. We have to get on! Monsieur Goetzi resides in the Serpent Quarter. Forward!"

At the entrance to each main square was a pedestal supporting the image of an animal, from which the quarter took its name. Merry Bones took the lead again, and having found the statue of the serpent, he set a course between the two ranks of mausolea indicated thereby.

When they had passed through the gateway into the square, the impression of immensity overwhelmed our Anna's mind as she was confronted by streets radiating in every direction, grafted on to other streets, while the principal thoroughfare plunged into vertiginous depths.

Each tomb, viewed at close quarters, was a considerable monument. Some, doubtless enclosing members of the vampire nobility, had the proportions of royal palaces–and there were not merely hundreds of them, but thousands! Each mausoleum bore a name, inscribed in black letters beneath its main entrance. The majority of these names were unfamiliar, but some could be found among them whose presence in that place explained many enigmas posed by the history of ages past, and also by that of the present: the names of evil misers whose scandalous wealth is the misery of entire nations; the names of courtesans, the obscene ruination of morals and patrimonies; and the names of those glorified by the title of "conqueror" in imbecilic poetry and slavish art because they crushed the weak by force and cemented their renamed atrocities with tears, shame and blood!

More than once, while passing before one of these ostentatious temples, where some illustrious scourge of humanity lay asleep, our Anna wanted to go in–but every time, the voice of Polly Bird, impatient and quivering with fear within the coffin, would cry: "Make haste! It's a matter of life and death, and we have little time!"

They hurried on, but the road seemed endless. Streets were followed by more streets, tombs by more tombs, and on they went. They did not encounter a single living creature in that interminable journey.

Finally, however, Polly, who was keeping track of their road through the holes in the coffin, said: "We are nearly there. Hold me hard, for although I hate my master, his heart attracts me as a magnet draws iron, and I may try in spite of myself to throw myself into him." The noise of her writhing, as she bruised her sides against the iron walls, could indeed be heard from within the coffin.

"Halt!" she said, at last. "We have arrived. Here it is."

Monsieur Goetzi was neither a king, nor a dictator, nor a tribune, nor a humanist philosopher, nor the founder of a finance house. He was no Baron Iscariot or Baroness Phryne; he could not pretend to be part of the vampire aristocracy. He was a mere doctor, although he did not practice medicine. For this reason, his tomb was so shabby that comparison with the patrician sepulchers almost excited compassion. It was a meager chapel in the barbaric Greek style, only a little grander than St Paul's in London.

Its architecture was a trifle parsimonious, comprising no more than four or five hundred columns. It was ignominiously overshadowed on one side by the mausoleum of a Prussian prime minister, and on the other by the cathedral of an ancient Parisienne whose practice had been–and would continue to be–to drink the blood of imbeciles, making no discrimination between the sons of the virtuous and the sons of the villainous, provided that they had gold in their veins and plenty of servants.

At the center of the facade, on a tablet of black jasper, the name of Monsieur Goetzi stood out in feebly illuminated pale green letters, accompanied by several Greek characters.

Γωεθεε

Our Anna regretted that she did not have William Radcliffe on hand, who read Greek as well as a Turk. She was obliged to ask the surgeon Magnus–who explained to her, in spite of his grief, that the name seemed to be formed from two distinct roots, one derived from the noun earth and the other from the verb to boil.

"Volcano!" cried our Anna. "A good name for a scourge of mankind!"

"Open it and go in!" ordered Polly, still restless within the coffin. "Even a single moment's delay might expose us to the most frightful misfortune."

They went up the steps and through the peristyle. The great door was not locked, and they went in. A long nave extended into the interior of the tomb, flanked by a regal cloister, above which ran a double tier of galleries, the whole being capped by a Byzantine cupola. All the walls, pilasters and arches were made of that semi-transparent, amber-tinted stone that our Anna called "lunar." In front of the columns there was a closely-packed series of statues, all representing young women, which made a circle around a porphyry shell precisely positioned in the center of the nave.

All these young women extended their softly rounded arms towards the shell, collectively bearing an endless wreath. Before them, a rank of Ninevite tripods was set, supporting alabaster bowls in which some unknown liquor was burning, so pale that the spirituous flame seemed ruby-red against its background.

Within the central shell, Monsieur Goetzi was lying on his back with his arms tightly pressed to his sides. The miserable wretch was reduced almost to nothing: diminished, emaciated and shriveled like a damp parchment dried by the sun.

"O my dear master," cried Polly, performing extravagant contortions within her iron box, "were I not a prisoner, how joyfully I would come to your aid." But she added, without pausing for breath: "Go on! Don't delay! Tear out his heart–without making him suffer too much!"

I ask your permission now to use a rather offensive word; circumstances demand it. Nothing stinks like a vampire who is at rest in the freedom of his own house. Despite the numerous cassolettes which were burning, Monsieur Goetzi, now seriously inconvenienced, exhaled an odor so malignantly fetid that our companions would have been at risk of death by asphyxiation had it not been for the bottles of Epsom salts bought in Semlin. That was why Baroness Phryne made the fortune of so many perfume manufacturers!

Doctor Szegeli took up his bundle, but his hand trembled lamentably, and you will understand why when I tell you that the unhappy father had recognized his two daughters among the statues.

"Go on! Go on!" repeated Polly, "Every minute is worth a century. Destroy the heart of my unfortunate master, quickly and gently!"

Merry Bones was only an Irishman, but he was not afraid of work. He snatched the bundle from Magnus' hands and said: "May the Devil choke me if I can't cut out what needs to be cut. I've been a butcher's boy in Galway, so I'll do the honors."

"Go on, my boy!" said the voice of the coffin. "Finish the job, but do him no harm!"

Merry Bones rolled up his sleeves. Our Anna, deeply moved, gravely took up a position from which she could see more clearly. Edward Barton and Grey Jack stood watch over the coffin, which threatened to fly open at any moment. Doctor Szegeli stayed beside Merry Bones lest his advice should be required to direct the operation.

The young Slavonian painter, seated on his folding chair, made a sketch.

I would, of course, be embarrassed were I to describe with technical exactitude the surgical operation which was carried out. Perhaps, too, it would exceed the bounds of decency. It is sufficient for you to know that Monsieur Goetzi kept his eyes open and fixed throughout the operation. His body remained immobile, because it was reduced to such a pitiably meager state.

"If he had only been given twenty-four hours," said Polly, "my dear master would have been plump and fresh. Cut away! Cut deep! Oh, I am so deeply attached to him!"

When the patient's chemise was drawn apart, everyone could see a little round opening, like the one in the end of a quill, on the left side of his breast. Ruby-red blood was coursing therefrom, drop by drop.

At the moment when the mysterious mechanism of vampiral vegetation was uncovered and displayed, the cupola began to vibrate with sound and the walls, galleries and cloister acquired a voice. They made a kind of plaintive music as pale as the ambient light, the marble of the edifice and the uncertain flames flickering in the cassolettes.

Merry Bones plied the scalpel conscientiously and proved his talent for butchery. But beneath the slicing edge of the blade, not a single drop of blood sprang forth. Evidently, nothing but the heart itself was alive; its envelope was dead and dry.

"Pay attention, please!" said Polly. "My life is attached to that of my master by a small thread of nervous tissue, which you must cut before touching the heart. You will find eleven such threads in the pericardium: one for each of my co-accessories. My own thread is the first on the right. Can you see it?"

"I see it," replied Merry Bones, severing it delicately.

The former Polly received such a shock in consequence that the iron coffin jumped into the air. Meanwhile, the heart was completely exposed, redder than a cherry and in a perfect state of freshness. Our Anna, pressing her bottle to her nostrils, examined it curiously. She never neglected an opportunity to further her education.

"Is the stove getting hot?" asked Polly.

"Yes," replied Ned and Jack, who had been ordered to see to it.

"Then goodbye, master! I will weep long and hard for you... Take it out!"

Merry Bones took from Doctor Szegeli the iron ladle which had been sharpened with this object in mind and, adroitly inserting it beneath the heart, drew the organ out intact.

Monsieur Goetzi's eyes became dull.

The monumental music vibrating within the blocks of porphyry swelled up as if in a mighty groan.

"Quickly!" cried Polly. "Grill it! Burn the heart of my seducer! But above all, do not lose the ashes, for I fear that we shall have dire need of them. What time is it?"

Our Anna consulted her watch, whose hands stood at a quarter to noon.

"Everything depends on your swiftness," said Polly. "The route from here to the central square is long, and there is only the one exit. Turn up the heat!"

The heat was turned up. Everyone set themselves to blow on the charcoal within the furnace, and the heart of the vampire was placed on the brazier, where it soon began to crackle and smoke. Then it burst into flame. It burned like a plum pudding doused in rum–and while it did so, the body of Monsieur Goetzi dwindled within the shell. His eyes, animated by a horrid urgency, rolled and rolled.

The ladle became red hot. Merry Bones held on to it with the aid of his jacket, which he moistened and folded round the handle. The others continued to blow, urged on by the voice of the coffin.

The heart was reduced to ashes. That which remained of Monsieur Goetzi within the shell was an exceedingly scanty residue of transparent matter, within which a series of little dead things could be distinguished: a parrot, a dog, a bald woman, a bearded innkeeper and a little boy with a hoop.

The livid music had ceased to make itself heard. The cold flames had expired within the cassolettes. The statues of young women, having fallen noiselessly from their pedestals, were lying in the porphyry dust which made up the ground–and all around the vault, a great black cuckoo like that of the Dutch clock flew in circles, fervently beating its silent wings.

"The matter is concluded," said Polly, who had fully recovered her tranquility in the depths of the coffin. "I had a moment of vertigo, but it has passed. Now we must get out of here. You must have heard the saying of Doctor Samuel Hahnemann, who invented the doctrine of homeopathy: when I am well, I have no faith in medicines–but it's sure and certain that the best remedy to employ against vampires is the ashes of a vampire. Take two or three pinches of that of my master to serve our present purpose, and keep the rest in the ladle. What's the time now?"

"Four minutes to noon," was the reply.

"Forward! Shift your legs! Carry me!"

They left the monument at once, leaving the furnace and the sack of charcoal, for which they had no more use. Edward S. Barton and the hired painter carried the iron coffin, because Merry Bones had been ordered to protect their retreat by means of the soup-ladle containing the ashes of Monsieur Goetzi's heart. Don't smile: you shall soon see the extraordinary power of that medicament.

As far as Magnus Szegeli was concerned, the unhappy father had decided to carry the statues of his two daughters. Unable to manage it, because they were too heavy, he threw himself back upon the residue of Monsieur Goetzi and took time out to trample it within its container and subject it to the most shameful outrages. She had not the heart to blame him for that futile but legitimate vengeance.

They emerged into the street. Outside, all was as mute and immobile as before–but something had modified the uniform tint of the splendidly lugubrious vista. As the moment of awakening approached–the dawn before the night, as it were–mysterious lights and shadows sprang up among the ghastly enormities: colors endeavoring to be born. There was a hint of red in the depths of the pallid atmosphere, and the silence was confused by murmurs...

Our companions ran full tilt through the streets of Selene, incessantly urged on by the exhortations emerging from the depths of the iron coffin, where Polly rendered herself as breathless as a jockey at Epsom. In truth, they could already see that she was not at all in error. The murmur spreading through the silence was becoming louder; the vague red gleam was increasing in intensity; and the wingbeats of the great black cuckoo which circled above the fleeing company were beginning to make themselves heard.

At the moment when our friends reached the gateway marked with the statue of the serpent, that magnificently proportioned porphyry animal began slowly to uncoil, and its previously colorless semi-diaphanous scales acquired an indescribably rich green tint.

At that very moment, a vast rumble emitted by the principal dome filled the space with a series of harmonious vibrations, and all the immobile pallors which stretched to the horizon of the dead city in every direction came to life, flooded by an intensely vivid green hue. The lines tracing the junctions of the stones, which had been black, took on a scarlet tint like long zigzags of fire.

It was magnificent, but horrible—and as this sinister grandeur, darkening and reheating the limitless horizons, submerged thought in a sea of terror, Polly said: "Faster! Run! Your death-knell is about to toll, and you must flee! What's the time?"

"One minute to noon."

"Run! Run for your lives!"

They ran, panting, staggering, bathed by a cold feverish sweat which trickled from their burning bodies. They were in the middle of the central plaza when the crystal bell bestirred itself to sound the first chime of the twenty-fourth hour. The black bird beat its wings and launched a triumphant "cuckoo" into the air. From the top to the bottom of the great church, the open windows released a furnace-like glow which seemed gradually to embrace the entire atmosphere, while the deep green of the walls and columns was checkered with lines of fire.

The young women of the peristyle were writhing and screaming now beneath the claws of the tigers; the statues assumed lascivious poses upon their illuminated pedestals. Shadow and light, night and day, grace and terror were all mingled therein, confounded by infernal promiscuity. It was no longer a dream, nor a nightmare, nor a hallucination; it was the debauch of all those reunited entities, their battle and their tempest.

The bell of crystal continued to sound, and after each chime the black bird loosed its cry, which grew ever louder. In like manner, the blazing air flooded the prodigious architecture with strange radiance, their blocks of emerald cemented by fire.

At the twelfth stroke, the flames sculpted atop the cupola on the summit of the dome came to life, stirred and fanned by the beating wings of the black bird.

All the doors of the mausolea opened...

XII

Our companions, who were now running out of breath, did not know how to get out of the plaza, which was surrounded by a series of identical exits. Polly Bird, mad with terror, was still crying: "Run! Go on! Make haste!" but did not think to give them the necessary directions. They ran around the fatal circle as fast as they could, already exhausted and breathless, unaware that they were no longer making progress and repeatedly treading the same circular course.

"By the Gate of the Bat!" Polly cried, finally. "The portal is through there! Run, by Heaven and Hell! Your lives are hanging by a thread!"

They immediately raced into one of the six great squares forming the rose—the one marked by a statue of a bat. The other four, of which we have not spoken, were dignified by a spider, a vulture, a cat and a leech. I should say that Ned Barton, and Grey Jack even more so, fervently desired to let go of the iron coffin, which slowed their progress, but how could they get out of that abominable labyrinth without it? No exit was perceptible.

Meanwhile, the crystal bell proceeded to sound its last strokes. Throughout the city, immobility gave way to movement, silence to noise. Through every open doorway, the interiors of the mausolea could be seen, their inhabitants rising from their shells and attending to their toilettes. Some of them had already appeared at their thresholds. The men of considerable stature, but for the most part effeminate; the females, by contrast, were both tall and bold.

All of them, males and females alike, were molded in a green material, marbled with dark red, with yellow shining eyes and lips which burned and sparkled, like coals in a forge excited by the bellows. Long purple veils flowed from their shoulders, and it was easy to see by the ever-more-intense glow which lit up the air that each of them had a bloody puncture on the left side of the breast, at which a ruby-red droplet quivered...

Were they not yet fully awake, or were our fugitives under some protection? None of these frightful creatures had yet perceived them, although nothing hid them from view. Polly Bird no longer dared call out within the coffin for fear of attracting their attention. Our Anna commended her soul to God, because she felt sure that her poor harassed limbs would carry her no further. Ned was not in good spirits; Grey Jack, although he was English to the core, was all gooseflesh; Merry Bones himself felt the pressure of time building.

"Courage!" whispered Polly Bird, who saw them falter. "One last effort! We are very close to the gatekeeper's tomb. To obtain passage, it will be sufficient to throw a little of the ash of my defunct seducer into his eyes. Courage!"

But at that instant the black bird, with its wings spread, alighted in the middle of the flames in the punchbowl which crowned the great dome and launched its last "cuckoo." The final chime of the crystal clock had sounded, and a distant cry was heard, followed by the sound of a hunting-horn.

Then, before another second had elapsed, the cries and trumpetings were doubled and redoubled with magical velocity, and our fugitives were surrounded by a vast clamor.

The voice of the hunting-horns sounded above all else. The shouts were formulated in an unknown language, and there are no words to describe the harrowing sonorousness of the fanfare sounded by the horns. At the same time, from the four points of the compass, invisible drums beat out a call to arms and the crystal bell sounded a tocsin.

"We are two steps from the doorway!" said Polly Bird. "They are crying: The Sepulcher is violated! A vampire is dead!–but we're there. One last surge, and we're out!"

It was true. Our fugitives could already see the high wall of porphyry, a marvel among marvels, girdling the low, deep and narrow arch that was the only entrance to the immense city. They must have passed through that arch on their arrival, although they had no memory of it at all–and as they had already passed the last of the mausolea, there was no one between them and the great gaping portal, beyond which was the night.

But the clamor–the fanfares, the call to arms and the tocsin, mingled with all kinds of noise–was swelling and rising like a tide.

The din was deafening, and an innumerable mob of men, women, four-legged animals, reptiles and birds suddenly hurled themselves into the street from every exit. They were uniformly clad in red and green, with yellow eyes, and they filled the street within the blink of an eye.

"Kill! Kill! Gatekeeper, close the portal! Drop the portcullis and lower the bridge! Loose the dogs, the lions, the tigers, the crocodiles, the serpents! The Sepulcher is violated! A vampire is dead! There must be blood, blood, blood!"

It was an astounding sight–but there was not the slightest response from beside the portal to the vociferations of the crowd. The gatekeeper did not show himself at all. The portcullis remained suspended and the drawbridge stayed down. No dogs could be seen, nor tigers, nor crocodiles, nor serpents.

With your permission, I shall take time out to explain this. Each of the inhabitants of Selene took a twenty-four hour turn at taking charge of the unique gate. Today was the day when that duty fell to Monsieur Goetzi–and because he had a reputation for punctuality, his predecessor had stood down at the first stroke of the twenty-fourth hour. He was wrong to do so, and I expect that he was punished for his negligence.

For this reason, our fugitives had no one to bar their retreat–but, great God, their position was hardly any less precarious! The furious and tumultuous tide of assailants was growing with increasing rapidity. They were already abreast of their quarry, to the right and the left, when the voice of the coffin cried: "Look out, Merry Bones! Protect yourself!"

The brave Irishman turned around, and the breath from the hugely gaping mouth of a hurrying green vampire burned his face, while two monstrous dogs leapt snapping at his throat and a swarm of hissing reptiles slid between his legs.

The moment was critical–all the more so because he was simultaneously beset from both sides by the yelping, croaking, baying, roaring crowd, crying: "Kill! Kill!"–and the fugitives, spurred on by the voice of the coffin, took the bit between their teeth.

221

Merry Bones paused for no more than a quarter of a second, but it was enough to separate him from the rest of his companions, who were passing through the arch and leaving him all alone in the city of Selene.

She would never have consented voluntarily to leave anyone–even an Irishman–at the mercy of such cruel enemies, but Polly urged them on like a maniac, knowing the fate that awaited her if she were recaptured–and we will soon see that she had ambitions of her own, in her capacity as the sole heir of Monsieur Goetzi. Edward Barton and Grey Jack, obedient to her voice, passed over the drawbridge and through the arch, running like hares.

Anna followed them without knowing that she was saved, or at least outside the evil city. She alone turned around on the far side of the moat, and was able to take one last look, through the opening of the arch, at the most magnificent and infernal spectacle that any group of mortals had ever seen since the beginning of time.

Intrepid as She was by nature, She certainly did not regret the dangerous hour She had spent among those fantastic terrors–but a great dizziness took hold of her thoughts. Following the instincts of her poetic temperament, She retained the impression of those miracles wrought by a power other than God's: the moment of awakening, when the sepulchral fairyland had recovered its orgiastically violent colors, left a particularly vivid memory, like a wound.

The hole pierced by the arch in the thick blackness of the rampart gave her one last glimpse of it: the orgy, bounding and rolling in an ocean of green and red light. And beyond the confused movements of the populace drunk with rage, She saw again, as if in an already distant dream, the infinite landscape of tombs, domes and colonnades lost in sparkling vestibules...

But She could not see any sign of poor Merry Bones, who was by then utterly drowned in the depths of the crowd.

"God be praised," She said. "We have been delivered from great peril."

"Forward! Forward!" replied Polly. "We are not yet in a position to congratulate ourselves. There will be time enough to thank God when we have passed out of the girdle of shadows and can see the bell-towers of Semlin before us!"

I hardly need to add that in passing through the arch, our companions had re-entered the darkness which surrounds Selene on every side, like an impenetrable suburb.

They resumed their march, and those among them who could not help thinking of Merry Bones were very careful not to mention his name.

We, on the other hand, will focus our attention upon him.

XIII

222

Merry Bones was both surprised and annoyed by the furious attack launched upon him by the vampires, because he had thought that they were still some way behind him. Such miscalculations are easy to make when in combat with unnatural creatures; their normal agility and litheness far exceeds that of humans. His astonishment did not, however, prevent him from planting his head in the stomach of the giant whose breath had burned him.

The impact filled the mattress of his hair with a coldness so disagreeable that he promised himself that, even though he was not proud, he would only use his feet on other beasts of the same kind. In spite of the beautiful appearance of jasper, the breast of the villainous giant was as flabby and ice-cold as the belly of a fish.

The head-butt had been solid, however, and the giant, having been hurled backwards into the crowd, did not fall over until he had knocked down half a dozen monsters. That gave Merry Bones a little room for maneuver, and enabled him to look behind him.

A howling, moving wall already separated him from his companions; he was cut off, surrounded and abandoned.

"Just like the English!" he said to himself, his opinion of the most civilized of nations unjustly lowered by his misfortune. "But perhaps they have enough good sense to understand that an Irishman can always look after himself!" And he set himself to launch a fusillade of kicks in every direction, so numerous and so powerful that the vampires saw stars by the million.

Unfortunately, there was no one to enjoy that amazing spectacle: a simple domestic servant, keeping at bay a riot composed of all the vampires on Earth, driven to the utmost extreme by their fury. It is highly improbable, I admit, but quite true–and Merry Bones, while beating them back, even sang snatches of Irish songs and hurled vile insults at them. Such was the pardonable produce of his poor education.

In all fairness, though, they were simply too many. They came on, and they kept coming. The dogs, especially, demonstrated their wrath; the birds came at him with intolerable relentlessness; and when the spiders and the fetid bats joined in the fray, Merry Bones lost patience. It is not that master vampires are so very numerous–happily, they are not, or the whole world would be exsanguinated–but apart from the fact that they have their own doubles, each one has in his train accessories which can also redouble themselves. Every vampire functions as a great finance house or a noble family, maintaining as many as a hundred clients or servants–and the members of the vampire aristocracy never have less than fifty. That gave the city of Selene a variable population, which could re-enter into itself like the elements of a telescope or the various parts of a fishing-rod. It was exhausting; within that abominable meadow, swarming with life and direly in need of a thorough mowing, nothing could be done.

We have arrived at a moment when poor Merry Bones was seriously embarrassed. He had two dogs at each leg, three spiders on his back, a bat within each armpit and several dozen leeches distributed hither and yon about his body. Four great vultures quarreled over his eyes–and all the while, the green men struck out at him vigorously with all manner of weapons. That bravest of servants was, in consequence, severely inconvenienced.

Suddenly, he clapped a hand to his forehead; an idea had occurred to him. He had placed the soup-ladle between his legs in order to have the free use of his arms. You will not have forgotten that it contained the ashes of the burned heart of Monsieur Goetzi. Merry Bones remembered that Polly had praised the virtue of those ashes very highly. Desirous of seeing something of what they could do, he dropped to his knees in order to cramp the style of the vermin that were harassing him, then flailed his fists so heroically that he forced his persecutors to retreat a pace or two.

Having thus made room, he took up the ladle and thrust it beneath the nose of the first green man to press forward upon him again.

The effect was most satisfactory. The green man immediately exploded. What could, I suppose, be called a sneeze had dislocated and fragmented him, clothing and all, causing considerable collateral damage around him.

This result afforded Merry Bones such a welcome surprise that his determination to live was renewed. He ran through every oath known in the west of Ireland and planted the handle of the ladle in his plaited hair, where it was as firmly held as a nail embedded in oak. He briskly executed the steps of an Irish jig to the imagined tune of Lilliburlero, then signaled that he wanted to talk.

"Do you gang of snakes understand the Irish?" he said. "If you want me to quiet down, I'll agree not to exterminate you all to the very last one, but if you continue to annoy me..."

He was interrupted by a piercing din of male voices, female yappings, canine howls, bird-cries, reptilian hisses and shrill bat-calls. The gist of the clamor was: "You are our prisoner. The gate is closed now, the portcullis lowered, the bridge lifted. If we cannot defeat you by force, hunger will kill you and we shall feed your blood to our swine."

Poor Merry Bones was already beginning to feel the pangs of appetite. The thought of dying of starvation was parent to an entirely legitimate anger.

"We shall see about that, you hundred devils and more!" he cried, rolling up his sleeves. And, taking hold once again of his magic ladle, he marched resolutely towards the portal to the outside world.

No one impeded his passage. The mob kept its distance, laughing in a mocking fashion.

On arriving at the gate, poor Merry Bones found that it was indeed closed and barricaded. He tried to release it, but it would have been easier to shake the towers of Westminster Abbey. Disappointed by this mishap, he hesitated indecisively, and his embarrassment caused the rabble to laugh all the more heartily.

"He who laughs last laughs loudest!" snarled Merry Bones, who would have scratched his ears till they bled for a plan.

The riff-raff replied, from a distance: "You'll die of hunger, you dirty beggar! Hunger! Hunger!"

"Hunger! Hunger!" Merry Bones repeated, mimicking them–but in trying to mock them with a gesture popular among common folk, he was unfortunate enough to upset the soup-ladle and spill the ashes of Monsieur Goetzi's burnt heart upon the ground.

The vampires raise a howl of triumph to celebrate this accident, whose consequences were incalculable, and the horrible crowd shook with a new fury, Merry Bones could not help being a trifle disconcerted at first, but he patted his head three times and said with a broad Irish wink: "That's the idea! Let's see who'll be laughing now!"

The fallen ash had settled at the steel-lined foot of the closed door. While the tumultuous mob came forward again, Merry Bones scraped the ground, gathering as much of the powder as he could in his ladle and collecting the rest in a little heap.

The entire pack of bipeds, quadrupeds, birds and ophidians flung themselves upon him together. He picked out a fine hussy reeking of perfume and seized a handful of her blonde mane at the scruff of the neck. He did it so rapidly that no one could prevent him, and there was scarcely time for a curse to pass the virago's flaming lips. In spite of the bites, the stings and the blows of wing and bludgeon, Merry Bones' powerful arms bent her over until her mouth touched the little heap of ash.

You already have some idea of the violence produced by a vampire's encounter with the only substance capable of causing one to burst asunder. No sooner had the courtesan's lips of flame made contact with the ash when there was not merely an explosion but a veritable eruption, like that of Vesuvius or Etna. The steel-lined door was lifted from its hinges and thrown to an incredible distance; the portcullis shattered into a thousand pieces; the wall was reduced to a rubble which would have served as adequate filling for a road–and yet, by some curious fluke, the drawbridge itself remained intact, although its chains broke, allowing it to fall vertically to its usual place above the moat, as if for the express purpose of granting free passage to poor Merry Bones.

Do I need to tell you about the damage done to the mob? No–you can easily imagine it. It will suffice for you to know that Merry Bones suffered only a number of insignificant scratches, a few bruises and the scorching of a couple of outer layers of his woolly hair. He figured that he could easily get his hair cut the next day, and that what he had lost had not been worth saving.

"Nice trick, eh boys?" he said to the vampiral mincemeat that surrounded him. "Look after yourselves."

And he crossed the bridge, holding his sides to contain his laughter.

Despite his brilliant success, poor Merry Bones' troubles had not yet ended. Once the bridge was behind him, he was beset by deep, opaque and impenetrable night. He moved off immediately, striding out purposefully–but after several paces, surprised that he could not hear any noise, he turned around. He saw nothing.

The darkness was complete and the silence absolute. The only effect of his turning around was that Merry Bones lost his sense of direction, and he set off again at random, oppressed by terror of the unknown. He should have gone straight ahead, that much is certain, but the people of his country have weathervanes in their heads. Suddenly, without any apparent reason, he was seduced by a passing whim into turning right–and then, an instant afterwards, became convinced that he was heading back into Selene and turned left.

It is difficult to make progress in this fashion, and such was the case with poor Merry Bones, who hardly advanced at all. At the end of an hour, as he was changing direction for what was perhaps the twenty-first time, he collided with someone following a course at right-angles to his own.

"Blundering fool!"

"Ruffian!"

"Hey! Grey Jack!"

"Miss! Miss! That sluggard Merry Bones isn't dead!"

Following this exchange of words, a glimmer of light intruded upon the night and our Anna appeared, carrying a candle in her hand. It illuminated Ned, Jack and the iron coffin. They had lost Doctor Szegeli and the young Slavonian artist, minor characters whose eventual fate you will easily deduce when you know that the night was full of vengeful thirsty vampires who were looking for victims to devour.

Our Anna and her followers were lost, just like Merry Bones. Perhaps you are wondering how that came about, since they were accompanied by Polly Bird–who, as the former double of Monsieur Goetzi had become familiar with all manner of devilment. The reason is that the unfortunate Polly had fallen into a state of shock by virtue of the cutting of the mystical thread which bound her to her seducer and master. Such operations cannot be undergone without the general state of health suffering considerable effect. Subsequent events had been so terribly dramatic as to drain her strength. The air inside the iron coffin was not good, and the consequence of these combined circumstances was that the former Polly had fallen unconscious in her box, and all subsequent attempts to awaken her had been in vain.

A brief interval of rest allowed them to confer with one another. Merry Bones took advantage of this moment of leisure to free himself of numerous scraps of vampire flesh that were sticking to his hair and clothes. Our Anna examined this debris curiously, from the viewpoint of a natural historian. This was the outcome of her observations: She concluded that the density of vampire flesh is rather tenuous; it is soft and a trifle sticky; by night a pale green phosphorescent glow diffuses therefrom into the shadows; by day, on the other hand, it is dark green, marbled with red and black. In science, there are no unimportant details–and I give you this information, moreover, for the same price that it cost me.

The unanimous decision of the conference was that they had to pierce that crust of darkness by any means possible. They guessed that it could not be later than two o'clock in the afternoon; consequently, once they arrived at the frontier of the false night, they would find themselves in broad daylight again.

Merry Bones took up his place at the head of the column once again, and ordered the departure. After a long and monotonous march, a cry of gladness escaped from every bosom: "Light!"

It was no more than a faint twilight, but their joy at perceiving it was hardly less than that which would have been occasioned by absolute clarity. Our friends quickened their paces–until they stopped abruptly, frozen by terror.

Shades of green had suddenly appeared in the atmosphere. At the same time, a dull noise–reminiscent of the reverberations generated by a troop of cavalry–became audible. Long threads of livid shadow were sliding about them to the left and right.

"The vampires! The vampires!"

It was only too true! All the inhabitants of Selene who were still able-bodied had saddled up their dogs, their lions and their tigers, and that monstrous cavalry had already surrounded our unfortunate companions. Meanwhile, other villains, mounted on bats of various species, arrived by air amid the clatter of membranous wings.

It was hopeless. Merry Bones had left his famous ladle behind–they were finished!

At the very moment of the utmost desperation, while the bloodthirsty cohort ranged itself on either side of our friends, celestial music was heard in the distance; and–need I say it?–the darkness recoiled before that enchanted harmony, which seemed to bring with it the beloved light of day.

The vampire horde, after an instant's astonishment and indecision, was sent howling in retreat, like a hundred demons put to flight by the approach of a single angel.

It was indeed an angel of sorts that was coming.

Like actual angels, such adorable beings only appear in order to work miracles. There is not even any need to think of them or wish for them: their blissful presence is sufficient.

The Right Honorable Arthur *** (the one whom we called, in another country, and with adequate reason, "the unknown comparable to a god") had not come to the plains of Serbia to protect Anna and her companions. As in Holland, previously, he was studying the art of warfare under the direction of the respectable member of the Anglican clergy who accompanied him in the role of tutor.

He was here visiting the battlefields which had secured the fame, successively, of Suleiman II, the prince of Bavaria, Prince Eugene[65] and so many others.

Yes, it was the honorable Arthur–blond, rosy-cheeked and beardless–in his admirable comfortable carriage. While the venerable clergyman took his siesta after a substantial meal, the young lord, momentarily forgetful of his precocious labors, was singing "God Save the King" to the accompaniment of a guitar.

He passed by. He did not even see those whose lives he had saved.

XIV

Our Anna did not wish to return to Semlin. The company left the incontinent Danube and took a westerly direction in order to race, at last, to the assistance of the unhappy Cornelia.

Monsieur Goetzi was no longer to be feared, so the journey across the fertile but little-known fields of Bosnia–where the women dressed very becomingly–was perfectly agreeable. The Tina Pass provided a convenient way through its mountains. Once on the other side, they could see the haughty peaks of the Dinaric Alps, in whose bosom Castle Montefalcone nestled.

The iron coffin had now been empty for several days. Polly Bird's conduct while they had been in the city of Selene had been so admirable that there had been no opposition to setting her free. She had not abused the privilege. The immoderate use she made of alcoholic beverages whenever the occasion presented itself surprised no one, because English village girls have a taste for liquor, which is even shared by some young women of better birth. In any case, she wore male clothing, which made her frequent lapses into drunkenness seem less improper.

You will not have forgotten that she continued to play the role of Monsieur Goetzi's double, that being the only means that had to secure the passage of Edward S. Barton esquire, through the high walls of the inaccessible castle. Homer had employed a similar strategy in his immortal epic; the iron coffin would serve as a reduced version of the Trojan horse.

Physically, Polly had changed somewhat since the death of her seducer. She was diminished in every sense of the word and presented the image of a Monsieur Goetzi reduced by fatigue or illness–but she had nevertheless retained a self-important manner which displeased our Anna. Merry Bones alone had the gift of her obedience. There was no mystery in this–he planted his head in her stomach or applied a foot to her backside every time she did not fall in with his plans.

---

[65] Prince Eugene was Eugène de Savoie-Carignan (1663-1736), a son of the Comte de Soissons who entered the service of Austria after being refused an army by Louis XIV and fought the Turks at Zenta in 1697.

The evening of the sixth day found them in the mountain gorges, and the moonlight soon illuminated the imposing mass of the noble dwelling which She so famously described under the name of the Castle of Udolpho.

No lights shone on its ramparts, nor in the gothic windows of the main building. The ancient fortress would have seemed entirely dead had not a human form been visible at the top of the highest tower: a young woman clad in long white veils–or her shade.

"Look there! I know her!" said our Anna

And Ned, wringing his hands with emotion, cried: "O Cornelia, my bride! Is it you that I see, or only your beloved ghost?"

In order to bring their enterprise to a successful conclusion, our companions had to separate into two groups. Monsieur Goetzi, as we shall now call the unfortunate Polly Bird, would enter the castle alone with the iron coffin; this would be carried by two local men hired in the town of Bihacz, about which the waters of the river Una divide. Our Anna, Merry Bones and Grey Jack would remain on watch outside.

The moment of parting was cruel. Long voyages engender intimacy, and facing common dangers creates a strong sense of togetherness–and I have not hidden from you the fact that She had previously honored Edward S. Barton with the first sympathetic impulse of her innocent heart. When he left her– perhaps forever–She shed a few tears; soon enough, however, the exceptional vigor of her character took over and She said in a firm tone: "Go, Edward Barton, my brother and my friend, as I am obliged to call you. Be as prudent as you are brave in the midst of the unknown perils that will surround you. Remember that my best wishes go with you, and that I am ready, night and day, to fly to your aid."

She turned around and the iron coffin was opened. Edward Barton lay down inside it; the two men from Bihacz placed it on their hand-barrow.

Monsieur Goetzi, naturally, had the password. As soon as he had shouted across the moat–having no horn on him–and given the necessary signal to the sentry, he was allowed to approach. When he was asked what he wanted, he replied: "To see Count Tiberio, immediately."

"The Count is taking his evening meal," came the reply, "and this is not a good time to see him."

"Any time is good for the delivery of good news," Monsieur Goetzi riposted. "Go find the Count and tell him that the man who has arrived carries the iron coffin."

The servant obeyed. Monsieur Goetzi, left alone with Edward, crouched down to one of the holes and whispered: "All is going marvelously. Sleep– pretend that you are quite dead."

"I am fully determined to save my bride," Ned replied, "but it is stifling in here, on my honor!"

The return of the servant put an end to the conversation.

The Count was waiting for Monsieur Goetzi in his apartment. The hired men replaced the coffin on their stretcher, carrying it along numerous corridors, past several dozen rooms which would have been magnificent had their dilapidation not testified to their centuries-long abandonment. Monsieur Goetzi could not repress an infernal smile as they passed the remains which marked the former bedroom of the Dowager Countess of Montefalcone.

That entire part of the castle, now fallen into disrepair, reminded him of the expedition undertaken by his defunct patron, and he said to himself: "That was well done–but I shall do better!" You have already guessed, I suppose, that the confidence of poor Ned and our Anna had been terribly misplaced.

They arrived at last in a better kept area, where the wall-hangings had been mended and the furniture dusted. Count Tiberio Palma d'Istria was sitting–or, rather, wallowing–in an enormous armchair whose form was reminiscent of those used by the Doges. He was drunk, as he usually was nowadays after dinner. Letizia had cultivated his bestial habits in order to enhance her dominion over him.

Monsieur Goetzi entered, followed by his two porters, who deposited the iron coffin on the tiled floor. They were ordered to leave, but made no move to withdraw.

"Good evening, you old scoundrel," said Tiberio. "Is that the Englishman that you have brought us in the box?"

"Greetings, my lord," said Monsieur Goetzi. "Yes, it's the Englishman."

"Is he quite dead?"

"I am astonished that you are not already inconvenienced by the odor of the corpse."

Tiberio immediately pinched his nose, trustingly.

"Would you like to see him?" asked Monsieur Goetzi, turning towards the coffin.

"Certainly not!" the Count exclaimed. "I've just eaten; it wouldn't be good for my digestion. The Englishman must be worm-food by now, for you've certainly taken your time bringing him here, old fellow."

"He was heavy, and the road was long," Monsieur Goetzi replied.

"It's quite a stink! Let's get on with it. What did I promise you for your reward?"

"Signora Letizia Pallanti."

"Is that right, you old scoundrel? That's marvelous. I loved her like the apple of my eye, but everything passes, and she wears the wig of a dead woman. Oh, poor Countess Greete. That was a good joke! Now, I have a fancy to marry Cornelia, my pupil, so that I might possess her youth as well as her fortune... oh well, throw the Englishman into the oubliette. I give you Letizia–now go away. Tell them as you go to open another bottle and bring my pupil Cornelia to me."

Thereupon, Monsieur Goetzi left with the iron coffin, and Count Tiberio resumed drinking. Edward Barton, in spite of the discomfort of his situation, congratulated himself on the success of the ruse. He thought that he was now being taken to Cornelia, and that she would easily find a means of letting his friends into the castle. That had been the plan, and Ned's hope was strengthened by the fact that Monsieur Goetzi did not carry out Count Tiberio's orders to the letter. He relayed the command to open another bottle of wine but did not mention Cornelia at all.

How many corridors, drawbridges, staircases, hallways and occupied rooms were there between Tiberio's apartment and Letizia's? The beautiful Italian was lying in the Oriental fashion upon a pile of cushions. She had grown very plump of late. It was here that our dear Edward S. Barton obtained a better understanding of his situation!

"Have you brought him to me alive?" cried la Pallanti, as soon as she saw Monsieur Goetzi–and when he had replied in the affirmative, she lifted herself up from her cushions and cried: "O Heaven! How wretched the darling love must be in there! Open the box at once, so that I may clasp him to my heart and intoxicate myself with the sight of him!"

Monsieur Goetzi, however, demurred. "Gently! The young man is robust and resolute. If we set him free, he will make us regret it."

"Do you think," Letizia asked, "that he is strong enough to resist my charms?"

"I am sure of it. Have you forgotten that he is in love with Cornelia?"

"That sparrow!" she exclaimed, shrugging her capacious shoulders. "I'll wager she carries no more than a hundred pounds of good flesh!"

Monsieur Goetzi made a face and replied: "You can say that again. Such that she is, however, she is all the recompense I seek."

Ned thought that he had misunderstood. "Perhaps, after all, Polly is making a joke," he thought.

"It's a fair price," said the Italian woman, however. "I promised her to you and you shall have her, but not right away."

"Why wait? I'm in a hurry."

"Because we must first get rid of that imbecile Tiberio."

"That will take time," Monsieur Goetzi objected.

"It will be all over by tomorrow morning," Letizia replied. "If you're thirsty, ask for my eleventh chambermaid: sixteen years old, a rosebud! I took her from the farm this morning and you will find her blood fresher by far than Cornelia's."

Monsieur Goetzi's eyes sparkled. Edward saw it through one of the little holes. The scales fell from his eyes. He realized with horror that Polly was still a vampire and that he was in her hands.

"I shall not refuse the little peasant," Monsieur Goetzi replied, "for I have had a good deal of trouble during my journey and few opportunities to obtain a good meal–but I warn you that you must not have a false sense of security. You have enemies outside the castle."

"What enemies?"

"Miss Anna Ward and her servants."

Ned shivered between the encasing walls, but he had sufficient spiritual fortitude not to betray his displeasure by any intemperate exclamation. There was an interval of silence, however, between the Italian woman and Monsieur Goetzi. She seemed to be thinking deeply.

"Listen," she said, at last. "You must go along the subterranean passage to the north; it is the shortest of four, only mile long. When you come to the end, you have only to turn a rock mounted on a pivot and you will find yourself in open country. Diligently make your way back to the Englishwoman and her men and offer to take them to Cornelia immediately. Bring them to me, and I'll take care of the rest. You've heard me–now do as I say. In the meantime, I shall furnish my beautiful Edward with explanations, after which he will give me his heart and his hand with pleasure."

Our Cornelia's prison was on the topmost floor of the tower. It was not out of pity but because he feared that her beauty would be affected by excessive seclusion that Count Tiberio had allowed her to take her exercise on the roof-platform. There, in that narrow enclosure, surrounded by battlements, she dwelt alone with thoughts of her young lover and regrets of happiness fled. The vast panorama of nature elevated her soul while nourishing her melancholy. The prodigious vault of the sky which loomed over her–a splendid cupola of blue by day, a million diamonds suspended in its depths by night–banished her despair by relating it to God. This was the white apparition that our friends had perceived as they arrived at the foot of the mountain.

That evening, tired of contemplating the sky, she lowered her gaze to the earth and was startled to observe a fire on the neighboring mountainside. She had never seen anything like it before. Full of astonishment–and perhaps, already, of hope–she fixed upon that glimmer with all the strength of her young eyes, afraid that she might be dreaming. She thought she recognized Anna, her best friend; Grey Jack, the old servant at the cottage; and Merry Bones, her dear Edward's valet. A fourth person was standing before the fire, but while his back was turned, his face could not be seen. Perhaps it was Edward! It ought to be Edward!

"Edward! Edward!" she cried, with an unutterable surge of joy.

Alas, he whom she had taken for Edward was Monsieur Goetzi, who had rejoined his friends by means of the northern underground passage–and who, following his deceptive scheme, was attempting to lead them to their destruction.

Following the departure of Monsieur Goetzi, Edward S. Barton was alone with Signora Letizia. That cunning woman was now showing him evidence of the most tender amiability.

"Dear boy," she said to him in a soft voice, "do you not see that everything that has happened is the result of my love for you? It began at the time when, having set aside your studies, you came to spend your vacations at the cottage I was visiting with my student, Cornelia de Witt, who has me to thank for her brilliant education. I cannot look at you now, your lip shadowed by light down and dressed with all the charms of adolescence, without a flutter in my frail heart. Having been brought up to observe the strictest standards, I had every respect for convention, but I promised myself that I would put the prodigious talents God gave me to good use in recovering the fortune of my forefathers in order that I might one day be worthy to unite my destiny with yours."

Edward S. Barton was an Englishman, so he had spirit. Despite the utter horror which this kind of discourse inspired in him, he resolved to counter it with equally skillful trickery.

"In the embarrassing situation in which I find myself," he replied, in an insinuating tone, "it is very difficult, Madame, to entertain thoughts of love. The walls of this coffin prevent the uplift of my heart–and how can I yield to your charms when I do not have the pleasure of seeing them?"

Letizia reflected for a moment, struck by the justice of this observation.

"I agree that we would be more comfortable," she said, finally, "if you and I could exchange words of love while accommodated upon my cushions–but prudence forbids it. Anyhow, in modern times, marriage is not altogether a matter of sentiment; I ought to open your eyes first. You have believed up to this point that that little girl, Cornelia de Witt, was rich and that I was poor. Abandon that error. Cornelia has nothing, and I am a rich heiress. Know that I am of royal blood. I have a vague memory of my cradle, richly ornamented with lace sewn with strings of fine pearls. A woman, beautiful as the day, bent over me as I slept, watching for my first smile. It was my mother! And my mother was named Princess Loiska Palma d'Istria, the elder sister-in-law of Count Tiberio."

It made no difference to Edward, but in the interests of making himself agreeable, he exclaimed: "Can it be possible!"

"I have the documents to prove it," Signora Letizia replied, "legitimated and registered. Shall I tell you how a company of Bohemians who prowled around the castle stole me away from the kisses of the princess, my mother...?"

"I'm so thirsty," Edward interrupted–but, as astute as she was shameless, Letizia took a glass from her bedside table, which she filled with excellent wine, and a straw. Having inserted the straw into one of the holes in the coffin and submerged the other end in the glass, she said: "Drink as much as you desire, dearest. I am happy to satisfy my beloved's least desire."

When he had drunk his fill, she continued. "Shall I tell you about the futile efforts my parents made to recover their only daughter? Unfortunately, their inquiries directed them to the Bohemian coast! Now, on the day that the wretches who had taken me had been approaching the coast, they were overwhelmed by Liparian corsairs, and I had fallen prey to the conquerors. I was five years old, my honor was intact. Algerian pirates took me from the corsairs, and I was prepared for the seraglio. A young eunuch helped me to escape and I returned to Italy, but I did not know the name and address of my parents. By turns a boarder in the most celebrated educational establishment in Turin, laureate of the Academy of Cracked Pots,[66] fugitive, seller of antique earthenware potsherds to the English, reader to a cardinal, servant of one of the oldest eremites in the Apennines and assistant in the company of the famous bandit chief Rinaldo, I cannot believe that there was ever a youth so accident-prone as mine. This brought me to my fifteenth year. At that time, I found a man in rags dying in a thick wood. On seeing me, he gave a feeble cry and begged me to remove the shoe from my left foot. The requests of a man on the point of death are sacrosanct, so I obeyed, and he cried: 'It is she! God has granted that I can expiate the worst of my sins before I expire. You have a birthmark on the side of your foot beneath your ankle, young stranger. I recognize it, because it was I who snatched you from your cradle!' He then told me the name of my noble parents. I forgave him and he died in my arms. From that day forward, amid vicissitudes diverse and innumerable, my primary objective was to find my papers. My father had died of old age, laden with honors, and my mother had joined the saints in Heaven. Monsieur Goetzi, a dangerous but clever man whom I believed to be secretly a vampire, was very useful to me during my research. I encountered him at court. It was he who recommended me to take charge of the education of Cornelia, to bring me close to my uncle Count Tiberio–who desires, vainly now, to dispute with me the patrimony of Montefalcone–and it was I who placed Monsieur Goetzi close to you, so that he could teach you to esteem and cherish me."

"A nice gift!" said Edward.

"Judge me not!" the Italian woman pronounced, severely. "Love is my excuse. As for my pupil Cornelia de Witt, she's a conceited and ridiculous little fool, who has none but the beauty of the devil. She is not entitled to a penny of the heritage of the Counts of Montefalcone, I tell you. I shall take it all, as is my right, and the first use I shall make of my wealth will be to cover you in gold. Those are my terms. You are, of course, perfectly at liberty to reject my advances–but in either case, Miss Cornelia will be delivered to Monsieur Goetzi, who will drink her like a glass of lemonade."

XV

---

[66] Féval's reference to *l'Académie des Cruches-Cassées* could be more literally rendered as "the Academy of Broken Pitchers", but he presumably intended to imply more–or less–than an interest in archaeology.

We left Cornelia at the top of the tower in which she was held captive, watching from afar the fire beside which her friends were in conference with a stranger–who, seen from behind, she had taken for Edward. You know that this stranger was the former Polly Bird, who had now fully usurped the personality of Monsieur Goetzi.

I ought to tell you something of the plans formulated by that creature, lost by virtue of her close acquaintance with a monster. In spite of her native sex, she had resolved to marry Cornelia, by consent or by force, in order to possess the immense inheritance of the Counts of Montefalcone and attain noble status.

The pretended Monsieur Goetzi had just informed our Anna that he had completed his mission successfully and that Ned was safely installed in the heart of the enemy castle, but that he would need help to bring the adventure to a conclusion. Grey Jack and Merry Bones himself were taken in. During the expedition to the city of Selene, Polly Bird had given such a convincing demonstration of her loyalty they did not think to suspect her now.

Monsieur Goetzi, therefore, set himself at the head of the little troop, and guided them towards the mouth of the tunnel.

"Gather your courage," said the impostor, as he preceded our friends into the bowels of the earth. "A terrible night lies ahead of us."

Monsieur Goetzi had brought several torches made of resinous wood, which were lit–but their brightness was immediately swallowed up in the profound shadows of the cavern, only serving to illuminate a number of reptiles fleeing into the darkness here and there. In that darkness, a strange sound was born and died, rendering up a monstrous sigh.

"What's that?" asked our Anna, stopped in her tracks by a suffocating weight which oppressed her bosom.

"Go on," replied Monsieur Goetzi. "It's only Countess Elvina's old Aeolian harps, which went out of fashion and were put down here because there was no room in the attic."

She would have liked to ask more questions about this Countess Elvina, but Monsieur Goetzi was pressing on.

"Lift the torches!" Monsieur Goetzi instructed.

The order was obeyed, and the seeping walls of a vast subterranean chamber became vaguely discernible.

"Look up above your heads!" commanded Monsieur Goetzi, again.

They lifted their eyes. A high vault loomed above them, a huge round black hole at its center.

"What's that hole for?" asked our Anna.

"It's the entrance to Count Tiberio's oubliette," Monsieur Goetzi replied. "The victims fall through it into the pit–which you will find, if you care to look, directly beneath the hole."

"What?" cried our Anna, deeply offended. "Do such barbaric curiosities of the Middle Ages still exist? Has not the vivid enlightenment of philosophy annihilated all such horrors?"

Monsieur Goetzi gave a mocking laugh. "They are only too well remembered," he replied, "but I do not believe that anyone has made use of them since Countess Elvina."

She suddenly found herself in a Gothic hall of the most lugubrious aspect. Mounted on its tall fireplace was a Venetian mirror embossed with a representation of the passion of Our Lord. On the wall to the right of the fireplace, a white spot was visible amid the hangings of dark brown Cordovan leather: an ivory button. Monsieur Goetzi had a fat black cat in his arms, whose four feet he broke, one by one, with cold cruelty. "That's so he won't run away," he said. "You shall see something of its function. I shall put him in the same place as Countess Elvina. Watch the pussycat closely."

He placed the black cat—which was mewing pitiably–on a flooring-slab that was larger than its neighbors. The animal tried to move away, but could not do so by virtue of its broken feet. Monsieur Goetzi, laughing, walked to the wall where the ivory button was. He pushed the button with his finger; the slab swung down and the cat disappeared. Then the door opened, and Count Tiberio's henchmen came in, armed to the teeth.

Monsieur Goetzi pointed his finger at our Anna and her companions, saying: "Here they are–I deliver them to you."

This time, Merry Bones was powerless to resist; our unfortunate friends were put in chains and taken away...

You must now imagine a frightful dungeon, in whose depths our Anna is lying on some bits of straw, with a ring of iron around her neck. This was where her generous devotion had brought her!

"Young maid of Albion," said a gentle voice beside her, all of a sudden, "I am Countess Elvina de Montefalcone."

She raised her eyelids, which had been sealed by tears, and saw a pale woman kneeling beside her pallet. The woman was still young, although suffering had turned her hair white.

"What!" our Anna exclaimed. "Is it possible that you have escaped the perils of the pit?"

"That happened several centuries ago," replied the pale woman, with a melancholy but pleasant smile. "We must concern ourselves with the present now. I have come into your dungeon at the behest of a particular power, and it will be my pleasure to break your chains forthwith. Get up. Freedom is granted to you."

She read in our Anna's expression an ardent desire for a more detailed explanation, and she obliged, continuing: "A barbarous usurper has condemned you to death. The one you call Monsieur Goetzi–who is none other than the infamous Gertrude de Pfafferchoffen, my rival, whose soul has passed after several other incarnations into the body of the village girl Polly Bird–has sold you. Do you know that Count Tiberio and Signora Letizia, separated for a while by covetousness and concupiscence, are reconciled tonight? Why? Because the young midshipman Barton has utterly repulsed the unseemly advances of the Italian woman, and the beautiful Cornelia has humiliated Count Tiberio with her disdain. Reunited by a common desire for vengeance, the two monsters with human faces are resolved to put Monsieur Barton and Mademoiselle de Witt to death this very night."

"How can I save them?" asked our Anna, wringing her hands.

"God is great," replied the pale woman, "and you are free!"

Our Anna threw herself towards the door of her dungeon, which opened before her as if by magic.

She marched forward, sustained by an instinctive hope. At the end of the seventh corridor, she encountered a stonemason who was sculpting a pair of arms in a block of alabaster. The two arms seemed to belong to two bodies of different sexes, and their hands were joined in an affectionate clasp.

The sculptor, desirous of embracing our Anna, said to her: "How do you like my work, my beauty? It's a pleasant whim of the gross Letizia, who wants it to ornament the tombs of the young Englishwoman and Cornelia."

She fled in desperation, while the laughing sculptor continued his work. By her count, she must have run for several leagues through corridors without end and derelict rooms.

Finally, in the corner of a gallery, She perceived a light under a door–and at the same time, her ears caught the sound of voices, some angry and others plaintive. She gathered her strength, which had been depleted by fatigue. She opened the door and entered, releasing a cry of terror at the sight of her two friends, Edward S. Barton and Cornelia, in chains.

Cornelia's beautiful hair had been cut short; Ned had a rope about his neck. They now wore the characteristic costume of those unfortunates tortured to death by the Inquisition in former times.

Behind them was a man of ferocious aspect entirely costumed in red. The axe that he carried on his shoulder was sufficient proof that his profession was that of executioner.

In another part of the room, a second group was formed by Count Tiberio, Signora Letizia and Monsieur Goetzi. The last-named, obviously discontented, was claiming that he had been promised that Cornelia would be delivered up to his unnatural thirst, while Letizia was making fun of him and Tiberio was threatening to have his head cut off. They were all raising and lowering their arms excitedly, like the roguish knaves they were.

At the sight of our Anna, they smiled cruelly.

"Just look at the bluestocking!" said the signora.

But She, heedless of this remark, fell upon her friends and clasped them in her arms.

"What good timing!" said the atrocious Italian. "Of her own accord, she takes up the position in which we can kill three birds with a single stone!" She turned round to take a step toward the fireplace, and the movement revealed the part of the wall that had been behind her. That favored our Anna with a shaft of sinister enlightenment. In her distress, she had not previously recognized the chamber above the oubliette; now, she saw the embossed Venetian mirror, the Cordovan leather hangings, and the ivory button.

"We must fly!" she exclaimed, in bewilderment.

It was too late. The Italian woman touched the button and the slab swung away–but our Anna, Cornelia and Ned were miraculously held above the drop by a supernatural hand.

Countess Elvina, emerging unexpectedly from the gulf, cried out with the voice of Mrs. Ward: "Now then dear, what's all this? Eyes open! Do you intend to lie abed till ten o'clock on your wedding day?"

There was a loud noise in the corridor. William Radcliffe blew his nose; Mr. Ward told him to go look for a locksmith.

"Save them" Save them!" cried our Anna, who found herself on her feet, in her wedding dress, in the middle of her room, with the March sun steaming joyously through the windows...

Epilogue

It seems that Milady made the error of smiling, for Miss 97 stopped abruptly. "I take your meaning," she said, in a scandalized tone. "You think that our story will be concluded by that threadbare formula: It was a dream! Admit it! Well, that's where you're mistaken!"

She briskly drained the dregs of her last cup of tea and continued. "No, no, no, no! I would not trouble the gentleman for so little. It was not a dream.[67] In the first place, She had been subject to fits of 'second sight' since the age of nine, and her parents had taken care to conceal that gift or infirmity. Be assured that I do not mean to say that She had accomplished so long and so eventful a journey in a single night–but there are other things than dreams, as you will see. When She finally opened her door, Mr. Radcliffe and her parents were awestruck by the change which had overtaken her person. She looked at them distractedly and demanded to know what had become of Countess Elvina. They

---

[67] Féval could have used the excuse that it was all a dream to "rationalize" his story–although Ann Radcliffe never stooped so low–but propriety did indeed forbid the use of such a threadbare device. Féval's attempt to wriggle out of his predicament is as implausible as any of Ann Radcliffe's "explanations" for apparent apparitions, but he would not have been unduly troubled by that.

thought her mad, all the more so when She extracted a formal promise that as soon as the marriage was over, they would depart for Montefalcone, with the stipulation that they would go via Rotterdam.

"And immediately after the ceremony, they left, for she held to the bargain. I remind you of the letters received the previous evening; those letters were certainly not a dream, and they had offered a glimpse of what had become of Ned and Cornelia.

"Henceforth, I shall only give you the facts without imposing any interpretation on them. When they arrived in London, the first thing that struck our Anna's eyes was a poster thus inscribed:

MAIN ATTRACTION!!!
THE DEVOURING OF A YOUNG VIRGIN
BY THE AUTHENTIC VAMPIRE OF PETERWARDEIN
WHO WILL DRINK SEVERAL PINTS OF BLOOD AS IS HIS HABIT!
WITH THE MUSIC OF THE HORSEGUARDS
WONDERFUL ATTRACTION INDEED!!!

"She pointed out that poster to Grey Jack, but the old and faithful servant had no memory of it. The phenomenon which had served as the basis of this story was absolutely personal to our Anna.

"They crossed the channel. On disembarking at Rotterdam, She relocated the broken road where the young unknown comparable to a god had offered his regards to her for the first time.

"She stayed the night at the Ale and Amity, in the room with the stovepipe hole, the floral curtains and the battles of Admiral Ruyter. She recognized everything, down to the minutest detail."

"And the city of Selene?" asked Milady.

"Wait–let me tell it. They went immediately, as fast as possible, to Montefalcone, where they arrived on the day of Corny and Ned's wedding."

"Saved by Countess Elvina, I hope?" the terrible countess interrupted again.

"No," replied Miss 97, with a hint of embarrassment, "but there really was a local legend concerning that unfortunate victim of feudalism. Count Tiberio and Letizia undoubtedly nurtured the most perfidious designs against the affianced couple; that they did not dare to execute their plans was due to an intervention which I do not hesitate to describe as providential. The young Lord Arthur *** came to the locality, accompanied by his tutor, the respectable clergyman, to study at first hand the famous battlefield of Scanderbeg..."[68]

---

[68] Scanderbeg (or Skanderbeg) was the nickname of Georges Castriota (1403-1468), an Albanian prince who won a famous victory over Iskander Bey during the same series of campaigns that made John Hunyadi famous.

"And that was sufficient to frustrate the plots of the two villains?" Milady exclaimed.

"Yes, Madame," replied Miss Jebb dryly. "If I could only tell you the glorious, almost divine, name of that young nobleman..."

"And Monsieur Goetzi?"

"He had married the widow of a tradesman."

"But Selene! Selene, the dead city!"

"Certain things, Milady," replied Miss Jebb, gravely, "remain beyond our understanding, and even of that which you possess by virtue of your nobility. One must have the protection of a vampire to enter Selene, and there is not always one at hand. Our two newly-married couples went to Semlin with Grey Jack and Merry Bones—whose shaggy hair really was diminished by three quarters—and although they could not find Selene, they found the shopkeepers who had sold the stove, the charcoal and the iron ladle. There is, in addition, the fact that the disappearance of the surgeon Magnus Szegeli was notorious in the town, and the home of the Slavonian sketch-artist had been empty for three weeks."

At his point, Miss 97 got up, and made her final bow.

A few days ago, in Paris, I received the following letter from the county of Stafford:

Dear Sir,

She had the habit of adding justificatory and explanatory comments to the conclusions of her compositions. Everything is clear in our story except for that which concerns the young unknown comparable to a god.

I think that it would be as well to lift the veil; your book will thus gain in historical importance. This could be done by adding a postscript in which you would say:

"We have not dared to inscribe in these frivolous pages a name which filled the world with its incomparable brilliance: the name of he who put Napoleon Bonaparte in his pocket, and who surpasses other modern heroes as far as Achilles did his Greek and Trojan rivals, etc, etc"—a deft allusion to the statue which the nuns of Lourdes erected to His Grace, in a Greek costume which might be reckoned a little too high above the knee by common folk.

Or it could be a simple note, heavily underscored and worded as follows: IT WAS WELLINGTON!!! (with several exclamation points).

I, for my part, would prefer the latter expedient.

Yours truly, etc.

JEBB.

Marie Nizet: *Captain Vampire*

Marie Nizet's Le Capitaine Vampire, *originally published in Paris in 1879 by Auguste Ghio, was lost to sight for more than a century. The Bibliothèque Nationale has no copy, nor has the British Library or the Library of Congress. The book was rediscovered by Radu Florescu, a Rumanian scholar who had made something of a specialty out of researching the historical background of Bram Stoker's* Dracula *(1897) and the Voivode on which the eponymous character was modeled, Vlad Dragul, alias the Impaler. One of Florescu's successors, Matei Cazacu, appended a reprint of Nizet's novella to his own compound biography (in French) of the historical and literary figures,* Dracula *(2004), and included a chapter in his commentary speculating about its possible influence on Stoker.*

Cazacu's research into Marie Nizet's background revealed that she was born in Brussels on January 18, 1859–which means that she had not long turned 20 when Le Capitaine Vampire *was published, presumably having written it at 19. Her father, François-Joseph Nizet (1829-1899), was a lawyer whose numerous political pamphlets, of a fervently patriotic stripe, had won him an appointment as the joint curator of the Bibliothèque Royale; while occupying that position, he published various scholarly works in the fields of bibliography and history. Marie's younger brother, Henri (1863-1925), also embarked on a literary career as a journalist and novelist.*

Although Henri remained in Brussels to pursue his studies, Marie went to Paris to complete her education, where she cultivated a strong interest in Rumanian culture and folklore. In 1878, she published a volume of poetry entitled România; *Cazacu observes that many of its inclusions are based on native ballads celebrating the continual wars of independence fought against the Turks of the Ottoman Empire, but that her political commentary takes even greater offence at the treatment of Rumania by the "great powers" whose international conferences strove to settle "the Turkish question" in the 1870s–with the eventual result that Rumania became a pawn of Russian imperial ambitions in the Russo-Turkish war of 1877-78, which forms the historical background of the story told in* Le Capitaine Vampire.

Marie Nizet never visited Rumania; her knowledge of the country and its predicament was very largely based on information provided by two close friends: Euphrosyna and Virgilia Radulescu, the daughters of the late writer and fervently anti-Russian political agitator Ion Heliade Radulescu (1802-1872). Radulescu was considered to be the foremost 19th-century representative of Rumanian culture; he founded and edited the first Rumanian newspaper and played a leading role in the 1848 "Muntenian revolution," becoming a member of the provisional government set up thereafter. He was well-known in France, and contributed articles to many of the leading French newspapers.

For Marie, under the spell of Euphrosyna and Virgilia, Rumania became part of that Parisian land of dreams called "the Orient," to which many Parisian writers made imaginary pilgrimages, if not actual ones. She seems to have found it very easy to empathize with her friends' patriotism, and their indignation at the Tsar's abuse of his Rumanian allies. The centerpiece of her story–the fulcrum around which everything else is organized–is an account of the storming of the Gravitza redoubt on September 11, 1877, when several regiments of the Rumanian army were ordered by their Russian commander-in-chief to lead a dangerous assault that had a tremendous cost in human lives.

Cazacu, whose only focus of interest is the character of "Captain Vampire" himself, suggests that the inspiration for the novella might have come from one of Ion Heliade Radulescu's poems, Zburàtoral, which describes a young girl's sexual awakening in response to the visitation of an incubus. Nizet's novella has a very different theme, though, and the most obvious literary influences manifest in the novella are two of Charles Perrault's didactic fairy tales, known in English as "Cinderella" and "Little Red Riding-Hood."

In studiously echoing these moral tales, Nizet is not attempting to produce an "art fairy tale" of the kind beloved by some Romantic writers, but quite the reverse; she refers to the stories primarily to mock and deny them, calling attention by contrast to the fact that real life is not at all like a fairy tale. Although its plot has supernatural elements, and its antagonist is manifestly demonic, the eponymous monster is part of a more elaborate pattern of symbolism whose purpose is to bring out the horror of actual events. First and foremost, and in its very essence, Le Capitaine Vampire is a war story, and a very striking one. In its method and tone alike, it was way ahead of its time, and the principal reason for the book's rapid descent into obscurity might well have been its discomfitingly cynical treatment of the ugliness of warfare–a treatment that must have seemed more than slightly shocking as the composition of a young woman of 19.

The possibility of Nizet's novella's possible influence on Bram Stoker cannot be sensibly discussed without extensive reference to its plot, so that sort of speculation is best left to an afterword, where it cannot spoil the reader's enjoyment in advance. It is, however, appropriate to offer a brief consideration here of the earlier history of French vampire fiction, in order to identify the groundwork on which Nizet might have been able to draw in selecting and shaping her key motif.

Cazacu observes that Marie Nizet's text does not employ any of the Rumanian words associated with vampire folklore–he lists strigoï, vârcolac, moroi and nosferatu–but only the word "vampire" itself. He notes that the word is of Slavic origin, but that is unlikely to be of any significance; by 1879 it had become commonplace in French parlance and it is with its French meaning that Nizet concerns herself. Indeed, she makes no reference at all to vampire folk-

lore, although almost everyone else who wrote 19th-century French fiction fea-
turing vampires seems to have had some knowledge of the contents of Dom Au-
gustin Calmet's classic treatise on the subject, first published in 1746, even if
that information had been filtered through the popular collection Infernaliana
(1822; belatedly attributed, perhaps dubiously, to Charles Nodier).

Infernaliana's *selective recycling of Calmet's "case studies" includes a*
substantial chapter on "Vampires de Hongrie," *which is presumably responsi-*
ble for the fact that most 19th-century French vampire novels feature Hungarian
vampires rather than Rumanian ones. Nizet shows not the slightest evidence of
familiarity with Infernaliana *or its source, or of having taken any notice of such*
elements in later texts shaped under its influence.

There were, however, other significant inputs to the development of the
French literary mythology of the vampire, of which the most important was John
William Polidori's novelette The Vampyre *(1819), which was rapidly translated*
into French. The Vampyre *gave rise to several imitative works, including two*
successful dramatic adaptations, both entitled Le Vampire *and both produced at*
the Porte Saint-Martin theatre, in 1820 (a version adapted by Achille Jouffroy
d'Abbans, Jean-Toussaint Merle and Charles Nodier) and 1851 (a version fur-
ther adapted by Alexandre Dumas and Auguste Maquet).

Although it is highly unlikely that Nizet had seen the play performed, she
might well have read the script of Dumas' version in the 1876 edition of his col-
lected plays, just as she might easily have read a translation of Polidori's origi-
nal. Both texts feature male vampires, as Nizet's does, but this was relatively
rare in early 19th-century French literature; the texts she could have found even
more easily–including Théophile Gautier's nouvelle "La morte amoureuse" *(tr.*
as "Clarimonde", *1836) and two poems from Charles Baudelaire's* Les fleurs
du mal *(1857),* "Le vampire" *and* "Les métamorphoses du vampire," *employ*
the word in a psychosexual context with respect to female temptresses (although
Baudelaire's use of the masculine pronoun suggests that it is male lust rather
than the female object of desire that he is characterizing as vampiric).

The only other text Nizet is likely to have run across which features a male
vampire is Paul Féval's La Ville-vampire *(1867 as a serial), whose first book*
version was issued in 1875 and must still have been available for purchase when
she arrived in Paris. Although Féval's novella is a historical comedy parodying
the excesses of English Gothic fiction, it does have two features that are found
nowhere else prior to 1879 and which are reproduced in Le Capitaine Vampire:
the vampire's ability to be in two places at once, and an extensive exercise in
symbolism that makes vampirism a lurid exaggeration of various sorts of human
depredation, including those associated with warfare. The former is trivial, but
the latter may be more significant.

The word "vampire" was extensively used in a metaphorical sense before
1879. Baudelaire's use of it as a symbol of the male response to female sexuality
reflected a trend that eventually gave rise to the American use of the term

"vamp" as a description of predatory women–especially those featured in the cinema–but the more frequent and lurid application was in socialist rhetoric that represented capitalists as "bloodsucking" predators. Karl Marx's Das Kapital *(1869; French tr. 1873; English tr. as* Le Capital*) makes continual reference to proprietors as "vampires."*

Nizet gives no clear evidence of being a revolutionary socialist, in spite of being fervently anti-aristocratic and pro-proletarian, but Ion Heliade Radulescu had played a leading role in the local version of the wave of revolutions that swept Europe in 1848, and his daughters would certainly have been familiar with contemporary revolutionary rhetoric. This influence could have combined with that of La ville vampire *to make it seem very appropriate to Nizet to symbolize the ultimate Russian bogey-man as an aristocratic vampire.*

B.S.

I. The Insult

It was May 1877. The Russians were descending like locusts upon the magnificent country of Rumania, which had been surrendered to them as prey. The population of Iasi had quadrupled; troops were cluttering the railway lines and the Cossacks were invading Bucharest, despite a specific clause in the Rumanian treaty forbidding the imperial battalions access to the capital.

One hot afternoon, a number of peasants were sowing maize and barley in the vicinity of Bucharest. It is impossible for Rumanians to remain silent for an instant, and there was no lack of topics of conversation.

"They have no respect for anything!" said one young man, shaking his long hair. "They trample the corn, break our ploughs and burn our trees like dead wood! God only knows what they won't do!"

"And then, we have to give them lodging!" said another.

"Right, Mitica," said a third to the first speaker. "It wouldn't be so bad if they didn't drink so much!"

"I have my sister to consider," Mitica Slobozianu replied, simply.

An old man with a white beard–a stereotypical *eternal father*–doffed his sheepskin cap respectfully and said, in a grave voice: "If Heliade [69] had lived, they wouldn't have got past Ungeny."

"Old Mani's right," the peasants said, "but it's not a good idea to remember Heliade just now."

Old Mani Isacescu paid them no heed, and said with a sigh: "Heliade! I knew him. Those were good times."

Alas, the good times are always those that are long gone.

---

[69] This reference is to Ion Heliade Radulescu (see the introduction).

"Our father Bismarck, who art in Varzin..." [70] Mitica intoned, nasally. "Bah! We'll have plenty of things to ask of *our father Bismarck*, of which he won't grant a single one."

"You seem very cheerful, Mitica–thanks to the *raki*?" [71] insinuated one of the peasants.

Mitica blushed. "Don't spoil my good mood," he sighed, ceasing to smile. "It'll go away by itself soon enough. Next Sunday I've got to go to the town hall–where, depending on how unlucky I am, I'll either be enrolled in the territorial army or the regular army. They'll cut off my hair, while I wait to lose my head! There you go!" Passing his hand through his Merovingian locks, he added: "It's a shame, though."

"To the town hall!" the peasants exclaimed, unpleasantly surprised.

"Yes–like everyone else unfortunate enough to have been born in the year of our Lord 1856."

A cry of anger erupted from every bosom.

"And suppose we don't want to!" Manoli said, with a gesture of defiance.

"Well, your wishes will be overruled," Mitica replied, the *raki* having reconciled him somewhat to his fate. "To war, my friends, to war! If the Turks take us prisoner, they'll cut off our arms and legs. That'll be very amusing."

"And my son?" cried Old Mani. "What will they do with my son?"

"Your son? My God protect him–and all the other *dorobantzi*.[72] Isn't he coming back today? Well, since he's a corporal, he must know a lot more than me, a humble conscript."

Old Mani did not reply. He turned away and resumed throwing maize to the wind.

"They'll send us to Dobruja," Mitica continued, with an ironic verve that excited his companions. "We'll sleep in the marshes with the toads and eat *mamaliga* made with plaster–that's good enough for poor devils like us."[73]

"What are you doing, father?" a familiar voice suddenly put in, causing the old man to shiver. "You're sowing corn for the foreigners and preparing straw for their horses!"

"Ioan, my Ioan!" cried Old Mani, hurling himself upon his son.

"Isacescu!" said the peasants, immediately forming a circle around he soldier, as avid as could be to hear the lie given to the bad news brought by Mitica. Alas, the *dorobantz* could only confirm it.

---

[70] Varzin was Bismarck's country estate in Pomerania.

[71] *Raki* is here defined as plum brandy [Nizet], although the term is often used more generally to refer to strong liquors of the region.

[72] The *dorobantzi* were a special corps of Rumanian infantry [Nizet].

[73] *Mamaliga* is a porridge made from maize, allegedly the staple diet of Rumanian peasants [Nizet].

Furious and exasperated, the peasants abandoned their work and took to their heels along the road, in the opposite direction to Bucharest.

"Say nothing to the women!" Ioan shouted after them.

Mitica and the *dorobantz* exchanged a few words.

"Are you going to Bucharest?" Ioan asked.

"And then I'll come back here," Mitica said. He added, with a smile: "Mariora's waiting for you."

"Poor Mariora!" sighed the *dorobantz*.

Mitica put his finger to his lips to command silence. Ioan made a sign to show that he understood, and remained alone with his father while his friend, whose robust cheerfulness was indestructible, went away whistling.

Ioan Isacescu appeared to be 22 or 23 years of age. He displayed all the distinctive features of his race; even if he had not been wearing the strange uniform of the *dorobantzi*, the slender and elegant figure, the olive complexion, the curly black hair descending over his forehead and–above all–the dark and profound eyes whose glare was unsoftened by their extremely long lashes, would have drawn from any Serb, Russian, Bulgar or Hungarian the possibly hostile and disdainful exclamation: "There's a Rumanian!"

The shadow of a moustache stamped his upper lip. The sole fault that an artist would have found with his face, which was otherwise perfectly handsome, was the extraordinary thickness of the eyebrows, which were almost joined together, and which lent his intelligent and pensive physiognomy a hint of wildness.

"Isacescu is proud!" said young women offended by the indifference of the *dorobantz*, who spared them neither a glance nor a friendly word. My God, no! Perhaps Isacescu's character was a little too serious, but he was certainly scornful of no one, and it was a cherished privilege to have him as a friend. In the territorial army, of which he was a member, the soldiers spent alternate periods of three weeks in their hearths and a week with their regiment. Old Mani Isacescu's flourishing fields gave scarcely any evidence of the brief absences of Ioan–who had succeeded, by means of his activity and economy, in doubling the little capital they possessed. Even his meager wages were put into his father's hands in full, and it was said that, although the Isacescus were not rich, they had a chance of becoming so.

The *dorobantz*, although brave to the point of temerity, hated boasting, and his horror of what one might call *staginess* had played a strange part in determining his future.

It was in 1876, at the time of the thaw. The Dimbovitza flooded the poor districts in the south of Bucharest and a great number of peasants, including Isacescu, had hastened to see the disaster. A pretty young girl of 16–who had not

246

read Schiller's *Diver* [74]–threw a flower into the river and challenged the young men to go after it. They immediately threw themselves into the muddy water like a flock of geese, to the great delight of the pretty girl, who laughed at the sight of them splashing about, trying to get the better of one another. Although he had heard the imprudent words of his neighbor, whom he had known since childhood, Ioan remained where he was on the bank. His severe gaze met the little fool's eyes, and she blushed. From that moment on, she loved Isacescu. At first, Ioan's response to that affection, so bizarrely originated, was lukewarm; he allowed himself to be adored by the young woman as a Hindu god by a Brahmin. One day, though, he was astonished to find that he loved Mariora Slobozinu, if not more, then at least in an altogether different fashion to the manner in which she loved him.

Old Mani leaned on his son's arm; they left the sun-drenched plain. The maize would certainly yield a double harvest this year. But the two Isacescus were not thinking about maize!

They went along a narrow sunken path, bordered on either side by bushes and trees whose roots projected from the earth, and they chatted as they walked.

"The country's independence will be declared within the week," Ioan said. "They'll have us fire our cannons, then they'll pack us off to Giurgiu." With a smile, he added: "Probably with a double ration of *selbovitza*." [75]

"Giurgiu!" said Old Mani. "Giurgiu's on the Danube!"

"Yes, it's on the Danube–the right bank. They don't want to tell us because they fear a mutiny, but we've figured it out." After a pause, he continued in a lower voice: "Father, when I'm gone, you'll go to see Mariora from time to time, won't you? I'll simply tell her that we're going to garrison Giurgiu–she doesn't know that Giurgiu's on the Danube, so don't tell her!"

Old Mani replied with a nod of his head, his black eyes gleaming beneath his white eyebrows. He pointed towards Bucharest and pronounced, in a loud voice, the malediction that the Rumanian people consider irrevocable: "*A curse be upon them, their dead ancestors and their unborn children.*"

The arm he had raised to issue the curse remained outstretched. Ioan shivered, and suddenly lowered himself to the ground, setting his ear against it. The

---

[74] In Friedrich Schiller's allegorical ballad *Der Taucher* [The Diver] (1797), a King hurls a golden goblet off a cliff into the sea, challenging his knights and vassals to recover it, and thus claim it for their own. A young page who accepts the challenge is dragged into the depths by a whirlpool. He returns, miraculously, after a magical underwater journey, but the King throws the goblet back into the sea and challenges him again, this time promising a knighthood and his daughter's hand as the reward for its recovery. The boy, fervent with desire to marry the Princess, jumps in for a second time, with the predictable result.

[75] *Selbovitza* is a kind of strong liquor [Nizet].

father and the son listened. A dull rumble reached their ears, similar to the steady gallop of a troop of horses.

"What's that?" the father asked.

"I don't know," the son replied. "It might be a cavalry unit passing by!"

The noise grew louder.

"They're horses," murmured Ioan, still leaning down to the ground. "Russian horses–I recognize their trot."

"Russians?" Mani repeated. "Which way are they headed?"

The *dorobantz* pricked his ears more attentively.

"Northwards," he said, finally. "They're coming towards us."

Scarcely had he pronounced these words when they saw a horseman appear a few hundred yards away, at the end of the path they were following–then another, and a third: an entire unit, as Ioan had said.

"Well?" said Old Mani, interrogatively.

"They're Cossacks, headed by a Colonel," said the younger Isacescu, whose eyesight had been honed on the streets. He was not mistaken; the Cossacks were coming down the sloping path at full speed.

"Let's get out of the way, father," Ioan said. "Here they are!"

The Russians had arrived within the range of an ordinary voice. The Colonel in command of them, having seen the two Walachians, cried out in strongly-accented Rumanian: "*Loc! Facetzi loc!*"–meaning "Give way! Get out of the way!"

The command was futile. The two Isacescus had their backs to a bank that was like a wall of earth. The Russians were riding three abreast, coming like the wind, and the path was no more than ten feet wide.

"*Loc!*" repeated the officer. "*Loc!*"

They could not go back any further. Ioan was about to reply when his eyes met the sallow face of the Russian Colonel. His terrible eyebrows frowned; he had just perceived a mocking smile in the greenish eyes of the officer, who was still howling: "*Loc! Loc!*"

The Colonel aimed his horse at the two Rumanians and shouted ferociously at old Mani: "Since when does a serf keep his cap on his head before a boyar?" With a rapid gesture, he lashed out with a slender horsewhip, which passed across the old man's forehead like a lightning bolt.

Bursts of laughter sounded behind the insulter; a cry of rage replied to them. Ioan, pale with wrath and brandishing his dagger, threw himself at the horse's head. He seized the bridle with his left hand, and was about to strike its rider with his right, when the latter abruptly pulled away and drew his sword.

The saber came down violently upon the hand of the *dorobantz*; a jet of blood sprang forth, but the dagger remained firm in Ioab's iron grip.

If the Walachian was strong, the Russian was skillful. Releasing a guttural exclamation, he jammed his spurs into the flank of his chestnut horse, which set off at a gallop, dragging the *dorobantz*–who fell, bleeding, beneath the hooves of the Cossack horses.

When he got up again, Old Mani was by his side. Ioan looked around, with a strange expression; blood was dripping from his fingers, reddening the grass, but he did not feel the wound. He only saw his father, knowing and understanding but one thing: his adversary was out of reach! He calmly folded his arms across his chest and watched the Russians recede towards the horizon.

When the last soldier had disappeared from view, and the sound of the last horseshoe striking the ground had ceased to echo in his ears, he murmured in a dull voice: "For what you have just done, man with the yellow eyes–what you did to my father, and what you did to me–I swear, here before God, to repay you a hundred times over!"

II. What Boris Liatoukine Was

That same May evening, a joyful sound of conversation and clinking glasses leaked out of one of the rooms in the Hugues Hotel, the most aristocratic in Bucharest. A crowd of young Russian officers, who had come straight from Iasi, were disporting themselves there.

The floor was strewn with the shards of broken bottles; merely by the manner in which these amiable young men downed the glasses of Rumanian wine that they were served, they were recognizable as Muscovites. The open windows gave passage to clouds of tobacco smoke and dozens of corks, with which the officers took pleasure in bombarding innocent passers-by.

"Who cares?" said Yuri Levine. "It's nice here! There are trees–which are in leaf, as in St Petersburg. I've always liked trees and leaves." The young Hussar seemed to be endowed with a sensibility that was quite rare among persons of his sort.

"Well, that's a fine thing to say at Countess M***'s ball!" exclaimed a tall fellow, whose name was Bogomil Tchestakoff. "Personally, I could never stand *green foliage and cool shade*, as my venerable aunt would put it–she has literary pretensions and claims that my aversion to nature is evidence of a moist throat and a desiccated heart." He drained the contents of his glass in one gulp. "These Walachians produce excellent wines!"

"Same goes for these little pastries," added a fat Pole, whose mouth was full. "They're very strong on little pastries."

"So you reckon, Bogomil," put in one Stenka Sokolich, who appeared to belong to the order of wading birds, "that we ought to exert ourselves to stay here for as long as possible?"

"Archduke Nicolas will see to that," said Bogomil, winking, "thanks to the pretty ladies..."

"Oh, the women are another thing!" cried Igor Moïleff, a sort of Petersburgian Don Juan. "They have primitive virtues, these little Dacian girls!"

"Oh, have you been tempted?" asked the Pole, with a loud laugh that he took pains to make dirty.

"Oh yes!" sighed Igor, negligently. "What else is there to do in an occupied city? And believe it or not, I was rebuffed–for the first time!"

"The first time, eh?" cried Stenka Sokolich. "And the Princess Sarolta K***, who..."

"She was an Ambassadress," Igor interrupted, impatiently. "I don't count Ambassadresses, myself."

"Oh, don't get upset–we believe you. Tell us your story instead."

Igor leaned back lazily in his armchair, lit a cigar and began: "This morning, I was innocently taking a stroll along what these good Walachians call the Chaussée–which I, personally, call 'under the lime-trees'–when I noticed a girl trotting along in front of me, whose figure didn't displease me and who seemed to be young. I could tell from her clothes that she was no boyar, so, assuming that things would be easy, I increased my pace. 'Mademoiselle,' I said to her, in French. She turned around. She wasn't exactly ugly, although she was as dark as a chestnut! She looked at me with fearful eyes, murmured a few words in that diabolical lingo they jabber hereabouts, and turned her heels towards me with no further ceremony. I fell into step with her. 'Mademoiselle,' I said again–and I summoned the assistance of my multilingual expertise–'*ia lioubliou tebia! ich liebe dich! io t'amo!*' Oh, but in vain–Russian, German and Italian were equally futile. She was deaf! In Petersburg or Berlin, a girl of her sort would have understood me even if I were speaking Chinese! I was wary of approaching too closely–she was escorted by an enormous dog that was looking at me sideways. I took the risk, though–and the beast opened its eyes! I wanted to talk to the beauty, not the dog. 'Muscha!' she said, suddenly. As I went to take her hand, the dog pounced–I had to let go, damn it. She didn't bear me a grudge, though–as soon as she got away from me, she called off her Cerberus, just as it was about to devour me."

"Bah!" said Bogomil Tchestakoff, "Liatoukine, who has exceedingly beautiful relatives here, will find us some palace where the cellars are well-stocked and the girls pretty. He's an invaluable man!"

"So where is Liatoukine, then?" they exclaimed, in chorus.

The emphasis with which they pronounced the name allowed the inference that Liatoukine was, at the least, a sufficiently important person not to cause well-born men to blush.

"You know very well that Liatoukine is everywhere," said Yuri Levine. "He has the gift of ubiquity, just like the good God of Archimandrite Samourkassoff."

"Bah! Since I've been with the regiment I've heard no stories of any other sort," said Bogomil. "I've grown tired of it. Do you believe such tales, the rest of you?"

No," said Sokolich, whose Mephistophelean profile advertised his skepticism. "Despite his funereal aspect, I take Boris Liatoukine for an honest fellow, no more stained by Diabolism than this stout Pole here. Except that this is what a trustworthy old officer told me:

"It was in the Crimea. Remember that Liatoukine is older than us, and over 45. Liatoukine was in command of a Cossack regiment. You know that he doesn't have a soft heart. All Cossacks are thick-skinned, it's true, but Liatoukine plied the knout so often and hard that one day, when he found himself in an out-of-the way spot with his men, they stripped him naked, intending to freeze him to death–yes, freeze him to death! The funny thing is that Liatoukine didn't make a move to defend himself. On the contrary, he smiled. Water cascaded down on him, and when he had the appearance of a pretty crystal statue, the Cossacks, glad to be rid of their Lieutenant, got back on their horses. When they arrived back at camp, the first person they saw was Liatoukine, fully dressed and not even chilly. One of the Cossacks went mad, and Liatoukine had the rest–who would surely have died of fright without his intervention–executed by a firing-squad. Ever since then, he's been known in the army as *Captain Vampire*–a nickname he's kept even though he's now a Colonel."

Bogomil and the Pole burst out laughing.

"That's not all," Sokolich went on. "You know that Liatoukine has the reputation of being a lucky man. One evening–it was last winter, I believe–little Count M*** went back to his estate. A charitable friend was waiting at the railway station to tell him that Countess Malgorzata had gone to the theater with Liatoukine. Bad news! The Count ran to the Opera House; Malgorzata was there, in the flesh, with Captain Vampire at her side! M***, afraid of a scandal, swallowed his rage with his supper, but first thing the next morning, he presented himself at Boris's lodgings–where he was astonished to discover a companion in misfortune! Prince S***, whom you all know, was saying: 'Don't try to excuse yourself, sir! Yesterday, as Saint Isaac's chimed midnight, you were found in intimate company with the Princess!'

" 'You're mistaken, my Prince!' cried the bewildered M***. 'It was my wife that the gentleman took to the Opera; I saw them, as midnight sounded at the station.' And they started bickering. 'It's me!–no, it's me!–it's me!' A fine subject for discussion! Liatoukine, profiting from this altercation, refrained from clarifying the issue, and do you know how it finished? The two husbands fought a duel against one another!"

This Rabelaisian anecdote excited a general hilarity. The officers let loose that good Homeric laughter, which has suffered so much abuse from romancers, and which never sounds so well as when it bursts out at someone else's expense.

"Isn't it said that he's been married?" asked Boleslas Brzeminski.

"Twice over!" said Stenka Sokolich, who could have compiled the chronicles of St Petersburg's scandals. "His first wife was a tall, stiff Pole—one week of marriage and *crack!*—no more Princess Liatoukine."

"She died?" asked Brzeminski, who was not quick on the uptake.

"Absolutely. The second was more durable—that one lasted a month. One fine morning, all St Petersburg learned that Liatoukine was a widower once again. It was whispered abroad that the two women had been strangled and that they both bore a little red mark on the neck—the vampire's teeth, you know..."

"Damn! That makes the blood run cold!" said the Pole, only half-jokingly.

It is unnecessary to add that several more bottles had been drained to the last drop during Sokolich's story.

"So he isn't coming, then, dear Boris!" cried Bogomil, yanking the cord of a bell despairingly.

A waiter appeared. "What do your lordships desire?" he said, speaking French with a Hungarian accent.

"Liatoukine, my friend! Yes, we've lost him, and we'd dearly like to find him again," said Bogomil, shifting in his chair.

"But..."

"No buts, my lad! We need Liatoukine—he's a Russian boyar. Find him!"

"It's just that there are a great many Russian boyars here now," the waiter replied, with a tentative smile.

"Ah!" said Sokolic, smoothing down his moustache with his thumb. "Does that displease you, perchance?"

And they repeated, in various tones: "Liatoukine—we want Liatoukine!"

"Here he is, gentlemen!" said a voice that caused them all to start, as if impelled by a spring.

Liatoukine was standing in front of them.

As Sokolich had said, the newcomer had a funereal aspect. He realized, with surprising exactitude, the legendary type-specimen of the Slavic vampire. His figure, unusually long and thin, projected an enormous shadow behind him, which merged with the darkness of the ceiling. With a gesture redolent with a slightly cold dignity, he offered a fleshless hand charged with rings to the young officers, and deigned to take the seat that was respectfully offered to him. His hair and beard, which were intensely black, made the livid pallor of his long face stand out, its stern and glacial lines seeming more reminiscent of a marble monument than any human physiognomy. The soldiers had nicknamed him "Captain Vampire;" a stronger mind might have labeled him a *perfect gentleman*. The eyes, which seemed the only living things in that impassive face, displayed a singular feature: each eyeball, iridescent as a topaz, had a vertically slit pupil, such as one observes in animals of the feline family. The power of that gaze was such that no one could sustain it.

The ladies of Petersburg said that Liatoukine had the evil eye, and hastened to touch iron when he approached.

Liatoukine spoke sparingly. His voice had a metallic quality, which served him marvelously well in battle, but which resonated strangely in a drawing-room. No one had ever seen him laugh, and when he smiled, his features took on an expression of ferocity to which his oldest friends had not yet become accustomed. He had received a precious gift of nature, which his comrades envied him: that of drinking wine as others drank water. A large amethyst which he wore on his finger prevented him, they were convinced, from getting drunk. Having a great deal of influence, he had few declared enemies; his town house in St Petersburg was a customary meeting-place for Ministers and Ambassadors. He had published a highly-esteemed treatise on strategy, and the Tsar sometimes sent him on missions to Vienna, London or Berlin. To sum up, Captain Vampire was an officer of great valor; he had distinguished himself in the Crimea and Khiva, and Archduke Nicolas's staff officers whispered that he would be a General before the campaign ended.

As to the rest, his life was shrouded in mystery, and no one knew any more than Stenka Sokolich.

A witness would have been struck by the change that Liatoukine's presence had brought to the manner in which these young hotheads expressed themselves. *That dear Boris* had become *Colonel*; familiarity had been transformed into deference.

Liatoukine slowly drained a large glass of Cotnar wine, and surveyed his companions with his mesmeric gaze. "Gentlemen," he said, in his sonorous voice, "the boyar Androcles Comanescu has done us the honor of inviting us to the party that he is giving at 11 p.m. in his palace in the Strada Mogosoi. Ten o'clock has just sounded; we have time enough."

Liatoukine got to his feet, as stiffly as an automaton. The young men bowed and followed the Colonel, very happy to be able, at last, to parade their graces before the eyes of Rumanian ladies, which they promised themselves to dazzle.

Yuri Levine and the Pole formed the rearguard.

"He's very generous, this Cococescu!" muttered Boleslas, starting off by mangling the name of his Amphitryon.

"Shut up!" said Yuri. And, taking Brzeminski by the arm, he picked up Liatoukine's glass in his gloved fingertips. "Look!" he said holding the glass up to the lamplight.

"Pooh!" said the Pole.

And Yuri threw the glass out of the window.

III. Mariora

Four or five miles from Bucharest, on the far side of the Baniassa Woods, a little white house stood in the middle of a tiny garden. The garden, where various plants vied to outgrow one another, was very narrow. The tile-roofed house seemed to be smiling through its small white-curtained windows. It all had an air of cleanliness and grace–which is not rare in Rumania, whatever people might say. Travelers halted instinctively in front of this cheerful habitation, and those who asked about the owners were informed: "They're the children of the late parish priest: the Slobozianus, Mitica and Mariora." And if the superb maize-fields round about caught their eyes: "Those are the Slobozianus' too–for as far as the eye can see, everything belongs to the Slobozianus."

While the Russians whom we have just left were drinking strong Cotnar wine and painting their friend Liatoukine in the darkest of colors, five or six young Rumanian women were gathered in the garden of the children of the parish priest. Some among them qualified as beauties, and none was straightforwardly ugly. They all wore the magnificent national costume, which retains echoes of Italy. Their double aprons of multicolored wool, the Byzantine embroideries that decorated their silken sleeves and the gold Turkish coins that shone in their brunette hair–invariably gathered into a thick plait–testified that they belonged to the families of wealthy peasants.

A joyful babble emerged from this pretty company. To tell the truth, they were gossiping about their neighbors, as people do in every village in the world when evening approaches–and God knows how Moldo-Walachian tongues wag!

"These Russians!" said a tall young woman of 20. "They think we're their slaves and they have a right to offend us."

"Zinca got married yesterday," said another. "They tried to carry off the husband."

"Bah! They couldn't carry off anything large." A loud burst of laughter greeted these words. Addressing a young woman whose clothes seemed slightly coarser than those of her companions and whose jet-black hair only bore red ribbons faded with wear, the speaker went on: "What did you say to the bold stranger?"

"Me? Nothing," said the young woman in red ribbons. "I didn't even understand what he said. I walked faster, that's all. In any case, I had my dog, which would have defended me."

"She's a savage, that Zamfira!" exclaimed Ralitza, a brunette.

"I hate the Russians!" murmured the one who had just been addressed as Zamfira.

"No," said the daughter of a wealthy farmer. "Zamfira's just faithful."

"Oh, faithful! Has the little one got a fiancé, then? Is it Stanciù the blacksmith or Stroïtza with the dancing bear?"

Zamfira blushed and made no reply, but a tear trembled on her eyelashes.

"One can't put on a show of being difficult when one has gypsy blood in one's veins," Ralitza put in. "Who wants a gypsy for a wife?"

"I know someone," said the oldest of the group, "and I forbid you to tease poor Zamfira–who's as good as you or me–any more."

Zamfira smiled and looked up, her eyes full of gratitude for her protector, who squeezed her hand gently.

"Was he handsome, at least, your Russian?" said Katinka, the farmer's wife.

"I don't know," Zamfira said. "I barely glanced at him."

"Ah! I would have known, myself," her interlocutor riposted. "Did he have black hair?"

"And yellow eyes?" said a soft and melodious voice from behind the young women.

The owner of the cottage, Mariora Slobozianu, had just appeared on the threshold.

Where are you, Rumanian poets too little known in the West–Heliade, Bolliaco, Alecsandri [76]–that you might tell us what a pretty thing this Mariora was?

Alecsandri would have cried, on seeing her: "Her hair is like the silvery rays of the Moon in summer, and her eyes recall the limpid mirror of a mountain lake!" Which, translated into vulgar language, signifies that Mariora had blonde hair and blue eyes.

She seemed, among her dark-complexioned companions, to be a daughter of the North astray beneath the serene skies of these southern climes–but her dainty feet, ever-ready to dance the *hora*,[77] her extravagant gaiety, bursting out on the slightest pretext, made her recognizable as an authentic Danubian. Her gaze had the calm profundity of the eyes of infants, and her smile was so sweet that it had finally captivated the heart of the wildest man in the neighborhood: Ioan Isacescu.

Mariora was leaning against the vine-clad wall, in a picturesque and slightly studied pose, the rays of the setting Sun brightening the vivid colors of her clothes, whose weave contained more threads of silk than strands of wool. Alas, the pretty Walachian had more than one fault. In all her life, not one serious thought had ever crossed her foolish mind, which was entirely occupied with the thousand trifles that have the privilege of delighting the sophisticated women of Paris and the female savages of Guinea to an equal extent.

Mariora was a coquette.

Her coquetry was fundamentally and entirely innocent; Mariora never dreamed of doing any harm and sought only to please Isacescu, whom she adored. She was considered by other young people to be a being of a superior kind; light conversation ceased when she approached, and she was held in re-

---

[76] Unlike Ion Heliade Radulescu, the Rumanian poets Cezar Bolliaco (1813-1891) and Vasile Alecsandri (1821-1890) were still alive at the time when the story is set. Alecsandri similarly played a significant role in the revolutionary upheavals of 1848.

[77] The *hora* is a Rumanian folkdance [Nizet].

spect as much on account of being the daughter of the late parish priest as the fiancée of the dreaded *dorobantz*.

Mariora was well-protected. She never went to Bucharest without the accompaniment of Baba Sophia, an aged female relative the priest had taken in, and the young boyars "returning from Paris" knew that anyone leaving the house of the sister risked meeting the brother's dagger or the fiancé's revolver at the corner. Only Lord Relia Comanescu, Mitica's foster-brother,[78] was admitted to the intimacy of the Slobozianu household; his mind was imbued with the caste prejudices of the previous century, and never even suspected that Mariora was pretty.

For her part, Mariora admired no one but Ioan Isacescu. He was poor, or nearly so, while she was rich; he possessed six miserable *pogones* [79] of land, while the Slobozianu estate covered an area of more than 50 hectares, all of which Mariora, an unconscious egoist, considered as her own property–a notion of which her brother, Mitica, did not think it necessary to disabuse her. Imperious and willful as she was, though, with regard to all those who surrounded her, a slight movement of the poor *dorobantz*'s eyebrows was sufficient to render her docile. Their wedding was to be celebrated within the year, although all the gossips in Baniassa were shaking their heads and muttering that, marriage or no, it would all end badly, and that Mariora was not the wife that Ioan Isacescu needed.

Perhaps that was true, alas. Mariora had the charming faults and caprices of a noble lady of Bucharest, which might prove rather embarrassing baggage beneath the roof of a simple peasant like Ioan. The wife of the parish priest–who had, incidentally, married beneath her–had devoted herself to educating her daughter in a plethora of small superfluous perfections, while neglecting to cultivate the solid qualities by means of which the young woman would easily have found employment in the position that she occupied. The end-result of this was that she had pretty pink fingers that did not know how to make cheese, and that she sang *doïne* [80] divinely, although it required more than courage to consume *mamaliga* that she had prepared. She seemed far less suitable for Isacescu's

---

[78] This relationship of *frère de lait*, for which English has so better equivalent than "foster-brother," plays a significant role in 19th-century French fiction. It had long been common practice in continental Europe for aristocratic women to "farm out" their children to wet-nurses rather than take on the ignominious burden of breast-feeding. Most European aristocrats of the 18th and 19th centuries thus had "foster-siblings" of much lower social status, with whom they were connected by peculiarly intimate and frequently enduring bonds. The practice was a boon to novelists desirous of forging connections between the social classes that would facilitate their plotting.

[79] A Rumanian *pogone* is slightly less than half a hectare [Nizet].

[80] *Doïne*–the word is plural–are Rumanian folksongs [Nizet].

humble hearth than the sumptuous drawing-rooms of some boyar; she had long since confided the duties of her own household to Baba Sophia and Zamfira.

What was Zamfira? Oh, almost nothing. She and her father lived together in little hut they owed to the generosity of the Slobozianus. The father labored, sowed crops, weeded the garden and gathered the harvest on Mitica's behalf; he daughter helped–or, rather, replaced–Mariora, and still found the time to weave nets and mats, which she sold in Bucharest. She was honest, according to supposition, although the question had scarcely been tested. She had had the misfortune to be born to a gypsy mother, thus suffering from a kind of proscription that may have struck her as unjust, but she never complained. She was very gentle, and when she wept, she was so quiet as to be scarcely audible. If Mariora was reckoned a pearl, Zamfira might have been called an angel.

Zamfira was devoted to Mariora; Mariora might have loved Zamfira if the gypsy had not had those poor frayed ribbons in her hair. There was a story attached to those ribbons, and they were the cause of Mariora frequently subjecting Zamfira to unmerited reproaches and wounding jeers. One day–it was about a year previously–Mitica had brought them back from the Mosilor fair, which is held in Bucharest during the week before Pentecost.

"Red!" the discontented Mariora had cried. "Why red, given that I'm blonde?"

Mitica smiled and did not reply. The following day, Zamfira appeared at the *hora* with the famous ribbons in her hair, to the great annoyance of Mademoiselle Slobozianu, who would not speak to her brother for a week, while complaining loudly that she did not want a Bohemian in the family. The continued sight of these ribbons exasperated Mariora, who set about making Zamfira into Danubian Cinderella; they had faded now, and Mariora had sworn that Mitica would not replace them.

Mitica Slobozianu loved Zamfira, not as the young men of Bucharest were habituated to loving gypsy girls, but in the manner that a brave and worthy girl–which is what she was–deserved to be loved.

Zamfira was not a beauty–her complexion, of a very pronounced bronze color, immediately revealed her suspect origin; her hair was as coarse as horsehair (Mariora called it prickly); she was short and two years older than Mitica–but such serene generosity was readable in her large black eyes that, on seeing her beside Mariora, people asked themselves whether the less pretty of the two might not be the more beautiful. Those eyes did not know how to lie.

"Why do you love Zamfira?" the young women said to Mitica. "She's neither pretty nor rich–and besides, she has pagan blood beneath her dark skin. A gypsy! They're old at 20!"

"I love her, first of all, because she loves me," he replied, simply, "and then because she's good–which can't be said of all of you, who have sharp tongues and empty heads."

Unfortunately, the tender affection that Mitica bore for Zamfira had not in the least diminished the young man's hearty appetite for *raki* and dancing.

Mariora's question regarding the Russian's eyes had caused her companions to shrug their shoulders.

"I thought it was only cats and owls that have yellow eyes," said Katinka the farmer's wife.

"Well, so much the better for you, my dear," said the priest's daughter, dryly. "There are things that it's better not to know."

"What do you mean?" cried the assembly, with one voice.

"I mean... I mean that I don't feel disposed to endure your aggravations this evening, and that you should have let me rest."

"Oh, I get it," said Ralitza, in a mocking tone. "The handsome Ioan Isacescu."

"It's Ioan all right!" Mariora murmured, ill-temperedly. Then, after a pause, she added: "Ioan! It's true–he'll come."

Something was evidently troubling her; her nervous fingers were twisting a sprig of box-wood from the hedge, and she was staring at the tips of her feet, presumably in order that her friends would not see the tears poised to escape from her eyes.

Florica, the raspberry-seller, begin to sing:

"The yellow bird takes flight,
"Cleaving space with its beating wing;
"One might think it a golden arrow
"Flying overhead!"

"*The Yellow Bird*–what a stupid song!" said Mariora. Who has ever seen a yellow bird cleaving space?"

This abrupt observation was exciting hilarity among the young women when Zamira, who had been searching the horizon with her eyes for some moments, put a hand on Mariora's shoulder and pointed to the Bucharest road, saying: "Ioan!"

Mariora shivered, and darted an anxious glance at the gypsy, while the playful group took flight, snatches of *The Yellow Bird* mingling with their bursts of laughter.

"Zamfira," Mariora said, suddenly, "I've told you nothing!"

Zamfira opened her mouth to reply, but Mariora was in her fiancé's arms and Cinderella slowly and reluctantly stole away.

As lithe as a cat, Mariora stood on tiptoe to match the *dorobantz*'s height and cover him with kisses. "You're very late!" she said to him, in a tone of gentle reproach, and drew him into the house.

Night was falling slowly, filling the corners of the room with shadows. "Baba Sophia!" the young woman shouted–but Baba Sophia was gossiping with some neighbor or other. Mariora had to light the enormous brass lamp–which was almost an object of luxury–herself.

While loading the table with eggs, fruits and a jug of *braga*,[81] which would comprise the couple's supper, Mariora babbled incessantly about God knows what. There were things that made no sense and meant anything at all, things that had been repeated since the world began and that people would never tire of hearing–except that the young woman did not seem to want to give Ioan time to reply. An attentive observer would have remarked that she was even seeking to avoid his gaze, which never left her.

Suddenly, she released a cry and seized Ioan's right hand. "What's that?" she exclaimed. "Blood! Are you hurt?" She lifted his blood-stained hand to her lips, while her eyes, full of anxiety, interrogated the *dorobantz*.

Ioan hesitated; he hated lying to her.

"It's a gunshot," he said, with an effort. "My rifle went off in my hands."

Mariora, who could not distinguish a wound made by a firearm from one made by a bladed weapon, did not perceive Isacescu's embarrassment. "Oh!" she cried, bathing the festering wound liberally. "Gunshots are dangerous! Almost as dangerous as going to war, no?"

"Not exactly," he said, forcing a smile that he tried in vain to make cheerful.

"War!" Mariora continued, pensively. Suddenly fearful, she added: "But there's war here. You'll never go to war, will you?"

"No," said Ioan. It was the second time he had lied.

"Because I wouldn't want that!" she cried, shaking her head in a mutinous fashion. "I need you, whatever this villainous Tsar that we don't know has done to us. Let him fight against the Padishah by himself, all alone. We have other things to do! Getting married, for example. When? Oh, the sooner the better, for I warn you that I'm getting tired of waiting. Aren't you?"

"Mariora!" he exclaimed. That was all he was able to say. There was both tenderness and reproach in his voice.

A few words from the innocent girl had reawakened the bitter thoughts that her caresses had lulled. Isacescu was thinking about the future, and about the insult he had suffered on the road–and a strange intermittent hallucination showed him his new enemy standing between himself and his fiancée. For a moment, he thought about telling her everything–his fateful encounter on the sunken road and his departure for Giurgiu–but they both had a secret, and Mariora said to him, in that slightly sulky fashion that she knew how to render charming:

"My handsome *dorobantz*, nothing can cheer you up today. Have you run into a *zmeu* [82] in the woods?"

---

[81] *Braga* is millet beer [Nizet].

[82] A *zmeu* is a fantastic creature that plays a considerable role in Rumanian superstition [Nizet]. It is a shapeshifter, although it usually appears in human guise–often with a precious stone set in its head–and often flies through the air,

"Yes," said Ioan, shuddering.

Mariora thought that he was joking. "What? Tell me about it, then," she said, smiling. "What does a *zmeu* look like? Does it have horns and wings, as Baba Sophia assures me?"

"No," said Ioan. "This one had yellow eyes and..."

"Yellow eyes!" Mariora interrupted, anxiously. "You've seen the man with yellow eyes?"

"Yes," Ioan replied, calmly. "And you've seen him too, apparently?"

"Me!" she cried, blushing. "Holy Mother of God, no! Are there really men with yellow eyes?" She plunged her hand into the soldier's thick hair and continued, murmuring like a turtle-dove: "I've never seen hair as fine as yours, Ionitza. It's so soft! It's lovely."

But Ioan remained insensible to these caresses; his apparent calm concealed a violent internal agitation.

Mariora saw Ioan's eyebrows quiver. "Oh, don't look at me like that!" she said, trying to pull away. "It makes me feel ill; there's too much black in your eyes."

"It's true that there's a great deal of black," he repeated, mechanically. There was a pause. Then he went on, coldly: "Mariora, has someone been here?"

"No one, my love, no one... except for the boyar Relia Comanescu." She added: "He was very boring; he talked about nothing but wine and maize."

"No one? Are you quite sure about that, Mariora?" The *dorobantz*'s features were contorted; his words, stamped with an unaccustomed hardness, frightened the priest's daughter.

"How you say that!" she cried. "Who do you think came?"

"A man with yellow eyes," Ioan said.

Mariora attempted a burst of laughter, which sounded so false even to her that she was terrified. She was about to reply when a voice sounded gravely in her ear, murmuring: "Mariora, it isn't right for you to hide something from your future husband."

It was Zamfira, who had just come in. Without taking any notice of her friend's angry start, she went to sit down on the other side of the room and silently set about weaving her rushes.

Mariora, red with shame, dissolved into tears.

"All right–yes, I'll tell you everything!" she sobbed. "Everything–on condition that you don't look at me while I speak!"

Ioan Isacescu would have accepted other conditions as well; he did not understand and made every effort not to want to understand. He was very pale, but he made an affirmative nod.

---

sometimes spitting fire. It is a symbolic manifestation of pagan evil, often featuring in folktales as the thief of something vital–which the story's hero must recover–or as a sexual predator.

Mariora wiped her tears, sat down beside the *dorobantz* and put her arm around his neck. Then she looked at him timidly, as if she wanted to borrow a little courage from his loving eyes.

"This is what happened," she began, in a very low voice. "This morning, Zamfira and Baba Sophia went to Bucharest, leaving me alone here. All the men were in the fields. I wasn't doing anything–I was thinking about you!–when I heard the gallop of an approaching horse.

"I ran to the door, expecting to see the boyar Comanescu, whom we were expecting. It wasn't him; it was a Russian officer. He dismounted. I thought he wanted to speak to me and I went towards him. Oh, I shouldn't have gone towards him–but how could I know? Eventually, he pointed to his horse, which was panting, and said two words: 'water, horse.' The way he spoke, which was anything but polite, shocked me; nevertheless, I went to fetch water, assuming that he couldn't speak Rumanian very well. I was mistaken, Ioan–that man expresses himself better than an Oltu riverman! While the horse was drinking, I observed its master. Jesus Christ!"

Mariora went on: "If I live to be a hundred, I won't forget him! He was tall, so pale and thin that he could have been taken for a dead man. It seemed that I could hear his bones rattling–but what frightened me most of all was the yellow gleam in his round eyes. When the horse had finished, I turned to go back in; to my great astonishment, the man followed me. I told him that the house wasn't an inn. He replied that it was all the same to him and continued following me. I didn't dare say anything; there was a sepulchral tone in his voice that made me shudder. He sat down at the table as if he owned the place and ordered me abruptly to sit down in the chair opposite. I was terrified; I no longer knew what I was doing; I obeyed.

"He stared at me fixedly for about ten minutes. I had an urgent desire to run away, but I felt my strength diminishing–and I had noticed, besides, that he had set himself between me and the door. Finally, he got up. I got up too. His eyes never left me. He came towards me. I drew back, and kept going backwards–but the wall was there. I closed my eyes, for I had just felt a cold hand grip my arm–which had the same effect as if a snake had touched me.

"He picked me up, effortlessly, went back to his seat at the table, and sat me down on his knee, rudely. I was afraid of irritating him by futile resistance. 'Look at me,' he said.

"His will seemed to have become mine. I looked at him, just as he instructed–but, as his back as to the window, I could see men sowing barley in the distance, far away in the fields. It was to them that I looked for my salvation, but my screams wouldn't have been able to reach them. I told myself that the only thing that I could do was to put myself in God's hands and I prayed. The man didn't budge. But I couldn't pray for long; a strange numbness overwhelmed me by degrees. It seemed to me that I was falling asleep. I mustered the residue of my will-power to resist that drowsiness, which was bound to be my ruination, but I couldn't do it, and my dazed head soon lapsed on to the man's shoulder. Then..."

"Then?" Ioan broke in, in a strangled voice–and his fingers gripped Mariora's wrist with so much force that his nails sank into her flesh.

"Then," she said, "Relia Comanescu came in–I was saved!"

Laughing and crying at the same time, she buried her head in Ioan's bosom. "Ionitza, Ionitza!" she said.

He let her go. He looked at her with a strange smile. It was as if he had not seen her for some time, and was astonished to discover her in his arms. "Relia Comanescu!" he murmured. "Whatever danger he finds himself in, and whatever service he demands, that man may count on me!" He went on, immediately: "And Mitica? Where was he while this outrage was perpetrated upon his sister?"

A soft voice, which was more regretful than accusatory, sighed: "In Bucharest."

"In Bucharest? When his presence was required here?"

"He was dancing the *batuta* with his comrades," Zamfira went on, in utter confusion. "They had been drinking *raki*... perhaps a little too freely."

Ioan shrugged his shoulders and addressed Mariora. "Do you know this man's name?" he said.

"No. Comanescu appeared to know him; he pronounced his name two or three times, but they were speaking in a foreign language–and besides, I was so distressed that I couldn't take it in. *Ine*... It ended with *ine*, I think."

Ioan knew that one Russian name in four terminated thus. He made Mariora give him a detailed description of the Russian officer; the more she said, the more certain he became that his adversary of the sunken path and Mariora's insulter were one and the same.

"This man will bring disaster upon us!" said Mariora. As if frightened by her own words, she drew closer to Ioan, who repeated her words in a dull tone: "This man will bring disaster upon us."

"Heaven preserve us!" said Zamfira, moved by her superstitious pity to get up and light a candle in front of the sacred images.

Ioan Isacescu had scant faith in the power of candles, though. "Mariora," he said, suddenly, "Why did you want to conceal what had happened from me?"

The young woman had not been expecting such a question. She seemed to be embarrassed, and twisted the corner of her apron between her fingers.

"I don't know," she said, eventually. She was not lying this time. She did not know–but her reply did not satisfy Isacescu, whose features took on the painfully ironic expression that caused the girls of the neighborhood to say that the handsome dorobantz was not unfamiliar with the kind of *zmeine* [83] that are manifest as lovely female demons.

---

[83] *Zmeine* is the plural of *zmeu* [Nizet], although Nizet subsequently employs *zmeï* in that capacity.

Mariora guessed what Ioan was thinking. "My love," she said, with dignity, "did you think my intention was to deceive you?"

Ioan's only reply was to take her by the hand.

"To deceive you!" she went on. "I shall be a long time dead before that shameful notion crosses my mind. To deceive *you!* If I were ever unfaithful, my handsome *dorobantz*"–she shook her head in a melancholy fashion–"would it hurt you very much?"

"Yes," said Ioan.

"Would you die of sorrow?"

"No," he said, firmly. "I'm stronger than sorrow."

"Ah!" Mariora formed a slight pout of disappointment, which might have had Ioan laugh on another occasion. "But you would surely kill me with your big sword–me, and the other!"

"You, no–the other, certainly."

"But what must you think of me, and the silly things I say!" she cried, all of a sudden. "Oh, pardon me! My poor head's aching and I no longer know what I'm saying from one moment to the next. There's one thing that terrifies me: that man, as he left, told me that I would see him again! I don't want to see him again!" She was speaking forcefully. "I'm frightened! You're coming back tomorrow, aren't you, Ionitza? You won't leave me again?" She added, in a murmur: "I think he'll come back!"

She clutched Ioan's clothing and fear was readable in her haggard eyes, which were staring into the void. "What will I do when you're not here?" she said.

"Not give any more water to strangers' horses," he replied, with a smile that calmed her.

"I won't leave you alone again," said Zamfira, making every effort to appear cheerful. "This terrible Cossack won't get the better of both of us!"

"Do you think so?" said Mariora, timorously.

Baba Sophia came in. Darkness had fallen. Ioan Isacescu said farewell to the two young women–and, while Mariora was pledging eternal amity to Zamfira for the thousandth time, the *dorobantz* walked away into the moonlight.

Instead of taking the path that led to Old Mani's hut, though, he took the road to Bucharest.

IV. A Tragic Ball

The boyar Androcles Comanescu had supported every cause, belonged to all political parties and served every government. He was reputed to be one of the richest landowners in the country, and Domna Rosanda–a Serb who had brought a marvelous beauty, which was fortunate, as well as a considerable dowry, which was even better, to their marriage–had taken it into her head to make him a Senator. Comanescu, carefree by nature, let his ambitious wife have her way; she, with a view to the approaching elections, was already busy sending cartloads of *braga* to the neighboring villages, intended to make certain of the peasant vote.

Domna Rosanda was a masterful woman, to whose subtle influence the poor boyar was—so to speak—unconsciously submissive. Her maternal dream was to see her daughters shine at the Court in St Petersburg one day, and the noblewoman's avowed desire became, by degrees, the secret desire of her feeble spouse. Besides, it was not without a vague sentiment of pleasure that the boyar saw rough-mannered Cossacks circulating in the streets of Bucharest, and handsome Hussars laced up like maidens. Androcles—who, like others less naïve,[84] was readily led astray by seductive appearances—sincerely believed that he was acting patriotically in welcoming the Russians as liberators.

An opportunity to be agreeable to these new allies soon presented itself, and Comanescu was not prepared to let it escape him. A certain statesman, of short stature but immeasurable ambition, had given him to understand that it would be appropriate for some noble inhabitant of Bucharest to organize a party, to which the principal Russian officers *passing through the capital* would be invited. Androcles had understood; under the pretext of following a suggestion, which was actually a disguised order, he yielded his palace to German upholsterers and decorators. A week later, high society, the staff of various embassies and the Russian officers *passing through the city* were crowded into the huge reception-rooms in the Strada Mogosai; Comanescu was giving a ball.

The Rumanian ladies were wearing dresses made in Paris, modified to suit the tastes of Bucharest—which is not the same thing as good taste. They were admirably beautiful, to be sure, these quasi-Oriental women, and the sight of them drew enthusiastic exclamations from the Russians, but how much lovelier they would have been if they had only been able to leave their family jewels—which sparkled in their hair, on their arms, in the pleats of their skirts, and even in the satin laces of their dancing-slippers—in their caskets!

Even the men seemed enamoured of jewelry, and their breasts proudly bore the insignia of more-or-less fantastic orders. Rumanians love everything that glitters, whether it be gold or gilded brass.

The ladies did the honors of their native land with perfect grace. They offered Turkish cigars to the foreigners with their dainty fingers, poured out Tokay such as Count Andrassy [85] never drank, and offered them rose jam made by

---

[84] There is a pun here; *autres moins naïve* [others less naïve] is phonetically identical to *autres moines naïve*; although the literal meaning of the latter phrase is "other naïve monks" *moines* is also used abusively to mean "bed-warmer." It is difficult to convey, in translation, the sarcastic disdain with which this entire sarcastic passage is saturated.

[85] The Hungarian count Gyula Andrassy (1823-1890) was the first Premier of Hungary; his tenure lasted from 1867-71; he is named here because Tokay des-

nuns. Yuri Levine sighed with satisfaction; Boleslas, Stenka and Bogomil thought they had been transported into the Mohammedan paradise, and wanted to convert to Islam. Never had invaders been better received by the invaded. Everyone was speaking French, which is the aristocratic language of Rumania, and anyone who had had the untoward idea of pronouncing a few words in Rumanian would not have found a dancing-partner all night. Beneath the windows of the mansion, however, the people were speaking the forbidden tongue. What were they saying? No one cared.

The principal Russian officers, among whose number was the sinister Liatoukine, surrounded the little Minister, who hopped about and gesticulated with a typically Southern vivacity. His speech was so rapid that the guests, who were listening with a perseverance bordering on indiscretion, could only catch such phrases as *cross the Danube* and *Rumanian army*.

There was little dancing, much drinking and a great deal more talking. The gentlemen chatted about the issues of the *Romanul* [86] that they were reading in the window-bays; they commented on Rosetti's latest editorial, and the widely-remarked absence of the English Ambassador, who had made his excuses. The ladies, thinking that they were *being political*, offered excited critiques of the costumes of Princess Elisabeth, and one old noblewoman claimed that the ex-Prince Cusa had an even grander air about him than Prince Charles. Malicious tongue suggested that she was in a better position to know that than anyone else.

Domna Rosanda was triumphant. Her two daughters, covered with gemstones, sparkled like sunbeams on the arms of their dancing-partners, who gave the impression that they were not ignorant of the fact that they were dancing with millions. The Serbian had showered so much affection on the heads of Epistimia and Agapia that she had not enough to spare for her son, Relia, the sole male descendant of the illustrious family of Comanescu.[87]

---

sert wine originated within his domain, and it was therefore assumable that he had the pick of it. He was a close friend (and reputed lover) of Elisabeth, Empress of Austria. This paragraph—as is obvious even in English—is replete with sexual innuendo.

[86] *Romanul* was the title of a newspaper founded in 1857 by Constantin A. Rosetti (1816-1885), a literary man and political leader much influenced by French culture and political ideology, who played a leading role in the revolutionary upheavals of 1848. The paper was closed down in 1864 because Rosetti opposed the first ruler of united Rumania, Prince Alexandru Ioan Cusa, but Cusa was ousted in 1866 and publication was resumed. In the war that forms the background to Nizet's story, both Rosetti and Cusa's replacement, Prince Charles (or Carol), took part in the historic Danube crossing.

[87] The names of the Comanescu children are ironically significant, in a manner typical of transfigured fairy tales (the reader has already been notified of the likelihood of such resonances, and will find more in the next chapter). The two

Relia–or, less familiarly, Aurelio–was little known in Bucharest. He was freshly arrived from Paris, where he had shone but dimly in his studies. He was, all in all, a very gentle and timid boy, not Parisian at all, who professed a respect for his mother that was not far removed from dread. In the Latin Quarter, the way he had of lowering his gaze had earned him the nickname *"Mademoiselle Aurélie."*

Domna Agapia, who was scarcely 16, was already in search of a husband. Her brown hair, red lips, dazzlingly clear complexion–very rare in Rumanian cities–and little black eyes lively with malice made up a face that was attractive, despite the irregularity of its features, and had no lack of originality. Some thought her pretty, others thought her ugly; in truth, she was both at the same time. She had a way of chattering which might have passed for intelligence if the cheerfully plump girl had not posed as a sentimentalist. Furthermore, she was subject to caprices that were impossible to satisfy and fits of anger that made her rip her handkerchiefs and beat her chambermaids.

Domna Epistimia, who was pale, thin and lanky, replicated her mother's cold and correct beauty. She was a true Princess. There was no spontaneity in her. She had learned to think, to smile and to speak as she had learned to dance, to curtsey and to push back the train of her dress with a flick of her fan. Her voice, which she knew how to render sweet, was attractive; her gaze, intense and piercing, was off-putting. She was a creature of contrasts; beneath her satin skin and velvet skirts, she concealed a hard heart and a quarrelsome and calculating mind. She was not in the least stupid, in any respect, and knew how to conduct an intrigue.

By the time midnight drew near, Epstimia had succeeded in taking possession of Colonel Liatoukine and was promenading him majestically through the dense crowd of guests. The Rumanian was not talking; the Russian did not breathe a word. They passed like shadows, and the gallery observed that they had a great deal of *distinction.*

"ugly sisters," Epistimia and Agapia, derive their names from *episteme* and *agape*, the former signifying rationally-derived knowledge and the latter being the name given to the Christian "love-feast," so they are being drawn in archetypally contrasting terms. In French, "Relia" is not so much reminiscent of reliability as of something rebound, like a book, while his full name, Aurelio, means "golden;" the fact that the boy's family nickname–he has another, far more telling, as the next paragraph will reveal–retains a faint echo of *Cendrillon*, the French version of Cinderella, may be coincidental, although he is certainly cast in a Cinderella role relative to his sisters. Alas, the next "ball" to which Relia gets to go will bring him into contact with an extremely uncharming prince, whose invitation to dance is a vicious one. The aftermath of that encounter is certainly not a wedding from his point of view.

The Colonel's *distinction* had a slight smack of the cemetery. His pallid face took on a greenish tinge in the light of the chandeliers; his eyes, deep-set in their orbits, gleamed like an owl's, and the silver braid of his uniform, set in horizontal lines across his breast, gave him the false appearance, from a distance, of an ambulatory skeleton–which did not give the lie to the sinister rumors laid to his account.

Such as he was, Captain Vampire attracted the gazes of women, ever avid for mystery and violent emotion; more than one pretty noblewoman was jealous of Domna Epistimia.

Princess Agapia was monopolizing Igor Moïleff, whom she was bombarding with such questions as: "What flower do you like best? What's your favorite color? Do you prefer Turkish tobacco to Latakian, or black horses to bays?"

Igor replied, rather awkwardly, that his favorite plant was tobacco, that, as regards colors, he found *bay* enchanting, and that he never mounted any but Turkish horses. This did not prevent Agapia from finding him infinitely intelligent and his judgment very sound.

"Personally, she said, "I love sunsets, Chinese furniture, the song of the nightingale and vanilla cream, but I adore poetry." Putting on her best squint, she asked: "Do you like poetry, Monsieur?"

Igor could only reply affirmatively, and God knows whether he lied.

"Perhaps you *are* a poet?" the Princess suggested.

"Not as far as I know."

"One is sometimes one without knowing it," the plump Agapia sighed, lifting her eyes to the ceiling.

But this was not the case with Igor and the Princess resumed her own enumeration. "I love..." she said–and might have ended up confessing that the objects which partook of her affections included gilded epaulettes and fine moustaches, if she had not suddenly been made to turn around by a quivering movement imparted to her dress.

Boleslas Brzemirski was there, blushing with confusion, having caught his foot in the pink silk train that the Princess was dragging in her wake. He muttered a few unintelligible words. Agapia gave a slight nod of the head and gathered in her dress with dignity.

"Who is that officer walking with my sister over there by the buffet?" she asked Igor. "The pale one with the strange eyes?"

She was no longer paying attention to Boleslas, but the Pole came back from the buffet, where he had spent the entire evening. "Him?" he said, bowing more deeply than the young woman's age and rank required. "That's Captain Vampire!"

Agapia and several other ladies released little cries of fright.

"Yes, Mesdames," the Pole repeated. "That's Captain Vampire!"

Igor studied Brzemirski's luminous face and haggard eyes apprehensively. "Go back to the buffet," he whispered in his ear–but the Pole was not listening.

"As you can see, he's died and been resurrected at least three times."

"What nonsense!" said an Ambassadress.

A diabolical notion came into Boleslas' head. "Would you like Captain Vampire to tell you the story of his successive resurrections himself?" he asked.

"Certainly! That would be amusing!" cried Agapia–and before Igor could say a word to prevent him putting such a strange project into execution, Boleslas advanced upon Boris Liatoukine, in as straight a line as he could contrive, given the quantity of liquid he had absorbed.

Liatoukine saw him coming and smiled.

Liatoukine's smile was hideous, but what might have alarmed Count Brzemirski on an empty stomach scarcely intimidated the drunken Polish Hussar. Boleslas planted himself resolutely in front of his adversary, put his hands on is hips, and said, in a bantering tone: "Liatoukine, my good friend, they claim that you were frozen to death by your Cossacks at Sebastopol. Is that true?"

These singular words had been pronounced so loudly that the greater number of the people present heard them. Individual conversations immediately ceased and all eyes focused on the group formed by the two officers and Princess Epistimia.

The Pole, at the risk of losing his equilibrium, balanced himself on one leg and continued: "And that one day, you were found at the same time in company with Countess M*** and Princess S***. Is *that* true, eh?"

Liatoukine did not move, but he was no longer smiling. The expectant crowd held its breath.

The Pole went on again: "And that you've been married twice, that both your wives died within a month of marriage, and that they both had their necks wrung?"

Boris felt Epistimia's arm trembling upon his own. He, however, remained calm, and said in a clear and firm voice: "This man is drunk! Come away, Madame." He took a step to remove himself.

The Pole, with a single bound, pounced upon him.

"Ah! It must be true, Boris Liatoukine!" he cried, in a voice choked with anger. "There! There! Look, everyone!" His fingers brushed the Colonel's sleeve. "There's blood there!" He howled in exasperation: "Get away! You reek of murder and the tomb!"

Liatoukine did not even glance at his sleeve, and the large red stains there that had just been pointed out, with more astonishment than horror. He drew himself up to the full height of his tall frame in front of Brzemirski and his eyes stared into the enraged eyes of the Pole. The latter tried to speak, extended his clenched fists, and fell stiffly to the floor.

Then there was a general, every-man-for-himself panic.

Agapia screeched like a peacock and buried her head in Igor's epaulette. Epistimia let herself fall gracefully into Liatoukine's arms. Her example was followed by a great many ladies, who fell, according to their preference, upon the breasts of Russians and high dignitaries. A pretty Ambassadress ran partially aground upon an old Senator, while chance brought together two divorced spouses, who let chance have its way. Androcles Comanescu, who did not want to put himself at risk, stood aside and suggested *separating the combatants*. A Hungarian Countess demanded the police; Domna Rosanda, with greater foresight, sent for a doctor.

A few ladies, bolder than the rest, went to Brzemirski, who was lying unconscious on the floor, but as he was neither handsome nor interesting, they did not stay long. Relia went from one group to another, murmuring excuses, but it was hardly worth the trouble; the mothers did not want to hear and drew their daughters away.

The doorways were too narrow to allow the passage of everyone trying to leave; people pushed and jostled. The servants ran around agitatedly and the rumble of carriages carrying guests away was heard outside.

Prince G***, who had claims to intelligence, put it about that it was a lot of fuss over a drunken Pole. The suggestion was not a success; the Prince seemed vexed and followed the crowd.

No one stayed in the immense and resplendent room except for Brzemirski's four friends and Domna Rosanda—who, still dressed in her ballgown, was wasting her smelling-salts on Boleslas. The Oriental essences could do nothing, though. The Pole was dead.

Liatoukine had disappeared.

The officers looked at one another. They were all very pale.

"Apoplexy!" said Igor, to break the silence.

"No," said Sokolich. "It's something else."

"What, then?"

"Who can tell, damn it?"

Bogomil, the most strong-minded of the group, shrugged his shoulders. "He owed me 500 rubles," he moaned, mournfully.

Meanwhile, Domna Agapia was writhing in her bed like one possessed. "Dobry, Dobry! Light! Do you think I can remain in darkness when there's a dead man downstairs?"

The serving-woman withdrew, after bringing a perfumed candle, and Domna Agapia continued her lamentations. "That Pole," she sobbed, "has just died, in the middle of a ball, right in front of me, at my very feet! It'll make me ill, that's for sure! The other officer was very pleasant—yes, very pleasant! He reeked of wine—he was drunk, the lout! The other one had nice eyes... yes, blue eyes! Aren't they dirty, these Poles—ugly and ill-educated? Oh, I hate them; I curse them... yes! The other..."

"Shut up, Agapitza," said a muffled voice emanating from the next room. "One prays for the dead; one doesn't insult them!"

Agapitza, who had recognized her mother's voice, hastened to obey and went to sleep, still waving her closed fist threateningly at poor Brzemirski–who had not, however, done it on purpose.

Domna Rosanda, sitting next to her elder daughter's bed, said: "He has more than two million rubles."

Epistimia, who was propped up on her pillow smoking a cigarette, repeated "Two million rubles!" distractedly. Her eyes followed the smoke that was forming a sort of cloud above her brunette head.

In a room on the floor below, the four Russians watched over their friend's corpse.

By noon on the following day, all Bucharest had heard what had happened during the night. People started out by recounting the thing as it had occurred. Then, they said that the Pole was a rejected suitor who, in order to avenge himself, had committed suicide before the eyes of the insensible Epistimia. They finished up swearing that Brzemirski had been murdered by a Russian Colonel who was the Princess's fiancé. The last version, being the most exciting, was considered the only true one.

The Pole, who no longer had any family, was buried without ceremony in the Catholic cemetery on the Serban-Voda Road. With every day that passed, talk of his tragic end diminished, and the worthy tongues of Bucharest soon forgot his name.

V. The Baniassa Woods

Independence! *Boom*! *Boom*! From the Ister to the Carpathians, Rumania was free! Cannon salvoes, fireworks, a speech by the Prince: the festivities lacked nothing–not even, this time, the enthusiasm of the people, for whom the government had sugared the pill, and who swallowed it with a very good grace.

The *raki* ran in torrents; in every country inn, the *babuta* and the *piper*– which was merely a frenzied cancan–ran their course, and–may God pardon me!–the Rumanians, in their gaiety, taught the Russians to dance the *hora* to the accompaniment of infernal gypsy music. Enormous seesaws, which bore no resemblance to those made for children, delighted the young women, lifting 20 people at a time and howling on their pivots. The streets were reminiscent of the galleries of an ant-hive. Along the Chaussée, the hubbub was indescribable. The Chaussée was a huge thoroughfare planted with lime-trees, which began in the fashion of the Champs-Elysée and ended in the manner of the Bois de Boulogne–except that, here, the Bois de Boulogne was called Baniassa. Elegant folk rarely went as far as Baniassa, whose promenade had fallen from grace and had been abandoned; they preferred the blinding dust of the interminable Chaussée to the outmoded shade of the woods.

This evening, the plebeian element had invaded the aristocratic domain, and the beautiful ladies, indolently extended in their Viennese carriages, made progress, less by virtue of being pulled by their horses as being pushed by the vulgar folk crowded into the interstices between the vehicles.

The Comanescus' emblazoned calèche proudly carried the Princesses Epistimia and Agapia, accompanied by their mother, who distributed charitable advice to them from time to time.

"Agapitza, my child, sit up straight–Decebale Privighetoriano is looking at you. Eight thousand hectares of agricultural land and property in Hungary."

Agapitza sat up, and put on a majestic air.

"Epistimia, my dear," the noble lady continued, "straighten your hair–what if the Colonel comes?"

Epistimia passed her white hand over her temples and darted a haughty glance at the surrounding crowd.

Meanwhile, Decebale Privighetoriano–pearl-grey gloves, pince-nez, Mexican trousers–sniggered in a friend's ear. "Look at that fat Agapia–built like a tavern-keeper! I'm told she weighs more than 80 kilos. I know a little actress at the Bossel theater who looks more like a Princess than that lumpen girl!"

No Colonel being on the horizon, Epistimia became impatient, and dug her pointed heels into her sister's feet; the latter had been too well brought-up to make the least grimace under the eyes of a boyar who owned 8,000 hectares of agricultural land. None of these three worldly souls spared a thought for Relia, whose fate–scarcely respectable–was to become a simple *dorobantz*, and who was leaving for Giurgiu within the hour.

Lost in the multitude, on foot, were Mariora and Ioan Isacescu, Zamfira and Mitica Slobozianu.

Zamfira had been weeping. Mitica wore the uniform of the *dorobantzi*, and his cheerfulness appeared to have stayed behind in Baniassa. Ioan was distraught. Mariora was the only one chattering in her usual fashion, not without an occasional sideways glance of annoyance at Mitica and the gypsy girl, who were speaking in hushed voices. Mariora could not hear what they were saying, which was a great pity.

"Giurgiu!" she said, laughing. "What an odd notion, their sending you to Giurgiu! Myself, I thought the *dorobantzi* never garrisoned any towns except those where they live."

"Not always," Ioan replied, fearful of saying too much.

"Will you be in Giurgiu for long?"

"I don't think so," he said, fiddling with his belt-buckle.

Mariora clapped her hands. "So much the better," she cried–but added, sadly: "I'll be very bored while you're away."

"Do you think so?" he said, with a half-smile.

Mariora released a deep sigh and lifted her eyes heavenwards.

"My father will come to see you often. He..."

"Your father! He's not you! That isn't the same thing at all!" she cried, blushing.

Ioan squeezed her small hand gently within his own, and they walked in silence for a little while.

"And we aren't married yet!" said Mariora, peevishly. "If we had been, I would have come with you to that nasty place, which I hate!" She went on, mysteriously: "Listen–I'm jealous of Giurgiu."

"Jealous? Of Giurgiu?"

"Yes–don't laugh. I'm jealous, and I have many promises to demand of you. So listen!" She slipped her arm under that of the *dorobantz*. "First, I want you to be bored as often as possible, so that you think about me all day long..."

"But if I think about you..."

Oh–that's true!" she said, smiling. "You won't be bored. So be it! I demand that you keep company with Mitica as little as you can, because Mitica..." She frowned, and added in a whisper: "It's the *raki*, you see!"

Ioan smiled, and attempted to speak.

"Wait–that's not all. You'll write to me every day–and you'll prevent Mitica from writing...to *her*."

"Mariora!" he exclaimed, in a reproachful tone.

"That's all right, isn't it?" she murmured, in a coaxing voice.

"No," said Ioan. "I can't do what you ask of me. Zamfira and Mitica love one another, just as we love one another. We'd draw the wrath of Heaven down upon us if we as much as thought of hurting them in such a cruel fashion. What would you say if your brother wanted...?"

Mariora guessed the rest of the sentence. Impatiently, she exclaimed, a little too loudly: "You're not a gypsy!"

"What's that?" said Mitica, whose head–entirely shorn of its long black locks–appeared over the young woman's shoulder.

"Nothing... nothing... I was talking about those gypsies over there, with their dancing bear."

Mitica enjoyed embarrassing his sister; an ironic smile played upon his lips. "Be careful, little sister," he said, significantly. Dropping back a few paces, he rejoined his companion.

"Mariora," said the *dorobantz*, "let's not talk about Mitica and Zamfira."

"Yes, let's not," she sighed. "They're very boring."

"Mariora," he continued, taking her by the hand without paying any heed to her abrupt remark, "there's something I've wanted to give you for some time... something that constantly reminds me of you."

"My Ionitza!"

"It's not of any great value," he went on, in a emotional voice, "but it was my mother's–she traveled a lot in her youth, as you know, and she brought it back from Constantinople..."

At that moment, Mariora felt something cold sliding along the length of one of her fingers. She withdrew her hand excitedly–and saw, to her surprise, a pretty ring that shone like gold.

The ring was made of copper. A jeweler would have laughed through his nose at anyone who wanted to sell it, but an antiquary would have thought himself lucky to be able to place it in his collection. Large enough to cover an entire knuckle, it was elaborately engraved; mingled with the Byzantine arabesques was a phrase in Greek or Turkish–Ioan could not tell which. The ring was worthy of attention by virtue of its strangeness; it was very old, and there was probably no other like it.

(I know that *the ring* is a hackneyed gesture, but, from Kamchatka to Senegal, fiancés have piously conserved its usage, and however it may displease the reader avid for novelty, Mariora received Ioan's copper ring joyfully.)

"It's pretty, Ionitza, it's pretty!" she repeated. "Is it gold?"

"I don't know," Ioan said, "but I don't think so."

"Yes, yes! I can see that it's gold!" insisted Mariora, who was a great believer in intrinsic value. "I'll never take it off–never, my Ionitza!" And, without worrying about what anyone might say, Mariora kissed the *dorobantz* in the middle of the Chaussée.

"In your turn, my beloved," Ioan said, "would you promise me...?"

"Anything you wish," Mariora interrupted, devouring her ring with her eyes. "Anything at all!"

Ioan Isacescu's features took on a wild expression. His famous eyebrows bristled and his hand went instinctively to his belt as if in search of the hilt of a dagger.

"Mariora," he said, with a hiss in his voice, "keep away from the Russians. God has cursed them! If you see that man again..."

Mariora went pale; she passed her hand vaguely over her forehead, and murmured, as if she were talking to herself: "That man! That's true... I'd forgotten him! But *he* won't forget me! He'll come back! He said that he would come back! Oh, my God! And you're going away. Mitica's going away, everyone's going... but *where* is everyone going?"

Light was probably dawning in her deceived mind–the cruel truth had probably been revealed to her in its entirety–when a cry of horror escaped her lips. Her wide-open eyes were staring at a fixed point within the crowd, towards which she extended her arm.

"The man!" she cried. "The man–there he is!"

"Where?" said Ioan, attempting to clear a path through the throng.

"There! I can't see him any longer. Oh there, to the right, next to Relia Comanescu. He's mounted on his chestnut horse. Domna Rosanda's talking to him–he's smiling. Do you see him? Why is Relia dressed up like a *dorobantz*?"

Ioan did not reply. He had just recognized his adversary of the sunken path.

Liatoukine was here, insolent, fêted, surrounded by his friends. Domna Epistimia was offering him her hand. Androcles Comanescu adopted a humble attitude in his presence. The noblewomen favored him with their softest smiles and their most ceremonious greetings.

"It's him!" murmured Ioan, though gritted teeth. "It's him! And I can't sink a dagger into his cowardly breast! I have to kill that man, though–I've sworn to do it! His name–who will tell me his name?"

But none of the common people knew the name of the foreign Colonel.

"When he passes close to me," Mariora sighed, near to fainting, "I go cold."

Mitica and Zamfira drew nearer. "Look, Zamfira," said Ioan, seizing the gypsy by the arm. "Look! That's the man who dared to insult the wife of Ioan Isacescu, the one who... the one against whom you must arm yourself and defend her. Do you understand?"

Zamfira crossed herself rapidly. "They say he's a vampire!" she said.

Mitica was silent. Ioan's simple words were translated, for him, into bitter reproaches, covering his forehead with a blush that he tried to hide beneath his military cap.

The Comanescus' calèche and Liatoukine's chestnut horse had disappeared in whirlwinds of dust in the direction of Bucharest. The four young people had arrived at the second roundabout on the Chaussée. It was nearly 7 p.m.; the air was warm and humid, and light grey clouds were missing in the north, which would hasten the dusk. Ioan saw them and stopped.

"We'll have to part here," he said, in a definite tone.

"Oh, no, Ionitza!" cried Mariora, dissolving into tears. "I don't want to leave you. I'll go with you as far as the station. I'll..."

"It's a long way to the Philarete Station, my poor love," he said, very gently, caressing the tearful Mariora's blonde hair. "The train leaves at 8 p.m.–see how the other *dorobantzi* are hurrying!"

Mariora tried to insist.

"Besides," he went on, more severely, "it's getting late, and even if you both walk quickly, you won't get home before it's completely dark."

"Ioan's right," Zamfira put in. "They have to leave us." Her eyes sought Mitica's.

The latter seemed prodigiously embarrassed; he was rooted to the spot, tugging at the feather in his cap as if to detach it. All of a sudden, he pulled himself together. "Zamfira! Zamfira!" he cried, hurling himself upon her. Placing his head on the gypsy's shoulder, he burst into tears.

Mariora, who had never seen her brother weep, stood there bewildered, not knowing what to think. "What's the matter?" she exclaimed. Then the contagion of the example took hold of her, and she started crying too.

Ioan ran from one to the other, rallying Miteca's courage, addressing words of consolation to Zamfira, and–most of all–making every effort to calm Mariora, who was crying even harder, although she was ignorant of the dangers her fiancé would be running, and had no reason to do so.

Besides, Ioan seemed more irritated than emotional. "It's getting late!" he repeated, incessantly. "We have to go!"

Finally, they all resigned themselves to following his advice. A kiss, a squeeze of the hand, a few words murmured in the ear, a lot of tears—and it was all over. Mitica, sensing that emotion was getting the better of him, heroically followed in Ioan's footsteps.

The latter lingered beside Mariora. "Walk very quickly," he said to her, with a singular agitation. "Follow the main road, avoid the sunken paths and don't leave Zamfira's side. Do you understand? Don't leave Zamfira's side!" He emphasized the repeated words.

"I'll do as you say, Ionitza. Goodbye—come back soon, and don't forget me!"

"*Adio!*" cried the *dorobantz*, one last time—and the two soldiers went on their way towards the city, while all the Rumanian expressions reserved for such occasions resounded behind them: *La revedere! Cale bunà! Remaì sènàtos!* [88]

"He's gone!" said Mariora, when the crowd had swallowed up the two friends' white uniforms. "I've never seen Ionitza going away! How sad departures are!" A vague astonishment distressed her features. "Gone, gone!" she repeated. Her eyes could not tear themselves away from the spot where she had seen Ioan Isacescu vanish. "Come on, Zamfira, let's go," she sighed. "We've no more business here!"

The gypsy, however—who also had a heart, although Mariora seemed to have no suspicion of it—was lost in thought and did not reply.

"Well, what is it now?" said Mariora, acrimoniously. "Come back down to Earth, my beauty; think about the cheeses that are waiting for you, and the clouds that Ioan pointed out to you."

Zamfira's sky was so very dark, alas! She turned her eyes, which were full of dolorous surprise, upon Mariora. The latter, who presumably wanted to be forgiven for her ungracious manner, put her arm around the gypsy's waist, and they went back along the Chaussée in silence.

Zamfira was dark, Mariora was fair; Mariora knew that Zamfira served her as a contrasting foil, and she collected the flattering remarks of the handsome gentlemen whose paths they crossed with a secret pride.

Baba Sophia was an incorruptible guardian who did not permit anyone to play with fire; she only had to catch sight of a young boyar's moustache to start marching at a military pace, and Mariora had to follow suit whether she liked it or not. When her aged relative's skirts were not brushing hers, though, Mariora would take her revenge and would prick up her ears to listen—and a well brought-up girl, who appears not to understand anything, can still hear! When she compared the laudatory words of these brilliant unknowns to the slightly la-

---

[88] These formulas are the equivalents of *au revoir, bon voyage* and a French expression translatable as "stay healthy" [Nizet].

conic severity of her future spouse, the comparison was not entirely to the latter's advantage.

The Chaussée, its noise and its strollers, no longer existed for poor Zamfira, whose excited imagination was evoking the most frightful scenes. There were terrible battlefields covered in corpses; there were towns in flames, their entire populations massacred. She heard the roar of cannon, the galloping of horses–and she thought she could make out Mitica's voice, rising above the imaginary racket, calling to her. She wanted to run to his aid, but Mariora's arm, which was holding hers, suddenly brought her back to a less cruel reality.

"My God, Zamfira!" her companion said, in a tone of lamentation. "It's ridiculous to run like this! When you're on your own, you don't walk so quickly that officers can't follow you!"

Zamfira slowed down, but she remained silent with regard to the unjust reproach, which was no kinder by virtue of coming from the mouth of Mariora Slobozianu.

Five minutes later: "My God, Zamfira! You're doing it on purpose. We'll never get out of the woods before nightfall. If you don't hurry up, I'll go back alone and Ioan will say that I was right!"

Zamfira bit her lip; her reserves of patience were exhausted.

A certain angry glance, which Mariora noticed, told her that a third observation of the same sort would probably be less well-received–but an evil genius seemed to have taken upon itself to counsel the priest's daughter that evening. She told herself that if Zamfira was angry, it was cause for rejoicing. While these ugly thoughts were circulating in her pretty head, she and her friend–or, rather, her victim–arrived at the entrance to the Baniassa woods. At the same moment, a group of young women irrupted into the principal thoroughfare; they let out cries of joy on seeing Zamfira and Mariora–to whom the unexpected encounter seemed extremely unwelcome.

"Hey, Zamfiritza! Hey, Mariora!" cried Ralitza, the brunette we have already met. "We're going back through Baniassa–are you coming with us?"

"I can't stand that little Ralitza!" Mariora muttered between her teeth. "She puts on airs, although she only has sandals on her feet." Zamfira was just about to accept the brunette's proposition when Mariora said, impertinently: "Speak for yourself if you wish, Zamfira, but I warn you that I won't accompany you where you want to go."

"But Ioan..." the Bohemian objected, timidly.

"Ioan couldn't foresee everything! You're free, and so am I. I know a pretty path that will spare me the tedium of keeping company with silly girls of your sort."

A German author of the 17th century said, in speaking of Rumanian women: "They are not, in truth, very good, but they are strong-minded, thinking much and saying little." The observation is quite just, save for the second point about saying little. That must have changed over time.

The young women knew that they would ruin everything by getting angry, but they lashed out with tongues, to such good effect that Mariora would have given her necklace of *rubias* [89] to take back her words.

"Oh! So the society of peasants like us doesn't suit you any more, my girl?" cried Katinka. "Someone must have made you a Princess."

"You're in a great hurry to be on your own! Ioan Isacescu hasn't left Bucharest yet, and you're already thinking of replacing him."

"It's done!" Ralitza put in. "Tell us, then, my beloved Mariora–what's you're new gentleman called? Konstantin? Nicolas? What?"

"Is he a handsome boyar, darling? A handsome boyar with pockets full of *galbeni* [90] and a mouth full of lies?"

"I'll bet he's an officer," said Florica.

"A Russian officer, hey, girl? One of those who talks *lubliubliubli?*"

"That's worth more than a simple soldier who's only got the uniform on his back and the love in his heart!"

"Aha!" said Ralitza, making a rapid movement to seize the hand that Mariora was hiding under her apron. "He's generous, your officer!"

Ioan's ring was revealed to all eyes, and was soon being passed from hand to hand, despite Zamfira's pleading and Mariora's invective. Scarlet with anger, Mariora tapped her dainty foot on the round and snatched the ring from the fingers of her jeering companions. "Give it to me!" she cried. "It was Ioan who gave it to me!"

The gleam of the copper and the delicacy of the engraving misled the young women as to the actual value of the metal.

"Ioan! Ioan!" they said, shaking their heads incredulously. "No peasant like your Ioan could have made you a gift of a ring that must have cost more than a hundred *leï*."[91] A hundred *leï* is the estimated cost of any glittering or unfamiliar object among Rumanian village women.

"Zamfira! Zamfira! Tell them that it was him who gave it to me!" cried the exasperated Mariora.

Zamfira's testimony carried more weight than her own, and she went on, indignantly: "Oh! You put less credence in my word than that of a gypsy! I know that you hate me–I know that you're jealous of me because my Ionitza..."

A burst of laughter, emitted with astonishing unanimity, drowned out poor Mariora's irritated voice.

"Your Ionitza! Your Ionitza! A fine bird, truly, for making us jealous!"

"Three hectares of land where wheat won't grow because the soil's too damp!"

---

[89] *Rubias* were gold coins minted in the Ottoman Empire [Nizet].
[90] *Galbeni* were gold coins [Nizet].
[91] A *leï* is equivalent to 100 francs [Nizet], or four pounds sterling.

"A hut whose roof lets the rain in, because Old Mani's too mean to have it repaired!"

"A rickety table, three chairs and two threadbare rugs for furniture, and what crockery! Great God!"

A smile brightened Mariora's features. "Ioan Isacescu isn't as poor as you think," she said, with dignity, "for I own nothing that doesn't belong to him."

She was truly beautiful when she spoke thus, and that unexpected reply appeared to have put a cap on the caustic verve of the disconcerted young Walachians, when little Ralitza, a true demon in petticoats, struck an ingenuous pose, biting the end of her thumb. "On that account, Zamfira isn't any poorer!"

A vivid blush covered the Bohemian's cheeks. She sensed that Ralitza's words were the first lightning-stroke of a storm that was about to descend upon her head.

Mariora went pale. "Zamfira!" she said, in a taut voice. "Zamfira! Ah, while the slightest breath of life animates Mariora Slobozianu, Mitica will never be the husband of Zamfira Mozaïs!" Taking a step towards the gypsy, she added: "You intend to be mistress of the Slobozianu household, do you? You want to have your own land! Tell us, then, what became of your sister Aleca?"

"Ale...Aleca?"

"Ah! You no longer remember Aleca, who was taken from behind by a Magyar magnate after he had espoused her, as one espouses the daughters of your race?"

"Aleca is dead!" said Zamfira in a dull voice, "and my father forgave her."

"And your brother, the renegade, who used to watch our flocks and now sells silks in Smyrna; your brother who named himself Serban and called himself a *Yezidee*;[92] your brother, who was born a Christian and is now no more than a pagan dog... if he isn't already dead and damned."

All that was true, alas; Zamfira could raise no objection, and large tears formed in her eyes.

"Mariora!" she begged.

Mariora was inflexible. "And your mother," she went on, spitefully. "That Nadejda, whom anyone could see dance for fifty *bani*." [93]

"My mother!" cried Zamfira, trembling with indignation.

Mariora fell silent momentarily. Then, with an attitude of inimitable disdain, she turned on her heel and said: "You, become Mitica's wife, when your own father probably doesn't know who you are!"

---

[92] The Yezidees are a Kurdish sect based in Armenia and the Caucasus. Their quasi-Manichean creed–presumably descended from Zoroastrianism, but having incorporated Christian and Islamic elements–sometimes used to be mistaken by ignorant commentators for devil-worship.

[93] A *bani* is equivalent to fifty *centimes* [Nizet], or slightly less than a shilling.

A general "Ooh!" of disapproval greeted these injurious words. If Zamfira had not held them back, the young women–who were by no means reluctant to take Mademoiselle Slobozianu down a peg–would have proved to the latter that their hands were not as light as their tongues.

"Little coward that you are!"

"It's a good job your brother isn't here to give you an answer!"

"An answer–along with another thing you deserve."

These epigrams were confused, like rifle-shots fired at a distance. Mariora went red and pale by turns. "Goodbye!" she said, in a changed voice. "We'll meet again!" And she went with a determined stride towards a copse that stood on left-hand side of the road.

"We'll meet again! That's what the city gentlemen say when they want to play with pistols after a drinking-session," said Katinka.

"Choose your weapons!" said Florica, putting her hand on her hip.

"Choose your time!" Ralitza continued, throwing back her head in such a fine parody of a braggart that the entire company sent a loud outburst of laughter echoing through the forest.

"Mariora!" cried Zamfira. "I don't want you to, but stay with us, in Ioan's name–or let me come with you!"

"She doesn't give a damn about Ioan Isacescu!" said Katinka, clicking her fingers above her head.

Mariora disdained to reply and plunged further into the bushes. Clematis and honeysuckle had invaded the place and were climbing the trunks of old beech trees. Mariora had difficulty making headway through the hectic confusion of the creepers. With her hands extended in front of her, she forced aside the rebellious branches, which sprang back to caress her face. She wanted to get as far away as possible from Ralitza and Zamfira, and the continual tickling of the foliage drew murmurs of impatience from her. Finally, the laughter faded into the distance, and the gypsy's plaintive voice, intermittently calling "Mariora! Mariora!" became less and less distinct.

Mariora was alone–alone in the Baniassa Woods at 8:30 p.m.–long after sunset!

The first thing that she did was to study the sky. A light southerly breeze had dissipated the grey clouds that were worth as much as a tart reprimand from Zamfira. Mariora seemed satisfied by the results of her observation; she redirected her gaze from the sky to the ground: thickets everywhere, save for a scarcely-perceptible path between oaks that had seen Michael the Brave [94] pass by.

---

[94] Mihai Viteazul, or Michael the Brave (c.1558-1601) was Prince of Walachia, Transylvania and Moldavia; he was the first to unite the territories comprising modern Rumania, and thus became a significant hero of 19th-century Rumanian nationalism. He joined a Christian alliance against his former masters, the Turks,

"Finally!" she sighed.

That "finally" signified that she was very glad to be rid of the company, all the more so because it had not been easy for her to get away.

"The Sun set some time ago," she said to herself, "but the Moon's about to rise, and will light my way. What pretty flowers! Nine o'clock hasn't sounded yet; I have time to gather a bouquet." And she set about plucking may-blossoms pitilessly, taking them somewhat randomly from the left and the right. She stopped occasionally and shook her head, as if to chase away an unwelcome thought; then she resumed her task with a kind of fervor. One might have supposed that she wanted to bring down on the innocent clematis the residue of her wrath, which she had not been able to pour upon the head of the Bohemian girl. The flowers that she had picked, unselectively, piled up in her apron.

Meanwhile, darkness was falling rapidly beneath the thick vault of the forest.

Like children, madmen and poets, Mariora had a habit of thinking aloud–a bad habit to nurture! She raised her head, and said, in a mildly commanding tone: "Where's that Moon that I'm counting on, then?"

With the good will that denotes the finest character, the Moon, thus summoned, hastened to display its plump red face within the dark blue of the sky.

"Ah!" said Mariora, who seemed to find it entirely appropriate to be immediately obeyed, even by the moon. "It's pretty, the Moon! Prettier than the Sun!" Then she added, by way of qualification: "Except that it never ripens the maize."

A ray of the moonlight that was powerless to gild the corn slid through the branches to strike Ioan's ring. Mariora studied it, admired it, turned it around in every direction–without, however, the ring recalling anything of the person who had given it to her.

Suddenly, she shivered; a familiar noise sounded close by. "Cuckoo! Cuckoo!" sang the bird.

She stood still, with one finger lifted and her mouth half-open.

"To the right? To the left?" she murmured.

"Cuckoo!" the bird repeated.

"To the left!" she cried. "An evil omen!"

She made the sign of the cross three times, in the Oriental fashion. Having perceived the ill-met bird perched on top of a wild cherry-tree, she picked up a little pebble, which she threw at the bird. It flew away, still towards the left, sounding its pitiful "Cuckoo!"

"Accursed creature!" said Mariora, letting her disconcerted gaze wander around her. Her eyes encountered the results of the pillage she had undertaken.

"That's no bouquet!" she said, woefully.

---

and fought numerous battles against them; in one of them, he captured the citadel of Giurgiu.

She let go of the corner of her apron, and the poor flowers went rolling at her feet.

"They were ugly!" she said, to console herself. Seized by a sudden resolution, she took a hundred paces in the direction of the village. But the young woman's courage diminished in inverse proportion to the deepening gloom. She began to find the Baniassa Woods much less pretty, and darted furtive glances at the bushes; but as she was afraid of nourishing her vague terrors by confessing them to herself, she attempted to drive them away by doing what the bravest folk do when they feel ill-at-ease: she began singing at the top of her voice.

Instinctively, she chose words full of pride and temerity; she boldly intoned the proud response of the architect Manoli in the popular ballad of *The Monastery of Argis*: [95]

"There is nothing here on Earth
"To match our ten master masons;
"We'll build the most beautiful monastery,
"A monument to glory..."

Her voice faded away. "I'm cold!" she said. Indeed, the temperature was descending towards that degree of coolness which ordinarily succeeds the intense heat of the day in Rumania, and which occasions the interminable fevers that have become a sort of national malady. But it was not the fever that was making Mariora shiver, and she launched into a long monologue, which a slightly less extravagant way of behaving would surely have spared her.

"Where are they now? Zamfira is wicked! Perhaps I did the wrong thing in not staying with them. I don't want her to marry Mitica, though! Yes, but I might perhaps have been too...too hard on her. I should have been able to make her understand with more tact. After all, it's not her fault that she loves Mitica! Love...that has come to me, of its own accord! Yes, but she has to avoid Mitica, and not reply to him if he speaks to her..."

"Will you go that far?" her conscience said to her.

---

[95] *The Monastery of Argis* (or *Argisch*) is a Rumanian folk-ballad based on a 13th-century legend, in which a company of master masons, headed by the celebrated Manoli (or Manol), undertake to build an unparalleled monastery for Prince Radu the Black on the bank of the Argis river. Radu threatens Manoli that if his masons do not succeed in realizing his dream, he will have him walled up in the monastery's foundations. Unfortunately, the work they do is continually undone by some mysterious agency, and Manoli is told by a disembodied voice that the monastery will never be completed unless the first woman to present herself the following morning is walled up alive in the foundations. It turns out to be his wife, Flora, so he resolves to trick the Prince with a charade–but Radu sees through the ruse and causes all the masons to fall to their deaths, leaving Flora to die in her makeshift tomb. The song is, of course, a rather ominous choice on Mariora's part.

A gust of wind set the leaves trembling agitatedly. Mariora went pale, and cocked her ear.

"I was wrong, definitely," she went on, after assuring herself that it was nothing. "It isn't Zamfira, it's me who has been wicked! It's no more her fault that Aleca let herself be carried away than it is that Serban became a Muslim or her mother danced for 50 *bani*! And me, in the presence of all her friends, I reminded her of it. Oh, I'm a miserable wretch!"

"Wretch," repeated the echoes.

"Poor Zamfira! She cried! But where can they be? I've been walking too–perhaps they're still not very far away. I'm very cold! It's so dark here! If I call out to them..."

She called out "Zamfira!" Then she waited.

"Zamfira!" replied the echoes, lugubriously.

Her own voice, coming back to her in modified form, chilled the blood in her veins.

"Zamfira!" she repeated, more feebly. "I won't do it again!"

"Zamfira! Again!" moaned the echoes.

"Oh!" said Mariora. "I'm afraid!"

Overwhelmed by discouragement, she sat down on the moist grass, put her head in her hands and began to weep. She had done it, alas! Night was closing in, and the wind was whistling in her untidy hair, to which leaf-debris was clinging. She wept like that for a long time, until she heard a sudden noise behind her, which made her get up. Making a whispered vow to light two fresh wax candles to the Virgin if she came back home safe and sound, she attempted to make her way back to the main road.

The main road was to her right, but the unfortunate girl was so troubled that she searched vainly to her left. She realized that she was completely disorientated, and began running straight ahead, no longer thinking of anything except finding the forest's edge. She was so sensitive to pain that pricking herself with her needle made her cry, but she did not feel the prickly holly-leaves that scored her hands and face–and when the moon, whose light was still her only guide, disappeared into the clouds, her ears perceived, along with the sinister *whee* of the wind, the beating of her own pulse.

Darkness and the unknown enveloped Mariora on all sides.

"Mitica! Ioan!" she cried–and terror lent a tone of profound desperation to the voice of the poor stray. But her brother and her fiancé were far away; they could not hear her.

She continued on her way in darkness, tripping on pebbles and bumping into tree-trunks. Will-o'-the-wisps emerged periodically from the marshy ground, their little blue flames seeming to wag accusatory fingers at the poor frightened girl.

For being disobedient! whistled the wind. *For being disobedient!*

Then, all the superstitions and legendary tales told by firelight came back into her mind. She gathered her exhausted strength.

"*Tata! Muma!*" [96] she called, hugging herself. But her father and mother were dead and unable to reply.

Mariora fainted.

When she recovered her senses, the Moon was shining with all its brilliance–but Mariora released a terrible cry and shut her eyes again.

Standing between her and the Moon was the spectral form of Boris Liatoukine!

VI. "Mademoiselle Aurélie"

Nicopolis [97] had just fallen under Russian domination, and a battalion of *dorobantzi* had been set to guard the western side of the town. *Bashi-bazouks* [98] had been seen prowling in the vicinity; there was fear of a nocturnal raid, and the soldiers had received orders to keep their eyes peeled and maintain complete silence. All the fires were put out; only one of the windows in the large white house that served as a temporary residence for the Rumanian commander, Colonel Leganescu, was illuminated by a feeble glow. Most of the soldiers were patrolling, weapons in hand; the rest were squatting on ground already strewn with shell-craters, testimony to the siege that the town had recently endured. Among the latter were the two friends from Baniassa.

"Two months gone by!" said Ioan Isacescu, shaking his head, "and no reply!"

"Bah!" said Mitica Slobozianu, who always found an explanation for everything. "Does anyone here care about letters to poor devils who ought not to know how to read? Do you have any idea what happens to our unfortunate scrawls? The Russians use them for lighting their cigars."

"Impossible!"

"When we took that infernal bastion over there... Lord Above, that was hot! I shudder to think about it..."

---

[96] These are the Rumanian equivalents of *mama* and *papa* [Nizet].

[97] Nicopolis, or Nikopol, a settlement founded by the Emperor Trajan at the beginning of the second century A.D., is nowadays too small to feature on the maps in Atlases, but it occupied a significant strategic position in 1877 by virtue of its situation at the confluence of the Danube and the Iatrus, on what is now the Bulgarian side of the border. It was the site of the first significant victory in the Russo-Turkish war; the Russians took the town on July 16, 1877 and retained it as a base during the siege of Pleven.

[98] *Bashi-bazouks* (*Bachi-bouzouks* in the French spelling) were Turkish irregular troops notorious (according to Webster's Dictionary) for "turbulence and cruelty."

"Well," said Ioan, "What do you mean?"

"What I said," said Mitica, clicking his tongue. "Hidden behind a wall, General K*** was sitting up with a cigarette in his mouth, while all of that was raining down on us. He asked Captain Xenianine, in a perfectly natural tone, for a match. A match! He might as well have asked for a fresh egg! The captain took a tinder-box from his pocket and a dirty piece of paper, folded like a letter. 'Are you sacrificing a *billet doux* for me, Captain?' the fat clown [99] said, simpering. 'Not one of mine, incoming or outgoing,' Xenianine said, unfolding the letter. '*Iubita mia,*' [100] he spelled out, with some difficulty. 'That's Rumanian, I suppose?' He proceeded to roll up the paper quite calmly, lit it and presented it to the general. *Iubita mia!* A love-letter! Perhaps it was one of mine–I always start off like that."

"Might she be ill?" Ioan suggested.

"Bah! Don't waste time constructing futile hypotheses. They don't send the letters we write; why should they pass on the ones addressed to us?"

"Hey, comrades!" Scarlatos Romanescu called out to them. "They reckon we'll see *bashi-bazouks* tonight."

"Proudly armed with their *yataghans*!"

"They can decapitate a man! Look at this!" He bared his arm, which bore a wound more than eight inches long. "But they'll pay me back, the bastards!"

At that moment, the illuminated window opened.

"Send Lieutenant Zaharios to me!" called Colonel Leganescu.

"Lieutenant Zaharios can't walk, Colonel."

"What? Is he...?"

"He'll walk if you order him to, Colonel–but it won't be very straight."

"He's still drunk?"

"Two days straight, Colonel–and he's gone back for more."

Leganescu let out an expression that was more energetic than decorous. "I need a secretary, though," he murmured. He seemed to be examining the faces of the *dorobantzi* beneath his windows, one by one. "Isacescu!" he said, suddenly. "Come in here–we've go work to do."

"Lucky swine!" cried a chorus of soldiers when the door had closed behind their comrade. "He won't have to deal with the *bashi-bazouks*!"

A tawdry tallow candle stuck in a bottle spread its uncertain light through a large room, in the middle of which stood a table loaded with papers.

"Sit down, my lad," said Leganescu to his improvised secretary, "And let's get on with it!"

---

[99] Nizet's *poussah* is a term derived from a sort of toy that simulates the motion of a tumbler; here, as with other terms of abuse used in this and other chapters, I have substituted something that has a similar flavor of contempt to the original rather than attempting to preserve unintended literal meanings.

[100] "My darling" [Nizet].

Ioan obeyed.

"To Brigadier-General Lupu..." the Colonel dictated.

For more than an hour, nothing was heard but the noise of the pen scratching the paper and the distant calls of the advance sentinels. Eventually, though, there was some animation outside. A horse dripping with sweat arrived at the threshold of the residence. Almost at the same moment, the door of the room opened, and a Cossack bearing an envelope sealed with the Imperial arms came in, with no more ceremony than if he were entering his guard-room.

Leganescu, who was somewhat resentful of the cavalier manners that the Russians had adopted, raised his head. "What is it?" he said, in Russian, in a distinctly churlish tone.

The Cossack bowed awkwardly. "It's a message from His Royal Highness Archduke Nicolas, addressed to Prince Boris Liatoukine."

"Prince Liatoukine isn't here. Go on, Isacescu! 'We are awaiting the fourth army corps, which...' "

"His Highness said that it's urgent," insisted the Cossack, "and ordered me to return immediately, without even entering Nicopolis. Can't someone carry...?"

Leganescu cut him of by rapping on the table with his snuff-box. "I have no *calaretzi* [101] here," he said. "They're all in the town." In Rumanian, he muttered: "How tedious he and his Archduke are!" He glanced sideways at his cherished heap of paper. "Isacescu, my friend, we've almost finished. Do you have any idea how to ride?"

Isacescu smiled. "You're forgetting, Colonel, that we Rumanians only quit the cradle for the saddle," he said.

"That's true!" Leganescu said. "Would you like to take care of this?" He threw the Imperial letter, with rather scant respect. "You'll find Prince Liatoukine over to the south–you'll have to ask, but someone will point you in the right direction. Hold on! You can use my own horse–take care of it, it's a thoroughbred!"

Ioan was eager to undertake the mission; the name of Liatoukine did not strike any chord within him. When he reappeared amid his brothers-in-arms, proudly perched on the Colonel's white horse, there was general astonishment.

"Since when did you join the cavalry?" several voices cried.

"Since five minutes ago." He gave them a brief explanation of his sudden promotion.

"Damn!" said Mitica. "You have all the luck! A little while ago, a secretary–now, an Imperial courier. You have your officer's diploma in your pocket, my dear chap!"

"I'd rather have a letter from Mariora!" he said, smiling, and he spurred his horse towards open country.

---

[101] *Calaretzi* are Rumanian cavalry [Nizet].

Meanwhile, on the far side of the town, four officers were walking in the moonlight. Three of them appeared to be in that state of merriment which ordinarily follows a copious meal lavishly washed down with fine wines. They were weaving from side to side, staggering somewhat, apparently aimlessly, when they saw a shadow coming towards them whose gait must have been familiar, for they aimed towards it and hailed it in these terms: "Hey! Yuri Mikailovich! Where are you going, all alone like that?"

"Nowhere, alas!" sighed Yuri Levine. "What about you?"

"Us?" said Bogomil, pursing his lips. "We're bored, and are in search of diversion."

"A rare commodity in these parts!" added Stenka.

"We're looking for a Rumanian," boomed Liatoukine's baritone voice. "A little Rumanian... to make him dance."

"That's a stroke of luck!" said Levine. Come this way. Over here, behind this hillock, there's one of our allies' sentinels–and you couldn't have chosen a better one, truly."

As if to confirm Yuri's words, an almost-feminine voice was heard sounding the challenge:

"*Cine e acolo?*" [102]

"*Prieteni!*" [103] called Liatoukine–and they went forward.

"Right!" said Bogomil, nudging his companions with his elbow. "I recognize the voice of the silliest and richest boy in Bucharest."

"What! Is that you, Comanescu?" cried Igor, feigning surprise. "Have they pushed irreverence to the point of giving you sentry-duty, like any common-or-garden plebeian?"

"Yao!" yawned young Relia, in an eloquently plaintive manner.

"Well, we'll relieve the sentinel," said Liatoukine, briefly.

"Impossible! I'm here by order of Colonel Leganescu."

Liatoukine was unwilling to allow the acknowledgement, at least in his presence, of any authority but his own. Relia's observation offended him, and he filed it away in a corner of his memory.

"And we're relieving you by order of Leganescu," Sokolich hastened to say.

"Ah, so much the better!" cried he young aristocrat, with an outburst of childish joy. Then, quite seriously, he went on: "Where, then, is my replacement?"

"Here," said Liatoukine, shoving Yuri Levine by the shoulders. The latter pulled a frightful face, accompanied a dull groan–but a glance from the Colonel reminded him that one did not trifle with the desires of Captain Vampire without severe consequences. He began standing guard without saying a word, while

---

[102] "Who goes there?" [Nizet].
[103] "Friends!" [Nizet].

privately cursing the ridiculous whim of his superior officer, which was going to cost him six hours of additional duty.

Bogomil and Igor had each taken Relia by one arm, although the latter seemed more sustainer than sustained. Liatoukine marched on ahead–he had the air of a man leading a flock of sheep–while Stenka formed the rearguard. In this formation, the four friends and the little Rumanian arrived without further interruption at Liatoukine's lodgings–which is to say, the house of the late Aga, which Boris had "repatriated."

In addition to sums derived from legal contributions, this functionary had received, while alive, revenues from a host of petty taxes, which he had instituted to his own profit. In his apartments, Oriental splendor mingled with European luxury; there were brocade divans and Venetian glasses everywhere. The whole place was only slightly damaged by bullets, which had, fortunately, spared the bottles of French and Spanish wines that the good Muslim–who had reputedly been extremely devout–had crammed into his cellars.

The Aga's wine-cellar was immediately put to pillage by the young madmen, who wanted to revive the suppers of the Hugues Hotel on a Sardanapalesque scale.[104] The startled appearance and gross *naïveté* of "Mademoiselle Aurélie," who had no inkling of the fate in store for him, drew tears of hilarity from the officers, and the impassive face of Liatoukine, presiding over the orgy, was reminiscent of the skeleton that the ancients exposed during their feasts in order that its empty orbits and rictus smile might remind the guests of the brevity of human life–except that the sight of Boris did not evoke any funereal notion in brains already disturbed by the onset of inebriation.

"And you studied at the Collège Mabille, didn't you?" Bogomil asked Relia, putting as much interest into his voice as he could.

"You're mistaken," said the young man, with a candid smile. "The Mabille isn't a college, it's a dance-hall. Actually, I was at the Lycée Louis-le-Grand..."

"That's right–Louis-le-Grand!" Bogomil said, unctuously. "That's what I meant to say."

"We went out every Sunday," Relia went on, seemingly disposed to tell the exciting tale of his experiences as a student. "We went as far as the Arc de Triomphe. We were very tired when we got back. It was very enjoyable."

Stenka raised his head. "Mademoiselle Aurélie" was still smiling, and speaking very seriously. "He's too stupid for words," Stenka murmured in Igor's

---

[104] Sardanapalus was the name given by Greek writers to the last of he great Sargonid kings, Asurbanipal (668-626 BC). He secured the Assyrian Empire by means of ruthless oppression, but also presided over a significant flourishing of art and literature, assembling a large library (whose archaeologically-excavated residue is now in the British Museum). Inevitably, he won a reputation in envious Greece–and hence in western legendry–for decadence and debauchery as well as magnificence.

ear. Then, addressing the schoolboy, he said, rudely: "Didn't your mother ever send you anything?"

Relia's face lit up. "Oh, yes! Pots of jam!" And the memory of these preserves absorbed his mind so completely that he did not see his comrades smile.

"I was talking about money," Stenka said, shrugging his shoulders, "not sweets."

"Money? Oh, we had no need of money at the school–they fed us, lodged us..."

"Fed! Lodged! Here's a boy who's easily contented," Igor muttered behind his moustache.

"But when I was at university..."

"How many mistresses did you have?" Liatoukine said, abruptly.

Relia jumped in his chair and reddened to his ears. "Oh!" he stammered. "I never..."

"Come, come!" said Bogomil. "No secrets among comrades. Was she beautiful, eh?"

Relia turned scarlet, and plunged his nose into his glass.

"Was she beautiful?" Tchestakoff repeated, in a thunderous voice that made the poor student quiver.

"Oh, yes!" he sighed, finally, without raising his eyes.

"And what was her name?" Igor continued, intent on analyzing this youthful romance.

Relia allowed the words to be drawn out, as it were, from between clenched teeth. "Athénaïs Beaubuisson,"[105] he articulated, in a whisper.

"Athénaïs!" cried Bogomil, in a piercing one. "That's a splendid name!"

"Athénaïs means..." the student began, thinking that an etymological definition might serve to deflect the course of a conversation that was subjecting his modesty to torture.

"We're not concerned with philology," Sokolich put in. "We're talking about love."

The terrible interrogation got under way again, and Relia decided to take the confessional route.

"How old was she?"

"About 30."

"Damn! She was ripe!" Bogomil exclaimed.

"Pardon?"

---

[105] Even in a text that is unusually frank, in its own sly fashion, this surname–which translates as "lovely bush"–is a trifle crude; Relia is presumably as blissfully unaware of the *double entendre* as he is of his intended role in the unfolding orgy. It is unsurprising that his archetypal image of womanhood should reflect the goddess Athene rather than Aphrodite.

"And did you see her often," said Tchestakoff, who rarely had difficulty maintaining his *sang-froid*.

"Oh! Not as often as I would have liked—once a month, when I went to pay the rent. I'd rather have paid the rent every day!" cooed "Mademoiselle Aurélie" in his softest voice.

"Pay the...*what*?" said Bogomil, who did not understand.

"The rent," young Relia repeated, complacently. "She was my landlady—in the Boulevard Saint-Michel, No. 55."

A gesture from Liatoukine stopped a loud burst of laughter on their lips, which would have shaken the windows of the room. Igor swallowed two large glasses of *selbovitza* one after the other; Stenka pulled the tips of his moustache; Bogomil's face disappeared under the peak of his cap. A beatific smile brightened Relia's features as he shut his eyes, to improve the passage through his imagination of the majestic silhouette of Lady Athénaïs Beaubuisson.

Stenka was the first to control his suppressed hilarity. He bowed to Relia, and said: "Well, my boy, you're stronger than I am. When I was at Heidelberg, where I scribbled essays in philosophy before making notches in the skin of my peers, I never got as far as domesticating my landladies—although it's true that they were older than 30 and I never went to pay the rent."

"I drink to our friend's *amours*!" said Bogomil, raising his glass. "To Madame Athénaïs Beaubuisson!"

"Boulevard Saint-Michel," Igor continued.

"No. 55," added Boris, maintaining his invariable grimace of a smile.

The glasses suspended their ascendant movement at shoulder-level. The three officers' mouths remained open; it was the first time that a pleasantry of that sort had ever escaped Captain Vampire's thin lips.

Relia wriggled in his uniform; unable to do anything but respond in kind, he seized the bottle of *selbovitza* that he found in front of him, mechanically, and drank directly from it.

"By the way," said Igor, gently retrieving the bottle from Relia's hands, "how do you say 'I love you' in Rumanian?" He added, thinking of a stylish little girl:[106] "It's bound to cost me some day, if I don't know how."

"*Eu te, iubescu*," said Relia.

"*You tay, youbesk!*" repeated Igor, jaw-wrenchingly. "A beautiful language, but a bit hard!"

"Comanescu, my friend, it would be very obliging of you to sing us one of your country's sings—a *doïna*—so that we can judge the genius of the idiom," Bogomil said, assuming a wheedling manner.

---

[106] Nizet's *fillette au chien* is a *double entendre*; I have given the seemingly-intended meaning, since "little bitch" would normally be rendered *fillette du chien*; both *fillette* and *chien* have other slang applications, widening the potential range of implicit meaning.

Domna Rosanda's teachings had borne their fruit, however. "Oh," said "Mademoiselle Aurélie," with a disdainful pout, "*doïne* are what the peasants sing."

"It's unnecessary to sully your aristocratic throat with plebeian airs," said Sokolich, sententiously. "In any case, we're not that fond of songs, are we, Colonel?"

Liatoukine sketched out a negative gesture.

"Since you won't sing," Bogomil, making himself more and more persuasive, "the least you can do is dance for us."

"Me, dance!" said Relia, with an ingenuous laugh.

"Colonel Liatoukine has expressed his intention to write an opuscule [107] on the various Moldo-Walachian dances, and he's counting on you to initiate him into the mysteries of the *hora*, which you shall dance for us forthwith."

"I can't dance the *hora* all alone," poor Relia replied. "It's a round dance."

"Oh well, you have the *batuta*, the piper and God knows what! There's plenty of choice."

"The *batuta*! The piper!" cried "Mademoiselle Aurélie." "But they're drunkards' dances!"

"Why should hold that you back?" Bogomil riposted, filling Relia's glass to the brim.

"Let's go, Monsieur–the piper!" [108]

The little Rumanian turned to his interlocutor, intending to protest–but Captain Vampire's gaze froze the words on the student's livid lips.

"Do you know what this is?" said Sokolich, setting before the bewildered young boyar a long lash made of hardened and creased leather. "We call this plaything a knout." He added, in a detached manner: "We make use of it in caressing the epidermis of recalcitrant soldiers."

Reflexively, Relia passed his delicate fingers over the thick stock of the instrument.

"It strikes hard," Bogomil said, with conviction.

"Monsieur Comanescu," Captain Vampire's strident voice resumed, "I'm not accustomed to giving the same order twice, you know."

Relia went pale, and tears came into his eyes. "But, Colonel..." he ventured. The little Walachian's attitude was almost supplicatory; he was reminis-

---

[107] An opuscule is, literally, a "little opus"–in this case, a brief essay.

[108] Although *piper* is featured here (at least ostensibly) as the name of a dance–previously advertised as a crude Rumanian version of the cancan–the term is replete with significant meanings in French. Derivatives of the verb *piper* are mostly used with reference to catching birds by means of a sonic decoy, and, by extension, to all manner of beguiling deception and confidence trickery; more crudely–and far more relevantly, in the present context–they include a slang term for fellatio parallel to the Anglo-American "blow[-job]."

cent of a lamb at the mercy of a pack of wolves. With smiles on their lips and their formidable knouts in their hands, the Russians surrounded their victim and only seemed to be waiting for a word from Liatoukine to make use of their weapons.

"Let's go, little one, jump to it!" said Bogomil, ostentatiously lifting his whip. But Relia did not budge, and slowly shook his head. The Slavic blood he had inherited from his mother had not entirely annihilated the passive courage that is one of the dominant traits of the Rumanian character.

"One, two, three...hop!" howled Sokolich. The thong of the knout was already brushing Relia's hair.

"No," he said, in a firm voice.

And the knout came down.

In response to that degrading contact, Relia leapt to the other side of the room, his fists clenching convulsively. His blue eyes–ordinarily so soft–flashed, and with an energy that his frail and sickly appearance would scarcely have suggested, he cried:

"Cowards! Are you not ashamed to attack a child?"

The epithet "cowards," so justly applied, brought the fury of the Russians–already excited by successive draughts of alcohol–to the boil.

"Oh, you refuse to recognize the power of our will!" they shouted. "Well, we'll show you how heavy our Muscovite arms can be! As we crush you, so we shall one day annihilate your miserable country, and all the men of your execrable race, if they aren't prepared to meet our demands!"

Under the frenetic impulsion of the bandits, the knouts clove the air and traced blue lines across the unfortunate young man's limbs. He was unable to defend himself.

Liatoukine, who had not abandoned his habitual indifference, came towards the damnable group, and moderated their ardor with a gesture.

"You're striking too hard, gentlemen," he said.

Liatoukine's words and attitude exasperated the poor Rumanian. "And it's you," he cried, "that my father welcomed into his home like a son! Oh, you're even viler than your hired assassins!"

Liatoukine's eyes sparkled. "Don't add insult to your other sins, Monsieur," he said, gratingly. "You might have the opportunity to repent of them."

Relia fell silent. His gaze was caught and held by an enormous mirror, broken in several places, which was facing him; his features suddenly expressed a sentiment that partook of both joy and sorrow.

"I may be small and weak," he said, in a voice tremulous with hope, "but I'm not so completely forgotten and abandoned that I can't find a friendly soul to pity me and a powerful arm to protect me! Help me, Isacescu, help me!"

VII. O Frailty...!

The hiss of the whips died away. An unknown man of taller stature and coarser features had just appeared next to the exhausted and bloodied Relia Comanescu. His left hand was crumpling a wad of papers, and his right hand was extended, in a gesture replete with nobility, between the young man and his executioners. The man was evidently strong, and conscious of his strength. Without taking stock of the influence to which they were obedient, the Russians recoiled from him like jackals before a lion.

Relia had recognized Ioan; Ioan had remembered Relia. Ioan had repaid the debt contracted by Mariora, and the boyar's lip brushed the peasant's tanned fingers.

The *dorobantz*'s extraordinarily calm gaze surveyed the entire company, to various degrees. Not a muscle quivered in his face; one might have thought that no hatred had ever subverted his soul–and yet, his enemy was in front of him, nonchalantly perched on a divan, within range of his dagger! Ioan could see his enemy, though.

"Which of you is Boris Liatoukine?" he asked, coolly.

"That's me," said Captain Vampire, sitting up straighter. Ironically, he added: "Is your memory so short that you can't recognize me?"

The Imperial missive slipped from the messenger's fingers.

"Oh, yes, I recognize you," he said, with a bitter smile. "A Rumanian's memory is trustworthy, as is his *khanjar*! [109] But I did not know the name of the monster who takes pride in insulting old men, beating children an violating women!"

"My boy," said Bogomil, slapping Ioan on the shoulder and causing him to take a step backwards to avoid contact with the drunkard, "you're not very polite, and you talk like my Archimandrite uncle. No more of your pious sermons, I beg you; it's not Lent any more and morality gets on my nerves!"

An irritated glance from Liatoukine imposed silence on Tchestakoff.

"Are you alluding to the Slobozianu woman?" Boris said, calmly, picking the Archduke's letter up with the point of his saber. He continued, addressing his companions in debauchery: "It's to do with Mariora, gentlemen."

"Mariora!" exclaimed Igor, smoothing his moustache. "I knew her–a lovely sprig of a girl!"

"I knew her too–*she* wasn't shy!" said Stenka, performing a pirouette.

Ioan thought that he was in the grip of a horrible nightmare. The name of Mariora, which he produced as if it were that of a goddess, tripped from the

---

[109] I have used the most usual English spelling of "khanjar," although Nizet probably intended to use a calculatedly-Westernized spelling in rendering it *kangiar*; the weapon in question is a short curved dagger originated in the Islamic world.

mouths of these libertines accompanied by epithets! So they knew Mariora! Where and when had they known her?

This flood of questions was rising to the dry lips of the *dorobantz* when Bogomil, sticking both hands in his pockets, advanced towards him again, studying him with an impertinent curiosity. "Is it you, my boy, who is engaged to marry Maruschinka?"

"It is me!" said Ioan indignantly, "and I forbid you..."

"Well, I congratulate you–sincerely, I congratulate you," Tchestakoff repeated, with a false bonhomie–and he turned his broad back to resume his place.

Igor got up in his turn, and said, with the disdain that stamps the least movement and most insignificant remark of a great lord, from the heights of his nobility: "It's a great honor for you!"

Stenka's word became much clearer.

Ioan's knees buckled; a red mist passed before his eyes. "You're lying!" he cried, crushing the officer's arm in his own despairing grip. "You're lying!"

Stenka calmly disengaged his arm and elevated his shoulders. "I'm lying?" he said. "Just ask Liatoukine."

"Tell me that he was lying, and I'll believe you," Ioan said, in a muffled voice.

Liatoukine slowly offered his right hand to the *dorobantz*. "Look!" he said.

Shining amid the opals, the emeralds and the diamonds was the humble ring of Byzantine copper that Ioan had given to his fiancée!

"That isn't Mariora's ring," he said. He remembered the last letter of the Greek inscription had borne a particular mark–a little cross that he had engraved there with his dagger. He examined the ring minutely, and let Boris's hand fall back. The little cross was there!

"Mariora!" he cried, in a heart-rending tone. He darted a mad glance at all the men surrounding him, and released a frightful burst of laughter. "Oh, Mariora!" he repeated. Reflexively, his hand sought that of Relia, to whom the sight of his great anguish seemed strange, since he was weeping like a child. He was no longer thinking of vengeance. Mariora was dead to him; henceforth, his life would be purposeless, loveless...

And around the desolate pair, the Russians sniggered.

The sound of raised voices had attracted a dozen Cossacks. Liatoukine pointed them towards the two Rumanians.

"Twenty-five lashes with the knout for the little one," he said. "Fifty for the big one."

The next day, there was a singular agitation in the Rumanian camp. The officers, who took great pains to disguise their anger, conversed in hushed voices, while the soldiers–less circumspect–muttered death-threats at the mere appearance of a Russian cap. The rumor was running around that a Russian Colonel had had two *dorobantzi* whipped.

293

"The truth can sometimes be unbelievable." This line of poetry is nowhere more applicable than in Russia.

A roll-call of the *dorobantzi* regiment was effected immediately; two men were absent! Colonel Leganescu, to whom the duty fell, organized a rigorous enquiry, whose results established that, in addition to the ignominious punishment they had suffered, the two soldiers were still subject to imprisonment, which would last until the superior authorities ordered the unfortunates to be set at liberty. The place of their incarceration could not be ascertained.

This serious incident had the effect of enlivening the animosity that the Rumanians had nurtured towards their allies since the beginning of the campaign. The grievances of the Moldo-Walachians were certainly serious; they had not been spared humiliations of any sort. The Russians' ill-will manifested itself on the least pretext, and questions of precedence were invariably resolved in their favor; they had given the nickname "tin soldiers" to those whose military valor would save them a month later!

Several Rumanian officers from the same regiment as the injured parties challenged Russian officers to duels, and the clashes of swords and pistols behind the fortifications lasted more than three days.

In a solemn meeting that took place in Leganescu's quarters, it was decided that a demand for reparation would be addressed to Archduke Nicolas. General Cerneanu attempted to obtain an audience. Leganescu composed the request with typical Rumanian brio, which is better suited to a dash of eloquence than a simple Colonel's report, and the secretary Zaharios, who had recovered the use of his legs, inscribed the names of Aurelio Comanescu and Ioan Isacescu in his finest handwriting.

Cerneanu, having received the letter granting him an audience, presented himself at the Russians' general headquarters, not without having made several cuts in Leganescu's manuscript. In various passages, the latter, attentive to legitimate indignation, had neglected the principles of courtly politeness that one must employ in addressing Archdukes.

The interview did not last long. From the moment that the Russians received a Rumanian officer, all ceremonial formulas were suppressed; a Cossack *shoved*–for want of a better word–Cerneanu into a low-ceilinged room, which served an antechamber, and after half an hour's wait, the General was introduced into the Archduke's apartment.

The Archduke's apartment bore a strong resemblance to those of the corrupt Aga of whom mention has been made. There were a great many *objets d'art*, and luxurious furnishings of exceedingly various provenance, assembled in haste. All these broken beautiful things gave such a strong impression of being elements of booty that the sight of them only gave rise to thoughts of sacked towns.

Not far from a table, on which were set a few pamphlets on strategy, the petty apparatus of a smoker and a glass of water, Nicolas Nicolaevich was lounging in an armchair that had belonged to an English businessman resident in Nicopolis. The Prince did not appear to be more than 45 years old; an expression of calm hauteur, which impressed all those who came in contact with him, was spread upon his features, which were much more regular than those of the Tsar and Archdukes Constantin and Michael. He was listening to the monotonous voice of a blond and rosy-cheeked aide-de-camp, who was reading an article from the *Golos*.[110] The reading did not seem to interest His Highness very greatly; he was yawning with Muscovite off-handedness.

"Enough, Xenianine, enough!" said the Prince, on perceiving the General's epaulettes. Xenianine fell silent and got up to leave; a sign from the Archduke immediately re-nailed him to his seat.

"What is it, Monsieur?" Nicolas said, raising his head slightly towards Cerneanu, in the dry tone he used to address everyone except his older brothers.

The General bowed, respectfully, but without any servility. His gesture displeased the Archduke, who thought the old man's dignified behavior irreverent.

Cerneanu explained, in a few words, the purpose hat had brought him to the Archduke's headquarters. The Prince interrupted him with a slight gesture of impatience.

"I know, I know, Monsieur," he said, putting out his hand. "Is that your report? Give it to me."

In the Russian army, the knout replaced or forestalled the reports that the Prince hated. The Archduke riffled through Leganescu's voluminous screed and his eyebrows slowly came together; he was annoyed.

"Well, Monsieur," he said, passing the report to Xenianine, "what is there to complain about? The two men are guilty. One, according to his own admission, abandoned the post that had been entrusted to him by one of your own officers. The other spoke words injurious to Prince Liatoukine–who, by only having a restricted number of strokes administered, has shown himself to be very lenient."

The Archduke imparted powerful shaking movements to the English businessman's armchair as the sentences fell from his lips like pebbles on a zinc plate–but the arguments that he thought worthy did not appear forceful to the Rumanian General, who resumed calmly: "I will point out to Your Highness that the sentinel Comanescu was relieved by Prince Liatoukine himself, and that Corporal Isacescu was forced to rescue his comrade from the ill-treatment to which Russian officers were subjecting him before the very eyes, and with the approval, of the aforesaid Prince Liatoukine."

Cerneanu's logic was a sovereign irritant. Nicolas Nicolaevich understood that he was dealing with someone cleverer than he, and that, if the discussion

---

[110] *Golos* means "Voice;" the word appears in the titles of numerous Russian periodicals.

continued much longer, his adversary would undoubtedly win a victory. In order to avoid a conclusion insupportable by his personal vanity, His Highness took the course of raising the pitch of his voice and becoming violently angry.

"Those are details, Monsieur!" he cried. "Details that are of no importance to us! There was wrongdoing, as I hope you will certainly admit; in consequence, there must be punishment!"

The armchair creaked and water from the glass sprayed the wall–but archducal extravagance did not have the power to move Cerneanu, who went on calmly: "The dishonorable nature of the punishment, however..."

The Archduke leapt to his feet.

"This is a joke, Monsieur," he said, setting off to stride across the entire length of the room. "The dishonorable nature of the punishment!" he repeated, sarcastically. "Should your compatriots have been awarded the Cross of St George, perhaps?" he shouted, striking his spurs against the floor-tiles in his fury.

The General, who had not been invited to sit down, endured the Archduke's sarcasm with remarkable coolness. "Among my people," he said, gravely, "the officers have too much self-respect to venture to raise their hands against their inferiors."

Nicolas Nicolaevich sank back into his armchair with a burst of bitter laughter. "Among your people, Monsieur–your people! My opinion is that your people tend to forget what they are!"

The armchair swiveled around. In response to a gesture from the Archduke, who was disposed to light a cigar, Xenianine's nasal voice sounded again, in the midst of a profound silence, to observe in Russian that the enemy was attacking within the town.

Cerneanu sensed that he was reddening to the hairline under the insult inflicted upon him, and his hand, tremulous with indignation, let the velvet door-curtain fall behind him.

The entire Rumanian camp assembled in front of the old General. On seeing their faces, full of anxious impatience, Cerneanu shook his head sadly.

"Oh, men!" he said, with an accent whose bitterness was indescribable. "What are we doing on this side of the Danube?"

A fortnight after that characteristic scene, a company of Cossacks returned the two heroes of this deplorable adventure–which was on the point of causing an abrupt breach in the amicable relationship between Alexander II and Charles I–to their company.

Relia Comanescu, dazed and dejected, was slumped on his friend's arm. His badly-scarred wounds were causing him to suffer cruelly and he fainted in front of General Cerneanu, who was his cousin in the British sense–which is the same as the Rumanian sense.

Ioan Isacescu, on the other hand–whose robust constitution rendered him less sensitive to physical suffering–was marching proudly, with a smile that was almost joyful. A Cossack observed that he had taken his 50 strokes of the knout cheerfully. He seemed to have undergone a complete transformation; he had the inspired expression of a visionary or a martyr, and his eyes were, so to speak, fixed on something inside himself.

Mitica marched straight towards him, while he slid his fingers over the horny hilt of Old Mani's dagger. "For Liatoukine!" he said. Then, half-drawing the *khanjar* suspended from his belt, he murmured: "For Mariora!"

VIII. Saint Alexander's Day

Eventually, time always soothes the sharp pains that translate into plaints and sobs, but mute pains are beyond its beneficent scope.

Ioan no longer mentioned Mariora's name.

The *dorobantzi* and the *caletzi* were encamped around Pleven. They met ambushes at every step and were perpetually involved in skirmishes, but these multiple dangers were no match for Ioan's ardent boldness. He took up the most perilous positions and often embarked on scouting missions behind the Turkish lines in the middle of the night, at the risk of being killed or taken prisoner.

His superiors held that courage in great esteem; it brought them valuable information about the lie of the land, the hazards of the terrain and the enemy positions; his peers compared him to Codrean,[111] and invariably spoke of him with admiration. Sometimes he came back from his solitary expeditions laughing silently, as had become his habit, his rifle reeking of burnt powder even though no Muslim had been seen in the vicinity.

"Isacescu knows well enough why he laughs!" the soldiers said, nodding their heads in a particular way.

He had a singular manner of fighting. In mid-battle, he would suddenly pause, his finger poised on the trigger of his rifle, his eyes fixed on some point on the horizon. The memory of Mariora would return to his heart; he saw her as a little girl, running through the maize with her blonde hair in disorder; he heard her voice, her infantile voice, saying "*Ionitza meù*" and he listened. Then the hammer would fall, with a dry click, and a man would fall in the distance. Russian or Turk? How could anyone tell?

His words were as bizarre as his actions. In one forward engagement, the barrel of his revolver ran into the breast of an Ottoman. "Why should I kill this man, who has never done me any harm?" he said, aloud–and, without even see-

---

[111] Codrean is allegedly the hero of a Rumanian ballad [Nizet], but the word simply means "forest" in Rumanian; if it had an acute accident on the e–there is none in Nizet's text–it would mean "forest-dweller," which would be more easily transferable to a particular individual.

ing the pitiful tears running down the poor Turk's cheeks, he lifted up his weapon, took aim, and fired–and a Cossack slid from his horse.

Isacescu burst out laughing.

"Ah, the hazards of battle! I *am* the hazards of battle!"

He ran around the battlefields without fear of *bashi-bazouks* and Cossack marauders, a muffled lantern in his hands, examining and handling every cadaver.

"What are you looking for, comrade?" someone said to him.

"I'm looking for someone I'd rather find standing up," he replied.

One day, in the heat of battle, he had an impulse to flee, to return to Rumania. He took a few steps backwards, then came back to face the Turkish gunfire. He captured one of their flags–but heroes who have 50 lashes on their record are given no medals.

General Cerneanu, to whom the Tsar had sent a prodigious number of Crosses of St George, regretted not having the power to award one to the brave *dorobantz*; by way of compensation, he gave him a handshake, less banal than the Muscovite decoration.

Mitica pounded his own cross repeatedly, and when it was no more than a slug of metal, he threw it in the river Vid, crying: "I don't want their filthy gold!"

Cerneanu saw the gesture and heard Miticas's exclamation, but he did nothing about it; soldiers and officers alike hated the Russians.

On the morning of September 11, the old General, who was the idol of the Rumanian army, brought his troops together and addressed this short speech to them:

"Men, there's a black dot yonder, hidden in the mist; it's called the Gravitza Redoubt. We have to take it. We'll have shellbursts above our heads, bayonets in front of us, powder beneath our feet–the redoubt is mined–and behind us, Archduke Nicolas. It seems that today is the Tsar's birthday. It's a matter of regaling His Majesty with a fine spectacle. I must see you all killed rather than retreat–that's the Imperial order. Believe your old friend–we're doomed! It's not pleasant to have to tell you that, but you've seen others do it and you'll die stoically in the breach, like the sons of Rumania that you are. Put your affairs in order immediately, and if you have any money, deposit it at headquarters; it'll be sent to your relatives. Can I count on you?"

"We'll follow you, General," the unanimous voices of the soldiers replied. On every face, though, the enthusiasm of the warrior was replaced by the bleak resignation of the condemned.

Relia, however, was devastated. He was fearful and timid, as the majority of children are whose mothers do not love them. Death terrified him, just as darkness did. His heart was tender, accessible to common sentiment; he had understood that devotion is a rare plant, which often grows better in plebeian hearts than in those the boyars call *well-born*. This poor, essentially inoffensive, creature felt that without Ioan Isacescu, he was nothing but a leaf thrown into the course of a torrent, and he had devoted to his savior a friendship and idolization that manifested themselves in complete submission and eternal protestations of childish affection.

"Brother!" he cried, hurling himself into Ioan's arms. "We'll be massacred."

"Yes," Ioan said, impassively.

"I have some poison. Do you want some? It'll be quick, and we'll suffer less."

"Yes."

Relia handed him a little packet full of white powder, which he had taken from his belt.

Ioan tipped it all out into a water-filled ditch.

"What! What are you doing?"

"My duty. It's our last day–let's not be cowards."

"Oh–but the Turks will do terrible things to us."

"No worse than others have done to us."

"I'm frightened, brother. You won't leave me, will you?"

Ioan remembered that those same words had once been spoken to him by Mariora. "No," he said.

Relia sighed. "Oh, you're lucky to have courage. I'm afraid of the crows, brother!"

"When the crows arrive, the pain is ended."

"I don't want to be buried here," the child groaned. "I want to go back to my own land–Rumanian ground! Who will take me back to Rumanian ground?"

"Me."

"You?" cried Relia, with an incredulous smile.

"If you die, I'll carry your body to headquarters, and you'll be able to sleep in your native soil."

"Oh, is that true, Ioan? You'll do that! And me–what shall I do for you, useless creature that I am?"

"When I'm dead, you'll take my large dagger with the horn handle, and you'll search out Liatoukine."

Cerneanu gave the order to sound the call to arms.

Mitica, who had been helping to carry the wounded into the wooden huts that served as temporary hospitals, buckled his belt hurriedly and seized his rifle. A feeble voice close at hand murmured the word "*Frate!*"–the Rumanian word for brother, so sweet to the heart of a Rumanian far from home. Very surprised to hear a Walachian word from the mouth of a Turkish soldier, Mitica drew nearer.

"Brother," the wounded man repeated, lifting himself painfully on to his elbow, "are you from the Rumanian land?" *The Rumanian land*, in the strict sense, is Walachia.

"I'm from Bucharest," Mitica replied.

A sudden joy illuminated the dying man's disfigured features. "From Bucharest?" Letting his head fall back on the cartridge-box that served him as a pillow, he sighed: "Bucharest is so magnificent!"

"I'm from the neighborhood of Baniassa."

"Baniassa! Do you know old Mozaïs, Aleca and Zamfira, then?"

"Do I know Zamfira?" Mitica exclaimed. "If I ever get back there, I'm going to marry Zamfira!"

The Muslim's dull eyes recovered a little of their sparkle. He studied Mitica attentively, saying: "I've never seen you before."

"That's not surprising, comrade!"

Blood was running freely from the dying man's breast; his fingers were designing vague symbols in the air. "Well," he said in a scarcely intelligible voice, "will you go to old Mozaïs...and...tell him...that..."

"Your name–quickly, what's your name?" Mitica said, insistently, feeling the unknown man's hand growing cold in his own.

"I'm... I'm..." His lips kept moving, but he could not articulate another syllable.

He died, taking his secret with him.

Mitica remained beside the body, pensively, for a few moments. He lowered the mysterious *Osmanli*'s eyelids and wrapped him in a dirty linen sheet; then, very thoughtful and annoyed with himself, he hastened to rejoin his regiment.

The *dorobantzi* set forth into the mud and the mist. The mud was thick, and made their march difficult; the fog was dense, and penetrated their clothing. Their mouths were shut. Their eyes were aflame. Did the Russian Emperor's dreams show him what was in those men's eyes?

Sometimes, a murmur ran through the ranks; a few ironic voices would cry "It's Saint Alexander's day!" and then everyone would fall silent.

They advanced in this manner for about an hour. Gravitza could not be far away; the noise of the cannonade was not so dull; the first projectiles were cleaving the damp-sodden air. The daylight was merely a grey twilight. The soldiers advanced at hazard.

Where was Gravitza? To the right or the left? No one knew.

"This is the beginning, men!" cried General Cerneanu. "Hold fast, and remember..."

"That it's Saint Alexander's Day?"

"No! That you're Rumanians!"

A violent fusillade burst forth; an atrocious clamor became audible.

"What's that, General?"

"A regiment dying."

"Where?"

300

"To the left, in the valley; follow me, men!"

Relia stuck fast to Ioan's side, mentally reciting the prayers that Domna Rosanda had taken the trouble to teach him.

"You're frightened, little one," said a Corporal with a scar on his forehead.

"I want to get out of here!" sobbed "Mademoiselle Aurélie," rolling his startled eyes.

"Well, we're getting out, my lad, sooner than we might wish!"

"Hurrah! The dead go quickly!" cried a Sublieutenant from Leipzig. "We're dead, or very nearly!"

"*Ajutatzi! Ajutatzi!*" [112] These despairing cries rising up from the valley re-ignited the Rumanians' anger.

"Throw away your rifle," Ioan said to the distraught Relia, "and give me your hand."

Relia obeyed mechanically.

Brave *dorobantzi*! They hurled themselves into the valley, more ardent than the *zmeï* of legend! The slopes were slippery, the men rolled over one another. It was raining lead. The incessant Turkish musket-fire tore frightful holes in their ranks. What did that matter? Comrades were in danger; they had to be saved, or, at least, one had to die with them! Smoke combined with the fog. Blood and mire mingled. Dead men–dead men everywhere! The valley slowly filled up. A bullet struck the regiment's ensign. "The standard!" cried a dying voice. "Protect the standard!"

Mitica took possession of it; whining bullets passed through the tricolored pleats of the flag.

"The Turks shall not have the standard," he said. The explosions succeeded one another more rapidly; little by little, the air was clearing.

"Well, men?" said a voice in the mist.

"Well, General, there's a trench... it's ours!"

"The nation shall know your names, my lads, and Europe shall know the nation's name!"

Relia did not have a single scratch. He was astonished to find himself alive. "Is it over now, Ioan?" he said, fearfully.

"Not yet. After the trench, the redoubt."

"Oh, my God! And...are there still Turks within it?"

"Of course! If there weren't, the redoubt would be taken!"

"Mademoiselle Aurélie" resumed trembling; Ioan drew him on.

The Rumanians scaled the opposite slope. They were no longer thinking about Saint Alexander's Day; they were thinking about the fatherland, positions to be taken–of all the ingredients of glory, in sum.

"Hey, Mitica Slobozianu! I've got a graze here that'll get me a Sublieutenant's epaulettes."

---

[112] "Help! Help!" [Nizet].

"The taking of Gravitza! What a great story to tell at parties, eh?"

"Unfortunately, no one will believe us–we've told too many lies!"

"Our scars will shut the mouths of the incredulous."

"When I become an officer, I'll marry a city girl."

He was not even to marry a peasant; a Muslim bullet put a permanent end to the young Walachian's proud ambitions.

They were truly splendid in an attack, these "tin soldiers"! How they climbed! And how they died, with smiles and jokes on their lips! They really were, as they said to another with legitimate vanity, *the Frenchmen of the Orient!* Within a quarter of an hour, the redoubt would surely be taken. The first rank had arrived at the top of the hill crowning the Turkish earthworks.

Suddenly, a cry–a howl of rage–emerged from thousands of throats, which struck the Tsar's ears from afar. The *dorobantzi* recoiled in consternation...

"Damnation!" cried General Cerneanu, in a voice that had nothing human in it. "There's a ravine between the redoubt and us!"

"I told you, General," Ioan said. "We'll cross the ravine."

"We'll cross the ravine," a powerful echo repeated.

At that same moment, a plaintive moan was heard from Ioan's side. Relia's grip relaxed.

"Ioan," he murmured. "The crows..." And he fell, as if struck by lightning, at his friend's feet.

Ioan remained motionless. His eyes went from the wounded man's face, already pale, to the silhouette of the redoubt, outlined in black against the brown. He hesitated between the duty that called him to his companions and the friendship that retained him at his adopted brother's side. A sigh from the unfortunate child sealed his decision. He loaded and fired his rifle one last time. While rapidly making the sign of the cross, he said: "My God help hem and pardon me!" Then he added: "I'll come back!"

He lifted Comanescu–who weighed hardly any more than Mariora–effortlessly. "Put your arm around my neck," he said to him.

But Relia did not put out his arm.

By clutching with one hand at tufts of grass and lump of rock, and digging his heels into the damp clay, Ioan managed to keep his balance, and regained the valley floor. Beneath a projecting block of granite, he perceived a few feet of ground carpeted with moss, which was scarcely dirtied; judging it to be a fairly safe shelter, he deposited his burden there.

There was not a drop of blood soiling Relia's white shirt; had it not been for the pink foam seeping from his lips, one would not have suspected that he was wounded.

Ioan parted the *dorobantz*'s clothing. The bullet had pierced the chest in the vicinity of the heart; the wound was slightly moist, but all the blood was in the pleural cavity.

Ioan shook his head. "A mortal wound that doesn't bleed!" he murmured.

Hastily, he improvised a dressing that he knew to be futile, and set about crawling between the corpses, carefully feeling the officers' belts. He soon came back with a flask half full of *selbovitza*. He unclenched Relia's teeth with the aid of his dagger, and introduced a drop of the beneficent liquor into his mouth.

The young man moved convulsively, and put a hand to his breast. An expression of indescribable terror overtook his features. "The crows!" he stammered, and fainted again.

"Let's go!" said Ioan to himself. "One Rumanian doesn't abandon another."

Loading his friend on to his strong shoulders, he began slowly climbing the other slope of the valley. The descent had not been easy, but the ascent was painful. Ioan was continually bumping into irregularities in the ground, and more often still into body-parts clinging to old tree-trunks. He provided a target for the Turkish carbines; one bullet went straight through his cap, from back to front, another through the sleeve of his uniform. The slightest false step might have sent the courageous Walachian tumbling in a fatal fall, but a mysterious power seemed to be protecting him. After half an hour of anguish and extraordinary effort, he reached the top of the slope.

When he saw that he was in open country, he felt that he was safe. Presenting the flask to the unconscious Relia's tight lips, he examined his friend's discolored features with fraternal affection.

"Poor boy!" he said. "Another ten minutes and he'll be finished." A tear, quickly wiped away, glistened in the soldier's eye. "He was good, but he wasn't brave," he added, as if to justify his moment of weakness.

A few horses–poor riderless beasts–were wandering in his vicinity. Murmuring the magic word *puiu*,[113] well-known to Rumanian cattle and horses, he went up to one of them, which seemed to him more vigorous than the rest, and capable of undertaking a long trek. The horse whinnied and offered itself to the caresses of a benevolent hand.

Then, lifting Relia in his arms as mothers do with little children, Ioan set his feet in the stirrups, and the horse set off like an arrow, carrying the two riders. The gallop was so rapid that the horse's shoes hardly seemed to touch the ground. The redoubt receded to the horizon, and Ioan soon perceived the outlying fires of the Russian encampment. He reined in his ardent mount in front of the door of a pretty cottage, which he took to be a hospital.

"Hey! Hey! What's this?" said the churlish voice of a Cossack.

Ioan spoke Russian well enough, having learned it in Nicopolis. "Open up– it's a wounded man."

"A Russian?"

"No, a Rumanian."

"We don't want any wounded men here–the Tsar's in the house."

---

[113] A friendly sound familiar to Rumanians [Nizet].

"But you can surely see that he's dying."

"All the more reason! It's Saint Alexander's Day; the Tsar is here, as you've been told. We're not receiving dead men. Go away!"

"Where shall I go, then?"

"To your own lot. They're over there, mimicking our general headquarters as best they can. There's some sort of Colonel they call Leganescu."

In other circumstances, the Cossack's insolent words would have rebounded, metamorphosed into blows with the flat of a saber, upon his own barbarous spine.

"At least give me a cart," Ioan persisted.

"There are no carts here! Go away, as you've been told!"

And the Cossack slammed the door.

Ioan knew the Russian character well enough not to be astonished by these inhuman proceedings. He made a gesture of disgust, dug his spurs into the flanks of his horse, and the fantastic ride became even more so, by the uncertain light of the rising Moon, huge and pale in the mist.

The cool of the night and the repeated leaps of the chestnut horse, an impetuous emulator of Calul Vintesh,[114] were more successful than the *selbovitza* in reviving the spark of life that still animated Relia. He recognized Ioan, smiled, slid his fingers into the dorobantz's belt and closed his eyes again with a sigh.

Poor Aurelio! Ioan thought, pressing his friend to his bosom. *The empty space he leaves behind isn't very large in the hearts of his family! Who loved him? Whom has he loved? Me—and me alone! While he's dying here, his mother and sisters are running from ball to ball, listening to the ridiculous flatteries of the Russians who have killed him. His father doesn't even know what people call him!* "He's a boyar! Ah, poor little boyar!" he cried, aloud, in a tone in which pity was laced with slight disdain. His face suddenly darkened; his gaze, which was almost hard, came to rest on Relia's feminine traits. "And in 50 years time, this child would have been my master!"

He lost himself in his reflections—and, while telling himself that a boyar was a very little thing, unworthy of being carried in the arms of a son of the people, and that men were all equal before God and circumstance, he arrived at the Rumanian headquarters. Relia did not seem to want him to dismount, though; his hand would not let go of Ioan's belt.

"We're among friends," Ioan said, taking his foot from the stirrup.

Relia did not reply, and continued to hold his companion back. Ioan then realized that he was dead.

---

[114] A famous horse of Rumanian legend [Nizet]; *Cal* is Rumanian for horse, so the legendary horse's given name may have been simply Vintesh, but I have been unable to track down any original reference. (Cazacu's version of the text misprints Calul as Caiul.)

At the sight of the corpse, Colonel Leganescu bared his head, with the respect Rumanians show to that which has been a man. "His name!" he asked, in a soft voice, as if he feared to trouble the dead man's sleep.

"Aurelio Comanescu, from Bucharest," Ioan replied.

"Cerneanu's cousin! The one who..."

Ioan interrupted him. "Yes," he said, and added, simply: "I'm the other."

Leganescu slapped his forehead. He drew the *dorobantz* nearer to the nightlight, which gave birth to more shadows than brightness in his tent. "That's right!" he said. "I remember you!" He paused, then resumed: "My boy, forgive me for the harm I did you, indirectly, by sending you to that incarnate Beelzebub."

"On the contrary, Colonel–I thank you."

Leaving Leganescu to his astonishment, Ioan departed, after depositing a last kiss on Relia's cold forehead. Then, as he had said he would do, he set off again for Gravitza.

The ravine had been crossed, but the redoubt had not been taken. "Curse it!" he cried.

The odor of blood and gunpowder caused him instantly to forget Relia, Mariora, perhaps even Liatoukine. He threw himself into the battle, thrusting with his saber, taking aim and firing, with a kind of desperation. He was terrible thus, and the Turkish corpses piled up around him.

He caught sight of Mitica's tall figure in the distance, defending the Rumanian eagle, removed from its staff, against a furious attack. That vision lasted two seconds before everything before his eyes became confused.

In spite of General Cerneanu's incontestable skill and the unbreakable courage of his soldiers, the Rumanians were visibly losing ground. Strategy could achieve nothing in the face of that thunderous artillery; it required men—men who would have formed a wall of flesh thick enough to impenetrable to bullets.

Cerneanu tore his hair and, while still exhorting what remained of his troops, he murmured: "We won't make it! We won't make it!"

"Hurrah!" a voice suddenly shouted, resounding like that of an angel of salvation in the besiegers' ears. "Colonel Boris Liatoukine's bringing us reinforcements!"

All eyes turned, and all hopes too, towards the Cossack regiment that was emerging from the mist like an army of phantoms in a dream–and while the Rumanians greeted the unexpected apparition with repeated cries of *Traiéscà Russia!* [115] Ioan, suddenly reclaimed by the idea of vengeance, murmured: "Liatoukine! Before the present hour is over, my dagger will have seen the color of your blood!"

---

[115] "Long live Russia!" [Nizet].

Despite the profound obscurity of that fatal night, in spite of the distance that still separated him from Liatoukine, he recognized his adversary easily by his tall stature and his strident voice, which rose above the various noises of battle like the blast of a clarion.

Ioan reloaded his revolver, even though he did not expect to make use of it. The accomplishment of what he considered an act of justice was solely reserved for Old Mani's knife. He loosened that terrible weapon–which was nothing but than a long *yataghan* snatched from the hand of a *bashi-bazouk*–in its leather scabbard.

Rumanians are as indifferent in religious matters as they are strong in superstition. Ioan signed himself more by habit than devotion. "Boris Liatoukine is dead," he said.

Clearing a path through the ranks of the *dorobantzi* and the Cossacks, stepping over the heaps of uniforms, beneath which a few items of bloody debris still stirred, he succeeded in reaching Captain Vampire.

"It's me!" he said, with a hateful stare that would have disconcerted a man less sure of himself than the Colonel.

The latter studied him coldly, apparently neither annoyed nor surprised. "I've been expecting you," he said, dismounting. In a casual manner that the fine gentlemen of Bucharest would have admired, he threw the bridle of his horse to an aide-de-camp.

"Leave us, Dmitri Nikitich," he said. He turned towards Ioan. "Come with me," he said. "This place is scarcely appropriate for conversation."

Ioan followed him, with his revolver in one hand and his dagger in the other. Contact with these weapons heated the Rumanian's feverish fingers, and the sharpened point of the *yataghan* caressed Liatoukine's clothing.

There aren't two cowards here, Ioan thought, recoiling slightly. *I don't want to stab him in the back!*

When there were no longer any but dead men around them to serve as witnesses, Liatoukine turned. "Well," he said, "what do you want with me?"

"What do I want?" Ioan cried, in a voice broken by sorrow and anger. "He asks what I want! Will you efface the brand from my father's forehead that your whip imprinted there? Can you render my honor intact, which you threw as a bone to the dogs who flatter your odious whims? Can you give me back my Mariora? Can you do that? If so, I'll forgive you."

"Cut it short!" said Liatoukine, nonchalantly brushing off the mud that stained his clothing.

"Mariora! All the gold in the world cannot repay me for my Mariora!"

"Pooh!" said the Russian, with a gesture of indifference. "If it's gold you want, you can have it." And he made the rubles in his belt clink.

This new insult changed Ioan's wrath into a furious madness. He leapt towards Liatoukine with a raucous cry. "I want the last drop of your blood, the last breath from your lips! I want your life!" he howled.

"My life?" repeated the impassive Prince. "That's easily said, my boy!"

"No more words, Boris Liatoukine! One of us will die, I swear! Defend yourself!"

Ioan applied the barrel of his revolver to Liatoukine's breast. The latter shrugged his shoulders, an enigmatic smile playing upon his features.

An explosion resounded, the blade of the dagger glittered in the sinister rays of moonlight, and Captain Vampire, still smiling, collapsed without uttering a plaint or releasing a sigh.

The warm sensation of the blood that ran in rivulets over his hands only served to excite the Walachian's rage. The Byzantine ring caught his eye; it was very tight–Liatoukine had been wearing it for more than three months. Ioan, unable to remove it quickly enough from the dead man's finger, cut it away; he placed it, all red as it was, on his own finger. But his vengeance was unsatisfied. This man, normally animated by the noblest sentiments, had taken on the manners and the passions of a tiger. He fell upon the cadaver and his fingernails raked its scarcely-chilled flesh.

His *yataghan* was plunged into the Prince's heart three times over.

"For Mani Isacescu!" he howled, in a savage voice. "For Aurelio Comanescu! For Mar..."

He did not finish. The hiss of bullets was audible. Ioan slumped on top of the body of his enemy.

The following morning, when the Rumanian stretcher-bearers came to recover the wounded, Ioan Isacescu was still alive. He was taken to the ambulance; he had a bullet in his chest and another in his left knee; the latter could not be extracted.

A violent traumatic fever overwhelmed the wounded man; the physicians said that he would have to endure atrocious suffering. When typhus broke out in the hospital, Ioan was one of the first to be infected by it. For three weeks, he was prey to the most intense delirium. The grimacing face of Boris Liatoukine never left his bedside. Captain Vampire's mutilated hand was suspended above the victim of hallucination, who believed that he could hear the sound of drops of blood falling upon his forehead one by one. Soon, the sheets, the curtain and everything else appeared red to him.

"Liatoukine!" he cried. "He's here! Chase him away!"

When he leapt from his bed, it took three strong men to wrestle the madman to the ground. His incessant cries disturbed the sleep of the other invalids, and he was relegated to a distant room. One night, it seemed to him that Captain Vampire cut off his little finger and tore away the copper ring. Then a gentler chimera came to abuse him: Mariora took him in her arms.

He regained command of his senses on All Saints' Day.

"Well, my lad," the medical orderly said to him, with a broad smile, "so we've finally woken up!"

Ioan looked up at the brave man. "The redoubt?" he stammered.

"What redoubt, my boy?"

"Gravitza."

"You're talking Ancient History! It's a long time since that was taken."

"Ah!" said Ioan, putting his hand over his yes, as if to collect his vague memories. After a pause, he added: "Where's Mitica Slobozianu?"

"What rank of officer is he, my son?"

"He's not an officer–he's a soldier."

"Oh, then we don't know," the fellow said, rearranging Ioan's pillows.

"And Prince Boris Liatoukine–where's he?"

The orderly squinted slyly. "Prince Liatoukine?" he repeated. "He's not dear to your heart, is he?"

"Who told you that?" cried Ioan, propping himself up on his elbow.

"You did, my boy. 'Liatoukine! He's here! Chase him away!' " The orderly imitated Ioan's distraught voice and gestures.

"But after all," the impatient *dorobantz*, "what's become of him?"

The orderly protruded his lower lip and slowly shook his head. "The crows that soar over Gravitza are the only ones who can tell you," he said. In a whisper, he added: "That's a blessing, too; Prince Liatoukine was an evil man."

These words were lost on Ioan. "Damn!" he cried, going slightly pale.

The copper ring was no longer on his finger.

"What a pity!" he said, after a moment's reflection. "Some *bashi-bazouk* must have stolen it." A bitter smile depressed the corners of his mouth. "And I'm not wearing it any longer!" he murmured.

IX. Captain Vampire

"*Noël, Noël*, the Christ is born!" sang the silvery voices of the children parading an enormous decorative paper lantern through the city streets. The lantern was cut into the shape of a star and fixed to the end of a pole; it was supposed to represent the guiding star of the Oriental Kings. It projected a broad beam of blue-tinted light upon the thick snow that crackled rhythmically beneath the hurried footsteps of the little Magi.

The cold was very intense. The Russian wind, the *crivetzù*, had begun to blow, threatening from time to time to extinguish the star–to the great delight of the children, who huddled more urgently within their warm sheepskin coats, letting out little cries of joy and bursts of laughter. The young boyars clustered around Christmas trees loaded with splendid toys were certainly not laughing as heartily as these sons of peasants defending their paper lantern.

At last, that was the opinion of a man who was making painful progress along the Bucharest road. The unfortunate was lame in the left leg, walking with the aid of stick.

"I too used to sing, and I too used to laugh!" he sighed, sadly, as the little Rumanians passed him by. Abruptly, he pulled the peak of his cap over his eyes. Seeing a company of peasants on their way to a celebration, he left the path and slipped behind a stout oak. He did not want to be recognized. Alas, who could have guessed that, beneath the rags and tatters which scarcely covered the poor cripple's body, was Ioan Isacescu?

The *dorobantz*, whose wound still rendered him unfit for military service, had been sent back home. His home! When he had left it, young and full of hope, happiness and love, all prosperity had been resident there; he had come back disillusioned, prematurely aged, reckoning the past as a dream and refusing to believe in the future. What was he going to do in Baniassa? See Mariora again, hear her weep, forgive her and then marry her? No! He would seek out Old Mani and take him to Transylvania, where they would attempt to live, if not happily, at least in tranquility.

"My father!" he murmured, in an affectionate tone, on finally seeing the paternal hut outlined in black against the snow-covered ground. "I still have my father! He's not expecting me. What a joy it will be for him–and what a consolation for me!" He raised his head, with a proud smile. "He'll ask me for his dagger," he continued. " 'Your dagger is at Gravitza,' I'll reply. 'Prince Liatoukine didn't want to give it back to me!' Father won't say anything, but he'll think that I've done well."

Ioan arrived in front of the cottage where his life had run so smoothly; his heart was beating violently and he paused to study it. There was not a glimmer of light in the windows, nor a wisp of smoke above the roof. The door was hermetically sealed. The hut had a sad and abandoned appearance–like that of the master who had returned to it.

"Father!" Ioan called, knocking gently on the door.

But there was no response.

He's asleep, Ioan thought. "Father!" he repeated, more loudly. "It's me, your son."

The same silence. Ioan was aware of his increasing anxiety.

"He must be here, though," he cried. With a vigorous kick, he forced the worm-eaten door open. He went in. The cottage's only room was empty; it was redolent with the acrid odor given off by old unused furniture and uninhabited apartments. He had no means of generating light, and set about exploring the room by touch. All the objects over which his fingers wandered were familiar; he recognized the little brass lamp, the sculpted frames of the holy images– everything, including the poor stool that was still set to the right-hand side of the misshapen table. These things were in their places, just as he had seen them in earlier times, but it seemed to his that they were covered in dust.

"My father's no longer here!" he cried, sorrowfully–and he slumped on to the stool. He put his head in his hands and remained motionless for some time. He did not think; he simply listened to the distant barking of guard-dogs.

Suddenly, he got up again. "I'm a fool," he said, in a firm and almost cheerful voice. "My father's at some neighbor's house, celebrating." He sang "*Noël, Noël*, the Christ is born!" in a falsetto voice, then added: "It's Christmas Eve–I'd forgotten that."

And he thought of Zamfira.

He readjusted the broken door as best he could, seized his staff and headed for Mozaïs' dwelling.

The father and the daughter were not there. Overcome by fatigue–the poor cripple had been walking all day and had scarcely eaten for two–and feeling more alone than before, he had reached that degree of exhaustion, more physical than mental, at which one can no longer aspire to anything but rest, wherever one might be. He lay down in the snow and closed his eyes.

He could not sleep; Mozaïs' hut was too close to the Slobozianu house. He wanted to see the threshold that he had worn never to cross again for one last time, but his half-frozen feet, clad in sandals worn down by Bulgarian soil, refused to carry him. He dragged himself along with his hands, bloodying his knees on stones rendered trenchant by the extreme cold.

When he perceived the windows that had once framed the elegant silhouette of Mariora so gracefully, he became almost afraid of finding something in his heart other than sentiments of disgust and indifference.

"It's finished," he murmured, laughing silently. "Ioan Isacescu no longer loves the mistress of Boris Liatoukine!"

He attempted to get up, in order to retreat more rapidly from a place whose appearance no longer invoked anything in him but shameful and unhappy memories. Suddenly, he shivered and lay down again in the snow, silently; a feminine shadow had just appeared on the doorstep.

"Wait for me, Father!" said a voice that was serious but soft. "I'll be back in a minute."

Ioan recognized that voice. "Zamfira! Zamfira!" he cried, reaching out towards the gypsy.

The sight of the black form crawling at her feet drew an exclamation of surprise from the young woman, who stepped backwards abruptly.

"Zamfira!" Ioan begged, lifting himself up on to is knees. "Zamfira, it's me–Ioan Isacescu!"

"Ioan!" she cried, launching herself toward him. Then she began jumping for joy and clapping her hands like a child, repeating: "Ioan's come back! Ioan's come back!"

"Too late!" murmured Ioan, sourly. He did not notice Zamfira's strange expression as her gaze seemed to search behind him for something that was not there.

She fell silent. Taking the *dorobantz*'s hand, affectionately, she sighed: "Poor Ioan. You know, then?"

"I know!" he exclaimed. "Shut up, Zamfira–don't speak her name!"

"Whose name?" Zamfira asked, astonished

"Whose name?" he repeated, forcefully. "Wretch! The infamous name–*her* name! I know everything, I tell you!"

"Alas!" Zamfira resumed, humbly. "Don't accuse her–rather pity her..."

"I despise her!" he cut in, with an explosion of anger.

"I'm more guilty than her," the gypsy went on, in tears. "It's my fault. She wanted to come back alone though Baniassa. A few thoughtless words she'd spoken, without meaning any harm, had offended my pride. I didn't want to follow her. Oh, I'm so sorry!" She drew him toward the house, adding: "Come with me, Ioan."

He recoiled sharply, withdrawing the hand that Zamfira had taken in her own. "No!" he cried, vehemently. "I'll never see her again. I don't know her any more. I don't love her any more! Do you hear, Zamfira? I don't love her any more!" He repeated the words with a ferocious laugh.

"The poor child isn't here," the gypsy murmured, shaking her head. "Living close to Baniassa became impossible for her. Sudden terrors seized her continually–the image of that man followed her everywhere. She called out for you incessantly in her delirium–you alone could defend her, she said. Oh, forgive her! If the ring..."

"Enough, Zamfira!" he cried, imperiously. "That creature is a stranger to me now. Stop your pleading–it's useless."

"Oh! My God!"

"I'm going away–far away," he continued, more calmly. "Some place where I'll be able to till soil that has never been dirtied by her impure contact. I shan't be taking any memory of her, or any love for her, with me. I'll pick up my old father and..."

"Your father?" Zamfira echoed, in sorrowful surprise.

"I'll pick up my father," Isacescu repeated. Then, he suddenly asked: "Where *is* my father?"

"What? You don't know? Your father..."

"Well, spit it out."

"He's dead."

"My father's dead!" he repeated, in a confirmatory tone. "I thought so." Gravely, he added: "Fortunate are the dead!" No tear glistened in his eye; he had scarcely any regret in his heart. Why should he weep? Who would he be mourning? Old Mani? Did he not envy the absence of thought and the eternal insensibility of the dead?

"Goodbye, Zamfira," he said, resolutely–but as he rapidly drew away, the gypsy's tremulous voice called out to him.

"Ioan!" she cried. "Where's Mitica?"

"I don't know," he replied, mechanically–and he disappeared into the swirling snow that the *crivetzù* was releasing upon the village.

311

He went straight to the cemetery, opened the gate–which was retained by a simple latch–and cried in a wild voice that resounded strangely in the silent night: "Rest in peace, Mani Isacescu! Your son has avenged you!"

For eight hours, Ioan lived like a pariah, dragging his misery through the splendors of Bucharest. Camp life had hardened him to corporeal suffering; he spent the night in a deserted alleyway were dogs were making rounds instead of patrols. When daylight came, he resumed his aimless wandering through the mazy streets.

He sought out the busiest places; the incessant hum of voices and the continual circulation of pedestrians eventually numbed the host of dark thoughts pressing upon him like a swarm of black butterflies behind his prematurely-wrinkled forehead.

Boyars and common people alike gazed at the crippled soldier with the tattered uniform and the scarred face, with respectful commiseration. Wretched as he was, he seemed to them to be greater than the *Domnù* himself; had he not shed his blood for the fatherland? Without any inkling of the naïve admiration that he excited, however, Ioan marched on and on, still fleeing from his memories.

One evening, he went to Philarete Station with the determined intention of rejoining his regiment in Bulgaria. The train was about to leave, and Ioan had to make an effort to place his left leg on the footplate of the carriage. Only then did the awareness of his infirmity come back to him.

"The fine crippled scout!" he cried, with bitter laugh, while the train steamed away in the direction of Giurgiu. He left the station, and, being thirsty, headed for the public fountain.

While he drank long draughts of icy water, a poorly-dressed little girl came up to him with her *cofitza*.[116] She raised her eyes timidly to the *dorobantz*, seemingly desirous of taking his place. With her disorderly blonde hair, the child reminded him of Mariora. She went away trembling, with tears in her eyes and the empty jug in her hand.

"Hey, little girl!" said the soldier, ashamed of having allowed himself to be carried away by a ridiculous impulse of anger. "Come here. What's your name?"

His voice, suddenly softened, reassured the child, who came forward smiling.

"Sperantza," she replied.

"Sperantza!" Isacescu repeated, pensively. He filled the cofitza himself and slipped his entire fortune into Sperantza's fingers: a single *gologan*! [117] Then, without listening to the little girl's *multziani*,[118] he headed into the metropolis.

---

[116] A water-jug [Nizet].

[117] A coin of the smallest denomination, akin to a French *sou* or a English farthing [Nizet].

[118] Literally, "many years"–a formularistic expression of gratitude [Nizet].

I must put an end to this! he said to himself. *I can't get that woman out of my head. I see her face everywhere, even in the features of an unknown child who doesn't resemble her at all. I feel that she's here, perhaps close by; I feel that I shan't have a moment's rest while that creature is alive. I've become feeble and cowardly. I...* He paused then went on, forcefully: *I've killed the lover; why haven't I killed the mistress?*

That same night, Zamfira's sleep was rudely interrupted by the sound of a clod of earth thudding into her window-pane; she got up hurriedly and thought she recognized Isacescu's voice calling to her.

"Is that you, Ioan?" she asked.

"Yes, it's me!" the *dorobantz* replied. He added, abruptly: "Where is she?"

"Mariora? In Bucharest, Strada Hagielor, No. 8," said Zamfira, in a single breath. She joined her hands together and went on: "May Heaven bless you, Ioan Isacescu! You're going to do a good deed."

May Heaven pardon me! he thought. *I'm going to commit a crime!*

The next day was January 1. The Sun rose splendidly into a clear sky and spangled the silvered cupolas of the churches with its golden rays. The breeze seemed a mere caress, and flocks of wild sparrows were twittering gaily as they pecked at the grain which the Rumanians had not neglected to sew on the thresholds of their houses, in order to attract prosperity of every sort. An air of happiness and contentment that one scarcely ever saw in Bucharest any longer blossomed again in the faces of the early risers. One might have thought that everything was smiling and welcoming the new year–which would, they hoped, be less fateful than its immediate predecessor.

While the city awoke around him, Ioan was leaning on the balustrade of the Vacaresci Bridge; he was contemplating, with a typical Eastern European vagueness of expression, the little blue waves of the Dimbovitza lapping against the sparse grass on its banks. He was holding his combat revolver negligently in his right hand, when a sudden twitch of his arm caused him to drop it into the river. At the same time, a child's voice beside him murmured: *Bunà zioa, frate.*[119]

Ioan recognized Sperantza. The little girl's friendly greeting touched him. He groaned weakly, but the combined influences of the beautiful sky–which had been cloudy for such a long time–and the solemn festivities of the day had reopened his heart to generous emotion. He remembered that Mariora had once said to him: "If I were ever unfaithful, Ionitza you would surely kill me with your big sword...me, and the other?"

"You, no–the other, certainly," he had replied.

Liatoukine was dead; Ioan would spare Mariora.

---

[119] "Good day, brother" [Nizet].

A crime always seeks its criminal! [120] he said to himself. *Isacescu has never been the name of a murderer.* He picked Sperantza up and hugged her fervently.

"My friend," she said, "you're hurting me." She adopted a serious attitude, which contrasted with her usual pert expression, and went on: "I like you a lot. Where are you going? I'll go with you."

"Where am I going, my poor child? Alas, I don't know that myself!"

Sperantza opened her eyes wide. "Haven't you got a house?" she said.

"Not any longer."

"Your father? Your mother?"

Ioan shook his head.

"They've been put in the ground, haven't they?" she said, gravely. "That's because they're dead, my friend."

"Yes, they're dead," Ioan repeated, mechanically.

Sperantza had an idea. "Come with me," she said. "I'll take you home." She added, by way of explanation: "It's not very big, but you don't take up much room."

"May God protect you, Sperantza," he said, tenderly. "Wherever you're going, I'll go!"

Sperantza seized his hand. He let himself be guided by her, happy to follow her and hear her chatter. Sperantza immediately began to tell her story. Her mother made flowers for the shops in the Strada Mogosoi; her father worked at the gasworks; they were poor; they had once been rich, before they came to Bucharest. Sperantza had been born "on the other side of the mountains;" she could read and write, well enough to count and manage the household budget, even though she was only seven. She had a bird, a dog "of her very own," and she also had a friend. "A grown-up friend!" she said, with proud satisfaction.

As they turned into the Strada Tarieri, Ioam suddenly stopped. "Where are you going, Sperantza my darling?" he said.

"Home, my friend. Strada Hagielor, No. 8," the little girl replied, trying to drag Ioan onwards. "Jesus Christ! How pale you are! Are you ill?"

"No. But, Sperantza, your father and mother aren't the only people who live in that house..."

"Certainly not, my friend. There's Mariora Slobozianu, who..."

"Mariora Slobozianu!"

"Do you know her? She's my grown-up friend! She's very beautiful. Come on, I'll show her to you."

Profoundly disturbed by the effect that Sperantza's words had had on him, Ioan understood that his old love was not yet extinct in his heart, and that it would only require Mariora to look at him to dissipate is anger.

"No, Sperantza," he said, in a barely-intelligible voice. "I won't see her!"

---

[120] A Rumanian proverb [Nizet].

"Why not?" the little girl persisted. "She'll like you just as much I do. Besides, didn't you say that wherever I was going, you..."

"That's true!" Ioan said, interrupting her. Sperantza had rendered him as fatalistic as a Muslim. *Let's go!* he thought, as he walked slowly beside the little girl, who led him along the Strada Hagielor. *What must be, must be!*

Sperantza's house was a Byzantine construction, of a sort still found in the quainter quarters of Bucharest. Ioan and his guide went through a narrow passageway, which ended in a square courtyard planted with box-trees and holly bushes.

"Wait!" said Ioan to Sperantza, as she was about to run to her mother to announce the arrival of a new guest. "Take me to...your grown-up friend."

Sperantza obeyed, and Ioan climbed the frail spiral staircase that led to Mariora's room, with a firm tread.

"She's in here," said the child, pointing to a door painted rose-pink. "Shhh! She's talking–listen!"

"No, Baba Sophia," said a voice that reminded the *dorobantz* of an era of lost happiness, "I'll only go back there when Ioan comes back."

"Ioan," whispered Sperantza, "is the name of a soldier she loves and who'll marry her when the war is over."

Ioan dated sideways glance at the child. "She loves this soldier, you say?"

"And how! She never wants to talk about anything but him."

"You know, little one," he said, with an ironic smile, "This Ioan–it's me."

"You!" Sperantza bounded towards the rose-pink door.

Ioan held her back. "Leave me alone, now," he said to her. "I've a great many things to say to Mariora."

Sperantza, who was neither obstinate nor curious, ran down the stairs, letting out little cries of joy.

Ioan did not want to give himself time to reflect. The key turned in the lock; he went in.

"Isacescu!" said Baba Sophia.

"Ionitza!" cried Mariora.

Two bare arms slid around his neck; a flood of blonde hair inundated his shoulders and ardent kisses were showered upon his forehead. In the middle of the room, Baba Sophia was kneeling down, praying fervently.

She embraced Liatoukine thus! Ioan said to himself. That thought brought all his hatred flooding back.

"Get away!" he said. "Get away, vile creature!" And, seizing a handful of Mariora's loose hair, he forced her to look him in the face. "Vile creature!" he repeated. Then he threw the poor stupefied girl across the room.

Baba Sophia leapt to her feet like a tigress. "Wretch!" she yelped. "How dare you...?"

Mariora clapped her hand over the old woman's furiously-pursed lips. "Be quiet, godmother," she begged. "Ioan is mad!"

"Mad!" he murmured, taking a step towards her "Yes, I was, when I believed your words and your sworn promises, which were nothing but perjury—when I allowed myself to be abused by your caresses, which only served to better hide your perfidies! I was mad when I loved you, Mariora! Now...I know...I've seen...!"

"Oh, my God!" sobbed the young woman. "But what have I done?"

Baba Sophia, her patience exhausted, put her arms behind her back and said to Ioan, with false calmness: "Listen, Corporal Isacescu—if you've only come here to reel off pleasantries of that sort. my opinion is that it's a great pity that you didn't stay where you were, like so many brave boys of greater worth than you!"

"Then you're a worthy accomplice of the other one," retorted Ioan, paying no heed to the gorgon's invective. "He too asked me what he had done. Do you know how I replied to him, Mariora?"

"Ioan," cried the priest's daughter, grabbing the *dorobantz*'s hand.

"Get away, I tell you," he repeated. With insulting sarcasm, he added: "Do you take me for Boris Liatoukine?"

"Boris Liatoukine!" Mariora repeated, slowly. "I don't know him."

"Oh? You don't know Boris Liatoukine—the man with the yellow eyes from the Baniasa Woods?"

Mariora shuddered. "Indeed, my Ionitza," she replied, tremulously. "I dream about him, I..."

Ioan interrupted her in a thunderous voice. "Your hand! Show me your hand!"

Mariora mechanically exposed both hands to the pitiless gaze of the *dorobantz*.

"And the ring?" he said.

"The ring?" Mariora stammered, quite beside herself. "Yes...that's true. He took it, my love—he took it!"

"Ah! You finally admit it!" he cried, with a bitter laugh. "He took it!"

"I couldn't...Ionitza!" Her tears were choking her; she covered her head with her apron. "All this because the ring is lost!" she groaned.

"It was only copper anyway, your ring!" the terrible godmother resumed. "We're only talking about your peddler's trinkets! Leave my god-daughter be. She's much too beautiful for a cripple like you. If you no longer want her, just tell her straight out, without such jeremiads! We'll have suitors flocking round, of better quality than the son of *your* father!"

Baba Sophia paused to draw breath.

"Me, marry Boris Liatoukine's mistress!" Ioan cried, indignantly. "You're dreaming, old woman!"

At these words Mariora raised her head again; her tears drying up, she advanced towards Ioan and stood before her fiancé, cold and pale. "I don't understand," she said, softly.

"You're the mistress of Boris Liatoukine," Ioan repeated, harshly. "Do you dare to deny that it's true, wretch?"

"The mistress..." Mariora stammered, astounded. She leaned on the back of a chair for support; her lips were pale, her eyes lit up. "Who told you that?" she demanded, quivering.

"Liatoukine himself."

"He lied!" she cried, in a voice vibrant with anger. "He lied!" she repeated, going to the gilded frame that enclosed a richly-illuminated representation of the Virgin. "I swear before these holy images."

"Which tells you that he lied!" Baba Sophia added, having recovered her breath. "Where do you get these fine notions, eh? To set about slandering the honor of honest women! It'll be a fine day when a beardless adolescent can come preaching morality to old Sophia! Haven't I always set the little one the strictest example of virtue? There's plenty in the village can remind you of that if you've forgotten."

"I don't believe you, Mariora Slobozianu," Ioan murmured, without raising his eyes.

Mariora made an effort to hold back her tears. Meekly, she presented her forehead for the *dorobantz* to kiss. In a voice stifled by sorrow, she said: "Good-bye, then, my beloved–and may the Supreme Lord pardon you, as I do!"

Ioan did not budge. *If Liatoukine lied*! he thought. *Oh, that would be Heaven!* "I want to believe you, Mariora," he said, "but...I saw that ring on Liatoukine's finger."

"It was in the Baniassa Woods," Mariora replied, simply. "We were alone: he took my ring."

"And afterwards?"

"That's all!"

"That man would not have spared you!" he said, shaking his head.

"Listen," she said, lowering her voice mysteriously. "That man is not a man: he's a vampire. He has two pupils in each eye. His gaze puts you into a strange sleep that ends in death. The saints were protecting me from the heights of Heaven: midnight chimed, a cock crew in the distance... What could he do to me then?"

Although belief in vampirism and the evil eye did not appear to him to be indisputable articles of faith, Ioan considered Mariora's bizarre explanation as the sole ray of light that might dissipate the grey shadows among which his hope was lost. Mariora innocent–that was the future clarified, happiness restored, life with all the joys that make all sorrows supportable.

The dignified attitude and limpid gaze of his fiancée succeeded in convincing him. "Then...it isn't true?" he said.

"It isn't true," Mariora repeated, forcefully.

While they stood there side by side, embarrassed and hesitant, Baba Sophia cried: "There we go! It's all over! Corporal Isacescu, should we send for the priest? Yes or no?"

"Get on with it, Baba Sophia!" Ioan replied, gaily, taking Mariora in his arms. "If your legs are as agile as your tongue, it'll soon be done!"

"Corporal Isacescu," Baba Sophia replied, putting her stiff hand on the *dorobantz*'s shoulder, "I forgive you for all the villainous things you said to me." And, abandoning herself unreservedly to exuberant joy, the old godmother began capering around the room like a mad goat, while Mariora, kneeling before the holy images, gave thanks to the Lord.

Happy people have no history. The happiness of the two fiancés was not quite complete. The memory of Mitica soared like a black bird above their dovecote. Ioan made several trips to the Ministry of War, but when the officials learned that Mitica Slobozianu was only a simple soldier, they replied: "Ah, then we don't know," like the medical orderly at Pleven.

Ioan persuaded Zamfira that Mitica was a prisoner in Constantinople and that he would come back as soon as the peace treaty was signed. People easily believe what they wish to believe, and every night, as she went to sleep, Zamfira told herself that the following day would bring him back.

How many times had Ioan to start the story of his adventures all over again? Mariora never tired of hearing him relate the moving scenes of the taking of Gravitza; the sad demise of the boyar Relia, "who only talked about wine and maize," brought tears to her eyes, and when it was a question of Liatoukine's death, she kissed the hand that had embedded the dagger in the breast of the man with yellow eyes.

Now that Captain Vampire was no more, the thickets of the Baniassa Woods had lost the ability to terrify the priest's daughter, and the proposal that she should return to the village was accepted unanimously.

The month of January was taken up with preparations of every sort. It was decided that the newlyweds would live in he Slobozianus' house, and Mariora sent to Bucharest for a quantity of useless items of furniture that were necessary to her, and which cluttered very corner. Baba Sophia complained of the abomination. Enough wardrobes to contain the linen of 20 families! Enough chairs to seat the entire National Assembly! In her day people had thought themselves lucky to be able to squat on a smooth floor!–and so on. To which Mariora replied that the past was the past, that one could stuff drawers full of fine linen and invite the mayor to dinner.

The marriage date was irrevocably fixed as February 15.

On the evening before, while Ioan was waiting in the office of an advocate in the city, to whom Old Mani had entrusted his money, Zamfira and Mariora were busy arranging the latter's trousseau: aprons with multicolored stripes, richly-embroidered bodices and gold-spangled waistbands all dazzled the eyes of the enraptured Baba Sophia. "Princess Elisabeth would look like a bourgeois next to you, my girl," she said to the future Madame Isacescu—who, bustling about and scuttling like a mouse, replied to her godmother's admiring comments with loud peals of laughter.

Three curt raps on the entrance-door caused a scalloped skirt to fall from Mariora's hands. Who could it be at this late hour? Mariora, whose particular memories rendered her less than valiant, took refuge in the thin arms of the worthy Sophia, who was rooted to the spot. Zamfira took it upon herself, as usual, to act.

The frail staircase groaned beneath a heavy and measured tread. The door of the room opened noisily and the gypsy reappeared, leading a man of tall stature and stern features, wearing a Cossack uniform.

It did not require much to reawaken Mademoiselle Slobozianu's old terrors. The young woman's fear reached its peak when the Russian came towards her and, greeting her by name, presented her with a large oblong box studded with iron nails and carefully sealed. Mariora, pale with fright, backed up against the wall.

"What is it?" asked Zamfira, bravely taking the box from the hands of the singular messenger.

The Cossack made a gesture to signify that he did not understand; the gypsy translated the question into Russian.

"A wedding gift," replied the Cossack, heading for the door.

"And from whom does it come?" Zamfira persisted.

"Forbidden to say!" the incorruptible courier said, laconically, as he disappeared down the stairs.

"There's some devilment in there!" said Baba Sophia, shaking her head. "That box has a suspicious appearance. If you'll take my advice, little one, you'll only open it in the presence of your husband."

Mariora's apprehension overcame her curiosity; she praised her godmother's foresight, and the three women spend the rest of the evening formulating and tearing apart the most improbable conjectures. The mysterious box, which was quite heavy, was weighed up, turned round and sounded out. At the least agitation a clinking noise could be heard, as if a metal object were clinking against the walls of the coffer; then the ear perceived another, fainter noise, like a coin brushing against the wood. The box evidently contained two objects.

Mariora slept badly; she dreamed all night of serpents escaping from a half-open casket, hissing as they did so. When Ioan came, before dawn, to visit his future spouse in private, Baba Sophia gave him a voluble account of the previous evening's incident, not without spicing her recitation with dramatic details that were very stimulating to the imagination.

Ioan had the box brought to him, and introduced a hook into the lock. In response to the instrument's efforts, the cover sprang open.

A quadruple cry of amazement went up. The box contained Mariora's copper ring and Old Mani's *yataghan*. The ring was completely oxidized and a thick layer of rust covered the knife's blade, but the name of its owner–*Mani Isacescu*–was still legible, crudely engraved on the horn handle.

"There!" said Baba Sophia, triumphantly. "Didn't I tell you that the Devil was inside!"

The entire village was present at the wedding feast, which went admirably well, thanks to the culinary talents of Baba Sophia, who surpassed herself.

Sperantza's mother had taken charge of Mariora's dress, and the latter, who doted on western fashions, had replaced the crown of boxwood that traditionally adorns the heads of Walachian winter brides with a magnificent garland of orange-blossom–which she wore proudly, as she had the right to do.

Little Ralitza made the whispered observation that the married couple did not seem very joyful.

"Hold your malicious tongue," said one of her neighbors. "The grass hasn't yet grown over his father's grave and her brother is probably in the arms of the world's bride."[121]

Even so, Ralitza's observation was not without justice. Mariora kept her eyes perpetually lowered, and scarcely made any reply to the conventional pleasantries addressed to her from all sides of the table. Ioan contemplated the Greek wine in his glass with a bleak expression; through the gilded liquid he could distinctly see Liatoukine stretched out on the ground, white-faced, with a dagger stuck in his breast.

"Well?" said Madame Isacescu, interrogatively, when the two spouses finally found themselves alone.

"Listen, darling," said the ex-*dorobantz*. "One of the man's friends must have read our name on the dagger's hilt and sent it back to me."

"That's possible," Mariora said. "But what about the ring?" she added, shaking her head.

"Ah, the ring...that's true!" Ioan murmured, disconcerted. Then, embracing his wife affectionately, he said, suggestively: "Tell me, Mariora, whether we really have to think about this today?"

Mariora smiled, and they gave it no further thought.

The days went by uniformly and rapidly for the two newlyweds. Ioan, for the sake of his peace of mind, had given up trying to find the key to the enigma represented by the ring and the dagger, but Mariora, who was fearful that the presence of the accursed objects might bring them bad luck, confided her anxieties to Baba Sophia.

"We should throw this rubbish in the Dimbovitza," the duenna said to Ioan.

---

[121] A Rumanian expression signifying Death [Nizet].

He refused. Putting the things carefully away in a drawer, he said: "It's important to keep them."

The repeated insistences of the godmother were reinforced by the supplications of the god-daughter, who declared that she would only feel perfectly happy when the ring and the *yataghan* were gone. Ioan was even more fearful of Baba Sophia's nagging than his wife's tears; he consented to bury the box, the ring and the dagger in a deserted spot in the Baniassa woods. Baba Sophia shut up, Mariora recovered her smile, and everyone thought that they would be liberated forever from the odious memory of Captain Vampire.

Mitica's absence being indefinitely prolonged, Ioan resolved to approach the Minister of War directly. An audience was immediately granted, and Mariora asked her husband for permission to accompany him. While putting on her best clothes, Madame Isacescu delighted herself with the thought of being able to repeat to her astounded neighbors: "The minister asked us...the minister replied to us..." and so on. And when Baba Sophia had cast a final eye over Mariora's costume, the two young spouses took the road to the city.

A spring breeze was floating in the air. April had reddened the chilly buds peeping timidly outside their envelopes. Storks and swallows were flying overhead, and violets embalmed the silken grass, in which the eye searched vainly for the humblest of flowers: the white daisy, which is not common in Rumania.

Mariora and Ioan were walking side by side in silence, fearful that words might disturb the gentle ecstasy that the spring morning had poured into their souls, when the advance sentinel of renewal suddenly released its dutiful signal, a joyful "cuckoo!"

Since the adventure of the Baniassa Woods, Mariora had sworn an implacable hatred for the avian omen that had never promised her anything but misfortune, but Ioan did not partake of his wife's prejudice.

Well, *ibita mea*," he said, teasing her gently, "what does the bird say?"

"It doesn't say anything," she replied, with all the seriousness in the world. "It's neither to our right nor to our left–it's over there, in front of us. Do you see it flying away?"

"And that signifies...?"

"Nothing–absolutely nothing. Don't laugh," she added. "That song reminds me of terrible moments, and that bird has always been the precursor, for me...of Liatoukine."

"But, since Liatoukine is dead..."

A gesture from Mariora cut Ioan's words short. "Let's never speak of that man again, Ionitza," she said.

Eleven o'clock was chiming as they arrived in Bucharest. The minister's office did not open until noon. As they went along the Strada Mogosoi, Mariora, who felt obliged to erase the disagreeable impression the encounter with the cuckoo had made on her, suggested that they visit the Sarindar Church. A marriage was being celebrated there–a boyar marriage, at which there would be splendid ladies' dresses, and officers' uniforms making up the couple's cortège, in the presence of the metropolitan Archbishop, who was officiating in person.

A good omen! Mariora thought, reassured. *We'll see Mitica again.*

Dragging Ioan through the crowd of spectators who were filling the church, she got a position as close as she could to the *catapeteasma*–the icon-adorned door separating the nave from the bema. From where they were, neither Ioan nor Mariora could see the faces of the bride and groom. In any case, the bride's beauty was of scant importance to Madame Isacescu, who only had eyes for the white satin dress, ornamented with lace and rivulets of jewels. The ex-*dorobantz*'s gaze never left the groom. That tall figure, that stiff stance and, above all, that uniform, were not unfamiliar to Isacescu.

"Where have I seen that man before?" he asked himself, waiting impatiently for the officer to turn around.

The ceremony was marked by a rather amusing incident. A political–one might almost say historic–person of note had been charged with holding the nuptial crown suspended above the bride's head, as is the custom in Orthodox marriages. The bride was tall; the statesman was short. The latter, feeling that his gravity was compromised, was standing on tiptoe and making desperate efforts to maintain his balance, to his own embarrassment and the extreme joy of the jeering public, which no longer idolized him.

"Who's getting married, then?" Mariora asked a woman of the people, who was chattering much more freely than the sanctity of the location should have permitted.

"Jesus Christ, little mother! You're obviously not from the city, to ask me a question like that! No one's talked about anything except this marriage for a month. I don't suppose they adore one another like turtle-doves, but *he* has two million rubles, and the good graces of the Russian Emperor; *she* owns lots and lots of land...it goes on forever."

"But who...?" Mariora persisted.

"I'm getting there, chicken. Prince Androcles Comanescu is marrying his daughter Epistimia to General Boris Liatoukine, so they say."

"That's not true!" Ioan retorted, forcefully. "Boris Liatoukine is dead!"

"Oh yes?" the old woman sniggered. "You're soft in the head, my lad! Dead! The dead aren't so hearty!"

The ceremony finished as the shrew pronounced these words, and the married couple, followed by their cortège, headed slowly towards the exit door, which was wide open.

Mariora fell unconscious into her husband's arms.

Next to Epistimia, who was moving forwards haughtily and scornfully, marched Boris Liatoukine, in the grandiose uniform of a Russian general: Boris Liatoukine, who was said to have died at Gravitza on September 11, 1877, Saint Alexander's Day!

Hardly having the strength to support Mariora, the motionless Ioan–his mouth agape, his eyebrows bristling and his eyes haggard–was the personification of Terror.

Captain Vampire's clothing brushed against Ioan's. The resurrected man's eyes flared; his ironic smile became ferocious; he raised his gloveless right hand.

The little finger had been cut off at the third knuckle!

Then the cortège continued on its way; the church emptied little by little, and complete silence was re-established.

"I killed him, though!" murmured the paralyzed Ioan. "I'm sure that I killed him!"

Eight hours later, Domna Epistimia was dead, and the Isacescu family, abandoning Baniassa forever, moved to Craiova.

Epilogue

Ioan Isacescu became what one might appropriately call a prosperous landowner. The reasonably large sum amassed by his father permitted him to acquire 15 *pogones* of arable land in the vicinity of Craiova, which he cultivated himself. His wife's wealth was invested advantageously, and all his tenants said that, if all its landlords acted as fairly as "the cripple," Rumania would be one of the most delightful places in this wretched world.

Ioan, believing that "it is only to see that masters have eyes," still traveled to Baniassa once a month. Mariora never thought of accompanying him. She had sworn to die without ever seeing Bucharest again. She made the sign of the cross at the merest clink of a Russian spur; the sight of a Cossack caused her to fall in a faint. Ioan had forbidden everyone to mention the name of Liatoukine in front of her. She had learned to cook *mamaliga* and to make cheese; she did not gossip with the neighbors, for which her husband praised her a great deal, and she had no more bitter words for Zamfira, who had brought her father to live with her in Craiova.

No news had ever been received of Mitica. Zamfira remained unmarried; her red ribbons faded to yellow. She brought up Mariora's children.

Baba Sophia grumbled and stormed all day long; she was forgiven her continual nagging on account of her age.

Old Mozaïs was completely senile; he spent entire hours crouched on his doorstep, incessantly murmuring "Serban Yezidee! Serban Yezidee!" while shaking his head. Then he suddenly got up and grabbed his staff. "Where are you going, father?" his daughter asked him. "To Smyrna!" he replied, in a firm voice. He took a few steps outside, then came back to lie down in the dust, repeating his terrible refrain: "Serban Yezidee!"

Domna Agapia ended up marrying the 8,000 hectares of young Decebale Privighetoareano. Decebale shuttled back and forth between Bucharest and Paris, beat the Princess, debauched her chambermaids and bought diamonds for pretty ballerinas. Mademoiselle Comanescu wepts night and day; she became very thin, and when she threatened to return to her father, Decebale offered her his arm to take her to the railway station. She then became a permanently resident in Vienna, where luck reacquainted her with her blue-eyed dancer, Igor Moïleff, who carried an interesting wound very gracefully. He desired to console Madame Privighetoareano. The poor Princess was deeply perplexed; Decebale, willingly excusing his own peccadilloes, showed himself to be not at all indulgent of his wife's.

The Comanescu Palace became the terrestrial paradise of priests, igumens [122] and Archimandrites, who always found a good meal, good lodgings and a cash donation there. Domna Rosanda threw herself wholeheartedly into devotion; the rosary replaced the fan between her fingers; she wore somber dresses, spoke through her nose and planned to build a church.

Androcles alone was happy. He had shed two tears over the graves of Aurelio and Epistimia. "We are all mortal!" he said, with an appropriate delicacy. Then he passed the back of his hand over his moist eyelids and returned to his business affairs. He constructed a sugar refinery in the Vlasca district, which formed a counterpart to his wife's church. In the Senate, he featured among the mute orators. His glory was at its apogee; the Order of the Rumania Star was conferred upon him, at the same time as the confectioner Capsa and the brewer Opler, two persons well-known in Bucharest.[123]

As for Boris Liatoukine, he paraded his insolence in the drawing-rooms of St Petersburg again. All the talk was of his strange adventure. The ladies bemoaned the fate of the unfortunate Princess Liatoukine–the third of that name– and not one aspired to succeed her. The superstitious old dowagers claimed that Prince Boris was well and truly slain at Gravitza; the Liatoukine whom the Tsar has elevated to the rank of General was, according to them, merely the Prince's cadaver, temporarily reanimated by a breath of infernal life.

Some of Captain Vampire's friends attempted to solve the mystery. Misfortune overtook them all. Liatoukine challenged Bogomil Tchestakoff and struck him dead. Stenka Sokolich, wrongly suspected of producing nihilist propaganda, was deported to Siberia. Yuri Levine was stripped of his rank; he was rumored to have gone insane.

---

[122] An igumen (Nizet has *igoumêne*) or hegumen is the head of a relatively small Orthodox monastery–the equivalent of an abbot in the Roman church; the head of a larger and more important Orthodox monastery is known by the more familiar title of Archimandrite.

[123] These two characters are "rigorously historic," according to Nizet's brief footnote, but I can only identify one of the two families: the Capsas were notable confectioners and restauranteurs from 1856, when Anton and Vasile Capsa founded a confectionery in 1856, until well into the 20th century.

J.-H. Rosny Aîné: *The Young Vampire*

J.-H. Rosny Aîné is now generally reckoned to be one of the most important pioneers of French scientific romance, second in rank to his much more popular and far more widely-known predecessor Jules Verne. His short story Les Xipéhuz *(1887),[124] which takes place a thousand years before Babylonian times, and in which primitive humans encounter inorganic aliens with whom all forms of communication prove impossible, became an instant classic. His novel,* La Mort de la Terre *[The Death of the Earth] (1910),[125] which takes place in a distant future when the planet has all but dried out, prompted Henry Davray, H. G. Wells's French translator, to label Rosny as the "French Wells."*

This was further established when another novel, La Force Mystérieuse *[The Mysterious Force],[126] about the destruction of a portion of the light spectrum by a mysterious force—possibly who, for a brief moment, share our physical existence—came out in 1913.*

J.-H. Rosny Aîné was the principal pseudonym used by Joseph-Henri-Honoré Boëx, who was born in Brussels in 1856. In the beginning, the pseudonym was simply J.-H. Rosny, but he decided after some years of near-fame to share that pseudonym with his younger brother, Séraphin-Justin-François, and it remained a joint enterprise for a decade and a half, until the two fell out and decided to separate; because both of them wanted to maintain the limited but significant prestige attached to the pseudonym, they divided it into two, becoming J.-H. Rosny Aîné (the elder) and J.-H. Rosny Jeune (the younger).

After the serial publication of La Légende sceptique *in 1889,[127] there was an evident hiatus in the publication of Rosny's scientific romances, although* Vamireh [128] *certainly warrants consideration as a literary extrapolation of late-19th century discoveries and (mostly mistaken) theories in paleoanthropology. The novel was serialized in 1892 in the early issues of a new periodical, the* Revue Hebdomadaire, *whose editor was probably pleased to acquire a contribution by such an up-and-coming writer, who had already published in many of the prestigious periodicals of the day.*

---

[124] Included in *The Navigators of Space & Other Alien Encounters*, translated by Brian Stableford, Black Coat Press, ISBN 978-1-935558-35-4.

[125] Included in *The Navigators of Space*, q.v.

[126] Included in *The Mysterious Force & Other Anomalous Phenomena*, translated by Brian Stableford, Black Coat Press, ISBN 978-1-935558-37-8.

[127] Included in *The Navigators of Space*, q.v.

[128] Included in *Vamireh & Other Prehistoric Fantasies*, translated by Brian Stableford, Black Coat Press, ISBN 978-1-935558-38-5.

The editor of another new periodical, Le Bambou, was also sufficiently interested in Rosny to be willing to serialize work of this sort in 1893, beginning with the prehistoric novel Eyrimah [129] (reprinted in book form 1896) and continuing with an account of unknown human races surviving in a remote part of Asia, "Nymphée".[130]

During the remainder of the two brothers' partnership, only four short scientific romances and one further prehistoric romance appeared under the J.-H. Rosny name. The brief sardonic prehistoric romance, "Nomaï" [131] appeared in the Revue Parisienne in 1895. "Un Autre Monde" [132] (Revue de Paris 1895), which extrapolates—rather uneasily—an idea sketched out in "La Légende sceptique," was almost as ground-breaking as "Les Xipéhuz." No more prehistoric or scientific romances appeared in print while the two brothers' partnership lasted—or, indeed, for two years thereafter, in spite of the fact that H. G. Wells had demonstrated in the interim that scientific romance could be popular, as well as interesting in its extrapolations.

But despite of his "poetic passion" for science and speculative thought, Joseph Boëx seems to have resolutely refused to embark on any further ventures of that kind between the publication of "Un Autre monde" and the formal termination of his literary partnership with his brother.

We can only speculate as to the role Justin Boëx might have played in dissuading his elder brother from experiments in scientific romance while they were sharing their pseudonym, but it seems highly probable that their collective change of status to "J.-H. Rosny de l'Académie Goncourt" also had much to do with it. In spite of the fact that the Goncourt Academy had been conceived as a protest against the conservatism of the official Académie, its members were nevertheless defensive of their own aesthetic credentials.

Oddly enough, the first Prix Goncourt, awarded in 1903, did go to a work that some might consider to be a scientific—or, at least, metaphysical—romance, La Force ennemie [Enemy Force][133] by John-Antoine Nau (Eugène Torquet), but it was the work of an already-respectable writer who never did anything else of a similar ilk, and the Prix Goncourt was never subsequently awarded to anything of that sort, or to anything else that might be considered a "genre" novel rather than a "literary" novel. Rosny seems to have felt, once he was appointed to the Académie Goncourt, that he was somehow obliged to shun such work as unbefitting a writer of his status. He did, however, eventually bor-

---

[129] Included in *Vamireh*, q.v.

[130] Included in *The World of the Variants & Other Strange Lands*, translated by Brian Stableford, Black Coat Press, ISBN 978-1-935558-36-1.

[131] Included in *Vamireh*, q.v.

[132] Included in *The Navigators of Space*, q.v.

[133] Published as *Enemy Force*, translated by Michael Shreve, Black Coat Press, ISBN 978-1-935558-49-1.

row the speculative premise of La Force ennemie *for adaptation to his own speculative context in one of his more interesting exercises,* La Jeune vampire *(1920), here translated as "The Young Vampire." It is interesting, in that, in contrast to Rosny's other stories in which entities from other sectors of "the fourth universe" interact with ours, it imagines an internal manifestation akin to diabolical possession—except that the "possessor" is not seen as actively evil or malicious, in spite of the fact that it imposes a subtle metamorphosis of its host body, which compels it to seek vampiric nourishment.*

B.S.

I

"There is some truth in all persistent beliefs," said Jacques Le Marquand. "I mean beliefs that relate to precise and oft-repeated facts."

"Such as witchcraft...."

"As a whole, I deny that, because it includes too many imprecise facts, and also because it varies immoderately—but modern science uses many practices similar to those of sorcerers and witches; consequently, it's ridiculous to deny that witchcraft rests, at least partially, on an experimental basis. I don't insist on that, because I've only studied the matter superficially—but what would you say if I were to affirm the existence of a phenomenon akin to vampirism?"

"Science doesn't deny it!" exclaimed Charmel, mischievously. "It merely transposes it from human beings to a species of bat...."

Jacques Le Marquand shrugged his shoulders and continued: "I knew a vampire once...in the district of Islington, in London, between 1902 and 1905—and I learned recently that she is still alive. What's more, she's married; she even has four children."

"Who will be little vampires! Charmel interjected, gravely.

"Vampirism doesn't seem to be hereditary," Le Marquand riposted, with even more gravity.

The young person of whom I speak was the third daughter of Mr. and Mrs. Grovedale, and she was distinguished from her sisters because she was much prettier. At the time that I knew her, she was even fantastically pretty. What I mean by that is that she combined her beauty with something extraordinary—I should say supernatural. To begin with, her face was exactly as white as that sheet of paper—which ought to have rendered her a trifle alarming, but, for one reason or another, didn't make her alarming at all. On the contrary, she was, as our neighbors say, *fascinating*. Evidently, her eyes, hair and mouth compensated for the excessive pallor or her skin. I don't know which was most tempting: the bush of flames that grew from her skull; her pathetic eyes, immense and avid; or her lips, as red as a *Canna* flower.

She hadn't been as pale as that for long—a little more than five years. Her mother explained that she had died—*literally* died. Two doctors had certified her death. In accordance with English custom, the cadaver was preserved for some time. On the third day, it began to decompose—which didn't prevent the fact that on the morning of the fourth day, Evelyn Grovedale revived. She presented particularities that were interesting to scientists and disquieting for those around her. Her memory was greatly disordered; she only spoke at infrequent intervals and in an incoherent manner; she showed no affection for her family. Although her intelligence was co-ordinated, one might have thought that Evelyn was two people. With respect to the present and events that followed her death she spoke in the first person; with respect to earlier events, she made reference to an indecisive personality. Furthermore, her memory only seemed to serve to guide her through life, not for any return to her past self. When she decided to grant caresses to her relatives, she did so ardently, but in a bizarre fashion.

With time, she reverted almost to normality. After some hesitation, rebellion and fear, she seemed to *accept* the story of her past, as one accepts rules of conduct or as one adopts a belief.

This is the moment to mention an abnormal phenomenon that occurred shortly after her resurrection. Father and Mother Grovedale, the two daughters and the little boy, who all had florid complexions, became paler, and languished to various degrees. Her father was the worst afflicted. Her mother simply seemed tired, as did her older sister, Harriet. As for the younger daughter, Aurora, she seemed to be afflicted with chlorosis, and little Jack seemed incapable of following his lessons at school or doing his chores in the house; he was always drowsy and slept nineteen hours out of twenty-four.

The Grovedales, being unimaginative folk, made few conjectures; the family doctor manifested some surprise, but limited himself to giving various names to the epidemic of pallor and administering an assortment of pills and potions.

In the spring, all the symptoms eased. The mother and Harriet became almost vigorous again; Aurora recovered her strength; and young Jack, without succeeding in studying, slept no more than fifteen hours out of twenty-four. This coincided with the persistent presence of one James Bluewinkle, a young man built like a wrestler, who conceived an inordinate passion for Evelyn. The Bluewinkles and the Grovedales yielded promptly to the solicitations of the lovers; they were married before the end of April. They took a "trip" to the continent and came back to take up residence in London.

Following Evelyn's departure, the amelioration observed among the Grovedales was rapidly augmented. Everyone, in fact, recovered—even the child, whose ration of sleep declined to ten hours. On the other hand, James Bluewinkle acquired a 'pale complexion'. Endowed with the stomach of a lion, he consumed pounds of rump steak, leg of lamb, chicken or goose every day, but his vitality weakened. A succession of physicians failed to discover any cause. In the end, a homeopath had a vague intuition and prescribed a rest cure in isolation in a sanitarium in Ipswich.

The effects of this cure proved prodigious. James Bluewinkle recovered his strength. By way of compensation, Evelyn sickened and became anemic. After a few days, she sought refuge with her family—with her grandmother, since Harriet and her mother felt "uncomfortable". Aurora and the boy began to go pale again.

In their innocence, they continued not to understand it at all. They scarcely felt the slight astonishment that one feels when confronted with insignificant coincidences when, on James Bluewinkle's return, their illness vanished as if by enchantment.

You might expect that the husband would now fall back into languor, and you would not be mistaken. A month after his return from the sanitarium, he had become weak and pale again. Less candid than the Grovedales, he conceived anxieties—almost suspicions—and began to study his wife.

She led a methodical life. Her tastes were simple. She spent little; she dressed elegantly but without ostentation; she ate sparingly. On the other hand, James fulfilled his various conjugal duties fervently, but without any of those exaggerations that can sap a man's energy—especially a strong man. Nevertheless, it seemed that after Evelyn's kisses—and I mean simple kisses—he was gripped by a kind of torpor. Then, without his quite knowing how, an idea occurred to him that might well have been an *instinctive memory*.

One evening, without his wife's knowledge, he drank two cups of exceedingly strong coffee, in order to resist the lethargic somnolence that overtook him every night, and pretended to go to sleep, as usual. For a long time, nothing abnormal occurred. Eleven o'clock, midnight and one o'clock chimed successively.

Finally, Evelyn's respiration, regular until then, accelerated. At first, the young woman remained motionless; then she sat up very slowly. Bluewinkle sensed that she leaned over him. Two warm and silky lips made contact with his neck. It was a strange sensation, voluptuous and disturbing at the same time. The lips aspired something, with infinite gentleness. Gradually, he felt himself growing weaker. An irresistible numbness overwhelmed his consciousness. He knew that if he waited another minute, he would fall into a leaden sleep, in spite of the stimulus of the coffee. With a limp gesture, he pushed Evelyn's head away, and his throat taut with anguish, exclaimed: "Vile creature!"

A sob burst forth in the darkness, and when he switched on the electric lamp he saw Evelyn, prostrate on the bed, trembling in every limb.

"Vile creature!" he repeated. "What have I done to you, that you should kill me?"

"Their eyes met. The young woman's pupils ere quivering; her entire face expressed a mysterious terror. As if in a dream, she replied: "I can't do otherwise...I'd *die*!"

Suddenly, Bluewinkle had an inspiration—one of those inspirations that come from the utmost depths of being and are born of extraordinary contacts. He became certain that Evelyn Grovedale was a vampire.

We sat in silence for a minute, under the spell of a mystical *aura*. Then Charmel slowly shrugged his shoulders.

"What does that certainty prove?" he asked.

"I'll tell you tomorrow," Jacques Le Marquand replied, after consulting his watch.

II

The next day, Jacques Le Marquand continued his story in these terms.

The sentiment that initially overcame Bluewinkle was one of horror and dread. Soon, though, Evelyn's tears moved him, for he had a tender heart and she seemed charming in the luminous disorder of her hair.

"It's an aberration!" he said. "You wouldn't die at all!"

"I'd die," she repeated, in a profound tone.

He sensed that she was perfectly sincere, and became thoughtful again. His conviction remained firm: Evelyn really was a vampire, but in a manner somewhat different from that related by tradition. James, who was something of a philosopher, knew that traditions embody elements of symbolism and legend. In this instance, it was not necessary to believe in vampires emerging from their tombs; that was the contribution of the spirit of the macabre and popular puerility. One could believe, on the other hand, in some organic oddity, followed by apparent death—which was strictly applicable to Evelyn's case. Not only had she been taken for dead, but her metamorphosis revealed itself by an excessive pallor and by the disturbance of her mind.

"The proof that you wouldn't die," he resumed, "is that you've spent the greater part of your existence quite innocently."

"My existence!" she murmured, in a grim tone. "Was it really *my* existence?"

That question did not entirely surprise Bluewinkle; he knew that the young woman's memory exhibited singular features. Nevertheless, his attention was more excited than usual: Evelyn had never been as precise.

"What do you mean?" he asked. "Do you suppose that the Evelyn Grovedale of old and the present one are not the same person?"

She did not answer immediately. Her lips were trembling. She looked up sat James with a gaze full of supplication and suspicion. Finally, as if carried away by an irresistible impulse, she whispered: "They are two different people!"

Her tone frightened the young man. He paused momentarily, as if bewildered, then said, hoarsely: "Then what? The old Evelyn Grovedale would be *re-*

ally dead...and the one that I have before me...where did she come from? It's the same body, though!"

"Yes, the same body...but *only* the same body."

"Try to explain yourself clearly!" he exclaimed, with a convulsive agitation. "The same body...and another soul?"

"Another *being*."

"The terminology isn't important. There would be a stranger living in the body of Evelyn Grovedale...a stranger incarnate therein."

"I don't know."

"How can you not know? Since you're sure of not being Evelyn, you must be the being incarnate in her body."

She shook her head, meditative and melancholy. "I can't answer you. I don't have the words to say what I'd need to say. I only know that the memories I find in this body—the memories of *before my arrival*—aren't mine. Yes, I know that...."

"How? Do you have other memories that contradict Evelyn's?"

"I have other memories."

"Of what?"

"I tell you that I don't have the words to explain them...and this brain has no images to enable me to recall my own past. They're memories of another world! They're there, apart....oh, how I sense them!—but I can't reach them."

"At any rate," said Bluewinkle, in despair, "you have a memory of the moment when you *invaded* Evelyn's body."

"I don't have any!"

James got up, and, having regained some strength with the aid of a cordial, sat down by the young woman's beside, successively enfevered by certainty and reassured by doubt. As is only natural, he sometimes wondered whether Evelyn might be mad—but if madness could explain her words and actions, it could not begin to explain the very real effect manifest upon himself.

"Explain to me," he said, fervently, "how you lived, after your death, until the moment when you met me."

"I lived on them!" she confessed. "And during your absence, as well."

With a long shudder, he remembered little Jack's pallor, and that of young Aurora.

"Then, if I hadn't come along, you would have killed those poor children!"

"No," she said, swiftly. "When one of them became too exhausted, I switched to the other. I'm not wicked...I'm unfortunate...I struggle against myself...I know that I'm doing wrong...but I also know that I'm in constant danger of death, and the temptation becomes irresistible...."

She spoke with a humble and coaxing grace, which touched Bluewinkle profoundly. He studied those eyes in which such a passionate flame burned, and said to himself: *That's not a wicked creature!* Then, seized by an ardent and somber curiosity, he said: "But what is it that you take from us?"

331

She looked away, hiding her face in the pillow; nevertheless, he heard her sway: "Your blood!"

He had half-expected that reply. In consequence, he was only slightly shocked, and he went to examine the place where Evelyn had set her lips in a mirror; he saw nothing but a faint—very faint—pink patch. "That's impossible!" he declared. "Blood doesn't filter through the skin like that...."

"Do you think so?" she said.

He postponed the problem until later and retorted: "Then again, you hardly eat anything. If you ate, you could give up this horrible thing."

"I can't eat much. Beyond a certain quantity, *your* nourishment poisons me."

"How did you come by the idea of absorbing blood?"

"It seems that I've always had it. I only have to place me lips of the skin. Straight away...."

She concluded with a gesture, and sighed. He no longer knew what to believe. Ideas were whirling in his head like dead leaves in a forest. As he had interrogated Evelyn, he had become accustomed to the fantastic, and no longer had a precise view of the limits that separated it from quotidian reality. There was also the darkness, the cordial, that strange and dazzling creature...he was living in a dream.

"You know that you're doing wrong. Are you repentant?"

"I have great regrets."

"So you love Evelyn's parents, sisters and brother?"

"I don't love them at first...affection came afterwards."

"And me?"

"Oh! You...very much!"

He felt moved. Evelyn's seductiveness reappeared in its entirety.

"Do you consider me to be a member of your species?"

"Yes," she said, passionately. "*Wherever I come from*, I belong to *humankind*. I know that I'm a stranger in this world, but I also know that I'm a woman—and I love my new life...especially because I live with you...."

In the state of excitement in which Bluewinkle now found himself, which was comparable both to the intoxication of alcohol and that of opium, there was almost no room for astonishment. The beyond seemed to him to be very simple, the supernatural intricately confused with the natural.

"You don't miss your other life?" he asked.

She shivered from head to toe; then, in a striking tone, she said: "I'm afraid of my other life! I sense that I underwent an adventure so terrifying *there*...that my soul was *obliged to depart*. It's inexpressible, and frightful. And what does it matter, since I love you?"

She had pronounced the last words in a voice so pure, tender and human, she was so beautiful, and her beauty so intoxicating, that James could no longer see anything but an adored wife. He seized Evelyn's head; their lips sought one another in an avid kiss.

At first it was delirious; everything was erased by an immense love…then, the strange weakness that Bluewinkle knew only too well took possession of his flesh and his mind; he felt faint. He only just had time to extract himself from the embrace.

Then he saw, distinctly, a moist redness overflowing the gap between Evelyn's lips, and red trickles on her silvery teeth.

"Blood!" he cried. "*My blood!*"

Evelyn uttered a long moan.

III

When James woke up the next morning on the divan in the "parlor", where he had slept lethargically, it required some time before he was able to separate illusory and real ideas. Then he was gripped by a mystical dread and a bitter disgust. Pity mingled therein when he saw Evelyn again.

She was no paler than usual—that was impossible—but in a few hours, she had grown manifestly thinner. Her eyes were sunken, full of an anxious fire, and her cheeks seemed hollow. She was agitated by a continual tremor, which sometimes extended to shivering. On seeing her thus, James forgot his fears. He could not believe that that tormented creature was of an essence other than his own. And the haunting quality of supernatural tending to dissipate, he began once again to think that Evelyn must quite simply be ill—except that the illness from which she was suffering, unknown to conventional science, had been reported in an inexact manner by tradition.

Was it curable? Strictly speaking, it could be classed among the neuroses, since, after all, neuroses confer certain abilities that are not observable in balanced individuals, and since they also often involve unusual appetites.

James tried to put questions to the young woman as methodically as possible. She replied meekly, consistently and without contradiction. In fact, once the point of departure was admitted, she said nothing absurd. She limited herself to affirming once again the fact of her anterior existence and the impossibility of expressing that form of that existence in words, or of suggesting it with the aid of images dependent on her current body.

As she was growing weaker and more feverish by the hour, James decided to obtain the advice of a physician specializing in neurology. In fact, he was distantly acquainted with the Scottish Charcot, Percy Coleman, who listened to him with all the more interest because he assumed him to be afflicted by madness as soon as he had described the first nocturnal scene—and even more so when he had described the second.

Even so, Percy Coleman consented to examine Evelyn. The young woman's spectral pallor interested him immediately, and rendered him jovial—for he had a mania for abnormalities. She refused at first to tell him anything; then, in response to James's pleading, she seemed to abandon herself o destiny, and repeated without variation what she had previously revealed.

The illustrious neurologist listened, rubbing his hands enthusiastically. "No lacuna, no fissure," he remarked. "All in place, all in order. Let's look at the machinery...."

The machinery delighted him too. The reflexes were functioning marvelously. All the organs proved impeccable.

"Delicious!" the wise man murmured, licking his chops. "Now, let's pass on to the nub of the drama."

He had a great deal of difficulty persuading Evelyn to embrace James. In spite of the brevity of the kiss, the experiment was decisive and astounded the specialist.

"A leap into the unknown!" he said, in a semi-whisper. "A plunge into the gulf! Not even a prick, and the blood passed through—which flatly contradicts everything we know about tegumentary osmosis. This little phenomenon will stir the pond for the frogs!"

His joy, muted at first by surprise, swelled his face; he looked at Evelyn with a mixture of avidity and benevolence. "Madame has acquired all my devotion," he declared. "I shall spare no sacrifice to restore her to health—none! If she requires human blood, it shall be given to her cost free!" With a little laugh, he added: "We'll club together is necessary. We have no shortage here of young men—and even young women—devoted to science."

This visit seemed to calm Evelyn at first. She consented to take peptones and a stimulant prescribed by the physician, and her attitude was meek, obliging and resigned. James was also relieved. As he knew little about medicine he had a great faith in the mysterious power of therapeutics. He promptly abandoned any idea of the supernatural; his mysterious dreads became negligible. The evening that he spent with Evelyn was, at times, quite charming. He abandoned himself to hope, and his young love came through the storm stronger than before.

Gradually, the young woman's frissons resumed. She curled up in her armchair, staring straight ahead with a sad and almost haggard gaze. She was getting visibly weaker.

"What's the matter, darling?" James asked.

"I'm tired."

He went to her and gently put his arm around her waist. She let him do it; her long hair spread around the young man's neck. When he tried to kiss her, though, she withdrew her lips.

"Never again! Never again!"[134] she moaned.

---

[134] Rosny has "Never more!"—which might be a calculated echo of Edgar Poe, but I have assumed that it is simply an imperfect command of the English idiom.

He insisted, drawing her toward him with the generous strength of love, but she resisted—and when he succeeded in attaining her red mouth, no caress responded to his own. The struggle exhausted the young woman, though. She made one last attempt to get away; her eyes closed; she smiled weakly—and then her head fell backwards. She had fainted.

He tried in vain to reanimate her. Her pulse seemed inert; the beating of her heart was imperceptible; no breath was exhaled through the parted lips....

Then, in desperation, James sent for Percy Coleman.

The neurologist appeared at about midnight, accompanied by a gigantic adolescent with auburn hair and a complexion the color of York ham.

"Hulloo!" exclaimed the scientist, tapping his companion on the shoulder. "Here's a rude fellow for you—a glorious servant of science. He's not the sort to be parsimonious with a few armfuls of blood."

The fellow agreed with infantile and colossal laugh.

"The young lady will need a healthy appetite to tire him out," added Coleman, to whom the evening port had communicated a generous gaiety.

He was taken to Evelyn's bedside, and understood at the first glance hat the situation was serious. The stimulus of the port evaporated on the spot. He leaned over the young woman and sounded her chest with a stethoscope. As he did so his cheeks stiffened and a keen disappointment appeared in his sharp eyes.

"My God!" he muttered. "That would be a damnable loss to science and Percy Coleman."

"She isn't dead!" cried Bluewinkle, gripped by terror. "Tell me that she isn't dead!"

"No, she isn't dead," the practitioner replied, "But she's sunk into a diabolical lethargy—and we'll need a large slice of luck to get her out of it."

IV

In spite of the ingenious care of Percy Coleman, Evelyn's lethargy persisted for several hours. Toward dawn, however, after a long application of induced electric current, a movement of her eyelids was perceived, soon followed by an almost-imperceptible heartbeat.

"She's *coming back*," the neurologist declared, mopping his brow—for he was sweating like a stoker. "Can we keep her, though?"

James had watched that interminable struggle against death, miserable and powerless. All sentiments other than love, pity, hope and despair had disappeared from his soul. He almost forgot the strange scenes enacted between him-

---

I have made similarly slight adjustments to one or two of the other phrases Rosny renders in English, but most of them are entirely satisfactory.

self and his poor wife. At the doctor's words, he started convulsively, and precipitated himself toward Evelyn.

"Stop!" said the doctor, peremptorily. "She hasn't as much strength as a newly-hatched pigeon. The slightest clumsiness could snuff her out—and you're in a state of frightful clumsiness."

In addition to the young giant, two interns had come; they carried out all of Coleman's instructions with celerity and precision.

"Enough current!" said the latter. "It's time to regulate her breathing."

The older of the interns inserted fine flexible tubes into the sick woman's nostrils, connected to a complex machine that the second internal started up by means of a lever. Percy regulated the speed by means of summary indications. After a few minutes, a regular palpitation of the chest was discernible; then Evelyn's eyelids opened slightly, and her eyes, as if impregnated with darkness, moved feebly from side to side.

"We've brought her back from abyssal depths!" whispered the neurologist. With a perplexed expression, he watched that abnormal body return to life.

While taking pride in his methods, particularly the artificial respirator, he felt that he was surrounded by a vast hazard. Every action was a risk—and Evelyn's awakening, far from facilitating the task, rendered it more awkward. He had no idea what to do. The young woman's weakness seemed excessive, and did not seem to be entirely natural. An intervention was indispensable—but what intervention?

Gradually, the shadow had quit her pupils. Evelyn could see again. First of all, she perceived the doctor leaning over her, then one of the interns—but these images seemed to leave her indifferent. As soon as she distinguished Bluewinkle, her lips trembled, and she was heard to whisper "Darling!"

"Bother the man!" muttered Coleman, in a low voice. "He's making her agitated…excessively agitated! We'll have to put him into a cell for twenty-four hours…what did I say!"

Evelyn's eyelids had closed again; a dolorous cease appeared between her eyebrows; then her breath seemed to slow down.

The neurologist continued soliloquizing. "Blood! It's blood that she needs! I'll bet a thousand pounds to a guinea." Addressing himself to the colossus, he said: "David, my lad, take off your waistcoat and roll up your sleeve."

The other obeyed, calmly and methodically—but then Percy was seized by doubt. Should he inject blood into the invalid? Or was it necessary for her to extract it directly from its source?

In itself, the injection seemed preferable, but in exceptional cases, Coleman observed the principle of rejecting logic and holding strictly to proven methods. Now, Evelyn had never absorbed blood indirectly….

He replaced the syringe that he had just taken up, examined young David's arm and applied Evelyn's lips to the place that he judged most favorable.

The effect was prodigious. The eyelids reopened instantly, and the pupils became animated; then her breathing accelerated. Scarcely a minute had gone by, and already one had the impression that energy was returning to the exhausted organism in waves.

Meanwhile, James Bluewinkle had moved surreptitiously to the bedside. At first, an ardent joy appeared on his face—but as he watched Evelyn's resurrection, another sentiment was born, which made his limbs shiver: the idea that his wife was drawing life from the veins of another man rapidly became unbearable. He leaned over; his jealous gaze encountered Evelyn's....

With a long sigh, she thrust the arm of the young colossus away and turned her face to the wall. As on the previous evening, James heard her murmur: "Never again! Never again!"

Attentive solely to the movements of his patient, Percy Coleman took no account of the psychology of the drama. He thought it a slight delirium, or simply a reactionary phase. "We'll start again in a little while!" he declared.

A sob replied to him; the young woman's shoulders shook convulsively; then she turned round abruptly and extended her arms to James. "Forgive me!" she said, in a faltering voice. "I didn't know what I was doing."

Exasperated, Coleman authorized the young man to draw nearer with a gesture. Evelyn embraced him desperately, stammering words that were tender and enigmatic by turns. Finally, she allowed herself to fall back, stammering: "I could have been so happy...why is it impossible? I can't do it any more...I have to go back. Oh, my darling, it's so terrible...so terrible!"

Her speech was becoming increasingly indistinct. It was in an exhalation that she breathed: "Farewell!"

"She's fallen back into the abyss!" exclaimed the neurologist, furiously. "That was well worth the trouble of five hours hard work...."

James had sunk to his knees beside the bed, like a guilty man—and a desperate one.

"Get out of the way!" cried the physician, rudely. "Perhaps there's something to be done other than weeping...."

The examination to which he devoted himself brought his exasperation to a head. Evelyn was in exactly the same state in which he had found her before midnight. At first, that state appeared to be stable, but Percy soon formed the impression that events were moving on. Life was decreasing with every passing second; after ten minutes, the most delicate observations ceased to reveal any sign of it.

"This time," he muttered, "there's only one more thing that we need, and that's a miracle...and what miracle, eh, David?"

He waited a little while longer, patiently renewed his investigations, then he took a very slender tube out of his medical bag, full of a transparent liquid and sealed at one end by a fine membrane, which he pierced with a needle.

"The last shot!" he said, peevishly.

He inserted the tube delicately into a nostril and waited. Gradually, the liquid took on an opaline tint.

"That confirms it!" the neurologist muttered. "She's on *the other side*...and it's a damned shame!"

James had collapsed, sobbing. Then he shoved Coleman away brutally. Leaning over, he stared at Evelyn steadfastly, in a dolorous stupor. Suddenly, he was seized by a tremor; his pupils dilated and he cried out, in a strange voice: "Look! Look! *Since she died, she has become less pale.*"

V

Coleman, who was making ready to leave, with the indifference of the practitioner and the acrimony of the disappointed scientist, turned round, shrugging his shoulders—but as soon as he had looked at the cadaver, he had to yield to the evidence.

"Marvelous!" he muttered. "This woman is a mine of anomalies!"

In spite of the double lassitude of a sleepless night and continuous work, he spent another half-hour carrying out various experiments. They told him nothing.

"She's gone, irremediably!" he reaffirmed. "I'll come back later. For the moment, I have a brain as thick as suet pudding. I'll send a fresh intern, if you want."

"I don't want anything!" James Bluewinkle replied, churlishly. The presence of the neurologist and the others had become unbearable. If he had given in to his irritation he would have thrown them out.

"All right," said Coleman. "I'll send him all the same—at about ten o'clock in the morning. And you'll see me again before noon, of course. You mustn't only think of yourself, young man—you must think of science."

James was full of a boundless scorn for science and scientists. He sat down at Evelyn's bedside and did not give another thought to Percy or his acolytes. At any rate, they did not take long to disappear.

For a good hour, Bluewinkle remained deeply immersed in grief and remorse. Beneath his muscular envelope, he concealed a sensitive soul, inclined to the malady of scrupulousness. Not only did he exaggerate immeasurably the small wrongs he had done Evelyn, but he added others to the list that were imaginary. In particular, he accused himself for not having been able to reassure the young woman, and even more for the furious impulse of jealousy that had taken possession of him while she had been drawing life from David's veins.

"I killed her!" he sobbed. "She was better than me."

Through the mirage of memory, everything that had seemed abominable to him now seemed touching. Poor creature! Gentle, fearful and tenderly submissive, she reproached herself for the grim fatality that condemned her, as if it were a crime. She would have liked so much to live like other people! What pity he ought to have had for her! And now....

"Forgive me, Evelyn!" he whispered. "It wasn't you, but me who didn't know what I was doing!"

He had lifted up her white hand; he placed a long kiss of grief and repentance on it. The little hand was cold, but singularly flexible. Moreover, no trace of rigidity showed in her face. Only her stillness was funereal. It also seemed to the watcher that Evelyn was even less pale than before. There was a kind of sketchy tint, a sort of *rosy dawn*, on her slender cheeks and temples, At no time had Evelyn ever seemed to him so charming, even in the dreamy hours when summer sunsets had attenuated the lividity of her face.

Gradually, an unfamiliar emotion mingled with James's disturbance. It was a slight oppression, the sensation of a breath, of a mysterious *aura*, and then an indescribable *envelopment*, the passage of some imponderable vortex.

"I'm not alone!" murmured Bluewinkle, suddenly. "Something redoubtable is happening here!" He had never had such a sentiment of the immense and profound life that envelops feeble creatures. Shivering, he was convinced that an extraordinary event had just occurred.

At first, his certainty remained in a "formless fog". James was like a man who hears the distant rumor of a multitude—it draws nearer; one knows that it signifies something; one perceives obscure words, plaints, threats, objurgations....

That was how James perceived the invisible drama.

Suddenly, it all became clear, and, covering his face with his hands, he stammered: "Evelyn is *no longer* dead!"

He shuddered like a tree in a storm.

His agitation lasted barely a minute. It was followed by a strange calm, which did not lack sweetness. James resumed contemplating Evelyn. She was still motionless, but the *rosy dawn* was accentuated. There was now a gleam in her cheeks comparable to that of snow on mountain peaks at the moment when the alpenglow[135] is about to disappear. There was no doubt in James's mind; he waited, with a hypnotic faith, for the young woman to wake up. Already he seemed to perceive a vibration of her lips—and he experienced no astonishment when the rhythm of her respiration elevated her rib-cage.

"Evelyn!" he called, in a muted voice.

She did not wake up immediately. She seemed to be sleeping profoundly and calmly. When he had called her several times, her eyebrows contracted; she ended up opening her eyes.

---

[135] Rosny inserts a footnote here to explain that the alpenglow—*Alpenglühn* in the original—is the name given by the Swiss to a glimmer that sometimes reappears on the mountains after nightfall.

He was immediately struck by the expression in those eyes—a particularly innocent, even naïve expression. Besides, there as something in her entire face that James had never discerned in his wife's face.

"What's the matter?" he stammered.

She looked around in alarm, without seeming to see Bluewinkle. Suddenly, though, a blush of modesty invaded her cheeks, and she exclaimed; "Where am I? Why am I here? My mother...."

That voice troubled James tenderly. He was gripped by a kind of shame. "Don't you recognize me?" he said, extremely softly. "I'm James—your husband...."

"My husband!" she protested. "I'm not married. Oh, sir...if you're a gentleman...fetch my parents...."

She spoke with a passionate vehemence and sincerity, partly concealing her face under the bedclothes. James genuinely felt like a stranger; the respect of his race for womanly modesty filled him with a sentiment of unbearable embarrassment.

"My darling," he said, "it's three months since we were married by the vicar of St. George's. Surely you haven't forgotten...."

She did not reply. Her forehead contracted; her gaze had become interior. Then she whispered: "That's strange! I recognize you, and yet I'm sure that we've never met...and yet...I see you...oh, what a dream! What a frightful dream!"

Nothing could surprise Bluewinkle any longer. He was literally adapted to the fantastic. As if he were asking the simplest thing in the world, he asked: "Are you the real Evelyn Grovedale?"

"Am I the real Evelyn?" she said, dazedly. "Who else would I be?"

"I don't know...I can't tell! I assume that you're Evelyn—but have you any memory of what has happened to you in the last six months?"

At first, the young woman's amazement seemed to increase; then her brow furrowed. A shudder of terror shook her entire body.

"Six months?" she murmured. "Has it been six months? I don't know...but I remember now...I've been away...far away...in a frightful place...."

VI

These words bowled James over, and filled him with a frenetic curiosity. They were, so to speak, *the heart of the mystery*. Whether they expressed a reality or an illusion, they bound Evelyn's destiny and his own destiny together with a thrilling intensity.

"Forgive me," he said, in a voice that was both hoarse and soft, "if I'm tiring you or tormenting you—but it's my duty to question you. Your future and your happiness are at stake. Everything that you say to others and to me, even to your mother, will appear so strange and so incredible that your liberty will inevi-

340

tably be threatened. No one will be ready to believe you. I alone am capable of hearing you indulgently, trustingly, with the most ardent desire to know the truth—so I implore you to suffer my presence for the necessary time, and to answer me without reticence. It's absolutely necessary!"

She listened to him, gravely and sadly, reassured by his tone and his gaze.

"I want to!" she said, with a slight shudder.

He reflected, His excitement was disciplined; he had recovered the self-control that Anglo-Saxons possess almost to the same degree as the Japanese, and combined the methodical mentality of his race with a mysticism amply justified by the circumstances.

"You say that you don't know me," he continued, coolly. "*Are you sure of that?*"

"Quite sure," she replied. She too was forcing herself to be calm; her tremulous lips betrayed her agitation.

"Consequently, you don't admit that we're married...you don't admit that we've spent nearly three months together...."

"I'm absolutely certain of the contrary."

He opened a cupboard and took out a wad of letters and a large piece of parchment. "Here are the letters you've written to me," he said. "Here is our marriage certificate."

She inspected the letters avidly, and then the certificate, trembling with emotion.

"I recognize my handwriting!" she said, in a stifled voice. "I even recognize the text of the letters—but it wasn't *me* who wrote them!"

"Your parents, your sisters, your brother, your friends—everyone, in sum—will confirm that you are my wife. Everyone will tell you that you have lived in this house since our marriage. Try to summon up your memories; try to look into your inmost depths...."

She uttered a sort of moan. "I swear to you that I have never been your wife."

"Consequently, you don't remember any of the events of our engagement or of our life together?"

"I remember perfectly the events of *your* engagement and your life with *someone else*," she replied, alternately going very red and very pale.

"And how can you remember that?"

"I don't know. It's within me, like a dream...like something in which I might have participated in a strange and mysterious fashion...or, rather, like something that might have been combined with me, by some kind of supernatural intervention."

Large droplets of sweat were covering James's forehead. "You can see that other person in your parents' house, then" he went on, "before the vicar of St. George's, and, finally, in this house? You also know that I've been ill and that

341

she was the cause of it. You know that she fell ill in her turn, and that she was cared for by a doctor...you must know the doctor's name?"

"Doctor Percy Coleman," she breathed.

"My God!" he exclaimed, raising his hands toward the ceiling. "Is it possible that you have such exact memories of another person, and of a person that you have never seen? Doesn't it seem infinitely more natural to believe that the person in question is yourself?"

"More natural, perhaps...untrue, definitely!" she cried, in a tone of such certainty that James started—but he had resolved not to take any account of his impressions.

"Can you tell me the approximate date when the last terrestrial events that you remember occurred? I mean, your memories concerning the true Evelyn Grovedale."

She reflected for a few seconds, and replied: "I don't know whether it was the twenty-seventh or the twenty-eight of March, exactly—but the twenty-eighth at the latest."

James went to fetch a *Daily Mail* that was lying on a table, and showed her the date. "The second of October 1903!" she exclaimed, in amazement.

"Consequently, for more than six months *you have had no consciousness of yourself*. Isn't that absurd?"

She was breathing hard. A glimmer of distress sparkled in her dilated eyes.

"I've been *out there* for six months, then...." she said, dejectedly.

"But think about it: your body was here...everyone will tell you so."

She remained bewildered. A fearful expression covered her charming face, and the furrow that was hollowed out between her eyebrows testified to her mental tension. "It's terrifying," she stammered. "But how can it be helped? I've been away for six months, then, and my body didn't go with me!"

"And your body was alive!"

She hid her face and uttered a sigh. "Poor creature that I am!"

"Come on," James murmured, with the utmost tenderness. "Can't you tell me *where* you've been?"

"Alas, no!" she sighed, trembling from head to toe. "I would search in vain for a way to tell you, or to give you the slightest idea. It resembles nothing that you know, nothing that my body knew. It's a frightful place, where I never ceased to suffer."

"Were there other beings there?"

"There were all sorts of beings."

"Including human beings?"

"Beings like me." A sort of glimmer passed over Evelyn's face. "Yes...like me...*as I was out there!* Beings that resembled human creatures, and yet were different. Oh, I sense now why my body remained here."

There was a pause. James felt that he ought not to prolong that poignant interrogation any longer. Given the invalid's state of weakness, that would have been cruel.

"You need to get your strength back," he said. "I'll call a doctor, and I'll also ask your parents to come. Nevertheless, I would still like—and, on my honor as a gentleman, purely for your own sake—to ask you for a favor. Since you know what has transpired between me and *the other*, you're not unaware of why I initially consulted Coleman—well, I'd like you to consent to apply your lips to my hand for two or three minutes, and to do you know what."

She hesitated, her cheeks invaded by a pink flux; then, touched by Bluewinkle's respectful attitude, she nodded her head.

"Nothing.....absolutely nothing!" said James, when he took his hand away. And, examining the young woman's lips, he added, with a long shudder: "*It was a different creature!*"

VII

A quarter of an hour after Bluewinkle's telephone call, Dr. Coleman arrived in a state of vehement agitation, which he did not take the trouble to hide. He brought the giant David and a plump girl with chubby cheeks, who displayed dimples whenever she smiled deep enough to bury banknotes in.

"By God and General Kitchener" he exclaimed, "you're not playing games with me? The young lady is really alive?"

"She's alive," James replied.

"David!" cried the neurologist. "This is enough to make all the occultists in the Empire sick with joy. But I shan't believe any of it until I've seen it." Addressing James, he added: "Is she weak?"

The young man made an evasive gesture.

"She must be weaker than a fly in November," Coleman affirmed. "I've brought provisions, as you see." He pointed to David, and the chubby girl. "A veritable little barrel of blood!" he muttered. "It seemed to me yesterday that our interesting invalid manifested a little repugnance at drinking from our friend David. Modesty, eh? She'd doubtless prefer a feminine liquid. By Jove! Annie won't miss a few glassfuls!"

"I don't think Evelyn has any need of that," said James, exercising constraint.

Percy darted a suspicious glance at him. "You haven't got in before them?" he exclaimed, in a reproachful tone.

"I would have done had it been necessary, but...."

"Good! Good!" sniggered Coleman. "We'll soon find out." He had been frowning, but as soon as he saw Evelyn, his face cleared. "Good day, my joyous phenomenon, my delicious anomaly!" he said. "Bless your heart!"

He drew nearer, with the air of an angler who fears seeing some extraordinary fish escape, and gently took hold of the young woman's wrist. "Seventy-six!" he exclaimed, after a pause. A pulse as regular and as healthy as my chronometer!"

Her heartbeat and breathing turned out to be no less regular. Percy observed as much with a mixture of satisfaction and anxiety. "Too bad! She's absolutely normal, this morning...and yet, her complexion...where has she stolen this color?" Gradually, his face became sullen. He scowled even more when he had finished his examination. "This is stupid! One would think she's just anyone...."

"At any rate," David remarked, "she seems devilishly weak."

This observation brought a hopeful smile back to Coleman's lips. "That's true," he said, rubbing his hands together "It's high time to restore her strength." He leaned over amiably. "Would you prefer David or Annie?"

A vivid blush covered Evelyn's cheeks. "Neither of them!" she whispered.

"Neither of them?" said Coleman, irritatedly. "You're off your head. You need to get your strength back, I tell you. Annie, my bonny lass, lend us your arm...."

Annie produced a round arm, pink and plump.

"Fresh as a spring, and as healthy as Highland air!" said Percy, in an insinuating tone. "Ah, you'll get your strength back!"

But Evelyn turned away.

"She *can't*, any longer," James put in, having watched the scene without saying anything, in order to confirm his own conviction.

"What! She can't do it any longer!" exclaimed the neurologist, whose face had gone purple. "Are you making fun of Percy Coleman? I can't answer for her life if she persists in this absurd refusal!"

There was a pause. Coleman strode back and forth, his eyes gleaming. James waited, desirous of a conclusive solution, while David and Annie maintained the ruminant attitudes of two young dull-witted Anglo-Saxons.

After walking for a minute, Percy recovered his self-composure. "Madame," he said, with as much softness as he could put into a naturally harsh voice, "What I ask of you is indispensable. Before prescribing remedies and a dietary regime, I need to know where you're up to. You need to understand—and I'm sure that you'll obey!"

A small frisson shook Evelyn's shoulders. Then she turned round, with a slight air of resignation, beckoned to Annie and applied her lips to the pink arm.

"That's a good girl!" said Percy, tenderly.

When Annie withdrew her arm there was a reddish mark there, but neither the examination of that mark nor the examination of Evelyn's mouth revealed the slightest trace of blood. Coleman's disappointment was terrible. He looked alternately at James and Evelyn, as if he were looking at a pair of crooks or fraudsters. He ended up saying, in a choked voice: "There's *nothing left*, then?

She's no more ill than David and no more abnormal than Annie? And for that I've broken promises to the Duchess of Mousehill and Lord Fathead? That's disgusting! It's disastrous. Goodbye!"

He hardly needed to slam the door.

Scarcely had he gone out than the maidservant came to announce Mrs. Grovedale. That excellent creature came in with an impetuosity that belied her voluminous build and threw her arms around Evelyn's neck, while James withdrew discreetly. It was only necessary to see Mrs. Grovedale for five minutes and hear her proffer a few sentences to understand the innocence of her soul. Evelyn returned her hug fervently and kissed her tenderly, but she quickly came to understand that it was impossible to confide in her.

"Darling!" cried Mrs. Grovedale, breathlessly. "Poor little thing! My little flower! My love! You aren't ill?"

"Just a little indisposed. And father?"

"Father's in Liverpool, my little turtle-dove—something to do with nickel. He won't be back for a week."

Words without number sprang forth from the old lady's lips—English words, duller, more insipid and more incoherent than the words of a Botocudo.[136] Evelyn listened to them as one listens to the chirping of a sparrow; they reminded her of the immense and delightful simplicity of childhood, but they confirmed her decision her to keep her redoubtable secret to herself. Pensively, she let the maternal voice run on; she could respond at random, without any fear of being called to account. Evidently, James was right. Everyone to whom she confided her adventure would think her demented. One is always alone in the world, but, for having touched the *beyond*, she was more alone than others! Bluewinkle alone was capable of understanding...and so little!

She sighed, while Mrs. Grovedale made her drink a cup of beef tea[137] brought by the maidservant. Then she fell into a melancholy reverie. What should she do? What was destined to become of her? She was both a maid and a young wife at the same time. A part of her being incontestably belonged to Bluewinkle. The part in question conserved memories that made Evelyn shudder, and which she found revolting. Her marriage seemed to her to be a violence perpetrated on her person during a profound sleep—but, in spite of everything, James was not guilty of any crime! She wanted him to be, though; she was overwhelmed by shame at the thought of this stranger who knew her so intimately and who did not know her at all!

Several times, she was on the point of begging Mrs. Grovedale to *take her home*; every time, she recoiled from the idea of furnishing the excellent creature

---

[136] An Amazonian tribesman.

[137] Rosny inserts a footnote to explain that "beef tea" is a kind of soup, although that is not quite correct as a description of Bovril, which is what Evelyn would probably have been given to drink.

with explanations. She could have lied, but lying disgusted her. She finally allowed her mother to leave without having made a decision; then she had the chambermaid help her dress and lay down on a chaise-longue to wait for James.

When he appeared, Evelyn's anxiety increased to the point of becoming intolerable. He was extremely embarrassed himself. They both felt even further apart than they had before Mrs. Grovedale's visit, but James had not recovered the dread and disquiet inspired in him by *the other*; this one appeared to him to be younger and more charming—*virginal*. And he was subject to a passionate infatuation.

She felt humiliated, galled and full of resentment—all the more so because James' physical appearance was to her liking.

"It's atrocious!" she said, eventually. "It's impossible—utterly impossible—for us to live together. It would drive me mad!"

VIII

James listened sadly. He understood, sensing how shocking the situation must seem to her, and was bizarrely ashamed himself, as if he had treated her dishonestly. All of that only increased his passion for Evelyn. That intelligent young man—but straightforward in the bluff British manner—experienced sentiments more complex than a Parisian trained by refined company and overly subtle reading. It was the fault of circumstances. It could not be helped that he had made love to that charming body; it could not be helped that the body in question had been "rejuvenated". And there was a considerable attraction—an innocent temptation, but both equivocal and invincible—in the fact that Evelyn was both his wife and another woman. One may be Anglo-Saxon to one's fingertips, but one retains the ancient instinct of patriarchy all the same.

After all, he thought, *it's really her that I thought I was marrying! She belongs to me at least as honestly as my fortune!*

He was too much of a gentleman to assert his rights. He replied deferentially. "You're free. I'm incapable of exercising the least constraint upon you. But after all, you don't know what you'll think and feel in future. I respect your first impression, which is noble, but it's not possible to undo what's done; there's no reason to think that the situation won't end up imposing itself upon you. I am, after all, your husband. And of all possible solutions, the most honorable...."

She interrupted him with a feverish gesture. "The marriage is void! Even if I loved you—and I believe that to be impossible now—I could never live with you without a new marriage!"

"Listen," he said. "There are many ways to arrange things and await developments. Since you don't want to live with me, you can return to your parents, or you can live alone in our home. I'll find the necessary pretexts. I'll go travelling. But what I ask you humbly is to see me occasionally, in company with your family, if you wish, or meeting me in public places. I have an absolute need to *try my luck*."

"And why do you want to *try your luck*?" she asked, bitterly.

"Because I love you."

"You didn't love the other, then?"

"I want to be sincere: I loved her. But understand me rightly: I loved her as one loves almost everyone…without knowing her well—and with a certain horror…quite natural, don't you think?"

"Yes," she agreed. "Quite natural. Except that you know me even less well."

"Well, I don't think so. The details of your character certainly escape me, but I sense your pride, your purity, your horror of deceit. That's the core of a moral nature! Finally, ever since human have existed, something has *dictated* that we also love other people for their physical nature…that's much older and much more powerful than we are. It's a law! We ought to accept it."

This argument was too well adapted to the English mentality for Evelyn to find anything to contradict it. She lowered her head, and repeated, meditatively: "We ought to accept it!" She continued: "So be it. I can't refuse to see you occasionally. I'll do it dutifully, on condition that it doesn't last too long."

"You can fix the time yourself."

"Would three months be sufficient?"

"Yes," he sighed. "Three months will be sufficient…."

There was another pause. Bluewinkle had got up to look out of the window. His heart was heavy. More than anything else, the idea that Evelyn would leave their home was unbearable. Eventually, he said: "You're still too weak to move house. This is what I propose. I'll leave on a journey this morning. The cook and the chambermaid are excellent creatures, on whose god conduct you can depend. Your family can come to see you as often as you wish. Thus, everything will be correct and comfortable."

He is, after all, a gentleman, Evelyn thought. And she offered him her hand—but as soon as she touched his fingers, she blushed deeply; the same shame and rancor that she had felt so violently a little while before seethed in her breast.

The little hand was swiftly withdrawn. James left the room, pensive and miserable. He made preparations for his departure, and did not see Evelyn again all day.

They were dismal hours. He was prey to that *inert* chagrin—if one may put it thus—which ravages men of the North so profoundly. At the same time, he suffered mentally. His state of mind would have been abnormal for any man; it was intolerable for a young Anglo-Saxon who had always lived under a regime of moral discipline in which even the unexpected scarcely gave rise to any contradiction. He was frightened by the bizarre aspect that each of his regrets or desires assumed, and the implications that his slightest actions took on. All of that added to his regret at leaving Evelyn, and made him feverish. At times, he had a desire to depart for the ends of the Earth, to bury himself in the white deserts of the South Pole or the sandy deserts of torrid Australia.

At dusk, he called for a cab and went to bid adieu to his companion. He found her lying on the chaise-longue, still somewhat weak, but so fresh and so bright, with her beautiful child-like eyes, that he felt overwhelmed by love.

"Farewell!" he said. "Be happy."

"How can I be?" she said, in a soft voice.

He felt a chill in his heart. He could not help thinking it unjust that this creature, who was so obviously akin to him, did not love him at all, while the other, who had come from the depths of the beyond, had loved him.

When he was in the cab, he leaned out of the window. Evelyn was there, behind those windows!

If she would only move the curtain aside....

He hoped for that; darting a long glance of appeal at the casement—but there was no movement.

The hackney plunged into the mist.

IX

James embarked on a continental tour. Meekly, he visited the museums, monuments, theaters and landscapes that his guide imposed on him. He inscribed the market value of famous paintings, the age of churches, the height of towers, the breadth and depth of rivers, the cost of hiring carriages, the population of cities and the importance of ports in a travel journal.

These efforts scarcely distracted him at all.

He thought about Evelyn Grovedale while the guardians of tombs or temples were giving him precise information about heroes, saints, relics and the apparatus of worship. He also thought about her while the apothecaries of Poquelin were waving around their vast syringes, Phaedra was enticing the son of Theseus or the swan was towing the boat of the mysterious Lohengrin. Even the champagne could not succeed in numbing his pain.

He terminated his voyage in Florence, whence he returned directly to London, just as melancholy and even more amorous then when he had left.

He had given notification of his return and the time of his arrival. A thick yellow fog blanketed the city, through which one could see a small red sun, like a blob of sealing-wax.

Evelyn was sitting beside a fire of Wallsend, a bituminous coal that burned slow and hot, throwing off long flames apt to give rise to daydreams. She was, in fact, daydreaming, full of her young, sad grace, illuminated by her long hair, in which the shades of wheat- and oat-straw were mingled.

She seemed less nervous, but much more resigned. James's presence did not seem to displease her overmuch. In fact, it almost amused her. So they talked, softly and monotonously, of the innocent things that British conversation involves. Evelyn remained distant, though.

As he was about to withdraw, she said: "I mustn't abuse your good will; I'm planning to return to my parents' house this evening."

"That would make things very difficult for me," sighed Bluewinkle. "And what will you tell them? It would be better if I lived on the first floor and you took the ground floor. You wouldn't see me, except for a few minutes every day. I'll use the pretext of business matters and eat in town."

"That would be terribly inconvenient for you."

"Not at all! What would inconvenience us, while we can't reach a definitive resolution, is a separation that would be incomprehensible to your parents and everyone else. I beg you to think about it, at least for a few days."

She knew that he was right. She was fearful in advance of her mother's candid questions, and especially of the discontentment of Mr. Grovedale, who had a keen and almost tragic sense of respectability.

"Since you wish it, and it inconveniences you less than my departure," she said, after gazing pensively into the long Wallsend flames, "I'll stay here for a while longer."

A fortnight went by. As James got up earlier than Evelyn, it seemed natural for him to take the tea, eggs, bacon, toast and orange marmalade of the first meal alone. He lunched and dined out.

To keep up appearances, Evelyn granted him conversations that she found less disagreeable than she had feared. Little by little, they returned to discussions of their incredible adventure. It was, in truth, the cause of their separation, but it was also an exciting secret—something that rendered their destiny unique among all human destinies and made them accomplices of a sort.

Evelyn knew perfectly well that she would be able to tear herself away from that honest overgrown boy, but every time she thought of the possibility of being his wife she blushed like the Comtesse Aimée de Spenssi, of whom Barbey said that "from her forehead, cheeks and neck to the nacreous parting of her golden hair, all was infused and inundated with a vermilion blaze."[138]

Evelyn had now completely recovered her strength. She went to see the good Mrs, Grovedale, young Harriet and young Jack on a regular basis. Her health had never seemed more solid; her complexion could compete with the freshness and glow of a baby's—one of those dazzling babies who roll in the emerald grass of Hyde Park or the verdant squares of the West End. She began to suffer abrupt fits of illness, however, most frequently early in the morning, but sometimes also in broad daylight, in the middle of a walk, while reading or visiting.

---

[138] Rosny provides a reference to *Le Chevalier des Touches*, a novel published in 1864.

One afternoon, Mrs. Grovedale, seeing her very pale and unsteady on her feet, became agitated. "You're not well, you poor little thing!" she exclaimed. "You've gone as pale as that saucer." She spoke emphatically, waving her arms like a windmill. Evelyn confessed to her bouts of illness.

As she listened to her, Mrs. Grovedale gradually passed from dread to hope. "Darling," she said, in an inspired expression, "I think it's time you saw a physician—or perhaps you'd prefer a female doctor?" She was almost smiling—she had a comically tender and mysterious expression. Seeing that Evelyn did not understand, she shrugged her shoulders. "What do you think?" she said. "We'll go right away—we'll go to Mrs. Tinyrump's—it's on the other side of the square. Mrs. Tinyrump knows all about ladies' troubles, and...oh Lord, how I'd like...."

She did not say what it was she would like, and drew Evelyn beneath the oaks and copper beeches of the square to Mrs. Tinyrump's residence.

The lady was at home. She had hair the color of a fox's coat, the muzzle of a hamster and an affable smile. She instantly understood Mrs. Grovedale's telegraphy and interrogated Evelyn, who had gradually become very pale.

An examination was deemed necessary; Mrs. Tinyrump carried it out minutely; then she shook her head with a sibylline expression, and said: "One can't be sure, Mistress—not yet! But I'd swear...." She lowered her voice to offer her prognosis, and Evelyn began trembling from head to toe.

When James came home that evening, he came to make his customary visit. He saw the young woman slumped in an armchair, her face moist with tears and her eyes full of an inexpressible despair. "What's the matter?" he asked, solicitously.

"Oh, it's so horrible!" she moaned. "So horrible...!"

She burst into sobs, her face leaning on her arm, and he stood there, anxious, astonished and curious. As she did not respond to his questions, he decided to wait.

Finally, the sobbing ceased. There was a long silence. Nothing could be heard but the murmur of the fire, the muffled chime of a church clock and the rolling of a cab in the street outside. Bluewinkle contemplated her flexible, semi-recumbent body, the scattered tresses of her hair and her white neck, which was occasionally shaken by a tremor.

"Well?" he resumed, gently.

She raised her head. Her mouth was grimly set, her face haggard, her large eyes full of a feverish flame of terror. Suddenly, she said, in a low and concentrated voice: I'm afraid...I'm going to have a child!"

As he leaned forward, gripped by an obscure joy, she cried out, in a delirium of terror: "Another woman's child...a child of the other world!"

For three months, Evelyn led a frightful existence. She had the continuous sensation of being prey to mysterious and hostile forces; she knew the fears of sad creatures who, in long-gone centuries, had believed themselves to be possessed by demons. More alone now than before, her malaise seemed to have no remedy, and those who loved her the most—even her mother—were totally incapable of understanding her pain. There was no one but James!

For several weeks, his presence was intolerable to the young woman. She did not even offer her hand to him any longer. She listened to him in silence, prostrate; she scarcely said a word to him, on his arrival and departure—and her aversion increased on the days when she had a sharper sense of her own injustice.

After the third month, the affliction and the disgust persisted, but they were mingled with resignation. Evelyn yielded then to the need to confide in someone that is a dominant and irresistible trait of social beings. She explained the nuances of her torture, and tried especially hard to make him understand the struggle that was going on within her, in which she so clearly discerned an extraterrestrial influence.

"Oh!" she cried, one evening in February, when London was deep in snow. "I feel so sharply that I'm condemned, and a slave."

He listened with a patience that never wavered. While watching the silvery flames fall through the gap in the curtains, he ventured to say: "It's your child too, though!"

"No, no!" she said, vehemently. "It's not my child!"

"Think about it," he went on. "Perhaps it wasn't, to begin with, or only slightly—I don't know! But it's more so every day. For many months, has it not been nourished by your blood? Isn't it your strength that sustain it—your life that gives it life? Think of everything that it will have received from you, when it finally sees the light of day!"

These words made an impact. She remained thoughtful for some time, and then objected—but with less disgust and bitterness: "Isn't that worse?"

"Perhaps, if it were an abominable creature—but why should it be abominable?"

"Because the *other* was!"

"No!" the young man replied, forcefully. "She was strange, undoubtedly, but I can assure you—and, by consulting the memories that she has left in your brain, you can convince yourself—that she was a good creature, worthy of being mourned, and even loved!"

"That's true," Evelyn murmured. For a few minutes, she felt almost reassured—but she suddenly went white and her lips quivered. "And what if the child is a vampire?" she cried.

James went pale in his turn—for, as time went by, he felt himself increasingly subject to paternal tenderness. "That's not likely," he replied.

From that evening on, Evelyn no longer exhibited any aversion. She received him amicably; their conversations were sometimes prolonged for more than an hour. Winter passed and spring sent its petty enchantments to weave the leaves of trees and the corollas of flowers; the equinoctial storms roared in the chimneys. Then the date approached that would mark a double deliverance for Evelyn.

It was the end of May. The evenings were interminably prolonged in the London firmament; Big Ben, atop the Houses of Parliament, scarcely sounded the hour twice between the last glimmer of twilight and the silvering of dawn. Evelyn spent one frightful night, when her entire being was racked by tortures...and in the morning, a little boy uttered his first cry. Except, instead of being red and frog-like, like his peers, he was fantastically pale, and his features were already thinned out.

"What a love!" cried Mrs. Grovedale, at all hazard. "And the very image of you, darling!"

That was true, but Evelyn did not see the shape of the face; she was terrorized by that pallor, which was truly *not of this world.*

"A phantom!" she whispered—and she dared not take the new-born in her arms. However, her fatigue was so great, and she felt such a sense of deliverance, that she sank into sleep. It was a very long sleep, scarcely interrupted by a brief awakening during the evening.

The next day, when she woke up, she perceived a young woman who came to pick up the child and offer it her breast. "Mrs. Tinyrump doesn't want you to nurse," said Mrs. Grovedale. "You need to get your strength back."

Evelyn made no response, hypnotized by the spectacle of the little mouth, which had gripped the nurse's dark areola. Tense minutes went by. The thin face was seen to tremble. The mother gradually felt herself overtaken by a subtle and profound joy. Eventually, she said: "Give him to me!"

The nurse held out the new-born. Evelyn never stopped gazing at the tiny lips. She was smiling broadly, her heart palpitating with happiness: the lips were full of milk.

James had been waiting anxiously since the previous ay. When Mrs. Grovedale had shown him the baby, he had been shaken by a great tremor; he recognized that prodigious pallor only too well. Confronted by the frail creature, he felt the dread and horror that had afflicted him before Evelyn's *return.* He spent an anguished day and a miserable night; his heart was full of tenderness for the child, as it was full of love for the young mother. It was the moment of destiny. If the poor mite could only nourish itself on blood, what kind of life would he lead? Undoubtedly, it would be necessary to resign himself to losing Evelyn forever.

He was thinking about these things when the chambermaid came to clear away his breakfast, which he had not touched, and said to him: "The mistress would like to speak to you, sir."

He dared not go down right away; he was like a gambler who hesitates before risking his stake....

When he went into the bedroom and saw the baby in Evelyn's arms, he breathed more freely. The young woman's face was peaceful, her eyes bright and devoid of fever. When James came closer, she whispered: "He's a child like any other!"

With an imperceptible gesture, she pointed to the nurse, who was sitting at the back of the room; for the first time, he felt a frank pressure respond to his handclasp.

Pleasant days followed. In the generous light of June, to the perfume of the pollen and verdure that rose up from the garden through the large bay-windows of he bedroom, the gradually felt the supernatural adventure becoming more remote. Terrestrial life gripped them again and consoled them; the evil past became a dream.

One afternoon, when they had talked for longer than usual, sunset took them by surprise. A furnace lit up in the distance, among the trees; flocks of birds, flying through the gaps between buildings and walls, settled on the branches, among the shoots, and on the crests of roofs, whistling cheerfully.

James had taken Evelyn's hand—and, as she did not withdraw it, he said to her in a low voice: "Why won't you be my wife?"

She did not reply immediately; she was meditative. A simple and naïve energy animated her; she knew that she could live for a long time with the tender, overgrown boy, but she sensed obstacles rising up within her, and she sighed.

"I can't give you an answer yet."

They reached the month of July. Apart from his fantastic pallor, the child remained normal. The nurse, who he had almost frightened at first, became affectionate toward him. He rarely cried. He had large grey eyes, a trifle flat, which already seemed to recognize people and objects. James adored him and Evelyn, in spite of resurgences of dread, was attached to his singular little person. "He's not like other children, though," she sometimes said to Bluewinkle.

He affirmed the contrary and—good Anglo-Saxon as he was—he forced himself to believe it, as a matter of paternal duty, for love of conformity, and perhaps also because he sensed that his chances of being loved by Evelyn depended upon it.

Their intimacy grew firmer. One morning, when he said something affectionate to her, Evelyn replied: "But you know that I don't consider myself to be your wife. What can we do to get married?"

He tried to reason with her. He showed her that they were married in the eyes of men and that, in consequence, their mutual consent was sufficient for the marriage to become real and irreproachable. She would not give in; she had a pathological need for some sanction.

James racked his brain for a solution to this bizarre and irritating problem. First he thought about a divorce, followed by a new marriage, but that solution required lies to which Evelyn would never consent, and which the young man also found repugnant. By dint of reflection, he came up with another idea.

"Wouldn't it be sufficient," he said, "if a priest *confirmed* our marriage?"

"Yes," she replied, "that would be sufficient."

James then went to see the vicar of St. George's, with regard to whom he resigned himself to disguising the truth. By no means a subtle man, the vicar understood that it was a matter of an eccentric woman who was excessively scrupulous. He was an overfed clergyman, inclined to indulgence by the temporal requirements of religion.

"We must not pass judgment on our neighbors lightly," he said. "Scruples are appropriate to elite souls. What you ask is not specifically provided for, but it's not prohibited. The fee, of course....." He coughed and looked at Bluewinkle.

"The fee is not a problem," the young man replied, placidly.

This response having a decisive virtue, Evelyn and Bluewinkle appeared before the vicar of St. George's, who gave them a jolly little sermon on the duties of marriage and concluded: "Evelyn Grovedale has already been given to this man, in this very church, and James Bluewinkle has taken Evelyn Grovedale into his care. They have promised to take one another, for better or worse, and to love one another for richer or poorer. I remind the wife that she must obey her husband, and the man that he must protect his wife; may the Lord's blessing be upon their marriage!"

After which James poured three pounds sterling, seven shillings and sixpence into the right hand of Mr. Blackfoot, pharmacist and sexton.

The beautiful weather tempted them to take a cab all the way to Epping Forest, where Old England retains immense oaks and fabulous elms. The wandered beneath the heavy branches, sat down on the hospitable moss, consumed roast beef, Yorkshire pudding and ale in an old-fashioned tavern—and that evening, turning toward the setting sun, before giant clouds in which fables, legends and chimeras sparkled, she was the virgin who allows her hair to fall upon the shoulders of her beloved, and he the conqueror who carries away the gilded fleece.

There were mornings and there were evenings. The past was behind them, like a dream; James wondered whether all of it, in fact, might have been a dream.

One morning, as he was thinking that, Evelyn still being asleep, he saw the nurse on the back garden steps.[139] She was gently rocking young Walter, whose glaucous eyes were looking at the trees with a terribly meditative expression.

James felt a pang of affection for the little creature, and took him in his arms. He walked across the lawn and the badly gradually began to smile: a smile that astonished James. *It's certain*, the father thought, *that the boy isn't like any other child....*

He felt a quiver of anxiety. The days of yore returned. He saw the first Evelyn and her livid face. He relived the maddening night on which he had discovered the secret. Then he found himself next to the dying woman again; he saw the strange cadaver....

What if Walter hasn't only inherited her pallor?

He had stopped beside a privet. His eyes met the attentive gaze of the baby, and the idea occurred to him of carrying out an experiment. He introduced the tip of his ring-finger into the pink mouth. Immediately, the lips closed. James experienced, albeit feebly, a sensation that he knew well. He waited for two minutes—and when he withdrew the ring-finger, there were delicate pink droplets.

"He's a vampire!" he whispered.

And he trembled with fear.

He was not mistaken. Young Walter Bluewinkle is indeed a vampire and, for a long time, his father has not confessed that to anyone, even to Evelyn. He is, however, an inoffensive vampire. He merely enjoys the ability to suck blood through the pores of the skin, without the skin suffering any damage. He also has an exceedingly precocious intelligence, which is attracted to the mysteries of the beyond.

Percy Coleman, whom James was finally obliged to take into his confidence, when the infant fell ill, would not trade Walter for "a church made of gold". It is said that the neurologist owes a prodigious discovery to the young vampire, which he will soon reveal to Old England and which will turn biological science upside-down even more profoundly than radioactivity revolutionized physics and chemistry.

---

[139] Rosny inserts a footnote here: "A great many houses in London have a small garden in front of the street façade and another garden on the side of the other façade."

Jean Ray: *The Heir of Dracula*

The original series of pulp magazines which eventually became Harry Dickson *began in Germany in January 1907 under the title of* Detektiv Sherlock Holmes und Seine Weltberühmten Abenteuer *[Sherlock Holmes and His Most Famous Cases]. Published by Verlagshaus für Volksliteratur und Kunst, also responsible for* Texas Jack *(a Buffalo Bill imitation, 1906) and, later,* Lord Lister *(a Raffles imitation, 1908),* Detektiv Sherlock Holmes *was likely written by Theo von Blankensee and Kurt Matull (the creator of Lord Lister) and a team of anonymous scribes. It eventually ran for 230 weekly issues, ending in March 1911.*

The fact that the name of Sherlock Holmes was actually used on the cover created some concern about the wrath of Sir Arthur Conan Doyle's lawyers, and with No. 11, the series was retitled Aus den Ge-heimakten des Weltdetektivs *[The Secret Files of the King of Detectives], even though, inside, the main character was still called Sherlock Holmes. Doctor Watson, however, was soon replaced by a younger and more dynamic man named Harry Taxon. In 1908-09, a number of issues were reprinted under the new title* Harry Taxon un sein Meister *[Harry Taxon and his Boss], giving the limelight to the younger assistant. The covers of the first 125 issues were painted by the renowned, Pomerania-born artist Alfred Roloff, a member of the Berlin Academy.*

Sixteen issues of the original German series were then adapted into French, between October 1907 and March 1908, by publisher Fernand Laven of La Nouvelle Populaire *under the title* Les Dossiers Secrets de Sherlock Holmes *[The Secret Files of Sher-lock Holmes]. That title appeared only on the first issue and was immediately changed to* Les Dossiers Secrets du Roi des Détectives *[The Secret Files of the King of Detectives] with No. 2. Like in Germany, however, the protagonist inside was still identified as Sherlock Holmes, but his assistant was Harry Taxon from the start.*

In December 1927, Dutch-Flemish publisher Roman-Boek-en-Kunsthandel (which also published Buffalo Bill, Lord Lister *and* Nick Carter*) launched a Dutch translation of the original pre-WWI German series, this time entitling it* Harry Dickson, de Amerikaansche Sherlock Holmes *[Harry Dickson, the American Sherlock Holmes]. The Dutch series lasted 180 issues, until May 1938. The Dutch publisher decided to sever all connections to Sherlock Holmes. Their first issue was a translation of No. 49 of the German series. The detective was re-christened "Harry Dickson" (this was the first time that the name actually appeared), and his young assistant Harry Taxon became "Tom Wills."*

Some scholars have speculated that that name "Harry Dickson" was a logically derivation from that of "Harry Taxon."

Others have remarked upon the similarity be-tween "Harry Dickson" and "Allan Dickson," the star of Allan Dickson, le Roi des Détectives Australiens *[Allan Dickson, the King of Australian Detectives], a short-lived but popular French pulp series created in 1906-07 by Arnould Galopin, the author of* Le Docteur Oméga, *under the pseudonym of "Max Dearly."*

Finally, others have noted the existence of a 1913 movie serial by René Plaisetty entitled Les Aventures de Harry Dickson, *in which the eponymous detective hero was played by Edmond Van Daële. However, that serial no longer exists. Some have claimed that, to name his hero, Plaisetty combined the names of two then-popular singers, Henry Dickson and Harry Fragson, not forgetting Harry Taxon, already known to the French public.*

Whatever the origins of the name "Harry Dickson," in 1928, Ghent-based Belgian publisher Hippolyte Janssens decided to translate the Dutch series into French, for publication in both French-speaking Belgium and France.

Janssens' new French-language edition was also entitled Harry Dickson, le Sherlock Holmes Américain *[Harry Dickson, the American Sherlock Holmes]. It began in January 1929 and lasted 178 issues, until April 1938.*

We do not know the identity of the first writers who were hired by Janssens to translate the Dutch magazines into French, who penned the first 19 issues and thus set the style for the rest of the series. (Some have speculated that Gustave Le Rouge might have been amongst them.) We do know, however, that a contract dated 1929 was signed between Jenssens and Belgian writer Raymond De Kremer, who also lived in Ghent, hiring him to translate subsequent issues of the Dutch series into French, starting with No. 20.

Raymond De Kremer (1887-1964), better known today as Jean Ray, was already a prolific writer and journalist who had authored numerous stories for young readers, as well as comic strips, detective and horror stories, in Flemish-language magazines under the nom-de-plume of John Flanders. His tales of the fantastique, written in French under the pseudonym of Jean Ray, have since become horror classics. They include the novels Malpertuis *(1943) and* La Cité de l'Indicible Peur *[The City of Unspeakable Fear] (1943), as well as short story collections such as* Les Contes du Whisky *[Whiskey Tales] (1925),* Les Cercles de l'Epouvante *[The Circles of Terror] (1943) and* Les Derniers Contes de Canterbury *[The Last Tales of Canterbury] (1944).*

Scholar Hervé Louinet claims that Ray edited, translated and/or adapted 148 issues of the French Harry Dickson *series, from No. 65 onward using mostly the titles and the covers by Roloff as starting points for very loose adaptations of the originals. It is no exaggeration to say that Roloff's covers, which had been purchased in bulk by the Dutch from the German publisher, greatly contributed to the success of the series. The very month after Janssens discontinued using them, the French* Harry Dickson *was cancelled.*

The adventures of Harry Dickson *have delighted several generations of French readers. Because most of them were penned by an acknowledged master of the fantastique, they are more fantasy-oriented than the traditional* Sherlock Holmes *canon. The best and most fondly remembered* Harry Dickson *tales are not those where the great detective fights a spy ring or a blackmailer in true Holmesian fashion, but the ones which pit him against some monstrous fallen angel, a mad scientist or some larger-than-life villain, in the true traditions of the pulps. What the intellect lost in logic and deduction, the readers gained in pure entertainment and fantasy.*

J.-M.L.

1. The Man Who Begged to Die

The appalling event was scheduled to occur in the small and charming Hanoverian village of Hildesheim. A scaffold was to be erected on the tiny square in front of the municipal prison and, there, the head of the terrible Ebenezer Grump, the so-called "Red-Eyed Vampire" who had terrorized Germany and a large part of Europe for over two years, would at last fall. These nightmarish events are still whispered about today.

During those two years, the human monster had wandered the working-class neighborhoods of Berlin, Hanover and Hamburg, bloodily taking the lives of more than 60 women and children.

Occasionally, he would take a small "vacation," traveling further afield to Holland and England, leaving hideous traces of his passage behind. The vile creature killed for the sheer pleasure of watching his victims' blood flow; his pleasure came from seeing their suffering as they died.

The Berlin Criminal Brigade had mobilized its top operatives in vain; equally in vain it had solicited the assistance of the police forces of Munich, Weimar and Hamburg. All of them had come up empty-handed as the monster continued his bloody exploits, seemingly unconcerned by the all the forces of order that were hunting him.

But then, he made a mistake that proved to be his undoing: he went to London and killed a young woman and her fiancé in Epping Forest, and then, cut the throat of a baby in broad daylight on the football pitch of Peckham Park, while mortally wounding the child's nanny. These ignoble exploits attracted the attention of the famous detective, Harry Dickson. Just as the hideous fiend was mutilating the body of a barmaid in Commercial Road, Dickson fell on him and broke his jaw with a shot from his revolver.

Even so, the beast was able to escape under the cover of darkness. A feverish pursuit followed through the south of England and across the sea, when the Vampire was able to stowaway on a German cargo ship. It continued through the worst sectors of Hamburg, until finishing in Hildesheim, when Dickson was able, at last, to bring down the horrible Ebenezer Grump.

During his trial, the monster freely admitted to the crimes committed in London. As to the rest, he insisted that the German police had but to solve them, just as the British police had done.

With braggadocio, he stated that he was honored to have been captured by the great Harry Dickson, and not by a "nobody" from the Criminal Brigade. When all was said and done, he was sentenced to having his head chopped off.

The crowd was incensed when, after the trial, a group of medical scientists and anthropologists requested that mercy be shown to Grump, and that instead, he be locked away in an insane asylum for the rest of his natural life.

The powers-that-be were terrified of the public's reaction if such a thing were to occur, so the doctors' request was promptly denied, and Grump's miserable life was turned over to the executioner.

Capital punishment was rare in Germany. The executioner in Saxony still used an axe to carry out his grim task; but in Prussia, the guillotine was used to take the heads of the condemned.

An ancient death-machine that dated back to the days of Napoleon was pulled out of the cellar of a museum in Hanover, cleaned up and serviced, then sent along to the small, picturesque town.

Calm and apparently resigned, Grump awaited the dawn that would see the end of his days in the single cell of the municipal prison, requesting special meals, cigarettes and the newspapers, all of which he claimed were his due as a condemned man.

Grump will be executed in three days time. Please come at once.

Ziegenmeyer
Prison Warden, Hildesheim

Harry Dickson crumpled the telegram with an air of discontent. He was quite busy in London; his assistant, Tom Wills, was still suffering the aftereffects of his terrible adventure in the Newcastle mines and was unable to provide him all the help he required.[140]

However, the suffering face of the young man was what pushed him to accept the Warden's request.

"A short voyage to the Continent will do you some good, my boy," said Dickson, a bit brusquely.

Tom looked at him with gratitude.

"I don't deny that I would enjoy it, but I don't like stopping work. And the villains in London have made much of that recently."

"I doubt we'll find ourselves unemployed where we're going."

Tom picked up the crumpled telegram.

"Is it just an invitation?"

---

[140] This refers to the events of No. 73, *Le Monstre Blanc* (The White Beast).

"I don't think he'd have us travel so far simply for the unique pleasure of watching Grump's head fall."

"Of course not... Do you think there's something more to this 'Red-Eyed Vampire' affair? If I was Harry Dickson, I'd go," the young man said with a mischievous grin.

"And if I was Tom Wills, I'd already be packing my bags so I could go with my Guv," replied Dickson in the same tone.

The detective avoided discussing the case during the journey, but Wills thought that his employer seemed curiously pensive.

When they arrived in Hamburg, and were in Dickson's favorite café, sitting with enormous steins of beer, while the detective puffed on a new Bavarian pipe, his face relaxed a bit and Tom felt brave enough to question him.

"Guv, you seem to be bothered by something."

Dickson looked at him, intrigued.

"What makes you say that, my boy?"

"This morning, while you were dressing, I heard you mutter to yourself twice: 'It's a terrible mistake.' "

"And what did you think I meant by that?"

"Well, from the tone in which you said it, I'd say the fault wasn't yours."

Dickson put out his hand and pinched the boy's ear.

"That's not bad at all. Indeed, they're going to make a serious mistake in cutting off that monster Grump's head."

"I don't understand. Do you want him locked up in the insane asylum?" asked Tom, astonished and indignant.

"Not at all; I'm as eager as anyone to see him die on the gallows, but I would have liked them to wait a little."

"For how many more days?"

"Days? Did I say days? I wasn't that specific; perhaps months, a year, even more... I'm not sure."

"But why?" Tom could not believe what he was hearing.

"Because I have the feeling that the mystery surrounding this business hasn't yet been solved."

"But surely, the death of that monster will end it all."

"It should, but it won't. I surprised Grump just after he'd committed his final crime. He escaped using incredible wiles; in fact, my considered opinion is that he should have escaped me for good. During the chase, he showed a kind of genius, until we got to Hamburg. Once we were here, he turned into a total imbecile and it was easy to grab him in Hildesheim. You could almost say that the thug had suddenly lost all his intelligence as soon as he set foot in Germany."

"And what do you make of that, Guv?"

"That someone with a superior mind was giving Grump instructions in England and that, by returning to Germany, he disobeyed this 'someone,' who withdrew his aid and delivered him into our hands."

"Is there anything in what Grump said that led you to believe that, Guv?"

"Not Grump, no, although I thought him shrewd before I met him. But once I did, he struck me as a brute, resigned to whatever happened to him, even going to the gallows. I couldn't say anything openly, because the Criminal Brigade sees the world only in black and white. However, I discreetly tried to make them understand that they would do well to hold off on the execution."

"Why? What are you hoping for?"

"That's a good question, Tom. What do I hope will happen? All I can say is that I've just got a kind of vague feeling about it. Could someone really have been directing Grump to commit his crimes? There certainly wasn't any proof of that, and Grump himself vehemently denied having ever had any accomplices.

"That's probably why I felt a bit irritated when I received the Warden's telegram—and was almost tempted to ignore it.

"Now, my boy, you'll just have to accept that I don't know anything else and that any further questions are useless.

"Look, there's a band getting ready to play! I see the music for a piece by Wagner on the piano, let's just enjoy it."

It wasn't until late afternoon of the following day that the two detectives arrived in Hildesheim. The sun's last rays gave a golden glow to the beautiful facades on the Brunnen-Platz; the townswomen, just as they had always done, were filling enormous, blue ewers with water from the fountain, while their men smoked their huge pipes on the terraces of the cafés and beer halls, surrounded by the haze of smoke and the smell of beer and wine.

"You could almost believe yourself in a different world," said Tom with a contented sigh. "Everything here is so calm and serene that I can't help wonder if we didn't take a wrong turn and wind up in a place where no one is set to lose his head at dawn tomorrow."

Suddenly, from inside one of the inns, a voice called to them:

"Can it be? Is it really Herr Dickson himself and young Herr Wills who always follows him like his shadow?"

A small, round man with the rosy, smiling face of a cherub waddled towards them and held out his hands in greeting.

"Why, if it isn't the good Doctor Poppelreiter!" responded Dickson, taking the two outstretched hands warmly in his own. "Just seeing you here tells me that the beer in Hildesheim must be amongst the best in Germany!"

"And in Austria and all the other countries of the world," finished the little man. "Come and have a drink with me. I imagine such high-class gentlemen are drinking wine? Kellner! Bring us two bottles of Hocheimer and some ice!"

"Have you come to see Grump die?" asked Poppelreiter. "It's thanks to you, Herr Dickson, that we'll be finished with that monster for good. And, it's also thanks to you that the glory of his capture rubbed off on the modest Chief of Police of our little town: your friend and servant, Doctor Poppelreiter!"

Dickson said nothing to disagree with his friend and patiently listened as he went over all the minute details of the infamous trial.

Tom was only half listening, instead enjoying the charming sight of evening casting its blue shadow over the Brunnen-Platz.

"Oh! What a splendid old house," he suddenly exclaimed, pointing to a house that looked like a lacework made of stone.

Poppelreiter looked to where he was pointing and frowned slightly.

"Frankly, Herr Wills," he said quietly, "the people around here would prefer it to be smashed to pieces, rather than be admired by visitors."

"That would be a crime!" exclaimed the young man in surprise.

"From your point of view, perhaps that seems the case, but not from that of my fellow citizens. We call it the 'Gespenster-Haus,' the haunted house. And you'll notice that this part of the Platz is deserted at night. None of the cafés do any business at all as soon as it starts to get dark and it's all because of that monstrosity of a house."

"Why does everyone think badly of it?"

"To be honest, it's all very mysterious. It's belonged to the same, ancient Transylvanian family for 200 years. They take care of the necessary repairs and they've even furnished it comfortably. But no one has lived in it all that time! Once a week, the notary who is paid to look after it comes with two servants who take care of cleaning it, and they rush off as soon as they're done. Everyone says that the owner, Count Dragomin, leaves it ready for the ghosts to use.

"They've never been interested in renting it out or selling it. As magistrate, I dislike them doing something that so upsets the people here."

Harry Dickson looked at his timepiece and stood up.

"My dear Poppelreiter, I hope that you'll excuse us, but we're going to take a look around town before paying a courtesy call on Warden Ziegenmeyer."

"Of course! I'll see you tomorrow, although it will be under far less pleasant circumstances."

Fifteen minutes later, the detective and his assistant were being announced to the Director of the Municipal Prison.

For a bureaucrat who was only used to dealing with minor criminals, the responsibility of watching over the Red-Eyed Vampire and getting him safely to the executioner's scaffold had been a major worry.

That was Tom Wills' first impression as they were approached by a man with a gray complexion, his features drawn and large dark circles under his eyes. Clearly, this was the product of many a sleepless night.

"Good evening, Warden," said Dickson, cutting short a pompous speech of welcome. "I don't suppose it's to either praise me, nor simply a desire for me to witness an execution, that you've called me to the continent."

"It is certainly not, Herr Dickson!"

Herr Ziegenmeyer hesitated several seconds, then went to the door, looked out to be sure no one was listening, and, with a mysterious air, returned towards his visitors.

"Herr Dickson," he asked, "do you believe that Grump is insane?"

"Not for a second."

The Warden nodded his head in agreement.

"That's what I think as well. I've never met anyone as clear-headed as that vile, brutish creature. But for the last few days, he's been acting in the most incomprehensible, bizarre fashion and I no longer know what to think.

"My duty should have been to alert my superiors. But I was afraid I'd be rebuffed and that they'd dismiss my concerns as foolishness. In my business, more than in most others, being ridiculed means the end of you."

Nodding his head, the detective made it clear that he understood completely.

"Well, Herr Dickson, for the last few days, Ebenezer Grump has been afraid!"

"He has a good reason," interrupted Tom. "He's about to die."

"But not at all! It's just the opposite! He's afraid that he won't be sent to the guillotine!"

"Perhaps, it's just that he prefers a rapid death, rather than a slow, agonizing one inside a lunatic asylum," suggested Tom.

"That's where you're wrong, Herr Wills, because Grump, who has a good life here, and who seems to have adapted quite well to the special conditions accorded those condemned to death, begs that his execution not be put off any longer.

"His guards have heard him muttering over and over, 'It would be horrible! I must be dead before he gets here!' "

"Have you asked him about it?" Dickson wanted to know.

"Of course, but all he does shake his head and look terrified. The night before I sent you that telegram, he asked to see me.

"I've never seen a man look more overwhelmed by fear. He said, 'I want someone to bring me wild garlic flowers right away!'

"I shrugged my shoulders and answered, 'That's just a whim, Grump, and I have no idea where we'd find such a thing.'

"He responded excitedly, 'They're in the woods outside of town! I'm begging you, Warden; I need them before the night is out! If I don't get them, it will be horrible! Despite what I've done, I don't deserve this!'

"I was going to refuse his demand, when suddenly he whispered, 'Get Dickson to come! I have something to tell him... It's not a lot, but it would be worth his while. For the love of God, please get me those garlic flowers!' "

Dickson's expression had become so somber and worried that the warden suddenly stopped his recitation with an astonished air.

363

"I hope you found him those garlic flowers," said the detective, almost aggressively.

"Well, after that, I could hardly refuse..."

"Thank God," said Dickson.

"Good lord! You seem to understand something about this madness, Herr Dickson."

"Madness? Not in the least. I could even say that this shines a new light on everything.

"Herr Ziegenmeyer, I would bet that something else strange, incomprehensible even, happened during the night following Grump's demand."

The Warden leapt from his chair, his mouth open, eyes round, the perfect picture of astonishment.

"How did you know that, Herr Dickson? I insisted that my employees remain completely silent, and they are all extremely loyal and responsible."

"No one told me, but everything you've said made me believe it. Someone undoubtedly tried to enter the condemned man's cell!"

"That's it! And in the most astonishing way! In the middle of the night, the guard who was sleeping in the prisoner's cell was woken up by an odd noise.

"To his horror, he saw a giant shadow on the wall. He turned towards the window and saw an indistinct form blocking the moonlight.

"He jumped up, but immediately saw the most hideous face pressing itself against the iron bars; he threw himself back, terrified. Just then, Grump woke up. He also saw the monstrous apparition. That's when the guard saw him grab the garlic flowers and rush towards the window.

"The thing that was there had barely seen the flowers before it began to scream so horribly that the entire prison was woken up. Then, it disappeared.

"Alerted, I organized an immediate search. The window of Grump's cell is 10 meters above the ground. There was no trace of a ladder or rope, but near the road, we found some drops of blood.

"What were we to make of it all? When we asked him, Grump would only say, 'He came! My God! I hope they take my head quickly!' "

"Get me a good lantern and a ladder," ordered Dickson.

Once in the courtyard, the detective began to carefully examine the walls by the light of the lantern.

"Two daggers were enough," he finally muttered, "but still, he must have been good climber."

"What are you saying, Herr Dickson?" asked the Warden.

"Just that with the help of two strong daggers pushed into the mortar of the walls, the night creature was able to scale the outer wall, then this one as well. It was an extraordinary feat!"

"But, tell me..." began the Warden.

"There's nothing else I can tell you, Warden. Take me to see Grump."

The murderer was stretched out on his cot, eyes wide open, staring at the weak lamp that barely lit his cell. He immediately recognized Dickson, and his ugly face with its broken chin, twisted into a semblance of a smile.

"They're chopping off my noggin' tomorrow, Herr Dickson," he said. "I'm really glad that you're here! And that's no lie!"

"Why is that, Grump?"

The man made an odd grimace.

"Tomorrow, at the foot of the gallows, when I'm certain I'm about to die, I'll tell you everything."

"Why not tell me now?"

"No! There's still tonight to get through, and a lot of things can happen during a whole night! On my eternal soul, I swear to you, Herr Dickson, I'll tell you everything I've got to say, but on the condition that my death is certain."

"This man is insane," muttered the Warden.

"No!" replied Dickson firmly. "*He is completely sane!*"

The detective remained silent, deep in thought, for several minutes before saying,

"Give me some of your garlic flowers, Grump."

The condemned prisoner laughed joyfully.

"At last, you understand! Here they are, Herr Dickson... But, now you have to promise me something..."

"What's that?"

"*Promise me that I will be guillotined tomorrow!*"

Dickson considered this request in silence.

"I promise," he finally said, slowly.

"God bless you, Herr Dickson," whispered Grump as Dickson walked away.

"What do you think of all that?" stammered the Warden once they were back in his office. "It's not at all... regular!"

"Well put, Warden. I'm glad you called me, and I think that your superiors will be too, later on. If I succeed—and I have to succeed—there will be a promotion in all this for you, sir, and a big one!"

"If you say so, Herr Dickson," responded the Warden, his face lighting up. "If you say so, I'll just have to believe you..."

II. The Haunted House

Tom went to bed around 10 p.m., but barely an hour later, he felt a hand vigorously shaking him awake.

"Sorry, my boy," his employer said, "but that will have to be enough for tonight. We've got work to do."

"We're going out?" asked the young man, seeing that the detective was wearing his hat and coat and was rooting around in his suitcase, from which the clanking of metal could be heard.

"A pliers, skeleton keys and lock picks," murmured Dickson as he took stock of what he needed.

"Guns?"

"No, but don't forget Grump's flowers."

"I know you've got your reasons, Guv, but this seems pretty peculiar to me," said Tom, as he hurriedly got dressed.

"I do, Tom, and I'll tell you what they are in due time. Oh! Take the rope ladder and climbing hooks."

"You sure that's all you want?" asked Tom a bit sarcastically.

"No! I'm going to need your eyes to see in the dark!"

All was silent in the small hotel, and Dickson and his assistant left without being disturbed, soon finding themselves in the street just as the last cafés were turning out their lights.

"Let's hide in the shadows for a minute, Tom," said the detective. "Look! There's Doctor Poppelreiter heading home full of beer. I don't want to be seen by anyone, even him."

When the streets were empty of any other sign of life, Dickson and Tom again set off in the dark, heading north. Hildesheim wasn't particularly large, and soon the two smelled the fresh odor of the countryside.

Fifteen minutes later, they passed the last outlying houses and found themselves on a wide, paved road heading off towards the horizon.

"Where are we going in such a hurry?" wondered Tom.

"Nowhere!" answered Dickson with a small laugh.

"What an answer!" said Tom, annoyed.

"Actually, we're simply following the line of telegraph poles."

The road entered a small wood and Dickson stopped next to a pole that grouped together several main lines of wires.

"Reinforced concrete," he muttered. "I thought that might be the case. Throw the rope ladder, Tom, and try to get it as high as possible."

Although Tom had practiced the maneuver frequently, it still took him several tries to succeed. At last, the hooks grabbed onto a cross bar and held the ladder firmly.

"Now what, Guv?"

"Take the pliers, Tom, climb up and cut all the wires."

"Why…"

"First, do what I tell you; we don't have a lot of time. I'll explain once you're back on the ground."

With no further hesitation, Tom climbed to the top of the tower, reached the circuits and started cutting through the copper wires. It wasn't long before the last one fell to the ground at Dickson's feet.

"Can I know why?" Tom asked as soon as he had climbed back down and began to carefully roll up the precious ladder. "I'd say Hildesheim is pretty much cut off from the rest of the world."

"Good guess, my boy! Harry Dickson can now make good on his promises!"

"Which ones, Guv?"

"The one I made to Grump that he'll be guillotined tomorrow morning. As long as it was possible to telephone or telegraph to Hildesheim, that wasn't a certainty."

"Would they have pardoned him at the last minute?"

"Possibly, but the bigger risk was that the execution would have been postponed."

"But only yesterday, you told me that this execution was a mistake!"

"True. But now that Grump wants to talk, that's no longer the case. And, Grump will only do so if he's sure he's going to die."

Tom would have liked to know more, but Dickson seemed to be in a hurry to return to town.

"We've got another job waiting for us, Tom, and it's not as easy as cutting a few wires. We're going to make an unusual visit."

"I thought that might be the case, given that you had me bring along our burglary tools!"

"And don't forget about our garlic flowers!"

"Can I at least know where we're going?"

"Of course you can, my boy! We're going to enter the building that so fascinated you this afternoon; the *Gespenster-Haus*—the haunted house!"

"That's the cat's meow, Guv! Do you think we'll trip over any real ghosts? That would be hilarious."

But Dickson wasn't laughing; in fact, he looked extremely serious.

"It's not totally out of the question, Tom. I don't know if it's truly a ghost, but right now, I don't know what to call the creature that's been wandering in the night, let alone how to fight it."

"Does the house have something to do with the Grump business?"

"I'm sure of it, Tom. Unfortunately, I've only known it for a few hours; otherwise, this whole vampire business would have finished in a much greater victory for us. It was only after we arrived in Germany that I asked myself why, after escaping from England, Grump came to Hildesheim, instead of going to ground in a big city like Hamburg where he'd landed?

"While I was chasing him, I assumed he was a man who was running away. But that wasn't it at all! He had a goal and that was Hildesheim!"

"But there are lots of other houses in this town besides the haunted house!"

"Yes, but that's the only one where you need garlic flowers to get inside!"

Tom made a gesture of frustration.

"I'll do what I always do, Guv," he sighed, "follow your orders without understanding a thing!"

"My poor boy, I have to tell you that, right now, I don't understand a thing myself! Are you worried about stumbling along the uncertain path that's unfolding in front of us?"

"I've always come through all right in the end when I've done what you asked of me, even when I haven't understood," Tom answered, contritely.

"Don't worry, Tom," Dickson said, warmly. "All you have to know is that you're taking part in a great exploit of justice and humanity!"

They had finally re-entered the town. The church bells began to toll the hour.

"Midnight!" said Tom with a shiver. "The witching hour, the most sinister time of night!"

Harry Dickson made no response, as he was himself moved by the deep sound of the bells high above, slowly ringing out 12 times.

The streets were dark and deserted, poorly lit by weak electric bulbs that had been set into 100-year-old streetlamps.

A kestrel flew from the top of a tower, shrieking as it gave chase to some small prey, while a dog howled mournfully in a garden. A lonely lamp flickered in the middle of the Brunnen-Platz, looking like a single star in a stormy sky. It did nothing to chase the shadows, and only served to make the gables of the old buildings seem gloomier and the windows look more like dead, staring eyes.

"These houses all look like something out of a nightmare," said Tom. "That one looks like it's going to jump us!"

"That's the one that we're looking for, Tom," answered his boss, softly.

"The haunted house," said Tom in a whisper. "It looked just like a charming dollhouse this afternoon... But it's sure ugly right now. I think I'd rather we visited it politely in broad daylight."

Harry Dickson was no longer listening; he had already climbed over the high wall and was standing in front of the heavy oak door. One by one, he tried his skeleton keys in the lock, then sighed with discouragement.

"I never expected so much trouble from a lock this old," he muttered, "unless... Ah ha! I should have thought of that; it's bolted. But they're so close to the lock that I didn't notice right away."

"Our ghosts are pretty careful," said Tom.

The detective looked carefully at the high windows.

"The ladder, my boy!" he ordered.

"Do you see a way of climbing this miserable façade, Guv? And what about the shutters? They look like they're made out of wood that's hard as iron."

"What about that kind of porthole over on the side? The hooks of our ladder should go into the frame like a hot knife into butter."

The detective was right, and, after a few failed attempts, the ladder at last held and was ready to be climbed.

"Should I break the glass?" asked the young assistant as he prepared to climb upwards.

"If there's no other way, then yes."

Tom climbed as nimbly as a monkey, and, once he reached the porthole, he gave a cry of satisfaction.

"It's not a fixed pane of glass, Guv, only a small window. It opens in on a hinge!"

Dickson watched as his assistant easily slipped inside the ill-famed building, then quickly followed behind.

As he pulled the ladder up through the window, he saw that Tom was on the spacious landing, already listening for any noises in the shadows.

"Did you hear something?" asked the detective.

"No, not really. But this silence seems somehow more frightening than any noise."

Dickson had to agree that the young man was right. There was something unidentifiable, hostile and even terrifying that seemed to linger in the heavy atmosphere of the abandoned house.

"Let's start in the bedrooms," he said, shaking off his dark thoughts.

There were seven of them, all empty and echoing in dusty silence.

Taking all their precautions, the descended the large staircase with its beautifully carved banister until they reached the ground floor.

The style changed drastically. The weak light of their pocket torches enabled the detectives to see expensive-looking antiques standing in the shadows.

"Nothing particularly ghostly here," said Tom, with a tinge of disappointment in his voice.

Dickson was standing immobile in the middle of the room, his gaze fixed on a shadow.

"Tom!"

"Yes, Guv?" the young man answered, startled that the senior detective should raise his voice so.

"There are candles in the candelabras. Light them all; I need to get a better look."

"But aren't you afraid someone will see us?"

Harry Dickson laughed so loudly that it echoed throughout the whole house.

"The filthy creature who lives here has been seeing and hearing us since we arrived, but trembles in fear at the thought of coming anywhere near us," he said, as loudly as he could.

Tom struck a match and set out to obey the detective's orders. Soon, everything in the room began to emerge from the shadows.

It was a salon decorated in an old-fashioned, severe style. The stagnant, heavy atmosphere was heightened by the smell of the heavy, dusty draperies, wood kept polished by the mysterious cleaners and a vague odor of rats and mice rotting behind the wainscoting.

Dickson was pacing nervously around the spacious room, his earlier air of calm seeming to have deserted him.

Then, he again spoke with the same loud bravado he had used earlier, once again surprising his young assistant.

"Did you think we'd find someone here, Tom? Well, it's true that we're not alone. But knowing that and finding him are two different things. And yet, right this minute, he's somewhere nearby, listening to us, perhaps even mocking us the same way he's mocked all the police in Europe and expecting to continue to do so for a long time to come."

Tom couldn't believe what he was hearing.

His boss was talking like a crazy man. He wondered if the haunted house had taken a new victim: the great detective!

Suddenly, the young man recoiled in fear. He had just fixed his eyes on the chimney, where one of the candles had brusquely gone out, without leaving the least trace of smoke, as if an invisible hand had snuffed it between its fingers. Another candle immediately followed, and shadows flickered on the walls.

Dickson seemed not to notice, however, and continued to speak:

"And yet, I, Harry Dickson, have promised to capture this unknown monster and I'm willing to use methods that the Criminal Brigade wouldn't approve or respect."

A third candle went out.

The detective spoke like a man who had lost his mind, making large windmill circles with his arms, movements that were repeated and amplified on the shadowy walls.

A fourth candle was snuffed out and only two small flames remained to illuminate the vast salon.

Tom found himself unable to stand it any longer and an unspeakable terror began to take hold of him.

"Guv," he whimpered, "let's get out of here. This is beyond us and you're not well…"

Dickson met his eyes. The detective may have been moving around the room like a man possessed, but his gaze remained clear and Tom thought he even saw a twinkle of humor in the piercing eyes. He also realized that the older man had a plan, and his confidence came flooding back to him.

His boss clearly had something in mind. Too bad if the candles were snuffed out so mysteriously, it was all part of Dickson's game!

When the fifth candle went out, Tom, despite his newfound confidence, couldn't keep himself from trembling. The room was filled with the shadows created by the single, small, flickering flame of the remaining candle. It was impossible to see a thing in the darkness of the furthest corners, and the young assistant detective felt as if a malevolent presence was very close by. He looked towards Dickson and waited.

The great man was totally still, as if he was carved from a block of marble. But his eyes burned brightly.

"Come over to me and don't leave my side," whispered Dickson so softly that Tom was barely able to hear him.

Just then, the last light went out, and opaque shadows took over the haunted house's salon.

"Don't move an inch, no matter what happens," murmured the detective into his assistant's ear. Tom gripped his arm fiercely in response.

Several interminable minutes passed in absolute silence, and then Tom smelled a vague odor nearby that reminded him of an old oil lantern.

"Don't move, Tom!"

He had needed the warning to keep him from recoiling in panic.

Two points of light surged towards them in the dark. At first, the two detectives saw only the lights, but soon the totality of the abomination could be made out: It was two fiery eyes that fixed them with a terrifying intensity.

"The Red-Eyed Vampire!" stammered Tom, feeling as if he was going to faint.

Dickson moved slightly next to the younger man, who noticed that the oil smell had intensified.

A bit of time passed and the eyes remained immobile, their gaze fixed and frightening. Tom thought he heard his boss make a disdainful sniff. Then, Dickson spoke,

"Yet, I'll get you, Vampire. How? Because I have methods that the police don't! Because I, Harry Dickson, believe you exist, phantom! And, because I am armed with *wild garlic flowers*!"

Brusquely, the eyes disappeared and Tom had the impression that he heard a distant sigh.

"I'll force you to leave your grave and I'll chop off your head!" yelled Dickson at the top of his lungs.

Tom couldn't believe his ears; Dickson was raving.

But, no... What was that sound? A cry of rage and terror rang out, then howls and frantic sobs that turned into a mournful moan that disappeared into the distance.

Harry Dickson sighed with relief.

"You can light the candles now, Tom," he said in a calm voice. "Let's light our pipes as well, to help us get rid of the horrible smell of garlic."

"Why did you bring those stinking flowers?" asked Tom as he struck a match.

"I'll explain it to you one of these days when we're a bit more relaxed, my friend. It's childishly simple. Just know for now that the odor that you smell proved two things to me."

"Will you tell me?"

"Of course! First, the Vampire is a real, flesh and blood man, and second, he doesn't live in the haunted house, but enters and leaves by a passage that it won't take me long to discover.

"The fiery eyes were infantile. It's insulting to use something like that on us!

"No, my dear boy, any real air of terror that this house had is gone; in fact, it was barely even booby trapped. Let's get out of here. It's almost dawn and Grump is ready to die."

"But what about the bolts that are thrown from inside?" asked Tom.

Dickson started to laugh.

"I already know how that was done; by using a simple electrical wire!"

Tom was attached to his ghost and begged his boss to look around the house one last time.

"If you want, my boy," agreed the detective. "Meanwhile, I'll finish my pipe. But I've already found everything there is to find here."

"But you barely looked at all!"

"And that was enough. Go on. You can have ten minutes."

At the end of that time, Tom returned repentant and downcast. The two men rapidly returned to their hotel.

"I told you, my boy. I'd wager you came up empty handed during those ten minutes."

Tom moaned.

"You're right. Less than empty, except for an old top hat thrown onto a chair."

"Bah!" said Dickson.

Later on, the detective would admit that in treating Tom's discovery with such disdain, he had made an irreparable mistake.

III. A Strange Execution

It was a dull, grey dawn...

The small town awoke from its odd nighttime dreams with difficulty. A man was set to die at a specific hour, surrounded by other men who would not offer him the least bit of aid, other than to make sure that the blade sliced through his neck cleanly. Blood would flow in Hildesheim, a place where nothing but beer and wine had flowed for as long as anyone could remember.

Herr Ziegenmeyer, the Warden, had not slept a wink during the entire night. This was to be the first execution that he had ever seen, and he would surely find it difficult. That is, unless the condemned was pardoned at the last minute; something that had been known to happen. But, as the Executioner had not yet arrived, nothing could even begin.

Meanwhile, Herr Ziegenmeyer and his assistant, Herr Zipfel, calmed their nerves with a small glass of their favorite cordial.

At 4:20 a.m., the top of the flag staff on the prison tower was just visible in the milky light.

What if the Executioner didn't come? The two bureaucrats almost hoped that this would be the case.

They listened intently, then sighed as the sound of a motor suddenly interrupted the morning's silence. It approached, then stopped in front of the gate. The entrance bell was pulled, and a prison guard rushed to let a small truck into the courtyard.

A thin man with a bilious complexion stepped out from behind the wheel. With a bad humored grunt, he approached the two bureaucrats and handed them a thick wad of papers, which Herr Ziegenmeyer took with a trembling hand.

All seemed to be in order; the official papers had arrived.

The bilious man was Herr Otto Liebe, the Executioner of Hanover; the condemned man, Ebenezer Grump, was to be delivered into his hands. Liebe was not in a good mood. He waited impatiently while the Warden read through the official documents, then spoke in a voice that sounded like chalk scraping a blackboard:

"I'm on my own. My two assistants let me down because they got themselves drunk! They're not going to get a pfennig for this execution. So, Warden, you need to get me two carpenters right away so I can get my machine ready."

"But that isn't my responsibility!" cried Ziegenmeyer.

Otto Liebe wasn't going to allow something like that to dissuade him.

"Re-read the notice from the Criminal Bureau; the Warden is expected to provide me with any assistance I require, so I'm within my rights to ask you to find me someone to get my machine ready."

The Warden remembered that two of his jailors were carpenters in their spare time. They were hesitant at first, but promises of good recommendations and a bonus at the end of the year soon swayed them.

The timber of justice was pulled out of the back of the truck. Two spindly supports were set up, while a few blows from a hammer adjusted a column of dark wood. Liebe arranged various rods and other metal pieces. Herr Ziegenmeyer turned away as a heavy steel triangle was hoisted upwards between the two arms of the sinister contraption.

Reed baskets were then pulled out of the truck and set in place. Liebe nodded with evident satisfaction.

"That'll do the job," he said. "It's old, but hasn't been used much."

Then, he fell back into surly silence.

The bell at the gate was rung again. The officials had arrived: two observers from the criminal court, Herr Doctor Poppelreiter, a court clerk and some other bigwigs. There were no journalists, except for the reporter from the tiny local paper. Indeed, the news of the execution had not been released to the press by order of the Criminal Brigade.

Poppelreiter was disappointed, as he had hoped for a bit of publicity in spite of everything. With an embarrassed air, he turned towards two men who arrived in a hurry.

"Good day, Herr Dickson. Good day, my dear Herr Wills! I don't think you'll have long to wait. Look! The device is in place and the Executioner is ready to pull the lever!"

The loquacious Chief of Police was preparing to launch into a long discourse when the Warden appeared and led the two detectives away.

"He must be awake by now, Herr Dickson, but I was waiting for you before officially telling him that his pardon had been denied."

The visitors' footsteps echoed somberly as they made their way down the long corridors, where the sounds of snoring could be heard through the reinforced cell doors.

"Here we are," said the Warden in a low voice, as he signaled a jailor to open the door of a small cell, set off by itself at the end of the gallery.

Grump was awake and already partly dressed. He listened to the fatal news with indifference, but when he saw that Dickson was standing behind the others present, his face lit up.

"Herr Dickson, you remember what you promised me, don't you?" he demanded.

"I do."

"Then walk beside me while I take my final steps. That should be long enough for me to tell you what you want to know."

Dickson nodded his agreement.

The condemned man quickly finished getting dressed, then allowed his wrists and ankles to be shackled. The Warden asked if he had anything further to say, and Grump congratulated him on the general quality of the prison.

Then, as fast as the shackles could allow, the walk down the long corridors began. Two guards helped support the prisoner, and Dickson stood as close to him as he could.

Grump himself seemed the least affected in the entire group, even whistling a little tune. When he saw the awesome machine of death in the courtyard, he showed not the least fear.

"I've only seen pictures of these things, and they didn't give me a good idea of what it really looked like," he said.

Suddenly, he paled and Dickson rushed towards him, but Grump brushed away any assistance.

"It's not that," he muttered. "But we have to do it quickly... *He's here!* I feel that he's here, Herr Dickson!"

"Where is *he*?"

"Is your promise still good?"

"Yes!"

Grump trembled like a leaf in a storm; however, the detective realized that it wasn't the fate that awaited him that put him in such a state.

"Listen... Listen... Dickson..."

He was almost on the guillotine, his foot touching the base.

"I am not the Red-Eyed Vampire... *The real monster is Vet...*"

He stopped as if the grip of some madness and started to scream:

"Hurry! Kill me, Herr Dickson! Hurry! You swore it! In the name of God, you must! Please, Herr Dickson! Hurry!"

There was then a scene that was so unbelievable and which happened with such rapidity that describing it takes longer than the events themselves did.

Dickson suddenly raced forward and, with a massive shove, pushed the Executioner out of the way, crying:

"Arrest him! I order you to arrest this man!"

Tom immediately rushed to carry out his boss's demand and jumped on Otto Liebe.

"Hurry, Harry Dickson!" yelled Grump.

The detective turned horribly pale, but, with a firm hand, pushed Grump into position and locked the wooden collar to hold the man's head steady.

Then, he pulled the handle which released the blade.

A sharp whistle was followed by a dull thump and the crowd murmured in horror.

Dickson wasted no time in looking at the blood spurting from the severed neck, running instead towards a group of men who stood bunched together.

"Do you have him?" he demanded.

"But, Herr Dickson," stuttered the Warden, "I don't understand."

"You don't need to understand! Did you arrest the Executioner?"

Tom was furious in his defeat.

"It was the fault of the two guards who held me back... The fellow's gone and this is all that's left of him."

He handed Dickson the tall hat that executioners were required to wear while performing their duties.

The detective cried out in anger.

"That's the hat that was in the haunted house! My God, I've just made the biggest mistake of my career!"

Just then, the bell at the entrance gate rang out frenetically.

Two police officers got down from their horses, which were covered in foaming sweat. The men stood frozen in stupor before the bloody guillotine.

"What's happened?" they demanded.

"What was supposed to happen," responded the Warden, coldly.

The two messengers looked around with shocked expressions.

"At 3 a.m., just when Otto Liebe and his assistants were leaving Hanover, the order came from Berlin to delay Grump's execution. We tried to telephone you, Warden Ziegenmeyer, but it was impossible. All communications with Hildesheim were cut.

"Instead, we left on horseback, sure that we could get to Liebe in time and not wanting to risk a problem with a motor.

"But halfway here, we found Liebe and his assistants dead on the road; killed by gunshots. Just before we got to town, we saw that the telephone wires were dangling, clearly cut by the guilty party!"

Harry Dickson was no longer listening. He rushed from the prison with Tom right on his heels; as soon as they reached the street, he began to run.

"Quick! We've got to get to the haunted house!" he ordered his assistant.

As they got to the corner of the Brunnen-Platz, they saw some early risers looking at the building with terrified expressions.

"What's happening?" cried Dickson.

One of the spectators, a mason in blue overalls, pointed a finger at the top step of the porch.

"That looks suspicious to me," he said.

A rivulet of blood ran from under the door and congealed on the blue stone steps.

"Someone's gone to tell the solicitor who watches over this cursed place," the man continued. "Look, here's his clerk, Herr Nussepen. Now we should find something out."

A sickly-looking man in an ill-fitting jacket took hurried, mincing steps as he approached them. He was yawning and rubbing his eyes, which were still red from sleep.

"Dear Lord," he stammered when he saw the blood, "what abomination has this appalling place brought upon us now?"

His hand trembled as he reached for the door handle, and he looked as if he would faint.

"I can't do it," he muttered. "Besides, in a case like this, we should wait for the police to arrive. I don't have the right to go in before they do."

Harry Dickson was impatient.

"I am the police, Herr Nussepen! Open this door immediately! We might still be able to save whoever is inside."

"But there's no one in there!" cried the clerk. "Unless it's… it's…"

"Ghosts, no doubt," snarled the detective. "Now hurry up! This isn't the time to act like a fool."

"Look! Herr Doctor Poppelreiter is coming!" said the mason. "Now you can be sure that someone from the police is here!"

"Herr Dickson," said Poppelreiter as he arrived, out of breath, "I saw you run off and realized that something important linked to the bizarre events of this morning must have happened in town."

Dickson pointed to the pool of blood that had coagulated on the steps.

"What do you think about this, my dear colleague?"

"Heavens! Will our small town be spared nothing?" he lamented. "Ah! Herr Nussepen! You must be here to open the door for the authorities. But, why isn't your employer here himself?"

The mason answered before the clerk could open his mouth.

"I'm the one who first saw the blood, so I ran to ring the bell at Herr Ameise's door. The maid looked out the window, then went to look for him. When she came back, she looked surprised. She told me that Herr Ameise wasn't in his room, but his bed was still warm as if he'd just gotten up.

"She looked everywhere, but couldn't find him, and wondered if he'd gone to the prison to watch the execution of the Red-Eyed Vampire.

"Then, she said I should go and get Herr Nussepen instead."

The man would have kept talking if Harry Dickson hadn't made it clear that he had no time for anything further. Herr Poppelreiter took the key from the hand of the trembling clerk and slipped it into the lock. The door opened with a loud creak.

The vestibule was gloomy, lit only by a weak shaft of daylight coming from a high, opaque window on a nearby landing.

Tom was following Herr Poppelreiter and felt nauseated at the metallic odor of fresh blood. Dickson pushed the door wide to allow as much light as possible to chase the shadows.

A body blocked the entryway; its head was bent onto its shoulder, giving it the sad air of a broken doll. It had been almost completely severed and remained attached with only a few thin threads of skin and sinew. Blood had flooded from it and covered the tiles in a massive pool.

"But... but... That's Herr Ameise, the town solicitor!" cried Herr Poppelreiter. "My God! This horrible crime must have been committed less than an hour ago! The body is still warm, despite the loss of blood."

Herr Nussepen, the clerk, cried out in shock and fainted dead away.

Although he could appear ridiculous, the Chief of Police also was able to get things done when it was necessary. He gave brief, precise orders to the officers who had come running, sent for a doctor, a photographer and an ambulance.

When he had finished, Poppelreiter realized that Harry Dickson had not moved an inch, but instead stared around as if he was a mere spectator.

"Herr Dickson," he said, "no one can shed a light on this mystery better than you. Would you like to come to headquarters to help us?"

Dickson shook his head slowly.

"There's nothing more to be done," he said.

"What do you mean? Such a horrible crime! Do you know who did it?"

"Of course!"

Herr Poppelreiter cried out in astonishment.

"Then tell me so we can catch him before he escapes!"

"That's a different story," said Dickson, signaling that the Chief of Police should follow him.

They walked into the salon, where the shutters had been opened so that a bit of weak morning light could enter the sinister room.

"I believe that this is our man," explained Dickson, pointing to a large portrait hanging on the wall.

Poppelreiter stared at the painting. It showed an austere, bearded man wearing a dark-colored, velvet cape. The beard was long and black, trimmed into a point that hung onto his chest, his expression was cruel and somber, and his eyes were reddish in tone and, due to a trick of the painter, seemed to follow the viewer around the room.

"Who is that?" demanded Poppelreiter.

A timid voice responded:

"That's Count Ion Nedelcu Dragomin, the last heir to the title and a descendant of the notorious Vlad Tepesch, the Impaler, better known as Count Dracula of Transylvania."

Harry Dickson turned and saw that the solicitor's clerk, Herr Nussepen, had regained consciousness and was pointing at the portrait with a trembling finger.

"And where can we find this gentleman?" asked Poppelreiter.

"Where? But... That's to say..."

The poor scribe seemed puzzled by the question.

"...But, Count Dragomin has been dead these past 200 years!"

The Chief of Police scratched his chin and turned towards the great detective, more perplexed than ever.

"Did you hear that, Herr Dickson! He's been dead for 200 years!"

"I don't doubt that," said Dickson dryly, "but it doesn't change a thing that I've said."

"But that's insane, Sir! How can you say..."

Dickson signaled that the Chief of Police should be quiet.

"Herr Poppelreiter," he whispered, "in order to catch a flesh and blood murderer, I first need to vanquish a large number of ghosts, and I guarantee you that it won't be easy."

He then turned towards Nussepen, who was sitting on the edge of a chair in a state of near collapse.

"My dear Herr Nussepen," he said, "can you tell me the history of this house?"

The poor clerk looked at him in fear and shook his head.

"That's a secret that the Ameises have passed down from father to son for centuries. Nothing has been written down. Herr Ameise was a fine man, but he would not allow us to speak about it. All that I know is that it's the property of the Dragomins."

"The last of which died two centuries ago!" interrupted Dickson.

The employee nodded in agreement.

"That's absolutely true… And now, Herr Ameise is dead as well, without leaving the least instruction on what is to happen to this house!"

"That's not what's important here," said Poppelreiter. "We'll seal up the whole place and none too soon either! It's been nothing but nuisance for far too long."

"I'm afraid, oh, how I'm afraid," whined Nussepen, as tears streamed down his face. "Can I go, Herr Doctor? I can't stay in this accursed house for a minute longer; my heart can't take it."

He finished his lament with a sharp cry:

"He's killing me! The red eyes! The red eyes!"

Then, he fell to floor with a thud.

"He's been wounded!" yelled Tom Wills, who had run to his aid. "Look! His cheek is bleeding and there's a fresh cut!"

"It looks like a gash that was made just this second!" grumbled Poppel-reiter.

Dickson had also approached the man and was looking all around him.

"Here's the knife!" he said. "And it's a very old one, too."

He pulled an antique weapon from the chair where the clerk had been sitting minutes before.

"It must have been thrown with great force," remarked Poppelreiter. "He got off lightly; look, the blade has blood on it."

"Handle it carefully," said Tom, "maybe we can get some fingerprints from it."

Dickson started to laugh.

"The person who handled that knife isn't the least bit worried about fingerprints," he announced.

"Almighty God!" shouted the Chief of Police, "Herr Dickson, look at the portrait of Count Dragomin! The knife in it is identical to the one you're holding!"

Dickson mulled the information over.

"Very clever," he muttered. "Maybe too clever by half."

The Chief of Police stood looking at the detectives with a perplexed air.

"Herr Dickson, when that knife was thrown, there were only four of us in this room: you, Herr Wills, Herr Nussepen and me!"

"So, look for the guilty party amongst us. The process of elimination will show us who it is right away."

"That's not what I was trying to say," said Poppelreiter. "I was just trying to draw your attention to the supernatural elements of the attack, and nothing more."

"Now that's what I call the voice of wisdom," said Dickson. "In fact, you're forgetting the fifth person present. And, that fifth person is the killer!"

"But who is it?" cried Tom and Poppelreiter at the same time.

"Why, it's Count Ion Nedelcu Dragomin," answered the detective somberly.

Harry Dickson and his assistant were ready to leave Hildesheim.

"Not counting Grump, that makes four deaths in one morning that he can add to his tally," said Dickson.

"Who are you talking about, Guv?"

"The Red-Eyed Vampire, of course, Tom!"

"But we saw him executed right in front of us!"

"We most certainly did not! And it's my own fault that I didn't get him when I had the chance."

"What do you mean?" asked Tom, stupefied.

"The tall hat, my boy! He left it behind when he was dressing. That Executioner who escaped you because those idiot guards grabbed you... Well, Tom, that was none other than the Vampire himself!"

IV. The Trail of the Dead

Afterwards, Harry Dickson himself would admit that the period of research that followed the dramatic events at Hildesheim was filled with uncertainty and false starts.

In vain, he contacted all the offices of the German Criminal Brigade to find out what he could about any names beginning in "*Vet...*"—that single syllable that Grump had had time to utter before he died. Hildesheim and the surrounding area were investigated in such detail that all those whose surname began with *Vet* soon cursed it.

Only Dickson's worldwide prestige and sterling reputation ensured that the Criminal Brigade kept the case open, as they refused to believe that there was anything left to investigate in the Affair of the Red-Eyed Vampire.

However, there was one discovery that disconcerted not only the German authorities, but the great detective as well. It turned out that Grump was a descendent of the Dragomins!

"I assume that we want to keep this information confidential?" asked a highly-placed German official when Dickson showed him proof of the strange connection. "The Dragomins were warrior princes in Hungary, and Germany would like to make sure that their reputation remains unsullied."

"I'm sorry, Your Excellency," the detective responded icily, "but my duty is above such political considerations, no matter how understandable they might be. I serve all of humanity and I have to keep that in mind. I'll just keep hold of this evidence."

"My government," began the German official, "will compensate your services richly, Herr Dickson..."

The detective stood up.

"I don't believe that we have anything further to say to each other, Your Excellency," he said in a voice that was even colder than before. "If I thought that this paper held nothing but curiosity value, I would gladly throw it into the flames this minute. However, to the contrary, I believe that it will lead me, if not to victory, then at least along the right path. Farewell, Sir..."

After that, Dickson returned to England, accompanied by Tom Wills; both of them were more than a little disappointed by the direction events had taken.

"I don't believe that the Vampire will rest on his unholy laurels," repeated the detective over and over again. Tom was so distressed to see how severely his employer was affected by his defeat that he forgot to ask for the promised explanation of the odd way he had undertaken things in Hildesheim.

Events were soon to prove the great man correct.

One evening, Tom had been sent by his master to handle a small affair passed on by Scotland Yard, and was late in returning. Harry Dickson wasn't overly concerned, because the young man wasn't in any particular danger. However, as the hours passed, he began to lose his habitual calm.

Suddenly, the telephone rang. Tom was calling and his tone was fevered and anxious.

"Guv! Do you know who I've been following for over an hour? Count Dragomin! Yes! The one from the portrait! It really is him, and what's strange is that I started tailing him right when he walked out of the door at the house of Mrs. Cosima Lamb in Bunhill Row."

"What? The poor pensioner who was mysteriously murdered last week?"

"That's the one, Guv!"

"Where are you now?"

"Our man can take credit for making me run! He took the trolley, then the bus, then came through the tunnel in Rotherhithe Street. Right now, he's in a little club called "Pretty Molly," and I'm calling from the telephone box on the corner so I can keep an eye on the door... Come quick! He just came out and I'm going after him!"

The phone suddenly went dead.

Dickson frantically jiggled the hook, hoping to hear something more, but in vain. Tom was gone.

"That boy has been seriously reckless," he muttered to himself as he slipped a revolver into his pocket alongside his flashlight and burglary tools. "Tom doesn't have the strength to battle a creature like that. I don't have a minute to lose."

He ran out the door, just as a taxi turned into Baker Street; the detective flagged it down and leaped inside.

"Step on it!" he yelled at the driver. "There's a pound tip if you go as fast as you can!"

The motor burned rubber on the streets of London, and, as he stepped out in front of "Pretty Molly," he had to admit that he couldn't have arrived any quicker.

He found a trail left by Tom Wills near the telephone box and was able to follow it along the famous back alleys alongside the river, past the Lavender Pond dock, his expression becoming graver as he went along.

"He's leading the boy a merry chase, and it stinks of a trap."

He lost the trail at Durand's Wharf, where it seemed to totally disappear. The detective sighed in frustration; it was a very bad sign.

Stymied, he looked around.

The night was black as a brigand's heart and rain threatened to fall at any moment. A strong wind started to blow along the river, making the flames of the gaslights flicker. Limehouse was in front of him, hostile and menacing with its dark cargo ships, barely lit by smoking gasoline torches.

Suddenly, a mighty clamor caused him to turn his head; it came from alongside the river and Dickson ran towards it. He saw nothing but the oily waters, but the cries became louder and shriller.

The detective took his flashlight and directed its light towards the river's edge. It was the huge, blue rats of the London docks, the terror of the district, fighting over some prize. At first, the rodents were frightened by the light, but soon again took up their battle.

"I wonder what they're doing," murmured Dickson. Pushing down his disgust, he slid down the bank, kicking at the vile beasts as he went.

The rats ran off, protesting loudly but leaving behind the object of their dispute. The detective recoiled in horror when he saw that the horrid creatures were fighting over a human ear!

"Where did this macabre debris come from?" he wondered as he looked around him.

A few yards away was an old, crumbling dock; Dickson headed for it and quickly discovered the opening of one of the large sewer pipes that released waste into the Thames to flow down to the sea.

"This is their lair."

He had barely set foot into the tunnel when a repulsive odor made him gag. He recognized it immediately; there was a body nearby.

He didn't have to look for long. A branch of the sewer was blocked by a skeletal cadaver that had been horribly mutilated, leaving little but a few bloody strips of flesh behind.

When the detective aimed his flashlight into the farthest corner of the sewer, he immediately saw another body sprawled there. Dickson ran towards it and the rats fled, screaming.

The body was naked, but the detective's hands found it to still be warm.

"Tom!" he screamed.

But there was no answer.

Feverishly, Dickson turned over the body and moaned at the sight of the painfully bruised head of his faithful assistant.

But it wasn't the time to be emotional. Dickson took off his coat, wrapped the naked body and lifted it to his shoulder, then hurried out of the dank sewer pipe.

"Ahoy!"

A green light bounced around on the Thames' turbulent waters; it was a River Police skiff.

Fifteen minutes later at the police dock, Tom regained consciousness.

"He isn't badly hurt," confirmed the police surgeon who had cared for him. "He got knocked on the head with a truncheon; but if you'd come a few hours later, Mr. Dickson, the rats would have done him in for sure."

"Do you have anything that will help us find the perpetrator, Mr. Dickson?" asked the officer in charge.

The detective shook his head gloomily.

"Unfortunately, I don't. This fellow's not going to let us take him easily I'm afraid."

Slowly, Tom came to his senses.

"He'd reached the water's edge," he mumbled, "and suddenly, I couldn't see him anymore. I walked to where he'd disappeared and someone bashed me on the head... Ouch! It hurts!"

"We need a car to drive us home!" ordered Dickson.

As the car crossed London, the detective sat forward with a start.

"Tom, my boy, this was all arranged in advance! The man with the black beard was following you when you thought you were following him! In Burnhill Row, he only pretended to come out of Mrs. Lamb's house in order to grab your attention. He made sure you had enough time to call me so that I would be lured out of the house."

"What for?" asked Tom groggily.

"He must want the papers proving the Grump-Dragomin connection," bellowed Dickson. "Driver! Hurry! Don't worry about getting a ticket, I'll take the blame!"

In the vestibule of 221B Baker Street, the two detectives ran into their housekeeper, Mrs. Crown, who was carrying a tray of tea and biscuits.

When she saw Tom with his bandaged head and wearing the ill-fitting clothing loaned to him by one of the policemen, she almost dropped her burden from the shock.

"Mr. Tom!" she cried. "What's happened to you? Where have you been? Just a while ago you ran into the house and called out to me in an odd voice that you didn't want to be disturbed... You ran up the stairs so quickly that I barely saw the back of you..."

Dickson and Tom didn't give her the time to finish before they bounded up the stairs themselves.

"Our man is good, you've got to give him that," groaned Dickson. "Don't forget that he had your clothes and keys, Tom… We're lucky that Mrs. Crown fell for his disguise; otherwise, he'd have done the poor woman in!"

"Ah ha! Just as I expected!" he added as he saw his office in a shambles, the drawers all pulled out and papers lying all over the floor. The detective gave a bitter laugh.

"But the point is in my favor; he did all this for nothing."

"So he didn't get what he was looking for?"

"He did not! Still, I admire his audacity and the rapidity of his actions. In fact, I'm almost grateful to him for coming, because now that the creature has shown himself, we can start with a warm trail."

Dickson wandered around the room, then stopped in front of an open window.

"He must have searched for a long time, but when he looked out this window and saw our taxi arriving, he took off into the night"

The detective bent over a mark on the windowsill.

"He removed his shoes so that he could climb the drain pipe… See the clear print of a foot wearing rather common socks… But, what's this?"

Dickson had cried out in surprise after collecting several grains of earth that he examined closely.

"Dried moss… Strange… Very strange…He must have walked through a mossy forest in those socks."

Hurriedly, the detective went to his worktable to look at his discovery beneath a microscope.

"Tom, here is what shows us the path to follow. Pack our things and look at the railroad timetable."

"Where are we going, Guv?"

"Dover, then Ostende for the Ostende-Vienna express!"

"You've learned all of that from those grains of earth?"

"Of course, my boy! But you should really speak of those 'grains of earth' with a bit more respect, because they come from a grave, and probably a very illustrious grave!"

"What grave?" asked Tom, so surprised that he forgot all about his horrible headache.

"The grave of Count Ion Nedelcu Dragomin, of course!"

"The Red-Eyed Vampire?"

"Exactly, Tom, the Red-Eyed Vampire," answered the great detective in a voice that was firm and bore no sign of irony.

V. A Cry in the Storm

When they arrived on the Continent, there was a thick layer of fog in the air. Tom morosely watched as the ghostly trees glided past the window; Harry Dickson decided the time was right to provide his assistant with some answers.

"I'm going to give you a lesson in the supernatural, my boy," he said. "Don't give me that look of disbelief; modern science is far from stripping away the veil that obscures ancient sorcery.

"The science of necromancy is real and our savants are barely beginning to make timid incursions into it, but most of the time, they wind up defeated and terrified. Clearly, belief in vampirism is as old as the world and, in certain countries like Bulgaria, Hungary, etc., it's not even close to disappearing."

"What is a vampire?"

"It's one of the living dead, Tom, terrifyingly dead and evil. Superstition has it that, on moonless nights, a vampire comes out of its grave to attack the living and feast on their blood. A few years ago, in the area around the Bulgarian village of Gabrova, they suspected that a rich peasant who had been dead for years was a vampire and came back at night to slake his thirst with his neighbors' blood.

"Amazingly, the authorities allowed the townfolk to open his tomb; this is what the journalists who were there said happened: *The dead man, a certain Grushka, lay in his coffin, completely untouched by any decomposition. The corpse had a pink complexion and looked as if it was sleeping. However, it was icy to the touch, stiff as a board and clearly dead. The terrified, angry crowd insisted that a stake be driven through the thing's heart.*

"The report goes on to say that the deceased writhed hideously and that blood flowed from the open wound. Ever since, the village has been spared any further vampire attacks. These facts aren't unique, and the author's account has the ring of truth.

"Popular belief in these horrible crimes from beyond the grave is also increasing. And, in these countries, they also say that a person who is killed by a vampire *becomes one himself!*

"That, Tom, is why Grump so desperately wanted to be sure he died beneath the guillotine's blade! He was terrified he would be killed by his vampiric partner and be forever cursed.

"I understood that immediately, and now that I know Grump was a descendent of the Dragomins, I appreciate his terror even more.

"Imagine his horror at recognizing the Executioner as the Red-Eyed Vampire; if he died at his hand, he would become one of those foul creatures of the night. So, I kept my promise and I executed Grump myself."

Tom listened open-mouthed, his mind invaded by a nameless horror.

"All that in this century of science!" he said with a shudder.

Dickson shrugged.

"Again, I ask you if you believe that science can explain everything. No, I admit that in these tales of monsters, there is a big dose of superstition, but there are many things we still do not understand."

"But what about the garlic and the dirt from out of the grave?" asked Tom.

"For each evil, there is a remedy. Garlic is the major protection against the fiend's depredations and causes him to flee; you can see it in the eaves wherever the vampire is feared. As to the earth of the dead, that shows a particularly clever subterfuge used by the blood suckers.

"The shadow of the cross locks the vampire into his tomb so that he can't escape… Therefore, the creatures sought a different way out and succeeded; by rubbing dirt from the grave into their shoes, they are always walking in their own burial ground, and the cross is powerless against them. That's the legend at least."

"OK," replied Tom, trying to lighten the dark tone of the conversation, "so they really shouldn't be burying their dead with shoes!"

"Well observed, my boy," said Dickson with a smile. "Popular belief is never logical in cases like these. It's accepted that anyone who brings shoes to a vampire is immediately richly rewarded by him, so there is always someone eager to lend assistance; just as there are always those willing to sell their souls to the Devil!"

Tom shook his head sorrowfully. After a few moments of silent reflection, the great detective continued:

"There were several events that set off what happened, but the most important is the fact that the criminal we've been following so relentlessly is himself convinced he is a vampire!"

"Why do you think that, Guv?"

"Many clues point in that direction, Tom. There is his wariness of garlic and the presence of graveside dirt in his shoes. Mostly, there was his desire to take the place of the Hanover Executioner so that he could kill Grump himself. He clearly wanted to punish him by turning him into an accursed creature of the night for all eternity; I don't know why yet, but we'll find out.

"This conviction that he's possessed of supernatural abilities gives him self-confidence and certitude in his success, so much so that he's afraid of no one and nothing. However, his last actions lead me to believe that he's not happy about what I'm doing. It seems that a seed of doubt has been planted and that's the first step towards his defeat."

At the junction at Linz, the detectives left the Express to take the train towards Prague. They made a brief stop in the picturesque city, and then joined a convoy on the road to the Bohemian Mountains.

That night, they changed clothes so that no one looking at them would believe them to be foreigners.

Harry Dickson and Tom Wills had become Herr Guttman, a toymaker from Nuremberg, accompanying his son Ludwig to the mountains to help him recuperate from ill health brought on by too many late nights at his studies.

Eiserharr wasn't really a village as much as a hamlet of no more than 50 hearths grouped together at the edge of the great forest of Bohemia.

The humble community wasn't served by any rail line, and the road leading to it was barely capable of being traveled by coach, for it was pocked by many potholes and gullies. The surrounding area was difficult to farm and industrial development was nonexistent. Therefore, no one thought it was worth the trouble of making it easier to reach Eiserharr, whose inhabitants survived by poaching game in the forest and fishing in the streams and marshes.

The summer sun was slowly setting as the two travelers walked along the road.

"My feet are going to fall off," complained Tom Wills as he looked ahead at the road that seemed to lead endlessly off into the distance.

"Look at that smoke drifting into the sky," replied Dickson. "I bet some wild rabbit took its last breath right before landing in a pot over there."

"I hope you're right, Guv!"

The road curved and, once they'd gone around that, the little hamlet appeared before the two voyagers like the Promised Land.

"That low house that looks a bit less dilapidated than the others is probably the Inn," suggested the detective.

Just then, a tall, thin woman with a tanned face appeared on the doorstep and looked at the approaching strangers.

"Good evening, Madam. Is this the Inn?" asked Dickson.

The woman nodded her head sadly.

"If you want to call it that, Sir, although not many use it, in this deserted place."

She turned towards the interior and called out.

"Darko! There are guests!"

A man with a withered but friendly face came at her call and ceremoniously invited the visitors to enter.

"Calling this an Inn is a bit grand," he said, taking up where his wife had left off. "We do have a room where travelers can stay, but it hasn't been used in years. Still, we can't have you spending the night out under the stars! If need be, my wife and I can sleep in the stable."

Dickson and Tom were moved by the hospitable greeting of these poor people. Soon, while the wife was busying herself in the kitchen, they began to feel quite at home, enjoying a stein of the excellent Bohemian wine.

"I hope you'll do us the honor of dining with us tonight," said the detective as the hostess served them a delectable rabbit roasted with wild herbs and refilled their steins.

Darko, flattered, didn't wait to be asked a second time and sat next to his clients at the best table in the house.

"I hope it's not indiscreet of me to ask what brings you to this forsaken place?" he asked.

Dickson laid out the story of Tom's supposed illness.

"My son needs fresh air and tranquility; that's why I looked for an out of the way place, far from the usual spa towns and other touristic sites."

The innkeeper nodded in approval.

"It's true that our region is beautiful, but much of it is not suited to those in search of real rest like you. Half a league from here, right in the middle of the forest, there's a castle…"

The innkeeper's wife interrupted him.

"A castle!" she said bitterly. "It's nothing more than the lair of brigands, all in ruins. The middle of an almost impenetrable forest is right where it belongs! No good Christian should set foot near it."

"Quiet, woman!" said her husband. "I wasn't planning on telling these gentlemen that they should go there and ask for a room. I don't like the place any more than you do, but I wish you would talk about it a bit more courteously, if only out of respect for poor Lady Miloska."

His wife nodded her head slowly in agreement.

"Yes. Poor woman, living all alone in that horrible manor haunted by terrible ghosts! Poor woman. Poor Miloska!"

"You mean to tell us that a woman lives in the middle of the forest in a haunted castle?" asked the detective sardonically.

The innkeeper remained silent for a few minutes, then a large sip of wine loosened his tongue.

"It's the old castle of the Count Dragomins who used to own this land. Lady Miloska was a very distant cousin of the family, but she's their only descendant. Some of us think she owns the place, but others swear she's only the custodian. In any event, she's very kind to the poor folk here, and even though her own resources are likely quite limited, she does what she can to help those more in need than herself."

"Tell me about the ghosts," said Tom excitedly. "I love stories about haunted houses!"

Darko sent a dark glance his way.

"The stories aren't happy ones, young Sir. The last Count Dragomin… Well, he's been dead these 200 years…"

"And he comes back at midnight dressed in a white shroud and wearing chains!" laughed Tom.

Darko shook his head.

"If only that was it… No, Count Dragomin is a vampire."

"It's horrible," moaned his wife.

"He's been seen, not often, but still seen, in the forest near the accursed castle," the innkeeper continued in a heavy voice. "And there have been victims!

"Rido, the miller! Strohl, the unfortunate vagabond! And others as well. He savagely killed them, stealing all the blood from their poor bodies."

"And what has the law done about it?" asked Dickson.

Darko shook his head sadly.

"We're just poor peasants here, and the Dragomin name still carries power... They accuse us of making up stories and even threaten to lock us all up in an insane asylum."

"What about this Lady Miloska?"

"She cries. She's done what she can to help the families who have been hurt by the monster... Everyone has complained. I beg you, though, when you leave here, don't talk about any of this; we have enough problems with the authorities."

A loud roar echoed through the room.

"My God! The storm has come!" said the innkeeper's wife, making the sign of the cross.

A violent burst of wind blew against the door and the shutters, which shuddered as if a hand was angrily beating against them. In the nearby forest, the trees sighed beneath the gusts.

Darko's wife lit a candle that had been blessed by the local priest and placed it in front of a picture of the Virgin Mary, then began to pray. Tom and Dickson remained silent, listening to the noise of the terrible storm outside.

Through cracks in the shutters, they saw brilliant flashes of lightening, and from the sound of the thunder, it must have struck very close to the house. The floor even vibrated beneath their feet.

The rain began to fall with such ferocity that the openings in the doors and the roof allowed a fine mist of water to form inside the building.

Suddenly, Harry Dickson turned his head to listen.

"Someone is calling from outside," he said.

The woman held her hands towards him in supplication and the innkeeper began to tremble.

"I beg you, Sir, don't go outside! The night spirits are trying to lure you to them. You will never return if you go!"

A sharp cry rose above the noise of the storm.

"It's the Vampire!" cried Darko's wife. "Don't go; by all the Saints in Heaven!"

But Dickson had already stood up, because he heard a human voice begging for help.

With a firm hand, he turned the key in the door.

The wind entered so forcefully that the candles were blown out and the glasses were swept from the table.

"Don't go!" the woman cried one last time in the darkness.

But neither Dickson nor Tom heard her; they were in the midst of the fury of the elements. The rain surrounded them with such force that it felt as if they were held back by a physical being. The wind forced them to bend almost to the ground to move forward. But they persisted, and move forward they did.

"Help! Darko! Darko!"

The cries had become weaker and were filled with a piteous anxiety.

"Walk against the wind!" cried Dickson with all his strength. The voice came from farther down the road.

Tom lit his electric torch, but the light barely pierced the huge wall of driving rain.

"Over there!" he cried suddenly. "There's something lying in the middle of the road... My God! It's a woman!"

With a leap, Dickson was by the side of the poor girl, who was lying motionless on the ground. He lifted her in his arms.

"Back to the inn. Let's hurry! I think she's injured."

The return trip was even more difficult. Dickson trembled beneath the weight of the woman he carried and they were blinded by the rain and the frequent flashes of lightning. Tom led the way, stumbling as if he was drunk. At last, the vague contours of the inn appeared before them.

"Open up, Darko!"

"Are you human or are you demons?" asked a trembling voice from within.

"It's your guests! For the love of God, hurry up! We've got an injured woman with us."

After a few seconds of hesitation, the bolts were finally drawn back. Once the detectives had entered, Darko relit the candles.

Very carefully, the detective laid the unconscious woman on the innkeeper's bed and got his first look at her. Although she was still young, she was thin and drawn, giving her the appearance of being much older than she was. She was dressed in a style that was old-fashioned and her entire being spoke of endless misery and sorrow.

"It's Lady Miloska!" exclaimed Darko and his wife.

"She must have fallen and hit her head against a rock," said Dickson as he carefully washed a large wound that the young woman had on her forehead.

"Unless..." began Darko without finishing the sentence. His wife merely nodded her head fearfully.

The detective felt for the injured woman's pulse.

"She's got a fever," he murmured with a frown.

"She's saying something," interrupted Tom. "Listen, she's talking in her delirium."

The young woman had become agitated. Although her eyes remained closed, her lips were moving rapidly. Suddenly, she gave a terrified cry and began to speak in a dialect that neither Dickson nor his young assistant could understand.

But Darko and his wife understood and began to shudder in terror.

"What is she saying?" Dickson demanded.

Darko sighed sharply.

"It's awful," he whispered.

"What is?"

"She said... She said... that Count Dragomin... the Vampire has returned!"

VI. The Castle of Terror

A clear, bright morning had arrived on the heels of the storm. The sun was shining on newly blossomed flowers and bird song filled the misty forest. It was if the terror of the previous night had never existed.

Pale, but recovered, Lady Miloska walked out of the inn followed by Dickson and his assistant.

"I owe you my life, Herr Guttmann," she said to the detective in a voice that was rough, but with a diction that indicated a refined education. "I hope you will do me the honor of being my guests, even though I do not have much luxury to offer you."

"I accept your hospitality, my Lady," answered Dickson. "Besides, I studied a bit of medicine in my youth and I can help you care for that terrible wound you've received."

The young woman shuddered, something that was not missed by the detective.

"I fell," she murmured.

Harry Dickson watched her intently; he knew that she was lying. He had carefully examined her injury and knew it had been caused not by a fall, but by a blow from a blunt object.

"At any rate, you have to be careful that the wound doesn't get infected," he said. "Once we're back at your home, I'll bandage it more effectively."

She smiled in gratitude and Dickson noticed an expression of infinite sadness cross her emaciated face.

The road climbed uphill and, after a difficult walk, they reached the edge of the forest. Miloska chose a path that neither Dickson nor Tom had noticed, as it was so deeply hidden by thick brush; she signaled that her guests should follow her.

The forest closed behind them like the gates of a prison and, suddenly, it felt hostile and menacing to the intruders.

"It feels like the forests one reads about in fairy tales; the kind inhabited by monsters," said Dickson, laughing. "I keep expecting to run across an ogre!"

Miloska shuddered.

391

"Dear God, don't say such things, Herr Guttmann!"

"Why not?" continued the detective in the same light tone. "I'd love to see one of them try to stand up against a modern automatic pistol!"

Miloska looked at him in admiration.

"On the condition that one knows how to use such a thing," she answered, smiling.

Harry Dickson laughed out loud.

"My son and I are shooting champions! We've taken the top prizes four years in a row. Hold on!"

Something moved high above them at the top of a tree; slowly, the American pulled his revolver from his pocket, raised it and shot.

"Got it!" exclaimed Tom excitedly.

There was the noise of something falling through the branches; then, with a thud, a small falcon, cleanly shot through the head, fell to the ground.

Miloska made a surprised cry.

"That's wonderful!" She blushed and added, "You make a fantastic body-guard, Herr Guttmann!"

"At your service, my Lady," the detective responded gravely.

She turned her head and continued to lead them through the woods.

The forest became ever denser and more sinister; unpleasantly surprised, Tom moved closer to his boss.

Suddenly, the three of them stopped: a piteous cry had broken the sylvan quiet.

"What was that?" asked Tom.

"My God… It's… I think it's a kestrel… We have many of them nesting in the ruins of the castle's tower."

"Is that so?" Dickson asked nonchalantly. "I always thought they were nocturnal."

Miloska didn't respond, instead, bending to loosen a bramble that had become tangled in the hem of her dress, but the detective noticed a blush appear on her pale cheeks.

"She's a bad liar," he said to himself. "Poor woman… What terrible secret is she hiding?"

"Well, it's an unpleasant bird," opined Tom, returning to the kestrel. "I've never heard such a depressing sounding cry."

The trees started to thin out and a small clearing opened up before the travelers. A small shrine stood in front of an ancient oak tree; as they passed before it, Miloska piously crossed herself.

At the far end of the expanse of grass, the grey and ochre mass of the castle was visible. After walking a hundred meters further, the three stood in front of the somber, medieval ruin.

Dickson and his assistant were silent, struck by the strange, almost surreal aspect of the crumbling walls and the high towers, with their impressive cornices and the massive portcullis that defended the long corridor of mossy stones, that they crossed to arrive at the large courtyard, overrun by weeds and invading grass.

"Look! There's a tiny light," cried Tom. "It's like being in a fairy tale!"

Miloska smiled wanly.

"That's the sanctuary lamp. It burns in the chapel, keeping watch over the tombs of the Dragomins."

"I'm fascinated by antiques and old traditions," said Dickson. "Can I take a look at it?"

Miloska nodded her approval.

"Please, excuse me for a few minutes. I'm alone here in the castle and I'm afraid I can only offer you meager provisions. But I'd like to fulfill my duties as a hostess as well as I'm able.

"The castle, or what remains of it anyway, is open to you. Make yourselves at home. The chapel has several interesting sculptures and the gallery of paintings behind those vaulted windows hasn't been completely looted of the family portraits. Hopefully, the time in this depressing place will not pass too slowly for you, gentlemen."

She turned, and her sad, outdated dress dragged through the weeds as she left them.

"To the chapel!" ordered Dickson in a low voice. "And keep your revolver ready to shoot, you hear me, Tom?"

"Do you suspect a trap, Guv?"

"A trap? No. But I am thinking about the fact that that poor woman was attacked, and the cry of that supposed kestrel."

The great detective silently crossed the dark sanctuary, making brief stops in front of the tombs with their crumbling stones destroyed by lichen and other destructive weeds.

Suddenly he stopped dead in front of a large gravestone and read:

"*Count Ion Nedelcu Dragomin, 1670-1728.* For a 200-year-old tomb, this one strikes me as being in damned good shape," he said in a sarcastic tone. "What are these? Air vents? Not something you'd expect to find in a place like this, huh, Tom?"

"This stone isn't attached!" exclaimed Tom. "Look, Guv!"

The young man had accidentally kicked a protrusion on the slab, which seemed to tremble slightly.

Tom gave a more energetic kick at the protrusion and a strange phenomenon occurred: the stone pivoted, revealing a dark cavern which contained a large, open, empty coffin at the back.

"Let's have a little light, my boy!" ordered Dickson. "I think we're going to find something interesting in here."

"This coffin isn't old," said Tom when he examined it. "And look, it's all upholstered! It looks like the bench in a first-class train carriage. You'd sleep pretty comfortably in there all right."

"And someone was sleeping here, Tom. Not any later than last night either!"

"But who?" asked the young man, shocked.

"The Red-Eyed Vampire, of course! Who else but he? And legend insists on it: a vampire must return to his tomb before the first cock crows. Only, the living dead who sleeps in this tomb likes his comfort."

Dickson examined a handful of dirt that he gathered from the inside of the coffin and whistled.

"Identical," he muttered. "Tom, my boy, I think we've been sniffed out by you-know-who. Our fake Nuremberg personas were pretty useless. The monster is not only here, he beat us to the punch!"

"But we left London right away and without saying a word to anyone!" protested Tom.

"He probably traveled on the same train and kept an eye on us the whole time."

"And, is Miloska...?" began the younger man; but Dickson shook his head.

"I'm convinced she's a good, young woman who probably knows certain things, but who has suffered horribly. I think that, in a few days, she's even going to look at our arrival as providential, because we're going to free her from a terrible nightmare."

"So, the end is near?"

"Very," affirmed the American.

After putting everything in the chapel back into place, they left and headed towards the castle. They climbed up the massive staircase and walked through an enormous, shadowy hall decorated with antique hunting trophies, and then pushed open a heavy door of black oak.

A long gallery plunged in a dim, green light greeted them; rats fled their footsteps and, in the corners, they could hear the dull flapping of wings from the nocturnal creatures they had deranged.

"Sinister," muttered Tom. "Oh! We're in the painting gallery."

" 'Paintings' may be a bit exaggerated," said Dickson in a low voice.

Indeed, in the dilapidated, gilded frames, there were some tattered remains of long ago paintings. Here and there, through a thick coating of dust, one could see a pale spot that was a face or a metallic shadow that had once been a coat of armor or a sword.

Slowly, the two detectives made a tour of the lamentably abandoned gallery, then brusquely, Dickson grabbed hold of Tom's arm.

"This portrait... Oh!"

There was horror and rage in the detective's voice.

Tom followed his boss's gaze and, in his turn, had to force himself to control his nerves: isolated from the other canvases, alone in the middle of an empty wall covered in shreds of moss, in a solid, ebony, gold-leaf frame, a portrait stood out from the shadows.

The two men had immediately recognized the ascetic, black-bearded face, the burning, terrifying red eyes...

"Count Ion Nedelcu Dragomin," murmured Dickson.

"It's an exact copy of the one in the haunted house," added Tom. "My God! It's almost as if the eyes are alive. Look how they're following us, Guv... I wonder if there's not some kind of trick to it."

Carefully, the young man approached the fearsome portrait to examine it more closely. Suddenly, Dickson ran forward, grabbed him and pulled him back with such force that the two men almost lost their balance.

Something incredible and frightening had just happened; a diabolical light had seemed to bring the portrait to life. The eyes were burning with a brilliant red glow and the arm had come out of the painting, while the knife in its hand was making an arc through the air.

"In the name of God!" cried the American. "If you had been in front of that damned painting, that blade would have gone straight through you!"

Tom trembled like a leaf, but his boss had recovered his calm.

He noticed a nearby weapons display, grabbed a heavy sword that hadn't been totally destroyed by rust, and approached the painting himself.

"Careful, Guv!"

"Don't worry, my boy," Dickson laughed. "We're just going to get him to repeat his routine."

The detective used his long blade to tap the floor in front of the painting. Suddenly, it gave a bit and once again the portrait became animated and the dagger whistled past his face.

"A simple system of counter balancing weights sets off a mechanism hidden behind the wall," explained the great detective. "It's the victim himself that activates this death machine, or rather it's his weight on a specific plank of flooring. God knows how many poor souls have been murdered over the years by this infernal portrait."

"And it's survived for centuries?" asked Tom, but Dickson shook his head.

"I don't think so. I think that it was carefully restored, oiled and brought up to date last night."

"But what about the luminous eyes? Is that a recent, electric addition?"

"Not at all. The painted eyes are simply encircled with small rubies that change angles and sparkle with the mechanical movement. That explains the devilish apparition in the salon of the haunted house in Hildesheim."

"Does Miloska know that this thing is here?"

"I don't think so... In any case, we need to make her aware of it. Come on. We're going to find her. I would imagine she's getting a meal ready."

Indeed, the smell of cooking was wafting up from the west wing of the castle where Miloska normally lived.

After a bit of exploration, they pushed open the door to a huge, ill-lit kitchen, but were surprised to find no one there.

Harry Dickson walked around the room, looking at everything.

"Here's an omelet that's in a bad way," he said, pointing to a large pancake that was quickly drying out in the fire.

"She doesn't seem to be the world's greatest cook," admitted Tom.

"I would say something happened to distract Miloska from her duties as hostess, my boy."

"Lady Miloska!" cried out Tom, as loudly as he could. Nothing but echoes responded.

The detective's face showed concern.

"Her disappearance isn't a good sign," he said. "The monster has his back against the wall and he's going to act with lightning speed if we don't do something to stop him."

"Is Miloska's life in danger?"

"It is because she'll never give in to the Vampire's demands," said Dickson with conviction.

"What demands, Guv?"

"To hand the two of us over to him."

Tom looked up, suddenly startled.

"The kestral's cry!"

Dickson turned pale.

"The Vampire is calling her! I'm positive that that's his signal. I noticed her reaction this morning when I caught her in her little lie. Quick, Tom, we've got to finish this business once and for all, or we're done for."

They circled the moat, then ran towards the forest, not even paying attention to the burrs and thorns that tore at their clothes and flesh. They could see the clearing that they'd crossed that morning ahead of them.

"She's there, Guv!" said Tom, breathlessly. "Over by the shrine... My God! Look who's closing in on her!"

Miloska, white as a sheet, pressed herself against the portrait of the saint as if she was begging for her protection. From out of the brush, a man slowly approached her.

A man! No, it was a wraith! It had a dark, hate-filled face in which burned two hideous red eyes!

"The man from the portrait," muttered Tom, anxiously. "It's him..."

"Count Ion Nedelcu Dragomin, the Heir of Dracula, the Red-Eyed Vampire!" said Dickson; then, he took his young assistant by the arm and pushed him behind a large oak to hide.

Just then, Miloska raised a trembling hand and her face showed a nameless horror.

"You… You've returned," she moaned.

The man made a strange cry.

"Say, rather, that I have come home at last! That I have come to stay and take back what is mine!"

"Count Dragomin," begged Miloska, "will you never stop your life of infamy? God…"

"Don't speak that name!" howled the Vampire. "I am the Devil incarnate! As to my life, it will never end. I cannot die. I have walked the Earth for 200 years!"

"Dragomin!" wept Miloska. "My poor cousin, you are mad… You think that you are Count Ion, dead for two centuries, and that you are living his accursed life."

"I *am* Count Ion Dragomin, the last to bear the name. I am more and more convinced that I am he, not only in spirit, but in flesh and blood. Go to see his tomb, cousin; it's empty. Or rather, it is occupied by me."

"Enough!" she cried. "I no longer want to hear your blasphemous language."

"Little fool! You will obey me! And you will pay dearly if you refuse. In less than three years, I have wiped out 60 lives. I drank the blood of my victims, because I am a vampire, just like my ancestor. Obey me or I will have yours as well, Miloska!"

The poor woman could do nothing but cry and moan.

"Tonight, you will put the two strangers into the blue room, the one where there is a secret corridor leading to the painting gallery."

"I won't do it!" insisted Miloska. "These good travelers saved me from your clutches yesterday when you attacked and abused me…"

" 'Good travelers!' " snarled the horrible creature. "Ah! That's a laugh! Let me tell you who these two really are: the elder is the executioner of Hildesheim and the last head he cut off was that of Ebenezer Grump!"

"Heavens!" yelled Miloska, covering her face.

"Yes, my dear cousin, your brother Ebenezer!"

Miloska stood up straighter.

"It doesn't matter. My brother paid for his horrible crimes and I prefer to know that he is dead rather than continuing his life as a criminal. I will not just hand you my guests, no matter who they are. That, I swear before God."

Dragomin's face was hideous to see.

"Very well," he growled. "You're a Dragomin and I know you won't change your mind. I'll get the strangers, no matter what you do, my pretty cousin.

"But you know too much about me to live; your last moment on Earth has come.

"You might as well know that the executioner who was meant to kill your brother was me. Dead by my hand he would have remained accursed for all eternity, a vampire. The demon that you're sheltering under your roof was stronger than I, and it was he who put an end to Ebenezer's life, letting him die at peace, the wretch!"

"Then, may God bless and protect this man," cried Miloska.

"Despite your prayers I'll get him, as well as his young acolyte. He almost had me, you know… Luckily, Gepensterhaus was there to offer me asylum. Hah! I'm still laughing about it. That imbecile Ameise, the solicitor, was inside just at the same time that I walked in the front door. He saw me dressed as the Executioner and started screaming. I had to get rid of him, of course, even though he served me well."

"Monster!" wept Miloska.

"And now, my girl, I'm going to slice open your lovely white neck and take pleasure in knowing that that damned Harry Dickson…"

"Harry Dickson?"asked Miloska?

"That's right, I should introduce your guests to you: they're Harry Dickson and his assistant, Tom Wills."

Miloska started to laugh hysterically.

"As much as I want to live, I'm almost happy to die. Kill me, Dragomin, but now I know that I will be avenged!"

"Never!" growled the Vampire as he threw himself at her.

"Yes!" thundered a powerful voice. "Get your hands up, Dragomin!"

The Vampire cried out in terror and released the young woman, then began to run towards the castle.

"Don't set foot outside the clearing, Dragomin, or I'll shoot," said Dickson as he raised his revolver. "Three more steps and you're dead."

The Vampire howled in rage and despair.

"Not another step!" ordered Dickson.

Dragomin leapt towards the trees and a single shot rang out. The Vampire roared in pain, then collapsed. A trickle of blood seeped out of the hole in his temple.

"Just like the falcon this morning," murmured Tom as he laid Miloska, who had fainted, gently on the grass.

"Dead!" said Dickson as he stared at the hideous cadaver. "Now, my boy, you're going to meet up with one of our old acquaintances. Pull off that black beard."

Tom did as he was asked and immediately jumped in surprise.

"The solicitor's clerk! Herr Nussepen!"

"Yes," said Dickson. "But he was Count Dragomin all along!"

"There's not much left for me to explain, my boy," said Dickson as the express train pulled out of the station in Vienna and headed north.

"The Dragomins were poor, but their last heir, Ion Nedelcu, learned of the existence of an old house they owned in Hildesheim, where two centuries earlier, another Count Dragomin had hid his criminal activities after fleeing from Bohemia.

"The Ameises were held to secrecy, even from the families heirs, so Ion couldn't find out what he wanted to know.

"So, he went to Hildesheim and got himself taken on as a clerk by the solicitor.

"There, he managed to learn his ancestor's secret: that he was a vampire.

"What kind of dark, hereditary insanity overcame him? Taking on someone else's personality isn't something that is well understood, but it does occur. Thus, the young man, who had adopted the ridiculous name of Nussepen, believed he had become a vampire himself. He began to thirst for blood. He was able to commit his crimes with rare impunity, because he made frequent voyages on behalf of his employer and left a trail of blood in his wake.

"He managed to get a hold of all the works on vampirism so that he could make sure to conform to all the traditions.

"Then, he lured his cousin Grump into his insanity, and Grump, in his turn, began to kill.

"But he didn't have the true madness of his cousin, nor his intelligence. He wound up being captured by me, and Ion abandoned him, but he was still worried in case Gump betrayed him. While Grump was in prison, he threatened him with eternal damnation.

"Grump believed him. Why did the vampire fixate on his cousin? I haven't completely illuminated that point, but I think that it was something initially insignificant that later grew to huge proportions for the Dragomins."

"But what did that mysterious name *Vet*... that Grump muttered as he died mean?" asked Tom.

Harry Dickson started to laugh.

"We were fools, my boy, and I accept all the responsibility for it. If I'd understood it at the beginning, we could have been spared quite a lot of trouble. *Vet*... it's the first syllable of *vetter*, German for cousin!"

"So Grump was telling us that the vampire was his cousin?"

"Exactly, my boy! As they say, the Devil is in the details!"

399

www.ingramcontent.com/pod-product-compliance
Lightning Source LLC
Chambersburg PA
CBHW020255030726
47499CB00001B/207